Lew & Karen McIntyre, Authors, LLC
11891 Knollcrest Ln
La Plata, MD 20646

Library of Congress Control Number: 2016921080
Lewis F. McIntyre, La Plata, MARYLAND

Tags: Ancient History, Rome, China, Parthia, Religion, Christianity, Judaism, Buddhism, Silk Road
ISBN-13: 978-0692820803

DEDICATION
AND
ACKNOWLEDGMENTS

This book is dedicated to my wife Karen, who has steadfastly supported this effort for twenty years. She has been tireless as a source for new ideas, a fearless editor and critic, without whom, this book would never have been completed.

I wish to acknowledge the many people who helped me through this long effort, particularly the help and guidance of Prof. Nicholas Sims-Williams, Emeritus Research Professor of Iranian and Central Asian Studies at the Department of the Languages and Cultures of Near and Middle East, the School of Oriental and African Studies (SOAS), University of London, UK, who helped me capture an accurate picture of Central Asia of the time.

I also wish to thank my very professional editor Hildie Block, my cover designer Fiona Jayde, and my fellow alumni and authors Gary Knight, George Galdorisi, Cap Parlier and David Poyer, who guided me through the pitfalls of first-time authorship.

Others helped in many ways and small: Vinny DiGirolamo, my carpool partner of many years ago who brainstormed the beginning of this book with me while stalled in innumerable traffic jams on the Washington, DC Beltway; Carol Mattingly, whose enthusiasm for my first draft spurred me on to finish this; Jan Foley, a most enthusiastic beta reader who contributed many small pieces to make this story flow; Dave Becker, Jim Watters and all of my many other "beta" readers whose kind and enthusiastic comments kept me going through the long publication process.

LEWIS F. McINTYRE

THE EAGLE AND THE DRAGON

A Novel of Rome and China

CONTENTS

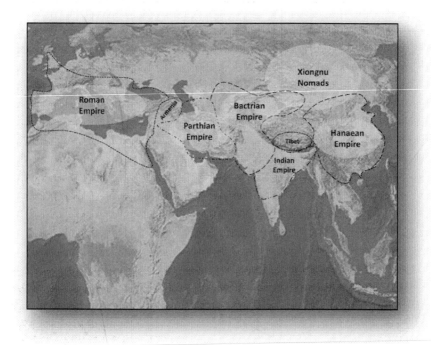

The World of 100AD

THE PAST IS PROLOGUE: CARRHAE, 53BC

Marcus Lucius, centurion of III Cohort, *Legio III Crassiana*, stood at attention, bareheaded in the blazing sun, hands bound behind his back. His mind struggled to find a way out, waiting their turn to die before a jeering mob of Parthian soldiers. No, not today. But how?

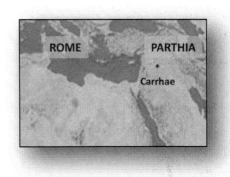

Marcus' heart swelled with pride for the doomed remnants of the shattered *III Cras*, formed up on the sands of Carrhae. Unable to wrest victory from the Parthians, they had chosen to show them how Roman soldiers die, with dignity and courage. To a man, the five hundred who had survived the battle had chosen last night to march to their execution, formed up in ranks with gaps marking the places where men and whole centuries no longer existed... all that remained of Marcus' cohort was less than fifty men, out of five hundred.

"Gods take the incompetent Marcus Licinius Crassus – he led us into this disaster," muttered the soldier behind him.

"Be still! This is not yet the end," Marcus hissed over his shoulder.

He heard the centurion of the last century of II Cohort, outwardly stoic, give a hoarse, choked order, the last he would ever give, and the crunch of feet on sand as his century marched forward, someone softly calling cadence. They halted, then went to their deaths eight at a time with barely a sob or a groan, presenting their necks on the gory chopping blocks to face their untimely end... no one begged for mercy. The heavy, coppery stench of blood clogged Marcus' nostrils as it pooled in front of the blocks, slowly soaking into the sand. The swish and thunk of the scimitars, the drone of flies gathering for the feast, and the mocking laughter of the Parthian soldiers filled his ears. He would soon have to give the men of III Cohort behind him their final order, to march forward and die.

He had no plan, but he was never very good at accepting inevitable fate. He considered his options as he toyed with the ropes binding his hands, to the sound of the butchery to his left. *I will not go like a lamb to the slaughter!*

When Marcus was a child, his father, a carpenter, had made him increasingly difficult puzzles where he had to free a key from a wooden block, or untangle rings that could not be disentangled. There wasn't a puzzle that Marcus hadn't been able to solve. They all began with one starting point somewhere, like the knot behind his back, and there wasn't a knot he couldn't untie. Even behind his back. The next move would then present itself. Like one of those puzzle boxes his father had made for him so long ago, the first piece fell into place as the knot loosened.

Marcus shivered from the horror, despite the sweat running down inside his baking leather corselet, drawn out by the merciless Syrian sun. His mind raced the beads of sweat down his back as he worried the knots binding his wrists. In the distance behind the Parthian soldiers, he could see the gold and blue canopy shading King Orodes from the sun as he observed the executions, accompanied by his senior officers and some foreign ones in unfamiliar battle gear.

One of the foreign soldiers stepped out from the canopy, the crowd of Parthians parting before him, his bright yellow cloak swirling in the hot wind. An obviously senior individual, a commander of some status. He came up to another foreign soldier on Marcus' left, by the Parthian officer observing the execution. By age and carriage Marcus determined that one to be something of a short and stocky centurion like himself, clad in blue, thickly quilted battle gear, wearing a black conical helmet. As the senior officer approached, the man presented his fists together stiffly before his face, and bowed his head low, holding it until the senior acknowledged him. A salute of sorts. Respectful, not subservient. His next move began to form.

Watching the foreign soldiers from the corner of his eye, he gave no hint as he worked the rope free from his wrists and dropped it to the ground. The soldier behind him subtly swept it away with his foot, not knowing Marcus' intentions. Indeed, Marcus himself wasn't sure. But as crazy as the half-made plan seemed, he couldn't remember a time when one of his plans had failed. He kept his head front, wrists still behind him.

The bearded Parthian officer strutted up to face Marcus Lucius, flanked by the two foreign soldiers, peculiar looking men with unfamiliar features: thin narrow eyelids perforated by dark eyes set in a bronze-colored skin. The senior man's yellow cloak had a fine sheen to it, unfamiliar to Marcus, with finely-detailed dragons embroidered on it.

It's time. Heart thudding, Marcus turned to the two foreigners and slammed his unbound hands together in front of him, as he had seen them do, and bowed deeply to the senior.

The Parthian officer gasped and took a step back in surprise, reaching for his sword, but the foreigner restrained the man's hand firmly and barked something unintelligible. The Parthian relented, glaring at Marcus. The foreign officer waited a moment, then acknowledged him with a grunt.

Marcus straightened up, returning the man's intense narrow-eyed gaze. The man said something in his own language, and Marcus said the first thing that came to his mind in return: *"Morituri te salutamus!"* We, who are about to die, salute you. The gladiators' salute. One of the soldiers behind him gave a choked laugh, which brought a smile to Marcus' lips, unbidden, his piercing blue eyes twinkling.

The foreign commander chuckled also, giving him a wry smile in turn, nodding his head several times in approval. He stepped back a few paces, summoning the Parthian and his subordinate to join him. They conversed intensely for several minutes while the executioners to Marcus' left lolled on their bloody swords, confused by the delay.

After a few minutes, the Parthian officer came back. Marcus was so focused on controlling his emotions that he missed the first few strongly-accented Latin words the Parthian officer spoke. "…yer Roman barstids! Look today yer lucky. Friends from east think yer worth more to them alive than dead. You and remaining soldiers march with them. Pack fer long walk!" He paused and looked into Marcus' eyes, almost smiling. "Crazy Roman barstid. Crazy brave Roman barstid!"

The paradigm had shifted, the executioners were dismissed and the remaining men were roughly unbound by grumbling Parthian soldiers. They marched themselves back to their encampment to eat and sleep for the first time in days. The next day, Marcus negotiated with the Parthians to retrieve their battle gear along with their cohort and century standards. He then ordered the remnants of III Cras to form up and march out of the death camp, re-equipped with a motley collection of damaged swords and ill-fitting blood-stained helmets, carrying their wounded on litters, led by a squadron of the foreign soldiers on horseback. They were heading somewhere east, he judged by the sun, not west and home to Rome, but they were alive and going as soldiers. Someone picked up their marching song, and the whole troop joined in:

Sive sequimur aquilas, sive progredimur ad cornices soli,
Nostra superbia est in legione
Et pugnans peditatus est domus genusque.

Whether we follow the eagles, or we go to the ravens alone,
Our pride is in the legion,
And the infantry is our family and home!

The verses quickly deteriorated to unofficial lyrics dealing with their officers, wine and women, amidst the rude gestures of the Parthian soldiers sending them off.

CHAPTER 1: ROME, 98AD

The sun shone through windows set high in the Senate's Curial House, creating shafts of sunlight in the dusty air. The sunlight reflected off the four-tiered blue-veined marble benches lining each side of the long walls, on which about a hundred senators sat, their chalk-whitened togas emblazoned with the wide purple laticlavian stripe of their rank.

On the top row sat Senator Aulus Aemilius Galba. Sweat dampened his tunic underneath the woolen toga in the July heat as he waited for the arrival of the *Princeps* and the diplomatic party, his mouth dry in anticipation. A large fly buzzed noisily near his head, trying but failing to distract him from his concerns. *This could be the day I lose my flagship and all that I have.* He thought of the clean lines of the *Aeneas,* her pleasant way on the waters. But she was in far-away Alexandria, mortgaged to the masthead to rent shipyard space a year in advance to construct her sister ships on the Red Sea, the note due in months. *And if this doesn't happen today, I can't pay it. Tens of millions of sesterces... I bet it all on this one deal. Bankrupt, I could lose my seat in the Senate, even our home.*

He thought of his new wife Livia. *Would she stay with me? Young and beautiful, she could do better than a bankrupt balding senator. She says she would stay... but maybe I should make it easy for her. Divorce her, return her dowry, let her start over with a better prospect.*

The *Princeps* should propose the funding today, and the mortgage will be paid. *Should! His staff assures me that he is enthusiastic about the plan, but none will make a commitment for him.*

Aulus sighed. *This is not the first time that I have bet everything on one throw of the dice. Everything that can be done has been done, deals made, bribes paid. If he proposes it, the Senate will pass it. The Fates will now determine the outcome.*

In the front wall, massive latticework doors stood partly open, admitting a view of the *Forum Romanum* below. Outside, trumpets blared to announce the *Princeps'* arrival. Aulus rose with the rest of the Senators to greet him as he entered, wearing a solid purple toga and accompanied by an administrative assistant in a white tunic, followed by twenty-four Praetorian Guardsmen acting as lictors. He took a seat on an ivory curule chair on a small dais, and the administrative assistant took his place by a basket of scrolls next to him. The Guardsmen took their places behind the dais, remaining at attention.

Aulus eyed the fifteen-foot marble statue of the Goddess of Victory, painted in life-like colors rising over the dais, holding aloft the olive branch crown in one hand and a sword in the other. *Wish me luck, my Lady Victory!*

Nine men and one woman, with eastern visages seldom seen in Rome, then entered, inexplicably wearing Roman garb, the men in plain white togas, the woman in a yellow *stola* ankle-length gown. They came to stand beside the *Princeps* on the dais.

Twenty other men from the Distant East, clad in multi-colored silk robes, hair bound up in black intricate buns, entered and smoothly rearranged themselves in two rows facing the *Princeps* Trajan. One man stepped forward and approached the dais. He brought his hands, concealed by the broad sleeves of his cloak, forcefully together in front of his deeply bowed head in a salute, and held that pose stoically until Trajan acknowledged with a slight nod. The man dropped his hands, head still bowed, and backed away. The group then seated themselves fluidly on the floor, cross-legged, their expressionless eyes respectfully focused downwards.

The *Princeps* stood straight as a lance, his slender face leathery from years in the field as a military commander.

"Conscript Fathers and the people of Rome! A century and a half ago, three of our valiant legions suffered a great tragedy at Carrhae, stricken from our military rolls after defeat by the Parthians, and believed wiped out to a man. But not all were wiped out. Some were taken to the land of the Han as mercenaries, to guard their far-flung borders. Those survivors took wives, and raised their children as Romans, however far from home they were. And their children, in turn, preserved among themselves their *Romanitas,* our language and our customs.

"Today, the Hanaean Emperor has honored us by sending our children back to us, as translators for his delegation seeking diplomatic association. Standing before you are the sons and daughters of Carrhae, accompanied by the representatives of their emperor. They have brought us a great gift!"

A military trumpet blew shrilly and drums began to beat as a contingent of Praetorian Guards marched stiffly into the Senate Curia, carrying four battered cohort standards on eight-foot poles, their *phalerae* battle awards long faded by time. The Guards halted in front of the dais and did an about-face, grounding the standards with a solid thud.

"I give you the standards of the lost cohorts of Carrhae, coming home with the descendants of the survivors who bore them!" The Senators applauded enthusiastically amid cries of "Hear, hear!"

As the tumult subsided, the emperor continued, turning to address the Roman-clad Hanaeans to his right. His administrative assistant turned to pick up eleven scrolls from the scroll basket by his side.

"Our administrators have researched your ancestors. They found each of them recorded in the rosters of the legion, all citizens of Rome. You are the descendants of those valiant soldiers, to the fifth and sixth generation. As the offspring of a citizen is a citizen by birth, I present to you official proof of citizenship, as *cives Romani.*"

His administrative aid opened and read the inscription. "To all, be it known that the above named person is a citizen of Rome, with all privileges and responsibilities thereto, given this day, *Princeps Senatus* Caesar Nerva Trajan, son of the Divine Nerva, the August and Most Capable Ruler." As the aide called out their names and ancestor, each of the toga-clad Orientals came forward to receive a scroll, with a handshake and an embrace from the most powerful man in Europe. The last man called was Marcus Lucius Quintus, then finally the woman, Marcia Lucia, both descendants of Marcus Lucius, Centurion of III Cohort. At the conclusion, the Senators again applauded enthusiastically.

The last scroll was for Gan Ying, the lead member of the Hanaean delegation, who rose, walked to the center of the hall to stand stiffly, eyes expressionless, mouth downturned, head slightly bowed. The scroll was read, certifying that Gan Ying and his party were representatives of the Hanaean emperor and under the personal protection of the Senate and the People of Rome. One of the togate Hanaeans on the dais translated the reading into the peculiar sing-song language of the Hanaeans. Gan Ying then stepped forward and approached the dais. He once again saluted with his hands before him, head bowed, until the *Princeps* nodded again in acknowledgment. Gan Ying stood upright and stepped onto the dais to accept his scroll. He then stepped off and backed away, to resume his place on the floor at the head of the delegation.

Trajan continued: "Please be seated." There was a rustling of clothing as the Senators rearranged their bulky togas to take their seats. "As you all know, a member of our august body has been actively seeking to expand our Indian Ocean trade with a new class of merchant ships that will carry more goods faster and farther than any ship has done before. He has been seeking the backing of the Treasury of Rome for this venture."

This is it! It is happening!

"Senator Aulus Aemilius Galba, could your ships, if built, make the passage directly to the Hanaean lands?"

Aulus leaped back to his feet. "The gods willing, yes!"

"The sons and daughters of Rome have come a long way to us to represent their mothers' country. Would you be willing to carry them back, to represent in turn their fathers' country?"

"Yes!"

"Then let it be proposed before the Senate, that funding should be provided to launch this effort!" For the third time, the senators applauded amid cries of "Hail, Trajan!" The motion passed and Galba exhaled deeply.

The Fates had been kind today.

CHAPTER 2: THE JOURNEY BEGINS, 100AD

Gaius Lucullus, prefect of the First Cohort, entered the headquarters tent to meet with the *legatus* commander. He was unsure why he had been summoned, but he hoped that it would deal with a proposed meeting of the eastern legions in Byzantium. Such meetings were rare due to the great distances and long

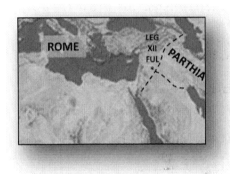

absences. As senior tribune of the *Legio XII Fulminata*, he was certain to accompany *legatus* Lucius Julius Maximus, or even represent him alone. The trip would take him halfway to Italia, and he could certainly argue for another month or so to visit his wife and family in Neapolis.

The guards saluted crisply, right hand across the chest, and his eyes adjusted slowly from the noonday brilliance of the desert to the dim lamp-lit interior. The headquarters tent was spartan, even ascetic. A curtained partition separated the consul's living quarters from the main body of the tent that served as office and command center. The *legatus* sat in a simple canvas campaign chair behind a desk of rough-cut wood, a wax tablet in his hands, clad in a plain white tunic with the broad purple stripe of a senator.

"Your Excellency," Gaius said, softly interrupting the *legatus* from his reading.

"My good Gaius, do come in, come in. I am pleased to have your company this morning," he said, putting down the wax tablet. The *legatus* rose, welcoming him with a warm handshake and ushering him to one of two chairs facing the desk. Having seen Gaius to his seat, the *legatus* seated himself, legs crossed, arms across his chest, an air of informality.

"Have you picked your delegates to the Byzantium meeting, your Excellency?" Gaius asked, almost immediately regretting his abrupt over-eagerness.

"I have. The tribunes Livius Osculus and Porcius Tullus will be going in my stead," said Lucius Julius with a slight smile.

Gaius nodded, swallowing hard to hide his disappointment. They were junior to him, but going as the legate's representatives. Perhaps if he had not asked so hastily?

"I didn't know you were related to a Senator," Lucius Julius said with a smile.

"That would be Aulus," Gaius paused, and then tacked on the full name to avoid the appearance of name-dropping. "...Aemilius Galba. He married my cousin Livia two years ago, so we are related by marriage. I hope he is not trying to post me to the Praetorian Guards," answered Gaius.

The *legatus* laughed. "You are too straightforward to do well in that posting. Has he hinted at that?"

"More than hinted," answered Gaius, relieved. "He suggested that he could arrange it last year when I was home in Neapolis with my wife Camilla and the children. But Praetorian Guardsmen are political pretty boys, not soldiers."

"Unfortunately, most of them are, and you don't want to turn your back on the ones that aren't. But the Senator has something better in mind for you." He slid the expensively-filigreed black wax tablet across the desk to Gaius.

Gaius picked it up and recognized Aulus' meticulous uncial script. He read the usual florid greetings between two senior people who didn't know each other, then stopped to read and re-read the last paragraph.

"You find it interesting?" asked the *legatus*.

"Hmm... I don't know where to start to ask questions."

The *legatus* retrieved a small bottle from the drawer of the deck. "It's not yet noon, but would you care for some wine?" he asked, offering the tribune a brass goblet. "I doubt if I could answer them, but go ahead."

"Yes, thank you, your Excellency," said Gaius, accepting the goblet while the *legatus* filled it, though uneasy about the unexpected familiarity.

"How is the wine? It is a local vintage."

The wine had a tart taste, most refreshing. "Very fine, your Excellency. But let me assure you," Gaius said with a chuckle, "I seldom indulge this early in the day!"

"I thought you would find his offer interesting. You have heard of the *Hanae*?"

"I have, but what is fantasy, what is real... I don't know."

Lucius Julius rose and walked over to a fine map finished in fine gold and rich colors, covering all of Europe from Britain to Judea, and on eastward to India. And beyond India, still further, and from the Hyperborean north far south into Africa. Gaius recognized the Mediterranean coastline, but that familiar part of the map seemed disturbingly small and far to the left. He pointed out the distant easternmost boundaries of the map.

"Gaius, the *Hanae* are very real," he said, "and they control an empire located about here. I presume you have bought some silk, or have at least seen it?" asked Lucius Julius. Gaius nodded. "The *Hanae* make silk. From, of all things, some sort of spider or insect, it is rumored. We trade indirectly with them for that and for many other things, by ship through India." His finger traced the route on the map. "A long trip, but not too bad, the sailors say. Our traders tell us that the *Hanae* are our equals in art and science, population and size of territory. We expect they are militarily strong as well. We need to know more about these people. They may be potential allies, to serve as the anvil to Rome's hammer against the Parthians. On the other hand, it might be better if Parthia and ourselves settled our grievances to ally together against the *Hanae*, as they might be more formidable than either of us alone. We don't know. In any event, only a few thousand miles separate our borders now. That gap could close in our lifetime." Lucius Julius returned to his seat, and took another sip of wine. "You've had an excellent career so far. Risen to cohort command, elected tribune of soldiers by the men. That's quite an honor. The troops do not pick their leaders because of family connections. A gifted fighter, leader, and orator, with extensive experience in combat. Senator Aulus Aemilius is offering you an opportunity for you to master new skills in diplomacy and politics."

Gaius' heart sank. "Your Excellency, politicians make poor soldiers and soldiers make poor politicians. The two are incompatible."

"Nonsense, Gaius. As a legion commander, politics will be your business. As a field officer, you have been trained to fight. As a potential commander, we must teach you when not to fight. We maintain our empire with just thirty-six legions," Lucius Julius sighed. "And almost all in the wrong place at the wrong time. The legions hold the Empire together with politics, the art of the possible, the science of perceptions. We use force when necessary, like we did thirty years ago to put down the Judaean rebellion. That message was not lost on our Parthian friends, who had helped instigate the uprising."

He paused, then continued in a softer tone, "But for every display of force, we have to manage our forces to make fighting unnecessary, and guarantee that any fights we do take on will be victories. That way we look invincible, even when we are vulnerable. And that is the job of the commander, Gaius." The legate lowered his voice still further, sounding almost fatherly.

"The Senator needs you to accompany him to grasp the military and technical aspects of this mission, to learn how the Hanaeans handle armies, organize their cities. In short, you will be a soldier, a scholar and a spy. So, again, do you find his offer interesting?"

Gaius was flattered and interested at his nomination to be his cousin's military aide, but the task was clearly daunting. "Yes, your Excellency. How long would this mission be?"

"It is hard to say, Gaius, but I would expect it to be two or three years."

Gaius' heart fell, the idea of a family visit becoming more and more remote.

"Aulus Aemilius expects me in Alexandria around the Ides of March. Do you know when he expects to leave?"

"You will have to ask him that when you get there."

Nothing to negotiate! Getting to Alexandria by then would mean weeks of hard riding, and it will be unlikely that he will give me two or three months to go to Neapolis. Three years cut off from Camilla. So bargain hard, make him give me a reason to turn this down.

"Aulus… Senator Aulus Aemilius asked for me and such as may accompany me. How large a group might I take?"

"A small group. Two, to be precise. You and one of your choosing. That's all I can spare. Do you have anyone in mind?"

"I have one man, your Excellency, that I insist accompany me. That man is Antonius Aristides."

"Aristides! The *primus pilus*? Not only am I losing you, my best cohort commander, but the legion's first lance as well! From the same cohort! Why him? Why not one of the younger tribunes?"

"We have served together since I was a green subaltern on the Danube. I see things from the commander's perspective. He sees things from the soldier's perspective. I need one person that I can trust totally. He is that person."

"Well, I hope we don't have any action here the next year or so while we put the First Cohort back in order. Very well." The legate scribbled on the scroll on his desk, then dropped a glob of hot wax onto it and sealed it with his iron senatorial ring. He picked it up and blew on it to cool it. "Very well. I have inked in both your names to the imperial order assigning you this task." He passed the scroll to Gaius. "You may now read your orders."

Gaius accepted the scroll, the highest quality Augustan papyrus, reading quickly: *From Caesar Nerva Trajan… skip all the titles…* Legatus *Gaius Lucullus… what,* legatus? *Must be a mistake! Accompany the Senator Aulus Aemilius Galba, and proceed to the kingdom of the Hanae… assist him in his actions as my personal emissary… my greetings and best wishes to the King of all the Hanae… two talents of gold* as *my personal token of respect.* Gaius calculated in his head, about five hundred thousand *sesterces. It is the intent of the Senate and the people of Rome to gain in mutual knowledge of each other's lands, cultures and language… our two kingdoms to be united forever in friendship. Report to me personally upon your return. Given this day, the Nones of February, in the Eight Hundred and Fifty Third year of the founding of the City of Rome, Caesar Nerva Traianus, Imperator Senatus Consulto, etc., etc…*

At the bottom was the flourishing signature of the Emperor himself, and his personal seal. At the left was the *legatus'* signature and seal.

"Very well. Do you accept these orders, Gaius Lucullus?"

Gaius' thoughts whirled in his head, delaying his response. *Imperial orders signed by Trajan? That is way above my cousin's wax tablet letter request. And promotion to legate! I don't think I ever had any choice in this matter. But Camilla? My being gone so long?*

"Y..Yes, your Excellency!"

"Very well. You are now a *legatus* without a legion, but if you have any success, I am sure we can find you one. Just remember, there are no posthumous commands, so try not to get killed along the way!" Lucius Julius chuckled. "Don't worry, this looks like an easy trip. See the *librarii* clerks on the way out. They will prepare your promotion to legate, and imperial orders to requisition supplies and transportation as needed. Check in with Quintus Albus, the legate of the *III Cyrenaica* in Alexandria. My correspondence will go through him, so no loose ends due to missed mail. Keep me posted on your itinerary as far as Sabaiae.

"Good luck, Gaius. Oh, and one more thing... I wish I were twenty years younger. I'd make the trip myself!"

They shook hands, then Gaius Lucullus turned briskly to depart the *Praetorium* for the *officia,* where the *librarii* clerks had already prepared the promotion, properly sealed, travel money and a year's advance pay totaling twenty thousand *sesterces.*

Antonius was dozing on his bunk in the centurions' tent when Gaius patted his boot to awaken him. "Special assignment on imperial orders, Antonius. You're going with me to the land of the Hanaeans as my aide-de-camp," he said grinning, knowing the reaction he would get.

He got it. Antonius hurled himself erect, wide-eyed at the news. "Begging yer pardon, sir, but yer have signed me on as what? Where?" The centurion fumed, angry and confused at leaving a prestigious position for some political adventure about which he knew nothing. "This legion is fallin' apart an' here we are skippin' off ter visit some mythical land? On imperial orders, no less? Me young tribune, people get their heads lifted from their shoulders muckin' about with politics they don't understand. Yer free ter go, of course, and the gods go with ye, but why take me? I got no head fer that work. Me, I'm a straight-talking, sword-slinging, foot-sloggin', mud-lovin', whoremongerin' soldier what's got two years to me *diploma* an' me equestrianship. Beggin' yer pardon, but please let me stay on here and turn these miserable ragamuffins into soldiers of the Empire. I was just gettin' the hang of talkin' with these Judaeans an' Syrians. Yer don' want me muckin' up some court floor with me muddy shoes. I'd be an embarrassment ter yer, *tribunus*." Antonius' Latin grew even coarser when he was upset.

Gaius Lucullus smiled at the centurion's consternation. "Go on with yourself, Antonius. I wouldn't expect so much noise if I had asked you to crucify yourself. You just named all the good reasons why I want you along.

You're a straight-talking, sword-swinging, foot-slogging soldier. Just what I need. I do regret having signed you onto this journey without telling you about it. But I had about as much choice in these orders then as you do now. The *legatus* was nicer about it, of course, *Senatus Populusque Romanum* SPQR stuff, but in the end, the ambassador had picked me to fulfill these imperial orders and I was going whether I liked it or not. Oh, and promoted me to *legatus* to sweeten it. So in fine Roman army tradition, *profluit ex satio,* it has all flowed downhill. Who are you going to pick for the new *primus pilus?*"

Primus pilus, the "first lance", was the senior centurion of the legion, the most coveted position a humble foot soldier could hope for. He represented his soldiers, supervised their training, and advised commanders on tactics. He was loved and feared by the troops, despised and needed by the officers. The first lance was critical to the legion. Antonius took this responsibility seriously, and if he had to give it up, he would give it up to someone capable.

"Well, it ain't goin' ter be me *optio* second in charge, *legatus*," said Antonius, accepting the inevitable. "Lad don't have the backbone ter take on the orficers on their own terms. Maybe more experience, he be strong enough, but not yet. Maybe Lucius Ratullus, in Third Cohort..."

Gaius Lucullus smiled and left the crusty Greek centurion to his devices. *This could be good for Antonius. This assignment really doesn't look particularly difficult. Language will be the biggest problem, but other than that, we will be going in with official paperwork, representatives of Rome. Espionage can get one killed, but if it we limit ourselves to watching troops train, and maybe observing a few real battles, that isn't quite the same as riffling through secret files or meddling in court intrigues. Maybe start a dictionary and grammar, some maps, some names. And bring all this back to the emperor in a nice report. Antonius could figure prominently in the report and retire properly with a nice bonus. He deserves more than just forty acres in some barren place no one else could farm.*

But what about Camilla and the children?

CHAPTER 3: THE BULL AND THE DOVE

Gaius Lucullus and Antonius rode with a *vexillatio* detachment of cavalry to Alexandria from Syria. They arrived in the early morning, skirting the city walls on their way to the fort west of the city where the *Legio III Cyrenaica* was garrisoned.

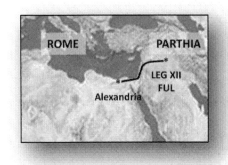

"Seems a shame not ter at least go through the city after three weeks of travelin'" muttered Antonius, watching the low walls roll by on his right.

"I think after three weeks of traveling, if this *vexillatio* went in the east gate, it might be hard to get them out the west gate and on the road again," said Gaius, grinning. "It's been a long trip."

"Worst was Judea. You'd think if yer'd lost the war as bad as they did thirty years ago, they'd not keep tryin' ter fight on. Bandits and rebels! Me shoulder blades was itching, thinkin' I was goin' ter stop an arrow with 'em!"

"Well, that was why we didn't go alone," said Gaius with a wry grin.

After another hour, the stone fort came into view. Riding in through the gates, they exchanged amused glances about the lax security.

"Guards saluted us, *legatus,* but they never asked who we was nor what we was doin'," quipped Antonius, scowling.

"I guess you just come and go as you please here. Rough life here in the *III Cyr*, stuck on the outskirts of 'the Pearl of the Mediterranean.' Let's check in with the *librarii* at the headquarters *officia* over there," said Gaius with a wry smile.

They dropped off their well-worn horses for a much-needed rest at the livery, conveniently next to the *officia*. Antonius arranged for fresh mounts for tomorrow, then they walked over to the building. "Let's get checked in and refreshed. I am going to the *praetorium* across the street to make an appointment with the *legatus*. Let's get together after lunch and I'll let you know the schedule."

"Right, sir! I'll be stayin' at the centurions' quarters. I got some former messmates from the Danube there, if they're still here."

"To be sure," replied Gaius. "Have your parade dress kit laid out handy, I will let you know when our meeting with the *legatus* will be then. Hopefully not today, and certainly not in this traveling gear."

They checked in, apparently expected when they identified themselves. Antonius was given a shell inscribed with a number to identify his bunk in his quarters, and headed off, lugging his gear. Gaius was given a swarthy Egyptian slave, clad only in a white linen kilt, to carry his baggage and escort him to his quarters. They made a brief stop at the *praetorium* across the fort's main east-west street, the slave waiting outside. There Gaius found mail waiting for him, another one of Aulus' elegant wax tablets, and most importantly, a letter from his wife Camilla, written on expensive paper, scented with her perfume and rolled in a tube, sealed with the family crest. And mercifully, the young soldier informed him that the *III Cyr legatus* was with the governor in Alexandria, and would not be available till mid-morning tomorrow. On a whim, Gaius got directions for the Library in the city. "Easy to find, sir, just follow the camp road to the Moon Gate on the western side. The big highway inside they call the Canopic Way, the Library is a huge columned building, maybe a quarter-mile on the right, opposite the Temple of Poseidon," said the young soldier. "Can't miss it, it's a popular spot. I like to read the Greek love poems."

Gaius smiled and nodded at the lad. Some Greek love poetry could get pretty explicit, and he suspected that appealed as much to the soldier as did its iambic pentameter.

In his quarters, he changed from his dusty battle gear worn the past several weeks, the leather dark with sweat and salt-stained, the helmet and body armor in need of polishing. He handed them to the slave, and slipped his sweat-soaked tunic over his head to add that to the pile in the man's arms. The slave nodded wordlessly and left to tend to his gear.

Gaius went to the fort's bath area, took a massage from another Egyptian slave in the pool area, then returned to his room, clad only in a towel. He snagged an apple from a bowl of various fruits and sat down on his bed to read his correspondence. Aulus' wax tablet was inscribed with directions to his villa on the west of town, fortuitously also on the camp road. He wanted Gaius to join him at sunset on the night he arrived. And the Twelfth had thoughtfully passed on the letter from Camilla, forwarded in Maximus' own handwriting.

He was slow to open his wife's letter. He opened his locket to gaze at a tiny miniature painting of Camilla, not two inches across. It captured her carefully-done blonde hair and shy smile. It was his most valuable possession, done at great cost during his last extended time home. He hadn't been home since then, a year and a half ago.

He finally unrolled Camilla's letter and read it. She was her usual effervescent self, going on about the children and their progress. Gaius Secundus was almost ten, and making great progress in oratory and Greek. Lucia Luculla was eight and a terrible tomboy. Gaius started to compose an answer, but decided to wait to ask Aulus about a trip home before departure. Three years! He hoped he might be back before his son turned fourteen and donned his man's toga.

Antonius checked in, refreshed himself and changed into a light white tunic. He then went to find the Third's travel clerks. He had begun some research on this area before detaching from the Twelfth. Each legion's *librarii* maintained, among everything else in their files, maps, travel reports, travelers' and merchants' accounts of various areas near their area of responsibility. While the Red Sea was far removed from the Twelfth's area, the legion was responsible for providing *vexillatio* detachments for security at the customs entry point at Coptos and the two main Red Sea ports, Myos Hormos and Berenice, and had all the necessary information to get them there. Antonius chuckled to himself, as he thought of the riff-raff the Twelfth had scraped up to meet their annual commitment of a century of troops to support them. Both ports had naval squadrons stationed there. Piracy was a day-to-day occurrence in the Red Sea, attracted by the gold and silver going out and valuable trade goods coming in. Antonius wondered what sort of security would be on the ship, what sort of weapons? Perhaps he should think about helping train the crew? Questions to ask later. Right now, he wanted to confirm what he learned in Syria with local information, and get a feel for booking passage on the Red Sea, if perhaps their ships were elsewhere.

Antonius approached a *librarius*. "Lad, I'd like ter be getting' information on shippin' through the Red Sea."

The *librarius*, a blond-headed youth of perhaps nineteen, did not appear to shave regularly as yet. But he came alert at Antonius' words, looking up from the pile of wax tablets on his small desk. "Are you embarking at Myos Hormos or Berenice?" he asked.

"I don't know yet," answered Antonius.

"We can get you up the Nile and overland to either port. We have passes for the Imperial Post riverboats as far as Thebes, then caravan passes across the desert on the new road. You can make your own arrangements, of course, but this is safest, fastest and cheapest. It's how we keep up the garrisons there."

"What about shipping out from there ter, say, Sabaea?" asked Antonius.

"You're pretty much on your own for that, sir. What few troopers as come and go there, go by way of the merchants. Go down to the Western Harbor, and find the Tavern of the Bull and Dove. Bull and Dove is at, lessee, the Street of the Lampmakers and Avenue of Astarte. Sort of behind the temple of Poseidon, about three blocks. Just ask. Everyone knows where it is. The merchants hang out there and they have some sailing schedules posted. The best of the lot is Hasdrubal, a convoy master from Tyre. *III Cyr* tries to make most of their arrangements through him. He's expensive but supposed to be first-class..."

"Anyone to avoid?"

"A devil named Ibrahim bin Yusuf. Unfortunately, no one seems to know just what he looks like, except he's pock-marked. Been wanted since before I was born, and the price on his head gets bigger every year. Took four passengers on a little outing south of here on the Red Sea a few months back. Of course, they never did make their destination. The men were found floating off the beach, face down; the other two was wife and daughter to one of them, never seen again. Probably slaves to some Bedouin now. They was a patrician family, too. Real high-born. If you hear the name, just let the urban cohort know right away, though he's almost certain not to be seen in a place like the Bull and Dove."

"Keep it in mind. I be off now."

"Well, when you get more information I can get you there easily. Good luck downtown."

A niggling doubt intruded in Antonius' mind. *It almost seemed like he knew exactly what to tell me, as though he had rehearsed just that answer. Who, what, when, where. But no, he is just a young enthusiastic lad, wantin' ter show off what he knew.*

Antonius knocked on the door, interrupting Gaius' revery. Gaius opened the door, still wearing just the towel, and Antonius immediately noticed his sad expression. "Excuse me, sir, did I interrupt somethin'? Yer lookin' glum, sir. Bad news?" he asked with a look of concern; Gaius seldom allowed bad emotions to show.

"Oh, no, Antonius, concerned about my family, that's all. I won't be seeing them for a while." He cleared his throat. "We have an appointment with the *legatus* at mid-morning tomorrow, and Senator Aulus Aemilius would like us to meet him at his country *taberna* this evening. In the meanwhile, I thought I would visit the Library here. An opportunity to learn something about the Hanaeans there, I am sure. Would you care to join me?" He seemed to be regaining his usual good humor.

"I'll be checkin' on some travel things in Alexandria, sir, or I'd be glad ter join yer. But we can ride in an' back tergether. As fer the Senator, such things make me uncomfortable, I think I'll just return to the fort, if yer don't mind."

"Nonsense, Antonius. The three of us are going to spend a lot of time together for the next year or two, so you might as well meet him now as later. You'll find him a most affable sort of person." Gaius shrugged on a fresh white tunic.

Antonius grumped, but acquiesced.

They walked over to the stables to check out horses and set out for Alexandria, the fresh cool sea breeze in sharp contrast to the broiling desert heat that they had endured in body armor for the eight hundred mile trek from the Twelfth's camp.

"So you think you'll learn something about the Hanaeans at the Library, sir?" he asked Gaius as they rode along.

"They have hundreds of thousands of books, from every language. If it's written down, it's in there."

"And if yer can find it, sir." Antonius chuckled.

"Yes, and I am hoping they have assistants for that."

"Just be careful how many questions yer ask, sir. Someone might notice, someone we don't want ter meet."

"To be sure. Good counsel, centurion."

Alexandria loomed into view shortly, alabaster white against the deep Mediterranean blue, its famous lighthouse on Pharos towering over the city. As they watched, the top of the lighthouse flashed briefly but brilliantly, and within a minute, it flashed again, and then again, piquing Gaius' curiosity. "I wonder how it does that?"

"Don't be knowin' sir, but they got real marvels here, temple doors what open by themselves, some little steam engine that spins so fast yer can't see it."

They entered the western Moon Gate to the Canopic Way, the two mile colonnaded thoroughfare through the center of the city. The main thoroughfare was easily fifty paces wide, broader by far than the most spacious avenue in Rome, with carts, wagons and horses, and an occasional camel, proceeding with an order that would never be found on a Roman street. Opposite the Library, they found a livery for the horses.

"All right, Antonius, you go your way - what did you say, the Bull and the Dove? – and I'll go across the street to the Library. Be back here about sunset."

"Right, sir and enjoy yer visit."

Antonius dived into the city stews north of the Canopic Way. He had not liked turning down Gaius' offer to join him in the visit to the great Library. But he was Gaius' centurion, and first things first... he had to get a feel for the details of the first part of the journey, let the *legatus* deal with what they would find when they got there.

The streets were narrower by far than the broad thoroughfares of the 'uptown' Alexandria, and not paved. Water from discarded baths, night pots and the gods only knew what else, pooled in muddy puddles in the streets. Drunks staggered across the streets or dozed in alleyways, although it was just after noon. Vendors hawked their wares under tents in many languages... some Antonius understood, some he recognized, and some he had never heard before. He rounded one corner onto Astarte Street, and two men erupted from the doorway of a bar, landing in the fetid mud with a splash. As a crowd gathered, they both came to their feet facing off against each other with short daggers. On the periphery of the crowd, he heard men begin to take bets on the two... "The short fat one, five to one. I've seen him fight..."

Antonius pressed on, not glancing backward at the sounds of the fight. Further up the street, women of every race were propositioning passers-by from the balconies of apartments on either side of the street, ranging in age from barely children to well past matronly, from flaxen-haired Germanic-looking *maadchen* to ebony Nubians. Well, at least he could tell Lucullus that he got in to see the whorehouse district.

At last the neighborhood improved a bit as the alley opened out onto the Street of the Lampmakers. The peddlers in human flesh and misery gave way to vendors in pearls, wine, glassware and fine cloths. A shabby merchants' *taberna* loomed into view, a wooden signboard with a faded painting of a bull and a once-white dove announcing it as the Bull and Dove.

Antonius entered the swinging door, his eyes blinking in the dark. He took a rough chair by a table near the rear. This kept his back to the wall, and his eyes on the bar and the front door. Next to him was a rough curtain of dark cloth, that might once have been red, and in the candlelight behind, servant girls washed dishes. The smell of charcoal and cooking mingled with stale wine and Egyptian barley beer. To his left, some well-dressed men in Arabic garb argued explosively in Aramaic two tables over, their hands gesticulating violently. Other patrons in shabby garb sat alone or in small quiet groups, one fondling a girl who appeared to be a professional.

"Wine or beer?" a servant asked, giving the table a perfunctory wipe with a filthy rag.

"Wine. Watered by half." *Keep yer wits about yer. This place smells like trouble.*

"Sure." The servant, a skinny type from somewhere in Asia Minor, returned with a bowl of red wine, Egyptian style. Antonius tossed some copper coins on the table. "I understand this is the place to come for shipping information," asked Antonius.

"Shipen... Inform? No speak...much Greek."

"That's all right. Nothing." *The boy just speaks enough Greek to serve the customers,* Antonius growled to himself. "All right," he repeated again in Aramaic, waving him off. *Should have spent more time learning that accursed Aramaic. This don't seem like much of a merchants' shipping office, just yer basic dive. Think the kid just steered me wrong. I'll just have some wine and move on to see the sights in town. Shoulda gone ter the Library.*

A weasely-looking man slipped out of the shadows, and took a seat opposite him at the table, uninvited. "Looking for shipping information, are you, my Lordship?" He said in Greek, with a rasping Nabataean accent.

"Off with you. I am just enjoying some afternoon wine," Antonius replied.

"I can get you a day trip for you and girlfriend. I can get you girlfriend if you have not. Very romantic… and cheap."

"Not interested. Bugger off!" Antonius was getting distinctly annoyed. *Weedlers like this are tryin' ter set yer up fer bein' robbed or kilt.* He put his hand on his dagger, loosening the strap on the thigh sheath.

One of the well-dressed men who had been arguing loudly turned slightly to watch the exchange. Dressed in the thick white robes of the Arabian style, he had a green headcloth which draped to his shoulders, an intricately braided headband holding it place. He barked something to the weasel in a language Antonius did not recognize; the weasel gave him an irritated look and scuttled off to find someone else to annoy.

The man turned to Antonius and smiled widely. "My apologies to you, great sir. Such scum bring great disgrace on the good merchants here at the Bull and Dove." He spoke nearly flawless Greek, with the slightest of accents that was difficult to place.

Antonius was only slightly grateful. More than once, he had seen such weasels used to earn someone's trust in such situations, trusts quickly betrayed.

"He paddled off quickly when you challenged him. He must know you. Are you in the shipping business?" inquired Antonius.

"I own but a few antiquated craft that ply only the safest of waters. But I would be happy to put these vessels at your disposal, if it is within my capability to ascertain your destination."

"I get seasick easily. I actually was just sightseeing, and this looked like a place for a quiet bowl of wine. A cut above the places on Astarte Street."

"Are you with the *III Cyrenaica*?"

"What makes you think I am under the eagles?"

The Arab laughed pleasantly. "You are either in the army, or you are a gladiator, and that is not a popular sport here in Alexandria. Or maybe an oarsman on a trireme. No one else has such a physique! And judging by your age, I would expect you to be a centurion, maybe a senior one. I know most of the Third's centurions, and don't recognize you, so I presume you are new. May I refill your bowl to welcome you to the finest city in the world?"

"You're very observant. I'll take another bowl, watered, please."

"So from where do you hail?"

This guy is good, too good. A Parthian spy, perhaps? "Up north. Vindebona on the Danube in Noricum with the *XX Gemina*." *All the better for being partly true. Just not recently. Skip the more recent tour opposite Dura Europos on the Syrian border.*

"I understand it is quite cold up there."

"In the winter. Sometimes cold enough to freeze the river over. But the summers are nice. Rough country, the mountains come right down to the river's edge, thickly forested on both sides."

"When did you arrive?" asked the Arab.

"Just yesterday. But forgive my rudeness. I have quite forgotten your name." *Forgot nothing! The bastard never gave it, just been pumpin' me for information.*

"Oh, but please forgive me. It was I who forgot to introduce myself, I am Ibrahim."

Antonius went cold inside and struggled to bring his breathing under control, not betraying his recognition of this name. "It is a pleasure to meet you, sir." In the dim light, he could make out a pock-marked face behind the wiry gray and white beard. Somehow, he had expected someone more obviously evil, more like the denizens of Astarte Street, than this urbane and obviously highly-educated Arab. And he certainly hadn't expected him to give his real name. No wonder this man had so easily lured a patrician family to their death. *If he was this man, if that story were true.* His mind spun, as he sought a way out of this dilemma. His senses tingled, remembering what the lad had said: *Go to the Bull and Dove. Find Hasdrubal and avoid Ibrahim. Had that innocent-looking lad just set him up, and for what purpose?*

"And your friend?" asked Antonius, nodding at the second man at Ibrahim's table.

"He is a fellow merchant, but wishes to remain anonymous. We are supposed to be competitors, but sometimes we collaborate on the side. It would not matter to you, but walls have ears in this place. You understand, I hope." The second man looked at Antonius and nodded politely, saying nothing.

Antonius took the man's face in at a glance, while trying not to appear to pay him too much attention. *It may be important to remember what Ibrahim's anonymous friend looked like. Black beard, dark hard eyes, square leathery face, like someone who spent a lot of time in the sun. Fortyish, medium build and stout, not gone to fat. Cowl covering his head, apparently not wanting to be recognized.*

"And you are...?" asked Ibrahim.

"Antonius." He had to offer him something to keep the conversation going, then find a reason for getting the hell out of here and back to the safety of the camp, without revealing his suspicion of the man's identity. "Forgive my evasiveness, my good Ibrahim. I wished to know with whom I spoke. How did you come to be such a wealthy merchant prince?" *When in doubt, flatter. And Greek is such a good language for flattery.*

"My father was a sailor, who died several years ago leaving me my poor flotilla."

"So.... to where do you sail?"

"Here and there. I carry people and cargo as best as I can handle."

"Any trouble with pirates?"

Ibrahim's eyes grew sharp as he returned Antonius' gaze. "No more than any other merchant. I have lost some ships and crews, of course. Most sad," said Ibrahim with a smile.

"Some passengers, too?" *Watch his reaction.*

"There have been some passengers lost, yes."

"On one of your ships?"

"No, on a colleague's ships. Very sad. A lot of attention from the authorities on us poor merchants, as though this were our fault."

"Hmm, sure did attract attention. Especially since they were a very high-born family, close friends and relatives of Trajan himself." *A crock of manure, that bluff. Will he buy it?* "Understand the emperor was real put out. Wants to know what's going on down here in Alexandria, personal report and all." *Give the line a good tug, see if he bought it.*

The waiter came up, noting Antonius' empty bowl. "Another, sir?"

Antonius affected a small slur to his speech. "Yes. But this will be my last, as my purse is running low and I must be back in camp by nightfall." *Pretend to get a little drunk, then give him a reason to let me walk out of here alive. Hm, yes, maybe this will work.*

"Oh, do not worry, my good Antonius. It would give me great pleasure to buy you this next bowl." The Arab laid a leather bag on the table. Several silver *denarii* spilled out through the bulging open mouth. He casually picked out four *denarii* with his fingertips and separated them from the rest. When the waiter returned with the bowl, he slid them across the table. "This bowl is on me, for Antonius, my good Roman friend. So…when may this report go out?"

"No idea… I just got here, and picked this up from conversations with my messmates today. Expect a lot more attention, especially if any more Romans start disappearing around here." *There, that might let me get back safe. Or not.* Antonius finished his bowl of wine, noting that it was not watered, then stood up. "I need to be getting back."

"Please sit down again, Antonius. At least let me buy you another drink. Waiter! another!" he gestured at the skinny servant, sliding more *denarii* across the table.

Alaia jacta est. The die is cast. If he buys this crock, I get to see daylight tomorrow, and explain all of this to Lucullus. Or wind up in some Alexandrian alley, my purse and dagger gone, my throat cut, no one knowing what happened to me.

Ibrahim sat silently, stroking his beard, his eyes turned inward for a moment.

"No, thank you, my good friend Ibrahim, I must be back before sundown. By the sun's angle, there's perhaps an hour's worth of daylight left."

Ibrahim rose with him, bowing to him graciously with his arms spread wide in supplication. A huge gold chain around his neck swung free, glinting in the late sun streaming through the door. "It is a pleasure to talk with one as astute as yourself. I look forward to our next meeting."

"As do I. Such time as we get together again."

To his great relief, Ibrahim accepted his departure, and Antonius affected a stagger as he rolled unsteadily to the door.

"Would you like someone to accompany you? The back streets of Alexandria can be dangerous for the unwary stranger."

"Uh, no, thanks. I'm a rough, tough centurion, built like a bull. I'll be fine."

As Antonius left, Ibrahim returned to his seat scowling. He snapped his fingers at the weasel who had first accosted Antonius and said, in Aramaic, "Yakov! Go thou and be as a shadow to yonder man. If he not depart to *III Cyrenaica's* encampment..." he drew his finger beneath his bearded throat.

"So be it, master." Yakov rose and slipped out the door.

"What makest thou of that man?" whispered the other man about the table, hiding his face in his brown cowl.

"I do not yet know. He was not drunk, therefore he is a liar. Yet some parts of his story may be true. And if parts are true, then perhaps the part about the report also. What fate can place that report in my hands?"

"You shall have it, the gods willing!"

CHAPTER 4: THE LIBRARY

The Library was a massive four-story building two blocks long by four wide, finished in exquisite white marble with a broad granite stairway leading up to a tall colonnade. *A temple of the soul of man*, thought Gaius, as he walked up the steps to enter into its cool interior, brightly lit by windows high in the roof.

Gaius halted just inside the doors and looked around in awe. Ten huge well-lit rooms, each framed by green marble columns, divided the library, each room dedicated to a specific discipline of learning carved into the massive white marble sill over its entrance: geometry, logic, mathematics, astronomy, history, rhetoric, grammar, physics, mechanics, and medicine. Within each room, he could see stack after stack of pigeon-holes lining each wall from floor to ceiling, each pigeon hole containing a single scroll, its title dangling on a string. Dozens of people sat at tables, quietly reading, writing, or taking notes on wax tablets.

"Can I help you, sir?" asked an elderly man in Greek. He was balding, gray of hair and beard, clad in a Greek-style tunic.

"Yes, you certainly may. I was hoping to gain some information here on a specific topic, but the resources here are so vast... I am overwhelmed," said Gaius, his gaze leaping from shelf to shelf holding the huge amount of information just in the immediate area.

"Yes, most people are, the first time." The old man chuckled. "I am Demaratos of Cos, and I serve as a guide. What information do you seek?"

A moment of caution crossed Gaius' mind. Antonius was right; it would not be wise to reveal too much of his mission here. "I am seeking information on lands to the east. A partner of mine seeks to invest in the silk trade."

"Ah, yes. Silk is becoming popular now. What would you like to know?"

"Ah, where does it come from? How does it get here, and how is it made?" The answer to these should lead to the *Hanae*, but without asking about them specifically. And silk was extremely popular and of widespread commercial investment interest.

"Please step this way." The old man's Greek had the inflection only a native speaker could offer.

Demeratos led him to the room dedicated to history. "I will be a few minutes. Please have a seat there by the window." He gestured toward an empty desk.

Gaius took a seat at a table, next to some people on an adjoining table arguing occasionally over the meaning of a word or phrase written on a stone tablet in tiny chicken-track script somehow impressed into it. Eavesdropping, he learned they were translating an alien script, written in a long-dead language.

Gaius idly picked up a scroll on the table, the *"Periplus of the Erythraean Ocean."* Greek for 'Sailing Instructions for the Indian Ocean.' *Hmm, could be worth looking at.* The document contained information on dozens of ports around the sea, the quality of their anchorages, land marks, tides and currents. More information described the kings of each port, types of currency used, trade goods, and reliability and nature of the inhabitants. *Skip the nautical and mercantile stuff.*

The scroll had a map, similar to the one in Maximus' tent. On the point of the southern coast of Arabia was Arabia Felix, in Greek as Eudaemon Arabia, with a line connecting it to India. The scroll said that ships went from Arabia Felix to India from June to September, with the Hippalic wind, blowing from the southwest. Six months later, this wind reversed, allowing a return trip.

There was little information beyond India. There were trading centers beyond there, but it seemed necessary to transship in India to get to them. And it did mention the *seres*, another name for the Hanaeans, but didn't say much about them. *But this scroll indicates that a lot of people know their way around the Indian Ocean, the western part, anyway. Latin won't be common there, maybe not even Greek. What do we do about money? The scroll says they take gold or silver, but do they recognize Roman or Greek coins? Will they argue about how much it is worth? Hmm… Hopefully, my cousin has thought of these things as well.*

Demaratos returned with a handful of scrolls. "Oh I see you found the missing scroll. It seems that someone recently has been inquiring about many of the same topics, as these scrolls, too, were scattered about on three reading tables. Perhaps your investment partner has some competition?"

"Perhaps. Let us see," answered Gaius.

Demaratos departed, leaving him to read. The first scroll did in fact mention the *Hanae* and their role in producing silk. Not one but two trade routes connected the land of the *Hanae* to the Roman world. One was by sea, by the ports in the *Periplus*. The second, which he knew slightly from his time in Syria, was overland, thousands of miles that wound north of India starting in Parthia. Not a good route for a Roman soldier who wanted to keep his head attached to his shoulders! But he had the name of the capital of *Hanae*: the eastern terminus of the Silk Road, Changanos.

But who else wanted the same information?

CHAPTER 5: A SIMPLE COUNTRY TAVERN

Antonius cleared the Bull and Dove as rapidly as possible. The cool evening air touched his face, which felt as though it were aflame. He was not as concerned with where he was going so much as he was with placing distance between himself and the Bull and the Dove. He was almost certain that he would be followed, and he was not going to return down Astarte Street. It was too easy to wind up dead there. Especially if someone wanted him dead. Like Ibrahim.

You fool! You stupid fool! Why didn't you talk this over with Gaius Lucullus before you charged out into the stews of Alexandria? Antonius berated himself savagely. A few hundred miles south of here, Roman power would begin to fade. Only their wits would keep them alive, and if his wits today were any example, they were already doomed.

It was nearly dark now, and he did not know exactly where he was. Off to his left, he caught the glare of the Pharos lighthouse. Facing that way would be north; going away from that should eventually bring him to the east-west Canopic Way, the Temple of Poseidon and all the other important buildings, along with the livery which held his horse. Ambush would be difficult on that thoroughfare, especially if he maintained a brisk pace to stay ahead of anyone following.

The February evening cooled off quickly. By the time Antonius reached the Canopic Way, his tunic, damp from perspiration, was chilling rapidly against his skin. The main avenue was well-lit with lamps every few hundred feet, making the livery easy to find.

A block behind, the thin weasel Yakov followed him unobtrusively in the flickering shadows.

At the livery, Antonius retrieved his horse. From the saddlebag he rummaged out a clean tunic and his faded old *sagum*, his red wool army cloak that was so good at keeping out the chill. He rinsed his body with water from a bucket, dashing cold water on his face to ease the throbbing in his head from the cheap wine. He changed into the fresh tunic, wrapped himself in the *sagum* and warmed himself by the evening fire, waiting. As the warmth began to seep into his chilled limbs, the door burst open, and in came Gaius Lucullus.

"Sir! I..." Antonius stammered into silence, while his heart skipped several beats. *Could he have any idea?*

"Very well, my good Antonius," he said with a smile, "I hope you had as interesting time as I did." He turned to the servant running the livery and handed him a handful of *sesterces*. "Here's for my gray, over there. And for this poor bedraggled Greek, his animal also." The servant accepted the coins with a nod.

"I be thankin' yer kindly."

"So did your travel arrangements go well?"

"I'll be tellin' yer about it on ter way back. Some important things has happened. T'were best we be on our way though," he said, as he swung himself into the saddle of his roan.

"As well, then. Let us be off. We shall dine at Aulus' villa."

"I am hardly well dressed for a villa. Let me go on ter the camp, so as ter not be an embarrassment fer yer."

"Aulus' villa is hardly a well-dressed place. It is a simple traveler's inn, but with excellent food by repute." Gaius Lucullus wrapped his own *sagum* around his shoulder and swung onto his gray. The horse snorted as Gaius wheeled the horse, cavalry fashion, into the Canopic Way and set off at a brisk canter. "Hai, yup." Gaius whistled and spurred his gray up.

Antonius mounted his own horse and pressed his knees against the roan's sides, laying the quirt gently against the animal's flanks to catch up.

As the clatter of their hooves echoed off the walls and disappeared in the gathering dark, Yakov noted their disappearance. Strange that the two men should rendezvous precisely here. Very strange. The other man could only be an aristocrat, with his classic Roman features. The narrow purple stripe on his tunic identified him as *equites*, a knight of the equestrian class. Probably the second Roman officer from the Twelfth. He slipped back into the darkness to report all this to Ibrahim.

Only a quarter-mile separated the Roman soldiers from the city's border. Alexandria did not have gates, but turnstiles on a few key roads provided lip service to security. The sleepy sentries waved them through...it was quiet and no passwords were in effect. Outside of town, they slowed the two animals to a walk. Gaius regaled Antonius with stories of the magnificent Library, until, a mile beyond the turnstile, the brightly-lit inn came into view. "You know," he said, "The oddest thing, someone was looking for the same information as I, scrolls misplaced. Coincidence, I guess."

"Sir, I think...," Antonius began, but Gaius waved him silent as they approached the pathway paved with white stones.

"Later, Antonius, we are here." The lanterns illuminated a low white stone building with a broad porch and tiled roof. The pathway led from the roadway to the *taberna*, that portion open to the public. The pathway ended in a circle around a fountain, reflecting the light from torches around the entrance. A brass dolphin, captured in a frozen leap from the fountain's center, squirted water vertically from his mouth. The two men dismounted there, and two servants came out to lead their animals back to the sheds behind the building. "Water but no oats, please," Gaius called out orders to the servants. "They have been liveried all day and are full to bursting now."

The two men came up the step through the porch, and entered into the *taberna*. The building enclosed a generous *atrium*, perhaps forty feet long by twenty wide, in the center of which was another fountain, and on either side, cooking and serving areas with whole pigs, huge slabs of beef and lamb slow roasting on charcoal fires. Servants filled plates for the thirty or so guests who sat on benches or reclined on couches around the perimeter. Some were Romans, a few of whom wore the wide purple stripes of the senatorial class on their toga. The remainder were clad in the Greek style, just simple tunics as were Gaius Lucullus and Antonius. A handful were very unusual in their dress and appearance, multi-colored shiny silk robes and odd-shaped eyes. Antonius felt distinctly underdressed and acutely conscious of his low social status.

"Just your basic country inn, sir. I see, indeed," he grumbled.

"My cousin's place. She and her husband, Aulus Aemilius Galba, invested in this *taberna*, and had it restored inside and out. They are just now beginning to make money from this effort. There she is now. Livia!"

"Gaius!" A buxom red-headed girl of about twenty-five swept across the mosaic floor, her diaphanous white gown swirling about her. Her blue eyes twinkled in the lamplight as she enveloped Gaius in an enthusiastic hug. "You didn't tell me you were coming!"

"Livia, it is always a pleasure to see you. Only last week, my life was one of simple, never-ending border warfare with Judaeans, Syrians and Parthians, all trying to kill me," he said with a chuckle. "My life has gotten much more complex, thanks to your husband. For the next few days, however, I will be staying here in Alexandria. Please pardon my manners, Livia, this is my centurion, Antonius Aristides. My cousin, Livia Luculla Galba."

"Pleasure, me lady." Antonius muttered, offering his hand. He was very uneasy at social functions under the best of circumstances, having scant experience with such things. Now, the urgency to discuss the events of the day with Gaius Lucullus gnawed at him.

"Oh, is this the great Antonius Aristides, the Greek, about whom you have written so much?" she crooned through delicate lips, smiling at him but talking to Gaius.

Yep, me legate's very own pet soldier.

"Indeed it is he. He was *primus pilus*, the senior centurion for the legion. It took some doing to get the Legate to release him to accompany me on this latest adventure."

"Antonius, I can't tell you how many times he has spoken of you in his letters." Livia turned her beautiful high-cheekboned face toward him, her hair glinting copper in the torchlight. "Ever since he has been in the army as a subaltern, he has told me that he had learned this from you, or that you had saved his life in some dreadful battle, or how the two of you concocted some stratagem that carried the whole day."

Antonius blushed, uncomfortably aware of the intense gaze from her green eyes. He never knew that Lucullus had written home about him. "Well, I think I be learnin' much from him too, me Lady."

Servants pressed wine goblets into their hands. Antonius checked to make sure that this wine was well-watered.

"Livia, where is that errant husband of yours?" asked Gaius. "Is he taking good care of you?"

"Aulus? He certainly is, and we expect an heir to the Galba patrimony perhaps in August. He is seeing to the various guests...I'll fetch him." She rushed off.

Gaius turned aside to Antonius, and spoke softly through the side of his mouth. "Delightful woman. Always regretted being so closely related to her. She was a shameless tomboy when we grew up. Now she's married and pregnant!"

"Sir! I have somethin' that's really important ter talk ter yer about. I know you'll be wantin' to socialize, but it has ter do with some events in town today." Antonius took a deep breath. *Let's get it over with.* "I may have made some stupid mistakes that put us all in some danger. Or not. But yer need ter know."

Gaius Lucullus eyed him intently. "You are really serious, my good man."

Just then Aulus Aemilius Galba bustled up. He was a portly man, but not objectionably overweight, balding with graying hair at his temples. He was properly draped in a full toga, the wide purple stripe announcing his Senatorial status. A plain iron senatorial ring of the old style decorated the index finger of his right hand. With his girth and graying hair, he could easily have been mistaken for the younger Livia's father.

"Gaius, my cousin! Great to see you on this side of the Nile. I am so glad you accepted my invitation. I see you got my message at the Third."

"How could I turn down the chance to leave the most promising army posting I ever held, to go somewhere halfway around the world to a place I never even heard of?" He smiled, pausing while everyone chuckled. "Frankly, Lucius Maximus had to do some serious talking to convince me to come! And then, he had to give me the Twelfth's best centurion. Meet the best the Roman army has to offer, Antonius Aristides, our senior centurion, formerly *primus pilus* of the Twelfth Thunderbolt!"

"Pleased to meet you, Antonius." The Senator took his hand warmly. Antonius mumbled something in reply, feeling even more out of his social depth.

Aulus returned his attention to Gaius. "Well, when the good Emperor selected me for this ambassadorship, I could think of no one but you to accompany me. So much of this mission revolves around military assessments, and you have devoted your life to that. You can see things in a glance that I would not notice in a year. I have devoted my life to making money, moving things from one port where they are not needed to another that pays dearly for them."

"Well, it should be interesting. Really. So little is known of the *Hanae*. I know you were well connected with Roman politics, but Trajan himself... how did he come to pick you for his envoy? That's more than quite an honor," said Gaius.

"Well, I have been in the Indian trade now for several years. And every year we've put more ships in service, handled more pepper and silk, and plowed every *sestertius* back into the business. Our consortium of traders has opened a full-time trading mission in Muziris in India now, with bankers, insurance brokers, and shipfitters... everything we need at the distant end to make the trade profitable. With warehouses open year-round and buyers in-country, we can buy goods off-season inland, instead of paying premium prices in port at the peak of the sailing season. And this year, we are going with our biggest investment ever. Three big grain freighters, specially modified for the Indian Ocean trade. Two hundred and fifty feet."

"That's a lot of ship," said Gaius.

"I called in some big favors owed among my colleagues in the Senate, and asked the Senate to split the cost of their construction and outfitting. Of course, His Excellency Trajan wanted to know all the details of how we were going to spend fifty million *sesterces* of public funds on just three ships on a single trip."

"I'll bet he did," said Gaius, chuckling. "He has a... parsimonious reputation."

Aulus laughed, but Antonius looked askance at the apparent disrespect. "Come, come, most of us just say he's cheap! But thorough and honest. So we briefed him on what we had done up to now, and how this would all benefit Rome and maybe, with the big-bottomed ships, make it more of a two-way trade. He liked that point, but wasn't sure about funding private ventures."

"But then a few years ago, the Hanaeans sent a delegation to Rome. Needless to say, they got a huge reception in there, right up to the Senate and Trajan himself. The next I knew, I was the envoy to the Hanaean king, with five of the translators accompanying me for their return home. Not hard really... *quid pro quo* for the release of the fifty million *sesterces* for my ships."

"Fascinating! I am looking forward to traveling with you. And fascinating business in India. What do you trade there? I would like to know all about it."

"Oh, I trade a little bit of almost everything everywhere. It's protection, really. Everything goes up and down in price, but never everything at once.

India is good for pepper, ivory, artwork, saffron. Look at this!"

Aulus led them to an alcove in a nearby wall, where a delicately carved elephant's tusk in the shape of an elaborate ceremonial ship caught the dancing golden glow of the flickering lamplight. Exquisitely carved filigrees penetrated the tusk where, within, equally exquisite dragon's heads cavorted with grimacing gods and goddesses. "This is a good sample of their workmanship. Each of the figures inside is smaller than your fingertip, and was carved from the outside." Aulus admired his prize. "I shall also have to introduce you to a drink called tea, a hot drink. Marvelous on a night such as tonight, when the desert chill sets in. Someday all the world will drink it!"

"Amazing. Who arranges all this shipping for you?"

"I have a very good merchant master of fleets, Hasdrubal by name. He outfits and organizes all of my trading expeditions for me."

Antonius' ears pricked up at the sound of that familiar name. *Hasdrubal. Is this the one I was told to find? Wish that I had found him, rather than the one I was told to avoid.*

"Hasdrubal? Sounds Carthaginian."

"Phoenician. He is from Tyre in Lebanon."

"So what is involved in navigating there to India?" asked Gaius. "I looked at some nautical information in the Library today. Not being a sailor, most of the terminology was lost on me, except the part about two thousand miles of ocean to India. That's a long time to be out of sight of land."

"Well, it depends on the ship. About twenty days is typical out of Eudaemon to landfall in India. We hope our new ships will do it in much less, maybe two weeks. The sailing season runs pretty much from June to September, with favorable winds, not too many storms. After that the storm season starts and you don't want to be out sailing in that. The ships have to lay over and ride the reversed winds back in late fall."

He turned to Antonius. "It was a Greek who discovered that monsoonal wind centuries ago, one Hippalus. They call it the Hippalic wind. You know, you Greeks have a great seafaring tradition, going back to Homer and his ships on the wine-red sea. Far older than our Roman one. We are newcomers to the sea."

"Yes, sir. But Rome has made a business out of sea commerce, and yer have brought great new ideas ter sea travel." Here he was, first generation citizen, talking to a full Senator. What he most wanted to do was return to some dive like the Bull and Dove - minus Ibrahim and his friends - drinking cheap wine neat with other commoners. His tongue felt thick in his mouth.

"At ease, Centurion." Aulus recognized the man's discomfiture, and switched deftly from Latin to Greek. "If you can bear my Latin-accented Greek... you and I are partners in building this great Empire. We owe a great debt to you Greeks, for you taught us literature and philosophy, and laid the foundations for our government." The senator laid a magnanimous arm around the uncomfortable centurion. "There are senators whose families were slaves just a hundred years ago. Rome is an aristocracy, where government is by the *ariston*, the best man fit for governing. Each of us are the *ariston* for a particular task... you for fighting, I am sure. I am not sure of my *ariston*. It would have to be for making money, I suppose!" he laughed, taking a sip of wine. "I think I have made far more money as a merchant than I have made laws as a Senator! So be proud of your Greek forebears, Antonius Aristides, of-the-best-men!"

"Be careful of your invitation, Aulus Aemilius. This insolent Greek can talk the ears off a brass statue when you uncork his tongue." Gaius Lucullus also placed his arm also across the man's broad back, the up-from-the-ranks soldier pinioned in a half-hug between a multi-millionaire Senator and his legate.

Livia wafted in, to take her husband by his other arm and lay her head on his shoulder. "My dearest Aulus Aemilius, there are some members of the Alexandria council of citizens who wish to meet with you. Can I pry you from my cousin and his friend?"

"Certainly. Well, my dear Antonius," he extended his hand warmly, "please let me know when you retire. I will arrange for a *Senatus Consulto* declaration in your honor."

"I... I would be most honored, sir, an' thank yer, thank yer fer the many kindnesses."

"You're most welcome. And to you, good cousin. We must continue a more leisurely discussion of our upcoming trip."

"Yes, and congratulations to you on your new heir. I was afraid that at your age the tax collector would make off with all your *patrimonia* before you could produce one. Good luck!"

As the gallant old senator wandered off with his young wife, Gaius gave a low whistle. "That is quite an honor he is offering you, Antonius. Having the Senate bestow your equestrian status on you personally, rather than generally upon your group of retirees."

Antonius sighed. "Beggin' yer pardon, but I have never been so uneasy in all me life. 'T'would be easier to face a squad of Parthians bare-handed, than to do dinner party chat at this level of society. That man knows the Emperor personally... enough to joke about him!" The centurion hissed, trying to keep his voice low.

"You did well, Antonius. In fact, both he and Livia seemed quite taken with you. Aulus Aemilius does not make idle promises, by the way. He will put together the decree on your equestrianship, and he will make it happen. Be sure you give him a date, when you have one. That will probably at least double whatever you are worth when you are out."

A wandering servant refilled their glasses from a ceramic jug, a retsina wine pleasing to Antonius' Greek palate. Gaius motioned him toward a bench along the walls, in the shadows away from the crowd.

"Now, come here to this bench. You were intently trying to tell me something earlier…"

The atrium had a second floor balcony that ran around the inside perimeter, forming a covered porch on the first floor. Against the wall were rough-hewn wooden benches, to which Antonius and Gaius retreated. Oil lamps hissed softly, punctuating the darkness with amber.

Antonius revisited the events of the day, beginning with the directions from *III Cyr's librarii* to the Bull and Dove, his unplanned but somehow forewarned meeting with Ibrahim and his companions there, the improvisation about a fictitious report, and his hasty departure.

"S'truth, sir! If I have failed yer, if I have put this mission in jeopardy, give me leave ter fall upon me sword, an' I will do it now! Right here."

"I don't think our hosts would appreciate that. It would be quite messy." But he did not smile. "Were you followed?"

"In town, probably, but I didn't see a tail. But the ride out, after dark…no. I watched over my shoulder from the time we left the livery, and there were no riders behind. None."

"That's good. You were in terrible straits. You are fortunate to not have your throat slit, and be tossed into some alleyway to feed the crows. They pick up bodies every morning here, take them out with the trash. Killed for whatever…and not only were you at risk. A pursuer might very well have chosen to assault me, unsuspecting on the road with my sword unslung. Even now, one could lie in wait to assault one of the guests here, or even ransack the whole inn. It is lightly defended." He paused for effect. "My good Antonius. Be seated. Put it behind you. You erred in leaping into a task without thought, but that is your way in battle… you charge and think later. For if you thought, you would surely never go in that direction, toward all those men with swords and clubs and sharp sticks trying to kill you, but the other way, toward a warm fire and hot food and lively women." He laughed, and Antonius gulped and chuckled also, still rigidly trying to keep his emotions under control.

"We will be going into a strange land, doing things beyond our ken or experience. You and I must trust each other completely. We must discuss things with each other like we did in the legions, so that the danger that I can't see, you might, and the danger that you can't see, I might. Don't operate so independently that one or both of us is at risk. Didn't we have this discussion once before in Noricum, you as a newly made ranker and I as subaltern? You were less respectful in your choice of words to me, but you yourself taught me that wisdom."

Antonius blinked.

"Let's review the bidding. You met someone named Ibrahim, who made small talk with you. Right?" Antonius nodded.

"And Ibrahim may...or may not... be the Ibrahim the pirate you were warned of. Right?"

"Sir, he was pockmarked."

"Yes. Various poxes are common here, as is the name Ibrahim. Some ancestral figure common to both the Judaeans and the Arabs. But that is still a lot of coincidences."

Antonius nodded again.

"And as awkward as the situation was, you were wise enough to concoct a cock-and-bull story of a report about some Imperial relatives getting killed. Probably made him think twice about killing you... if he had the intention to do so. Right?"

Antonius nodded.

"You actually did well. Did you get him to buy you some wine?"

"Yes, sir."

"And you didn't wind up in an alley, or press-ganged onto some tramp galley pulling oars under a lash, or missing your purse?"

"No, sir."

Gaius laughed. "Count yourself lucky. I think you actually did well to keep your wits about you and get out alive. This area is not like the small frontier towns you are used to. People come, people go. People get lost here, and are never seen again. Just... lost."

"Stay out of town now for a while, especially that part of town, and don't go exploring any part alone. In the meanwhile, when we meet with the *legatus* of *III Cyr*, your reporting may be helpful, whether or not you met the infamous Ibrahim bin Yusuf." He slapped the centurion across his big shoulders. "Come, let us try some more good wine, rather than the rotgut stuff you drank at the Bull and Dove."

Gaius flagged a passing servant for more wine, and another servant to fetch two plates of roast lamb and onions.

"So this is how the other half lives, sir. I thought yer said this was just a simple inn. Just yer basic simple inn, run by a Senator making millions of *sesterces* in the India trade."

"Livia and Gaius Galba do this for fun. They love getting out of Alexandria for the desert and this old *taberna* gives them an excuse. And it's a cut above the Bull and Dove, I suppose. At least the wine here is better by your account. Tell me the truth...you actually found wine so bad even you could not stomach it?"

Aulus Aemilius rejoined them before Antonius could answer. "You must come meet some of our escorts." He took the two in tow to meet some of the foreign guests. "Gaius, Antonius, meet our Hanean representative, Wang Ming, his concubine Marcia Lucia, and her brother Marcus Lucius Quintus.

"Pleased to meet you," said Marcus, and "Pleased, also," followed Marcia. Their excellent Latin and their Roman names did not match their peculiar appearance: straight, shiny black hair in tight buns, slightly yellow skin and slanted, almond-shaped eyes... though Marcia's were a discomforting shade of blue grey that clashed with her appearance almost as much as her Latin. They were dressed in silk oriental robes of a wholly unfamiliar style.

Wang Ming said, "Pleased." He apparently had learned some Latin, but not well.

"Uh, pleased to make your acquaintance." Gaius offered his hand, but Wang Ming refused it, keeping his hands across his chest and offering instead a deep bow

"Are you two related?" said Gaius to Marcus and Marcia

"Brother and sister," said Marcia.

"How do you come to speak Latin so well, and have Roman names, and look so... so..."

"Foreign? We are fellow Romans, with a few detours. Our great-grandfather was one of Crassus' centurions at Carrhae. You have heard of that battle?" said Marcus

"Who hasn't, but that was a century and a half ago."

"He and several hundred survivors were taken back to *Ch'in* to serve as mercenary border guards, ending up in Liqian, which is the Hanaean pronunciation for 'Legion.'" He pronounced the words as '*shin*' and '*li-shan*', apparently in Hanaean. "They took Hanaean wives, but passed their language and Roman heritage to their children. Alas, there are but a few of us left."

Gaius noted that Marcus' Latin seemed a bit antiquated, like Ennius' histories from his school days. But of course, it would be. "So... how did you come to be here... in Alexandria?"

Marcus answered, "The Hanaean Imperial Court learned that we in Liqian spoke both languages fluently, and understood both cultures, and we became a prized commodity. We and eight others were brought to the court to be trained as translators for Gan Ying's expedition."

As if on cue, Wang Ming said, "Thank you, we go now." He then spoke to Marcia in a fluttering, bird-like speech, took her by the arm and steered her away.

"Friendly one, that! Marcia is married to ... him?" said Gaius, struggling to remember the unfamiliar syllables of the man's name.

"Marcia was made Wang Ming's concubine at an early age. He is a pig, but that is the Roman in me speaking. Anyway, we were translators for Gan Ying on his mission to Rome, where we met with Trajan himself."

"Really!" said Gaius.

"He issued declarations of citizenship for all of us Carrhae descendants before the Senate. Not that this will matter much when we get back to *Ch'in*."

"You refer to your home as *Ch'in*, but we call it the land of the Hanae. Which is correct?" asked Gaius.

"*Ch'in* is the name of the land. It is ruled by the Han people, but the land is *Ch'in.*"

Aulus interjected himself into the conversation. "Well, it is late, and my two soldiers must make it back to *III Cyr* by midnight, or sleep in the desert until the morning watch is posted. Gaius, will you and Antonius meet me here tomorrow afternoon? I want to take you to Alexandria to see one of my ships."

"We'll be here. Good night, Marcus. My regards to your sister, and to… her consort."

"To be sure. A pleasure to meet you," said Marcus.

At the second hour of the night, the two soldiers took leave of the villa, and rode back to the camp through the chill February desert, the stars crisp and brilliant in the clear sky. A quarter moon spread shimmers on the breakers of the sea to their right as the road led above a hill in the darkness. They arrived at their quarters in the camp around midnight.

CHAPTER 6: A DEATH IN THE CAMP

Shortly after first light, Antonius roused Gaius Lucullus in his sleeping quarters with a bag of Egyptian flat bread and some cold drinking water.

Gaius put on his tunic, then they supped on the simple breakfast. He was never talkative in the morning.

"Well done, Antonius," said Gaius, "That saved us a trip to the breakfast mess in the wee hours of the morning. Heavy-lidded army cooks are never pleasant company in the early hours, even to us officers."

Gaius donned his bright dress armor, buckling on the polished leather breast piece and the split-end leather skirt over his tunic, securing his bright red army cloak with a brass broach. He wiped a smudge from his gleaming bronze helmet and riffled through the scarlet plume to remove any dust. "Well, I was beginning to wonder if I would ever wear this piece of parade-ground gear again. Simple steel field armor has been our order of the day for the past few months. This dress uniform has been in my campaign locker for the last six months."

Antonius was similarly dressed, over a plain white tunic, but with more brass and bronze decorations.

"Yer looks mighty fine this morning, if I may say so."

"As do you, Antonius."

"I thank yer for the visit to the Senator's inn last night. That is a most impressive place."

"Well, we will have the opportunity for a brief stay there again soon. I think we can call it a business visit, so to speak," he said, fitting on the gilded helmet and adjusting its fit in a brass mirror. "I knew that he was into maritime trading, but I was amazed at the extent of his work. If his Indian Ocean ships are as good as he says, our trip should be pleasant indeed."

"Probably more pleasant that what Ibrahim had in mind."

"I wouldn't jest about that. Let's go, we have a morning appointment."

The sun was just presenting itself over the eastern horizon, red against the desert, when the two arrived at the *praetorium*. "Gaius Lucullus of *Legio XII Fulminata*, *legatus*, with appointment to see the legate of *Legio III Cyrenaica*."

"Yes, sir. *Legatus* Quintus Albus Pontus is occupied with his morning meeting. However, if you will sit here in the anteroom, this meeting will be over shortly." The young *librarii*, clad only in a white tunic, motioned them to some canvas campaign chairs by the wall, and returned to studying a scroll.

The two sat quietly, listening to the scratching of the stylus against papyrus as the young clerk carried out his duties. They could hear rumbles of voices from the meeting behind the wall.

The two soldiers studied the impressive polished floors of the *III Cyr praetorium's* anteroom, emblazoned with a mosaic of the shield-symbol of the *III Cyr*, an eagle bearing an asp in one claw and a lightning-bolt in the other. Antonius whispered to Gaius, "Nice quarters! But I wonder how long since they've deployed in a mobile field camp?"

"It's been a while, Antonius, maybe too long."

At last the meeting broke up, well into the second hour of the morning. The twelve camp tribunes, the *primus pilus* and the *praefectus castrorum* camp prefect emerged into the anteroom, laughing and joking.

"Hullo!" said one of the tribunes. "You can go in next, we've softened the old man up for you." Gaius smiled and waved in return as the group departed to their duties. *Pudgy around their waists. Political careerists in a soft post.*

The young clerk went into the commander's office with the scroll, then returned empty-handed. "You can go in now."

Gaius entered first, "*Vale!* Gaius Lucullus, legate, *Legio XII Fulminata*, sends greetings!" He said, slapping his right hand smartly across his chest.

Quintus Albus waved lazily, not rising from his chair by his polished oak desk. "Please, enter and sit down." He too wore his parade ground armor, his helmet on the right side of the desk. He completed his reading and rolled up the scroll, looking up and fixing them by eye. He was young, lithe, and with a full head of dark hair. About Gaius' age. "I am sure you find this quite a change from the frontier," he said.

"Yes, your Excellency. Quite a comfortable posting," answered Gaius.

"Sure, but drop the 'Excellency', Gaius. I am where you will be in a year or so, if the Legate Maximus' recommendation on your behalf carries any weight. In command, as I am. This is my first month here. Like you, I came from the frontier, *X Fretensis* in Judea. But at least here you can go to town without someone trying to put an arrow in your back."

"This command must pose its own challenges to you, Quintus Albus."

"Better than 'Your Excellency,' but shorten it further to just Quintus. I don't feel like being formal with you." He smiled, then continued. "You know, challenge is not enough to describe the experience. I had this legion fall out last week in battle gear. Not in the fancy parade ground crap, but real steel. Would you believe, even my centurions had rusty field armor! Hadn't been oiled in months, the leather cracked. Then we did some basic small unit drill. Nothing much, just run a few miles, then pair off centuries against one another in *testudo* formation, shields interlocked over their heads, some basic sword drill. Not one century finished the drill, Gaius! Not one! Half the men went down for heat. Complained they shouldn't drill the *testudo* in the hot sun." He shook his head. "We are going out this week into the desert. We'll sweat some pounds off these... soldiers."

"Sounds like you'd like to borrow Antonius. He was my first spear," Gaius chuckled, pointing toward his gruff centurion.

"And a damned good one, too, by reputation. I got thrown into this command without any of my own staff. Can I have him for a week?"

"Ho, ho! I'd like to loan him to you, Quintus, but we won't be here that long. We'll be heading south to the Red Sea, then out to the Indian Ocean."

"So now, this is more than the obligatory courtesy call?" queried Quintus, his curiosity aroused. "What takes you to India?"

"India and far beyond. However, that is another story in itself. I have some intelligence which may be of interest to you. Have you ever heard of some pirate by the name of Ibrahim? Ibrahim bin Yusuf?"

"That devil! Yes! There's a full talent of gold on that bastard's head. Sixty pounds worth. The Navy would like to crucify the son of a bitch to his own masthead if we could catch him. He jumps ships all up and down the Mediterranean and the Red Sea. Always knows just which ship to pull down. Never a whole convoy, just the pick of the litter. What do you want to know about him?"

"Antonius thinks he may have met him yesterday. At the Bull and Dove, a dive frequented by sailors and merchant marine types."

"Not bad work. You lads have been here less than twenty-four hours, and you have already been introduced to the most wanted man in Egypt. The Bull and Dove is a hellhole, Antonius. What makes you think you him there?" Quintus turned, fixing Antonius squarely in the eye, with a bit of a twinkle.

"Well, your Excellency, he introduced hisself ter me." The centurion expressed himself squarely, with no hesitation or uncertainty.

"Is that so? At the Bull and Dove, he just introduced 'hisself' to a Roman soldier he never met before?" He cocked his head quizzically, a smile playing across his lips.

"Yessir, yer Excellency. I wasn't in uniform or nothin'. Was lookin' fer information on shippin'. Din't he just kill some high-born Romans?"

"Well, seems like he did, and he is getting bolder than ever. Describe the man you met."

"Arab. Speaks very good Greek. About fifty-five years old, gray beard, actually kinda salt-an'-pepper, an' behind the beard, he is really pock-marked. Blue eyes, real intense, hooked nose. Strokes his beard a lot. Maybe five foot ten inches tall, one seventy-five or so. I'll skip the clothes. He was in Arab dress. They all look the same ter me."

"Hmm. How'd you know he spoke good Greek?"

"Yer excellency, 'tis me first tongue. Me great grandfather was a Greek tutor in rhetoric... a slave. Me grandfather was a freedman, me father earned his citizenship in the auxiliaries, and I am the first citizen by birth."

"And a great addition to the Principate you'll be, Antonius. So Greek is your native tongue. *Koine*, I suppose?"

"Aye, that an' classical. We bein' a family of tutors we pride ourselves on that." Gaius looked up in surprise. He had not known that Antonius spoke classical Greek as well as the *koine* 'dockyard Greek' of the Mediterranean.

"So you were making inquiries yourself in civilian clothes, in fairly good Greek. Maybe he mistook you for somebody's servant. Someone with some money."

"No, he seemed to know right off that I was under the eagles. A centurion, even. An' your *librarius* what sent me down there yesterday had alerted me to him."

"Back up. Someone here at the Third told you to go the Bull and Dove. At this camp? Who? And why?"

"One of your *librarii*. I don't remember his name, but I think I could point him out. I was tryin' to find out how shipping was arranged through the Third, an' he said they didn' do that. He tol' me how to arrange Imperial Post passes on our orders, as they do that regular here. But shippin' south of that was done through the merchants. He suggested that I look at schedules at the Bull and Dove, ter look for someone named Hasdrubal an' watch out fer anyone named Ibrahim. But the Bull an' Dove weren't no place to be arrangin' transport, 'cept maybe acrost the Styx."

"This is interesting. We just had two Romans killed and two disappear, and some cocksucker in this camp is directing a stranger down to that cesspit. The Bull and Dove, Antonius, is not one of the places I like the *III Cyr's* troops to frequent."

"What about that fellow Hasdrubal?" asked Gaius.

"You have me," answered Quintus. "That's a common enough Carthaginian name. One of the biggest shipping magnates in Alexandria goes by that name. But you wouldn't find him at the Bull and Dove. He could buy that dive, and twenty square blocks of the city around it. In fact, I think he's south himself now, setting up some big project on the Red Sea, last I heard. Hmm, I wonder if that bastard Ibrahim has penetrated the camp."

"Quintus, that may make some sense." interjected Gaius. "Antonius may not be much of a big-city fellow, but he generally knows to stay on the beaten path. He wouldn't go down there on his own unless he expected a bona-fide merchant's shipping office."

"Which I was, an' the Bull an' Dove weren't," added Antonius.

Gaius was glad to restore Quintus' confidence in Antonius' common sense. Anyone can be misled some of the time. And, if the misleading took place in the same orderly room where Antonius had lined up their lodgings and horses, the tipster would have known that he was in fact on Imperial orders. Which might be why Ibrahim would have been willing to expose himself a bit to a stranger?

"I think I need to bring the *quaestiones* into this." Quintus placed his fingertips together. "If they are not penetrated also." The *quaestiones* were a combination legal and police staff within the Legion, attached to the headquarters. "You won't mind spending a few more hours with them this morning, will you?"

"Not at all, *legatus*."

"Very well. Antonius, if you are lucky and we run him to ground, you may get a talent of gold." Turning to Gaius, he said, "Well, you have brought me mixed events this morning. A lead on a pirate, and a possible traitor in my camp. What else can we do for you?"

Before he could answer, the clerk opened the door. "Begging your pardon, sir, but there has been a death in the camp."

"Let me guess, a young *librarius*, right?"

"Right, sir... How... how did you know?"

"Commanders know everything. Antonius, care to bet that the dead man is your friend the *librarius*?" Turning back to the clerk, he said, "Fetch the *quaestiones*. Where is the body?"

"Under the stands, behind the *Campus Martialis*."

"I'll be there in five minutes," Quintus said, buckling on his sword. "Let's go see your friend, Antonius."

The *Campus Martialis* was a combination parade ground and drill field dedicated to Mars, the god of war, lying opposite the praetorium on the south side of the *Via Principalis* which divided the fort in half. Outfitted with seats, the field doubled as a sports field, theater and other such uses when not used for training.

The *quaestiones* were already examining the body when the legate and the two visitors from the Twelfth arrived. The young man lay face down by the field, his arm crossed under his face, one leg drawn up somewhat sideways, like a man asleep. A *quaestio* turned him over, and the young man's dead eyes stared blankly up to the morning sky. Someone had slit his throat from ear to ear, and the gaping red wound was in stark contrast to the blue pallor of his skin. His tongue protruded from the side of his mouth, and there was a look of surprise, frozen on his face for all eternity.

The legion's *medicus* knelt to examine him, attempting to move his arms and legs, examining his eyes. "How long has he been dead?" asked one of the *quaestiones*.

"I'm not sure, but I think he probably died before daybreak. The body hasn't begun to stiffen yet and that takes about eight hours... but he didn't die here. Not much blood. He was killed somewhere else and dragged here."

Quintus Albus nudged Antonius. "Don't tell what you know about this," he whispered. "Is he the one? Just nod."

Antonius nodded in the affirmative. It was indeed the young man who had directed him to the Bull and Dove. The man was too young and innocent to have been a conscious traitor. Perhaps picking up a *denarius* or two, steering people there to the Bull and Dove and other dives but not realizing the danger to them, or to himself. The traitor was still here, Antonius was sure, and he strongly suspected that he himself might indeed be the target. One of these five men could be the traitor. Or one of those in the gathering crowd in the field. Or even Quintus Albus. The hackles on his neck rose.

"Well," announced Quintus, "It seems we have yet another gambling death, or lover's triangle or whatever. Cupid's arrow struck deep last night. Who is this young man?"

"This young man is Lucius Servilius, your Excellency. Originally from Cisalpine Gaul, enlisted from the dockyards at Ostia. He hasn't been with us long. Six months, maybe."

"Bring me a report by noon today to the *praetorium*. Find out where he was killed, since it was apparently not here. Include in the report all of the people who entered or left the camp last night, and the times of their comings and goings," Quintus demanded.

"That may be difficult, your Excellency," mumbled one of the centurions. "This camp is more like a town than a frontier post. People just come and go. We don't keep records at the sentry posts."

"Correction. You didn't keep records. You do keep those records, starting now. One of the reasons for doing so lies at your feet. I will inspect those records myself tomorrow... and the next death in this camp may be the sentry who fails to keep those records adequately." Quintus continued: "I expect you to reconstruct from the sentries what little they may have observed of last night's comings and goings. They were awake, were they not? I know we post sentries, for I place my own seal on the watch bill myself." He was growing increasingly sarcastic.

Quintus turned to his *primus pilus*, who had just now arrived on the scene. "Lepidus! As you may notice, someone is dead. Murdered, in fact. I want you to examine our camp security and explain to me how this happened. Everything. The status of our sentries, who was on watch, how they were trained, what each saw. In writing. Tomorrow at the morning meeting."

Lepidus' mouth began to move in protest, then thought better of it. "Aye, sir."

Quintus wheeled to leave. "I shall be in my quarters. Bring his parents' address with your afternoon report. I shall have the miserable task of explaining to them their son's fate."

Two *capsularii* field medics arrived with a stretcher, a blanket stretched between two poles. They hoisted the dead Lucius Servilius onto it, and produced another blanket to cover him, shielding his unseeing eyes from the stares of the living. They led him away with the *medicus* to the fort hospital, while the *quaestiones* assembled to plan their questioning.

Gaius and Antonius followed Quintus, as the commander strode briskly away from the scene of the crime. Quintus Albus clearly expected his staff to take the lead in this investigation, examining for themselves how their shortcomings had led to this young man's death.

"There's not a doubt in my mind that this was foul play, and damned serious." Quintus was angry. "We lose perhaps a man a month to fights and murders of one kind or another here. Regrettable, but that's what you have when you have men of all social classes here, from every nation in the empire. Trained to fight, they fight. Over women, gambling debts, you name it. They confront each other, fight, stab each other or knock each other over the head. One gets killed." Quintus paused, "and sometimes both."

"But cutting a man's throat... that happens very seldom. The attacker comes by stealth, sneaks up behind someone, and kills the victim before he can cry out. The attacker is either someone trying to penetrate the guards, or an executioner killing coolly, deliberately and without remorse. I think it may have been the latter, especially since the body was moved. Ominous!"

The three took a light lunch in the *praetorium*, with Gaius sharing the details of the scope of the forthcoming expedition. They were in mid-meal when a centurion burst in, saluting.

"More bad news, your Excellency," said the centurion. "The clerks' office appears to be where the young man was killed, though the killer took some pains to slosh the blood away with a bucket of water. A lot remained in the corners and along the wall. And it has been ransacked, as though they were looking for something."

"The report on the four murdered Romans!" Gaius blurted out. "Antonius exaggerated a story about a report on their deaths while talking to Ibrahim, saying these were relations of Trajan himself, who had taken a personal interest in the case. He had hoped to make killing him sound very unattractive to Ibrahim."

"And Excellency, you're not going to believe the family name of Lucius Servilius. Nothing 'servile' about the Crassus *gens*."

Quintus gave a low whistle. The Crassus *gens* was an old line patrician family, going back to the founding of Rome itself. Their clan had produced generals and consuls, tribunes, governors of provinces. "A common *miles* is an odd occupation for such a distinguished family, Centurion. Enlighten me as to how Lucius chose such a career." It was not illegal for such an illustrious family to enlist as a simple foot soldier, just highly unusual.

"Appears he was disinherited, Excellency," replied the centurion.

"Maybe so. But disinheriting is not an uncommon thing among the blue-bloods. In any event, I personally know of ten men in Rome who would loan the young man a million *sesterces* on his name alone, just to be able to say they loaned money to a Crassus when he was down and out. Nine of them wouldn't care if they were repaid or not." Quintus tapped the desk with his spoon. "So what's he doing here, as a common foot soldier?"

"Appears there was a falling out with his father over a girl he wanted to marry. She may have been... a Christian, sir, if you'll pardon the expression.

Anyway, she died afterwards, or was killed by someone, or the authorities. His messmates aren't sure, 'cause Servilius didn't talk much on this. After he was disowned, he denounced all his family's possessions, and went to work in Ostia as a common stevedore. Guess he found that kind of life too rough, 'cause he enlisted with the legions a year later. Been a good soldier, kept his class well hidden. Only one lad really knew his background, and he didn't want to talk about it much."

"Hmm, and well he shouldn't. A high-born patrician serving that far below his station... he's lucky if a slashed throat was all he suffered." The four soldiers nodded in assent. The Roman society was an upwardly mobile society, with many senators having barbarian or even slave forebears not three generations back, like Antonius. But the lower classes were not as quick to welcome interlopers from the upper classes in their midst. "Any chance he was a... Christian, also?" Quintus asked.

"No one knows for sure. He didn't have any of the cross signs or fish symbols of the cult. He wasn't actively religious for any of the gods or goddesses either, but frankly, most of the troops just think they're swear-words anyway."

"Well, seems like we have a good reason for his dying as he did, though it is most ominous. Did you find anything missing from the *officia*?"

"They're inventorying as best they can with the other *librarii*. I'll have them find out if any report is missing."

Quintus turned back to Gaius and Antonius. "Good job, Centurion. Dismissed!"

"Aye, sir!" The man turned on his heel and left as briskly as he had entered.

"What do you think, Gaius?" said Quintus, returning to the remains of his lunch.

"I defer to my centurion. He knew the lad. What do you think, Antonius?" said Gaius.

"It sounds, like what yer Excellency said... ominous."

CHAPTER 7: THE DOCKS OF ALEXANDRIA

Gaius and Antonius departed the *III Cyr* encampment in the afternoon on horseback. Gaius was pleased to note that the sentry challenged their departure, demanding their name and unit. Despite the ugly business of the morning, Quintus Albus had decided Gaius and Antonius had

little to add to the investigation that they had not already given, and it might be to their advantage and safety to remain for the duration at the Senator's inn. In any event, the accommodations were less spartan.

They arrived there in mid-afternoon, and found Aulus preparing a covered cart. Gaius privately gave him a quick overview of the ominous events of the day, which concerned him greatly.

"You mean to tell me, you think someone in the camp administration directed Antonius to the Bull and Dove deliberately to meet Hasdrubal – who by the way really is my shipping master – and 'avoid' Ibrahim whom he just happened to meet, and then was murdered the very next day, and someone searched the legion files?"

"That's what it looks like, cousin. What we don't have is a good reason for any of that. But let your bodyguards know there may be trouble," answered Gaius.

"I don't know as I can provide better security than *III Cyr*, and whoever did that apparently had no trouble penetrating theirs."

"We're not sure their security was that good, though I expect it has gotten significantly better fast, but our disappearing seemed to be a good idea."

"Well, I'm still not satisfied. If it is Ibrahim, then he can find us here easily, if he wants. But no matter now, I will tell them to keep an extra lookout, then we can head off to the city so I can show you the kind of ship you will be traveling on."

Aulus left and came back a few minutes later. "They've doubled the guards. Not much, but the best we can do for now. Let's go see a ship!"

They mounted up on the waiting carriage and departed for the city with Aulus's servant driving the two-horse team eastward along the coast road to Alexandria. After a while, the Pharos lighthouse came into view, flashing brilliantly at intervals, though it was still ten miles distant.

"Do you know how that works, cousin?" asked Gaius, pointing at the lighthouse.

"I've been up there," answered Aulus. "The engineer showed me around, and it's an amazing piece of machinery. I don't understand all of it, but the flash comes from a rotating mirror, aimed at the horizon, reflecting sunlight from another mirror above it, tracking the sun. A handler leads a donkey around a walkway on the perimeter, in time to a waterclock to keep everything in step. They adjust everything just before daybreak for the sun's movement. The rotating mirror is double-sided, so at night, fires from below are reflected from the bottom side. Day and night, it can be seen from thirty miles at sea."

"Quite a nice piece of work," answered Gaius.

Aulus continued on, "So have you been on any ships, Antonius?"

"Troop transports on the Danube. Hundred-footers, big enough to carry a century, their ten mules an' kit. Not enough room ter turn around without hitting yer messmate though, an' smelled awful, 'cuz everyone pissed in the bottom of it, beggin' yer pardon, sir."

Gaius laughed. "Well, I think you'll find these ships a bit more comfortable."

The coastal road led along the north side of the city, next to the beaches of the western Eunostos Harbor. The soldiers watched the water aswarm with luxury pleasure craft ranging from small day-sailers skittering along the water like water bugs, to mammoth pleasure palace yachts lolling at anchor. The beaches were full of scantily-clad people enjoying the sun and water, strolling, playing ball games, swimming in the surf, or just taking naps in the sun on blankets. Men and women wore mostly brief tunics, some men just a loincloth, and some women a loincloth and a cloth covering their breasts, with a lot of attractive midriff in between. This caught Antonius' eye, and he gave a low whistle. "That is some amazin' good womanflesh there. Dressed as they are, are they … er, perfessional women, Senator?"

"No, Antonius, I doubt it, though some might be, at a price that would take your breath away. That's just normal beachwear here in Alexandria. Leaves a lot of skin for the sun to turn a nice shade of tan! This is the Eunostos Harbor, playground of the rich."

They reached the Heptastadia, and clattered across the mile-long causeway connecting the mainland to Pharos Island north of the city. All along the causeway, their cart passed bullock trains pulling strings of carts filled with grain and other bulk cargo to the heavy shipping on the Ptolemaic quay, fuel for the lighthouse's nightshift. An occasional wheeled squirrel-cage crane rumbled along, its tall lift lowered to the horizontal.

Aulus continued acting as tour guide. "The Heptastadia divides the bay into the Eunostos Harbor that we just passed, and the Great Harbor on the east, for commercial shipping and military. Smaller freighters and fishing fleets use the city docks on this side. Heavier shipping, such as mine and the *Classis Alexandrina*, the Alexandrian Fleet, use the dockyards built along Pharos's flank on the other side of the bay, up ahead on your right."

To the immediate right of the Heptastadia, along the edge of the island, they could see a concrete dock, with a dozen quays extending up the bay to the protected shelter of a rocky promontory. Along the first four quays rode the galley warships of the fleet. Alongside the remaining quays, one and sometimes two massive ships were moored amidst a forest of man-powered cranes to feed their empty holds from the queued-up bullock trains.

"The fleet headquarters are in the base of the lighthouse at the far right of the island up ahead, by the Great Harbor entrance beyond that rocky promontory," said Aulus, pointing at the massive building.

From where they were on the Heptastadia, they could easily make out the details of the huge lighthouse, built like a layer cake on a large square base the size of a fort, a tapering square second section going up perhaps two hundred feet, an octagonal third section, then a short circular tower capped by the light itself and a conical roof. It was, by any measure, the largest and highest structure that they had ever seen.

"My ship is in the fourth quay, next to the warships. It's a typical grain freighter. Keeps Rome's people fed, and a well-fed population is a happy population. Sailing season is about to open up at the end of the month, so everyone is loading."

At the end of the causeway, Aulus's driver expertly wheeled the cart briskly to the right, proceeding down the access road onto the fourth quay, smooth concrete like the dock. On the right, a nest of black triremes were moored nose-on to the quay, between wooden walkways that separated the ships their entire length. On the left, at the far end of the quay, a massive grain freighter was moored by the starboard side to massive bollards, with space left over to accommodate another ship of the same size on the inside berth. The harbor smells of fetid water, dead fish, seaweed and sewage filled the air, and gulls wheeled raucously in the sky, vying for various pieces of offal.

"This is the Ptolemaic Quay, it gives you a great view of Alexandria's buildings, beaches and waterfront," announced Aulus. The white buildings of the city gleamed in the afternoon sun.

The cart rolled past the triremes, their gunwales even with the level of the quay. The ships, black and red with gold trim, rode restlessly in the choppy port seas, arrhythmic clatter of rigging on masts beating time with the chop of waves trapped between the docks and their hulls. Over their quarterdecks aft, high sternposts rose and arched gracefully forward over each ship, each identically decorated in a carved white-painted papyrus bloom. And on the bow, just above the waterline and just aft of their wicked bronze ram, a pair of evil eyes glared at the dock, as though the boat intended to ram the structure that restrained it.

"Their papyrus bloom stern figures are the emblem of the *Classis Alexandrina*," Aulus explained.

Antonius and Gaius noted dozens of sailors visible on the deck of each ship or on the quay, working at various maintenance tasks, others lugging supplies below decks, or just strolling the deck, gazing back at them.

There was no man in the Mediterranean world that was quite the equal of an oarsman on a Roman galley. Most stood six feet tall, over two hundred pounds. In sailor fashion, the men shaved their heads bald, their faces clean-shaven, though some sported long mustaches that drooped down their cheeks. They wore white linen kilts with huge leather belts, bare-chested, huge pectoral muscles glistening with oil to protect them against the sun.

Antonius took note of the massive oarsmen that powered these warships. "S'truth, it seems a bull can really beget a child from a woman. Look at those sailors, sir!"

"I wonder what they feed those boys?" asked Gaius, incredulously.

"I think pretty much whatever they want to eat, Gaius," answered Aulus. "Those men row like hell or fight like hell, as needed."

Continuing down the quay, the cart pulled up to the aft companionway ladder of Aulus's grain freighter, opposite the last of the warships. The ladder, riding on roller wheels on the dock, scaled her black flanks rearing ten feet above the level of the dock. Two masts and a maze of rigging towered a hundred feet above their heads. Over the raised poop deck, the sternpost curved upward and forward to host an intricately carved white goose with a wingspan of ten feet, in full flight over the deck. While the galleys rose and fell with each choppy wave, the freighter sat like a wall in the water, the waves breaking ineffectively against her bulk.

It was the largest ship either soldier had ever seen. Looking down the length of the hull, a second companionway ladder could be seen servicing the bow of the ship fifty paces away. And everywhere above them, a web of rigging tied something to something else, and everything to the deck.

Aulus cast an affectionate glance along the ship's fine lines. "Gaius Lucullus! Is she not the grandest ship you have ever seen? This is the *Aeneas*, my first venture, and I am the heavily-mortgaged owner of her. That goose in flight on her sternpost over the quarterdeck, that is the emblem of the Galban shipping enterprise." Gaius and Antonius nodded in admiration.

"I have three ships like this under construction in Myos Hormos, the ones I told you about last night, jointly funded with the Senate. Ships of this size have never been used for the Indian Ocean trade, so it is an investment of equal interest to the Empire and to me, as well as transport for our delegation. The three are being completed in the yards there, but still require rigging, sail manufacture and fitting, trimming of the mast and so forth. And sea trials.

Since this trade will link three continents, I have chosen to name them the *Europa*, the *Asia* and the *Africa*. We will be going south to monitor their final stage soon."

As Aulus was elaborating on his shipbuilding efforts, an alarm bell began to clang on one of the galleys directly opposite the *Aeneas*, interrupting the discussion. Still seated in the cart, the men turned to watch as sailors sprang into action, quickly putting away whatever tasks they had been performing. Some leapt to tend the lines at the bow and stern, others disappeared below decks to man oars. On the quarterdeck aft by the steering oars, an officer of the deck was crying out commands that carried clearly: "Signal in the air! Get underway at once to conduct armed operations! Captain to the bridge!"

Aulus pointed to the naval headquarters building by the lighthouse. From a mast at the top of the first level of the building fluttered multi-colored flags, snapping in the breeze. "Don't worry, this is a drill. The Prefect Admiral of the Fleet does this on a daily basis. Today it's the *Danuvia's* turn."

The sailors executed what appeared to the soldiers to be a well-orchestrated dance to ready the ship for sea, punctuated by shouted orders from the officer of the deck.

Down the quay jogged about twenty marines at a brisk double-time, dressed in light naval armor. They turned down onto the wooden walkway by the *Danuvia*, their sandaled feet thudding across the gray weathered wood and down the wooden gangway to the deck of the ship, where they fell into formation. As the last marine came aboard, sailors cast off the gangway with a thud onto the dock, and the bow lines landed with a splash in the water. The stern line handlers tugged fiercely, pulling the ship by its bootstraps from the dock sternfirst. As the bow cleared the pilings, the oars emerged, backed water and yawed the bow to port with an asymmetrical stroke to line up parallel to the quay. Below decks, the monotonous beat of the drum timing the strokes began its steady rhythm, and the oars gave a forward stroke. The ship surged forward, and white foam began to break around the ship's ram. Armed and alert, the warship began a graceful turn toward the eastern exit, her painted eyes glaring wickedly ahead searching for its foe, racing for the breakwater and open sea, her signal flags snapping in the breeze on her bare poles.

"Well, he'll make it easy. She has a bone in her teeth already," smiled Aulus, watching the white foam break around her bow and form a vee-shaped wake. Wind caught the breaking crests and tore away white spindrift.

"That was well-executed," said Gaius Lucullus, admiringly, as the *Danuvia* rounded the breakwater and turned into the open sea. Neither Gaius nor Antonius had had much contact with the Navy throughout their career. However, the discipline and flawlessly executed timing of the galley's sortie bespoke considerable training, which had impressed both the soldiers.

The *Danuvia* in the distance met the rollers of the open Mediterranean, her bare poles pitching against the blue sky.

"The legate an' I agree, those was the biggest youngsters I has had the pleasure to see. I bet they'd make a great wrestlin' team!" said Antonius, obviously enjoying the show.

"They do, and remind me to tell you a story about them! So let me show you two my ship. I think you will find this a bit more comfortable than your last troop transport, Antonius," said Aulus, dismounting from the cart and walking along the dock toward the distant bow.

"Our ships will be similar to this one, a bit bigger, with a third mast aft just about there," Aulus said, pointing to the deck above them. "My shipbuilder is on new ground with that rig. He isn't sure about how it will handle. He'd rather leave it off, but I think we can shave days off a long trip with just a few more knots of speed."

They continued walking forward along the dock adjacent to the ship. Antonius leaned his head back to gaze skyward through the complicated rigging, estimating the yardarm to be at least seventy-five feet up.

"We hoist the mainsail and main topsail here. With all sheets to the wind and a fair breeze, our ships can cover as much as two hundred miles in a single day, fully loaded. But right now, it's the winter season, and sails are being refurbished."

They continued on to the bow companionway ladder, under the foremast, inclined at a jaunty forty-five degree angle.

"Yer Excellency, what is this odd… mast, yer call 'em?" asked Antonius.

"That is the bowsprit that carries the *artemon*, a small sail rigged to that yardarm there. It helps bring her head around."

"Hail, Aulus Aemilius, and please bring your party aboard!" A black-bearded figure hailed them in Greek from the elevated quarterdeck above the stern. "You are expected!"

"Hail, Appollonius, and we shall do so, now." Aulus responded, also in Greek, and turned toward his cousin. "That is *navarklos* Appollonius, captain of the *Aeneas*." He motioned the two men toward the forward companionway. "Grip the line, Antonius. It's sturdier than it looks."

Antonius seemed unconvinced. *Damned ships! Everything moves!* He grabbed the single rope accommodation line gracing the right side of the gangplank, and stepped up onto it cautiously. He swore as the gangplank's dockside wheels slipped under his weight and he momentarily lost his balance. Grasping the accommodation line in his white knuckles, Antonius proceeded gingerly up the gangplank, trying not to watch the choppy water slapping between the dock and the hull of the *Aeneas* beneath his feet. Gaius followed, a bit more at ease, and finally Aulus, who slipped effortlessly and casually up onto the ship, despite his bulk.

As they landed on the finely-finished deck planking, Appollonius greeted each with a handshake, and a "Welcome aboard." The landsmen found the *Aeneas* a steady, immovable platform. From the deck, they could watch the naval galleys swaying with the chop of the harbor current, but the *Aeneas* could well have been part of the dock.

"You'll pardon my empty ship, Aulus Aemilius. We have only a skeleton crew of caretakers aboard, now that repairs from the last sailing season are completed. Since we will begin preparations for the spring season in earnest in a week, I have given most of them time off now. Today there are only myself and ten men aboard," said Appollonius, scanning the mostly empty ship. "The crew will begin returning next week."

"You have always kept your ships in such immaculate shape, Appollonius. These two soldiers will be journeying with me out across the Indian Ocean. I thought I would show them the type of craft to expect," said Aulus. "But you know the *Aeneas* so much better than I, would you do the honor of showing them around?"

"Certainly." Appollonius turned toward the two soldiers. "You gentlemen will be traveling on the three finest ships ever to be built. Three masts, not two, and half again as much sail as this one. And fifty feet longer."

Antonius tried to picture a ship fifty feet longer than this one, without much success.

Appollonius turned his attention back to Aulus. "How is the third sail working for you?"

"We don't know yet. The rigging should be completed next month. Frankly, the shipbuilder is not happy. But the *Europa's* masts have been stepped, and that pretty much sets the design. *Alea jacta est*, the die has been cast, as we say in Latin. If I am wrong, and the ships sink on sea trials, I am out millions of *sesterces* and die in disgrace. But what else is new?"

"You've always been a risk-taker, Aulus, and always a lucky one. *Fortuna favet portuna*, fortune favors the bold, as you also say in Latin. Well, this ship doesn't belong in the same dock with your new ones but let's see what we can show your friends."

He led the men aft in their tour. Along the way, they passed something familiar to the soldiers, five-foot *ballistae*, four on a side, very similar to the army's wagon-mounted mobile crossbows.

"I see you found our weaponry! This ship was built for the Mediterranean trade, and is only lightly armed," Appollonius said. "Mostly we use incendiary bolts to set fire to a pirate's ship. If you do that, you've won."

Antonius was impressed, "No marines?" he asked.

"No marines. Our sailors can swing swords with the best."

Aulus added, "We will be adding still more capability to our Indian Ocean ships, because the waters will be more dangerous. Perhaps you can assist in training the crew?"

"To be sure, sir," answered Antonius, rubbing his hands over the smooth wooden guide, and the well-tended torsion spring of the lethal weapon.

They continued aft to the quarterdeck, a deckhouse the width of the ship extending to the stern, with steeply-pitched ladders to the guardrail-lined roof. "Here we have an elevated quarterdeck." Appollonius levered himself up the ladder to the roof followed by the three. "This gives us a better view of what is going on. The helmsman is here. And below deck it gives nice accommodations for the Master, Aulus Aemilius when he rides with us, and myself." The goose-winged stern ornament soared over the quarterdeck in frozen flight. "Good luck, there," he said, throwing his arm out in salute to the wooden bird.

Apollonius led them down the ladder back to the main deck, turning into a hatchway in the center of the quarterdeck leading to a small hallway, dimly lit. "Straight aft is the shipping master's cabin. My cabin is on the left, and opposite it is the navigator's." Apollonius opened the door at the end and held it while they entered the master's cabin.

That cabin ran the full width of the ship. The late afternoon sun streamed in through five expensive Egyptian glass-paned windows covering the entire stern. Only a few distortions upset the view of the harbor, looking aft to the dockyard and the Pharos lighthouse. The room was furnished with a large comfortable bunk, a reclining couch for dining, and a desk in the center under a hanging oil lamp. Apollonius laughed. "It is here the Master counts out how much money he made!"

"Maybe. If he pays off his creditors!" replied Aulus with a wry smile.

"How much do your ships under construction cost?" asked Gaius.

"Millions! And still more to fund the crew and line up the money for purchases!"

The size of this project was overwhelming to Gaius, who had been impressed with the one hundred twenty pounds of gold which he was supposed to deliver to the king of the Hanaeans, worth about a half-million *sesterces*. Now it seemed a pittance.

"You put together some sort of a consortium to do this?" asked Gaius.

"Consortium, yes, but I am still fronting over half the cost. I mortgaged this ship to the Aeliae Isidora and Olympias. They may be women, but they are the biggest shipping magnates in Myos Hormos and own the only shipyard there big enough to build my ships. I had to reserve space, paid in advance, before the Senate approved funding. But enough of that, that will be paid off. We will double our wealth in one trip, no problem. Continue the tour, Apollonius, and no more talk of mere money. What is gold, anyway, compared to a ship such as this? Just a shiny rock from the ground. These ships are a creation of the genius of man!"

The captain's and navigator's cabins were similar but smaller than the huge master's cabin, with wooden shutters instead of glass, propped up to admit the afternoon breeze. Appollonius allowed them to peer into his cabin, but not to enter. "It's a mess. I am working out our sailing schedule for the next season."

They went below to the second deck by a ladder that led to the officers' mess and quarters, smaller but still luxurious compared to a Danubian troop transport. They continued through the crew's quarters in the center section, penetrated by the two masts. A handful of men worked at tables with attached benches at various tasks below swinging oil lamps. Along the sides were wooden bunks, four high, berthing for about two hundred men... almost three centuries without crowding.

Apollonius continued his discussion of the technicalities of the ship, most of which were lost on the soldiers, as they peered down into the hold to the below decks cargo area to see lashed spare yardarms, extra timber, coil after coil of rope, the bones of the ship, the backbone of the keel. "Forward, dividing the two cargo holds and nearly dead amidships, is our water supply. When we are at sea, water is perhaps our most valuable resource. Landlubbers don't realize it, but seawater cannot be drunk... it is too salty. We must carry all our own water for a thirty-day period at sea... That gives us an extra fifty tons of ballast down here to keep us balanced."

Against the forward bulkhead was a brick oven, covered by gleaming white ceramic tiles and vented by a brass hood, surrounded by well-kept cooking utensils firmly lashed down.

"My good captain," interjected Gaius Lucullus, "what is the longest period you have spent at sea in a ship like this?"

"The *Aeneas* crossed the Mediterranean from end to end, from Spain to Alexandria, in about three weeks. Over two thousand miles, at an average speed of seven knots, without so much as a single break. There's not a ship that's come close to that."

Antonius winced at the thought. Two days was nearer his limit for time on the water, and he had found it far too long.

"So there you have it, from stem to stern, top to bottom. I could not show you more without getting underway," said Apollonius. "Aulus Aemelius, would you like to add anything?" The group climbed a ladder back up to the main deck and turned aft, returning to the quarterdeck.

"No, my good captain, that was most excellent. I thank you, sir, for your most informative tour of this splendid vessel. You may join us in the master's cabin or go about your many duties as you see fit."

"Thank you, sir, but I think I shall return to my perplexing schedule in my own cabin," answered Apollonius. "I thank you both for your patience."

"And may Poseidon bring you fair winds always upon the wine-red seas," answered Antonius, in flawless Ionian Greek, so different from his gutter Latin or dockyard *koine*.

"And you also," replied Apollonius, departing courteously.

"That's an excellent quote, my good Antonius," said Gaius Lucullus.

"Come in," said Aulus, ushering the group into the cabin, while Appollonius detached himself into his own. "Our shipping master Hasdrubal is in Rhodes for the holidays, but he has left some fine wine aboard. I am sure he will not object to sharing it. Antonius, too?"

"Please, yer Excellency," replied Antonius, reverting to Latin.

"Well, what do you think of the *Aeneas*?" asked Aulus.

"She is a true beauty. You cannot fail but to make a fortune on your trip if your new ones are anything like her. What a phenomenal venture you have put together here!" said Gaius.

"Cousin, I shall make a fortune or lose one. I have invested more heavily in this venture than anything which I have ever done. The ships are bought and paid for, and now all I await is the money from our consortium's bank in Rome to finance the remainder: retainers for the crews, supplies, and money for trading on our arrival. About thirty million more *sesterces*. The bankers will be busy with letters of credit on this one!" said Aulus, pouring each a bronze goblet of red wine. "Alexandrian. A good local vintage."

Aulus offered a goblet to Antonius, then poured one for himself.

The light was fading fast as the sun set over the Eunostos Harbor, framed fully in the stern windows. The Pharos lighthouse was already lit, its bronze reflector throwing its amber night beam into the gathering mist. The evening breeze was up, blowing the first harbor chill into the cabin through the open windows. Aulus lit a hanging lantern with a flint striker, trimming the wick till its friendly glow spread across the room.

"The sun sets quickly here in Egypt. No lingering sunsets like at home in Italy," he added, seating himself in the chair by the desk. "Please, there are folding chairs lashed against that wall. I am afraid we must tie everything down when not in use. It's very... nautical," he said with a chuckle.

"When do we plan to depart?" asked Gaius, savoring his wine.

"We must depart here not later than two weeks from now, up the Nile by boat, then overland to the port of Myos Hormos, about five hundred miles south of here. We must set sail from there by mid-April, in time to replenish our stores in Sabaea before striking out across the Indian Ocean with the June monsoon."

Gaius' heart sank, but he concealed his disappointment. *No point to even ask about a trip home.* "We can help with the overland trip, cousin. We can obtain, if you like, Imperial Post passes from *III Cyr*. It may be a bit austere, but the security will very good. We are carrying hard gold for the Hanaean court, no letters of credit for them! How many people in your party?"

"I like that idea, Gaius. I'll be taking my personal manservant, Lucius Parvus, and four *servi*, good bodyguards doubling as baggage handlers. Lucius handles all my finances and administrative work. He's good... very good. Efficient. Can you cover all of us?"

"We are all covered by Imperial orders, that will not be a problem."

Antonius volunteered the information he had gained the previous day, from the late Lucius Servilius Crassus. "Mail boat ter Thebes, then overland caravan with armed escort ter Myos Hormos. Two weeks travel at the most."

"That's about a week better than I could do commercially, and much better security. I will also be picking up considerable hard currency in Coptos. Please, make the arrangements, but let me know at once if there are problems. Shall we adjourn to the inn now? Livia is eagerly waiting to talk more with you two."

The three returned to the deck, the western skies ablaze as the sun sank below the waters to the west, and the light of Pharos casting an amber glow on the purple rollers. The evening mist began to dull the horizon to gray, as the black bulk of the *Danuvia* patrolled the harbor approaches like a nervous hound, her long sweeps propelling her centipede-like over the uneven sea.

And on the quay, a sailor with a narrow, weasel-like face, looked up from his work, carefully noting their departure.

CHAPTER 8: THREATS AND COUNTERTHREATS

A man darted swiftly from behind an Alexandrian alley, to cover his victim's mouth firmly with his left hand. His right hand guided the razor-sharp knife through the dense black foliage of the victim's beard, pressing its point firmly against the throbbing jugular, its blade across the windpipe.

The assailant hissed in the man's ear in sibilant Greek, "Not a sound. Struggle and you're a dead man." He increased the pressure of the knife blade ever so slightly to emphasize his words. "Nod gently if you understand."

The bearded man's head bobbed up and down slowly, twice. The assailant nodded his head to the alley. "We're going into the alley. Slowly." The knife-wielder glanced up and down the street as he backed up. No one seemed to have noticed the attack, or even glanced in their direction.

Out of the sunlight, he switched to guttural Aramaic, "Elibaal, Jeshua, quickly. Bind ye his hands." The two men emerged from an alleyway door with a rope and swiftly secured the man's hands behind him, then his feet, and gagged him with a dirty rag, before relinquishing his grip. Yakov and his assistant gracelessly placed the man face down in the alleyway muck, working the free end of the rope around the man's neck in a slip knot. Any struggle on the hapless victim's part would immediately threaten him with strangulation.

They wrapped the man in a large blanket, and the three nonchalantly carried him back out on their shoulders into the street and the sunshine, to be dumped in the back of a donkey carriage. The choke rope guaranteed that the bundle wiggled only slightly, then lay quite still, as the three clambered onto the seat with Yakov at the reins. Yakov whistled up the donkeys, clucking and snapping the reins, and they pulled into the streets.

They wandered the streets of Alexandria for an hour, mostly circling idly on a random course throughout the city. Whenever there were no observers, they prodded their bundle to ensure that it still moved or made a muffled, gagging sound, indicating it still breathed.

At last they came to an alley near the Eunostos Harbor, and turned down that one into another, and yet another, each filthier and more run down than the last. They pulled to a halt before a three-story apartment that had been abandoned due to a fire.

A matted, ragged blanket that had once sported four or five bright colors covered the doorway. The three dragged their bundle through the doorway and pulled the blanket behind them. In the dark, a single table sat in the middle of the room, incongruous amidst the charred, jumbled timbers from the collapsed upper floors. While the first floor windows were sealed with boards and blankets, light streamed in through the second and third floor windows, illuminating the stumps of floor joists protruding from the smoke-blackened plaster walls. A shadowy, robed figure sat behind the table. "Thou hast my package, Yakov. Is it undamaged?"

Elibaal smiled, "But for minor handling." He held out his hand. The gray-bearded man at the table slid three silver coins from his leather purse to the other side of the table, covering them still with his hand. "Let us then inspect the goods."

The three men undid the bundled man, removing the choke rope and foot hobbling. They left the hands bound and the gag in place, and helped the man to his feet. His eyes went wide as he recognized Ibrahim bin Yusuf. Ibrahim released his hold of the three silver coins and Elibaal took them, depositing one in his own purse and distributing the other two to Yakov and Jeshua. The three stepped into the shadows behind the bound man, who continued to glare at Ibrahim, who greeted his guest in Greek.

"Welcome, my good friend. It is unfortunate that we cannot meet as before, but you must understand the precautions necessary now. Not even you can know of my movements this time." He paused to clear his throat, and continued threateningly, "Perhaps, especially not you." He rose, placed his knuckles on the table and leaned forward. "I am sure you would like some cool water. I will release the rest of your bindings, but you must remember not to cry out or try to escape. Where we are, screams are not unusual, even at high noon. They would not be noticed."

The man nodded. "Releasest thou him, Elibaal," said Ibrahim.

Elibaal undid the man's hands, then his gag. Ibrahim passed him a cup of water. The man took some, rinsed his parched mouth of the foul taste of the gag, spat, and eagerly swallowed the rest. He hurled the cup away in anger.

"What is the meaning of this outrageous abduction, Ibrahim? Are we not comrades and allies? If you mean to do me in, you must do it quickly, or by every god in Canaan, I will have your miserable hide crucified atop the very lighthouse of Pharos before sundown!"

"I don't think that I would be crucified alone, my eager partner in crime. I have too many details on our mutual endeavors to share with our Roman friends in the event that I were captured. In any event, we are still partners in our greatest enterprise to date." Ibrahim returned to his seat, not taking his eyes off his guest. He withdrew a stiletto from his robe and proceeded to clean his fingernails.

"I felt it necessary to inquire into a recent death of a Roman soldier in the *III Cyrenaica* fort. I presume you know something of this incident." He completed the scraping of one fingernail and studied the deposit on the blade intently.

"Of course I know something of this incident. The young man had to die. I would have preferred to have done in the centurion that night also, your friend Aristides of the cock-and-bull story, but he was not in his quarters." The man was becoming sufficiently enraged that Elibaal and his companions edged closer.

"Why did you think that he had to die, my friend?" asked Ibrahim calmly, still picking at his fingernails.

"Because he could place me at the Bull and Dove. And the centurion could place you there. He saw me with you, though you were intelligent enough not to tell him my name. Even a Roman could deduce that perhaps we were both there - together."

"And how did he happen to be there, my friend?" asked Ibrahim, beginning the excavation of another fingernail.

"You know that as well as I do. We have used that drop for six months. My agent dropped off our rendezvous location to their travel clerk, and the clerk was to caution anyone who inquired of shipping arrangements to beware of you and to ask for Hasdrubal. Your agent could then come, give the sign and receive the location, and the clerk never knew what he did. It only cost us a few *denarii* a month to keep him on the payroll."

"But that day, not only did someone come into a Roman camp really looking for shipping information, but you, you Arab fool, you introduced yourself to that stranger. So don't blame me for the breakdown, Ibrahim, blame yourself. Had Aristides been an agent of the urban cohort instead of the idiot he turned out to be, you would be dead now."

"And you made sure that no one could connect me to you if that happened. Right?" asked Ibrahim, placing the stiletto on the table.

"One of us has to survive. It might as well be me," said the man with a mocking smile.

Ibrahim stood up abruptly, his chair toppling behind him. He grabbed the man by his expensive but mud-stained robes, twisting the collar into a knot around his neck, and forcing him to his knees opposite the table. Ibrahim seized the stiletto and placed the point just above the man's bobbling Adam's apple. He pressed until the tip penetrated the flesh, a trickle of blood running down the man's throat and over Ibrahim's clenched fist. "Arrogant dog! You have profited handsomely from our many enterprises and live freely to enjoy the fruits of our labors in the open as the first among equals in Alexandria. While I, the despicable pirate with a price on his head, skulk around the stews of Asia Minor, always glancing behind for the Roman waiting to bring me in. For harvesting what you send down to me, for sharing in the overabundance of trade that comes with this great Empire." He looked into his victim's eyes, wide with fear. "Did you think," continued Ibrahim, "that I was unaware that you might be tempted to offer me up, leaving you with your fine reputation, to enjoy your profits?" He paused, to let that sink in.

"I am not that stupid, my friend. I have witnesses to connect you to me in a hundred ways. I can show how you tipped the ships, your own and others, to me, how much you got from me and from the piracy clauses in your contract," he paused for emphasis. "And I know where the money went, and how your books balanced so you never showed a profit where none should exist. I know where your banks are, I know where all of them are. And if I should die or be captured, it is all written down, and my most trusted agents will ensure its delivery to the proper Roman authority. If I go to the cross, you go with me. And your family, your most respectable wife and children, will wind up on a Roman slave market." He released his hold on the man's throat and pocketed the stiletto.

The man came to his feet, nervously adjusting his robes, wiping the blood from his throat. "I did not mean to imply that I would betray you, Ibrahim," he stammered. "I meant to protect us both. If I erred, I erred on the side of protection."

"You did not protect yourself by killing that young man. You attracted more unnecessary attention. Had you killed the centurion as well, in the confines of a Roman army fort, the Roman interest would have become insurmountable, even more so than in the wake of your debacle with the four patricians. There is to be no more killing. We must keep our eyes firmly on our next target, Galba's new India traders. Do you understand?" he repeated. "No more killing."

"I understand."

He returned to his seat, and waved his left arm expansively. "Be seated, my friend. Yakov, Jeshua. A chair and some fine wine for my co-conspirator." A gracious smile covered his lips, as the two bodyguards produced a chair, wine and brass goblets from behind a half-burned roof timber. "A nasty cut on your neck, my friend. You should have it looked at very soon. Things get inflamed quickly here in Alexandria."

CHAPTER 9: MYOS HORMOS AND A VERY BAD DREAM

Gaius and Antonius stayed at Aulus's inn for a week while they made preparations for the journey.

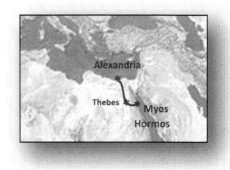

Gaius started several letters to his wife, all discarded, a waste of expensive papyrus paper. He decided to procrastinate further until they were in Myos Hormos.

In the meanwhile, Antonius went about the travel arrangements. Being on imperial orders, the centurion found it only moderately difficult to obtain the necessary passes for the Imperial Post for themselves, and another set for the Hanaeans. On the seventh day, he returned to Aulus' inn grinning, bearing the fourteen passes, with Trajan's and the Governor's signatures. "Here we be, me Excellencies! Signed an' official an' everythin'!" Aulus took those intended for the Hanaean party and gave them to Lucius Parvus, his administrator, for delivery.

The party celebrated with a final all-night tour of the entertainment of Alexandria.

The following morning, Aulus' party departed on the Post riverboat up the Nile to Thebes, the Hanaean party to follow later. There they left the boat for a military convoy over the Eastern Desert road to Myos Hormos, stopping briefly to pick up pre-positioned chests of gold and silver from the customs office at Coptos, the emperor's gift for the Hanaean king, and financing for trading enroute.

Aulus did not look forward to returning to Myos Hormos. He spent as much time there as he did in Rome or Alexandria, but he never found much to like about the disorderly town, made up of tumbledown mud brick buildings staggering around meandering alleyways. The smell of charcoal and dung cooking fires mingled with the smell of garbage and human waste. Myos Hormos had grown enormously in the past century, but without regard to any form of planning, sanitation or esthetics. And the weather was awful, especially now in the spring.

At the post station, Lucius Parvus rented a wagon and drove them a few miles along the road to the crest of a hill looking down into the Red Sea for their first view of the area. Although just a bit past dawn, already the heat lay oppressive on the bay, the sea steaming in the still, sultry morning. A hot wind blew in from the Arabian desert across the Red Sea, boiling humidity out of the Red Sea to deposit it like a wet, hot rag on the dirty face of Myos Hormos. Sprawling below them was a swarm of ships entering and leaving the port, mostly the triangular-rigged, low-slung native dhows, and a few larger ships. Aulus, sweating profusely, pointed at a shipyard about a mile away, where three huge hulls lay nestled against the dock, only one rigged with masts. "Our ships! They are nearly complete. Are they not fine, truly fine?"

Gaius smiled at his cousin. He too was feeling the heat and humidity. "Fine indeed. But where on earth do you find so much lumber here?"

Aulus pointed seaward at a freighter laboring southward towing a bundle of logs larger than itself. "See there? Lebanese cedar, the best shipbuilding timber in the world. Trekked overland across Judea and floated here under tow." A battered bireme galley, looking like it had seen one too many combats, labored out into the channel to intercept the ship. "That boat will take it in tow and bring it into port. That's one of our timber lighters. We got them cheap, retired from the Navy because they're liable to sink if they stay out more than a couple of hours. The boat is cheaper to replace than to repair."

"I'll bet rowing is hell inside that hull on this very hot day," said Gaius.

"To be sure. It is like this most of the time, stinking beastly hot and ghastly humid. Like the desert after a torrential rainfall, they say. And plenty of flies and mosquitoes," said Aulus, slapping at a swarm of tiny black midges around his arm. "Let's go down to our quarters, Lucius, and wash the desert off these good soldiers of Rome. Then I want to visit my ship. You and the other servants bunk up in the servants' quarters, refresh yourself and meet me at noon with the cart."

"Yes, my lord," said Lucius, clucking the mules into motion down the hill.

The road wound downhill steeply, requiring Lucius to apply the brakes several times with a squeal to keep from overrunning the mules. They drove past several nondescript houses and stopped in front of a large stone structure at the entrance to the shipyard.

"This is it, my lordships," said Lucius, dismounting from the cart with a leap.

The reddish tan sandstone structure was in the style of a Roman *domus*. Two scraggly brush plants contributed a sickly bit of grey-green color to the entranceway, which opened into the atrium with a nicely made pond gracing the center. Some greenery throve here and there in pots, paintings and frescoes decorating the walls. The massive walls did nothing to attenuate the oppressive heat and humidity, which wafted in with the hot damp air. Inside it was quiet, punctuated only by the droning of a particularly large fly somewhere.

A dark-skinned Nubian appeared, clad in a long flowing white robe with a cylindrical hat. He bowed and passed his hands over his face and chest in a gesture of obeisance and muttered his greeting. "*Salaam,* lordship. And lordships," he added, bowing in the direction of the other men. "Welcome. My name is Salawi, and I am head of this household. Did you have a pleasant journey, Lordship?" he said, in rather excellent Greek. Salawi's face was a shiny dark brown, almost black, the color of dark polished leather. His white teeth shone behind a full smile, and he seemed to give the impression of energy and efficiency.

"We did, indeed, Salawi. In fact, it was so pleasant that I am most glad that it did not extend another day in the desert. You seem to know me, but just to make sure, I am Aulus Aemilius Galba, guest of Aelia Isadora and Aelia Olympias, who have so generously given us their permission to stay here until our departure. This is my cousin, Gaius Lucullus, legate, his companion, Antonius Aristides, and my administrative servant, Lucius Parvus, whom I am sure you have met before. My other servants are outside, awaiting your household's directions to their accommodations."

"I am most pleased to be at your service, my lordships," Salawi said, bowing yet again. "May I offer you some wine?"

"Water, please, after the desert, and a bath," said Aulus, removing his sweat-soaked *kefira* from his head. "Lucius, you have done well this trip. Have the boys bring up the baggage, then they are free of duties. I want to bathe, meet with our hostesses, and visit the ship, then you too are done for the day."

Salawi returned with a silver tray holding six Egyptian glass goblets, each pearled with moisture. Aulus took his while Salawi handed out the remainder. Aulus took a sip, savoring the cool freshness, wondering where in this god-cursed heat the water was kept so cool, and fighting down a temptation to bathe in the chilled drinking supply.

"Thank you, Salawi. Are the Mistresses Isadora and Olympias here?" asked Aulus.

"We have sent runners for Mistress Isadora at her residence. I expect her by mid-morning. Mistress Olympias is overseas on business."

The Romans retired to their quarters and stripped off their sweat-soaked tunics. They reassembled in the atrium with towels about their waists, where Salawi was waiting with wine to lead them to the bath in a room on the far side of the atrium. The bath was tastefully tiled and ringed with perfumes and oils on shelves, the water warm.

After a lingering soak, the group returned to their rooms to change into the lightest tunics they had, and returned to the atrium as a stately, black-haired matron swept into the room, leaving the whiff of expensive perfume in her wake behind her billowing white silks. She took Aulus in an affectionate hug, kissing him on the cheek. "Welcome back, Aulus Aemilius!"

"Aelia Isadora! So pleased to see you! Our ships are well?"

"They are well. The *Europa's* masts are stepped, she's being rigged and is almost ready for sea trials. Hasdrubal is back, overseeing the final fitting out with your *navarklos*, Captain Demetrios. We will step the others after her sea trials, in case we need to make modifications."

"Your shipyard does fine work. There's no other shipyard here that could accommodate ships of that size."

"They were a challenge to my shipwrights, but they are the best on the Red Sea."

"Here is confirmation from your Alexandrian bank that we have deposited the agreed-on sum. I don't need to inspect your work, Isadora. We have done business before."

"I had word from the bank that you had done so. I brought the lien on the *Aeneas* to release to you. You can have your flagship back." She handed him a scroll, her eyes dancing with glee. "It has been a pleasure owning her, if only as collateral."

"It was a good thing government funding came through. Even after the Senate passed it on Trajan's request, there was always the fear that it would be cancelled, and I would lose my flagship trying to build ships I didn't have money to complete."

"We would have worked something out, Aulus Aemilius, I would never have taken your flagship. We all knew the urgency of your gamble. Someone always wants into our shipyard unscheduled, and your reserved time would not have stayed open long if you had to give it up. But my financial manager is a stickler for paperwork, so the mortgage was necessary."

"What is Aelia Olympias up to… overseas?"

"She is stealing one of your ideas, Aulus," she said, relaxing the formality. "She wintered over in Muziris to open our own warehouse as you did so wisely a few years ago, to buy cheap during the off-season."

"Imitation is sincere flattery. Oh, but I am rude. These are my traveling companions, Gaius Lucullus, legate, and Antonius Aristides, centurion. Gaius is my cousin by my marriage to the beautiful Livia, and Antonius is a long-time companion of his, both from the Twelfth Lightning Bolt up in Syria. Gentlemen, this is Aelia Isadora, she and her partner Olympias are the two richest shipping magnates in Egypt."

Gaius took her hand in both of his, "At your service, my lady."

Antonius was a bit more intrusive, though with all seriousness, "Charmed, me ladyship, and beggin' yer pardon, but how does a woman find herself in such a line of work?"

"You mean, what the hell are women doing in the shipping business?" she said in mock firmness, her eyes twinkling as Antonius came as close to blushing as he ever did.

"No offense, me ladyship... I'm sorry."

She laughed, a hearty deep laugh. "No offense, my good Antonius. You are not the first man to ask that question. In fact, some people think that every ship lost at sea, or every sailor swept overboard, is the gods' retribution for such an affront to the divine plan as us. Though ships and men have been lost long before I and Olympias took over our late husbands' business. And that is how it happened, Antonius... they started the business thirty years ago as partners, and we both took a great interest in how it was run, helped manage the books and schedules while we were raising our families. About fifteen years ago, they were both lost at sea, and we were surprised that their wills named us as joint co-heirs to the business. So we began by staring down the men, convincing them that we, not they, owned the business and had the final say. Some took more convincing than others." She sighed, then continued. "We both miss our husbands, they were wonderful men, but they put a great deal of trust in our business acumen, and we have tried very hard to not betray that trust. Thank you for asking, Antonius, and I assure you again, no offense taken."

"I am impressed, me ladyship. Truly."

"I understand it takes a lot to impress a centurion," she said, taking his hand with a smile.

Just then, Lucius Parvus arrived with the cart, and they took their farewells.

Lucius drove the cart to the dockyard where the *Europa* lay, nearly fully fitted out, with the *Asia* and *Africa* still under construction. The dockyard was silent and largely deserted as were the ships in the noonday heat. The trio made their way up the gangway. A big, bearded man in multicolored Phoenician dress hailed Aulus, and seized him in a familiar bear hug. "Aulus Aemilius, my good friend, what a pleasure to see you again. Salawi sent word that you had arrived. I trust you had a pleasant trip?"

"Pleasant enough. A journey more pleasant when completed," answered Aulus. "My friends, you must meet our sailing master, the great Hasdrubal, finest of the fine line of Phoenician sailors, whom I personally chose to command our merchant squadron. This is my cousin, Gaius Lucullus, legate of the *Legio XII Fulminata* and his centurion Antonius Aristides."

As Hasdrubal's eyes fell on the centurion, his heart thudded hollowly in his chest. *Like that crucifixioner's hammer so many years ago, thud... thud... thud... thud.* He struggled to remain expressionless while his mind spun wildly through scenarios that could link a drunken centurion in an Alexandrian dive to the richest merchant in the Indian trade. *Did he, does he recognize me? Oh, gods, is this a trap?*

"Hasdrubal, are you all right?" asked Aulus, concerned at the change in expression in Hasdrubal's face.

"I am sorry. It is the heat," said Hasdrubal, then fixating the centurion with a penetrating gaze, "Pleased to meet you. Have you and I met before?" *Better to confront this head-on than to stumble blindly in the dark.*

Antonius returned the intense scrutiny. "Aye, captain, I have heard so much about ye, it seems that I must know yer by sight as well, but I cannot place where we may have met."

This man is either a total fool or an excellent actor. "Perhaps we have met in a previous life. You know, some Greek philosophers believe we live our lives over and over again, transmitting our souls at death to another person, creature or deity. That belief is particularly strong in India. They believe that often, when you feel that you have met someone but cannot remember where, that you two have shared a common experience in a previous life." *Or a dive in Alexandria.*

"Perhaps so, me good sir. Perhaps so."

Hasdrubal toured the *Europa* with the men, with Aulus pointing out the similarities and differences from the ship they had visited in Alexandria. Most significantly, she was rigged with the controversial third mast. The *Europa* was more heavily armed, as well. She was fitted with eight five-foot *ballistae* on swivels, four on a side.

But while Hasdrubal toured the ship, pointing out the features of the ship which he knew so intimately, his mind grappled with the task at hand, determining if this was coincidence or a trap, and if the latter, who set it and how to avoid it.

The coincidence was that these two just happened to wind up shipping with the richest victim he and Ibrahim had ever staked out. Just coincidentally one of them is related to him. What was it that Aulus Aemilius had said? Cousins. After the centurion had just chanced to blunder into one of the few face-to-face meetings Ibrahim and he ever dared to have, with just the right code word to attract Ibrahim's attention. And a crock about a report of the deaths of four highly-placed citizens that he himself had ordered robbed and killed. Luckily, the report on that incident stolen from the officia *had not added up to what Aristides had said... indicating he must have been onto much more than he let on, but what? How much?*

The group went on touring the ship, Hasdrubal pointing out incomplete work, or work that had been done improperly and needed redoing. But he was speaking by rote, having prepared this tour for days. His mind was not on the task, but on Antonius.

"Beggin' yer pardon, sir, could it have been in Alexandria?" asked Antonius, as they rounded the bow of the ship.

"I'm sorry, I wasn't quite paying attention," replied Hasdrubal.

"Could it have been in Alexandria that we met somewhere? Last month. On the docks, perhaps, or somewhere downtown?"

A good shot. Hasdrubal shook his head negatively. "No, I am sure we did not, quite sure. I was in Rhodes, then came here last month." He returned to his patter of nautical terminology, but now his eyes had a most distant, glazed expression.

Crucifixion. Despite the noonday heat, Hasdrubal shivered as he recalled that one crucifixion he had witnessed. *The man staggered drunkenly as the Roman crucifixion team lay the heavy crossbeam on his back, tying his wrists to hold it in place.*

When they reached the place of execution, they lay the man down and drove nails through his bound wrists into the beam. Expertly avoiding the arteries which would cause his life to course out redly in just a few minutes. Thud, went the hammer, and the man screamed as the nail shattered his wrist. Then thud, thud, thud, thud. Again for the other side. Then they hoisted the cross beam with the man up onto the upright. They nailed the feet vertically through the ankle to the step. Thud, and another scream, thud, thud, thud, thud, thud. So nailed, he might carry his weight for days.

Crucifixion reduced the strongest, most defiant man to a pitiable, whimpering mass of tormented flesh. There were no martyrs at the cross. It didn't allow them.

The man tried to die defiantly. For most of the first day, he protested his innocence and hurled invective at the soldiers. He then fell silent, his chest rising and falling convulsively.

Throughout the night, he dozed fitfully, but lurched awake every few minutes. At sunrise the following morning, he stirred, staring about with his glazed eyes. After lunch the centurion gave permission to terminate the execution. A soldier broke the man's legs with a club with a sickening crunch. Unable to lift himself to breathe, he struggled desperately for a few minutes for air, then his chest heaved for the last time and life left him.

The man had been his uncle, Isdrubal, who had raised him from childhood when Hasdrubal's father had died. Isdrubal had the misfortune of knowing some fellow Phoenicians who spoke often of avenging the Roman rape of Carthage centuries before. These men had taken part in an attack on some Roman soldiers, and they and all the people they knew, including Isdrubal, were rounded up, tried and crucified. This despite the fact that Isdrubal had always believed that the benign Roman rule of law was the best thing that could happen to Phoenicia. Till the night when the soldiers knocked on the door and then, not waiting for the door to be opened, burst in with swords drawn. "You'll come along with me, sir. We have some questions for you." In Latin. Not Greek. Not Aramaic. Latin. *Just some questions.*

Hasdrubal, all of twelve years old, had watched every minute of the ignominious last thirty-six hours of Isdrubal's life, in the mud beyond the perimeter established by Roman lances.

"I said, when do you expect to get underway for sea trials? Honestly, Hasdrubal, are you sure you are all right? It seems as though the heat might have gotten to you," Aulus asked with concern, placing his arm on the Phoenician's shoulder. "Let's get you out of the sun here." They retreated to the master's cabin for shelter from the direct rays of the sun. Inside, it was even hotter and more stifling than the main deck, even with all the windows flung wide.

"Lie down here, my good Hasdrubal, I cannot have you become ill now. Whatever would become of our departure? We have only a few weeks until we sail. I want you to stay at my residence until you recover." He lay Hasdrubal down on his own cot, while Antonius gave him water.

Thud, thud, thud, the crucifixioner's hammer in his chest. "You'll come along, sir. We need to ask you some questions." Just the way they came for my uncle that night. So the trap isn't yet sprung, and a trap not sprung is a trap that can yet be avoided. But how?

CHAPTER 10: SUSPICIONS

The visit to the *Europa* was cut short due to Hasdrubal's sudden illness. Antonius felt that there was something very, very wrong here. Hasdrubal retired to his quarters, while Aulus and his companions returned to the residential *domus*.

Gaius and Antonius retired to their adjoining rooms. "Sir, may I talk privately with yer?" asked Antonius at Gaius' door.

"Certainly, Antonius. Come in, please." He gestured toward a folding camp chair in the corner. "Sit down. What's on your mind?"

"Maybe nothin'. Were yer watchin' Hasdrubal today while him an' me was talkin'?"

"Yes, closely. He seemed to genuinely recognize you from somewhere, didn't he?"

"Aye, that he did, an' din't seem ter like it much, either. Funny thing, I kinder recognize him meself" Antonius paused. "I baited him a bit, an' suggested we had met somewhere in Alexandria an' he got sick, real sick when I did that."

"It seems he started getting sick when he first saw you!"

"Been rackin' me brain ter figger that out. I'm sure I woulda remembered being introduced to the richest merchant shipper in Alexandria. Maybe I met him at the Bull an' Dove," chuckled Antonius. "That's where I was supposed ter meet him, according to the late young Crassus. But I met with Ibrahim bin- whatever, with his silent friend instead. I made a point ter remember that guy's face, an' ter think on it, I'd think it were him. But it wasn't his kinda place, and it don't make sense for a man like him ter be hangin' out with the biggest pirate in the Mediterranean."

"Tell me again what the stranger looked like."

"About same build, black beard, blue eyes, hooked nose. Looked ter be thirty or forty years old. Hard ter see more, he kept a cowl over his head, never said a word so I can't match the speech. Am I bein' too suspicious, sir?"

"Maybe. That describes a lot of men in Alexandria. You're right, the biggest shipping master in Alexandria is not likely to be hanging out in a dive with the biggest pirate in the Mediterranean. But there are some things here that don't feel right. That young soldier getting killed is connected to all of this, and someone wanted your trumped-up report badly. Don't get too far away from your weapons."

"Aye, right here," said Antonius, reaching back through the neck of his tunic to withdraw his army dagger. "Suspended right there between me shoulder blades."

"Look, tomorrow I am going down to the garrison. I want to see if there is any news from home or *III Cyr*. Anything developing up in Alexandria, the Third said they would keep us informed by military post. And I am expecting some letters from the Twelfth. Now, for you, here is my plan. I am going to assign you to Hasdrubal to train the sailors in fighting tactics. He won't like it much, but I suspect that Aulus's little fleet has attracted the attention of every pirate that can put a hull in the Red Sea. Aulus Aemilius has already suggested you train them on the *ballistae* and I am sure he will buy the rest of the program, even if Hasdrubal wants to stall you off. Size up the crew, work them hard at swordsmanship and see if we can have some fighting sailors. And keep your ears open. That will plug you into some of the shipboard gossip...but watch your back."

The group dined after sundown. The oppressive heat kept the meal small. Goat, roasted on a spit, some olives and figs, thin breadcakes, all washed down with unwatered wine was enough for everyone's appetite. Salawi seemed trying to be everywhere, but when finally the last of the light meal was cleared away and the wine refilled, he departed into the shadowy kitchen area, and the three men, alone at last, were free to chat. Aulus was bubbling with enthusiasm.

"Isn't she fine? She'll be taking to sea this week for sea trials, and the other two the week following."

"Cousin," asked Gaius, "Didn't the behavior of Hasdrubal strike you as strange? He seemed to become positively alarmed, then ill, at the sight of Antonius."

"He did indeed, but I am sure that it is the heat. And have you not seen someone that looks just like someone from your past...but is not? Or an event, where for a minute, it seems to have happened to you before, and you know the unfolding of events before they take place? Such was the case, I am sure."

"Sure was coincidental," said Antonius. "Got sick just when I mentioned meeting him in Alexandria..." Directing his attention to Gaius, he continued. "Sir, does he know about the Bull and the Dove an' the other goin' on with *III Cyr?*"

"He does, Antonius, I told him the next day at his inn. But thanks for not assuming that I had!" Gaius turned toward Aulus. "Hasdrubal... how long has he been down here?"

"Since January. No, he made a trip back in early February to visit his family in Rhodes, then to Tyre to check on the timber for the masts. But that was a short trip, I think the travel was longer by far than his stay in Tyre," answered Aulus.

"But not by way of Alexandria?"

"No, he went by Gaza and the coast road, much shorter that way. He hasn't been in Alexandria since before the winter solstice. Why?"

"Just wondering if he could have run into Antonius there. But I guess not." Gaius paused, then continued. "Cousin, please ensure that you do not discuss the matter of the incidents in *III Cyr* and the Bull and the Dove with Hasdrubal yet. It may be... premature. Tomorrow I will go down to the military garrison here. They should have news, if any, which may shed light on the incidents in the camp," said Gaius, hoping that his nascent distrust of Hasdrubal was not warranted.

The three continued chatting quietly into the night, drinking wine and batting mosquitoes, as the stars pierced the sky over the sweltering Red Sea port.

CHAPTER 11: A CAMP IN THE DESERT

Gaius Lucullus set off alone in the morning to the military garrison near Myos Hormos. Despite the heat, he went in battle gear, since this was a professional call on a contemporary commander. He mounted up on a frisky grey, one of several fine Arabian ponies Salawi had procured for them, and spurred it into a gallop.

The cohort-sized unit, cobbled together from *vexillatio* detachments from various eastern legions, was located to the northeast along the main artery between Myos Hormos and Coptos.

He crested the hill and looked down at the encampment, a small one about a tenth the size of a legion *castra*, definitely a non-standard unit. Rather than the orderly beige eight-man army tents arranged in an orderly grid, the wide multi-colored awnings of Bedouin tents sprawled about in barely perceptible order. He did recognize the walls of the encampment, and a wide, staggering row between tents which might be the *via principalis*, and the large tent on the south side of it might be the *praetorium*. Maybe.

To the east, several large strings of horses competed for the sparse desert vegetation, while a few dozen camels milled about on the western side, an unusual number of animals.

As Gaius approached the camp, he began to wonder if perhaps these were the *auxilia* native troops rather than the Roman. Most of the soldiers were dressed Bedouin-style, with white, full-length flowing robes, no Roman uniforms in sight. As he rode up to the eastern gate that gave way to the *via principalis*, the two sentries snapped to attention. Here Gaius finally noted some evidence of Roman army equipment, for about their waist were the *gladii* swords and bucklers around their Bedouin robes, and lightweight Gallic helmets. The two soldiers crossed their lances to block his entrance, and in a Latin so vulgar that it could only have been spoken by a native, one challenged his identity.

"Gaius Lucullus, *legatus, Legio XII Fulminata*, here to see the commander. On Imperial orders." He identified himself, waving the parchment with the Imperial seal. The two withdrew lances, and he cantered into the camp.

Beneath the open sides of the tents, he could hear all the familiar accents of Latin normally heard in camp, the nasally twang of Gaul, the harsh guttural pronunciation of Germania, the clipped syllables of the Roman lower class *insulae*, and occasionally the careful enunciation of someone with some formal education. The Roman army was indeed in, and underneath the tents, Gaius noted that the troops were doing those things that all Roman troops do in camp: reading watch assignments, complaining about duty, gambling, and comparing women. They just did not look like Roman troops. Under the tents, most were bare-chested with knee-length kilts of white linen, Egyptian style. Outdoors, most donned the Bedouin robe, although some hardy, heavily-tanned souls braved the sun's direct rays on their bronzed skin. Nowhere was there a proper uniform to be seen.

Outside what he hoped was the *praetorium*, he dismounted. His own uniform had attracted considerable attention, since he was the only one wearing one. Two troops appeared out of nowhere to escort his mount. A young tribune, perhaps twenty-five, lean, bronzed and tautly muscled, emerged wearing a linen kilt. Gaius saluted in a nonchalant sort of way, despite the disparity in rank: the young man, after all, acted like the commander. Gaius noted that the edge of the young man's kilt was decorated with a wide purple stripe. That meant socially, if not militarily, the young man outranked him.

"Welcome to Camp Charon!" the young man greeted him. "If you've a coin in your mouth, we'll ferry you across the Styx to Hades in Arabia on the other side, where it is really hot." He extended his hand, "I am Sextus Julius, a distant relative of much more important people in the Julian *gens*."

No wonder the young man acted like he could get away with anything. He was somehow related to the whole Julio-Claudian line of emperors down to the late but unlamented Nero.

"Gaius Lucullus, *legatus Legio XII Fulminata*, here on Imperial orders." Gaius said stiffly and formally. He did not like the unmilitary camp, and he did not like young tribunes flaunting their social status and higher connections, though those connections had done the young man little good in getting this assignment.

"Ah, yes, you have been preceded by a ton of mail, most of which was addressed to me about you and Senator Aulus Aemilius' mission. Come in out of the heat and sit down." He motioned to the camp chair, while he seated himself at his desk.

"Rufus!" A young red-headed soldier appeared from behind a curtain. "Water for the good legate!" He turned back to face Gaius. "You need water now," not asking.

"Please feel free to remove all or part of your uniform, as you see fit. As you have noticed, and probably do not approve, I have developed my own uniforms for desert warfare, and my own style of fighting. The Roman uniform here we call the *clibanus*, a bread-oven. For what it does to the men inside them, as you are discovering but will not yet admit. So we dress and fight here as the Bedouin do. They've been doing that in this hell-hole for longer than we have, so I reckon they know what they are doing."

Gaius thought that the young Sextus was certainly enthusiastic, and what he said made sense. The uniform had become stifling just in the short ride out from town, and it was still early morning. He removed his helmet, the leather liner and chinstraps black with sweat, and rubbed the pressure lines on his forehead. Any fight at noon, especially an all-day pitched fight, would probably kill more men from heat than from the sword. He savored the sweet water Rufus gave him. "I noticed that the camp was... unusual."

"Unusual! You should have seen it when I first got here. The previous commander of this detachment ran this camp like it was in Germania, with daily sword drill and three mile runs in full kit. He killed way too many of his men. Criminal! Dead from exhaustion, thirst and heatstroke. Combat out here is different, and he couldn't think of any new way that hadn't been done for centuries. Chasing Bedouin raiding parties on foot." Sextus' disgust was obvious. "With all those casualties, not once, in two years, did he ever close with an enemy. Not even close enough to chuck a *pilus* at them."

"And you?"

"I've been here nine months, and I'll probably be here a while more, the problem with success... I spent a month with the Bedouin *auxilia* here to find out how they fight, and how they beat the desert. Then I trained the men to fight like they do."

"The Parthians aren't coming down here to raid. They'd like to, for all the money that moves through this dung-heap, but they can't get here. No big army is coming up the Nile and across the desert to the west of us, either. It just isn't going to happen. The Bedouin is the threat here, and the Bedouin is a mobile raider. He lives on his horse, he strikes like lightning out of the desert, he steals what he wants and disappears back into the dunes. If you want to fight him, you fight him on his terms and his territory."

"So when I got back, I took all my centurions back there to train with them. We learned how to find water in the desert, what to eat, and what not to eat. Then we all got together and developed desert tactics and formations, and along the way almost everything Roman, except discipline, went away. We dress like Bedouins because that robe keeps you cool in the desert. We fight like Bedouin on horseback, or on camelback for the really deep desert work. We do everything the Bedouin does, but faster and better." The young man was smiling.

"Our first few engagements were inconsequential, except to the men we lost, but at least we engaged. Two months ago, we tracked down Ibn Sahaad, sixty miles east of here, and left twenty of his men in the sand. Missed him, but just barely. And only lost two men, one by an accident." Sextus could not conceal his pride.

"And these aren't your best legionaries here." Sextus looked knowingly at Gaius. "You can bet that when your legion's turn came to ante up a century or two for detached duty here, you didn't send me your best troops. You probably didn't send me a proper century, for that matter. You scraped the bottom of the barrel for the eighty worst slackers you could find, promoted one to centurion, sent them to me and hoped I'd forget to send them back!" The young man laughed and Gaius chuckled inwardly, for that very much described the process they had gone through last winter to assemble their "century" for detached duty.

"And I'll take them, because I'm a misfit, too. My family hates me because I hated the bullshit that went with life in Rome. Didn't understand important questions like who to invite or not invite to a dinner party. You know what? Misfits work out better here. They have fewer misconceptions to overcome. And these boys won't be misfits when I send them back."

Gaius Lucullus' initial distrust of the young aristocrat was replaced by grudging admiration. Sextus was innovative and able to make others innovate. That was no small trick. He might succeed in following in the tradition of his ancestor Gaius Julius Caesar.

"But I am taking up your time discussing desert warfare. What can I do for you, Gaius Lucullus?" He put his elbows on the desk, rested his chin on his linked fingers, and looked intently at his new-found comrade.

"Well, have you heard any indications of the piracy problems? We will be shipping south in about a month to Eudaemon Arabia, and on to India. We are particularly interested in one Ibrahim bin Yusuf."

"Well, he's active, all right. He is, I think, well south of here. He has been sighted in Berenice, and a few other obscure places. Always heading south. We think he has some secure basing areas at the mouth of the Red Sea, probably in Far Side Somalia with the Troglodytes and around Arabia Felix on the east. There are dozens of little islands he can hide out on. He's a fox, always one step ahead of the navy. What are you going to do in India?"

"We'll be pressing on to other business. But my cousin, Senator Aulus Aemilius Galba, has arranged our transportation to India. We will be traveling on the *Europa, Asia* and *Africa.*"

Sextus slapped the desk. "Oh, yes, and every pirate in the Red Sea wants one of those ships! Even some coming in from the eastern Mediterranean to go for your three big ships. You will, I understand, be carrying some huge sums of gold and silver."

Gaius nodded. Apparently Sextus had been reading his intelligence correspondence thoroughly. "I suppose. That's my cousin's side of work. Has any protection been arranged? Like galley escorts?"

Sextus shrugged. "I'd really like to help you out there, Gaius, really I would. But that would tie up at least two or three galleys for months, taking you down to Sabaea, laying over a few weeks and then deadheading back up. We have twelve ships, and I can do that. I'd very much like to give that order, because your convoy is a prime target. But really, every ship out of here is traveling with a fortune. If I ordered the navy to escort you, I'd have to order them to escort every single convoy that leaves here. And twelve galleys can't do that."

"How many of those other convoys have passengers traveling on Imperial orders carrying Imperial gold on an Imperial diplomatic mission?"

"Hmm… now that is different. Are you asking for an escort under those orders?" He clasped his fingers under his chin and fixed his gaze on Gaius.

"Yes. I need continuous escort."

"How far?"

"All the way to Eudaemon Arabia."

"I recommend, now that I'll be billing the Treasury for this service, that you keep escort as far as the Dioscirides, locally known as Socotra, the last large island in the mouth of the Red Sea. After that, you're in the Indian Ocean, and after a few hours, it is impossible for two ships to meet except by chance. We have a small service dock in Socotra for just this contingency, and we can drop the galleys off there, give the crews a rest, and return to Eudamon Arabia the next day. The navy will scream, but we are the senior service, and ultimately, they can't fail to support Imperial orders. Trajan is footing the bill, so there is no precedent to obligate me to support other merchants."

"So do I have the escort?" asked Gaius.

"You have them. Three ships, to Socotra. Tell Fabius Maximus, the *navarklos* at the *Classis Alexandrina* detachment, that I approved it… Here, wait." Sextus grabbed a square of papyrus from a box, scrawled the orders on it with a stylus, and folded it in half. He passed a stick of sealing wax through a candle flame and dropped a blob on the letter, sealing it with his ring. "Tell Fabius to come talk to me about any problem he has about this. And underway, do what Fabius tells you! As far as convoy rules go, the convoy master is the god of the sea to you, your shipping master Hasdrubal and his captains. If your ships break away from his, they aren't going to come looking for you, they're coming back here at best speed and you're on your own. Understood?" He looked Gaius squarely in the eye, and handed him the letter.

Gaius took the letter and returned the gaze. He had never had his opinion of a man change as drastically in as short a time, as his had over the outgoing Sextus Julius. Innovative, decisive … and he took a defeat in stride, confidently issuing orders to Gaius about convoy operations, when in fact the Imperial orders had given him no choice but to provide it.

Gaius accepted the letter and rose. "Well, I thank you, Sextus Julius, and I commend you on your ingenious desert tactics." He offered his hand to Sextus, who accepted the handshake. "And by the way… you were right about how we picked our centuries to support you. I helped picked the batch from the Twelfth last winter!" He smiled ruefully.

Sextus Julius smiled. "They actually weren't as bad as most of the rest. They're the senior century in the cohort."

Gaius winced. They had been his worst batch of thieves, ne'er-do-wells, and malingers, with a few cowards thrown in to boot. "Well, then I would hate to see your other *vexillationes!*"

The two parted in good humor, and Gaius mounted up for the intensely hot ride back to Myos Hormos. *I wonder where I can get one of those Bedouin robes. I think the kid is onto something there,* thought Gaius, as the sweat again filled up his leather breastplate. He contemplated writing the long-delayed letter to his wife.

CHAPTER 12: A CASE OF DYSENTERY

Hasdrubal took leave of the ship to stay at the residence with Aulus and his entourage, claiming a case of dysentery. This was a common enough disease in Myos Hormos, not serious enough to bring in a physician and his scrutiny, easy to fake. Hasdrubal made his tenth trip to the latrine that night, scurrying through the shadows.

It was amazing what one could learn on the way to the latrine. For example, he learned that they had lined up three galley escorts. He also learned that whatever had triggered memories in the Greek centurion's mind, they were fading rapidly. Hasdrubal was fairly sure now that Antonius did not connect him with that ill-fated meeting at the Bull and Dove.

He had to get word to Ibrahim, holed up south of here in some obscure fishing village, about this latest development. They had arranged a drop for information through the fishmarket, through a one-eyed old fish merchant. How the old man did it, Hasdrubal didn't need to know.

Tomorrow would be a good time to recover, and see if Gaius Aemelius would go over the schedules. As soon as he had the details, he would deliver them to his contact point, always a difficult balancing act. It might take weeks to get the information to Ibrahim, so he should not delay waiting for too many details. On the other hand, he did not want to send partial messages whose subsequent updates or corrections might not get through.

Hasdrubal stepped out of the stinking latrine into the steamy night air.

"Well, good evening, Hasdrubal. Do I detect some life now behind that beard?" asked Aulus, sitting by the pool with only a single lamp.

"Just a little, sir, and I hope that I am on the mend now. I think I may be ready to return to work tomorrow. We must go over the schedule for fitting out the ships, conducting sea trials and our departure plans at your earliest convenience," said Hasdrubal, still holding his stomach.

"Perhaps immediately after breakfast, if you can eat. We have good news... Gaius Lucullus did what I could not do, and lined up three galleys to escort us to the Dioscirides."

"The Dioscirides! That is good news indeed. If we got an escort at all, I would have expected Eudaemon Arabia and no further. And three! Gaius has done well." *Too well. This would place the hijacking far out to sea. Three days, then. I will send on whatever information I have by Friday.* "Well, your lordship, this illness has left me weak and tired. I will retire to my quarters tonight and hopefully sleep through for the first time in two nights. Goodnight, sir."

"And good night to you also, my good Hasdrubal. Sleep well and be well tomorrow."

The following morning Hasdrubal had indeed made a miraculous recovery, eating a heavy breakfast, and at mid-morning, met with Aulus and the three captains, Dionysius of the flagship *Asia*, Apollodorus of the *Africa*, and Demetrios of the *Europa*. Also present were the captains of the escort galleys, gathered to discuss the sortie plan. This was followed by berthing arrangements for the Hanaean party of six, Wang Ming and five translators, which had arrived overnight, divided up two per ship. Lucius Parvus, unaware that Marcia Lucia was Wang Ming's concubine, had assigned her and brother Marcus Lucius to the *Europa* with Gaius and Antonius, while Wang Ming and the translator Marcellus Albus he billeted in the *Asia* with Galba and Hasdrubal. Pontus Valens and Titus Porcius were to ride in the *Asia*.

"Lucius, that is good, we have these people nicely distributed, along with the gold and silver. But Marcia Lucia is Wang Ming's concubine, and I am sure he would prefer her company to that of Marcellus Albus," said Aulus, pointing out the problem.

Lucius picked up a stylus and prepared to correct the wax tablet, but Wang Ming intervened.

"No problem, Aurus. She stay with brother, I stay with you. Need no change now, maybe later," said Wang Ming.

Aulus noted the faintest of a smile on the girl's demurely downcast face.

CHAPTER 13: A CHANGE OF PLANS

Ibrahim read and re-read the letter the fisherman had brought him, sipping bitter beer in the hut overlooking the Red Sea. Unlike the sweltering upper reaches of the sea, here the breezes were warm but not humid, and blew steadily from the northeast from over the Indian Ocean.

The innocuous letter was written in the cursive Nabataean script:

"My dearest brother,

I hope that thou findest the weather to thy liking. Here the weather is humid, even more so than at Berenice. We had the opportunity to take delivery of our new fishing boat, and we are pleased with its speed, although the rig is most unusual. I look forward to the opportunity to join with thee in the fishing off Socotra, perhaps in the first week in June. I hear that the fishing is good there at that time of year, but I also hear that the sea to the west is full of dangerous sharks. I hope that we can avoid them. In our country, it is the custom for fishing boats to fly a red flag, to warn others to steer clear of their lines. Is that also the custom in Socotra?

I wish thee well, and await thy company soon.

Yasser

A plain letter, signed by Hasdrubal's code name. However, the letter informed Ibrahim that Hasdrubal had made a major change of plans, moving the rendezvous more than five hundred miles into the open ocean to the east to Socotra Island in June. This was due to some danger around Dehalak, their original rendezvous. Galba must have obtained naval escort.

Ibrahim stroked his beard. *I wonder what that dog is up to*, he thought. *The ship will be flying a red flag. That part didn't change.* He didn't trust Hasdrubal any longer, and had not for many months. Part of his instincts told him to call off the entire operation now, but he had made extensive and expensive plans. His reputation was on the line here... *Odd how much piracy is like a business. I have backers, the same as my victim, and they expect me to deliver.* He had been doing this business for forty years, and every once in a while, he remembered someone with whom he had sailed briefly a long time ago... "Just believe," he had said to Ibrahim. *Ah, but belief is denied the pirate. Too many lies, too many deceptions, and too many dead men and betrayed trusts. I hope when I make my fatal mistake, it will be at sea, my only friend.*

All right, in a way, the new rendezvous is to my advantage. Dehalak was well inside the mouth of the Red Sea, and the ships would have been depleted, replenishing the galleys with food and water. A seizure at Socotra, on the other hand, will be after Eudaemon

Arabia... with full water and plenty of food for the long trip across the Indian Ocean to India. So seizure just east of Socotra after they drop off the galleys.

Ibrahim had planned on rounding the horn of Africa and escaping southward to the Far Side. But with full water tanks and food... could he consider taking the ship all the way on its intended journey to India? He would have a hold full of gold, and all he had to do was to lose the other two ships... which would lose him, since Hasdrubal would haul them east at full sail, their standard procedure, and gave good cover to Hasdrubal. Who could fault a shipping master for escaping with two out of three ships and continuing on his journey?

But to modify the plan... He would be in one of the fastest ships in the Indian Ocean with tons of gold and silver in the hull, and if he went to north India, he would beat the news of the hijacking arriving with Hasdrubal at Muziris and no one would be the wiser. His gold was good anywhere, and there were places he knew that the Romans never went. He would be perfectly safe there. And from there...

"Just believe," the man had said to him years ago. He wished he could. But he certainly could believe in a ton of gold and silver in his hold, the finest ship ever built at his command, and the oceans of the world at his fingertips.

The ocean breeze stirred the palm trees in restless motion, and the sibilant hiss of the breakers along the white sand came like a distant song to his ears. They seemed to say, over and over again, "Just believe... just believe..." Ibrahim took another sip of bitter barley beer and tried to imagine a life without fear and distrust.

CHAPTER 14: TRAINING THE CREW

Antonius began training the crews of each ship in organized fighting tactics while waiting to sail. Each ship already had a contingent of Nubian archers, and Antonius prepositioned enough swords, helmets and shields to outfit another eighty men among the three ships.

The crews were a polyglot group. In addition to Greeks and Italians, brown-skinned Phoenicians and Berbers, red-headed Gauls and blonde Germans, they included Nubians and Ethiopians with shiny black skins, coastal Arabians with skins like leather, Parthians, Indians and various easterners with yellow skins and varying degrees of slanted eyes. There was one man of an unknown race and language, with skin the color of copper and long straight black hair done up in a topknot, recruited, along with a Jew, from a crew from Carthage.

Antonius solicited volunteers from among the crews for training on the *Europa*. He chose Greek as the best common language, hoping to pick up interpreters if needed.

Sailors tend ter be good individual fighters, but brawlers, mostly. I got ter teach them how ter fight like a team. He tried to fall out the men on deck, but was met by puzzled stares and indifference. *Barstids! They're pretendin' not ter understand me!* After his fourth attempt to kick some order into the straggling lines of men, one of the men piped up: "Hey, Roman! Most don't understand more than a word or two of Greek. You're wasting your fucking time."

Antonius stepped forward, flushed with anger and about ready to clobber the insolent sailor with his hickory stick, then reconsidered. He went nose-to-nose with the young sailor, glaring but elicited no flinching in return. He calmed his temper and hissed: "That is Centurion to you, sailor. Do you have a name?"

"Shmuel. Shmuel bin Eliazar." No 'Centurion', no 'Sir.'

This lad is tryin' me patience! "Where are you from, Shmuel bin Eliazar?"

"Tyre." Shmuel never blinked, never straightened up from his insolent posture.

"All right, Shmuel bin Eliazar of Tyre. What language would you recommend I use?"

"Aramaic."

"I'll tell you what, Shmuel son of Eliazar. I am going to make you my second in command. I am going to give you the instruction in Greek, and you get the men to carry it out, in whatever language you need to use. If they don't, I whip up on you, and you whip up on them. Understood?"

Still not blinking, Shmuel replied, "I am hard to whip."

Antonius was waiting for that insolent reply, and in a few quick moves, the young man was flat on his back on the deck with Antonius glaring down on him. Antonius extended his hand to help him up, but Shmuel attempted to wrestle the centurion down with him. Shmuel wound up face down on the deck, with Antonius pinning his right arm behind his back in a painful hold. "Maybe at the end of your training, you might be able to take me down, but not now. Tell them this is a demonstration of what they will all be able to do, if they pay attention. Tell them, and I speak enough Aramaic to know you said it right!"

Antonius helped him up, saving his new second a loss of face in front of the men he was to lead. Shmuel clearly seemed to understand that the centurion was not one with whom to trifle. "Yes… Centurion." He turned to the men and repeated what Antonius had told him, and the men seemed intrigued with what they had observed.

"Now fall them out in rows of eight men each, an arm's length between each man and the man in front and the man beside, no more, no less!"

The men fell into place, and Antonius, with Shmuel at his side, inspected each for wounds, signs of illness, and general condition, dismissing twenty for various reasons.

"Shmuel. Can you read and write?"

"Yes… Centurion."

"Get me a list of these by name, and where they are from. Pick a squad leader from each row, and work through them to get things done."

The rest of the day was spent in basic close-order drill, how to move as an organized group to the left or right, ending with conditioning exercises, windsprints along the two hundred foot deck. At the end, he thanked his *optio,* praising him and the deckhands for a good first day's work in broken Aramaic. After the men were dismissed, he waved Shmuel over to the rail.

"Good job, today, really. Thanks."

"Yes… Centurion."

"Centurion in front of the men. Between us, I am Antonius. You are Jewish, Shmuel, I think. How did you wind up in Tyre?"

"My family fled Jerusalem for Galilee before I was born, ahead of the war against Rome. I was born there, went to sea from Tyre. Were you there for that war…Antonius?"

"Before my time. I heard it was very hard on your people. I am sorry… war is horrible."

"Thank you for the thought. I did not know Romans apologized for anything."

"It helps, sometimes. I understand some Jews believe that touching a non-Jew makes them unclean, so I will ask your permission before I extend my hand to you, Shmuel. May I?

"You may. It is becoming harder and harder to be as observant as I once was." Shmuel gave just the faintest of smiles, and held out his hand. The two shook firmly.

After a few days, Antonius issued the men helmets, shields and wooden training swords. They mastered various lunges and parries, the use of the shield to throw the enemy off balance, how to merge left, sheltering the man on that side with your shield as well as yourself. Then on to various throws and hand-to-hand combat, how to disarm a man with a knife when unarmed, and other tricks of the trade. At the end of training, Antonius allowed the best five to beat him at hand-to-hand and lay him out on the deck, to howls of glee from their shipmates. Finally, they were issued the real swords, but only to put their names on them and learn how to sharpen and repair them. Their graduation exercise came right before sailing, with an on-deck parade and demonstration drill before Gaius Lucullus, the captains, and Hasdrubal.

"Well done, Antonius. You seem to have turned shark bait into sharks!" said Hasdrubal.

"They were easy to work with, and quick to learn. Hopefully we won't need their skills, but if we do, we won't find them wanting. I expect any batch of boarders would be pretty much like they were at the start, individual fighters that could be easily beaten and finished off."

In the course of the training, Antonius had discovered nothing untoward about the crew. And the discomfort he had felt about Hasdrubal on his arrival had evaporated. Perhaps Hasdrubal truly had been ill with dysentery. Indeed, he had frequently come onto the deck where Antonius conducted his training, to watch their progress, praising their professional manner as the defending crew swept a mock assault from the decks.

Hasdrubal had also learned where the keys to the armories were kept.

CHAPTER 15: UNDERWAY AT LAST

The convoy began their sortie from Myos Hormos a little after midnight in late April. Antonius and Gaius stayed up all night to watch the evolution.

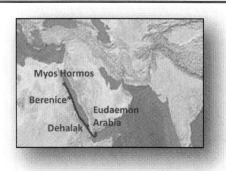

Their escorting triremes *Nilus, Tigris* and *Euphrates* slipped their moorings first, to clear the area and patrol the approaches to the harbor mouth. They paced north and south along the coast like nervous black watchdogs, their sweeps occasionally catching a glimmer of moonlight, kicking up phosphorescent sparkles in the water. Periodically, the flagship *Nilus* repeated the "all clear" signal, three sweeps of a torch. Well before dawn, satisfied no pirates lurked in the area, the three warships took station in a line abreast north of the harbor, blocking the downwind approach.

At dawn, the big sailing ships received their 'clear to sortie' signal, and they too slipped their moorings, beginning with the *Europa* with Gaius and Antonius aboard. Four longboats with twelve rowers each tugged the bow of the big ship out into the channel, away from dockside. When she was about a hundred yards out, Demetrios gave orders to deploy the *artemon*. The foresail luffed restlessly in the light morning breeze, slapping ineffectively, then filled with an explosive pop. Almost instantly, the head of the ship went down and she began to turn downwind. The skipper gave word for the big mainsail to be deployed from the yardarm until it too filled. The longboats cast off their towing lines, and the waters of the harbor began to gurgle overside as the ship picked up headway, making for the flickering torches that marked the harbor mouth.

Outside the harbor, the *Europa* sailed south about a half mile before heaving to, rocking restlessly in the ocean swell awaiting the *Africa*, followed by the *Asia* with Aulus and Hasdrubal.

With the sun low on the morning horizon, the *Nilus* hoisted signal flags directing them to proceed. As they made sail, the *Tigris* and *Euphrates* flashed by on either side like black centipedes scurrying across the water to take their station in the van of the convoy, white foam hissing across their rams. On each warship, above the ram, a bronze wolf figurehead was frozen in a perpetual leap, two feet above the water.

"I don't think they'll keep that pace up long in this heat!" noted Gaius to Antonius, listening to the rapid rhythmic beat of the timekeeper thumping below decks on the warships as they sliced through the water close abeam, their wakes breaking on the sheer sides of the *Europa*.

And no sooner had the warships taken station in the van, they shipped oars and deployed their diminutive blue square sails, set far forward, and now wallowed along gracelessly. The three merchant ships matched speed.

Gaius contemplated this climax of weeks of preparations - sea trials, fine-tuning the various riggings for tension and placement, followed by more sea trials. And after they were complete, endless supplies had been brought aboard, jugs of oil and wheat, spare timbers and lines. *I read a book once, of a trip to the moon by sailing ship. The moon could not be more remote than our destination across the Indian Ocean, with no place in mid-ocean for replacements. There had to be a spare in the hold for everything they could not do without!*

The ships had topped off the midships water tanks on the last day. Here Roman hydraulics ingenuity showed: the Myos Hormos port could water up to ten ships at once with only a few people. A cistern had been placed on an artificial hill about thirty feet above the dock, filled with water from an artesian well. From this, lead pipes ran to the dock, with wooden valves at each slip, fitted with leather hoses to be inserted into each ship's tank.

Finally, just before sunset on the night prior to departure, the money wagons had rumbled down the pier under guard by soldiers of the Myos Hormos garrison. Each chest had been opened, inspected by Aulus, weighed, resealed, receipts signed, then divided among the three ships and sealed into special holds. Each ship was carrying several tons of gold and silver, with a total value of fifty million *sesterces*.

Aulus, an ordained *auspex*, had then donned an olive wreath and conducted the official ceremonies, killing a sheep to carefully examine the animal's liver. Holding the liver aloft, he had declared the auspices good, and sacrificed it in the ceremonial fire. As he did, a flock of birds had flown overhead, heading south, a further good omen for the journey.

The first afternoon at sea was pleasant, the wind moderating the heat. Gaius joined Antonius, Marcus Lucius and his sister Marcia Lucia lining the starboard rails to watch the shoreline, stark barren red granite rock punctuated by an occasional outcropping of greyish-green shrubbery. The ship leaned gently with the wind, pressing its prow against the sea as it headed south. The water chuckled gently against the hull, brownish-green water breaking into silver foam, swirling aft in the wake, stretching for miles as a disturbed white trace in the water behind them, in which one of their escorts behind them rocked restlessly. The ever-present sun beamed down on the Red Sea, clearly highlighting details miles away on the coastline.

A pod of dolphins had chosen to entertain them, their smooth grey bodies sinuously weaving through the curling bow wave. The animals took turns broaching the surface in a smooth curling flow, barely disturbing the water. Occasionally one came close enough for them to hear their peculiar *chit-chit-chit*.

Marcia was quite taken with the graceful animals. "What sort of fish are those? They are so graceful!" It was the first time Gaius had heard her initiate a conversation.

"They call 'em... er, those are called dolphins. They have a reputation for saving people who fall overboard or are wrecked at sea. They push them to shore, sometimes for miles." Antonius answered her in formal Latin; the two had difficulty with his coarse soldier's Latin.

"They're beautiful. And it almost seems like they are looking at us when they surface."

Gaius smiled, as Antonius continued the conversation. "So how did you come to keep our language for more than a century?"

Marcus answered, "Our ancestors moved around quite a bit before they settled down to build a borderpost they called the Legion fort. The locals called it *Liqian* in Hanaean. The soldiers took local wives and raised families. Their boys were expected to grow up to be soldiers like their fathers, and needed Latin for that. They learned Hanaean from their mothers, to go to market and deal with the locals. Over time, the fort was replaced by a town, but kept the name."

"How do the locals get along with you?" asked Antonius.

Marcia smiled. "Pretty good, now. I was told that originally they didn't like us much. The only wives our ancestors could come by were prostitutes, or ugly or deformed girls, rejects that the community didn't want. But those women found a home in Liqian, families and children, and they were very happy. Now, we pretty much look and talk like our neighbors, and there is a lot of friendship between us. But we still keep ourselves a little bit separate."

She paused a bit to watch the dolphins cavorting alongside the ship, then returned to the conversation. "The Emperor Trajan is a remarkable man."

"I never met him, of course. Way above my station in life! But those who have, speak well of him. How did you come to meet him?"

"The Emperor personally met with all of us and the Hanaean delegates in private, before the public ceremonies. He is quite different from the Hanaean emperor."

"How so?"

"Well, just so much less formal. In the Hanaean court, there are ritual bowings, and specific times and ways to speak. We have only met Emperor He once, and were never in a position to do anything but listen. But when we arrived in Rome, we asked Trajan's staff how to go in to meet him, and they said 'Well, just go in, give a bit of a head nod, and if he extends his hand, give him a firm handshake. Look him straight in the eye." She laughed shyly, and her blue eyes twinkled. "We explained this to our leader Gan Ying who was ... a bit shocked at the informality."

Marcus interjected. "He adapted. He was a professional with experience in many countries. But he was uncomfortable through it all."

Marcia picked up the thread. "Emperor Trajan then invited us to sit and made small talk with us, had drinks and trays of food brought in. He sat with us, asked about the Hanaean emperor, our homes and families, and swapped stories with us. I never felt so at ease with such a powerful man in all my life!"

"Well, don't judge all our Emperors by his standards! He is one of the best, but we have had some bad ones," said Antonius.

"How did you come to have Emperors? There is nothing in our tradition about them, just the elected magistrates and consuls," asked Marcus.

"That came about around twenty years after your ancestors were separated from Rome." Antonius gave them a quick sketch of the events that followed Crassus' ignominious defeat, the civil wars that led to Caesar's rise and assassination, and more civil wars until the installation of his nephew Octavian as *Princeps Senatus*, speaker of the Senate, and *Imperator*, commander in chief of all Roman legions.

"We created a monster when we did it, half hereditary king, half military dictator, and no easy way to get rid of a bad one. Three died hard, and a couple more died at the hand of their successor." Antonius finished with a sigh. "And we have had some bad ones. Mostly, though, they only screwed with the upper crust, and left us on the bottom alone. How does your government work?"

"I guess hereditary king comes closest to describing it. The *Hanae* are the ruling clan, and have been for generations. Overall, they have been good. The emperor is the intermediary between man and the gods, and if he does well, the nation and the people prosper. If not... well, it can get turbulent... assassinations, maybe civil war to set things right. Like you, we have no orderly way to get rid of a bad emperor. For now, Emperor He is a kind and gentle man."

"But his court is not," said Marcia softly. Gaius thought he heard bitterness in her voice.

"So how did your expedition get to Rome? There surely were more in your party than just you six traveling with us," asked Antonius.

Marcus answered, "We left the capital Luoyang with twenty delegates and military escorts, led by Gan Ying, plus ten of us translators, We went overland to Parthia through *Da Yuan*... I am sorry, I don't know the Latin name of the place, between *Ch'in* and Parthia. When we got to the Parthian capital, they arranged shipping to take us south to Eudaemon Arabia. The ship abandoned us there, just left us stranded."

"Arrgh, yer were had by those Parthian bastards!" Antonius said reverting to his soldier's Latin.

"I am sorry, I didn't understand," said Marcia.

"It is I who am sorry. That brought my soldier's talk out! The Parthians sent you thousands of miles out of your way. They didn't want you to make it to Rome. Roman lines were only a few hundred miles from Ctesiphon. I know… I was on that line opposite them! You're lucky they didn't arrange for you to have an accident enroute."

"So they played us for fools?" queried Marcus.

"Like a harp, lad, like a harp."

"Hmm… that explains a lot, because the expedition began to fall apart in Eudaemon. The ship's captain told us we were in Rome and sailed off. Gan Ying was about to turn back when we found a building with the Roman symbols, we thought it was the Roman Senate! When they found out who we were, they booked us passage to Rome, with a letter to Trajan."

"So what happened afterwards to Gan Ying and the rest of the group?"

"They went overland to Parthia and back the way we had came. Trajan and Aulus Aemilius Galba persuaded them to leave five of us and Wang Ming, to get you to Luoyang. Ming is Marcia's consort, but he decided to stay on *Asia* with the Senator."

"So you are emissaries of Rome now?"

"Yes, we are your translators."

"Interesting. Will you be returning to Rome someday?"

"You have no idea what a long and arduous trip it is. We couldn't possibly do it again."

Turning to Marcia, Antonius asked, "Your – uh – consort, he is on Aulus's ship?"

"Wang Ming is not my consort, I am his concubine," she replied coolly.

"I am sorry, I think I intruded on your personal business."

"No matter. We are free Roman citizens on our father's side, but slaves of the Hanaean Court on our mother's." Her face clouded. Taking her brother by the arm, it was clear she wanted to leave and end the conversation. "We must go now."

"I hope we can continue," said Antonius, but they made no reply, and he turned back to the rail to stare at the coastline.

Gaius put his arm around Antonius' broad shoulders and smiled. "Not a full day underway, and you already had a fight with our female translator!" laughed Gaius.

"Women!" Antonius spat over the rail. "Asked about her life and she went off in a huff! What did I do wrong, sir?"

"Women never were your strong point, Antonius," said Gaius, still chuckling. "I think her life is none too pleasant. Her arrangement does not seem to be a good one, not one she wants to talk about, so just avoid that subject for now. We are going to have to get some details on court protocol from them eventually. Meanwhile, don't worry about it, you didn't say anything wrong. Remember those things the Germans used, sharp spears in a shallow pit with a matt over them, and a scattering of leaves? I think you just stepped on one!"

They talked about Egypt, and Gaius was surprised to learn that Antonius had read the Histories of Herodotus dealing with this ancient land, and had a scholar's grasp of that book.

"It's hard to imagine a common soldier reading Herodotus."

Antonius flushed. "Beggin' yer pardon, sir!" He stared off sullenly into the Red Sea.

"Antonius, please. I didn't mean to insult you. I knew you came from a long line of Greek tutors. It's just that you don't... seem like one."

"It does not pay, sir, to reveal all of one's skills for all the world to see," replied Antonius, in the formal Latin that he had been using with Marcus and Marcia. "I am indeed a common soldier, dependent on my messmates for my very life. And my most noble officers would not care to see a common soldier standing too far above the crowd. They would be... uneasy. Patricians from Rome's most famous families have served as common soldiers, as the unfortunate Lucius Servilius did, and they, too, found it prudent to blend in with their cruder messmates. Lest they wind up as he did." He spoke in perfect scholarly style, the accent and intonation perfect.

"I am truly sorry, Antonius. You have had my greatest respect since our first combat together along the Danube, so many years ago. And yet... this was a side of you I never saw."

"Arrgh, sir. Methinks we should have taken a boat trip sooner," Antonius said, lapsing back into the vulgar Latin. "... with nothin' better ter do than exchange bullshit about the meanin' of life... we never had time ter do this, remember? If we wasn't killin', we was tryin' not ter get killed, trainin' ter kill, or thankin' our lucky stars we dint get kilt. No offense intended, sir, an' none taken. But now yer got ter pay up... I want ter know more about yer. Where was yer born?"

"Fair's fair, Antonius! My home town, alas, is no more. I was born and grew up in Pompeii. My father was a well-to-do merchant there. He, my mother, brother and sister died there twenty years ago when Vesuvius blew up. I would have died there, too, but I was in Ostia visiting my uncle, Quintus Lucullus Mercator. My cousin Livia, Aulus' wife whom you met in Alexandria, is his daughter. When Vesuvius wiped out the town, he raised me as his own. So Livia Luculla Galba is more my little sister than my cousin."

"I'm truly sorry, sir."

"Well, many thousands of people died there. I guess the Fates had something in mind for me. I went back to Pompeii a few years ago. It's awesome...it simply isn't there anymore. The main road to town still has a mile marker for Pompeii, but then just disappears into a hill. The hill is all green, everything is grown back, but the town, my family, all my friends, are buried beneath it. Except for the road, you'd never know the town had ever been there. The forum, the theater, the baths, everything. Just... buried."

"Yer uncle Mercator... was a merchant? How did yer wind up in the army then?"

"Well, I guess I liked to fight a lot. I didn't handle being orphaned very well and resented the other kids with parents. I was a hellion, and my uncle Mercator finally sent me off to an old retired soldier, Commodus, who had commanded the *III Gallicae*, back when it really was in Gaul. He ran a military school for us wealthy ne'er-do-wells, spoiled rich kids who needed his approach to discipline... a major drawback to the upper classes, Antonius. Our children turn out terrible!

"So anyway, he had no qualms about beating any of us who didn't snap to his orders. It didn't make any difference whether it was Greek grammar, mathematics, sword drill, or athletics...you did it his way, or he put you on your butt. It was just what I needed to keep me from feeling sorry for myself. Some of the other kids didn't fare so well. He just returned them to their parents and refunded them their money. He wouldn't waste time on kids who wouldn't try. So when I turned seventeen the army seemed natural. Uncle Mercator funded my stipend when I joined, because I had no inheritance. I guess if it hadn't been for the army, I would have been one more broke high-born snot, sucking wine neat in the dives and telling the whores how much money I was going to inherit... someday. Hustling business deals on the docks at Ostia."

"Somehow, I don' think so, sir. Yer far better than that. Yer know, we watch the orficers an' we sees some good 'uns an' some bad uns. Yer one of the good uns. Yer take care of yer troops, an' yer care if they has a dry place ter sleep, an' yer lissen, when we tell yer how we think we should deploy. Yer allus lookin' down that patrician nose at us... but it's as big an act as me vulgar Latin. Yer trouble is...yer really care about people. An' people care about yer... that makes yer a great orficer."

Gaius was silent. He had never wondered if his men liked him or not. He assumed they did not, except maybe for gruff Antonius. He didn't think they hated him. He knew they respected him, and maybe feared him. But the idea that they actually liked him touched him deeply. Especially since the lives of so many had been summed up in a brief papyrus letter to a parent, a brother or sister, or even to a live-in harlot. "From Gaius Lucullus, *vale!* Your Lepidus, or Marius, or Cornelius was a noble Roman soldier who died valiantly..." He didn't have to write them, but he did, and how many had he written? The muster roll of a cohort of dead Roman soldiers, men who had died under his command. And in each, he gave some personal detail of the man for his family. The idea that these men felt affection for him...Gods curse it all, he had loved each of the hard-headed lot like a brother! His eyes grew hot and moist. "Thank you, Antonius... that means a lot to me."

The following day, Marcia sought out Antonius, standing alone by the rail. She stepped up beside him and put her elbows on the rail, her white Roman *stola* gown rippling in the brisk wind, along with her long black hair, now undone. "Hello, Antonius, may I speak?"

"But of course. I am afraid I offended you yesterday, and I want to apologize."

She laughed, a beautiful laugh like a bell. "My goodness, I wanted to apologize to you! I was terribly rude yesterday."

"Well, I'll accept yours, if you'll accept mine. There was something you didn't want to talk about, and I intruded."

"You didn't know. It is hard for me to talk about... Ming. To answer your question yesterday, he sometimes wants me around all the time, and then wants nothing to do with me for weeks. It is good for me to be away from him for a while." She said this while staring out to sea. Antonius could see she was having trouble talking about this.

"I am sorry," said Antonius.

"There is nothing I can do. Thank you for accepting my apology, I must go now."

"To be sure. May *fortuna* smile on you."

She smiled. "I don't think *fortuna* speaks Hanaean! But thank you." And she left.

The ships pressed southward, day after day at a snail's pace. Gaius, Antonius and Marcus met frequently to chat, but Marcia remained in her quarters.

As they sailed south, the humidity and temperature moderated. After two weeks they rounded Dehalak and turned eastward through the straits to moor at Eudaemon Arabia.

CHAPTER 16: TO THE OPEN SEA

Mostly weathered mudbrick huts and a few modest administrative buildings, Eudaemon Arabia was important as the last jumping off point into the Indian Ocean. Here, ships came to await the coming of the June monsoon to carry them to India, their holds laden with gold and silver. Here, the ships replenished food and water for the long weeks at sea, and the crew sought out gods to guarantee their safety, or easy women to ensure one last memorable port of call.

And here again the ships returned in December, the fall northeast monsoon blowing them back laden with spice and silk, cinnamon and pepper, ivory and animals for the Roman games. One by one they staggered back to port like drunks from a binge, heavy-laden, sails in need of repair, hulls leaking, masts jury-rigged after storms, to be repaired and dispatched up the Red Sea. The port earned a steady income servicing this trade, and a few people became very wealthy. But the streets were not paved with gold, though Sabaea was the legendary 'Land of Sheba' celebrated in Judean and Arabic legends about an ancestral monarch named Solomon.

There was an imperceptible Roman presence in Eudaemon, a *praetor externa* and a tiny staff to represent Roman interests with the ruling Homerite kingdom. The emissary had a few retired soldiers as guards, highly polished to add a touch of class. The residence was a whitewashed building at the end of a road lined by a colonnade of palms. The rear of the mission opened out onto a white beach, where the endless surf rolled in restlessly from the East.

Aulus, along with Gaius, Antonius, Hasdrubal, Wang Ming and the five Hanaean translators, arrived there shortly after the ships docked. Two of the guards stood at stiff attention beneath the golden eagle clutching the SPQR logo in its talons above the doorway, their lances blocking the entrance. Two bronze Roman she-wolves, their teats swollen with milk, were caught in mid-stride on marble pedestals either side of them.

"Senator Aulus Aemilius Galba of the Indian Ocean Flotilla, to see the Ambassador!" announced Aulus, in a commanding voice.

"Enter, sir, you are expected!" The lances snapped vertical and the two sentries rendered a crisp salute as the group entered into the cool interior. A fountain bubbled in the atrium, and the polished mosaic floor glistened with scenes from the *Aeneid*. The ambassador entered, clad in a fresh white toga, with a wide purple stripe.

Aulus embraced his old friend. "Marcus Pomponius, *vale*, you old devil! And how did you get such a desirable posting, on your way to power and influence? Most people would open their veins in their baths before coming this far for duty! Allow me to introduce you to my party: My cousin Gaius Lucullus, his centurion Antonius Aristides, both of *Legio XII Fulminata*, and my shipping master, Hasdrubal of Tyre."

Aulus then introduced the Hanaean party. "I believe you met our Hanaean party a few years ago. Wang Ming is our Hanaean delegate and this is his woman Marcia Lucia, sister to Marcus Lucius, both translators, along with Titus Porcius Quintus, Marcellus Albus Sextus, Pontus Valens Quintus, and Marcus Lucius Quintus, also translators. They may not look Roman, but then these days, who does anymore? Wang Ming is returning home with us, but knows only a little Latin. Best talk to him through Marcia Lucia." Wang Ming bowed to Marcus Pomponius politely, but said nothing, standing with his hands in his wide sleeves, out of sight across his chest. Marcia Lucia was clad in an Hanaean silk robe, decorated with flowering trees, silent, eyes downcast.

"Pleased to meet of all of you, for the second time," said Marcus Pomponius, beaming broadly and clasping each of the Hanaeans' hands in turn firmly in both of his. He turned to Aulus, "Aulus Aemilius, yes, we met these people three years ago, washed up on our shores when their Parthian captain sailed off without them. They found us here, thinking they were in Rome. Which they were not," he said with a chuckle. "But we got them there anyway." Marcus Pomponius paused, then continued, smiling at the group. "It is amazing how well they preserved their language and traditions from generation to generation. You know, they can recite more of Ennius and the plays of Plautus than I can. And they learned them all from scraps of memories written down by their ancestors, not the original books!"

"Interesting. I happen to have a set of Plautus' plays on my ship. I shall give it to them as a gift," offered Aulus. "I was in the Senate when the whole delegation was honored. Their story is truly remarkable."

"It made me proud to be a Roman, what they did."

"So... how did you come by this fine assignment?" asked Aulus.

"Well, this isn't bad duty, if you like independence. I get to meet the wealthy merchants like you, and occasionally do one of them a big favor... like get them into the shipyard for repairs ahead of everyone else! Those favors do pay off later, you know!" He laughed heartily. "How was your trip down?" he asked Aulus.

"As miserable as ever. I wish we could have just flown on a bird over that horrible piece of water. Not until we cleared Ptolemais of the Hunt did the steamy heat leave us. The escorts slowed us down, but these new ships promise to be fast. I am looking forward to getting into the open ocean and bending on all their sail. But now, perhaps lunch?"

CHAPTER 17: HIJACKED!

Antonius thought about going out to town with the crew the day before departure, then reconsidered. Gaius had retired with Aulus to the embassy to write their final letters to their wives, so Antonius just loafed around the silent ship with the in-port crew.

He was surprised to find Galosga, part of his security force, sitting cross-legged on the deck in the forward part of the ship. Galosga was always incommunicative and standoffish; many of the crew thought him a deaf-mute or slow-witted. However, he could understand a little Aramaic, if it was simple and spoken slowly and clearly, about as well as Antonius himself spoke that language. "Why thou not in town, drink, women?"

Galosga smiled, "No want. Drink no good. Make head hurt. Women, no money." Antonius was intrigued with the man, for he seemed so different, as though drinking and whoring were foreign to him. "Why not you?"

The question seemed innocent. *And why not me?* Before he left Syria, an afternoon's carouse was a welcome diversion. He remembered fondly the farewell that the other centurions had put on for him in Syria, the night before he left on this trip. Drinking silver *denarii* from flagons of wine while the rest of the centurions clapped and chanted "*Bibe, bibe, bibe!* Drink, drink, drink!" at an increasing pace, until he displayed the *denarius* in his wine-soaked teeth. But that was different there. Those were his friends and equals, lives owed each other in mutual debt, shared tents and meals and storms and fears and fights and narrow escapes, from the Danube to the Jordan. These sailors had their shared experiences too, but they were not his, and his not theirs. Maybe some day, but not today. He replied, "Not my people."

Galosga nodded his head, "Not mine."

Good explanation, as good as any.

Antonius tried to find out more about the stranger's home, learning that he had lived in wooded mountains far from the sea, but Antonius could not figure out where. Ending the conversation, Galosga spread out a blanket, distributing around him the contents of a leather bag from around his neck. They were mundane items: some animal bones in one corner of the blanket, some dried herbs in another, a sealed animal horn. Galosga took his knife from a belt sheath, and began to mash the dried herbs in his hand with the knife.

Antonius stared at the knife. In Noricum along the Danube, delicately fluted stone arrowheads and spear points were a frequent find as the legionaries dug ramparts for their camp. He had seen dozens of these tools, alone or intermingled with the bones of men or animals. But he had never known anyone, even the primitive tribes of the far north, who used anything other than metal tools. And he had never seen a stone-bladed knife attached to a handle, ready for use.

Antonius reached across the blanket to touch the knife, which Galosga handed to him. Antonius examined it carefully, turning it over and over. The stone blade seemed of recent manufacture, for the flecks on the side appeared fresh and the blade quite sharp. The blade was short, perhaps three inches, and securely attached to the wooden handle by sinew. The proportions seemed odd, for the handle was nearly twice as long as the blade and slightly curved. But when he hefted it in his hand for carving, it balanced perfectly. He returned the knife, "You make?" Galosga nodded. "Make another?"

"Cannot. No have... " he used his own language. "*Dawisgala.*"

"*Dawisgala?* Tool? Stone?" said Antonius, repeating the foreign word as best he could, and the Aramaic words slowly and carefully. Suddenly Galosga's face lit with understanding, and he shook his head affirmatively, "Stone!" It appeared to be some kind of a flint.

Galosga continued his preparations, and indicated that Antonius should sit beside him. The centurion smoothly seated himself into a cross-legged position next the man, aware that this was some type of religious ceremony. He watched in silence as Galosga opened a moss-filled animal horn and blew in it until a wisp of smoke curled up from inside, then filled the end with the dried herbs until they began to smolder. He fanned the horn with a large feather to spread the pungent smoke, while chanting rhythmically in his own language.

Galosga handed him the horn, and Antonius repeated the motions respectfully, imitating the rhythm of the chant, if not the words, then handed the horn back. Galosga set the horn down to continue smoldering. "For good trip," he said, smiling.

Well, I'll be damned. The man's praying for a safe journey.

The two sat in silence for a while, just contemplating the smoke as it curled up out of the horn. As the last wisp was tugged away by the afternoon breeze, Galosga put a wooden cap over the horn, and picked up the paraphernalia on the blanket "I thank thee," he said, with great care to say the Aramaic words just right.

Antonius nodded, "And I thank thee, Galosga."

Antonius took his leave for dinner and retired to his quarters. Since Gaius and Antonius were the senior passengers onboard the *Europa*, they had been given the spacious master's cabin to share. Antonius broke out a flagon of wine from the wine rack and poured some. *Arrgh, if I don' feel right sharing me last night in port with me mates on the ship, I'll share it with mesel' an' a fine bottle of wine.* He kicked his feet up on the other chair, and watched the sun set through the open windows of the cabin.

About ten that night, Gaius Lucullus, Marcia and Marcus returned with the captain Demetrios, and the in-port crew became active, making the necessary preparations to get underway at daybreak. The ships became alive with the sounds of boxes being opened and closed, cargo shifted, sails shaken out and checked, and lines checked for tension.

About midnight, the off-duty crew began to return, the shouts and songs of drunken men echoing up the pier as they staggered back. Antonius watched the swarm of men attempting to find their ship on the pier, dimly lit by guttering torches. There were some loud splashes and cries for help, as sailors mistook the pier side for the ship. Others, their arms about each other's shoulders, made it to the gangplank. However, the wiser ones crawled, rather than walked, up the narrow board to the ship.

Some of the sober in-port crew were dispatched dockside to help their shipmates aboard, but an hour later, there remained a stubborn bundle of bodies snoring on the dock, unresponsive even to blows of a club. Two other sailors reeled about the dock, unable to climb or be helped aboard. Finally some ingenious crewmen swung out the cargo boom with a net overside. The dockside crewmen loaded up the sleeping drunks, and manhandled the two ambulatory drunks into the net as well, to be hoisted aboard to the cheers of their shipmates. They swung the bundle into the forward cargo hold, where its payload could sleep off their overindulgence out of the way of the morning deck crew. Antonius chuckled, then turned to Gaius. "Looks like they had a fine night tonight."

Gaius laughed also. "Just remember, Antonius, these will be sailing our ship tomorrow!"

The thought was a sobering one... so to speak. There would be some agonizing heads tomorrow, sweating off their hangovers in the broiling sun.

The convoy got underway at daybreak, some of the crew moving decidedly slower than usual. By midmorning, the ships had formed up in their escort formation, *Tigris* and *Nilus* taking their turn in the van, and *Euphrates* in rear guard. The ships flew colored pennants, so that they could be easily recognized from miles away. The three warships each flew a long, thin pennant from their mastheads, the *Nilus* green, the *Tigris* blue and the *Euphrates* yellow. The merchant ships flew large square flags, the *Asia's* flag white, and the *Africa's* black. The *Europa's* red flag snapped smartly in the stiff breeze over the heads of Gaius and Antonius.

The first leg was southeast, to the headlands on the African coast of Far Side opposite Arabia. Then, as on the long leg down the Red Sea, they sailed by day, and anchored off sheltered harbors by night. However, the galleys set a much better pace, with one bank of rowers in the morning and another in the afternoon, sailing only in the heat of noon.

On the morning of the fifth day, the galleys got underway with greater than usual eagerness as the convoy left the African continent behind them. A hundred or so miles over water lay the big island of Socotra, where the galleys' escort duties ended. A double bank of rowers kept up a steady pace on the galleys, and the three big ships finally began to sail with more speed, deploying their topsails. The ships heeled a bit, meeting the swells with an abrupt impact that sent a shudder through the hull. The convoy opened their interval a bit, and a few hours after sunset, a baleful fire-lit glare loomed on the horizon, the lighthouse of the naval station at Veni Etiam. Somehow the name seemed appropriate after such a long journey. It meant, "I made it this far."

The sailing plan called for the galleys to detach at this point. The *Nilus* made the torch signals that instructed the convoy to proceed independently, and Hasdrubal in the *Asia* made the signal assuming command and directing the convoy to follow in his wake.

At last the ships were free to sail as they had been built. Although it was night, all three ships deployed all of their canvas to the fullest. Demetrios experimented with the tension of the sails, and aligned them slightly at an angle to the ship. He then gently turned slightly off the wind, increasing his heading to the northeast. Taking the wind more on the quarter than was customary, the ship heeled to port, and he played with the tiller, seeing just how far over he could nurse the ship. And the further over he nursed her, the faster she went. The portside was just ten feet out of the water hissing by overside, boiling in phosphorescent whiteness. The ship took the swells explosively with a heavy thump, plowing her bow into an occasional big roller which exploded in a shower of white in the moonlight and drifted back, floating like a cloud to spatter on the quarter-deck with the fury of a rain shower. Captain Demetrios rode the lunging freighter with all the careless abandon of a charioteer flogging his steeds onward around the *Circus Maximus*, continually trimming one sail or another to coax yet one more knot out of the wind. And, in the moonlight, the other two ships, visible as dark shapes and amber running lamps against the heaving, moon-sparkled sea, were the other chariots, likewise intoxicated with speed.

Gaius and Antonius stayed on the quarter-deck, fascinated with the change of pace and the sudden burst of efficiency of the crew. By first light, Demetrios was still at the tiller, the convoy stretched out in a line with the *Asia* barely visible two miles ahead, the *Africa* behind them by as far. Gaius estimated their speed at about eight knots, and this was still with a relatively light wind; the June monsoon had just begun and had not yet reached its full intensity.

Gaius and Antonius finally retired to their quarters with the sunrise, for it had been a long night. They became one with the motions and sounds of the ship... the constant rush of the water outside, the rhythmic thud as she muscled her way through another swell, followed by the patter of spray on the deck above. And the creaks of the finely fitted wood and the groans of the taut lines as the strains were transferred throughout the ship. And as each expected sound followed in its regular pattern, it became less and less obtrusive, until sleep overcame the two.

About four in the afternoon, both men awoke with a start, for the rhythm of the ship had ceased and the silence echoed in their heads like a shout. The deck was level, the ship not moving. Gaius gathered his tunic and ran to the side window. Sure enough, the ship lay dead in the water, wallowing back and forth with each wave. "We've stopped, Antonius. Let's get on deck! I hope we haven't run aground or broken a mast!" Gaius stepped out the door, then came back in immediately.

"Get your sword, Antonius. We've a ship alongside!"

"I think we would have been roused if there was a fight, sir. Perhaps they jus' came along some disabled ship ter render aid," said Antonius, nevertheless buckling on his sword.

"Maybe, Antonius. But that is also a good trick to get someone to stop."

The two stepped onto the deck, just in time for Antonius to watch a man climbing over the rail from the boat alongside. Clad in loose black pantaloons and a flowing jacket, with a turban and a scarf of dark blue partially covering his face. Antonius could see the cold blue eyes, the silvery salt-and-pepper beard, and the pockmarks. "That's him, sir! That's Ibrahim!"

He drew his sword with a hiss, as did Gaius. "To arms, men!" Antonius cried. "Drive them off the ship, those bastards are pirates!" The ships' officers on the quarter-deck called out commands to the crew in Aramaic, while Gaius called out to Demetrios. "You've been had. That man is bin Yusuf! Get your archers on deck quickly and we can sweep him clear!" Gaius was puzzled at the sad expression on Demetrios' face, shaking his head forlornly, as though Gaius was an errant child who just didn't understand.

Antonius charged on, expecting the crew to rally behind him. Only Galosga stepped forward, grabbing a marlinspike to aid his comrade. As Antonius leaped over the deck fittings and neared Ibrahim, the pirate gave a signal, and his bodyguards' swords flashed to the ready.

"Antonius! Look behind you! There's no one there!" the pirate said. Antonius gave a brief backward glance, to see that the three of them were rushing alone to their deaths. He stopped, turned and called to the crew. "Shmuel! Come on, damn you! It's not a drill! Get yer weapons and come, or

I'll cut your guts out mesel'!" A few of the crew, unarmed, stirred guiltily, but the officers barked more Aramaic, and they held their ground.

Gaius' stomach went cold as the reality of the situation came to him... This was a setup, planned months in advance. He pointed his sword savagely at Demetrios. "*Fellator!* You filthy cocksucking bastard! You surrendered this ship to him. Forget the goddamned pirate, I'll kill you myself! Traitor!" He began to bound his way up to the quarterdeck, but the crew surged forward to seize him from behind. He inflicted a nasty sword cut on one man's leg, but the mass of humanity bore him down.

Antonius looked at Ibrahim, then at Gaius, who had disappeared under a pile of bodies. "I'll settle with yer in a minute, barstid!" As he turned to charge to Gaius' rescue, one of Ibrahim's bodyguards unleashed a sling, and the whizzing egg-sized stone caught Antonius squarely behind the ear. His world vanished with a flash of pain and light.

CHAPTER 18: RECOVERY

Antonius was floating, his body weightless in blackness, as he slowly became aware of his surroundings. His mouth was dry, very dry, like paper, and he was aware of a pain behind his right ear, but very distant, like the mutter of a summer thunderstorm. Where was he, how had he gotten here? He continued to float, in and out between total blackness and awareness. Finally, he began to remember... Ibrahim, the treacherous handover of the ship, Gaius disappearing, buried under bodies, fighting to the end. Galosga coming to his aid, the other crew members quivering like whipped dogs. And something had hit him from behind, very hard.

He listened, restoring another sense. Water was rushing by somewhere, like in a pipe.

Sensation returned. He was aware of his left cheek pressing painfully against the wooden deck, like it had been there for some time. He opened his eyes, and to his shock, saw nothing but blackness. Fear seized him... he had known men to lose their sight from a blow to the head. He tried to lift his head... and the summer thunderstorm broke with full fury. Yellow and purple lightning flashed before his eyes as the pain crashed in on him, swelling in his head, nausea exploding in his stomach. *Oh, gods, don't let me barf now! I'll die!* He lay very still, and the pain carried him away, back to the drifting floating blackness.

He awoke again a long time later. This time, he was aware of dampness, of water trickling down his cheek, past his jaw. Without moving his head, he managed to catch a drop on his tongue. It seemed more like water, a bit salty, but not the thick acrid taste of blood. He opened his eyes again, and this time caught the grey outlines of his surroundings. He listened, and heard the breathing of someone else. He lay very still, eyes open, scarcely breathing for what seemed like an eternity, not wanting to raise the pain in his head again, catching drops of water with his tongue, probing his surroundings with his eyes and ears, trying to make sense of it without moving. At last, unable to continue with his face pressed against the floor, Antonius slowly, very slowly, raised his head. His head began to throb, and more flashes, this time red ones, flared in his eyes with each heartbeat. But it was not bad enough to take him off to unconsciousness again. As he raised his head, something wet fell from behind his ear, and landed on the deck with a plop. He reached for it, and as he did, his arm met resistance, and metal clanked on metal. Chains!

"Good morning, Antonius. I see you have rejoined the living! I was worried about you. I thought you might not. You took quite a blow to the head. Slinger's stone, I think, or a very well-wielded club. How do you feel?" It was Gaius, somewhere behind him. Antonius heard the clink of chains that didn't come from his own movement. Gaius must be chained up also.

"Hurts like hell, sir. An' where are we?"

"I think we're in the forward hold. Here, keep that wet rag on your noggin. But don't press. You have a solid lump the size of goose egg behind your ear, and until the swelling goes down, I can't tell if you've cracked that thick skull of yours or not. So don't press on it, and don't move around too much."

Antonius recovered the rag, and placed it behind his ear. He could gingerly feel the lump, easily filling the palm of his hand. "Ouch! I'm going to kill the cock-sucking *fellator* that did that."

"Well, you may get that chance. We've been down here about eighteen hours, and they sent down food and water. That's always a good sign. If they were going to kill us, I think they would have just thrown us overboard yesterday. Your big friend is on the other side of you, by the way, but we can't talk to each other much. He doesn't know any Latin or Greek, and I certainly don't know any Aramaic, or whatever else he talks."

"Name's Galosga." He raised himself slowly and very carefully to a sitting position. "Eighteen hours? Have I been out that whole time?"

"Every once in a while you'd groan, so I knew you were alive. Just as well you did stay still, that's the best thing after a head injury."

Antonius turned, very slowly, toward Galosga on his left. "Hullo, Galosga, you big ape. If yer din' listen ter ever'thin' I say, you wouldn' be down here. That'll teach yer!" Galosga was sitting cross-legged, and smiled to see his friend stir in the semidarkness.

The three were lightly chained. Manacles on each hand, the chains run through iron rings on the bulkheads. They were able to stand and walk, and use their hands to eat, but could not go far. "Where do yer pee, sir? I feel like I ain't, in a while."

"There in the middle, Antonius. Try to get it into the bilges, where it can run around the ship and be someone else's problem. It hasn't gotten too strong in here yet."

Antonius stood and relieved himself, then sat back down among the chains. Gaius handed him a dipper of water. "We're right by the water tanks and we can reach the valve, so water is no problem. Food's been sufficient... barely. Crew's leftovers. I saved you some, if you're hungry."

Antonius declined. "No, I'm not ready ter eat just yet. I'm afraid I might just bring it all up if I move me head wrong. Save it fer later. How come they din' just kill us?"

"I'm not sure. This looked like a well-planned setup, and once more, your instincts were right. Demetrios and our officers were in on this, and I suspect

Hasdrubal was, also. You and I have done this once or twice before, but if Aulus winds up in *Asia's* hold, he's going to get very scared fast."

"Yeah, 'member that German chieftain, what was his name, Arcintorix, I think. Surprised our century one night with a neat ambush, an' you an I spent 'bout a week in his cow barn. Had a nice daughter though... very nice!"

"Sounds like you got to know her well, Antonius!" Gaius chuckled.

"Right well, while yer were out shoveling cow shit fer her father that day, beggin' yer pardon, of course... she and I got ter be... friends."

"You're kidding, of course. Both of us were in chains, and you went after his daughter."

"'S'truth, sir!" Antonius began to laugh. "... Ouch!" the laughter had been a bit much, bringing another wave of pain through his head. The story was, however, quite true. "Oh, I wish I had me *capsula*! I have some willow bark in there. But it's in me quarters topside." One of Antonius' specialties was that of medical field orderly, or *capsularius*, from the brass metal *capsula* in which were kept clean, dry bandages, horsehair for suturing up wounds, and vials, and potions, and always lots of willow bark, famous for its analgesic properties.

"Remind me to ask the servant for some willow bark, when he brings us dinner." Gaius replied, then attempted to nod off to nap.

CHAPTER 19: CROSS AND DOUBLE CROSS

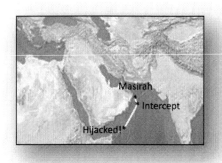

Titus had not taken the shipwrecked slave's story seriously at first. It sounded like an illusion from drinking too much saltwater in the shattered lifeboat. The slave had been picked up just off the naval station, raving about a rich convoy about to be hijacked to Parthia. He claimed he had been captured by pirates, and escaped in a ship's boat while they were careening the ship's hull in a harbor. He spun a story of the multi-millionaire Hasdrubal, in cahoots with bin Yusuf to plunder the richest convoys in history and escape to Parthia. Cornelius was just about ready to ship him back to Alexandria, when an official letter came from the garrison commander at Myos Hormos, informing him that such a convoy had just sailed... under Hasdrubal, with galley escort all the way to Veni Etiam. Cornelius, on a bet, had the slave carefully interrogated again, then questioned him himself.

"And that is a nice story, Philipus," said Titus, after listening to the tale and asking the same questions over and over. The slave had not slipped once. Even when Titus intentionally asked the wrong question, the slave corrected him. "Now what proof do you have that will stand up in a Roman court of law that this highly-placed person is in league with the devil bin Yusuf?"

Philipus stammered, "Your lordship, I overheard bin Yusuf himself say that Hasdrubal had all the incriminating records kept under a floorboard in his cabin. That's what I heard."

"Well, we shall just find out, shan't we," said Titus. He certainly did not intend to incite the ire of any high-placed personage like Hasdrubal. Hasdrubal may be a Phoenician, and he may not be a citizen, but he had millions of *sesterces* that buy a lot of support.

Titus Cornelius deployed with three liburnians at the time Philipus predicted, late in the first week of June, enjoying the clear air that went with the start of the summer monsoon. He took Philipus with him, just in case this turned out to be a ghastly mistake. Those ships shouldn't be going up this way, as the Myos Hormos letter had clearly stated their destination was India, not Parthia. Most likely, the liburnians would sweep back and forth, tracking east and west for a few days and return to port empty-handed, to send Philipus on his way home.

Titus Cornelius had no illusions about his position. This could be some sort of Parthian ruse, to draw part of the Roman squadron out to sea. The naval station at Masira was a Roman toehold on the southerly approach to the Parthian Gulf, with just twelve lightweight liburnians under his command. Titus had left the naval station on an alert state against that possibility, with orders to evacuate if that were the case.

On the sixth day of June, the lookouts sighted first one, then another, sail on the horizon, northbound, each with the distinctive triangular topsail of the heavy Roman freighter. "Hmm, Philipus," said Titus, scanning the horizon, "You've a rather high success rate for a refugee from a pirate ship's hold."

Hasdrubal cursed his luck for blundering into the three liburnians. "Bring me Galba on deck now, and get him into a reasonably clean toga."

The Senator was brought before him about an hour later. "Galba, do exactly as I tell you. I will do all the talking, and you will confirm everything I say. Everything." He blandished a short dagger. "We can outfight those light galleys, as you well know," he said, motioning toward the heavy *ballistae*.

"You bastard! I'll not cooperate with you!"

"Yes, but you must admit that we do have a good chance to escape those ships and if we do, I know that you would not want anything to happen to the beautiful, pregnant Livia, now would you?"

Aulus turned florid with anger, but fell silent.

"Ahoy! Heave to and state your business! And stand away from the *ballistae*!" the liburnian flagship hailed them. Hasdrubal gave the order, and the sails luffed on the *Asia* and *Africa*, hoisted to the yards by the brailes. "This is the *Asia*, out of Myos Hormos. How may I help you?" cried Hasdrubal, cupping his hand to focus his voice across the water.

"Stand by to be boarded. We are coming alongside!" Cornelius lowered the *corvus* boarding ramp gently onto the *Asia's* gunwhale, towering fifteen feet above the small liburnian's deck. The *corvus* was steeply inclined making the boarding somewhat dangerous as the two ships pitched and rolled restlessly. Nevertheless, about twenty marines clambered aboard, followed by Titus Cornelius and the slave Philipus, under the watchful eyes of the liburnian's *ballista* crew and the bowmen, who had each selected a crewman to shoot in the event the ship attempted to escape or repel the boarding party. Titus grudgingly gave the slave a hand to assist him up the steep incline.

"Hasdrubal of Tyre? And this is Senator Aulus Aemilius Galba, I presume." Titus appeared puzzled at the Senator's dirty appearance, then wrinkled his nose as he caught the man's unwashed scent. Hasdrubal interceded quickly. "I am he, and this is the good Aulus Aemilius. We are glad to see you as we had a most unfortunate experience with a storm. We have become separated from one of our ships, the *Europa*. Have you heard anything of her?"

"Nothing. Nor of a storm south. Where are you bound?" asked Titus.

Hasdrubal paused for a noticeably long time, then answered very measurably. "We were bound for Muziris in India, but we've been blown off course, and wanted to refill our water supply at your naval station before going on."

"You're most welcome to do so. And Senator, how has the journey been so far?"

"This has been a most miserable trip so far." The senator's gaze scanned the armed marines, the liburnian's artillery tower peeking over the *Asia's* gunwhale, the archers on deck and the two other liburnians laying to, covering the boarding party. He paused, then his face turned red as he bellowed: "Arrest this man. He is a pirate, in league with pirates!" Aulus twisted away from Hasdrubal, who reached for him with the dagger, only to have it fly from his hand with a blow from Titus Cornelius' broadsword.

Some of the crew moved to put up a token defense, but two went down with arrows in their chests before it even got started, and the remainder dropped their swords and daggers, raising their hands before the Roman marines.

In the master's cabin, underneath a loose floorboard, Philipus helped the boarding party find the books, records, letters and bank transactions that would convict Hasdrubal.

Hasdrubal protested that they were forgeries, but Titus was satisfied with their quality.

Five hundred miles south, Ibrahim looked northward, wondering if his plan had worked. Sending Philipus north a month ago had been a good insurance bet, but he would never know if it worked. Hasdrubal had done almost exactly as Ibrahim had expected, turning northward immediately for Parthia, three or four day's sail north, with two immensely valuable ships and tens of millions of *sesterces* in the hold. And that had been Ibrahim's clue to continue east toward India, improvising as he went. Hasdrubal no doubt intended to seize the *Europa* as well, if Ibrahim were to land at the pre-arranged rendezvous on the Far Side coast to transfer the booty to waiting transport and security.

But now he had bigger concerns. The sleek-barreled ocean swell, the thick humidity, and the electricity in the air signaled a big June storm. A very big one. To the south a band of tropical rain squalls exploded into the upper atmosphere, billowing white on top and ominous purple, like a bruise, underneath. The ship rolled drunkenly, as a crosswise swell propelled by enormous winds a few hundred miles south took the *Europa* broadside, causing her to stagger.

CHAPTER 20: A STORM AT SEA

The sailor came down to the hold, not with dinner, but with a key. He unlocked each man in turn while two sailors stood guard, holding back a bit in case the Romans tried to make a break. The three men rubbed their wrists and ankles, trying to get the circulation back into the pinched flesh.

"To what do we owe this honor, sailor?" asked Antonius, in Greek.

"Topside. Captain wants you," the sailor replied with a strong accent.

The three followed, Galosga and Gaius aiding the none-too-steady Antonius up the ladder through the hatch onto the deck. They blinked in the dim light of a stormy evening near sunset, clouds glowering gray and gloomy. A steady wind keened over the deck, humming in the rigging, spitting stinging spray from the crests of waves. Gaius noted that only the *artemon* and the mainsail remained deployed, half-furled by brailes. All the other sails were bound fast to the yard. The sailor separated Galosga from the Romans, and led them into the master's cabin, what had formerly been their quarters. He then left, slamming the latch shut firmly to keep the weather and water out. The stateroom was dark, the windows shuttered, glass removed and stowed. An oil lamp swung lazily from the overhead with the ship's motion, casting a fitful glow throughout the darkened room.

Ibrahim was seated at the desk. "Antonius Aristides. How pleasant to see you again! Come in, sit down, both of you," he said in Greek, motioning to the empty chairs.

"No, thanks, I'll stand. Been sitting all day," Antonius responded in Latin. He spat, working the thick gobbet of spit into the polished floor with his toe.

"Suit yourself, Roman dog." Ibrahim refused to change languages, and continued in Greek. "We have a bad storm coming, and I will not leave you to drown, chained in the hold of a foundering ship. However, make no mistake." His arm snaked out of his robe and a small knife flashed through the air over the desk to land with a quivering thunk, transfixing Antonius' spit inches from his big toe. "I have no qualms about killing you, and I may do so yet. But no man deserves to die in chains, alone, not even a Roman.

"We will need every man to work the ship, if we are to live," Ibrahim continued. "You two will work with my sailors, hauling lines and doing what you are told. If you try to make more of this than it is, I will throw you overboard. Understood?"

The deck pitched upward vertically and rolled to starboard, the ship shuddering as the bow stumbled back down into a big wave. The spray spattered over the quarterdeck above their heads. Ibrahim studied the two men intently, as they studied him. Then Gaius responded, also in Latin, "So be it. We shall talk later!" It was not a question.

Ibrahim produced two coils of rope from under the desk. "You will wear safety lines at all times tonight. That is not just for you, but for all the men as well. These waves can wash you over the side with no warning." He handed them the ropes, fitted with bronze hooks at the end. Outside, to give emphasis to his words, a wave broke over the starboard rail with a boom and a crash of splintered wood. Shouts of men could be heard in half a dozen languages, swearing as the water rushed about the deck. The ship staggered to port under the blow, buckling the men's knees as the bow plowed once again into a wave, and the load of water hissed off the deck. It was going to be a long night. "Now out!"

Outside, the darkness had grown much deeper, although it was just sunset. Rain spat fitfully, propelled by the wind into horizontal stinging pellets. The sails were now fully reefed, the bare poles and rigging moaning in the sustained winds.

The seas were mountainous, waves rolling by in slow, unhurried grace like passing elephants, plodding but unstoppable, as the wind ripped white spindrift from their tops. The *Europa* rode up and down the sides of these huge rollers, pitching and bucking like a tethered horse. And tethered she was, to a host of sea anchors deployed from her bow and stern. Occasionally she would catch a wave from the wrong angle and it would explode in a dark torrent over the gunwale, boiling fiercely, running down the scuppers and back out overside. Everything, the sea, the sky, the ship and the men themselves, was in shades of black and gray.

Gaius and Antonius were assigned to parties tending the sea anchors. These heavy leather baskets, six feet across, were let out overside and towed by heavy ropes to catch the drift and keep the ship's head around into the sea where she could best take the waves. Six sea anchors were deployed from the bow and two more from the stern. The heavy hawsers holding the deployed anchors, as big as a man's arm, were in full tension, as taut as if Poseidon's sea horses were towing the ship through the water. The Romans' job was to tend these sea anchors and ensure that they did not foul, replacing them as the storm carried them away. Replacements were lashed in place, ready to be thrown overboard.

The luckless *cybernetes* conning officer struggled with the tiller, trying to aim the head of the ship to take the next wave head on, where the ship's natural balance would cause it to ride up the wave. Only the largest waves broke green water over the bow. A full broadside wave, on the other hand, could roll the ship, and capsize her if she rolled far enough.

The wind, already strong, howled even louder, the rain and wind-whipped spray became a torrent, stinging the skin and blinding the eyes. It seemed that even the mountainous waves could not compete with this wind, which ripped their tops off to scatter them in white spray. Gaius and Antonius had never seen a storm like this. It had begun with the force of a terrible mountain gale, and gotten worse. Much worse, and still building. Speech had become impossible, and the rapidly gathering darkness limited visibility to just a few dozen feet or less. Staying on one's feet on the tilting, heaving deck became impossible without a firm grasp on some part of the ship, and the cold and damp began to sap the strength of all the men.

A particularly heavy wave struck the starboard bow of the *Europa*. The *cybernetes* had not brought the head about to meet the wave, and the ship rolled sickeningly to port, almost forty-five degrees, and the bow pitched up, up and still further up, as the men on the quarterdeck hunkered down to take the impending blow. At last, the wave broke over the bow, water roaring down the deck like an avalanche in the gloom, more heard and felt than seen. Antonius huddled down with Gaius in a corner and grabbed the strongest wooden object in sight. He checked his lifeline, which seemed so frail and thin, then also gave Gaius' a quick tug before the wave reached the quarterdeck.

At first Antonius thought the ship had foundered. The water poured onto him like a waterfall and did not end, but just kept pouring and pouring. He could not breathe, his injured head throbbing redly. At last, unable to hold his breath any longer, and sure that the ship had gone under, he released his hold on the stanchion and stood up, fumbling for his lifeline. As he did, his head broke out of the abating wave and he inhaled hungrily. He looked about in the darkness, and could see the dark shape of the ship's hull, her masts reeling against the sky, and other men on deck helping each other up. Still afloat! He went back to check the sea anchors, and noted that one had parted with the last surge, the three inch hawser unable to stand the strain of tons of seawater. He pitched the new anchor over the stern, taking care to clear the other lines.

Ibrahim had come on deck to relieve the *cybernetes*. He didn't like the way in which the ship had taken the last wave, and although Antonius could not see the facial expressions well nor understand the words, the gestures left no doubt what Ibrahim was saying to the young officer. Ibrahim gesticulated angrily in the direction the wave had come over the bow, and the way the wave had nearly swamped the ship. *He may be a murderous bastard,* thought Antonius, *but I'm damned glad he is taking the tiller tonight.* The *cybernetes* left the deck, and Ibrahim expertly guided the big ship's bow through the next several waves, breaking water over the main deck with a dull boom but no risk of swamping the entire vessel.

To port, another sea anchor hawser parted with a loud pop that could be heard above the storm's roar, the sailors ducking as the line whizzed over their heads in recoil. The portside group gathered up one of the spares and tossed it overboard, and as the new line snaked out overside, Antonius watched in horror as Ibrahim seemed to be seized bodily by some unseen god and snatched away from the tiller, flying through the air to follow the sea anchor overside! *Damned idiots! They didn't check to see if the hawser was clear!* It had fouled Ibrahim's lifeline, snapping it from its attachment, and the pirate was dragged bodily overboard to come to rest suspended, clinging to the hawser twenty feet overside. Only Ibrahim's strong arms kept him out of the sea which heaved like a slowly breathing monster below him. However, Antonius could see that the Arab would not remain there long. Either his strength would give out, or another monstrous wave would tear him from the line and fling him into the sea. He would be lost in the darkness if he didn't drown at once or be smashed against the hull.

In the meanwhile, rudderless, the ship began to careen against the waves. The portside crew gathered about the hawser, reaching futilely across the distance toward Ibrahim, while below him the sea foamed whitely below the stern of the ship. Antonius grabbed one of the young sailors and thrust him onto the tiller, indicating that he was to steer. *Don't know if he knows what he's doing or not, but he's probably going to do better than me. Hope someone comes up here soon and notices we're in big trouble!* Antonius located Gaius in the darkness, and helped him size up the situation. Antonius freed up his own lifeline, doubled it over, and handed the loop to Gaius. The two did not need to say much. Antonius made a jerking motion three times and Gaius nodded. Antonius then clambered out onto the taut hawser headfirst, inching downward hand over hand to where Ibrahim clung helplessly in the darkness. Seen from the deck, the hawser had seemed much more taut than when it sagged under Antonius' full weight.

They were two feet apart, face to face, when Ibrahim recognized him. He said something that Antonius could not hear for the wind. *It had damn well better be "Thankin' yer very much, yer Roman lordship, sir!" Arab bastard!* He felt in the dark for Ibrahim's lifeline, finding it of course parted, so Antonius had to bend a knot into the line. *This is gettin' complicated, what with not enough hands ter work this knot in the dark!* The ship stumbled and swayed, in the tell-tale lurch that preceded one of those monster waves, and Antonius' stomach sank with the downward pitch of the stern. *Oh, Poseidon! I bet yer thinkin' this is real funny like, real funny!* Antonius inched down to grab Ibrahim firmly, for that man was not secured to any sort of lifeline, and only the hands of the seamen on the quarterdeck secured the loop of his own. The two waited while the ship pitched up by the bow, settling the stern rapidly into the water. The distance separating them from the boiling water below narrowed to just a few feet, then bare inches, when the water came cascading down upon them from above. After an eternity of being unable to breathe, eyes squeezed shut against the salt water, the waterfall ceased and the stern reared upward like an unbroken horse, yanking the two men upward and away from the water violently. The two men clung to the line, waiting for the heaving motions of the ship and the sea to die away. Antonius could hear Ibrahim sputtering in the dark while he completed securing his lifeline to the bitter end of the pirate's. Now, if the men on deck had maintained their hold on his line, it doubled back and secured Ibrahim as well. He gave his line three sharp tugs as signal, and felt the line go taut. *They're pulling us in. Just work it back, slowly, slowly.* He inched back up the hawser, his hands and knees maintaining their grip, and Ibrahim followed. Antonius was dressed in a light tunic, so the waterlogged fabric did not bear him down. But Ibrahim was dressed in a traditional Arab gown. *That must really add some weight when it's wet.*

At last, he felt someone grab his ankles and pull him in. As he went in, he grabbed Ibrahim by the shoulders and hoisted him in as well. The two landed in a pile on the deck, breathing heavy, their arms and legs quivering from the strain, rope burns on their arms and legs on fire from the salt. *Oohh! I forgot about me headache*, thought Antonius, as his head throbbed heavily. Ibrahim grabbed him by his aching head, unaware, and shouted into his ear, "*Gratias tibi!* Thanks to you!" In Latin.

Now why did I go an' do that? But he knew the answer. He wasn't going to let a man die alone in a storm-tossed sea, any more than Ibrahim would let him drown chained to a hold of a dying ship. "*Davar!* Thou art welcome," said Antonius, shouting back, hoping the gale would hide his butchered Aramaic. The two laughed, slapped each other, and struggled to their feet.

Demetrios had taken the helm, while Gaius and Antonius continued to work with the stern sea anchors. The crew fought the storm all night, deploying additional sea anchors off the bow to keep the head around. After midnight, ghostly green fire began to dance around the tops of the masts and the rigging, occasionally making men look like apparitions as it wavered and dripped from their open mouths. Some took this as an evil omen, but Antonius took it as a positive sign that Poseidon was with them. Finally, dawn announced its arrival by a barely perceptible change from blackness to grayness. Shapes on the deck and lines in the rigging, previously indiscernible, could now be seen. The wind's steady howl abated for a few moments, and the constant drenching rain and spindrift let up. Both returned with their former fury a moment later, but the breaks became longer and more frequently thereafter. By midmorning, the hurricane winds had died off to gale force, and while the ship still tossed and pitched heavily with the huge gray storm waves, the waves no longer broke over the bow. Heaven and sea were shades of white, gray and black, the lower scud whirling by overhead like gray smoke against the darker leaden gray color of the higher clouds. Visibility was up to a mile or two, though there was little that the eye could see except the restless expanse of dune-sized waves spattered with stormcaps rolling across the dark sea.

The ship's officers inspected the ship, and finding no major leaks in the hull, secured the more exhausted of the deckhands to rest wherever they could find a dry spot. The remaining crew continued at their deck stations, tending sea anchors, posting lookouts and tending the injured around them.

Demetrios requested Gaius Lucullus assist in inspecting the ship and mustering the crew. Demetrios needed his engineering skills, and Gaius crawled in and out of the many dark nooks and crannies of the ship with the captain, looking for damage, leaks... or bodies.

CHAPTER 21: STORM'S AFTERMATH

"Come on, you men! Hold him! He's flopping around all over the place!" Antonius bellowed in Greek at the sailors holding the young man's shoulders. The man's face was white with pain, perspiration pearling on his quivering upper lip. The men shifted their grip and Antonius went to work, seizing the man by the leg and pulling hard until he felt the bones begin to grind again. The man screamed, a long continuous scream, but Antonius ignored it.

Suddenly he felt an almost imperceptible catch as the bones engaged inside the leg, damaged end mating with damaged end. Antonius worked the leg back and forth gently to see if it was holding. It was good, and he gave an exhausted sigh. The man stopped screaming, but continued to sob. Antonius gave him a friendly slap on the chest, "That's a good lad, you'll be running after the women again sooner than you know." The man managed a weak smile and a barely perceptible nod, and said something Antonius couldn't understand.

"All right, splint him up like the others, then give him enough wine to put him down solid. Who's next?" Antonius stepped back from the young sailor and stood, stretching and pressing his hands against his throbbing temples. His own wound was untended. He had worked without sleep through the night, first the fighting the storm, then tending the wounded.

"That's it. Everyone else is bruised or knocked about, no more serious injuries," said the quartermaster next to him, superintending the makeshift sickbay in the master's cabin. "Thank you. A lot of these boys would have lost arms and legs today." Antonius had forgotten the man's name and was too tired to care.

"Make sure they don't get feverish, or they might yet. I am going to find a place to lie down, if we're done." He had treated twelve men for serious injuries that morning, mostly broken bones, and a few ugly cuts that needed suturing. His *capsula* was out of horsehair and he had used most of his vinegar washing wounds.

Antonius walked forward to the galley area, hoping to find some food, his stomach reminding him that he had not eaten in days. The ship was riding with bare poles, tethered to sea anchors in a moderate, restless sea; the sails were haphazardly laid out on deck, sailmakers working to dry and repair them. Also laid out to dry were soaked coils of rope, bedding and clothes. Both steering oars had been cracked, the remains unshipped, lying on the deck. Rails were broken or carried away, fittings askew. The masts and yards seemed solid and the rigging in good shape, as far as Antonius could tell...

nothing sagged or seemed broken. Amidships, Antonius watched four sailors working the see-saw levers of the pump over the forward hold. He looked down to see five feet of dark water sloshing back and forth where they had been chained. He shuddered a bit. *I will not leave you to drown, chained in the hold of a foundering ship*, Ibrahim had said. Drown they certainly would have. The pumps began to take hold and water gushed noisily overside through a leather pipe with each stroke. Behind him four more men began setting up the aft hold for de-watering.

Gaius came over with some sailors lugging sea anchors. "Good morning Antonius! How are the wounded?"

"Doin' all right, sir. Didn't yer get enough sea anchor duty last night?"

"We're rigging the cargo hoist to use these as buckets along with the pumps. Your head?"

"On me shoulders, thuddin' like a big drum. I'm goin' forward, see if I can find some food, then get some sleep."

By the forward galley, cooks gave Antonius some sodden bread, which quelled the grumbling in his stomach. The forward cook stove was lit for the evening meal. Ten soggy dead goats, apparently drowned in their pens, were laid out for butchering.

The overcast had continued to clear to a bright blustery sunny day over a beautiful blue sea. Only the residual heavy swells, now running just six to eight feet or so, left a hint of the previous night's violence. Ropes were being strung across the gaping holes in the railings to prevent men from falling overboard.

Galosga had rigged his own cooking device near the galley, an odd tent-like arrangement of sticks and cloth about three feet high. He hung goat meat in long strips inside, and put in a bowl of smoldering wood, which burned with an enormous amount of smoke. "Galosga!" he cried out, "Good see thee. Make smoke, why?"

Galosga replied, but most of the words were incomprehensible. Galosga opened the tent, and pointed to the goat meat inside. *Odd way to cook. It doesn't seem to be hot enough.* Galosga opened a leather pouch from around his waist, and pulled out two long, flat pieces of what seemed like greasy leather. He handed one to Antonius and put the other in his mouth. Whatever it was, it was tough like leather, but as Antonius chewed, the flavor came out. *Not bad.* Galosga pointed to the tent and said "Tomorrow." *Hmm, got to remember this. I wonder how long he's had this piece of meat. Just carries it around in that pouch. Those ten goats can feed us for weeks, smoked like that.*

Marcus Lucius and Marcia came on deck in mid-afternoon, ecstatic to find Antonius and Gaius resting amidship on some piles of rope.

"Antonius! Gaius! You are alive! And free! We thought you were dead! But what happened to your head, Antonius?" cried Marcia. The ugly goose-egg protruded through the close-cropped black hair on the back of his head, purple with a bloody scab.

"Someone wasted a stone throwing it at me, but I broke it with me noggin."

"Sit down. Let me tend it for you, before it gets inflamed."

"Here, use me *capsula,* I think I have some stuff left over." He pulled out the rolled up pouch from the brass cylinder, and found some white dressings and the vial with a little vinegar remaining. Marcia dabbed at the scab with the vinegar-soaked cloth, while Antonius chewed on his last remaining piece of willow-bark. "I hate ter be losing me last piece – I mean to say, I hate to be losing my last piece of willow-bark. I hope we have some more medical supplies on board."

Marcia tittered at his language. "That's all right, I am beginning to understand your soldier talk better than when we first heard it." She finished binding up his head with the last piece of linen.

"Thanks! I had almost forgotten about this bump. I was tending some folks much worse off than me."

"You two look exhausted."

Antonius added, "We have been up for almost two days. Thanks for the fix-up, we can chat later when we can keep our eyes open."

Marcia smiled shyly, and helped roll up the bundle and put it back in the *capsula.* "No problem, get some sleep and tell us about your adventures tomorrow."

CHAPTER 22: NEGOTIATING WITH THE DEVIL

Gaius and Antonius staggered off to find a place to sleep on the second deck, and stretched out on the wooden planks for a few hours. But near sundown, they were awakened with a surly, "Captain wants you!" In Greek. In poor Greek.

Antonius was slow to respond, then asked, "Which one, the traitor or the pirate?" The sailor aimed a kick at the soldier which Antonius evaded, rolling away but catching the man's foot, bringing him down hard. The Roman soldier rolled on top of the sailor, grabbing him by the throat. "Don't kick me, sailor boy, unless you're ready to kill me! And if you think you are, better bring along a friend, because I don't think you can do it by yourself!" In Greek. In excellent Greek.

He held the man's throat gently, not choking, but with a firm grip on the man's Adam's apple. He looked the sailor in the eyes, making sure he saw total terror, then he said, "Arrgh, yer too young ter kill. Maybe termorrow," and rolled off him, stood up and extended his hand to help the stunned sailor up. "Now which one did yer say wanted ter see us?" This time in Latin.

The sailor stammered, coming to his feet as Antonius dusted himself off, as though they had just completed a training bout in a gymnasium. "Ib...Ibrahim!"

Gaius chuckled, and in literary Latin that he was sure that the sailor could not follow, said, "You seem to have adequately demonstrated a point of courtesy, my good centurion!"

"Aye, sir, one must first obtain their undivided attention!" replied Antonius in the same style.

Ibrahim had relocated his quarters to share Demetrios' portside stateroom. The master's cabin, no longer a sickbay, was undergoing repairs and cleaning, for the shuttered windows had leaked heavily. There was a lot of hammering, shouts and the sound of heavy timbers being fitted as the ship's carpenters rigged the massive replacement steering oars.

"Welcome, welcome, please dine with me tonight," Ibrahim said in Greek, opening his arms expansively. "Captain Demetrios would enjoy your company as well, but he hopes to be under sail before midnight. His other duties keep him on deck." He continued, apologetically. "I hope we can converse in Greek, since you both speak that language so well and my Latin is so poor." Two couches were in place for them to dine reclining, Roman style. He seemed genuinely glad to see the two, who nevertheless maintained their reserve. "You saved my life last night. Among our people, that leaves me permanently in your debt."

Gaius decided to come right to the point. This was a negotiating opportunity and one always wanted to put the strongest case on the table first. "To pay your debt then, you may return the ship which you wrongfully appropriated, and inform me of my cousin's whereabouts and health. You may then leave this ship alive, in return for your having saved our lives. I shall put in favorable word of that with the Roman authorities," said Gaius stiffly in Greek, tacitly accepting that as the conversational language.

"I expected no less from you, my noble Gaius! As to your cousin's whereabouts and health, I cannot say for sure. I have taken steps to protect him as best I can, but Hasdrubal has betrayed both him and me. Will you accept my hospitality? Perhaps we shall find a way in which we can endure each other, until I can set you on your trip again."

Antonius' face clouded and he seemed prepared to speak, perhaps unwisely, when Gaius touched his elbow. "We accept your hospitality, without accepting your right to this vessel. Perhaps we can better settle our differences on a full stomach. If you do not mind, we would prefer to eat at table, rather than reclining. That is a custom of the Roman aristocracy which makes my centurion a bit uncomfortable." Antonius was extremely self-conscious about dining reclining, since he often spilled food on himself or the couch.

"Certainly," said Ibrahim, taking two chairs from the bulkhead and placing them at the table spread with some flat bread, cheese, olives and a haunch of goat meat. Gaius reached for a knife and carved a slab of meat, as did Antonius and Ibrahim. There was no other silverware, so the two Romans ate as Ibrahim did, Bedouin style, wrapping the greasy dark meat into the flat bread with some cheese and olives. The two were quite hungry, having eaten very little for days.

With his hunger satisfied, Gaius began to think analytically about the next move. This was indeed a negotiating opportunity, and he began to set his priorities. The first priority was to determine what became of his cousin and the other two ships. Apparently, not everything had gone according to plan for Ibrahim. The second was to negotiate their status on board. And the third was to negotiate their ability to leave and continue their mission. Gaius did not really expect the release of the ship. It seemed best to lay out the easy objective first, and bargain down to the difficult ones last. "It seems we are both in each other's debt. We inspected the hold where we were chained, and found that we surely would have drowned last night. We both thank you, because you surely saved our lives as we saved yours, but may I ask you why? We appear to be more of a danger to you alive than dead, and few would have given their prisoners a second thought under such circumstances."

"You are most welcome. May I tell you a story that will clarify why I could not leave you in the hold?" asked Ibrahim.

"Please, feel free," answered Gaius.

"When I was a young man, I shipped in the Mediterranean as a deck seaman on the *Astarte*, a tramp freighter. The captain was a fool who insisted on making one more shipment, sailing in November after all wise Mediterranean skippers dock their ships and pay off their crews for the winter. I was heard criticizing him, and he put me in chains into the hold.

"The ship ran into foul weather, and the hold filled rapidly with water. There is nothing worse than drowning alone in the dark, with cold water inching up your body. Fear can add enormous strength, for I pulled my chains from the bulkhead with the water chest-high. Perhaps some rotten wood helped, for the *Astarte* was not well cared for. I scrambled out of the hold, the chains still about my hands, and went straight to the captain's cabin. I found him there, dead drunk, and killed him where he lay with my chains. Back on deck, the crew was in near panic with no one giving orders, the ship foundering. We could not abandon the ship, we had to fight the storm. I gave orders, sending people here and there. I was only a deck seaman, but I guess that some of what I said made sense, for the crew did what I said. One man objected, and I broke his jaw, the rest obeyed. We got her head around, and we saved the ship."

At this point, some of the cooks brought in another slab of goat, some figs, dates, and olives, and more wine. They set it on the table and left. Ibrahim began to serve each some more meat.

Ibrahim continued. "The next day, I held a council with everyone to determine what to do next. You see, we had dumped the cargo overside to lighten the ship. I could be forgiven for killing the captain, if I had been able to bring the ship in with a full load. But coming back empty, the owners would assume that we had killed the captain and dumped the cargo to save our own lives, and would treat us as mutineers. So I decided to take the ship as the pirate they would have made me out to be. Those who wished to sail with me could do so; those who did not, could leave. They all chose to go with me, even the man whose jaw I broke. We sailed together, some of us for forty years, though many are dead today.

"That is how I came to be what I am today, and that is why I will never leave a man chained in the hold to die in a storm. Now, Antonius, you must answer me: why did you save my life last night, for I also would appear to be more dangerous to you alive?"

Antonius chewed on the meat, pondering his answer. "Well, I remembered when you came on deck to take the tiller, I was really glad you were there. You might be a murderous pirate, but you're a good seaman, and we needed all the help we could get last night. So when you went over, all I could see was our losing the only person who could keep the ship and us alive. So I went down that rope and got you up." Antonius chuckled and continued, "I figured I could kill you myself later if I had to. But when I got out on that line, over that sea heaving below me in the dark, and that big wave broke over us, I wished I'd left you out there!"

Ibrahim laughed. "Well, I do thank you for saving my life. You may feel free to try to kill me later, but I do hope you will change your mind!" The man had a booming, expansive laugh, not at all the harsh barbarian the two had expected.

Gaius admired the workings of Ibrahim's mind. In other circumstances, the man would have been a successful admiral or businessman. Now here he was, a pirate, the most wanted man in the Mediterranean and Red Sea, and Gaius was enjoying the charming bastard's company! Well, on to the next. "Can you tell me what became of my cousin and the other two ships?"

Ibrahim replied, filling their wine goblets, handing one to each. "As best I can. As you may surmise, considerable planning went into this enterprise. As you may not know, Hasdrubal, the shipping master, is my long-time partner in crime, and was essential in setting this up."

Antonius interrupted, swearing. "That son-of-a-bitch! I knew he was involved in this!"

"How did you know that, Antonius?" asked Ibrahim, studying him with a cool smile.

"He was... strange, ever since he saw me, as though he knew me from somewhere. He was sick for two days after we met, nearly delayed the sea trials."

Ibrahim laughed. "Sick! I'll bet he was! And you did not recognize him?"

"Yes, but... Hecate take him! He really was with you at the Bull and Dove!" A flicker of anger went across his face, as he recognized the implications. "And you! You murdered that young Roman soldier!" Antonius rose, and was leaning across the table to grab Ibrahim by the throat when Gaius seized his arm.

"Down, Antonius!" said Gaius. "Down! Let's hear this out!" Gaius wanted to know the whereabouts of his cousin and the other two ships, and if he had to listen to Ibrahim brag about every Roman he'd ever killed to get that information, well, then so be it.

Antonius sat down, breathing heavily.

Ibrahim continued, unflustered. He didn't rattle easily. "He was there at the Bull and Dove, but it was he, not I, that killed that young man. Because you saw him there together with me. The young man was nothing more than a box where we left cryptic messages for our people to find us so we could meet under safe circumstances... he knew nothing more, and you inadvertently drew from him a message meant for Hasdrubal's agent, who was with you in the fort that day, supposed to meet with us at the Bull and Dove. When you showed up with the right code phrase, 'shipping information,' we thought at first you were that agent. I introduced myself, and quickly determined you were not, but we had to keep talking."

Ibrahim touched his fingertips together delicately. "Hasdrubal has grown more and more rash. Earlier in the year, around the winter solstice, he had some Romans killed on one of his boats, which was foolish, since there was no need. Your describing them as relatives of the great Trajan scared him senseless, that and some report which might eventually link the crime to him. So also without my knowledge or direction, he told his agent to kill you and the young man, and steal the report... but he could not locate you." The pirate chief looked almost sincerely concerned as he looked into Antonius' eyes. "Like you, I have no compunction about killing, and like you, I have done it many times. And, as I suspect also like you, I do not enjoy it, and I do not kill when it is not necessary. Otherwise, a drunken Roman centurion would not have left the Bull and Dove alive that afternoon. Your death in that quarter would have caused far fewer problems than that of the young man in camp... what was his name? Lucius Servilius?"

"You knew him?" Antonius growled.

"Young Lucius never knew me, but I always make it a point to know my people, even if they don't know me. My people recruited him on the docks at Ostia before the legion did. "

Gaius interrupted, "This is all very interesting, if it is true, but why are you telling us all of this? You know we will testify against you at your trial, so if you are planning to kill us, please get on with it, or we shall have to kill you."

"There will be no trial, for I am going far away from Roman law and justice. As for you, by all the gods of the desert, I swear I shall not kill you unless I find it necessary, which I have not done so, not yet. If you wish to kill me, feel free. But you shall find yourself in a long line, and none so far have been successful. May I continue to tell you what I know of your cousin's whereabouts? And, please, some more wine." He poured each man a fresh cup.

"Consider those of us who ply the pirate's trade as the wolves of the sea. We take down the lame, the weak, the unwary, but it is not in our interest to be greedy and devour the whole flock, or we would then starve. Or arouse the shepherd to take strong action and destroy us. So I take only a percentage off the top of your trade." Ibrahim smiled.

"Our plan was to take but one ship. Hasdrubal and the rest of the convoy were to continue the voyage with the other two, his cover as shipping master intact, to share in the insurance fees and in my generous share to him. Hasdrubal had the *Europa* fly a red banner, my signal. I planned to take it south to Africa along the Far Side, and offload the money to secure transportation. The officers, as you can see, were all a part of it and as for the rest of the crew... well, they just follow who leads. And who has the keys to the armory. Except for one who followed you, Antonius. You seem to have inspired him."

"And nothin' better happen ter him... I swear, sir, why are we listenin' ter this pirate crap? There's just me an' yer, we can take him..." As Antonius turned to Gaius, two silent figures emerged out of the shadows behind them, swords drawn.

"Oh, I forgot... please meet Elibaal and Yakov, my two most unworthy servants. I fear I was most discourteous to not introduce them earlier." Ibrahim smiled, again. "As I said, I am most difficult to kill, but you are always welcome to try." He snapped his fingers, said something in Aramaic, and the two bodyguards disappeared back into the shadows. "More wine? As I recall, you like it neat, Antonius."

Ibrahim placed the cup before Antonius, but he did not take it.

"So, Gaius," Ibrahim turned toward the senior Roman, "Hasdrubal double-crossed me as well as the Senator. As I was securing this ship, my lookouts observed his ships veering north towards Parthia, taking the rest of the fleet and two-thirds of the gold to Rome's greatest enemy. He would be most welcome in their capital at Ctesiphon." He leaned across the table and whispered in a conspiratorial voice, "And somewhat beyond even Rome's long arm, although you do have your agents there, too. I happen to know a few of them by name."

He leaned back again and continued in his normal voice. "And your cousin and all his servants, if they survived, would be sold on the block. There are quite a few Parthian nobility who would pay a good price to own a Roman Senator, to empty their chamber pots and other menial tasks around the house. And there would also be trouble waiting for me in Africa at my formerly safe harbor, which Hasdrubal had set up for me. So I chose to do the unexpected and continued east. Hasdrubal, in the meanwhile, may have encountered some Roman galleys, up near Masira. If he tried to double cross me, that was the only direction for him to go, so last month I planted an agent to be picked up by the Roman Navy at Masira, to tell them of his plot, and help them find the evidence if they intercepted him. I don't know what really happened. My agent may not have been believed, Hasdrubal may not have gone to Parthia, or the Roman navy may not have found him. But if they did, Hasdrubal would now be in considerable trouble, for the evidence clearly documented his many crimes, and told where to find the money. As for your cousin the Senator, I would hope that he is alive and continuing his journey, thanks to your vigilant navy. But if the trap did not spring as planned... well, I do not know what actually took place. I hope I answered your question fairly, Gaius."

Gaius put his hand to his chin. "A most interesting turn of events." He couldn't resist a wry smile. "I admire your straightforward way of dealing with people. You should perhaps learn to be more devious. Now what are you going to do with the ship and with us?"

Ibrahim sighed, and suddenly seemed old and sad. "Gaius, I am an old man. I have followed the sea for forty years, almost all of it as a pirate. Never have I had the opportunity to have a family, wives and children. Yakov, whom I adopted when he was a ten year old orphan cutpurse, is my only son. Had my life been different, I might have had more sons such as you two, and a home somewhere. But I have been a nomad on the water, as my father and his fathers before him had been nomads in the desert. I want to be somewhere where I do not need to look over my shoulder for the next danger. I have many accomplices and many enemies, but I have never had a friend. I want to know real friendship before I die, and perhaps wives and children. I can't do that here. Perhaps somewhere far east of here, where no one knows me. Our next stop is a place called Galle in Taprobane, south of India. You are free to leave there, both of you, and anyone else who wishes to. I will guarantee your passage back to Muziris in India. From there, you may continue on your way, or return to Rome as you choose."

Ibrahim got up and pulled two chests from a closet. "These are your personal possessions, including your weapons. You will find everything there, and if you are missing anything, please let me know and we shall try to find it. I have arranged accommodations in the officers' quarters below for you. You are free go about the ship as you wish. Please do not try to kill me, for I have grown to like you both, and I should miss you greatly... especially you, my gallant Antonius!"

It had grown dark, and the brighter stars were visible through the windows of the cabin. Ibrahim went to secure them, as the noise of men shouting and running to their stations filtered into the cabin. "It sounds as though Demetrios is getting ready to get underway. You'll pardon me... I think that I am tired and must rest. We must chat again."

CHAPTER 23: A THOUGHT OF SUICIDE

The master's cabin in the *Asia* was blazing hot, although the windows were open wide to whatever breeze stirred in the barren harbor at the southern tip of Masira. Outside, the pink rocks of the hills elbowed their way toward the brassy sky with no hint of vegetation.

A rivulet of sweat ran down Lucis Parvus' nose, where it hung, before plummeting to the wax tablet worksheets spread out before him.

Lucius set aside his stylus. "Sir, no matter how you calculate it, you personally lose twenty million *sesterces* if you delay to next sailing season. Mostly due to the increased costs, penalties, and those last three bargain loans we struck up in Alexandria. They looked good when we were certain to complete our expedition in a single season. But the interest goes from ten percent to a hundred percent if we don't repay the loan by the next winter solstice. We've been over these figures a dozen times already, sir."

"Hmm." Aulus's tunic was wet with sweat. A fly buzzed noisily somewhere in the cabin. "Well, I think we have no alternatives, Lucius. The officers and crew are compromised, from the captains on down to the deckhands. We can't go back for a new crew, train them and still sail this season, and we can't come close to breaking even if we wait till next year. Not with the *Europa* lost and ten million in gold and silver with her."

He sighed. "Lucius, I can't lose that much. My family, everything we worked for, it would be gone. All of you, my loyal *servi* and *servae*, auctioned on the block, your families broken up, sold to the gods know who... or what. All my homes and businesses and shipyards, gone. Nothing for my child but my leftover debts. You know what I must do, so please order up a splendid meal for us and the servants. Then draw my bath, take down my words to my family, and help me off quietly. Oh, and please, take this." He withdrew a rolled scroll from the desk and handed it to Lucius.

Lucius unrolled the scroll, and his eyes grew wide with surprise. *Manumitted! Free! He, his wife and children, and the four menservants... and their families. Free! This was his dream.* Then the impact of the Senator's words sank in. This was the old man's *testamenta*, his last will... he was going to take 'the pink bath,' slit open the veins in the crook of his arms and let his life ooze slowly out as he relaxed in a hot tub of water, falling asleep to slip over the edge of life quietly at the end.

"Sir? I can't accept this, much as it means everything to me and my family. You and I have put together too many crazy business deals in the past, we've gambled millions and won some and lost a lot. This... please, don't." His eyes filled with tears. "It's no different than some of the other deals. Don't you remember that olive oil grove and factory in Pompeii? How the owner was so proud of the fine trees that grew on the slopes of Vesuvius? 'It's the ash,' he said. 'Makes them really flourish.'"

"It wasn't the same, Lucius. We scarcely lost a million on that. And I'm old and tired. I should have let a younger man try this gamble. Hasdrubal took me for a sucker!"

"Well, sir, if you don't mind my pointing out, Hasdrubal took in a lot of others besides you. He was recommended by everyone, the governor, the city council of elders, even some of the other merchants he shilled. You were in good company, indeed... Aulus." Lucius was taking a chance. He had been his *servus* for all of his forty-three years, born into the household and risen to be his financial manager. Never, not once, had he called his master by his *praenomen*: not to his face, not behind his back. But he had his manumission papers in hand, and his master wanted to kill himself three thousand miles from home. What was Aulus Aemilius Galba going to do, get mad and whip him? Maybe that would at least steer him away from his planned course. "And maybe the papers the slave Philippus found are all a forgery."

But Aulus was nonplussed. "No, Lucius. They tortured some of the officers today and it didn't take long to corroborate the outlines of the story. The details will take months to verify, maybe years, but I suspect they will all fit. Titus Cornelius wants to know what to do with the crew, to take them into custody, or what." He paused, then chuckled, "That damned olive oil scheme. It's been twenty years. I had almost forgotten that one! How long did we own it?"

"About a week, until the eruption. It must be under twenty or thirty feet of ash now. Maybe we should go back and excavate it... fine ash now, for sure!" Lucius said, smiling.

"Hmm, maybe we don't have to excavate the grove. How high above the ground do my property rights extend? If property is buried under ash, doesn't it still lay on the surface of the ash? That sounds like an interesting case for the Roman courts! And an interesting surveying task. Maybe we can go into the olive oil business after all," said Aulus. "And thanks for calling me Aulus. You've always been more like a younger brother to me than a slave. We certainly have put together some crazy schemes, haven't we?"

Lucius rejoiced, for his master was turning his mind away from thoughts of suicide. "You know, you thought you were done for then. Not yet thirty-five and having to start over. But you did." But then he saw his master's face turn downward again. He had chosen the wrong words.

"No," said Aulus, sighing heavily again. "It's not the same. Twenty million isn't a million. And I had barely begun then, so starting over was hardly the same as now."

"You didn't think so then. And anyway, if you have lost twenty times as much today, you are worth far more than twenty times what you were worth then."

"I'm too old. Look, just call the boys up and let's get on with the celebration."

Lucius was fed up. He shouted angrily, "They're not boys, they are men, damn it. You freed them and you freed me, so call them yourself, and by the way, draw your own damned bath and open your own damned veins! I'm a freed man, and I'm too busy to waste my time on an impotent old fart who can't take a little setback. Don't pee in your bathwater!" He turned to leave, but Aulus put a hand on his shoulder.

"You have a good temper, but your tears betray you," Aulus said quietly.

Lucius turned to shout something again but collapsed to hug the old man, sobbing into his shoulder. "Master! Don't make me beg. Let me help you, and we'll see it through. Trust me, just one more time. I'll see you home to Livia Luculla Galba and your child, with a profit. Please!"

Aulus held him, patting his shoulder as if the newly-freed man were a child. "Now there, Lucius!" But his own eyes brimmed with tears. "I want to trust you, but what else can we do? We can't get a new crew this year, and can't afford to do it next year. What else can we do?"

"Go with what we have!" said Lucius, breaking away from the hug.

"What, sail with a crew that will throw us overside as soon as we're out of sight of land?"

"So? Then you just don't show up at destination. Lost at sea. Most of our notes have an escape clause for just that eventuality. Lost at sea, that's a write-off. Delaying a year, that's non-performance. Suicide, also non-performance. Your estate, and Livia, gets stuck with your debts. But if they kill you, the bankers get stuck. Of course, we're both dead, but one of us wants to die anyway, and I'll bet my life that we can make it."

"You crazy fool! Are you sure?" said Aulus, excitedly.

"Of course I'm sure! I negotiated those contracts, damn you!" Lucius was beginning to enjoy the amenities of being free.

"Go over those figures again, and tell me what my estate is out if we are lost at sea."

Lucius sat down again at the desk, erased the wax tablet with his thumb, and recalculated. The stylus scratched on wax for about five minutes, the abacus clicked rapidly, then he announced, "With some insurance payments on the ships that cover losses at sea, and assuming they cover the *Europa*, and counting the replacement costs of four manservants and one financial wizard, your estate is out a million and a quarter *sesterces*... a manageable sum. Livia likes Alexandria and that little *villa*, so I would suggest she dispose of the one in Ostia and reside there permanently. Assuming this terrible thing happens to us. Put that in a letter to her and I will have Cornelius deliver it with the next supply ship. It will get there before any bad news does."

"Lucius, I don't know what I would do without you."

"You probably would have taken a pink bath a long time ago and died a pauper. Now pardon me, but I am taking away all your sharp knives, and have Cornelius release the officers. I presume we sail on the morning's tide?"

"Make it so!"

Titus reluctantly released the officers. The navigators, who were academic types with no involvement, had been locked up separately for safekeeping, and treated gently. Hasdrubal was also separately confined, in chains. The other officers and the two captains had been thrown into the naval prison, and two flogged to assess the Greek sailor's story and the incriminating documents. It didn't require more than ten lashes to loosen their tongues, and they confirmed the conspiracy. This wasn't legally correct, since only slaves' testimony under torture could be accepted as evidence. But if some fat-assed *praetor* wanted to make a trip out here to Masira to question him, he could just do so. June was a perfect month for a *praetor's* visit, with the temperature hot enough to fry eggs on rocks - his sailors had done that, for a joke - and no rain since April.

"Your master is sure he wants these men released? You have that in writing from him?" Titus had asked, when Lucius communicated his request. Lucius had anticipated this, and had the necessary paperwork. Titus didn't like it, but it was the Senator's ship, his money and his crew. And his life. If the Senator wanted to risk all that, it too was his choice.

However, Titus had an insurance plan for the man, in the form of a talented artist among his marines. This artist was particularly good at making full color portraits and tiny, life-like cameos on ivory. The young man made a fair supplement to his wages capturing the likeness of his shipmates to send home to their mothers, wives and lovers... sometimes, sailors being what they were, to all three. And each likeness could not be more lifelike than if the subject himself had been captured in the two-inch white disk. Rusticus could work swiftly, from a charcoal sketch to the delicately painted final piece in just a few days. Titus was particularly fond of the full-sized portrait done of him in honor of his new command.

Titus displayed this work of art to the released officers, admiring the way in which Rusticus had captured his square jaw, the look of determination in his eye, and the stray lock of hair that fell, undisciplined, across his right eye. Behind him, battles that he never fought raged between galleys on a storm-tossed sea. The Senator's officers admired the artwork.

Then Titus had them each sit for a quick sketch by Rusticus. "I promise you each as good a portrait as this one," he said, strolling around them as Rusticus' charcoal scratched along the stiff paper. "And if the *Asia* and *Africa* safely return, I will deliver them to the addresses you have given me with my personal best wishes, complements of the Roman Navy and the far-flung *Classis Alexandrina*. On the other hand... rest assured, Rusticus can make many copies of these portraits in the next six months, and each shall be as good as the last. If the two ships do not return by the end of the sailing season, it would be best if you didn't either, for I shall distribute them to every naval commander from here to the Pillars of Hercules in Spain! You may change your names, but you had best change your face as well, or there will be no port safe for you if you repeat your treachery!"

The *Asia* and *Africa* set sail the following morning.

CHAPTER 24: A DEAL IS STRUCK

The *Europa* returned to her sailing routine with little break. Only the presence of Ibrahim was different.

Antonius and Gaius settled into their new quarters in the officer's section, just below the master's cabin. Not as spacious as their former quarters on the deck above, the spartan accommodations were more to their taste. They shared a single curtained-off cubicle with two bunks, two stools in the common area, with room for the two men to move around. Gaius dragged his campaign chest into the stateroom, and opened it to inventory its contents. It was all there: his field armor and his parade kit. His sword, a fine scarlet cloak and a faded wool *sagum*. Gaius gently removed the dress helmet, dusted the red horsehair plume and rubbed a smudge from the metal.

"That's a fine piece of dress armor there, sir. If I may say so, kind of dated. They haven't made helmets like that since Augustus' time," said Antonius, admiring the curve of the neck guard on the highly-polished bronze, with its gold and silver filigrees.

"No, they haven't. This dress kit was a special gift to me. I don't know why, but Commodus always thought I might amount to something in the army. So when I left his school to go to Noricum with my first legion, he made a gift of this to me. It was very special, because... he was murdered a few weeks after I left."

"Murdered? How?" asked Antonius.

"The bastard Domitian! Titus Flavius blood-sucking Domitian accused Commodus of treason during his reign of terror, inciting the students against him. As if we were any threat!"

Gaius wiped at his eyes, and choked a bit, then continued. "He taught us how to live like men, and he taught us how to die like men. The Praetorian Guards burst in while he was lecturing his students. They charged him with sedition and treason... the standard charge then. Who knows where it came from, or if it came from anybody at all?" Gaius sighed, "Commodus listened to their charges, then dressed them down like errant cadets. Their swords were dull and nicked, not held properly, armor not properly secured. Commodus could find something wrong with Julius Caesar! They didn't know what to make of that! He made sure that there were no charges against his students and dismissed them all home, with a big blonde German that he had captured in battle to escort them." He paused, swallowing hard to choke his tears to a halt. "And... he... went upstairs... and drew his bath... and read his Plato... about the death of Socrates.... and opened his veins!"

There was no other way to deal with an accusation of treason during the Emperor Domitian's reign of terror. To be accused was to be found guilty, and Commodus had fought too many fights on the Empire's frontiers to be found guilty and executed in disgrace. No, better to open the veins in the bath, and not have all of one's estate forfeit to the Emperor.

Antonius patted his shoulder, and Gaius returned the helm to the campaign chest. "His faith was well-placed, sir. Yer've done him proud."

Gaius secured the lid and shoved the chest beneath the lower bunk. He wiped at his eyes and stood up. "Sorry, Antonius, didn't mean to let my emotions rise up like that. But if I had lost that gear... it means a lot to me."

"I understand, sir. Whyn't yer take the lower bunk, an' I'll take the upper?" He slid his own campaign chest under the lower bunk as well.

The ship's carpenters' hammered and sawed, replacing the damaged fittings and railings. Gaius returned, for lack of anything else to do, to assisting the navigators, engaged in a long argument over their position. They knew their latitude from the sun and Polaris, but they did not know whether the storm had carried them east or west, or how far. The precise mathematics provided Gaius an escape from the decisions that he faced but couldn't make.

Later that afternoon, after tossing a log overside with a knotted rope, and counting the knots against a water clock to determine speed, he took a break to lean against the rail and take in the beauty of the blue sea which stretched unbroken to the horizon, unimpeded by haze. The ship was under full sail, leaning to port by perhaps twenty degrees. Occasionally a bevy of green flying fish would break from the crest of their bow wave, their fin-wings working furiously, buzzing like locusts while they spanned the fifty or hundred feet to the next wave, till they dropped into a glide to disappear into the water with a plop. Gaius had never seen such creatures before, and he watched, trying to anticipate when next they would emerge, when Ibrahim came to stand by him.

"Ah, today, the sea is so still and beautiful, it is hard to believe that only two days ago, we were fighting for our lives against her, Gaius. The sea can make all men brothers, even Romans and Arabs."

"But can she can make brothers of the lawful and the lawless?" asked Gaius, spitting.

"One must ask then whose law... the law of man, the law of Rome, or the law of God?" Ibrahim was sparring with him again.

"The law that says you don't take what doesn't belong to you."

"Perhaps you can explain to me how the Romans came to such power without taking from others. But I didn't come here to bait the good Gaius Lucullus, but to admire the open sea with him. And actually, I admire Rome." Ibrahim leaned forward, his elbows on the railing.

"So tell me, Ibrahim bin Yusuf, how did a desert Bedouin come to be a man of the sea?"

"Well, in our culture, all advantage goes to the first-born son. And I, as the fifth, was far removed from that. My father was a sheep-herder, and we traveled as nomads through the desert, not unlike traveling at sea. You learn the weather and the stars, and you learn to plan your next move carefully, for neither the sea nor the sand will forgive a mistake.

"When I was about twelve, my brother and I took some sheep into Jiddah to sell. Jiddah is one of the few seaports on that side of the Red Sea, with ships and boats of all kind there. Eve, the mother of all men, is buried there. And in the streets, so many different races of men, and so many languages. My brother kept yelling at me to pay attention, but all I could think of were those ships, their beautiful white sails full, leaving port. At last, I broke away and ran down to the waterfront, telling him to be sure to get his money's worth for the sheep. I gave him the slip, and one of the small boats took me on as crew."

"I knocked around the Red Sea for a while, then when I was fifteen we went up to Egypt. I went over to the Canopic Nile, and from there to Alexandria. There I fell in with the Mediterranean ships."

Gaius smiled, "And you turned pirate at twenty."

"That's right."

Another bevy of flying fish burst from the waves.

"May I ask you a favor?" continued Ibrahim.

"Certainly."

"Could your good centurion resume training the crew in swordsmanship?"

Ibrahim had asked the question in all seriousness. Gaius stared dumbfounded, then laughed. "Surely you jest! Train them to do what? To take yet another prize on the sea? Are you trying to turn us into pirates?"

"Perhaps. But that later. Seriously, I shall be continuing the journey as planned. I have spoken with the navigators, and they have agreed to continue in order to complete their survey of these waters. And I bribed them with a toy." Gaius pondered the remark, recalling the lodestone "pointing needle" that they had shown him just this morning. "We'll be heading into unknown waters after we leave Taprobane. We ourselves will be prey to whomever lurks in those waters. Antonius has done a magnificent job of forging the crew into a first-rate fighting force. Had they been able to arm themselves, I could not have taken the ship."

"Well, it seems then that they are sufficiently well-trained for your defensive purposes."

"A knife unsharpened quickly loses its edge." Ibrahim turned to leave. "Please consider my offer, and join me in my cabin for dinner tonight." The

Arab left, as silently as he had arrived, his white robes swirling in the stiff breeze.

Gaius returned to the rail to ponder the offer. What was the Arab's motive in this bizarre request? How did he benefit from Antonius continuing to train his crew? Obviously, he gained a well-trained crew, but he ran the serious risk of the two Romans turning that well-trained crew against him. Ibrahim had made the point repeatedly that the crew was not involved, only the officers. *They only follow those who lead,* he had said. And if Antonius leads, then they can be made to follow. A mutiny could be launched, but then what? Neither Antonius nor Gaius could sail this ship, nor could the crew, who sailed the ship under orders of the officers they would have to overthrow. The problem was aggravatingly interlocked, an Oriental Gordian knot that defied Roman logic. So why did Ibrahim want Antonius to resume training the crew?

Gaius wandered forward, where he found Antonius in company with Galosga. Those two had become inseparable.

"An' g'morn', sir. It's a beautiful day terday. Galosga! Say hello to Gaius fer me."

The bronze-skinned man smiled shyly, and said softly, "*Vale, dom'ne.*"

"And *vale tibi,* Galosga! That's very good. You'll be giving speeches before the Senate itself if your teacher of rhetoric keeps on with you!" Gaius clapped the man on the shoulder. "Antonius, Ibrahim wants you to resume training the crew."

"What the hell does he want ter do that fer? Is he invitin' me ter stir up a mutiny fer him? I'd be glad ter oblige him!"

"That's what I thought. Why the hell..." Gaius stopped. "Of course! I think you just put yer finger very close to the problem!"

"I did? How'd I do that?"

"He is inviting us to stir up a mutiny against him. We are an unknown quantity to him right now, and he is giving us the opportunity for trouble, in an area that he can control closely. He probably will have several of his own trusted spies in the crew with you. And he will know the instant you even hint of action against him. Because right now, you and I wander the ship, and he doesn't know with whom we meet or talk."

"So he's better off givin' me the opportunity ter start trouble under his nose, an' then it's back in chains again for both of us."

Gaius nodded. "Or worse."

"So when do I start me mutiny, sir?" laughed Antonius, resting his big hairy arms along the rail.

"You don't. Even if we could take this ship, we couldn't sail it, and all of the officers are his men. No, let's give him what he wants, which is a chance to observe. And you be extremely careful about what you say. Our necks are in the balance."

"Arrgh, Gaius, if'n yer don't mind me getting' personal an' all, yer know I'm the very soul of discretion! An' anyway, I hate ships!"

"Good. And continue calling me Gaius. Our stations in life count for nothing from here on. And be ready for dinner tonight. We've been invited to his cabin. Let's do it up right, dress armor, and show him two Roman soldiers!"

Dinner came, and the centurion and legate were the spitting image of the *vires militares,* military men, decked out in their finest parade kit. The crew looked at them in a mixture of awe, fear and disgust as the two strode in step, head erect, eyes neither right nor left, to the master's cabin. Antonius knocked at the door and announced in his finest Latin, "Gaius Lucullus, *legatus* of the *Legio* XII *Fulminata!* We send greetings from Trajan, *Imperator Senatus Consulto,* on business of the Senate and the People of Rome!" He did this in his best parade ground voice, so that every head on deck turned to watch. Ibrahim opened the door and admitted them. The late afternoon sun streamed through the cabin windows.

"Welcome," he said, bowing and making a little motion with his hand from his face, to his lips and chest. "You make a good entry. Nothing like a uniform to make you formal. You'll pardon my Greek, but my Latin is not up to your centurion's high standards." Still sparring.

The meal, one of the drowned goats and some figs and wine, was set on a low table on the floor, surrounded with pillows for seats. "Please join me in my humble fare. Though I left the desert forty-five years ago, I am a Bedouin at heart and still prefer to eat like one. We dined at table last night. Some wine?"

Tonight Antonius accepted the cup and sat cross-legged on the cushion. The wine was some of the captain's stock, a good Judean vintage.

"Please dine. And to acquaint you with our customs, please wash, and use only the right hand. In our country, we place a high value on cleanliness. The left hand is unclean, and not to be used at dinner. It is our custom." He dipped his hands in a water bowl and passed it with small hand towels to the two soldiers.

The goat was good, well-roasted. "We shall not be eating well by the end of the trip, I fear. And I make a point to never eat better than my men. They bear their hardships better when they know that they are shared."

"So it is in the field," answered Gaius. "The good leader cannot lead in luxury, while his troops suffer from cold, hunger and the weather."

"So it is. You Romans, for all your faults, are great leaders, some of you. I wish all were half as good as the best, and you would rule the world."

"Thank you. I will admit, however, that some of our leaders are the worst. Many of us long for the old republic, when our horizons were smaller but our people bigger."

"Perhaps. I know only the Rome of today. But there is more to be admired there than despised. But on to our task at hand. You know, Gaius, from the navigators that we may be at sea for twenty-five days. Maybe longer. And we lost our goats. We will be very hungry before we make landfall."

"Galosga may help there," said Antonius.

"Galosga? Oh, yes, that strange fellow. Where is he from?"

"West somewhere, way west. I can't make heads or tails of his language, but he has a little Aramaic. He has a way to smoke meat. It's tough, the way he prepares it, but it will keep a long time. He's got lots prepared already. Trouble is, everyone wants to eat all the goats now."

Ibrahim stroked his beard. "I will talk to Demetrios about him. If he can prepare some meat and we ration it, and get lucky with some fish, we may make it to Taprobane. Water, well, we will have to pray for rain, and ration what we have carefully. I am afraid that we will be a hungry smelly lot when we make landfall. Now you wonder why I extended my offer to Antonius to resume training for the crew," he said, abruptly changing the subject.

"I have some theories," said Gaius, while he gently restrained Antonius' left hand from reaching into the goat meat for a second serving. "I think you want to keep us under observation, so we don't stir up a mutiny."

"Or help put one down," replied Ibrahim. "It doesn't take much to stir up a crew on a long, dangerous journey. A mutiny at sea is a bloody thing, and on this trip would be fatal for everyone. The ship would almost certainly be lost, and the mutineers would die of hunger and thirst not long after they killed us. These men are strong and brave, and in their own way loyal, but if panic takes them, all will be lost."

"So now you do want our help in your piracy!" Antonius exploded. "Didn't I tell you, Gaius, that next he would be recruiting us into his efforts?"

Gaius was unmoved. "So how would we, two Roman soldiers, the two most hated people on the ship, help forestall a mutiny by two hundred sailors? I appreciate your high opinion of us, but even Roman authority has its limits."

"As I said, they follow who leads. And it is most important, at times like this, to not allow the crew to be idle. You would be my eyes and ears, helping me to spot trouble."

Gaius shrugged. "I do not want to risk Antonius' life in this regard. If trouble comes, it may focus on him first as the hard taskmaster. They could overwhelm him by sheer numbers."

"By not doing this, you may be risking his life more. We are going into unknown waters. Piracy is not confined to the Mediterranean and Red Seas. There I am protected, for I have a reputation. I have a rather formidable organization to defend me, and avenge me if necessary. There are very few competitors there that would continue an attack if I deployed my personal flag. Here, I am unknown, and the predator could easily become prey. This is a large ship, and large ships carry valuable cargo. But I have another reason, as well."

"Let's hear it," grunted Antonius.

"You'll get very bored over the next three weeks," smiled Ibrahim.

Antonius laughed. "Well, that's one of the better ones!"

Gaius' position was unmoved. "Ibrahim, I appreciate your situation, but it is one of your own creation. I cannot allow my centurion to participate in this effort without involving myself in the perfidy you have committed against my cousin, and against the Emperor. This ship, itself a valuable treasure, and the gold and silver in the hold, is not a fortune belonging to some abstract Roman treasury. A large part of this was funded by my cousin, and if he lives, he will lose not only all of his personal fortune, but his personal *dignitas*, his reputation, as well. He and his family will be bankrupt, thrown into abject poverty and exiled. The rest is money provided by the Roman people. Thousands of people will be impoverished by this action. If I were to assist you, then not only would I help you bankrupt my cousin, but if I lived, I would be tried for treason and my life would be forfeit. I would prefer to die with honor, against your hypothetical mutiny, or even leading it. After all, I am mastering the navigation of this ship. India is pretty big, and between the North Star and your lodestone, I think I could find it."

"Always the proper Roman, Gaius Lucullus."

"My ancestor was a powerful general in Caesar's time. It runs in the family."

"So what can I do to change your mind?"

Gaius leaned back and considered how to pitch this. "Well, it seems you have stolen more gold than you can swim with when you chose to keep the ship." He paused to let this sink in, observing Ibrahim's reaction. "You wanted out of the business, you said, and a chance to end your life doing simple things, like raising a family. Right?"

"That is my goal."

"You can't do that back west. If the Roman army and navy don't hunt you down, your patrons will, for double-crossing them. And going east, this ship will become a millstone about your neck, as you try to defend it in increasingly unknown and unfriendly waters. A millstone that will eventually drag you down and drown you. Right?"

"I will, for the moment, accept your premise."

"Now, as you know, we are traveling under Imperial orders to the land of the Hanae. And we have a letter, which I can't read, from the Hanaen Emperor extending us protection in his waters and entry to his ports. Which I am sure you're not aware of, unless you can read the peculiar Hanaean script. Marcus and Marcia can."

Ibrahim sat up with interest as Gaius continued. "Now I cannot let you get away with the ship and its gold. I could be criticized severely for letting you get away, but there is really little I could do about it. But if this ship winds up at its destination, and some of the money sticks to your fingers as ransom, well… Rome understands ransom. I continue the mission, the gold goes to the Hanaean emperor, and the ship is impounded there till we leave. And you get off with enough gold to find that little wife in the land of the Han and raise a bunch of little almond-eyed Bedouins. You may only get a fraction of the whole amount, but you don't have to split it with your patrons, either. And take Demetrios with you. He's not taking the ship back, because out of my sight or yours, he'll throw the bargain to the winds."

Ibrahim sat quietly considering. Gaius reached for the wine and offered it to him. "Another glass, Ibrahim?"

CHAPTER 25: UNDERWAY AGAIN

The *Asia* and *Africa* made an uneventful departure from Masira, but their new southeasterly heading put the monsoon winds more nearly on their beam. The big ships wallowed slowly, rolling drunkenly with the abeam seas, instead of the heady leap and plunge that they had enjoyed with the following seas and 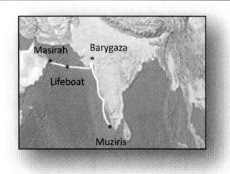 winds. Two helmsmen were posted to work the tillers, heavy with effort to counter the winds that continually tried to force the ships back to a northeasterly heading, though the third sail, properly rigged, took some of the work off the tiller. It was clear, with the seas and winds against them, that Muziris would be unattainable. They would have to land at Barygaza, and run along the coast to Muziris. The *Asia's* captain Dionysius considered this risky, as the seas would constantly force the ship dangerously close to shore, where they might easily fetch up on a hidden reef or shallows. However, Aulus insisted; there was no alternative.

Aulus was disconsolate, both with the loss of the *Europa* and with the loss of his cousin Gaius Lucullus. Aulus's wife Livia would be even more distraught, for they had been as close as brother and sister. Aulus had dispatched a letter to Livia from the naval station at Masira detailing the sad events, and urging her to not give up hope. But it was clear from the tone of his letter, despite many rewrites, that he himself had done so. Perhaps Livia would perform the rituals with *Bona Dea*, the Roman goddess of women, for his safekeeping. But Aulus feared the rituals would come too late, for it would be months before his letter would arrive in Alexandria.

The world seemed so vast, and the endless expanse of blue water so limitless, under a limitless blue sky. A hundred yards to port and slightly astern, the *Africa* kept station.

Aulus distrusted his crew, the captain Dionysius on *Asia* and his counterpart Apollodorus on *Africa*, all the officers, and even the deckhands. He suspected that at any moment they might turn on him again, steal the ship and throw him, his newly-freedmen and the Hanaean delegates overboard. Aulus's relationship with Dionysius was cool, formal and impersonal, and he never met alone with the man without Lucius Parvus and his bodyguards, all conspicuously well-armed. And Aulus kept a dagger, hidden in a back sheath, suspended behind his tunic. They could kill him if they wanted, but they would have to work hard to do so.

Three days out of Masira, the lookout in the masthead spotted what appeared to be debris in the water. Dionysius and Aulus went forward to catch a glimpse, their eyes straining against the sun glint. It appeared to be a small boat, similar to the ones they carried. As they drew closer to the bobbing craft, they could see a body, motionless, apparently dead. Dionysius excused himself to the quarterdeck, where he maneuvered the ship expertly alongside to investigate. They signaled the *Africa* to come dead in the water, and she pulled out of line, passing astern of the *Asia*, her sails luffing as she came into the wind.

Dionysius expertly laid the huge ship alongside of the boat, her sails trimmed to bring her to a halt on the windward side. Sailors clambered down on lines and rope ladders to secure the boat. "He's still alive!" one of them shouted, and they hoisted the emaciated body, as gently as possible, into a sling and up over the shear sides of *Asia* onto the deck.

The man was gaunt and severely dehydrated. White flecks of foam edged the sides of his ulcerated lips and unkempt beard, and his body was raw with blistered sunburn and saltwater sores. He could only quiver as they forced ladle after ladle of water down the man's throat, his Adam's apple bobbing furiously.

"Get him below! Get him out of the sun!" ordered the boatswain. The sailors carried him below in a makeshift litter.

The boat was hoisted out of the water on a jury-rigged rope cradle and swung, dripping and akilter, onto the main deck. The captain came forward to investigate, and attempt to determine from what ship it might have come.

The boat was not only similar to those on the *Asia* and *Africa*, it was identical. The boat was leaking heavily, the painter ripped out of the bow, but it was afloat.

"Dionysius, this boat appears to be from the *Europa*," said Aulus.

"That's hard to say, sir. Adib, the boatbuilder from whom we bought our boats, makes dozens of these, all alike. All I can say for sure is that it's one of Adib's boats. See, there's his mark. But any ship out of Myos Hormos, or even any passing ship needing a replacement, could have several just like it," said the captain, shaking his head. There were no markings on the boat to denote the ship that had carried it.

"Well, take care of the sailor. One of my bodyguards is skilled in medicine, and he will assist your crew and the ship's surgeon." *And keep an eye on them, too,* thought Aulus. He did not want the man killed to cover up more treachery, although it did not appear that much effort would be needed... the man didn't appear to have much chance for survival.

He indeed did not have much of a chance. Judging by the sunburn, he appeared to have been in the open boat for more than a week, possibly two. Whatever he had been drinking had run out several days ago, and he was delirious from drinking seawater. Whatever water they forced past his parched, encrusted lips seemed to ooze from the raw, festering blisters and saltwater ulcers. Nevertheless, every seaport had some epic tale of a sailor surviving for weeks, even a month or more, drinking rainwater or urine, and eating flying fish or seagulls.

The sailor remained delirious for a day and a half, and then seemed to become more lucid as evening approached. He was aware of his rescue, and croaked some Aramaic words, thanking his attendants. He rasped out his story, of how he had been swept overboard in a violent storm, but had found the dory towed astern the ship for that purpose. But a giant wave had swept over the ship in the darkness with such force that it had parted the tether. When the storm abated in the morning, he was alone and adrift, the ship nowhere to be seen. He had subsisted on water stashed in an amphora, replenished by rainwater from passing squalls. But the squalls had ceased, and he had been without water now for days.

The ship had been the *Europa*.

The bodyguard rushed aft to Aulus's cabin, interrupting him at dinner. "*Domine*, come quick, he's awake!" he blurted out, and ran back to catch the rest of the man's story.

Aulus with Lucius Parvus and his retinue, strode through the crew's quarters to the man's bunk, brushing past the captain, the surgeon and a group of attending sailors to the man's side. "Ask him about the two Roman soldiers!" Aulus demanded in Greek, to no one in particular. One of the sailors rattled off some Aramaic. The survivor seemed confused, and the sailor repeated the question. The man answered hoarsely, and the sailor translated, "He say, sword-man still alive when he go over."

"Sword-man? Who does he mean? Which one?" queried Aulus. More Aramaic, and the sailor said simply, "Roman sword-man."

Lucius Parvus interjected, "Antonius was training the crew to repel pirates. Maybe that's what he means."

"Antonius, alive? Then maybe Gaius is alive as well. Ask him about Gaius Lucullus. Did the ship survive?" asked Aulus, firing off questions. "How long ago did it happen?"

The translator tried to keep pace, but the sailor just shook his head. Dionysius joined the discussion. "He's a young deckhand, he probably didn't know or care about a high-ranking passenger like Gaius Lucullus. Certainly not by name. The ship could still be afloat, or it could have foundered in the storm. And he lost all sense of time days ago. He's been out a long, long time. Let's let him rest, and maybe we can learn more later."

"Hmm, you're probably right," said Aulus, edging away from the bunk to let the attendants care for the man. Next to the massive mainmast which stood like a pillar from floor to ceiling, he quietly asked Dionysius, "If the ship survived, where do you think he would head?"

"Sir, I think that storm was about two weeks ago, when we experienced some heavy swells and squalls. The worst of it passed far to our east, I think. So I think he's committed to somewhere in India, the Laccadives, or maybe Taprobane."

"And what was the plan, my good captain Dionysius?" asked Aulus menacingly.

"The plan was for us to seize these two ships under Hasdrubal's command and sail north. And not ask too many questions about things that didn't concern us. But do you want my opinion?" Dionysius said levelly, as honestly as possible.

Aulus nodded.

"Most Indian Ocean pirates hit near where we were hit. And escape south with their prize to east Africa. They beach it, break it up and loot it, and try to look like fishermen with a good catch coasting back up to Musa, Eudaemon or Cana in small boats. He's gone too far to the east for that. Still going to India, and no choice about it now with the wind at his back. Though I can't figure why."

Aulus listened attentively. He suspected the captain was being honest. "But why would Antonius be on deck?"

"Perhaps they outwitted Ibrahim Bin Yusuf, and took the ship back. That would explain the easterly heading, too," explained Dionysius.

"So if the ship survived the storm, then we shall meet in Muziris!" exclaimed Aulus, suddenly exuberant.

"Perhaps. *If* they survived, *if* they beat Ibrahim, and *if* they went there. Many ifs and few solid answers."

But at least Aulus had a ray of hope.

There were unfortunately no more answers from the castaway sailor. He died the following day, and was buried at sea, Phoenician style.

After several weeks, the convoy made landfall, anchoring far up Narmada River at Barygaza, with the assistance of heavy oared tugboats to tow them past the treacherous and shifting river sandbars. The ships refitted and resupplied, while Aulus's traders cut some good deals on a few tons of peppers, saffron, cloth and silks, and some truly beautiful ivory carvings. This would make their first installment to pay off Aulus's creditors. Aulus posted letters through the Roman trading station. One was to go overland to Muziris, posthaste, requesting that the *praetor externa*, the administrative official representing Roman interests there, detain the *Europa* and all her crew and passengers, if she was present, until Aulus's arrival. He might well arrive ahead of the letter, but it was the proper thing to do. The other two were posted to Rome via westbound ships: one went to Livia, and the other to his creditors in Rome, on the fruits of their first port call. They then set off southward to Muziris.

CHAPTER 26: A FRIENDSHIP IS BORN

Ibrahim accepted the arrangement in exchange for Antonius' training of the crew, no surprise to Gaius or Antonius. Demetrios passed word for the security team to form up in the afternoon, along with the Nubian archers led by a tall black man named Abdi. Abdi trained his own team of mercenaries, but would work with the crew to develop joint tactics against borders. When Antonius showed up, Shmuel at their head stepped forward in front of the men, very shaken. "We failed you, Centurion. I am responsible," he said in Greek.

Hmm, the young man is catching on. "How is that, *optio?*"

"We were unable to arm ourselves," replied Shmuel.

"Why not?"

"I went to the armory to break out weapons, but the keys were gone."

"I know. They were taken by the officers to prevent your responding. That is their responsibility, not yours."

"We should have attacked the pirates unarmed, but I could not give the command."

"Enough! That would have been suicidal. Get on with the training, and put that behind you. Since you feel in need of punishment, however, you may begin with laps along the deck, hard! The first man to throw up his lunch can take a break! Now go!"

The training went well, and the exertions seemed to sweat the shame of their failure from them. Afterward, Antonius went to stand by the rail. He enjoyed watching the vastness of the sea when it was in a peaceful mood. Marcia Lucia came up to join him, alone. "Good day, Antonius, and how is your head?"

"Better, I think, I haven't looked at it today."

"Allow me."

Antonius bent over and she removed the bandage and inspected it. "It's ugly purple, and still swollen," she said, pressing gently on the lump.

"Be like that fer a few days," he growled. "Is it hot? Any pus or oozing?"

"No, just a scab."

"Leave the bandage off then. Thank you, *domina.*"

"Antonius, I am not a high born lady! Please." She smiled shyly at him.

"Arrgh... never mind. I don' know exactly what ter say ter yer." He turned back to watch the sea. "Is this yer first time ter sea? I am sorry, is this your first time to sea?"

"That's all right, I understand you perfectly, you may speak however you are most comfortable… Yes, this is my first time at sea." She paused, then went on, "Captain Demetrios says that we will be continuing on our trip, and you have come to some understanding with the pirate."

"We are. As ter the understandin', Gaius Lucullus worked that out. It seems our shipping master Hasdrubal was in with the pirate, but double-crossed him too, an' took off with the other two ships."

"Took off? To where?"

"Ibrahim – that's the pirate's name – thinks Parthia. I hate ter say it, but I think those ships and everyone on them is lost. Including the Senator, Gaius' cousin."

Marcia watched the restless blue sea for several minutes. "I am sorry for Gaius' cousin," she said at last.

"Gaius doesn't talk about it much. Ibrahim had some scheme, in case Hasdrubal tried something like this, but I don't think it has much chance. I don't think we'll be seein' them again, I'm afraid." He watched the ship's vee-shaped bow wave course along beside them. "I guess – Ming, is that his name? – he's gone too."

"I won't miss him."

Antonius listened intently to what she said. He wanted to say more, but did not want her run off if he pried too deeply. He tried to think of something to say, but could manage no more than a non-committal "Hmmm…"

"I have never been allowed to speak to any man alone. I am awkward, and I thank you for bearing with me."

"An' I be thankin' yer for bearin' with me!" he said, with a big smile.

They spent the rest of the afternoon, talking about a lot of nothing, Marcia feeling a freedom she had not known since she was a child.

CHAPTER 27: PORT CALL IN MUZIRIS

The *Asia* and *Africa* coasted along the treacherous west coast of India, maintaining a safe distance from the strong currents and shoal waters that plagued that area. The winds were not favorable, and Dionysius continually changed the set of the sails to accommodate contrary winds. It took three weeks to cover the five hundred miles from Barygaza to Muziris, putting in frequently at the dozens of trading ports along India's west coast to trade and to replenish food and water. But after one memorable stop, the entire crew suffered dysentery the following day from the water. They put in at the next port, discharged their tanks, and replenished again. Fortunately the dysentery subsided, but the crew was more cautious about watering the ship thereafter. Finally the lighthouse off Muziris loomed into view. The crew put in for some much-needed rest, and Aulus went off to visit the *praetor externa*, a fellow senator named Lucius Sulpicianus, who had adopted the *cognomen* of Indiacus.

Muziris was a major trading station, with a strong Roman presence. Bankers, insurers, lawyers, judges, translators and merchants, clustered in a Roman-style enclave of warehouses, with apartments for the minor officials, and sumptuous villas for the more successful entrepreneurs and administrators. Within this enclave, Latin and Greek were the norm, and were it not for the fetid heat, Muziris could have been any trading town in the Mediterranean. Aulus and Lucius Parvus trudged up the muddy streets to Sulpicianus' sumptuous office.

The office was an imposing marble structure, with a colonnaded entranceway to a pleasant *atrium*. A servant rushed up to attend them. "Aulus Aemilius Galba of the *Asia* to see Lucius Sulpicianus Indiacus," said Lucius, introducing Aulus. The servant bowed and disappeared into a room on the side of the atrium. Aulus waited, admiring the fine statuary, the mosaic floor, and the excellent murals, with a selection of local flowering plants and tropical greenery providing accents above the bubbling fountain pool in the center of the atrium.

The servant returned. "This way, *domine*. Lucius Sulpicianus is expecting you."

He led them to a curtained entranceway and swept open the deep blue gold fringed curtain. Lucius Sulpicianus, clad in an elegant but lightweight toga, rose from his desk to greet the two. "*Vale*, Aulus! I expected you months ago with the first of the shipping. What happened? Prices go up every day, and selection down."

"You didn't get my letter from Barygaza?" asked Aulus.

"Barygaza? What the hell were you doing that far north? I thought you were supposed to come here directly." Lucius seemed concerned and sat on the corner of his polished desk, his arms crossed across his chest.

"It's in the letter you haven't yet gotten. I was certain that while I was lugging along the west coast, my letter would precede my arrival."

"Roads here aren't what they are in Europe, Aulus. They go out from the city, and then the pavement stops. Pretty soon it's nothing more than a path in the jungle. Things here are done in Indian time," Lucius shrugged.

So Aulus related his story, beginning with Hasdrubal's treachery and the hijacking of the *Europa*, the events at Masirah, and the finding of the shipwrecked sailor at sea. He then described his detour to Barygaza, and the slow, torturous journey down the west coast of India.

Lucius let a low whistle. "You're lucky to be here! *Fortuna favet portuna!* Fortune surely favors the bold! So you lost one ship and a few months of trading. And that's all."

"That's enough. This whole enterprise balances on a knife-edged margin. At least we got some good, if unscheduled, trading up at Barygaza. The merchants were falling all over themselves when they found we were not only early but buying... by the ton! We got some good prices there. And I'm not sure I've lost a ship yet, I just can't find it," Aulus laughed. Perhaps he was getting his sense of humor back.

"Well, I think you've probably lost it. We got word of the storm they must have encountered. It was an early cyclone. There's nothing like those storms in the Mediterranean, nothing like them on earth. They cover hundreds of miles of ocean with winds powerful enough dismast a ship, even one your size. Waves fifty feet high. They call these storms 'Poseidon's hammer'. A convoy of five just escaped the fringes of it, and lost two ships, to a man... just gone. I'm afraid the *Europa's* chances are not good, not good at all. The best thing for them is to go down in the storm. That's better than drifting as a dismasted derelict for weeks, while the water and food run out.

"But I'll send word to keep an eye out for her. If she survived, she could put in at hundreds of little fishing ports along the coast, or even passed you enroute. Or she could have gone to Taprobane, but that's a long haul for a ship after a storm like that. But because you're a friend, I'll send the letters and pay the outrageous fees to get word to these out-of-the-way places. But Aulus, you had better plan on what you're going to do without her. I'm sorry."

"Thank you," said Aulus. It wasn't the answer he wanted to hear, but it was probably true. He had hoped to find the *Europa* safe here in Muziris, perhaps damaged, but with Gaius safe and alive.

"And another tip. Don't go for pepper here. That's mostly picked over two weeks back. Take advantage of your capacity, and go for jewelry, silks, ivory, and other things you can transport in bulk. You can afford to depart late, and the merchants will come from a hundred miles away when they hear you're buying by the ton. Elephants are good, too. They bring a real big price for the animal shows in Rome, and most ships can't handle them. Take along a native *mahout*. They get wild at sea."

"Thank you for the tips. We're going to rearrange our itinerary, and I will need an armed escort to transfer gold and silver from the *Africa*. She'll be taking the merchandise back, while we go forward with the Hanaean delegation in *Asia*. Do you have a reasonably trustworthy official who needs to go back to Alexandria? I don't trust her captain out of my sight."

"Yes, I can provide you one. We're rotating some of our urban cohort back. If you'll transport them also, that will be muscle to keep any treachery at bay."

Later that day, Aulus met with *Africa's* skipper Apollodorus to lay out the plan. "Let's just get it out in the open, Apollodorus. You betrayed me once. But right now, I need you to get *Africa* back to Myos Hormos and the cargo dispatched for sale. I want you to work through Aelia Isidora and Aelia Olympias to do that, and they will extend credit, if necessary, for the twenty-five percent customs fees at Coptos. Don't let any money stick to your fingers."

"I have apologized before, Senator Aulus Aemilius, and I will apologize again. We were taken in by Hasdrubal, and I want to redeem myself. I will get *Africa* back safe and sound," said the captain.

"Good. And by the way, some of the Myos Hormos urban cohort is rotating back with you." *No need to tell him that the centurion of the guard knows what he has done. If Apollodorus arouses suspicions, the* Africa *may make it back to Myos Hormos without him on board.* "Have a safe trip, and if all goes well, I will pay you our agreed-upon commission, and ensure that nothing of this unfortunate incident ends up before the Sailing Board as part of your record."

CHAPTER 28: AN AFTERNOON'S DELIGHT

The major task ahead for the crew of the *Europa* in Taprobane was to obtain new steering oars. Demetrios conferred with Agathias, the ship's carpenter.

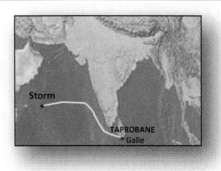

"I searched every shipwright, lumber supplier and carpentry shop in Galle. The biggest piece of raw wood that I could find was thirty feet. We need two forty foot pieces from a single tree, four feet in diameter. This is a small fishing port, the ships mostly Indian coastal lugs. They don't have anything that big," Agathias reported, shrugging his muscular shoulders in exasperation.

"Can we go without spares?" asked Demetrios

"Sure. And if we hit another storm like the last, the ship is lost and we're all dead men."

"Any alternatives?"

"There is a lumberman who will send a team of elephants to the mountains in the south part of the island, and bring back several fifty foot trees. But that's not going to be cheap or fast. Works out to twenty gold *aurei*, ten now and ten more on delivery, two weeks to go and bring them back, and another week for my men to shape the new rudders."

"Try to bargain him down."

"I did. That is as cheap as it gets."

Demetrios dismissed Agathias and brought the bad news to Gaius, who reluctantly went to the hold, unlocked one of the cash chests, and doled out the gold coins. Two thousand *sesterces* for a pair of steering oars! But there was little else to do.

The other repairs were quickly accomplished, and Gaius and Antonius kept a low profile in town. They were able to resume their workouts, running several miles daily along the beach to a sheltered cove, where they stripped off their linen kilts and dived into the ocean water, warm as a bath.

And they found a decent little inn, on the outskirts of town, smaller than the officers' mess on the *Europa*, with plain wooden tables and benches, but quiet and inconspicuous. No one in the inn spoke anything that Gaius or Antonius could understand, but the serving girl understood the eating and drinking motions the Romans made. She talked to the innkeeper, a short, very dark man who eyed them suspiciously, but prepared them a meal in a small black oven in the corner. She brought them their meal, rice with chicken curry with a sharp saffron flavor, and good wine.

At the end of the meal, Antonius handed the girl some bronze *sesterces*. She looked at them in bewilderment, and took them to show to the innkeeper. The man's visage became even darker as he frowned and shook his head negatively.

"What's wrong?" asked Antonius.

"They don't know what a *sestercius* is, Antonius. Offer them a silver *denarius* instead." Gaius smiled at the centurion's discomfiture.

"A *denarius*! For a meal like this! It was good but not that good!" exploded Antonius.

"Just give it. I'll give you a handful of *denarii* when we get back to the ship, because I don't think we'll have much use for our *sesterces* from here on out."

Antonius handed her the silver coin, and the dark man looked critically at it, bit it, and put it on a small scale. His face lit up in a smile, and he nodded affirmatively.

"What's wrong with a *sestercius* here, Gaius?" asked Antonius.

"A *sestercius* only has the value that Rome says it has, four to a silver *denarius*. It has no value of its own, just a chip of bronze with a pretty picture of somebody on it. They only use gold and silver here, so that conversion doesn't mean anything."

"Hmm, guess we're definitely out of the Empire."

They left and returned the following day. The innkeeper, no longer suspicious, beamed broadly at their entry and personally showed them to their seats. They paid in *denarii*.

Ibrahim fretted about the delay. This was far longer than he had planned to be here. He had hoped to stay only a few days, a week at the most, and escape before the ship's presence reached the king's ears in Anuradhapura in the north. Now he had to consider the possibility that the king would send someone down to Galle to investigate, perhaps with soldiers to seize the ship. How far could he trust his Romans?

The Taprobanean king had an agent in Galle to keep an eye on unusual happenings, such as the arrival of the biggest ship he had ever seen. Arriving unannounced, that in itself was most unusual, particularly for a ship of that size.

It wasn't unusual for a trader to call at Galle, although mostly they went north to Mannar, closer to the capital and the Roman *praetor externa*. But when they did call, they were scheduled a year in advance, to line up merchants to commit to lower prices. Even a small ship would do that, because without prior commitments, its merchants had only the choice of leftover goods, at higher prices and lower quality.

This was a huge, very expensive ship. A Roman trader, with only two not-very-inconspicuous Romans on board, and an Arab who seemed to be in charge. Of course, the ship could have been blown off course by a storm, but the winds would have favored Muziris more than Taprobane. Perhaps this could be just what it appeared, but then, maybe it was much more.

The agent tailed the Romans, oblivious to the people around them and very predictable in their movements. Every day, they left the ship for a run, though why anyone would run in the heat was itself suspicious, and every day, they dined at the same inn. So it was easy to set up the best of all ways to get information. He hired a Greek-speaking prostitute to proposition one of the men.

Gaius and Antonius returned to the inn to find a strange girl sitting in the inn at their table. She beamed a charming smile and said "I sorry... I move for you," and stood up to leave. "That's fine, that's fine. You can stay," said Antonius. She was a dark-featured, attractive girl with a red jewel prominent in her forehead. Long straight black hair, slender build. Her *sari* barely hid her full breasts, which attracted Antonius' immediate interest. Her brown midriff was bare, with another jewel in her belly-button. *I wonder if she has jewels in any other part of her body,* thought Antonius, feeling titillated. She had that professional look about her, and the innkeeper didn't seem pleased to have her on the premises.

"Oh, thank you. I wait for friend. You from ship here?"

Gaius looked like he had eaten something unpleasant, his jaw was set firmly, but he said nothing.

"Off the *Europa*. The big ship," said Antonius, eyeing her cleavage.

"Oh, that big ship! Where you come from?"

"Uh, we're Romans. Roman soldiers from Syria. This here is Gaius Lucullus, he's going to get his own legion someday, and I'm the meanest Roman centurion you ever met."

"Oh, I never meet centurion before. You from Rome?"

The innkeeper brought them their usual curry. "Ah, one for her, too. You are hungry, aren't you? Yes, we're from Rome." Antonius made hand signs to convey his intent to the innkeeper, who scowled disapprovingly but went off to get another.

"That richest city in whole world! You rich, too?" cooed the girl.

"Nah, soldiers like me don't get rich. Now, Gaius Lucullus there, he's rich."

She smiled at Gaius, but it was obvious he wasn't buying her charm. "And where do you come from?" he asked her.

"I come from Anuradhapura."

"The capital. Isn't that a better place to live than Galle? I understand that it's very fine, with beautiful temples."

"Very nice. But I not live there anymore." She seemed flustered, losing control of the flirtation.

"Your husband lives here, I guess. What does he do?"

"Husband I don't have. He... died."

"That's too bad. Have you been mourning him for long?"

The innkeeper brought the girl's food, and she seemed relieved to eat, free of Gaius' further questions.

They ate their meal, with Antonius solicitously observing her. She noticed and smiled. A delightful smile. She giggled and tried to contain her mouthful of rice. She introduced herself. "I Thani. You?"

"I'm Antonius."

"Anthonus?" She struggled with the unfamiliar syllables. "Have you seen town much?" she asked, stretching her breasts against her *sari*.

"Not much, I'd love to. With the right escort," answered Antonius.

"Oh, I very good escort." Antonius was rearranging his tunic, which had suddenly become uncomfortably tight.

"I think we'd both enjoy the tour, Thani." said Gaius.

"Oh, that won't be necessary, Gaius," said Antonius. "You've got things to do, and Thani and I will just tour the town and be back by nightfall."

"I'm actually free this afternoon, and I will take the tour with you and Thani."

Antonius scowled at him, switching to Latin to keep Thani out of the conversation. "Look, sir, I haven't had a woman since we left Syria. I been good, true ter me word. Just let me have few hours with her, that's all. Yer can see, she ain't no nobleman's wife. She's a street hooker, is all."

Gaius considered the soldier's words. "I'm just concerned about you messing with whores in a strange place like this. You wouldn't be the first to get your throat cut playing around with a strange whore."

"I ain't no dumb *miles*, I've been with hundreds of hookers an' I can handle mesel'. An' anyone wants ter take me, he's got a fight on his hand. I'm a big boy. I'll be back by sundown. Alone." Antonius was getting angry.

"Well, give me your purse. I'll leave you a few *denarii* to pay her off, and that will take away the temptation to try to roll you. Make sure she sees. And just have fun. Don't tell her the story of our lives."

Antonius conspicuously handed over his purse, and Gaius returned a few silver coins. Antonius reverted to Greek. "I just wanted to get Gaius to take my purse back to the ship. I don't like to wander around a foreign city with a lot of money. You come? Gaius is going back to the ship, aren't you, Gaius?" He glared at the legate.

Antonius and Thani stood up to leave.

"Yes. Have a good time."

Of course there was no tour. Thani led Antonius down a back alley to a small apartment where she kept her bed, a small statue, and several pieces of explicitly erotic statuary. Although it was daylight, she lit a small candle for the apartment had no windows and was quite dark. Antonius admired the statue. "Who is this?"

"Oh, that Lord Bodhisat. He live long time ago, taught us how to live good life."

"How do you do that?"

"I tell you later." Thani stripped off her *sari* to reveal a lean, nut-brown body. Her breasts were full, with tiny brown nipples.

The afternoon was one of delight. Thani was not like many prostitutes, who lay motionless beneath the man, waiting for him to finish. Nor was she like others, whose display of sensuality was crude and artificial. She was genuinely sensual, and savored the act of love as much as any man. She teased him to a peak, then kept him there suspended just short of climax while her own built. She then released him, to spend himself within her while she convulsed in her own ecstasy around him. And after a few minutes of cuddling in the dim apartment, she began to tease him to a second effort. She knew positions that Antonius had not thought possible. And then to a third, a dreamy sensual event that endured for an hour, sometimes slow, sometimes violent, that finally ended with a loud cry as Antonius spent himself again. Afterwards, they lay dozing in each other's arms, and awoke just before sunset.

"I have to go, Thani. Uh.. how much?"

"Whatever you want. Feel better?" she drew her knees up to her chin, purring in the bed like a kitten.

"Yes. You were beautiful" He handed her four *denarii*, all he had. She smiled.

"How long you be here?"

"Couple of weeks. We need to replace something broken on the ship."

"Where you go after?"

"We're going east..." he thought about Gaius' caution and began to sense some of Gaius' suspicion. "Away. Can't say for sure where."

"Will I see you again?"

"Uh, maybe. I have to go now, really." He ducked under the curtained doorway into the alley, checking first to make sure that there were no surprises waiting outside.

Antonius felt pleasantly relieved, but he also felt foolish, having pressured Gaius into letting him have the whore. But he hadn't told her anything. Anything at all.

Gaius was pacing the quarterdeck when, promptly at sunset, Antonius came strutting aboard.

"Have fun?"

"Sure did. Didn't tell her any big secrets, either." Antonius went to their quarters without further discussion.

Pali, the agent, considered the information the girl brought. Two Roman soldiers, one a *legatus*, a high-ranking officer, the other a centurion. If he remembered correctly, that was a senior ranking foot soldier. An odd combination. Going somewhere. The soldier had said 'east", and then refused to say more, just 'somewhere'. But where? East would be across the Bay of Bengal. Few traders ever ventured that way. Why would two soldiers be going east? Why would soldiers be coming to India in the first place? Traders, yes, but soldiers? Some urban cohorts came into big trading centers like Muziris, but they were just policemen. And the Roman ship, commanded by an Arab. This was strange enough to pass on to the king.

The king at Anuradhapura called the *praetor externa* to his throne room. Julius Ferrus bent his head, his grudging accommodation of a bow, and waited for the king to speak.

"What do you know of a Roman plan to invade my country?"

Julius was dumbstruck. "Invade your country? Why your Excellency, that would be the height of folly! Even if we could get here and take your country, you are far too distant to hold."

"Your statement has the ring of truth. At least I think you believe it. But even now, there is a Roman transport in Galle unloading soldiers."

"A Roman transport? Unloading troops? Preposterous!"

"The *Europa*. The troops are commanded by one Gaius Lucullus, from one of the Syrian legions. He is, I believe you call it, a *legatus*."

Ferrus' stomach turned flipflops. *A landing party in Galle? What in the hell was going on?* "That's impossible. Even our biggest freighters can only carry a few hundred soldiers, and are used only in the Mediterranean. There are none in the Indian Ocean. And a few hundred soldiers would not be enough to take Taprobane."

"But they could take Galle, and hold it while the remaining ships of the fleet discharge their troops in safety. Two more are even now in Muziris, I am told. These ships are about two hundred and fifty feet in length, with three masts. And well-armed, with the weapons you call *ballistae*

"Your Excellency, this is impossible. We must verify this information. Someone is trying to stir up trouble between you and Rome. Haven't you enjoyed most favorable relations with the Empire? Since your father's time, we have shared ambassadors, and trade that has been highly favorable to both our countries."

"Yes and now you want to make it more favorable to Rome and less favorable to me. But I will verify the information, indeed. This morning I dispatched an army of ten thousand men to Galle. If this is Roman treachery, I will feed the soldiers to the sharks, and post your head above my castle, after I have it torn from your body!"

The king swirled his royal robes about his brown body, rose and left. "Dismissed," he said, without turning his head.

Julius Ferrus swallowed hard, and left, weak in the knees and feeling quite sick. Two soldiers escorted him to the royal prison.

CHAPTER 29: SEDUCTION

Back in Masira, Titus Cornelius was preparing his report on the incident with the *Asia* and *Africa*. He had written and rewritten it several times, shading the reason for releasing the obviously guilty officers to Aulus. Legally, he had no legal alternative but to imprison them as mutineers and conspirators to piracy, and send them back to Alexandria for trial and execution. But this placed the ships in a bad situation, and made impossible demands on his limited food and water; these dictated yielding to Aulus's insistence. He had made a command decision, far removed from the advice and counsel of the commander of *Classis Alexandrina*. The commander might agree with his judgment; he might not.

Finally, he decided to just smudge the evidence a bit, outlining his suspicion, but denying any firm evidence to justify detaining them. This had to be done carefully; falsifying records could be dangerous. Finally, after a month, Titus felt that the report would hold together. The officers were done, anyway. He had enclosed their portraits, and conveyed his suspicions that they were involved in the mutiny, to the Shipping Board in Alexandria. That board would guarantee that they never went to sea again. So it all came down to whether the evidence was firm or soft, and that was a judgment call. He prepared one copy for the governor of Egypt, and another for the fleet commander.

Hasdrubal languished in the stifling prison. He was manacled with long chains to the wall of a cave carved into a rock wall, with an iron cage in front. The heat blasted in through the open mouth during the blazing July noon, and at night, the desert chill set his teeth chattering. He had only the now-filthy robe he had worn when captured, and a small blanket barely adequate to cover him. Food and water was just enough to survive, a piece of Arab flatbread for breakfast and a thin gruel with something that might have been meat for dinner, with more flatbread. A jug of water was provided in the morning, to last all day. Private functions were performed in a corner of the cell, which had become foul and fly-infested.

Guards were continuously posted outside the cell at four hour intervals. Most stood stiffly straight, their lances erect, and met his entreaties with stony silence. One young man, though, stood night watches over him. He leaned on his *pilum*, bored and distracted. The marine seemed willing to talk to him, to make the long night watch go by faster. His name was Francius, and he hailed from somewhere in southern Gaul, north of Marsala. He occasionally shared some water with the prisoner when Hasdrubal's meager supply ran out after dinner.

One night, Hasdrubal tried a new tact.

"Have you ever seen someone crucified, Francius?" asked Hasdrubal.

"No, I haven't. I understand it's not a good way to die," answered Francius. It didn't sound like a duty that he was looking forward to perform.

"I have. It's barbaric." He paused, then burst into tears. "They're going to take me to the cross, and I can't face that. It's all lies, lies, lies, but that Arab pirate set me up, and I'm going to die on that stinking cross. O Gods, I wish I could die, right now, rather than face that!"

Francius seemed genuinely moved. "Well, you're going to trial. If there's evidence for you, you'll be given an *absolvo*, a not guilty verdict, and everything will be fine. Trust me. You'll come off all right if you're innocent."

"Are you a citizen, Francius?" asked Hasdrubal, his eyes brimming with tears and his voice quavering.

"Yes. Since my grandfather's time."

"It's different for you, Francius. Citizens can count on justice. But me, I'm just another dirty Phoenician trader. I made millions and millions of *sesterces*, and almost as many enemies who will want to put me under. They'll all lie, just to get me out of the way, and I'll die in disgrace!" Hasdrubal collapsed in tears again.

Francius looked on sympathetically.

Hasdrubal looked up, his eyes red and rheumy from crying, his tears making watermarks in his filthy face. "Would you do me a special favor, Francius? I know you understand."

"What's that?"

"Would you give me your dagger? I can end my life right here, all over in a minute. No suffering, no humiliation, no listening to all those lies." Hasdrubal's eyes were bright and pleading in the moonlight.

"No way! I'd be flogged to an inch of my life!" answered Francius, shocked.

"Well, then, just do me with your dagger! Here," he said, struggling to his feet, his chains clanking. He spread his dirty robe, bared his chest and pressed it against the bars. "Just stick it in, right here, third rib from the bottom. It'll go straight into my heart! You can tell the centurion of the watch that I tried to grab you."

"No, Hasdrubal, I can't. Just trust the court. You'll be freed if you're innocent."

Hasdrubal sighed and retired to the corner of his cage.

The next night, Francius was on watch again.

"Here, I brought something to cheer you up," he said, pulling a chicken leg from his cloak. "Do you need some more water?"

Hasdrubal grabbed the chicken leg and devoured it hungrily, gnawing every scrap of meat and gristle off the bone. "Thanks!" he said, offering his jug through the bars for a refill.

He slurped the water thirstily, and said, "God, it's hard to believe how good food like that can taste. And I feel as full if I had just finished a big banquet. You appreciate the small things when you're in a place like this. You know, you should have seen the banquets I used to hold in Alexandria. Dozens of goats and pigs. Fine wines from all over the Mediterranean. Apples, pomegranates, figs, all the finest pastries. Have you ever had *baklava*?"

"No, I haven't. What is it?"

"It's made from filo pastry, fine and flaky. With nuts and cinnamons and honey. You have never tasted such a good dessert in your life." He sighed. "The parties I used to throw. Did you know the governor of Egypt and his wife used to come to all my parties? I spent a million *sesterces* on just one party one year. And it was nothing, nothing at all!"

And it was true. Hasdrubal was an extremely wealthy man, well-known among the Alexandrian party set.

"Well, with friends like that, you should have no trouble at your trial." Francius stopped slouching and sat down, reclining against the bars. He reached inside his *sagum* and pulled out a flask of wine. "I'll share some with you, if you help keep lookout for the centurion of the watch. He'll beat the hell out of me if he catches me sitting down on watch. Never mind what he'll do if he catches me drinking!" He took a healthy slug off the flask, and passed it through the bars. "You keep it inside there, and just toss it in the back where you shit, if he shows up. He won't see it in there. Here, help yourself."

Hasdrubal took a drink, and felt the warm glow spread through his body. "It reminds me of better days. But those party hounds aren't my friends. They won't do anything for me now that I'm in trouble. No, you know who my friends are?"

"Who?" asked Francius.

"Young men like you. I can't tell you how many young men like you I took off the street. I gave them responsibility, their own ship or a market, or an account, whatever they were good at, and in no time, they were making their own millions. I wish I'd gotten to you before you joined the navy, and before I got into this mess. You'd make a million *sesterces* the first year. I can tell. You're the ambitious type. Too bad I'm in here, and you're stuck in the navy. How much do you make?"

"Three thousand a year," Francius lied. It was actually closer to two.

"Too bad. You're worth much more than that."

A clink of sword on armor betrayed the approach of the centurion of the watch. Francius struggled to his feet, his face red, and was almost in a military posture when the centurion rounded the corner.

"Not talking with the prisoner, are you, Francius?" The centurion asked coolly.

"No, sir!" said Francius, his eyes forward, little beads of sweat on his forehead cool in the chill night air.

"Better not be! If you are, you better hope that stinking pirate throttles you before I get to you. Got it?" He cuffed the sailor across the cheek with a blow that sent him reeling, a trickle of blood running down his chin.

Francius clambered back to his feet. "Yes, sir!" he quavered.

When the centurion left, he sat back down.

"Bastard. Give me some more wine, Hasdrubal!" he ordered, sullenly.

"Are you sure it's safe? He might come back," said Hasdrubal, withdrawing the flask from the folds of his robes where he had hidden it.

"He won't come back. He never does. He just comes around to cuff some guard every night. It doesn't matter whether you did anything wrong or not, it's just your turn." He sniffed and wiped the trickle of blood from his cheek. "He's a stupid fucking bully!"

"I never tolerated bullies in my business, Francius. I believe if you treat a man with respect, he'll respect you."

"Yeah, well, I'm not in your fucking organization, I'm in the fucking navy." He stood up and resumed leaning on his *pilum*. "Keep the wine, though. I've had enough trouble tonight."

Francius showed up again the next night. Hasdrubal asked solicitously "Did you get in any more trouble over last night?"

"Oh, hell, yes. That *fellator* was waiting for me when I got off watch. He chewed my ass so loud that everybody could hear it in the whole camp, and then he beat the hell out of me. Look at this shiner!"

"I'm truly sorry. I don't want you to get in trouble for me," said Hasdrubal.

"Oh, I can see why your young men would stand by you. Here you are, getting ready to get crucified, and you're worried about me getting roughed up a bit! I wish you and I had met before. I've had nothing but trouble since I joined the navy. Stuck in a hellhole like this, working for people with brains like turds!"

He sat down again, nursing his resentment.

The relationship between Francius and Hasdrubal deepened. He regularly brought food and wine, and once brought paper so that Hasdrubal could write his wife, and sneaked the letter out to mail for him. He posted it inside his own letter to his family to forward on to Hasdrubal's family. Hasdrubal seemed like a genuinely decent man who had fallen on a hard time, and the idea of this decent fellow being crucified really bothered Francius. He wanted to do everything he could do to ease the man's misery. Their conversation turned to the fabulous places that Hasdrubal had been, India, even Parthia.

"You know, there are some people in Parthia that would clear me if I could get there," said Hasdrubal one night.

"Well, just have the court summon them to Alexandria. They'll come, of course."

"No, you don't understand, Francius. Roman courts won't summon people from Parthia, and they can't come. Relations between Rome and Parthia aren't good. No, the only way I could clear myself would be to go to Parthia, and then bring them to Alexandria. But I can't do that. Even though Parthia is just a few hundred miles by boat from here. There's no hope."

The next night, Francius showed up, looking smug. "Want to go to Parthia?"

"What do you mean?"

"Well, while the centurion of the watch was whaling me around the camp again last night, I thought 'What the hell am I doing here? Getting beat up every night, and not getting anything for it?' So I found a small boat and a pilot. We can just go to Parthia, you can set me up somewhere to make that million *sesterces,* and you can find those people who can clear you. What kind of businesses do you need doing in Parthia?"

This is better than I thought. He's volunteering to get me out, thought Hasdrubal. *Play it carefully, but for Baal's sake, don't talk him out of it.*

"Oh, Francius, bless you, but I can't let you take the risk! You'd be executed. And what about your family?"

"No risk. I got it all figured out. We have about four hours to go a mile to the beach, grab the boat and be gone. I have clothes for you, food, water. Everything is planned. And when I make a fortune, well, a million *sesterces* buys a lot of forgiveness. Especially with all your high-placed friends."

"Well, if you're sure" *Could this be a trap? Killed while trying to escape? No, this young man seemed too guileless to set that up.*

"I'm sure," he said, rattling the key in the rusty lock. He unlocked the manacles, and the two bolted out into the darkness.

They came to the beach where the boat lay waiting. The pilot was nowhere to be seen. "He'll be along in a minute. Here, hold my wine!"

Francius passed the wine flask to Hasdrubal, who took a swig, while Francius stripped off his uniform and rummaged in the back of the boat for the Arab robes he had hidden there. Hasdrubal studied the back of his head, and thought, *the young man's got me out of here, but he will be trouble later on. Best to end it now.*

Hasdrubal brought the wine flask down on the back of the young man's head with all the force he could muster. The flask shattered, wine and blood spattering over the man's back. The young man stumbled forward and rolled over. "Hasdrubal! What the hell..." his eyes were puzzled, as Hasdrubal brought the remains of the flask down again on the man's forehead. It opened a huge gash, but rebounded from the man's thick skull. Francius was stunned but unhurt.

Hasdrubal's heart thudded. He had ordered many men killed, but he had never seen it done, much less killed them personally. He had no idea how hard it was. And the young man was strong, in a moment he would be fighting for his life, and Hasdrubal was no match for him. He picked up a rock, and raised it high as Francius groaned, "Hasdrubal, why?" His eyes were pleading, watching the rock descend till it struck his skull. Bone shattered like broken pottery and blood spurted. Hasdrubal raised the rock, bringing it down again and again on Francius' bloody skull, until bone no longer splintered, and the stone sank into something soft.

Hasdrubal stood up, sick to his stomach, quivering, his heart racing. He felt something warm on his cheek and wiped it away. A gout of Francius' blood, with a splinter of bone in it. Hasdrubal doubled over and retched violently. *Think quick, the pilot is coming.* He rummaged through Francius' clothes for the sailor's dagger, and hid behind a rock. *Gods! What if he already came, and saw me killing him! Soldiers might be coming instead of the pilot.* Waves of panic and indecision swept him. *Why do I have to stay here? Why not just leave? No, the pilot knows where we're going. The Navy will have me by noon tomorrow.* While he was arguing with himself, the pilot showed up. Hasdrubal crouched lower behind the rock. *Let him find the boy. He'll bend over to see if he's alive, and then I jump him. God, what if he's young and tough? No matter. Just catch him in the back with the dagger.* His heart hammered, his blood ringing in his ears. He was sure the pilot could hear his breathing.

The pilot walked up to the boat, and about fifty feet away, saw the body of Francius half-in, half-out, motionless as the boat bobbed in the beach swell. "Francius!" he called out, and broke into a run. As Hasdrubal expected, he went immediately to the boat and bent over the young man, aghast at his shattered head. Hasdrubal came up silently behind him, and slid the dagger in between the man's ribs. He was surprised how easily it went in, through the robe, binding a bit as it stuck. Hasdrubal turned the knife a bit, and it slid in up to the hilt. The man, an old fisherman, straightened up, surprised. He tried to reach behind him to grab the knife, but Hasdrubal twisted it a bit. The man gasped, gagging and twitching spasmodically while Hasdrubal held him against the knife. He seemed to take a long time to die, but finally his breath rattled in his throat, and he collapsed in Hasdrubal's arms. Hasdrubal lowered him to the ground and lugged him into the boat, where he grabbed Francius' body and pulled it fully into the boat also. He clambered in and pushed off the sand with the oar. About a hundred feet off shore, he opened the sail to catch the night breeze. The boat leaned against the wind and the water began to gurgle past the rudder. Hasdrubal's pulse slowed as he set a course north to Parthia and freedom. The pilot's eyes stared sightlessly at the moonlight, and he tossed a rag over the bloody mess of Francius' head. *I have never killed a man before, and tonight I have killed two.* A mile out to sea, he rolled the two bodies, Francius' armor, and the bloody rags overboard. They bobbed lifelessly on the swell. *Too bad, I really sort of liked Francius. But it's better this way.*

The centurion of the watch roused Titus Cornelius a little after midnight. "Bad news, sir. Hasdrubal's escaped. The morning watch found the prison open, and the sentry missing!"

"What happened?" he said, sleepily, trying to focus his attention and chase the fog of sleep from his brain. He sat up and threw the thin blanket off. "What of the sentry?"

"No sign of him, sir. I caught him chatting with Hasdrubal the other night. Hasdrubal might have got him close enough to the bars to strangle. I don't think Hasdrubal could have overpowered him, though. Francius was a pretty strong lad. Gallic farm boy."

"Search the island. Get the word out, I don't want any boats leaving the island tonight. Post guards on all of them. And have three galleys ready to sail at first light!"

CHAPTER 30: WORD OF EUROPA

Asia and Africa were docked in adjacent berths in Muziris. *Africa* had purchased a huge quantity of spices, silks, artwork, and two elephants, loaded onboard and into the forward hold with great difficulty. From time to time, their angry screams could be heard a hundred yards away in the *Asia,* where Aulus and Lucius Parvus were doing

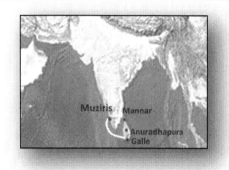

the books in the master's cabin, trying to eke out a profit margin from the voyage for the two ships. It was not looking good. No matter how Lucius worked the abacus, it came up the same: Aulus would only barely break even, not including a good bit of his own fortune sunk into the venture. The only hope lay in a generous bonus from Trajan for a successful mission to the Hanaean emperor. Their gloomy calculations were interrupted by some cries outside, jabbering in an incomprehensible Indian dialect. Aulus flung open one of the windows to the cabin and peered alongside the *Asia*'s hull to determine the source of the clamor. An Indian coastal lug was alongside, with the boat's master, presumably a fisherman, gesticulating to the crew on deck.

"Go topside, Lucius, and find out what that man wants. Probably trying to sell us some fish he caught. Get them to hold down the noise. We're having enough trouble making the numbers come out right." Aulus shut the window disgustedly.

Lucius disappeared through the cabin door, but returned, agitated, in just a moment. "*Domine! Domine!* Your lordship! Come quickly, the man has seen the *Europa!*"

"The *Europa*! Where?" asked Aulus, standing up and scattering the scrolls and wax writing tablets onto the deck.

"In port, somewhere in Taprobane! The fisherman hailed us, thinking we were the same ship he had seen there, and wondering how we had gotten here so quickly!"

"Taprobane! That's only a few days' sail from here. Let's go! I have questions for that man." Aulus hurried out the cabin door, with Lucius in close pursuit.

Dionysius was already on the scene when they reached the knot of sailors clustered about the midships rail. "Captain! Have that man brought on board immediately!" Aulus ordered. "Where's the translator?"

"Right away, sir!" Dionysius barked some orders and the sailors let down a rope ladder over the side. "The translator is over here. It's a very different dialect than what he's used to, but he seems to be able to make himself understood." Dionysius pointed to a slender, very dark man with a coal-black beard, clad in a dirty grey loincloth.

The sailor clambered over the railing, assisted by several sailors from the *Asia's* crew.

"Good! Ask him when he saw the *Europa*... the ship in Taprobane," demanded Aulus.

A flurry of incomprehensible syllables, some repeated questions, and the translator replied in bad Aramaic, which Dionysius translated for Aulus's benefit.

"Several days ago, a week maybe. She was in port in a town called Galle, I believe in the south part of the island. A small fishing village and local trading port, mostly."

"What sort of shape was she in?"

Again, the three way translation from Greek to pidgin Aramaic to Indian and back again.

Dionysius delivered the final translation. "He thought she was in good shape. Looking for some big timbers for some repairs, but he didn't see any signs of damage"

"The masts?" asked Aulus. "Did she have any damage to the masts?"

Back and forth again, and the Indian fisherman shook his head. "No," said Dionysius, finally. "He said the rigging looked good, although he couldn't tell for sure.."

"Hmm, I wonder what else they could need timber for? The hull? The steering oars? Ask him if her steering oars were in place."

Pause, then "No, they seemed all right. But if I might add, each ship carries a spare set of two. They may have replaced one or both of them at sea, and need replacements. I would. I would never go to sea without at least one set of spares. And those are hard to make. I wouldn't count on being able to make a set just anywhere."

"It's a possibility. Well, how long would it take to make them?" asked Aulus. "I want to know what our chances are of catching them still in port, Dionysius."

"I don't know, sir. If the wood is in hand, maybe a week or so. But the hard part is finding the wood. Those are big blades."

"Well, ask the translator if by any chance he knew anything about the crew?"

A moment later, the Indian sailor shook his head. "He doesn't know anything about the crew. They were all foreigners to him."

Aulus fished out a gold *aureus* from his purse, and handed it to the sailor. The dark man hefted the bulky gold coin, and his eyes went wide. "That's generous, sir," said Dionysius. "He probably doesn't make that much in a year."

"He's earned it," said Aulus, closing his leather purse. "Give him a good meal, him and all his crew, and bring the navigators and yourself down to my cabin. I need to know more about Taprobane. Have them bring every map they have of the place. It looks like *Europa* indeed survived the storm."

A few minutes later, Dionysius came into the cabin with the three navigators. Dionysius brought his *periplus* sailing directions, ports, tides, winds and local customs. The navigators were encumbered with several long scrolls, maps of Taprobane.

"Spread them out here on the desk" invited Aulus, while Lucius looked over his shoulder.

The senior navigator spoke first, unrolling one map. This map showed the coast of India and the ragged outlines of Taprobane. "Muziris, where we are now, is here," he said, pointing to the southwest coast of India, near the tip. "And Taprobane is here. There are several big ports, the best of which is Mannar, on the northwest coast opposite India. Mannar is the closest to the capital, Anuradhapura, here."

Dionysius volunteered. "That is the main trading port, and I believe you have a *praetor externa* in the capital."

"Yes, we do, and in a minute, I might remember his name. Go on. Where's this place...Galle? Where he saw the *Europa*?"

"Near the southern end of the island. There."

"My *periplus* mentions the port, but says very little else about it. Seems to be strictly a local trading port. The book does mention, however, that relations between the northern and the southern ends of the island are not good," added Dionysius. "And Ibrahim has a friend there, no doubt, well away from the capital."

"Well, let us set a thief to catch a thief," said Aulus, glaring at Dionysius. Aulus had still an intense distrust of the man, and the captain flushed under the insult. "If you were Ibrahim, what would you do now?"

"I was not privy to the plans between the sailing master and the pirate... sir!" he replied stiffly. "I was following the orders of the sailing master placed over me to divert the remaining convoy north. As I have told you repeatedly, I regret greatly having done so, for I am not a pirate, myself." He paused to regain his composure, then continued. "But if I were Ibrahim in Taprobane, I think I would offload my haul there, spread some of it around liberally to make good friends, and go elsewhere in India as a legitimately wealthy man."

Aulus considered his words. "What about going on further eastward with the ship?"

"Unlikely. Ibrahim is, by all accounts, a pirate of the Red Sea and the Mediterranean. He would find no friends and many enemies... the pirate would face serious trouble from other pirates, just as we may on the eastward leg. The ship would attract some serious attention."

Aulus turned to the navigator. "How far from Galle to the capital at... at...
"

"Anuradhapura, sir. About two hundred miles overland."

"He has then, at most, a few weeks' grace at the most. Let's lay course for Galle, then and see if we can trap him."

Dionysius interjected. "May I add some caution, sir? If Ibrahim is in port there, he likely has some local protection. Might I counsel that you stop first at Mannar, and notify the Taprobanian king?"

"I think not. We'll test ourselves against whatever local force he can bring to bear on us. Stopping at Mannar would add days to our trip, and the king might very well seize the gold himself. Lucius, leave word for *Africa* to remain here, continue trading till the fall monsoon shifts, then return home and pay off as many of our creditors as possible. As for us, to Galle, gentlemen! Let's sail at the next opportunity!"

CHAPTER 31: FIREFIGHT IN GALLE

"Antonius!" barked Gaius, roughly shaking the sleeping centurion awake in his bunk by light of a dim oil lamp a little after midnight. "Antonius, wake up, damn you!"

"Aye, sir," said Antonius, rubbing his eyes sleepily. "What the hell's goin' on, if yer'll pardon me choice of words?"

"What the hell did you tell that woman?"

"Thani? That was days ago... lemme see. I think I said she had a nice arse. Did, too." Antonius smiled dreamily.

"Well, the local king is marching his army south. He thinks Rome has invaded Galle with a couple of legions. Get your ass out of that bunk, Centurion. We have big trouble coming. Get your deck guards rousted out, and post a guard. Then meet me in Ibrahim's cabin in full battle gear in five minutes!"

Antonius' jaw dropped. "What?! Honest, I just said she had a nice arse. I didn't tell her nothin'... no' at all!" He banged his head on the low overhead getting out of the bunk and swore vehemently. "God cursed low hangin' shit! If yer don't trip over it on this bloody ship, yer bang yer head against it!" He began rummaging through his campaign chest for his battle kit, but Gaius was already gone.

Antonius entered the master's cabin, where Gaius, Demetrios, Ibrahim, and Abdi, the head of the Nubian archers, were studying a map of the city and docks, rudely drawn to no particular scale, but it gave them a view of the area they had to control. "Come in, Antonius. As you can see, it's getting serious out there."

"Sir, I am truly sorry. I swear I told that girl nothing... nothin' at all!"

"Let's deal with that later. Right now, we have two enemies. One is that mob on the docks, and the other more formidable force is a few days out. Let's deal with the nearest one first. Ibrahim, what does your local friend think?"

"He told me just hours ago that he had heard rumors of this. The king in Anuradhapura is moving several thousand men south to defend Galle against what he thinks is a Roman invasion." He paused, as chuckles murmured through the meeting at the incongruity, then continued. "And oh, by the way, subdue the local governor. The north and the south ends of the island don't get along. Galle's governor is building barricades against the assault but the townspeople blame us for this impending disaster. Fortunately, I had

Demetrios keep the crew close to the *tabernae* and brothels right adjacent to the docks, so when the riots broke out, we got almost everyone back, although one young man was beaten to death, and about five others have broken bones. The rest of the crew came to their rescue and pulled them out. Several locals were down, I don't know how bad, but I wouldn't be surprised if we gave better than we got. We are anchored several hundred yards out, but that does not stop them from shouting curses and throwing torches and projectiles at us. "

"But with locals dead and injured, they probably won't calm down too easily. They want revenge. How do the local authorities come down on this?" asked Gaius.

"My man thinks the provincial governor has been spoiling for a showdown with Anuradhapura for years, and sees this as a chance to give the king his comeuppance. The governor thinks that when the king's army shows up, the town will turn and stand with him."

"Does the governor have forces to control the mob?"

"His army was conspicuously absent during this riot. He wants to rally his townspeople to his side against the king, and he can't take the side of foreigners against them. At best, he will let us take care of ourselves. At worst, he'll join the mob and try to seize us. Word's out, too, that we have considerable money on board, and not well-gotten." Ibrahim sighed.

"What about our crewmen up in the mountains?" asked Gaius.

Demetrios answered. "That's our biggest problem. Half our carpenters went with the locals to the central forest to make sure they picked the best trees. They're not back yet, and I don't want to leave without them unless we absolutely have to. Not only would the mob tear them to pieces, poor bastards, but we can't get along without those shipwrights. Some of them helped design this ship, and they're irreplaceable."

"What about a rescue party?" asked Gaius.

"Not likely. We really haven't any idea where they are, and as little as we know the country, we could pass within a mile of them and never know they were there. Could we send a message to the king, telling them we are not invaders?" asked Demetrios.

Gaius answered, "Not until the king is already here, and we would face a large well-trained army instead of a local militia and a mob. If his answer is 'no' then we will have to fight our way out against much worse odds. We need to be gone when the king arrives. Antonius?"

"Let me see yer map. Do the king or the governor have any kind of siege engines? I mean catapults, onagers, or *ballistae*?"

Ibrahim answered, "Fortunately, no. This island doesn't do siege warfare. Every city depends on irrigation canals for water. Just block their water and they'll be out in a few days."

"Well, that's good ter hear. We can sit tight then, and hold the mob off the docks with the *ballistae*. We can reach them, but they can't reach us. And what does get by the *ballistae*, the archers can pick off, and what's left won't get on deck. So we just sit here, out of reach, and odds are, in a day or two, they'll turn their attention to the king's army. Now our big problem is bringin' them carpenters aboard."

"I don't know how we're going to that," said Demetrios. "Partly, because I don't know when they're going to come back. Hopefully, they'll get word of the trouble and slip in quietly and get word to us, then we can figure out what to do. On the other hand, the local lumberers may just truss them up and hand them over to the mob." Demetrios sighed. "Or kill them. If they aren't back by the time the king's army is on scene, then we'll have to assume the worst, and sail without them. They should have been back today."

"Very well, then," said Gaius. "We stand and defend ourselves, but do as little as possible to inflame the situation. Just whatever is necessary to keep them at distance. Antonius, how's the deck force?"

"Ten men on duty now, the rest in an hour. Abdi's archers are stringing their bows, and should be in position by now. Everyone is on twelve on, twelve off shifts, so we always have a rested force and good reserves, if we need them. They'll sleep with their swords."

"Good. What about the *ballistae*?"

"Manned and ready. I got a blank for the blacksmith to start makin' up some more bronze bolts. I figure we have enough bronze on hand to make a few hundred more bolts if we need 'em. The only problem is, I never had enough bolts to train them. They've fired a few wooden ones, but I don't like to train with them too much, 'cuz their weight throws the aim off."

"Good. All right, Demetrios. What else do we need to get underway besides our wayward carpenters?"

"Not much, sir. Just favorable winds and a good tide. Anchored out like this, I don't need boats to get her head around. Getting the anchor up can take an hour or more, but if I have to, I'll chop the hawser and go without it. I have spares for both cable and anchor."

"Very well. Gentlemen, the next few hours are critical. If we can convince the mob that we are too hard to get at, but otherwise no threat, I think they will drift off and start concerning themselves with the upcoming battle with the king. So... let's go to war!" Gaius dismissed the group, and left the cabin with Antonius.

"Not much of a plan, is it, Antonius?" asked Gaius, on the quarterdeck. The warm tropical night, the gentle breeze and the stars flung against the velvet night sky struck a discordant note with the angry mob and twinkling torches on the docks.

"Well, most plans fer situations like this are just pulled out yer arse at best, sir...you've done it before a coupla times. All we can do is buy time, but I think we can afford ter buy a lot of that. An' by the way, honest, I di'n't tell her nothin'! I wracked me brain, but whatever we said, about what we do an' all, is what I said with yer right there with me." Antonius was absolutely crestfallen at the thought that something he said might have triggered this disaster.

"Well, remember what I said about womanizing. See how much trouble you got us into?" But Gaius smiled again.

On the dock, the tenor changed, enough to be noticed on the ship. Instead of the roar of a mob, only a few voices, each speaking one after the other, carried across the dark water to the *Europa*. Periodically, the mob would roar its approval at what was said, and men could be seen, scurrying to and fro distributing swords among the men.

"Sir, I think it's gettin' a bit more serious down there. There's some leaders now, an' in a few minutes, it won't be a mob no more. We should get the *ballista* crews to push 'em back."

"You're right. It's getting close. But I want to wait just a bit longer, when they try to actually do something. If you can hit the foe right between the eyes when he is charging, you'll break up his attack. Right now, they're organizing but still milling around. If we push them back now, they'll just reorganize again out of range." Gaius kept his eyes on the docks, the starlight and torchlight glinting off his armor. "Like the good old days, right, Antonius? Waiting for a crowd of Germans to finish strutting their stuff, drinking their beer, and telling each other how brave they are."

"Yup. Thought them days was behind me on this trip. Well, I'm goin' ter check the *ballista* crews an' start havin' 'em pick their targets."

"Good. Plenty of incendiaries?"

"Of course. Lots of pitch."

As Antonius left, Gaius felt a shiver run through his body. He never understood how he kept his fear from showing before action, but no one ever seemed to notice but him. The dry mouth, the twisting stomach, the million what-ifs running through his mind that could spell the difference between victory and defeat... well, he was used to it now, at least.

Antonius inspected each *ballista*, and its crew, led by a ship's officer. There were four *ballistae* on each side, each with a five foot bow and a heavy wooden shield to protect the shooters against return fire. Massive rope torsion coils on either side of the track groaned and creaked, storing energy as the ratcheted firing windlass at the end was cranked to draw the bow back and arm the weapon. Two cranks on the pedestal locked it into the correct elevation and azimuth, so it did not require re-aiming after each shot. Pulling the trigger dispatched a four-foot bronze bolt to its target up to a thousand yards away. These bolts had enough striking power to splinter wooden fortifications at a quarter-mile. Their volume of fire made it highly likely someone moving unprotected in the target area would be fatally skewered.

On the side of each weapon was a sighting tube, pivoted to rotate through range marks. If the range had been estimated correctly, sighting the target through the tube guaranteed correct elevation angle… Antonius hoped. He had not had the opportunity to do accuracy checks, impossible while underway. Supposedly, they had been sighted in while in Myos Hormos, but Antonius had not done it personally.

The two midships weapons were configured as *polyboli* 'many-shooters' equipped with an automatic feed. Above the cradle, a dispenser held twenty bolts, fed from the top. When the firing windlass reached the end of its draw, it tripped a bolt from the feeder and released the trigger. The crew just had to keep the dispenser full and crank to launch ten bolts per minute.

Antonius came up to each weapon, and thoroughly checked the bow and rope torsion springs. A loose fitting could disintegrate explosively if it failed, potentially killing someone. He checked the tightness of the elevation and azimuth cranks, and the range settings on the sight tube; he had told them to use two hundred fifty yards. He then sighted to see the targets they had picked out. He made sure the incendiaries had plenty of water, sand and a blanket to extinguish any fires, and that each had a good batch of about a hundred bolts. He then gave the same speech to each crew in Greek.

"Make sure its trajectory is well clear of the ship's rigging. No need to damage or light off your own ship with a stupid shot. Take your time. If it don't feel right, cease shooting and call me. We don't need to bust one of these, they're hard to fix. You might kill yourself, too!

"*Polyboli* shooters, no incendiaries! It's too easy to light off the whole damn magazine and torch your own weapon. Single shooters at the bow and stern will use incendiaries; aim at the sides of the target to bunch them up, the *polyboli* will aim for the middle and pin them to the dock. Don't light the incendiary until you're cocked and ready to pull the trigger. If you have a fire, put it out quickly, or this whole ship might go up.

"Port side shooters, stand by and keep an eye out for boats approaching us from seaward. Keep your azimuth and elevation loose, you won't know where they are coming from if they come.

"Everyone, be safe! I don't want someone losing a hand in these rigs!"

The combination of dry bolts and incendiaries would quickly reduce the dockyard to flaming splinters in short order.

Antonius had just finished his inspection when the crowd's voice changed again. This time it was the sound of a charge, as the mob swirled down the dock, and began boarding the boats tied up there.

"Antonius! This is it! Push them back!" cried out Gaius from the quarterdeck. Antonius relayed the order, and two solid *thunks* dispatched their flaming projectiles on their arcing trajectories. The two incendiaries arced high and bright against the night sky like meteors, while the other two bolts were unseen angels of death, whistling through the air to the mob focused on the visible incendiaries. Both incendiaries plunged into the dock, where the men there had already cleared the expected impact zone. But in so doing, they bunched up in the middle, right in the path of the two dry bolts.

And on deck the midships *polyboli* kept up their rhythm. *Ratchety-ratchety ratchety thunk! Ratchety ratchety thunk!* The first volley had not yet struck their victims when two more volleys of seen and unseen death were launched, winging their way to the hapless mob. The milling and consternation indicated that the dry bolts had scored their mark, and the second and third volleys penetrated the mob's core. The fires lit by the incendiaries went unextinguished, and the next volley of incendiaries exploded in a shower of sparks and flaming pitch as the bolts impacted the dock.

Antonius, from amidships, was commanding the artillery. "All right now, they're breaking to the left now, trying to make to the streets. Let's cut off their escape and keep 'em bunched! Incendiaries, aim for that alley way. Close it off, set it ablaze. The rest of you, follow the mob and keep aiming for the center!"

The *ballistae* loosened their azimuth so they could swivel to follow the crowd, without losing the elevation that gave them their critical range. The dry bolts stopped to aim before that last fateful turn of the crank, while the incendiaries, having put part of the dock ablaze, cut off the crowd's escape. The dry bolts continued to plunge into the massed men. The people were in full panic now, never having seen such a devastating weapon. Some dove into the water, and others, finally realizing the folly of remaining in a tight knot, began to scurry alone across the firelit dock, past dozens of men who lay impaled. More and more began to take to the water.

"All right, now! Incendiaries, drop your aim a bit, and take out those boats! All of them!"

The boats were much smaller targets, harder to hit. Incendiaries hissed into the water, ineffective for the most part, but the rate of fire was such that one by one, each boat was eventually struck, its sail exploding in a sheet of flame, its men diving overside to the protection of the water.

By now, the battle for the docks of Galle had turned into a rout. The survivors were leaping through flames in terror to escape the whistling death, or diving into the water to swim to safety. And, since they didn't know the range of the weapon, they didn't know where safety lay. In ten minutes, the *Europa* had reduced the dockyard to a flaming inferno, as well as all the boats that had lined it. And, through the flames, the charred remains of what had once been men could be seen.

"All right, all right, enough already. Cease firing!" bawled Antonius.

The *ballista* crewmen stared in awe at their handiwork. None of them had ever fired these awesome weapons in combat. From a quarter-mile out, the *Europa* had started an inferno that destroyed the docks, killed at least thirty or forty people, and now the blaze, spreading from building to building, threatened to engulf the whole waterfront.

"Not bad, Antonius! Not bad at all! In fact, damn good shooting for beginners! I expect they'll be trying to bring some firefighters down to extinguish the blaze. Hold your fire, unless they try to regroup and re-attack. But I don't think you left them much transportation there," Gaius chuckled as the flaming boats bobbed aimlessly, flames licking up their rigging until masts and booms gave way. "Keep a sharp eye out to seaward, now. I expect that if they mount a re-attack, they'll try it with boats further out along the beach, and try to come in under cover of darkness. I'd give them about an hour to get around that far, if any of them have the stomach to try again."

Predictably, the town's firefighters arrived to try to stem the waterfront blaze. Warehouses began to explode as the flames found flammable oils and wine stores, and the firefighters scattered, thinking somehow that the terrible weapons on the *Europa* were responsible. But the *Europa* fired no more bolts in the direction of the docks, and the firefighters established a firebreak east of the waterfront to contain the blaze. There was nothing else they could do; they could not extinguish it.

And about four in the morning, a sharp-eared lookout caught the sound of voices and the thud of oars across the water to seaward. His sharp eyes strained against the starlight to catch the dim outlines of a mass of small boats approaching, coming into bowshot range, perhaps a quarter mile or less away.

Again Gaius gave the quiet order, Antonius bawled his command, and the seaward *ballistae* worked their terrible deeds. On this side, Antonius had removed the *polyboli* automatic feeders, so that all four positions could fire incendiaries. The boats saw the flames as the incendiaries were lit in their direction, and their consternation could be heard on deck as the first volley arced skyward to plunge into their midst, striking one boat. However, this was not to be as one-sided a contest as the dock had been. The intruders had slipped inside bow range, and a volley of dozens of arrows answered the *ballistae*. Crewmen scurried to shelter behind their shields as the arrows struck the deck like hail. One *ballista* crewman screamed, a shaft penetrating his forearm.

"Get him down! Get him down! And get another man in his place!" bawled Antonius, as the next volley of incendiaries traced out against the sky. Antonius noted that there was just a hint of dawn, and one boat, now aflame, illuminated the others. "Archers! Let's get some arrows in the air! Two can play this game! And use some fire!"

The Nubian archers were among the best in the world. Tall, dark, regal representatives of Africa, they served as auxiliaries to the Roman legions throughout Europe, Asia and Africa. Almost in slow motion, they took careful aim and twenty bowstrings thrummed in unison. And in that same surreal slow motion, they selected another arrow, took aim and fired and fired again. The third volley fired incendiaries, and twenty small sparks followed a higher, shorter trajectory than the large meteors from the *ballistae*. The clatter of arrows impacting the deck from the attacking boats became erratic as cries across the water confirmed that the Nubian arrows had found their mark. And now three boats were ablaze. The boats could now be seen clearly in the dimness, illuminated by their flaming companions. Some had turned around, others pressed on. The boats were close enough now that the *ballistae* no longer fired high arcs in the hopes of hitting someone, but leveled their deadly volleys in a flat trajectory at their intended victims with much greater force and accuracy. Another five boats burst into flame. And the Nubian archers pressed the rail, firing as individuals directly into the boats. Several boats bobbed aimlessly, their crews lying dead or wounded.

Some boats continued to press the attack, belatedly using incendiaries themselves. These lit several small fires on the *Europa*, but the highly flammable sail had been stowed before action, and the fires quickly extinguished. But the closer the boats came, the more accurately the *Europa's* bolts and arrows tore into them. Finally, at about fifty yards, the lead boat burst into flames, and the remaining four came about and broke off the attack, joining the others who had fled the action earlier.

This attack had lasted about half an hour, and by now it was grey dawn. They could survey the damage done overside. Twenty small boats lay burning, ten more bobbed aimlessly, their crews dead, wounded or having fled overside. Bodies floated in the water.

The *Europa's* crew had not escaped unscathed. Besides the *ballista* crewman, ten others had sustained arrow wounds, and two were dead. But compared to the carnage overside, it had still been a one sided action.

Ibrahim came down to look sadly at the damage. "So many dead. I have seen death so many times, and yet it never becomes familiar."

"I know that well, Ibrahim. They fought well," said Gaius, grimly.

"Demetrios! Put boats over and pick up the wounded. The dead as well! Let's not let the sharks feed on such worthy foes as these!" Ibrahim ordered.

The boats went overside and brought aboard their terrible harvest. Many of the wounded fought, thinking they would be tortured to death, but all were firmly but gently brought onto the deck with the help of a translator who assured them that they would not be harmed. And the dead were brought aboard as well, wrapped in shrouds and laid on the deck. The wounded were treated. By midmorning, Ibrahim and Gaius spoke with one of the least injured, a young dark man who had taken an arrow wound to the shoulder, little more than a knife cut.

Ibrahim addressed the young man through a translator. "I want you to go back to the townspeople of Galle, and take some of the wounded with you. Tell them we mean them no harm, but they should know that attacking us is foolhardy. We will set the entire town ablaze if necessary if they do so."

The young man was defiant. "Why you not go? Not wanted in Galle. Go!"

"We go when we are ready. We are not yet ready. Now have them send back one boat, unarmed, and we will return their dead and more seriously wounded."

As the young man was led away to the ship's boat being readied overside, Gaius couldn't help but admire Ibrahim's ingenuity. "What a stroke of genius. That will, I suspect, give them something to think about. Ibrahim, you surprise me. If you weren't a pirate, I think I should truly consider you a gentleman."

"The dead have fought their fight. They should be honored."

Billows of thick smoke poured from the remains of the Galle waterfront, fires still flaring from a few buildings. Against the blackened remnants of the dock, charred remnants of boats bobbed against the collapsed timbers.

The provincial governor came aboard with the boat sent to recover the dead and wounded. The boat came under a flag of truce, but he demanded that his four armed bodyguards escort him on board, despite the provision that they come unarmed.

Ibrahim, Demetrios and Gaius conferred on this, and decided that the boat was too small to carry a large boarding force. They agreed, but first arrayed the deck force, both as a welcoming committee and as a subtle warning. Antonius fell out the on-duty shift under Shmuel, and called them to attention as the governor and his guards clambered gracelessly up the rope ladder to the deck. As he recovered his footing on the deck, Antonius bawled out, "Sword...salute! Ready...to!" and the swords flashed upward in a Roman sword salute, arm outstretched, then fell to the ready position, forty five degrees downward. This was an ancient ritual that displayed the men's weapons, and their willingness to forego their use.

The governor was not impressed with the ceremony, and did not return the honor. He immediately confronted the trio in passable but accented Greek. "What hell you do here? Destroy my port, kill my people, stir up trouble with king! What hell you do here? These boats... my people's livelihood!" He sputtered in anger, unable to say anything more coherent.

Gaius replied, gently but firmly. "Your Excellency, you know that we were defending ourselves. That mob attacked our crew, killing one and injuring several. They rioted on the docks for hours with no sign of your urban cohorts. When they began to board their 'means of livelihood' to attack our ship, we defended ourselves, since you would not. And they attacked again, a few hours later, and still you did nothing. As for the king, perhaps you can enlighten us as to why he thinks we are invading your city. I understand you and he are close friends." He paused, waiting for a reply.

None came, so Gaius continued. "As you can see, had we wished to invade your town, we could have had it hours ago. So if you will be so kind as to inform the king of our peaceful intentions, that we will depart, and leave you two to your friendship."

The provincial governor was silent, glowering at the insolent Roman.

"Of course, should we succeed in finding your king first, perhaps we could tell him the truth personally. Taprobane profits enormously from trade with Rome, and I am sure that he would not want to jeopardize that trade, just because some provincial governor wanted to stir up trouble." Gaius folded his arms across his chest.

The governor's face betrayed a bit of panic. "I must defend townspeople, too," he said. "They acted in haste and fear. But I want you leave Galle. Now. At once. I settle with the king when he arrives."

Demetrios spoke up. "We would like to leave, also. But we cannot."

"Why not?" asked the governor.

"Some twenty of my most valuable crewmembers have not yet returned from a very important task ashore, procuring much-needed lumber for repairs. Had they been aboard last night, we would have sailed, and none of this would have happened. They are two days overdue. Perhaps you know of their whereabouts?"

The governor pondered this question, betraying that he knew very well where they were. "They are safe. But they are being held for the king's arrival."

"Too bad. I had hoped that they could be returned, and we could leave before the king arrived. Now it seems that we may have to defend ourselves against him as well. For that we shall need our heavy weapons." Gaius paused for effect in mid-bluff, then continued. "And I cannot promise that the rest of Galle can be protected from those weapons. You have seen what our light weapons can do."

The governor paused, obviously alarmed at what other weapons the ship might have at her disposal. "Perhaps for price. To cover cost of damage you inflicted on Galle. Then maybe I release them."

Ibrahim rejoined the bargaining. "Perhaps for the price we contracted for the necessary timber. *And* the timber, too."

"Of course, we can always wait for the king," added Gaius.

"I give you men, you leave?"

Demetrios joined in the bargaining. "The men and the timber. We will be gone within hours after their return."

"Your men here in an hour, and timber. Then you, gone!" Bested, he turned on his heel and clambered down the rope ladder to the boat, and disappeared below. His bodyguards followed over, then more men came on deck to claim the wounded and the dead.

True to his word, the governor delivered the carpenters and two partially-finished pieces of timber by barge late in the afternoon. And, true to their word, Ibrahim paid them the agreed-upon balance. They hoisted the timbers aboard, lashed them to the deck, and sailed at sunset.

CHAPTER 32: MURDERS FOR A POT OF GOLD

Hasdrubal made landfall at the dusty Parthian port of Hormirzad, on the north side of the Persian Gulf inside the straits of Hormuz, after spending about a week at sea in the small open fishing craft. He was dirty, he stank, and he was bone-tired, dozing only intermittently while single-handing the lateen-rigged fishing dhow.

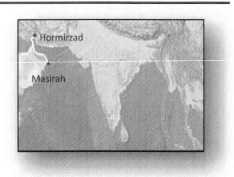

Late in the morning of the first day at sea, he had experienced an hour of sheer terror, as the distinctive blue-camouflaged sail of a Roman galley scout had passed within a mile or two of his boat, close enough for him to see the black hull as it pitched on the swells. He had doused his sails, but the galley continued on, dismissing him as another fishing boat. After that, nothing but endless sea.

Hasdrubal had inventoried the cache that the ill-fated Francius had put together. A handful of silver *denarii*. Probably all of the young fool's savings, given his meager income. Not even a hundred *sesterces*, all told. What a waste! Hasdrubal did not comprehend how some people could live their entire life within such narrow horizons.

But the food and water, intended for three, was ample for the trip, and Hasdrubal was a competent small-boat pilot. He sailed at night to avoid detection, picking his course by Polaris, and put in during the day at the various fishing villages and landings along the Arabian coast until he reached the conspicuous mountainous promontory marking the southern end of the strait. At this point, he struck out due north, covering the hundred miles of open sea by dead reckoning. He raised the Parthian coast, and headed westward along the shore until Hormirzad emerged from the sweltering monsoon haze.

Hasdrubal tied up the boat along the fishing docks, inconspicuous in his Arab burnoose. No one questioned him - just another itinerant fisherman. He made his way along the bustling alleyways of the busy town, past mud brick buildings in various states of repair until he reached the more affluent business district. Here he found the offices, and above them the luxurious apartment, of his contact in Parthia, Rani Ben Barca.

Hasdrubal stepped into the rear servants' entrance, where his disreputable appearance would attract less attention. A burly servant glowered at him, barking something in Parthian, which Hasdrubal didn't comprehend, and again in Aramaic, which he did.

"You there! Where the hell do you think you're going?"

"To see Ben Barca," answered Hasdrubal, with authority. The servant was taken aback, then laughed, mockingly.

"Sure, and I'm going to see the king of Parthia! Get your ass back out on the street, and don't come back until you've had a bath! You stink!" The other servants laughed at him.

Hasdrubal's ears burned. "YOU get YOUR ass upstairs, and inform your master that Hasdrubal is here to see him. And if my smell annoys your nose, perhaps I'll have Rani Ben Barca remove it from your face, as a lesson in manners! Now, go!"

The servant gaped at the impudent response, made a move toward Hasdrubal, then reconsidered. "You better be who you say you are, or I'll remove your whole head!" The man went upstairs, none too quickly. The other servants stopped laughing and stared.

"Go on about your business!" barked Hasdrubal, and the gaggle disbursed.

Ben Barca hurried downstairs from his apartment. "Hasdrubal, oh my, oh my! Upstairs quickly, and don't talk to anyone!" he hissed quietly. And louder, so all the servants could hear, "I am eager to see your catch of fish. I hope you'll sell at a good price."

Ben Barca slammed the door behind him as they entered the apartment. He dismissed his bodyguard, and waved the house servants away. "Here, sit. No, please, not on the sofa! It cost a fortune and you're... well, please sit on this leather chair here." He motioned Hasdrubal to a folding wooden chair with a leather seat.

Hasdrubal sat down, wrapping his stinking robes around him. "Rani, sorry for the appearance, but I've had rather a run of bad luck. I didn't bring the ships I promised."

Ben Barca sat himself down on the elegant white sofa, made of bleached lamb's wool. "I'll say! What happened to you?"

Hasdrubal lied adroitly, "Ibrahim turned the tables on me. Took the ship for himself and set me adrift in a small boat. I barely escaped with my life. I'm going to need some help getting back to Alexandria."

Ben Barca eyed him suspiciously, his hand nervously toying with the narrow beard that fringed his chin. His other hand tapped nervously on the sofa.

"Hasdrubal, I'm afraid you're going to need more help than that." Ben Barca paused, gauging Hasdrubal's reaction. "Much more. Perhaps Astarte can help you, but I cannot."

Hasdrubal looked surprised. "Why? You and I have helped each other out of tight spots in the past. A few hundred *aureii*, a change of clothes, and I'm on my way. I'm sorry the deal didn't come through as planned, but that wasn't my fault!"

"You don't understand, do you? You really don't, I think. But then, I could never tell when you were lying, anyway. The Romans were here, Hasdrubal... three days ago one of their galleys from Masirah pulled into port under a flag of truce. Their squadron commander met personally with the governor and told a slightly different version of your events. You're wanted for treason and a couple of other state crimes that the Parthians don't care much about. But piracy, conspiracy, jailbreak, murder... the Parthians took them really seriously. Do you want to tell me what really happened?"

Hasdrubal looked aghast. It was an admirable act. "Impossible! You know me, I could never do those things! It's a lie! Ibrahim set me up, I told you!"

"Well, I would believe you, but I don't see how even Ibrahim could get the Roman navy to corroborate his story to the Parthians. And take the risk of sailing into an enemy port under truce to warn them of a highly dangerous individual. They distributed your likeness, too. A reasonably good one, I might add. I recognized you right away. Who was the artist?"

"That son of a bitch!" sputtered Hasdrubal. "What do they say I did?"

"That you connived with pirates to hijack ships under your command, that you personally hijacked two freighters under Imperial orders, kidnapped a high-ranking Roman ambassador on a crucial mission, escaped from prison, killing a Roman marine and an Arab sailor. Stole a boat. Most importantly, the squadron commander, one Titus... Titus... oh what was his name, Hasdrubal?"

"Cornelius," Hasdrubal blurted, completely off balance.

"Oh, so you have met," said Ben Barca, smiling. "Well, Cornelius requested the governor pass on that Rome would view with concern your being sheltered in Parthia. Which, in non-diplomatic language means the consequences of your staying here are more expensive than the king sees as worthwhile. That was a stupid stunt, Hasdrubal. I thought you were bringing me a run-of-the-lot Indian Ocean freighter with the usual gold and silver, not likely to attract much attention. You hijacked not one, but two, top-of-the-line freighters with tens, maybe hundreds of millions of *sesterces* worth of gold, with a high-ranking Senator on board, on an Imperial mission. What do you think I would have been able to do with those ships, and what do you think the Parthians would be able to do with them?"

Hasdrubal glared sullenly. "Money can buy anything here!"

"Including trouble. The whole country is on a war footing now, and the question of war with Rome is no longer if, but when. And the king prefers it later to sooner, when he can win the big prize, Alexandria, and a truce that will kick the Romans out of Asia Minor."

"So? Fifty million *sesterces* outfits a lot of troops."

"Yes. And invites a Roman strike before Parthia is ready. That was stupid. You misled me, Hasdrubal, and you could have got my neck in the strangler's noose. That didn't happen, fortunately. Now on to your problem. Your face is going up all over the coast, and the border with Syria, as fast as the governor's servants can make copies. It's all over town, and riders have already been dispatched to the other coastal towns. There's a sizable reward for your capture, and you don't have to be breathing when delivered. Don't worry, it's not big enough to tempt me, but it is several years' pay to the commoners. The Romans identified all your banks, even a few I thought only I knew about. Anyone that extends you credit will forfeit his life."

"You know a lot about this," grumbled Hasdrubal. The seriousness was sinking in.

"The governor is a personal friend. In fact, I was visiting him when the Roman squadron commander called. He allowed me to remain. Particularly since he knows I know you. That friendship didn't keep me from being grilled for several hours by the captain of the guard at the palace. This house has been searched, once openly and at least twice covertly. So you can't stay here. You need to continue to look just as you do now, a disheveled dirty Arab. And keep your mouth shut, so your Phoenician accent doesn't give you away."

"What the hell am I going to do then? Sleep in the streets with the dogs?"

"I will take one last risk for you, Hasdrubal, and then I don't know you. Not here. Not for a long time to come. You met Gyges, my head bodyguard, when you came in?"

"Yes," said Hasdrubal, now humble and feeling increasingly afraid.

"He was expecting you. We have contacts with the lower strata of society as well as the higher. I have some friends that do some... smuggling and other less savory tasks for me from time to time. They're a rough lot, but would not live to spend their reward if they turned you in. And right now, you don't have enough money for them to rob. Gyges will take you to them. I'll loan, no, give you some Parthian silver coins, several hundred in fact. In memory of our past adventures. Don't stay in Hormirzad. And don't go west. Try to go up east to Bactria. You won't be expected up that way, and no one will even know you're wanted. There's a caravan going up that way in a week. Be on it, keep inconspicuous. And don't come back here. I'll have to turn you in if you do. I've already taken too great a risk."

Ben Barca clapped his hands. "Gyges!" The big servant appeared from the shadows behind the elegant drapes. "Take my friend here to our prearranged place. Then come back, pick one servant that saw him here, and cut out his tongue in front of the others. Let them know what happens if their tongues get to flapping!"

Gyges nodded.

"May the blessings of Baal and the Lady Ishtar be upon you, Hasdrubal. Goodbye... and good luck!"

Hasdrubal did not leave Hormirzad. He bribed one of Ben Barca's lower-strata mercenaries with a silver coin to arrange a low-class room for him. He settled in, bathed, as he really did stink, shaved off his black beard, and cut his hair short, almost Roman style. He knew he had not sat for any sketch, so any drawing circulated by the Romans would be from memory, by someone who did not really know him. After a week, he felt comfortable enough to go about the city without looking over his shoulder, and passed several soldiers and urban cohorts who did not look twice at him. If asked, he introduced himself as "Mehdi," a common enough name in Parthia, and avoided Aramaic in favor of Parthian, which he spoke not too well. But many outsiders in Hormirzad spoke worse... he blended in.

He would be going east, but not with just a few hundred in silver. Ben Barca had quite a bit of money, most of which he kept in the house.

About a month later, he went back to Ben Barca's house a bit after midnight, when all the neighborhood was shuttered and dark. He began banging on the door, and calling out as loud as he could, "Ben Barca, wake up, it's me, Hasdrubal! I need you!"

The night watchman opened the door shutter to get a glimpse of the loudmouthed oaf outside, believing him to be some drunken acquaintance of Barca. He was not Gyges, but an older slave. At the same time, a lamp flared in the upstairs bedroom and Ben Barca threw open a window.

"Shut up, you fool, you'll get us both killed. Bazarges, let him in and I'll be right down."

The door opened.

Hasdrubal brushed past Bazarges and felt in his pocket for a weapon chosen for just this moment. He pulled out a sack filled with lead balls, held it by the end, and struck Bazarges solidly on the right temple from behind. The blackjack worked as well as the street thug who sold it to him said it would... a crunching sound indicated that it had done more damage than he had hoped, and the night watchman crumpled to the floor. He would be out for a long time, perhaps forever. Hasdrubal then drew his dagger and waited for Barca.

Barca rounded the corner in a nightshirt, carrying a lamp. "Why the hell are you here? I told you to get out and never..." the words died in his throat as he eyed both the prone night watchman, laying in a pool of spreading blood about his head, and the shiny dagger in Hasdrubal's hand, pointed at his midriff.

"It seems I left something behind, some money I think. And don't call out for Gyges, because I'll spill your entrails on the floor before the words leave your throat. Anyway, I waited until he left to visit the brothel around the corner about half an hour ago. I want you to go quietly to where you keep your money, the big gold coins, not a few silver shekels."

Hasdrubal's body was hardened by years at sea, firmly muscled though a little soft with fat. Ben Barca's was the soft body of a merchant, who seldom did anything that a slave could do for him, other than eat or drink. He swallowed hard and nodded, "Follow me."

He led Hasdrubal upstairs to his bedroom and produced a small locked chest from under his bed. He fumbled around in his day clothing for a key on a thong he wore around his neck, and with shaking hands, finally persuaded the lock to open. "Here, take it all, and just leave," he said, as the gold coins glinted in the lamplight.

Hasdrubal picked a few up to inspect, and satisfied, put them back. "Lock it up, and give me the key. Then fetch me one of your slaves."

"Why?"

"To help me carry it, of course."

Ben Barca led him to the sleeping quarters for the servants. A youngish one stirred at the disturbance. "That one. He'll do"

Ben Barca woke him up, bade him to be silent, and the three went back to his bedroom. "Please be a good lad and help carry this chest to the destination this gentleman requests," he said. The lad picked up the chest, put it on his shoulder, and started down the stairs.

"Thank you for your gracious hospitality, Ben Barca. You owed me much more than you were willing to give, however." Ben Barca began to muster an answer but Hasdrubal's dagger penetrated deep into his throat. He died gagging, but did not wake the rest of the household.

He met the young slave at the door, where the lad was staring at the night watchman. Hasdrubal checked the man and determined that he was in fact quite dead from a massive head wound. "Say nothing, young man, and you will live through the night."

Hasdubal contemplated the pleasure he was beginning to take in killing. Not like his timid fearful effort with the young Francius, who helped him escape from prison and certain crucifixion on Masira. There was an awesome power in the act of killing, in seeing the eyes begging for mercy, then their light fade after the stroke they never understood. He regretted the many deaths that he had ordered, allowing others to feel the pleasure instead of tasting it himself.

At last they reached his poor accommodation. The slave carried the chest inside, and Hasdrubal flipped him a silver coin. "Thanks, you may go home now."

The slave, dumbfounded, looked at the coin and turned to leave. Hasdrubal grabbed him from behind and slit his throat. He was surprised at the amount of blood that gushed forth, and how long it took the boy to quit twitching. He carried the body out and dumped it in a creek that doubled as a sewer behind the building, and cleaned up the blood as best he could.

Slaves were always the first suspects in domestic murders. The authorities would believe the slave stole the chest, killed the master and night watchman, and fled. His body would likely not be found, or if found, not recognized.

Tomorrow, he would head east with a chest of gold to finance a new life somewhere.

CHAPTER 33: ON THE MEANING OF LIFE

The *Europa* sortied from Galle in early evening, with just enough light left to pick her way out to the open sea. It was not Demetrios' preferred time, because the night fell swiftly in the tropics, and there were still several hours before the ship would be clear of the rocks and shoals that lay not far away on either side.

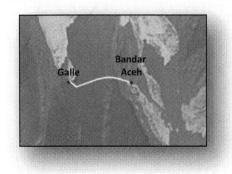

Demetrios put four boats over the side, ten rowers each, to begin the backbreaking job of towing the ship to open water. He posted lookouts with flaring torches on the bow, along with a man sounding for the bottom, periodically calling out the depth. Having made good their escape, there was little point in foolishly running aground in the harbor mouth.

The *Europa* was broad, her round bottom far below the surface. It took half an hour to nurse the ship to a sluggish crawl, the rowers sweating and groaning by torchlight in the tropical evening heat. Fortunately, the work was short-lived, for after about an hour, Demetrios gave the call to cast off the towing lines, and the exhausted men returned to the ship. The mainsail snapped and boomed as it filled overhead, and with full sail, the *Europa* bore down on the swells, the west wind on her stern driving her bow down into each wave. After three weeks in port, it was good to be underway again, especially after the last two days.

In view of the deck force's excellent work in the firefight, Antonius had given them several days off without afternoon training. Which meant, when his men were off, so was Antonius.

It was a splendid day ter be at sea, I can see why sailors like the life. Not another ship in sight anywhere, all alone on the open sea. The wind blew with just enough force to riffle up a few white caps on the dark blue wave tops, and the sky was dotted with just a few scattered clouds. The ship had, as the sailors called it, a "bone in her teeth," a white-cresting bow wave that trailed behind her in a big vee. Looking aft, Antonius could see white wake extending for miles behind her, as the ship leaned slightly into the wind. Stays creaked, somewhere some sailors were talking, and up on the quarterdeck someone shouted a command. Alongside, a pod of dolphins joined in the fun, cavorting in the bow wave, taking turns doing a graceful roll out of the water.

He was so lost in reverie that when Marcia came up beside him to say hello, he was almost startled. "Goodness, Antonius, I didn't mean to make you jump. What, have those dolphins followed us all this way?"

"Just lost in thought, Marcia," he said, turning to smile at her. "I don't think those are the same fish, or they must really like us. Where's your brother?"

The wind rippled her white ankle-length *stola* and she hugged a light wrap tightly about her bare shoulders. "He's not feeling well today. He gets a bit queasy the first day at sea, and he thought he would just stay in our quarters and nap for a while." She shook her long black hair, flowing free in the breeze. "I love wearing my hair loose, Roman-style, instead of done up in an Hanaean bun."

They watched the dolphins for a while, then Marcia cleared her throat a bit. "That was a terrible fight the other night. Quite a show! What are those things you were shooting?"

"*Ballistae*. The crews did very well, considering it was their first time in a real fight. We're sorry, Gaius and I, for not keeping you and your brother informed about what was going on. I hope that didn't catch you two by surprise."

"Captain Demetrios has been keeping us informed. He has been very good, and we usually take dinner with him."

"Good, we have been stuck with Ibrahim, out of necessity. But he can be quite a charming individual, surprisingly."

"Have you had any word on the other ships?"

"No, and not likely to. We are, as you know, going on to your home by ourselves."

"Thank you." She stopped to look over the rail. The dolphins seemed to have tired of their big toy, and were moving off in search of something edible. "My life is very confused right now. Wang Ming is not in my life, and may never be again. I feel free for the first time since I was twelve. But if he is lost, so are those two ships and their people. I can't be happy for that."

"Mmmh... twelve, you say. That is ... very young."

"I thought so, too. We were taken from our homes, when they needed translators and found that we could do nicely. We needed to learn proper court Hanaean, which is different from what we spoke. Like your soldier Latin, and what they speak in Emperor Trajan's court. They wanted people under thirty, because it would be a hard trip. But Latin is dying out in my home town after more than a century, there were only ten of us young enough, and I was the youngest. Ming just... took me, because he wanted me."

"You deserved better."

"Thank you, Antonius. Thank you for listening, and please understand, I can't talk any more about this right now. I am going back to my quarters, but please, you didn't offend me."

She touched his shoulder gently in farewell, but to Antonius, it almost felt like a hot coal. "Glad to help. Listen, yer need ter talk, or anythin', we're in the officer's staterooms. Or here."

"Thank you!" She turned and left.

I think she was about to cry. Mmmh. Don't even be thinkin' those kinder thoughts, soldier, she ain't yer type. Way above yer station.

Ibrahim invited the two Romans to his cabin, for what was becoming a traditional dinner together. Gaius could not help but like the wily old pirate, who despite his background, had an excellent grasp of philosophy. The dinners included some of the best conversations that he had ever had the pleasure of sharing. Even Antonius, though still wary of the man, was warming to his charm and wit, and all three of them now had shared the experience of combat, having fought together to save the ship.

An hour after sunset, they arrived at the cabin. Ibrahim had already lit the oil lamps about the cabin. He had prepared a roast lamb for the night. The dinners were rather predictable: either goat or lamb. The Romans longed for some pork, but had long ago learned that Ibrahim, like most Semitic people, had a strong aversion to that animal, and would starve before eating something he considered unclean.

They seated themselves on the floor, Arab-style, around a blanket with the food in bowls.

"So, Ibrahim," said Gaius, slicing off a piece of mutton, "that was a most generous thing you did, rescuing the wounded and collecting the dead. How does a pirate come to be so scrupulous?"

"Well, for me, death is part of my business, as it is of yours," said Ibrahim, sipping some wine. "You kill for Rome, I kill for myself. But none of us, I think, enjoy it. I have nothing to gain by killing one more person than I must to survive. Do you remember the first man you killed?"

Antonius watched Gaius intently, for Antonius certainly remembered that day.

Gaius' eyes faded as his memory took him back to the event decades past, recounting a story he had never before shared with anyone. *The armorer had reported three swords missing, and the* legatus *was convinced that they lay somewhere in the village around the legion's winter quarters near Vindebona. He had ordered a house-to-house search of all the residences, and I, new to the legion, led a centurion and an eight-man squad, including Antonius, on a search of the village. I knocked at each hut, politely inquired in halting German if we could search their house for contraband military supplies. I phrased the inquiry as a question, though it was not.*

The search had turned up nothing. The last hut was like all the rest, a rude structure of timber. As we approached it, a German emerged from the blanket covering the door. He was big, verging on fat, with dirty, reddish-blond shoulder length hair hanging in tangled strings. His beard and huge mustache were bushy and unkempt with greasy food stains. He crossed his hairy bear-like arms across his chest and stood defiantly in the doorway, icy blue eyes flashing fire. A long German sword hung at his side, stuck scabbardless through a twisted rag that served as a belt.

I began to speak, but the German interrupted. "Aus! Macht dich fort" he ordered, "Get out! Go away!" I took another step toward him, and the man dropped back and drew his sword.

Another subaltern might have dropped back and given the order to the centurion to take the man. But I was young and brash, and full of self-confidence. I drew my own sword and waved the centurion and the milites *back. The two of us circled, both smiling wickedly at each other, sizing each other up: me and the overweight but fierce-looking German.*

I had not intended to harm the man, who probably had just one too many tankards of that foul barley beer. We lunged and parried several times, then I thrust forward with a maneuver called "tickling the ribs," a quick thrust to the side, close to, but not quite touching the ribs. This usually caused the victim to step backwards, off balance and wide open for a stunning blow to the side of the face with the flat of the sword.

But the German didn't feint backwards. Perhaps he lost his balance, or had in mind a countermove. He fell forward across my outstretched sword. Surprised, I immediately drew the sword back, and as I did, I heard a sound like ripping cloth. The German looked up from his hunched-over position in surprise, straightened up and looked stupidly at his stomach. A line of red ran from rib to navel, and as he stared, a green knot of intestines erupted with a wet sloppy sound. The man dropped his sword and put his hands over his guts, trying to stuff them back inside, making mewing noises like a kitten.

"Take him, lordship. Put him down. It's the most merciful thing yer can do fer him now," Antonius hissed. A wound to the stomach was almost invariably fatal, but might take a week to kill, as the victim grew more and more feverish. It was an awful way to die.

A woman peered from the door, watching in horror, while around her ragged skirts clung dirty little children. Damn, did they have to come to the door now to watch this? I swallowed hard and did what I had to do: I buried my sword to the hilt in the man's chest, then wrenched it free. I felt the ribs splinter against the blade.

I will remember the look in the woman's eyes for the rest of my life, as she watched the man sink to his knees, a rivulet of blood staining his beard. The German gasped wetly, pitched over and died at her feet.

They found the missing swords the following day, in the armory, where they had been all along. An accounting error, said the armorer. Just an accounting error. "Yes," said Gaius. "I remember him very well."

They ate in silence, until Ibrahim broke the chill that had settled on the meal. "I fear I touched a nerve, my good Gaius. Please forgive me."

"It's all right. It's not one of my favorite memories," replied Gaius.

Antonius shifted his weight to relieve the pressure on his knees, still eyeing Gaius intently. "If it's the one I'm thinking of, Ibrahim, I was there, too. Gaius took it hard," he said hoarsely. "It should not have turned out that way, but it did."

"It is good to know that even the much-feared Roman soldier does not enjoy killing, either," said Ibrahim, smiling, as he poured them both more wine.

"Like you said, it's part of the job. You do what you have to do, and get it over with. And like you, I don't want to kill one person more than I have to. I don't enjoy it, and I've never met anyone who did," said Gaius.

"I have met a few what did enjoy it, an' they was as big a danger to their messmates as they was to their enemies," added Antonius bitterly, in Latin.

"That first one was a mistake," said Gaius, soberly. "One I wish that I could erase."

"I met a man once who told me he believed that past mistakes could be wiped out," said Ibrahim, sipping his wine.

"Nice trick! How did he propose to do that?" asked Gaius.

Ibrahim related the story. "I told you of the *Astarte*, the ship on which I began my career as a pirate. Just before that event, we were sailing from Caesarea, and a Jew was brought aboard, under Roman military escort. For some reason, he came up to talk to me while I was watching the sea go by, off-duty for an hour. Deckhands were not supposed to mingle with passengers, and he seemed to be well-educated, maybe even upper class. The Roman centurion seemed to give him very respectful treatment."

"So what did yer two talk about?" asked Antonius.

"Many things I didn't understand at the time. I was illiterate then, and also had no Greek, not enough to carry on a conversation. He switched to Aramaic for my benefit."

"Nice of him," agreed Antonius. "What did he want from yer?"

"Nothing, and that was odd. Just… to talk about the meaning of life, and life after death, mistakes, and setting straight the score. Something he called The Way. Of course, at twenty, I didn't think I had done anything wrong yet! My, how that has changed!" Ibrahim laughed. "The foolishness of youth!"

"Anyway, he sought me out every day for a week, until he got off in Myra to take another ship going to Rome. He was, he said, going to see Nero himself, as a citizen, to bring him to his Way – did I mention that he was a citizen?"

The two shook their heads negatively.

"He invited me to come with him to Rome, to help spread something I didn't even understand. I turned him down, but he said, 'May God grant you your greatest wish, young Ibrahim.'" Ibrahim paused to take a sip of wine.

"The next week there was that terrible storm, the one I told you about, when I came to command the *Astarte* as my first ship. He had booked passage out of Myra on a big Alexandrian grain freighter, the *Castor and Pollux,* which was lost in that same storm, foundered a thousand miles off course in Malta. A ship that size foundering feeds the dockyard gossip mill for months. I always wondered if he survived, what he had been trying to tell me, or if his god had in fact granted me my greatest wish. Bear in mind, I don't believe in gods. I lean toward the Epicurean philosophy that we are all just random atoms, dust in the wind, and gone when we are gone. But I never forgot him."

Ibrahim rose to light an oil lamp against the gathering gloom.

"Sounds like one of the stories that we Romans would attribute to *Fortuna,* the goddess of fate. What was this Way he was talking about?" Gaius said.

"He was a follower of a Jewish holy man, Jeshua bar Josef, the one some now call Chrestus." said Ibrahim.

Antonius sputtered, half choking and spraying wine. "Chrestus! Those cannibalistic bastards! You're lucky you didn't end up on his dinner table! Eaters of flesh and blood!"

"Easy, Antonius," said Gaius, refilling Antonius' goblet. "That's a much maligned myth against them. My tutor in Pompeii was a follower of Chrestus, and so were several others of my father's *servi.* That story has to do with a ritual they do, and maybe something with how they explain it. They have a dinner of bread and wine, and believe that this represents the flesh and blood of their holy man. Some *Chresti* will tell you adamantly that it really is, which is how that story got started. My brother and I sneaked a peak at one of their ceremonies one day, and watched... it was bread and wine just the same after they said their magic words as before. They were really a very gentle people, and my father liked them. He bought as many *servi Chresti* as he could, because he said they were a good deal... never lazy, never stole, and all he had to do was give them every seventh day off." Gaius laughed, and poured himself another drink of wine.

"Well, I hope your friend never made it to Rome, Ibrahim," growled Antonius. "Nero did some nasty things to them, un-Roman things. He blamed them for the big fire there thirty or so years ago, and hung them up in his gardens for torches. Women and children, right alongside the men. Brr!" Antonius shivered. "That's not right. Bastard was a perverted butcher. Anyway, many don't believe the story about their being cannibals and all. I knew a few, too, and they seemed right decent folk."

The leg from Taprobane to Bandar Aceh in Sumatra took thirty uneventful days. The ship beat her way ahead of the stiffening monsoon wind, but with no storms other than a few brief squalls. And Marcia and Antonius managed to meet alongside the rail, weather permitting, nearly every afternoon, sometimes alone, sometimes with her brother Marcus or with Gaius, sometimes even Ibrahim.

CHAPTER 34: A TOWN DESTROYED

Dionysius queried the *Asia*'s navigators: "Are you sure this is the right promontory? This area seems deserted." But they checked their charts and calculations, shook their heads, and assured him that this was indeed the harbor mouth, just two miles ahead. But it didn't seem right. They had raised the headland of the port of Galle at daybreak, and now, nearly three hours into daylight, the wooded promontory and beaches were clearly visible, but no fishing boats were yet out to ply the waters for the morning catch.

The *Asia* rounded the promontory an hour later, and sailed in eerie silence into a town destroyed. Smoke hovered in a thick sheet over the water with the morning mist, curling above demolished buildings from the dock all the way up to the center of town. Not a dog barked, not a person hailed the big ship. Dionysius reluctantly gave the order to lower sails and drop anchor. The crew stared over the rail, awestruck at the destruction. Only the cry of birds broke the silence.

Aulus requested Dionysius put ashore an armed landing party, almost in a whisper. He himself donned a military sword, making him a caricature with his portly figure in a tunic. Lucius Parvus and the body guards wore their weapons with greater credibility. Wang Ming insisted on coming along as well, impressively clad in padded Hanaean military equipment, a sword on his left hip.

"No need for you two to go ashore here, sir," said Dionysius deferentially to Ming and Aulus. "My men can handle it alone. There may be some considerable danger here."

"Thank you for your concern, Dionysius. But I fear that one of my ships may have wreaked this mayhem here, and I am responsible," replied Aulus, struggling over the side onto the rope ladder to the boat waiting below, followed by Ming.

"Well, I am coming with you, sir," said Dionysius, buckling his sword. One of the sailors handed him a helmet and shield. "Your *servi* could use some gear. Here! Helmets!" The sailors broke out more helmets from the armory and tossed them to Lucius and his crew.

They landed at the shattered dock, and noted with dismay the Roman bolts still embedded in the wood. "The *Europa!* Your friend Ibrahim did this!" said Aulus, wrenching one of the bolts from the charred wood and tossing it into the water.

Dionysius ordered the sailors into a defensive formation, the best fighters on the outside, with Aulus, Ming and himself in the middle, advancing up a main road leading into the town.

The buildings were gutted by fire, and bodies lay in various postures in the muddy road, others half in and half out of doorways... men, women and children, all dead violently. Flies buzzed noisily about the carnage.

"About three or four days ago, if I can judge by the smell. Bodies decompose quickly in this heat," said Dionysius grimly.

At the head of the hill, the road opened onto a small square. The townspeople had apparently been herded into the square and slaughtered en masse, for hundreds of bodies lay in heaps. Buzzards strutted and quarreled with each other for the remains, beating each other with their wings for the right to feast on a particular carcass. Many of the women had their wraps pulled up over their heads, exposing themselves... rape had accompanied the pillage. The men stared at one young girl, whose hair and dress indicated she might at one time have been quite attractive before death. "Cover her up!" Aulus ordered. A sailor almost tenderly unfolded her saffron *sari* from around her head and lowered it about her torso, covering her nakedness. Her face seemed serene, as though she had welcomed death when it finally came. She probably had.

Around the square, dozens of men's heads were impaled on pikes, their faces frozen in the grimace of the last terrible second of their life, eyes staring at the horrible square. Flies crawled in and out of noses and open mouths. "Take them down! At once! Down!" Aulus was becoming overcome with emotion and horror at the sight of so much wanton death. He had not had any military experience, and nothing in his life had prepared him for this awful sight. He felt violently ill, collapsed on his knees and retched uncontrollably, while Lucius attempted to comfort him. Dionysius remained close, uncomfortable that he might have allied himself with a human being that could cause such slaughter.

The sailors dispersed around the square, lowering the pikes, and shooing away the buzzards with curses and stones. Suddenly one shouted from across the square. "Got a live one here! Come quick!"

An old man sat cross-legged and silent, so still that the sailor had first mistaken him for dead. He cradled an old woman's head in his lap; she was quite dead. The man could have been anywhere from fifty to eighty years old, with white hair and beard almost like snow on his dark brown skin, his thin, almost emaciated body clad only in a loincloth. He finally looked up at the men around him and said something in the local dialect.

One of the sailors translated, not waiting to be asked. "He says if you're here to kill him, to please hurry." Dionysius fished in his pouch for a piece of bread, and took his leather water flask from off his shoulder. "Here," he said, offering them both to the man.

The old man resisted the bread, but not the water. He took the flask and drank thirstily, gagging and choking as he practically inhaled the sweet water, sloshing as much down his chin and brown chest as down his throat. A sailor grabbed the flask, trying to slow him down.

Having slaked his thirst, he took the bread and devoured it. Then he broke into tears, bending over the woman's body and pounding on the packed earth of the square with his fists, repeating the same words over and over.

"Says he's sorry, he's sorry, he'd tried to join her, but it was too hard," said the sailor. "Guess he was planning to die right here with her. Poor bastard. Must be his wife."

Aulus joined the group around the old man. "Ask him what happened," he said, softly, but his florid face displayed his tightly-controlled rage. "Ask him if the *Europa* had anything to do with this!"

The sailor and the old man exchanged words for a few minutes, then the sailor gave the gist of the story. "The king came for the devil ship... sounds like the *Europa*, maybe. He found the ship gone, he slaughtered everyone in the town. The elders had to watch, then he beheaded them, stuck their heads on pikes. This man and his daughter, her husband and grandchildren escaped into a basement. She... his wife... stumbled and fell in the street, and the king's men caught her. He and the rest hid in the shelter, but listened to the whole slaughter. He came out when it was over and found her body, two or three days ago... he's not sure. He sent his family along to another village and stayed here to die. Anyway, I think that is what he said. He speaks a different dialect than I do."

Aulus thought briefly, then asked why they called the *Europa* the "devil ship."

After a few minutes the sailor related more of the events. "The king was marching on the town, something about the *Europa*, but he didn't know what. The southerners do not like northerners, and they were looking for a fight with the king anyway. But they wanted the ship too, and some townspeople and local soldiers tried to take it. They never got close. She was anchored out, and fired big arrows at them... I guess he means the *ballistae*... and set the docks on fire and killed a few people. The local leaders decided to let the ship go. The king arrived the next day with war elephants and his best troops. Didn't take them long to destroy the town."

"So the *Europa* didn't do this?" asked Aulus, hopefully.

"No, at least not all of it," answered the sailor.

Dionysius interjected. "The crew couldn't take a town like this and do this kind of slaughter. Sounds like the king must have got wind of the gold in the ship and come down with his crack troops to seize it. And, if all this happened two or three days ago, he might not be far away. I recommend that we leave quickly."

"Agreed," said Aulus, recovering some of his sense of command. "But first we must do something for the dead. Ask him what funeral rites they do for the dead, our sailors will help put his wife away properly."

"They cremate the dead here," answered the sailor, not waiting to pose the question.

"Tell him we will help, but we must act quickly. Ask him if we could cremate the others *en masse*. We don't have time for individual pyres, but I can't leave these good people for the buzzards and dogs."

The sailor and the old man exchanged more words, and then the sailor said, "He would be most grateful. As for the others, one pyre would be fine."

"Good. Have some of the men help him with his wife's body, and the rest just pile up the dead and start one big fire," said Aulus to Dionysius.

"Yes, sir, but let us leave as soon as the fires are lit. The smoke will be visible for miles, and I don't want to bring the king back. I'll keep some men posted on the outskirts as lookouts, and if the king shows up, we're gone. You can either come with us, or take your chances with him. But I don't want my crew ending up like this," replied Dionysius curtly.

"Fine, Captain. I think I prefer your company to his." Aulus turned to the sailor. "Ask him if he would like to come with us after we take care of his wife. We're going east, and he'll be safe with us. Tell him we are another 'devil ship' like the *Europa*."

The old man's face brightened. "He says he used to sail east of here when he was a young man. He will sail with us."

It took most of the day to collect the dead throughout the town and assemble enough wood to dispose of the bodies. When all the bodies were counted, they had close to two thousand men, woman and children heaped in the square. They waited with the old woman's funeral until they were ready to light both pyres. They poured pitch around the wood to speed the flames, and lit them off. The old man sat cross-legged, expressionless, as the greasy smoke rose up from his wife's pyre and the flames consumed her body. After a few minutes, when it was clear that the fires were going to consume all the bodies, they tapped the man on the shoulder, and he quietly unwound himself, stood up and left with the sailors. As they reached the end of the square and started down the muddy road to the harbor, he turned and waved to his wife. A gust of wind caught the black smoke, which dipped and cavorted in the breeze. Then her pyre collapsed in a shower of sparks, and she was gone in a roaring inferno.

Very faint and far away, but discernible nonetheless, they heard trumpets announcing the return of the king. "Let's get back to the ship, we haven't a moment to lose," said Aulus.

CHAPTER 35: PREDATOR AND PREY

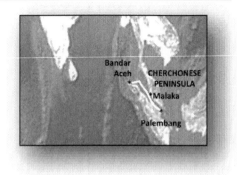

The Big Man had a name, given by his mother at birth, but few knew what it was, and none would dare to call him by that name if they did. From his town of Melaka the Big Man controlled the pirates that preyed on the trade in the Straits of Malacca. He was not physically big, a short, wiry Malay who had spent forty years in these straits. Illiterate and never having seen a map, he knew the straits with an accuracy that could not be captured on paper. The empire of Palembang, ruled by Hindu expatriates, controlled the southern side of the Straits. The Big Man controlled the northern side, depending on intelligence and well-paid informers to keep him posted on interesting targets of opportunity in the Straits. With only small boats at his disposal, he used stealth to make these tips pay off. The hapless victims of his attacks were quickly fed to sharks, or sold as slaves to the many buyers along the Straits. Palembang was not above buying his human cargo, to keep him as far to the north as possible.

The *Europa* made landfall at Bandar Aceh on the northern mouth of the Straits in early September, unaware that the *Asia* was just a few days' sail behind. It was unusual for a *Yavanan* Western vessel to call so far east, so word of such a large ship as the *Europa* spread quickly down the Straits. The Big Man was one of the first to learn of the *Europa*'s arrival in Bandar Aceh.

The *Europa* replenished food and water at Bandar Aceh, then quickly departed on a southeasterly course into the Straits. The *Asia* also docked at Bandar Aceh, arriving just a few days after the *Europa* had departed. The *Asia*'s crew expedited this loading, grumbling at the lack of shore leave, and the ship left after only forty-eight hours in port. It would be fortunate that they had not left earlier.

Demetrios, Ibrahim, Gaius and Antonius were on the bridge with a Hindu pilot and a translator, along with Marcus and Marcia, up for the view, as they coasted slowly under light sail, the lush green jungle slipping by in tropical splendor near to port. "So how long to Palembang, Captain?" asked Marcia.

"About a week," Demetrios replied. "Seven hundred and fifty miles, but it will be slow going. The monsoon winds don't favor this course, and are setting the ship against the northern coastline. However, the pilot assures us that except for the narrows near the eastern mouth, there will be little danger of grounding."

Ibrahim was studying a little bowl marked with eight Nabataean symbols arranged hexagonally around its rim, set on a little table. Filled with water, a little cork bobbed in the middle, pierced by a needle. Antonius looked at the thing curiously. "What's that fer? If yer goin' ter wash yer hands in it, yer goin' ter git stuck by that needle," he asked.

"That's an Arab trick for navigating when you can't see the North Star. The needle points to the north, so you can see we are heading southeast." The cork bobbed and swung with the gentle pitching of the ship, but uncannily pointed generally north most of the time.

"How's it do that?" asked Antonius. But Ibrahim just smiled and said nothing, until Antonius noticed that his iron dagger pulled it off north, and tracked it as he moved it.

"Lodestone! It's a bloody lodestone, that's all it is!" said Antonius.

Ibrahim laughed. "Now you know why Arabs refuse to use nails or metal fittings in their ships! We tell you Romans that mysterious deposits beneath the oceans will draw nails from the ship's timbers and cause them to founder. In fact, metal on the ship can cause the device to point incorrectly, and I spent the last several weeks finding just the right spot to put this to match Polaris. We have been trading along the east coast of Africa as far south as Azania for hundreds of years, and before us, Phoenicians had circumnavigated the African continent, from the Red Sea to Gibraltar and back to Egypt for Pharaoh Necho. We learned to do without Polaris south of the equator, and know of southern stars that serve nearly as well as Polaris in those waters."

Marcia had pressed close against Antonius, her bare shoulder against his bicep as she studied the device. "What is a lodestone?" she asked.

"Lodestones are natural magnets that attract iron. When you stroke a piece of iron with it, like that needle, it gives its spirit to the iron." Antonius stepped back to give her room, clearing his throat with a nervous cough.

"Did I get in your way?" she asked. He seemed uneasy; perhaps she had intruded?

"Er, no, *domina.* Just wanted er... ter give yer more room."

Twin-hulled fishing boats with lateen-rigged sails darted in and out of their transit. "Those boats seem to be awfully close," she noted, to nobody in particular.

Both Demetrios and Ibrahim were eyeing them closely, to make sure that none of them crossed their bow and collided. "They seem maneuverable enough," said Demetrios.

"Keep an eye on them, Captain. They seem very curious," said Ibrahim.

"They probably are," said Gaius. "They have never seen anything like this ship."

"Curious is fine, but keep an eye on them anyway."

The ship continued on the rest of the day. Sunset came abruptly with little twilight, and their wake broke phosphorescent greens and yellows behind them.

The next day, the boats, apparently fisherman, continued their game, like playful dolphins. The fishermen were friendly Malays, offering up prize catches of big fish, squid, and shrimp to the crew for a few coins, and Ibrahim became more comfortable with their presence. After a few days, it was not uncommon for them to clamber, spider-like, up a dropped rope to board the ship underway. No one onboard spoke their language, but they were smiling and cheerful guests who quickly earned disparaging names from the sailors in various languages: "Monkey", "Spider", "Slant Eye", "Boy" and "Fatso". The crew began to look forward to their daily visits for barter in what the Malays must have thought was a floating city. The crew took them below decks and, in the international language of sailors, taught them various dice games, gambling for their catch against tools, articles of clothing or a flagon of wine. The sailors whooped in delight when the Malays, often half-drunk, caught on to the game of chance and actually won something from them.

The pilot was careful what he said to Ibrahim and Demetrios, because he was in the Big Man's pay. And Ibrahim, of all people, should have been aware of what was happening, but he, too, found the Malays cute and harmless. Perhaps because they seemed so much like children.

The rain squall broke from a sullen tropical sky, pouring down like a deluge from a waterfall. From the quarterdeck beneath the big white goose figure, the *Europa*'s bow could not be seen, and the sails hung sodden and slack in the windless but torrential downpour. The pilot, through the Hindu translator, informed Demetrios and Ibrahim that further progress was not possible due to poor visibility and lack of wind. The two concurred; Demetrios obtained a depth reading from the leadsman, then gave the order to drop anchor. The ship lay dead in the water, two miles off-shore, and Demetrios posted watches to ensure that the ship did not drag anchor and run up onto the coastal shoals. He then struck the remaining crew to shelter below, with the tropical rain drumming on the decks above. The port holes were open to ventilate the humid living quarters, dark and fetid with the smell of two hundred wet, sweaty bodies huddled inside against the rain. Through the portholes could be seen grey cascades of water sheeting off the deck.

It was these open portholes that gave the crew their first and only hint that something was amiss. An alert crewman caught a glimpse of a Malay clambering up a rope to the deck, and as he peered outside, he saw dozens more clambering up the sheer sides of the ship. "Hey look, the monkeys want to get in out of the rain, too!" he cried, before a flung knife caught him the mouth. He turned, spouting blood, clawing at the knife which had impaled his tongue to his lower jaw, Shmuel just paces from him. At the same time the above-decks anchor watch dropped through the deck hatch, levering himself down, not bothering to use the ladder. "Secure the hatches! They killed the other watch!" he cried, and two sailors hustled up behind him to secure the open hatch with a timber. "Secure the port holes!" Up and down the main belowdecks area, portholes began banging shut, secured by latches.

The noise in the forward area attracted the attention of Gaius and Antonius in the officers' quarters aft, along with the Hindu pilot, Marcus and Marcia, and they stepped out into the crews' area. It was dark and sailors were fumbling with flint, trying to strike a light in the blackened area. Above their heads could be heard the splash-patter of bare feet running on the rain-slick deck. One by one, oil lamps illuminated the darkness, and Shmuel dispatched men to the armory to break out weapons.

Antonius caught sight of Shmuel bawling orders in the gloom. "We're caught flat-footed!" Shmuel spat, adding a Hebrew curse that Antonius understood perfectly well without knowing a word of Hebrew. "One man down on deck and one wounded below. Malays! They're raiding the ship!" From forward came the hammering sound of wood on wood, as the Malays tried to smash through a hatch.

"We can't stay here! Bastards will burn us out, and burn the ship as well. We've got to get topside. You too, Marcus, Marcia, stay in the middle of us." Antonius turned to Marcus and unobtrusively handed him his dagger, whispering. "If things go badly. Don't let the bastards take her alive." Marcus nodded, but Marcia had overheard and nodded also, full well understanding Antonius' intent. A tinkle of broken glass came from above, aft. "Gods take us, Ibrahim and Demetrios! And the navigators! Topside, in their cabin! Your men got steel yet, Shmuel?" bawled Antonius.

"Got steel, centurion, let's go!"

Ibrahim and Yakov were ready when the Malays, defeated by the locked cabin door, burst through the glass windows that lined the master's cabin. They had heard the tumult throughout the ship, and had taken up swords, exchanging knowing glances. The first Malay through the shattered window met Ibrahim's long steel blade. The weapon whistled, disemboweling the man, and Ibrahim turned to take the second man coming in, who had placed his hand on the window frame to draw himself through. He promptly lost it as Ibrahim's blade took it off cleanly at the wrist. He fell, screaming and streaming blood from the stump of his arm, to splash into the rain-pecked waters pitching restlessly below. Yakov held the port side windows, dispatching several more into the waters below. The Malays relented in their assault on the cabin, and Ibrahim took the break in the action to dispatch the wounded Malay with a thrust through the chest, heaving the man through the window and turning to Yakov. The two men had fought together for so long that they could read each other's thoughts. "Yakov! Forward and get Demetrios and the navigators in here. I'll hold the cabin!"

Yakov nodded and unbolted the cabin door. He nearly swung in instinct at his own sailors clambering up the ladder from the officers' quarters below, but Antonius' bellowed warning "Friendlies coming up!" from belowdecks penetrated his red battle-haze.

Demetrios and the navigators had fortunately shuttered their windows because of the rain. Hustled out by the sailors and Yakov, they crowded into the master's cabin, where the men quickly secured shutters against further raids.

The Nubian archers clambered up the ladders from belowdecks, eager for battle, followed by Gaius and Antonius. They conferred quickly with Ibrahim.

"Gotta break outa here, thank the gods we held this topside space. I don't wanna think about breakin' out from below decks. Let's break out the door there, archers first, an' lay down some covering volleys. Gotta watch our backs out the hatch, though. There's a bunch of 'em up on the quarterdeck above." Antonius spoke softly, quickly.

"Can you get some men up there through the rear windows?" asked Gaius.

"When we make our breakout. Topside bandits be lookin' forward, tryin' ter get the men comin' out the door. Shmuel! Yer got fifteen men in here, and Galosga's men belowdecks. Ten men follow out behind the Nubians, an' stay behind 'em, 'cuz them Nubian arrows ain't too perticular. The last five take down that shutter there, real quiet like, an' when we go out, go topside an' get ready ter go ter work. Galosga's men come up by the bow when we break out an' sweep the decks between us. Have some men relay the command so's we do it all tergether."

"Right!"

"We ain't got too long. They just tryin' ter figure out the best way ter regroup. Any idea how many?"

Ibrahim interjected. "About a hundred, maybe. Knives and swords, maybe slingers. I don't know about bows."

"We need to get the aft *ballistae* under control quickly," said Gaius. "Once we have them, we can keep any other boats from joining in the fun."

"Will do!" Antonius shouted down the hatch into the officers' quarters for the *ballista* crews to get ready. Then Shmuel levered himself up out of the ladder into the crowded main cabin. "Galosga's ready."

"What's the signal?" asked Antonius.

"Just yell Masada."

"Judean bastard!" said Antonius, grinning toothily and slapping him on the back. "Well, let's see if we can do as well as you Jews did." Masada was the name of a mountain fortress where the last of the Jewish rebels had held out for months against three Roman legions. "Ready to go to war?"

"Ready!"

"All right, Abdi, open the doors and let your archer have at 'em. Fire low, get their legs."

The Nubians notched arrows and drew their bows, taking aim at targets yet unseen. Two sailors slipped the timber from the door, swung them open and hit the deck as the first four Nubians let their arrows fly. They knelt down while the four behind them fired and then all eight fanned out through the doors, taking position either side of the door to fire again. Another eight archers filed through the door, and they began to set up a rain of arrows lengthwise down the deck, disciplined and remorseless. Their teeth showed in wicked grins, brilliantly white against their black faces glistening in the rain, as their arrows forced the Malays into a disorganized rout.

Back in the master's cabin, Shmuel assembled his men. "Watch your backs!" He slapped each one on the chest, "One, two, three..." he counted. "Remember your number! Odd men turn and cover aft. Even men form up and get ready to advance." He turned to the men by the window. "When they go out front, you go up. Watch going over the top! Ready?"

The men nodded.

Then Shmuel yelled "Masada!" down the hatchway to the lower deck to Galosga's crew far forward. Gaius and Antonius had buckled on their battle gear, and took position aft of the men erupting out through the door. Antonius and Gaius drew swords, slapped each other's steel helmet with the pommel, and Gaius said, almost as a prayer, "*Fortuna favet portuna!*"

The Malay pirates were not used to ships giving organized resistance. Most ships they raided were small merchants with a few armed men of mediocre skills. When the doors had first opened, they had expected the crew to emerge begging for mercy, perhaps offering money for their lives. They had not expected the volley of arrows from sixteen tall black Nubians. Their disciplined firepower had felled a dozen Malays before the pirates could retreat. The pirates on the quarterdeck, above and behind them, could have dropped down and engaged them, but they were too slow and indecisive. By the time the first one thought to do so, he was too late... he dropped into Shmuel's swordsmen emerging from the door, half of whom had turned to receive him. And the remainder never saw the second group of sailors clambering over the aft railing, not until the first Malay fell forward clutching a sword point erupting from the center of his chest. The quarterdeck was cleared, and forward, Galosga's men poured up out of the forward hatch. He had timed his outbreak a few seconds after the command, so the Malays were caught with their attention focused aft. And the archers kept up their fire, carefully aiming at the midships area to avoid casualties to their own. They picked off those who tried to escape the slaughter on deck by climbing into the rigging... those hapless Malays tumbled back down, their bodies studded with arrows.

As if someone had turned off a faucet, the rain stopped suddenly and the sun came out, beating down hotly on a deck running red with blood.

The *ballista* crews manned their weapons, training them outboard to take any boat in range under fire, manned or unmanned, while the disciplined sailors hewed through the confused mass clustered amidships. Some escaped, leaping overside into the water, but the Nubian archers, clustered on the rail, picked off many of them as they tried to swim to safety. There would be few survivors.

The Big Man watched from his boat. He could hear the cries of his men dying on the deck, could see their lifeless bodies tossed overside to the sharks. Although he was a quarter mile from the ship, bolts from the *ballistae* hissed wickedly into the water just yards from his boat. He grimly ordered his boat out of action, and was standing out of danger when he felt something strike him hard in the back, knocking him forward.. He tried to turn in his seat but could not; he looked down and saw two feet of bloody bolt protruding from his chest, the tip buried in the splintered wood of his boat.

It was the last thing he saw.

CHAPTER 36: RENDEZVOUS AND ARRIVAL

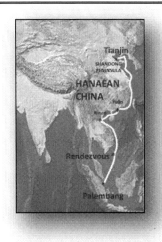

The remainder of the trip to Palembang was uneventful. Word of the *Europa's* routing of the pirates and the death of the Big Man spread quickly along both coasts of the strait, and other would-be pirates were content to watch the big *Yavanan* western ship drift slowly by.

The crew took care of their dead, burying them at sea according to each one's custom. Antonius and other medics on board cared for the wounded. Most of the wounds were sword cuts to an arm or leg; one man had a Nubian arrow lodged in his shoulder, and one had a leg broken in a leap from the quarterdeck. Overall five died and twelve were wounded seriously enough to be out of action for a while. Not bad, considering the intensity of the fight. Marcia sought Antonius out after he finished tending the wounded. "Your dagger. Thank you," she said, handing him the weapon hilt-first.

"Welcome and glad it wasn't needed," he answered, slipping it back into the empty sheath on his waist. "Does Marcus have a dagger?"

"Yes, he does, and he will keep it more handy in the future. Trouble comes quickly."

"He know how ter use it well? I kin teach him some."

"It would be good idea. Anyway, thank you. I must go now."

Antonius watched her walk off. She knew exactly what he had meant, that Marcus should kill her rather than let her fall into the hands of the Malay bandits. And she accepted that quite calmly and without argument. Courageous lass, that one.

The pilot saw no need to tell them that he had been in the pay of the Big Man. He went about his duties quietly, and the ship reached Palembang mid-morning of the following day.

Lateen-rigged fishing boats and lighters darted nimbly in and out of the harbor, the wide delta of a river the pilot said was called Musi. *Europa* slipped upriver under light sail as far as it was prudent, then dropped anchor.

Now just a few days behind the *Europa,* the *Asia* encountered the debris of the battle, bodies bobbing on the water, boats with bolts impaled in their hull.

"Seems like the 'devil ship' has been at it again. I wonder what annoyed them here?" noted Dionysius.

"Nothing that will annoy them, or us, again, I suspect. My cousin seems to be good at his work," said Aulus.

Wang Ming came up to join them. "Big fight! You friend ship?"

He had spent the past several months improving his Latin to the point that he preferred discussions without translators to help him out. He still had no concept of grammar, but he could now be understood, even if it sounded like baby-talk.

"Roman bolt in that little boat there. Looks like they tried to swarm their way onboard."

"Hmm," said Ming.

Dionysius had experimented with *Asia's* sails, using the brails to raise the sail to the yardarm on the lee side, lowering that side of the yardarm at an angle, improvising a lateen sail modeled after those used by the ubiquitous native dhows. That rig allowed him to sail much closer into the wind than he could square-rigged. It was a little frightening to the crew at first, not to mention to Dionysius and Aulus themselves, with the hull heeled hard over to leeward, the rail just five or so feet above the rushing water. Unnerving as it was, the ship didn't capsize, and it sailed considerably faster, maybe fast enough to catch up with the *Europa.*

The *Asia* docked in Palembang still a few days behind their quarry. The big ships were attracting considerable attention. Ming's language was common here, and he located an Hanaean pilot to take the ship to the southernmost Hanaean prefecture of Jiaozhi, in a land the locals called Nam Viet. The translators Pontus, Marcellus and Titus were happy to have some work to do, besides translating for Ming.

The *Europa,* ahead of them, had embarked its own Hanaean pilot in Palembang, with the help of Marcus and Marcia. The pilot consulted a scroll of strips of bamboo marked with the chicken-scratch Hanaean script, with Marcus and Marcia translating. The scroll contained sailing directions, sending them northeast until the constellation *Zhuwang* was directly overhead, then north-northwest to landfall, also at Jiaozhi. The Alexandrian navigators determined that *Zhuwang* was Taurus, and watched with interest as the pilot laid out a course on a detailed map of southeast Asia. They estimated the trip to take about ten to twelve days, maybe less depending on winds. Marcus and Marcia now stood four hour watches on the bridge, translating whenever the pilot was on duty. For the first time in months, they encountered many ships at sea, some half or more the size of *Europa,* heading north or south. Every few hours another sail emerged on the horizon, and if southbound usually turned out to be the big Hanaean ships which Marcus told them were called *chuan.* The *Europa* took the southbound freighters portside, sometimes close enough to wave and call out to their crews lining their rails to see the big foreign ship.

Antonius had seen little of Marcia since leaving Palembang due to her new responsibilities as translator for the pilot. Friendship with a woman was a wholly new concept to him. Friends were his messmates, officers like Gaius who could treat him as an equal, even Ibrahim, toward whom he was developing some affection. His mother had died when he was young and there were no sisters in his family. He liked Marcia's company, and admired her intellect, the only woman who had ever captured his interest in that area. And now her courage. But he was totally in the dark how to deal with her. Pondering these thoughts, he was jarred out of his reverie as she came up to join him at the rail to watch the brilliant blue sea slip by.

"Antonius Aristides, my duties have intruded on our talks! I have hardly seen you since Palembang," she said with a smile.

"Umh, me, too, been busy training the deck crews again, *domina.* Didn't mean ter avoid yer."

"Good, because I really enjoy our talks. I am hardly patrician, you know. I would prefer you call me Marcia."

"Well, uh, Marcia, jus' bein' polite an' all. Din't want to be uppity an' insult yer."

"I don't think you could insult me. But you are nervous. Yer back ter talkin' soldier's Latin." She gave a good rendition of his tortured grammar and pronunciation which made him laugh, breaking the tension.

"Damn all, not bad … Marcia. Not bad at all! Yer've been practicing."

"Jes' thinkin' how yer would've said this, is all… sir! Yer need ter teach me more profanity. Gaius thinks I swear like from a Plautus play." She laughed and smiled brightly.

Having lost all his unease, Antonius replied with a big grin, "That's probably about right. Yer people bin outer touch almost that long. But profanity lesson later, you teach me Hanaean."

"Are you sure, Antonius?"

"Sure, go ahead, try me."

"Well, let me start…" she rested her chin on her hands, thinking where to begin. "You know Latin and Greek."

"And some German, and my Aramaic is gettin' better."

"All right, forget all of them. Hanaean –*Han-yu* as we call it – is completely different. You know about grammar, gender, cases, tenses… so forget about them."

"How do you tell what you are talking about?" asked Antonius, puzzled.

"Word order. You know you can say '*canis homem mandet,*' '*mandet homem canis,*' or any other arrangement you like, and you always know that the dog is biting the man. Because of the grammar endings. In *han-yu*, it must always be 'dog bite man,' in that order, because if you change the order, you change who is biting whom. If you say 'bite dog man,' it means that the bite follows the man!" she laughed.

"Good with that, not too hard. Go ahead."

"Now *han-yu* has very short words, and only a few of them, so words have several meanings, and we use tones to tell them apart. Here is a phrase my mother taught me as a little girl, to learn to use them correctly. '*Mama qí mǎ. Mǎ màn. Mama mà mǎ.*' It means. 'Mother rode a horse. The horse was slow. Mama scolded the horse.' *Ma* uses three different tones for Mother, horse and slow. Try it! '*Mama qí mǎ. Mǎ màn. Mama mà mǎ,*'" she said very slowly.

Antonius took a breath and tried to repeat it. "Mamashima... mamamamama... ma, I think. I hope."

Marcia giggled. "We'll have to work on this some more." She repeated the phrase, with Antonius struggling to hear the subtle differences in pitch, then ending with about the same result. But after about fifteen minutes, Antonius got close to the right tones.

"That's great, you catch on fast!" She touched his shoulder, and for a moment her hand rested there, and he, for a change, did not pull away, savoring the intimate coolness of her touch.

Just then Gaius strode up to them. "Hate to interrupt your conversation, but Antonius, we need you aft. There's a sail behind us, and it might be one of our ships."

"Right. Thank you, Marcia, I really enjoyed it. Tomorrow, if yer can put up with me."

"*Shi shi,*" she replied. "That is 'Thank you' in *han-yu*. And I can always put up with you, Antonius."

But Antonius caught a glimmer of concern on her face. *If that is the* Asia *with Wang Ming on board...*

Antonius and Gaius strode aft to the quarterdeck, where Demetrios and Ibrahim were shielding their eyes against the sun. On the horizon, a tiny white dot bobbed, several miles aft.

"What makes yer think that white dot's not one of the *chuan* junks?" asked Antonius.

"Because it is white. Most of the junks' sails have been yellowish or even dark. We have the only white sails in this whole ocean, though ours are getting a bit grey after all the wear and tear," replied Demetrios.

"Hmm," thought Gaius, one foot on a bollard. "How long before they close with us?"

"Hard to tell. If he can get a knot or two of speed on us, five or ten hours."

"Any chance that ship could be hostile, still under Hadrubal?"

Ibrahim answered, "Hasdrubal wouldn't have made such a difficult journey into the unknown. His plan was to go to Parthia, sell the ships, and hand over the gold while keeping a good share of it for himself. It would make no sense for him to go east." He continued with a chuckle, "He's too damned lazy and greedy to do that!"

"What do you think, Demetrios?" asked Gaius.

"I agree, sir. These past few months have been the hardest sailing of my life, and a few times I wasn't sure we'd make it," answered the captain.

"Antonius?"

"Agreed, sir. If it's one of the Senator's ships, I would bet it's in his hands."

"All right, we have a consensus. Antonius, break out the *ballista* crews, but don't load any bolts until I order it. Even if it is Aulus Aemilius, he may be spoiling for a fight with Ibrahim. Demetrios, hoist the Galba house flag, so that he can see we are flying his colors. And ready a small boat to take us over as he draws near. I would like to parley face-to-face with him, or with whoever is onboard, before he gets in firing range."

On the *Asia*, Dionysius and Aulus also had spotted the white sail on the horizon ahead of them, and came to the same conclusion. They could just make out the triangular topsail now.

"That confirms it is *Europa*. Or a very lost Roman freighter!" said Dionysius.

"Agreed, skipper. What do you make of the situation?" asked Aulus.

"I suspect your cousin has regained control of the ship. The dockyard workers in Palembang confirmed there were two Romans and several Hanaeans on board. But also an Arab. They seem to be enroute to *Ch'in*."

Wang Ming joined them. "You ship? Bright white sail," he said.

"My ship, almost certainly. Top sail triangle," said Aulus, making a triangle with his hands. He had learned to speak slowly and in simple words to Ming. "We wonder if we fight when close."

"Prepare fight now, not need later, good," said Ming.

"That's good advice. Ready the *ballista* crews, and fire a few practice rounds, captain. We haven't used them at all, and *Europa's* crew appears to be pretty proficient."

On the *Europa*, they were surprised at the speed which the white dot closed the gap. In the space of two hours, the ship was just two miles astern, close enough for them to make out the rig of the sails. The square *artemon* foresail billowed out ahead, but the other two sails were rigged lateen style, and the ship sailed heeled over at sharp angle, white water curling under her bow. The *Asia* had three or more knots on them.

"I think we had better lower the small boat now, the rendezvous is going to be sooner than we think. Antonius, you stay on board in case there is a fight. Demetrios, you come with me. Ibrahim, you have the ship, and if you try to run off with *Europa* again, I'll hunt you down like a dog and feed you to the pigs." But Gaius was smiling as he said it… if he didn't trust Ibrahim, he would have brought him with him.

"Look, he is breaking the Galba flag also. I think he has seen our signal," said Demetrios.

"Good. Skipper, you still have the code books Aulus had made up when we started?"

"Aye, sir!"

"Can we tell them we are coming dead in the water and putting a boat over to come to them, or words to that effect?"

"Yes, sir!"

"Signal in the air then, and join me in the small boat with rowers!" Gaius was excited and looking forward to reuniting with his cousin.

"Signal in the air from *Europa*, sir. She is coming dead in the water and putting a boat over to us," cried Dionysius on *Asia*, looking up from the code scroll. *"Cybernetes*, take in some sail and slow down, be ready to come dead in the water when their boat is about a hundred yards off."

"Amazing. *Fortuna* has beamed her smile on us today, bringing our two ships to within a few miles of each other on a brilliantly clear day, in a gigantic expanse of ocean! On a cloudy day, we could have sailed past each other and not seem them. Send a reply that we are ready to receive them."

A few hours later, Gaius and Demetrios were relaxing in the master's cabin with Aulus and Dionysius, along with Wang Ming, having recounted their respective adventures. By no small coincidence, they had both chosen Jiaozhi as there next destination, the normal point of entry for foreign vessels into Hanaean waters.

"So the *Africa* got to go home early?" smiled Gaius, leaning back on his chair, hands behind his head.

"Yes. Hopefully we may break even, despite your ransom. I still can't believe you not only bought off that pirate, but you sound as if you actually like him," said Aulus quizzically.

"He would have been cheap at twice the price, considering he had the ship, the crew, and the gold and silver. And yes, he is actually a likable, interesting fellow. I hope you will have the chance to meet him when we dock at Jiaozhi."

"I'll have to think about it. What are his plans after that?"

"Leaving us, I guess… we haven't talked about it much."

"What is he going to do, set up another banditry and hijacking ring here in Asia?"

"He says he is out of that business. He wants to go back to shepherding, what he did as a boy in Arabia." Gaius smiled at the incongruity, but he did believe the old man was at least half serious. "He is in his sixties, and I think he is getting tired. And eventually, in this business, someone double-crosses you. The incident with Hasdrubal weighed on him a lot, even though he saw it coming."

"Well, that's one bastard we won't be seeing anymore. Feeding crows on a cross in Masira. I hope they don't puke eating rotten meat like him."

"Oh, I forgot to mention… that was Ibrahim's doing," said Gaius, slapping his thigh.

"How's that?"

"He arranged for one of his minions to be conveniently left afloat near there, with a story about a shipwreck and a hijacked flotilla heading north. He set that up a long time in advance, and planted evidence in the master's cabin in *Asia*. There, I guess," he said, pointing to a patchwork repair over where the Roman marines had pried up the floorboards.

"My god, that is brilliant! And that was about what happened! But why?"

"He expected Hasdrubal to double-cross him. He figured that if he did, there was only one place for him to go, and he had to go by Masira to get there. From what you related, it worked brilliantly."

"Well, I don't care for his line of work, but I have to admire the way his mind works. Amazing." Turning to Wang Ming, he said, "So Ming, this is our entry into your country. What do we have to do?"

"Inspection. No weapons, not allowed. *Ballista* take apart, put in box with swords. I put Emperor He seal on box. I seal money chests also, so no pilfer. They inspect everything else, any weapons they find they take. Then we get coastal pilot, go home."

"Sounds good. Well, Gaius my cousin, I am sending you back before it gets dark, along with a boatswain to help you rig the sails lateen-style. See you in a few days!"

Wang Ming interrupted, his face darkening slightly. "Woman Si Huar, I come boat, take her back ship."

"Sure, you must mean Marcia Lucia. Yes, of course, she is your concubine."

As the *Europa's* crew watched the boat return from the Asia, Marcia came back on deck beside Antonius. She had changed from the ankle-length white tunic she had worn earlier to an orange silk Hanaean robe, bound by a wide red sash. Her long black hair, which had been free to blow in the wind, was now done up in a tight bun, pinned firmly in place. She stood primly, hands on the rail, and said not a word, her eyes, now cold, staring off in the distance.

Antonius waited for her to speak, but for a long time she said nothing. Finally, she spoke, "I want to thank you, Antonius…," her voice choked a bit. "I have truly enjoyed your company and I will treasure our long foolish talks for as long as I live."

"Why, sure," answered Antonius. "But… yer just changing ships to be with Wang Ming. When we get to Luoyang, maybe we can meet to talk from time to time there."

"Yes, maybe." But Antonius knew from her voice that she did not think this likely. More silence. "You have been a true friend, and you will be a great gift to some woman someday… if you can stop wasting your time on cheap *lupae* whores." She smiled, but her blue eyes were brimming with tears.

Antonius wanted to hold her, to take away whatever hurt she was feeling, but he did not. "Tell Wang Ming ter take good care of you, or he can answer ter me! Remember, *Fortuna* favors the bold ones."

"Boldness is denied me… I have to go now, my noble Antonius Aristides." And she went back to her cabin, to await the inevitable.

Gaius and Demetrios clambered up the rope ladder lowered down to the boat, followed by Wang Ming. Gaius noted the concern in Antonius' face and went to stand beside him. Marcia came out of her cabin, accompanied by Marcus, also clad in Hanaean robes. Marcia went to Wang Ming without a word, head bowed, as submissive to him as when Antonius had first met them in Alexandria. Antonius wanted to strangle the arrogant bastard, but this was not his affair. Marcus went to stand on the other side of him, hissing "Please, say nothing!"

Wang Ming, grim-faced, spoke a few angry-sounding words to Marcia, who kept her eyes downcast to the deck. She turned without a word and clambered very awkwardly down the rope ladders until the sailors could guide her into the craft. Then Wang Ming left without a word and descended into the boat with her. The sailors pushed off, took oars, and they were on their way back to the *Asia*.

Antonius sadly watched the boat grow smaller. *Damn waste of a good woman on that bastard!*

A few days later, *Europa* and *Asia* docked in Rinan in Jiaozhi. Aulus and Wang Ming came aboard to seal the containers holding the stowed heavy weapons and money. Then the local magistrates inspected the ship, accompanied by Wang Ming, but did not touch the boxes with the court seal.

After the magistrates had taken care of everything, Marcus took Marcia's chest of belongings over to the *Asia* with Wang Ming. Aulus, Gaius and Antonius assembled in the master's cabin with Demetrios, Ibrahim having already gone ashore. Antonius did not wait for the proprieties; he asked Aulus immediately, "How is Marcia?"

"I am sorry. She has stayed in her cabin with Ming since she came aboard. I haven't seen her," answered Aulus.

Antonius grunted, then half-listened as Gaius and Aulus discussed various details of the upcoming leg. As they were breaking up, Marcus returned.

"How is she?" asked Antonius.

"I didn't see her," answered Marcus, his face angry. "Ming told me to leave the chest by the cabin door, the sailors would bring it in."

Ibrahim did not disembark the *Europa*, but continued on to Tianjin, saying conditions were better for shepherding further north. Gaius and Antonius were not displeased, and continued to let him use the spacious master's cabin.

For a month, they coasted easily along the Hanaean coastline, stopping briefly at Panyu and other smaller ports. Antonius had continued language lessons with Marcus, now the ship's only translator. The subject of Wang Ming was the topic of their first get-together.

"He's a pig. I said it once, and I'll say it again," said Marcus bitterly, spitting into the water overside.

"Can't she leave him?" asked Antonius.

"No more than a slave can leave her master. It's about the same. All the responsibilities of a wife, none of the benefits."

"I hate ter see her have ter live like that."

"As do I. But there's nothing to be done. Let's talk about something else."

So they changed the subject, discussing *han-yu,* the Hanaean court and its protocols, Luoyang and his home in Liqian. The subject of Marcia and Wang Ming never came up again.

Finally, the ships rounded the Shandong Peninsula to dock at Tianjin on the mouth of the Hwang He River.

CHAPTER 37: PORT CALL IN TIANJIN

It was a cold drizzly October day, wrapped in fog that condensed on the ship's rigging and dripped onto the deck. Dionysius had gone below after the last line went over, eager to get out of the chill damp, but Aulus remained on deck, peering down over the rail to catch his first glimpse of this strange new land, though he could barely see the bow from the quarterdeck. *I am very much the stranger here, in a way I have never felt before.* The waterfront was quiet, except for the restless slapping of the waves between the hull and the dark wood pilings… no more ships would be coming and going in this visibility, and the coolie stevedores preferred being inside near a meager fire.

Aulus shivered, then realized how long it had been since he had been cold…underway nine months across nine thousand miles of ocean, from the deserts of southern Egypt through the tropics off India to Palembang, and before that, two years shuttling between Alexandria and Myos Hormos with the fleet under construction. He hadn't missed the cold, he decided, wrapping his cloak about himself as he turned to go back inside to the meeting in the master's cabin.

The two captains Dionysius and Demetrios, Gaius, Antonius, and his newly-minted freedman and financial manager Lucius Parvus, were waiting inside, along with Wang Ming and four of the translators, Marcus, Marcellus Albus, Titus Porcius and Pontus Valens. Marcia was conspicuously absent. Aulus laid out their instructions.

"Fill up *Asia* and *Europa* here in Tianjin with as many Hanaean goods as the ships can carry, and use that excellent Hanaean iron as ballast. You can carry tons of it without taking up cargo space. Save about ten thousand *sesterces* in gold and silver for the return leg, in case you need repairs or have to bribe your way out of some port.

"I, Gaius, Antonius, Ming, Marcia and Marcus will depart for Luoyang by riverboat to conduct the diplomatic mission. Marcellus Albus, Titus Porcius and Pontus Valens will remain here as your translators, and Lucius Parvus, you will be in charge until our return. Wait for us until the Ides of April, no later. If we are not back, sail without us for Muziris, for the fall monsoon to Eudaemon Arabia. We will make our way back by Hanaean ship. If you have any of the reserve money left when you arrive, pick up as much frankincense as you can there. It is as cheap as dirt, doesn't take much space, and brings a huge profit in Rome. Marcus and Marcia will be with us in Luoyang, but the other translators will remain here. There is some sort of postal system we may be able to use here, and if we can, I will be in touch."

Lucius Parvus signed over to Dionysius and Demetrios several tons of gold and silver in sealed chests, worth ten million *sesterces*, for trading.

"If you buy wisely, you should be able to get back tenfold that amount when your goods hit the markets in Alexandria," said Aulus, smiling. "Now onto the most important in-port briefing I have ever given you. A mistake on your part in following these instructions could result in the ships, funds and goods being seized, and the crew possibly executed or sold as slaves, including the captains. Do I have your attention?"

Asia's translator Titus Porcius brought out some Hanaean documents, two on paper with an elaborate seal, and the rest on parallel strips of bamboo, bound together at the top and bottom of each strip and rolled up like a scroll. All were written vertically in the Hanaean script.

The paper documents bore the Hanaean emperor's personal red stamp. Titus translated them aloud to the group: the documents identified them as guests in *Ch'in* at the Emperor's personal invitation and under his protection, authorized to conduct business in compliance with Hanaean laws and customs. Each captain got a copy.

Aulus warned the captains: "Make sure that you keep these secure, and make sure that your watch officers know where to find them if there are any problems with the authorities. These carry the full authority of Emperor He. Use them only if there appears to be trouble brewing with local authorities. Consult your translators. They will tell you when it may be necessary to show these papers and to whom.

"The bamboo strip documents are routine documents that authorize you to buy and sell goods, and exchange money as necessary. Local merchants will exchange silver and gold coins by weight for Chinese currency, if you show them this authorization. You can't use our currency here to purchase anything."

Titus held up a long stack of copper coins, strung together through a square hole in the middle. "This is their small currency. They call it something that sounds like 'cash, about half a Roman penny each. Any silver coin, whether it is a shekel, *denarius* or *drachma,* will be exchanged for a thousand of these, give or take a little for weight. Gold coins will be exchanged for twenty-five of their silver coins, again by weight. Make sure the crews use only local coins while they are in port."

The final two documents stated that there were sealed chests exempt from inspection by the Emperor's orders.

Titus continued: "These sealed chests contain your weapons and *ballistae* parts. You are not to break the seal or open them until you are clear of Hanaean waters on the way back to Palembang. If they are found open, you will be in serious trouble. Perhaps fatal trouble that even the first document can't get you out of.

Finally, Titus cautioned the captains: "Make sure your crews understand that order is paramount in this society. Fights, brawls, arguments with locals, and beating up prostitutes will not be tolerated. You are barbarians to them, and your lives are very cheap. Be polite!"

At the conclusion of the in-port brief, Aulus, Gaius, Antonius and Marcus departed for the inn at which they were staying, while Ming departed for the governor's residence where he was staying with Marcia.

Antonius asked, "What happened to Marcia? Shouldn't she have been at the meeting?"

Aulus replied, "Ming said she was not feeling well today. But frankly, I only saw her once or twice in passing, and she would not talk, except a polite hello."

Marcus added "She didn't even get a chance to say goodbye to me, her own brother, when he took her. That bastard has her thoroughly under his thumb."

The four concentrated on ascending the steeply inclined road that led up a hill away from the dockyard. The portly Aulus was getting winded, and the conversation lagged. Fortunately, their baggage had been delivered earlier.

After about half an hour, they reached the inn that Ming had reserved for them. Grey granite walls on the first floor, highly finished, wrapped all around with a dark wood porch, and the black timbers of the wood framed second floor gave it an air of elegant austerity. Its odd-shaped curving tiled red roof dripped foggy condensate. The whole structure seemed to have grown from the mountainside.

Marcus went inside to locate the innkeeper. They emerged together, and the smiling innkeeper clasped his hands in front of him inside the sleeves of his dark grey jumper, smiled broadly and bowed, saying something in *han-yu*. Marcus said, "He is pleased to have such honored guests grace his humble inn."

Aulus returned the innkeeper's smile with a rendition of the Hanaean salute and a respectful head nod, and asked Marcus to thank the innkeeper for his gracious hospitality. Another torrent of *han-yu*, and the innkeeper waved them to enter and led the way. Inside the first floor was a sitting area with folding dividers, some plain white and others painted with elaborate scenes. He motioned to the group to sit, left, and returned with a tray of cups and a bottle. He poured each of them a cup of white wine.

"You have never tasted anything like this, sir," said Marcus to the group. "This wine is called *mijiu*, made from rice. You will find it quite delightful."

They each held their cups up to the innkeeper in a toast. He again smiled and bowed, seeming quite flustered at the attention he was getting, and left them to their drinks.

"Innkeepers do not usually attract such attention from high-ranking guests, unless something goes wrong," said Marcus. "He is quite enjoying himself."

The wine was clear with a clean aftertaste, quite unlike any white wine made from grapes. They finished their drinks and Marcus escorted them upstairs to explain their accommodations.

Each man had a single spacious room on the second floor. Huge waxed paper windows admitted light but kept out the weather. Thick draperies could be drawn across them if the weather was cold, or they could be folded back and the windows rotated open to admit the breeze on warm days. Directly below the window was a massive bed, built into the floor.

"This is a *kang*, which you will find pleasant on cold nights. This bed is heated with a flue, and the ceramic face gives off heat for the entire room. You will find it most comfortable," said Marcus.

On a small table, a washbasin and a ceramic jar was provided for washing. Behind a folding screen was a toilet with indoor plumbing. A large cabinet, complete with carved dragons cavorting along its sides and top, provided storage for their clothing. Their personal chests were on the floor in each room. It was, in all, the most stunning accommodations they had ever seen, but with the theme of elegant austerity that had marked the outside of the building.

Antonius was impressed. "Hmm, maybe we are the barbarians they think we are. These are nice quarters!"

Marcus smiled. "Dinner's at the twelfth hour. Give yourself time to freshen up. The bath is on the first floor to the back, and keep your hands off the girls! They are there to give massages and wash your back, not service your private parts!"

CHAPTER 38: FELLOW COUNTRYMAN

No one in Tianjin was more fascinated by the two big western ships than Ma. His name meant "horse," given to him by the Hanaeans because of his size and strength, and because it was as close as they could come to his real name, Musa. But that was a name he used only with the few countrymen from Arabia who washed ashore in this faraway port from time to time. Perhaps five that he could remember, in the twenty years that he had lived here.

The ships were clearly Roman, with their triangular topsail, but twice as big as any such ship he could remember from his youth, comparable to the larger Hanaean *chuan*, and thousands of miles from their home waters.

Ma hailed the crewmen in Aramaic as they came off the ship. They were glad to find someone with whom they could talk, though his speaking skills in his birth language were rusty from disuse. Musa introduced them to good bars, eateries, and the better brothels, to Hanaean rice wine, and to Tianjin's unfamiliar, but very good foods. The sailors, in turn, told him about the adventures of the *Asia* and *Europa*, the great pirate captain Ibrahim bin Yusuf, and his unlikely alliance with the Romans Lucullus and Aristides.

So it came as no surprise that in a few days, Ibrahim and Yakov visited Ma's boatbuilding shop. "Hello, brother, art thou well?" Ibrahim inquired in Aramaic.

"Quite well! I am Musa bin Ishmael, and thou art Ibrahim bin Yusuf, I presume?"

"I am he, and this is my trustworthy assistant Yakov. Our crewmen have been quite pleased to find someone here with whom they can talk, and to guide them to good places."

"It has been a pleasure. Thou hadst quite the adventures, I hear, in getting here."

"More than a few."

Musa took off his work smock and put away his tools, stepping back from the boat he was constructing.

"Wouldst thou two do me the honor of joining my family for lunch?"

"I would be most honored," replied Ibrahim.

The two ducked under a doorway screened by a cloth blanket, into the living quarters at the end of the boat shop. A woman of about thirty beamed a smile at his entry. They exchanged some words in *han-yu*, then Musa made introductions. "This is my wife Mei Ling, and my children Wo Fan, Han Ju and Kuei Ling." The boys ranged from eight to about fifteen years old.

Mei Ling brought bowls of rice, some soup and bottles of warm rice wine. He picked up the chopsticks and demonstrated how to use them. "They are tricky at first, but you either learn to use them or eat with your hands."

Ibrahim clumsily tried to follow Musa's demonstration, and eventually managed to get some rice into his mouth without getting any on his robe.

"So how did you come to wash up on this foreign shore so far from home?"

"Well, depending on whether you ask me or the captain, I walked off, or was thrown off, a freighter in Palembang twenty years ago, after I questioned too many of his orders. I got press-ganged onto an Hanaean ship going north, and wound up here. After a while as deckhand, I decided to try my carpentry skills in this boat shop. I build boats the Hanaeans call *sampan*, "three boards." That pretty much describes the construction. They come in all sizes, from ten foot poleboats to seventy footers with *chuan*-rigged sails. The locals like my work."

"How did you come to be married?" asked Ibrahim.

"I frequented the brothels. Mei Ling had the misfortune to be the youngest daughter in a large family, and they had sold her to a whoremonger at a very young age. I always treated her nicely, I became one of her 'specials,' and after I set up shop, I got the brothel master to sell her to me. It's been a good life for us, for her especially; most of her friends did not end up so well," he smiled, obviously content with his life. "So what are your plans?"

"I want to be a shepherd," answered Ibrahim.

Musa spewed wine as he choked uncontrollably in mid-swig. "Sorry! I must have misunderstood... a shepherd?"

"A shepherd. What I did as a boy."

"From what I understand, you are one of the richest, most successful pirate captains in three oceans, and you want to be a shepherd?"

"I do."

Ibrahim explained his disgust at his latest double-cross by Hasdrubal, and his desire to settle down and to finish his life the way Musa lived with Mei Ling, raising sheep and children. This path had been closed to him all his life.

"Well," said Musa, "I can understand why you would do that, but there is no money or status in sheep-herding."

"The Romans paid me a ransom in exchange for seeing them to their destination, so money I have, and the gods can have my status. Here, I can be free to do what I want to do, what I did as a boy, to live outdoors with no threats other than wolves."

"Well, if you want to be a shepherd, you will have to go west. The land here is spoken for... every square inch is devoted to growing food for people, and there is no room for grazing. West of Luoyang, into the grasslands, that is where you must go to raise sheep. If you are serious."

"I am. How far away is Luoyang?"

"Up river, about three hundred and fifty miles. By boat, ten days to two weeks, against the wind and current."

"Mmmh." Ibrahim stroked his beard. This was much, much further than he had expected to have to travel. He concealed his huge disappointment. Passage he could buy, but when he got there, he did not know the language, customs, writing, anything necessary to get started.

He wasn't good enough to fool Musa, who understood at once what was going through Ibrahim's mind. "I have business in Luoyang with one of my customers, who is special-ordering a large boat, and he has been wanting me to go over the design with him. I have been putting this trip off for months, but you gave me the excuse I need. You can travel with me, if you like."

"What about your business here? You cannot just drop everything and take off like that, can you?" asked Ibrahim.

"I have an assistant, a Mongol, who manages the shop and keeps the boat construction moving, and my two older sons are capable men. Mei Ling runs the family, and she is used to me being gone on long trips. Would it be just you two?"

"And maybe two others." Shmuel had formed a close tie with Ibrahim and Yakov, and claimed some shepherding experience as a boy. And Galosga and he were inseparable. If Shmuel were to jump into boiling water, Galosga would be right behind him.

"I have a nice thirty-foot sampan, which should handle the five of us quite well. Let me show it to you."

He led the two to the waterfront at the back of the shop. In the misty rain, his boat bobbed on the water. As he had said, it was square on both ends, odd by Western standards, with the stern three times wider than the bow and much higher; the whole boat sloping down to the bow. Two of the odd-shaped *chuan*-rigged sails were secured in place, and a long steering oar protruded aft of the stern. Amidships between the two masts was a barrel-shaped passenger compartment.

"This is one of my best sailing sampans. She sails very close-hauled, with a retractable keel for shallow water. We will be going to Luoyang along the *Huang He*, the Yellow River so named because it is so silty. When do you want to leave?"

"Whenever you are ready. I do not want to inconvenience you."

"No inconvenience. I will post a letter to my customer tonight, and it will arrive several days before we do. I will help set you up in the sheep-herding business, and see you off."

Ibrahim brought out his purse. "Let me reward you handsomely for this."

"No reward is necessary. When I came here there were people who helped me, and I had no money to offer them. Otherwise I would have wound up as someone's slave. In this country, *li*, social balance, is very important. So, no reward... put away your purse."

CHAPTER 39: A VERY UNHAPPY RELATIONSHIP

Wang Ming had booked the envoys' passage to Luoyang on a luxurious river *chuan*, about a hundred feet in length, high stern sloping steeply down to the bow, with three rhomboidal, heavily battened sails. She had individual cabins for each passenger, and a warm bath amidships aft of the galley.

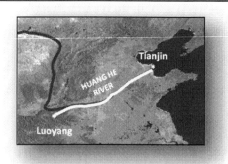

After touring the river *chuan*, Aulus, Gaius, Antonius and Marcus returned to the nearby *Europa* to say goodbye to their shipmates from the long cruise while their baggage was shipped down from the inn. The four were dressed in Hanaean clothing, baggy pants, knee-length smock and woolen robes, well-suited to the damp cold weather.

One of the first to meet them was Ibrahim, who embraced each with a big hug and kissed them lightly on the cheek in Arab style. "You three look like you are going native," he jested, though he was similarly dressed.

"This chill October makes a mockery of Mediterranean clothing," said Gaius.

Ibrahim announced the news: "I was fortunate enough to meet a fellow countryman who has lived here for many years. "

"How in the hell did he wind up here?" asked Antonius.

"Musa was stranded here twenty years ago, married, and learned Hanaean from his wife. He opened a boat shop around the corner and knows his way around. He has business of his own in Luoyang, and will take me and Yakov on his boat, and Shmuel and Galosga as well, near where shepherding country begins."

"Argh," growled Antonius, but with a smile, "I thought we were rid of yer Arab ass. I understand Yakov, but Shmuel and Galosga? I didn't think they were that close to yer."

"Shmuel wants to help with the shepherding. He did that when he was young, and he and Galosga are inseparable," replied Ibrahim. Ibrahim's Latin had improved considerably over the past few months, and he had no trouble with Antonius' speech.

"Well, I am going ter have a talk with them. They need ter go back home in April!"

And he went off to talk to them, to no avail. Galosga feigned difficulty in understanding him, and Shmuel said they wanted to see the new land. Antonius warned them that they were on their own, and if they missed the April sailing from Tianjin, they might very well spend the rest of their lives in *Ch'in*. They accepted the risk. He was seriously concerned for them, but he would not order them to not go.

He rejoined Ibrahim a bit later, Gaius and Marcus having gone off to see the captain, navigators and some other crew members. "No luck. They claim they just want ter go sightseein'. Damned fools are liable to wind up stuck here for the rest of their lives."

"I will do my best to help take care of them. Shmuel will be in my employ. He knows sheep, so he will teach both me and Galosga their ways. So it is not like they will be completely on their own," said Ibrahim.

"Take good care of them, I'm really close to those two lads. Here, I want ter give yer a gift." He pulled out his Roman army dagger, with the abbreviation "ANT ARIST PP LEG XII FUL" carved into the hilt. "This was given ter me when I stood up as *primus pilus* for the *XII Ful.* It's my initials, PP for my title, and the legion. Every time yer look at it, yer can remember how many times I wanted ter slit yer throat with it when we first made our acquaintances." He put the dagger back into its sheath, and extended it hilt-first to Ibrahim.

"I am truly honored, Antonius. I don't want to leave you without a blade, so please accept my own humble one in exchange," he said, presenting his own dagger. A humble blade it was not. The sheath was jeweled and beaded leather, the blade a rare and expensive watery Damascus steel that held an extremely sharp edge. The ivory hilt was engraved with flowing Nabataean script.

"My crew gave me this a few years ago. The script reads "Tooth of the Serpent," the name of the blade. Wear it well, and try not to cut yourself, it is very sharp," he said.

"We Romans know a bit about steel, so I don't think I will. Seriously, I am truly honored. I never thought I would ever consider you friend, but you are."

"We have saved each other's lives several times now. What may come in Luoyang?"

They took their farewells of the rest of the *Europa*, and returned to their ship, the *Xue Long* Snow Dragon. Wang Ming and Marcia were the last to board in the morning, just before sailing on the high tide. She walked ahead of Wang Ming, her eyes focused on the deck in front of her, till she passed by Gaius and Antonius. She looked up, gave the faintest flicker of a wordless smile, and resumed her downcast gaze the remainder of the way to their cabin. Ming was expressionless and said nothing to the two.

"Mmmh. He has her cowed. That's not the same lady we knew," said Antonius.

"To be sure. Marcus said he was a pig, and I can see why. It is unfortunate... she is a bright and witty woman."

Inside the cabin, Wang Ming's expressionless face turned dark.

"Did you think I did not see you leering at the Roman barbarians, Si Huar?" He used her Hanaean name, 'Western Flower,' in a voice loud enough to be intimidating but not so loud as to be heard outside the cabin.

"I was not leering, Ming, I was but ..." Her answer was cut short by a slap to her cheek.

"Do not argue with me! You have had airs about you since you returned from Rome, believing you are something special, with that worthless scrap of paper the barbarian king gave you. You lust after those Roman soldiers because you are the spawn of Roman barbarians and Hanaean sluts who could find no proper husbands! You are a whore and the daughter of a whore!" He slapped her hard again and she tasted blood.

Whenever these beatings began, she long ago had learned to retreat to a quiet spot, memories of her childhood before they took her away from her family and Liqian. Protestations were futile, they only made him beat her more. She closed him out, but this time she was surprised to find her quiet spot filled with memories of Antonius and their long talks. Such a delightful, awkward man, so embarrassed when he feared he might have offended her... the way he called her *domina*, 'lady,' placing her above him. Those were the only moments she had conversed with a man as equal in her entire adult life. She cherished those days on the *Europa*, when she thought she was at last rid of Wang Ming and his hatefulness. But that was not to be: the *Asia* had caught up with the *Europa*, and Wang Ming had caught up with her.

Wang Ming usually avoided leaving marks, but his anger surged with her acquiescence and he hit her solidly on the side of her face with a balled fist, sending her sprawling. The pain shocked her out of her quiet spot. He grabbed her roughly up, threw her on the bed, and hoisted up her silken skirt. He dropped on top of her, rutting like a goat until he grunted and spent himself. He then collapsed on top of her and fell asleep. As he began to snore, Marcia carefully slipped out from beneath him, to lay beside him in bitter silence as the ship began to rock gently and move away from the pier.

The next day, Marcia again briefly left the cabin, passing by Gaius and Antonius without acknowledging their greetings. But her downcast gaze could not conceal the blackened left eye.

"Marcus is right, the bastard's a pig!" Antonius was turning purple with anger at the thought of that gentle person being so roughly handled.

"There's nothing you can do, Antonius," said Gaius, putting his hand on the centurion's shoulder. "She is his concubine, like his slave. If he wanted to kill her, that is his right. It is unfortunate, but there is nothing we can do that wouldn't make it much worse for her. Let it be."

Antonius let it be, but not easily. He stayed in his midships cabin most of the trip, hoping he would not meet Wang Ming, or worse yet, hear him beating her. He didn't think he could let it go, no matter what came of it.

Gaius confided the incident to Marcus, and he confirmed that Ming beat her frequently. "He usually doesn't leave marks, though. People in the court disapprove of that as poor etiquette, making a dispute with his concubine public. Unseemly."

"Unseemly! What do you think set this one off?" asked Gaius.

"Who knows? He is likely just jealous of you and Antonius paying attention to her. He has a wife and about a dozen concubines. I hope he will pick another favorite some day."

"What would happen to her?"

"Nothing. Rejected concubines just stay on in court, getting old and crotchety. Some get bitter, but Marcia certainly won't miss his attention."

Gaius and Marcus stood by the rail watching the shoreline slip by. A northeasterly breeze favored their course, and the boat followed the river without tacking. The coastline was lined with dikes, and beyond the dikes, the country spread flat and treeless as if it had been planed smooth as far as the eye could see. On the vast plain, hundreds of workers busied themselves in the chilly weather, dredging irrigation ditches, tilling the fields under for winter, burning residue, and spreading winter fertilizer, which filled the air with its tang.

The river was alive with traffic, from little sampans polling along the shore fishing, to bigger boats going upstream and down, some with sails, some with oars.

Marcus looked lovingly at the countryside and the brown muddy river. "The Yellow River is the blessing and the curse of *Ch'in*. Like the Nile, it floods and makes the land incredibly fertile. But unlike the Nile, it has no schedule. It floods when it chooses, and devastates the land when it does. In some places the river level is higher than the land behind those dikes. We try to control it, but the river has a mind of its own. A century ago, its mouth used to be on the other side of the Shandong Mountains south of here. Then in one rainy season, it changed its mind, and came out this side where it is now."

"Must have been a devastating flood!" said Gaius.

"It was indeed," said Marcus. "Tens of thousands died, whole towns just wiped out."

"One wonders how you Hanaeans - I guess you are one now after all these generations, despite your Roman blood - how you Hanaeans survive and even thrive in such adversity."

"We've been doing it thousands of years by our legends, and yes, I am both, rather more Hanaean than Roman. Survival here involves accepting the will of the gods, which for us is to maintain order in all things, *li*. The emperor is the son of heaven, and he sets the standard for order. If he becomes disorderly in his conduct, then the gods express their displeasure in bad events like floods. If it gets bad enough, then we must choose a more orderly emperor."

"How do you do that?" asked Gaius, assuming there was some sort of protocol.

"We do it crudely. We have a civil war, and the strongest and most organized emerges as the new emperor. Then order reigns again, until disorder breaks out again," Marcus said with a grin.

"Hmm, sounds like Hanaeans are more like Romans than I thought. "

They went off on a discussion of Roman politics, since Marcus' understanding of Roman government from his ancestors ended well before the rise of Julius Caesar and the establishment of the Augustan Principate. "At first it didn't seem that big a change. Augustus Octavian was *Princeps Senatus,* speaker of the Senate, a constitutional position permanently assigned to him. He was *Imperator*, supreme commander in chief of all legions, and he could appoint all of the commanding generals, with the Senate's consent. It didn't seem that big a change from the Republic, some said it wasn't even a change. But when the *Princeps* became disorderly there was no way to stop him, and no way to remove him except by assassination or civil war. Just forty years ago, we had four emperors in the space of a year after Nero, and they all died violently! We are more alike than either of us would like to admit."

After a little over two weeks, the *Xue Long* docked in Luoyang. Antonius had come out of his cabin only to eat, and Marcia not at all.

CHAPTER 40: DESTINATION

Luoyang was gray with cold snow when they arrived in mid-November, with a biting wind from the northeast that drove the warmth from the bones. The gray sky and stone walls layered with snow brooded on the hillside leading up from the river to the mountain behind.

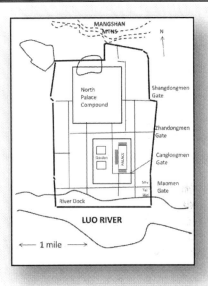

The riverboat had left the Hwang He River for the Luo River at their confluence, cruising through the hilly countryside for about thirty-five miles until the capital emerged from the fog around a bend in the river. A massive wall perforated by two gates fronted the river behind a wide stone dock. Rowboats assisted in towing the big riverboat alongside the dock, lines went over to bollards, and they were at their destination.

Wang Ming led Aulus and his party to the easternmost gate into the walled city. Aulus noted that the guards came to attention expressionlessly and raised their lances after Ming presented documents bearing text and a square red seal. Inside the city, another walled compound loomed on their left, but they turned right to a large building abutting the outer wall, where they maneuvered through still more guards inside. With each, Ming repeated the ritual with the same stoically respectful result.

Banners vertically inscribed with the inscrutable Hanaean script dangled from the ceiling between long cylindrical lamps that brightened the interior. Busy officials scuttled back and forth, carrying scrolls from office to office. Wang Ming led the entourage through several layers of officials of apparently increasing rank, until they reached Ming's intended contact.

He and Ming exchanged formal salutes, hands joined inside their cloak sleeves, accompanied by a bow, then burst into smiles, clasping each other's shoulders and engaging in an extended exchange of pleasantries. Wang Ming and this official apparently knew each other quite well, and they seemed intent on catching up on details of the court, and on Ming's adventures in the West during the past several years. Aulus stood silent, Gaius and Antonius at parade rest. Protocol demanded silence, except to answer questions put to them.

At last, Ming remembered the envoys, and introduced them to the official, pointing to each in turn and saying their names with a decidedly Hanaean pronunciation: "Aus Gawba, Gis Luk Lu, and Anjin Aris". Marcus he introduced by his Hanaean name, Si Nuo.

Then Ming addressed the envoys, first in his stumbling Latin. "This man see all safety for Emperor He, he give permission to enter palace."

After stumbling over a few technical terms, he recognized the limit of his Latin and switched to Hanaean for clarity, with Marcus translating: "This is Wang Tai, head of Imperial security. You must have his personal permission to be inside the Imperial compound." Marcus handed out three scrolls to Aulus, Gaius and Antonius. "Keep these with you at all times in the compound, and don't go anywhere outside your residential area without me as translator. These confirm your permission to be inside the South Palace."

Conspicuously, Ming had not identified Marcia as a translator.

Each of the Romans nodded in turn, accepted the documents, and Ming led them out of the building. Outside, some clerks, senior officials, and a few military officers were coming and going or sitting together in small groups, in what was apparently a hub of government. Marcus explained quietly what had just happened.

"That was the supreme military commander's office, the *taiwei*. The man with whom we spoke, Wang Tai, is a mid-level officer, commander of what you would call the urban cohort, several thousand men that guard Luoyang and the Imperial palaces. He is Ming's brother, hence the big reunion. Ming is a senior minister in the *situ*, the ministry of finance, the big building to the north of the *taiwei*. That position is what led him to be selected to accompany the westward expedition a few years ago. The interior walled compound is the palace itself, and foreigners require the *taiwei's* approval to enter."

They reached the enormous east gate of the palace compound, flanked by red columns with gilt capitals and pedestals, guarded by two green and red dragon statues snaking outward along either side of the broad thoroughfare. The thirty-foot palace gate, which Marcus said was the Canglongmen Gate, was always shut unless the Emperor was exiting. Built into each huge wooden door panel and guarded by soldiers called *sima*, however, were two smaller doorways, closed, that admitted foot, horse and carriage traffic into the South Palace.

The impassive *sima*, clad in a blue quilted uniform and conical helmet, examined each of their paperwork in turn. He then grunted and the door swung open to admit the party.

The door was big enough to admit a man on horseback, and as it opened, Aulus noted it was about two feet thick. He watched, admiring the engineering, as the massive door weighing several tons swung open effortlessly and silently, then closed behind them with a solid thunk.

They looked onto the vast South Palace compound, a quarter mile wide, the whole expanse paved with perfectly flat white stonework. Aulus observed the side of the building on their immediate right, elevated on a huge white stone foundation about a hundred paces in width, with a wide stone stairway. Just the side of that building was as big as the Curia in Rome.

On the far side of the compound, separated from them by a wide sunken road lined with low stone walls, were two more massive red and black columned structures with gilt decoration and lettering, with the unique dark green Hanaean-style curved tiled roofs. The buildings were separated by a garden filled with trees, now stark winter skeletons except for a few dark green conical pines, weighted with snow.

Ming led them on until they reached the central road, terminating in another gate on the north wall a half-mile away where some yellow-clad individuals were barely visible. There was no other discernible human activity, no sound except the sighing of the winter wind and the intermittent clanging of some distant gongs. The vast emptiness was overwhelming, the silence deafening.

The building on their right was a palace wider than the two buildings and gardens facing it put together, perhaps five hundred paces long with a central promenade easily a hundred feet wide. The promenade terminated in steps of the same width, flanked by dragons running down the stair walls. The roof was double-peaked, and a long horizontal inscription in gold Hanaean characters proclaiming something ran the length of the roof line. The walls were a dull red color with black, white and gilt trim, black columns flanking the huge entrance.

Not as long as Nero's mile-long Domus Aureus in Rome. But that was gaudily ostentatious and clustered in amongst a tumble of other buildings. This one just radiated quiet power and solitary majesty. The isolation made one feel like an ant, alone in a space larger than the Roman Forum, but devoid of people, uncluttered by statuary and dominated by that temple to their god-king!

They continued up the concourse until another narrower walkway on their right led them to the north side of the palace, similar to the south side they had seen on their entrance. They walked up fifty or so steps to enter the building through a wide columned portico, flanked by two grotesque lion-like figures snarling in frozen menace. No one challenged them.

Inside, the floors were gray polished granite, the walls blue at the bottom with gilt decoration and pinkish red above, the ceiling towering over them. Hanging banners proclaimed announcements in characters that were a silent shout to the Romans, illiterate in all but the most basic ones. The banners were interspaced with cylindrical lanterns about eight or so feet long that added illumination to the generous daylight entering through rice-paper windows overlaid with wooden grills. These windows ran the length of the hallway on their right. In the distance, a dark blue curtain blocked the corridor.

There was activity as individuals clad in blue and gray uniform robes quietly went about their business, but like outside, all was order and silence.

The three Romans tried to take this in stoically, without gaping at the magnificent simplicity of their surroundings.

About a quarter of the way down the corridor, a set of wooden stairs opened to their left, and they climbed up two floors to a residence area reserved for foreign envoys. Ming led them to a door which opened into a large sitting area, with highly lacquered black tables and chairs in the center on a yellow mat. The wall was lined with rice paper-covered windows and wood grillwork that admitted light but kept out weather. A door at the center of the far end gave way to one large private bedroom, flanked by two more doors leading to a shared hot bath on the right and a toilet on the left. Two doors on each side wall gave way to four more private bedrooms, small only in comparison to the huge first bedroom.

Ming and Marcus conversed in Hanaean for several minutes, then Ming excused himself. "I go now, your comfort here in room, Marcus explain."

Aulus attempted the Hanaean salute, fists pressed together in the sleeves of his Hanaean cloak, and gave a curt bow of his head while watching Ming. "I thank you for your hospitality, Wang Ming! *Vale!*"

Ming beamed, and returned the salute, "*Vale*, Aulus Aemilius!" and left.

"Welcome to the envoy's quarters," smiled Marcus.

"Not bad, not bad at all," admired Gaius, examining the fine lacquered table. "I take it you are going to insist on the larger bedroom, cousin?"

"Well, I am Trajan's envoy, so I guess, yes, I will. I hope you three will be comfortable in your spartan accommodations," answered Aulus with a chuckle.

Their traveling chests had already been brought up from the riverboat, set neatly in the living area. They each lugged their own into their bedrooms.

They inspected their bedrooms, heated *kang* beds like they had seen in Tianjin, but more spacious with woolen blankets, a silk decorative coverlet and silk pillows. These beds were heated by some sort of hypocaust system, rather than their own fireplace. Probably charcoal, judging by the faint tang. There was a cabinet for hanging clothes, and a chair for sitting, with several lamps. Each room had small translucent windows that admitted ambient light from the hallways.

After a few minutes of organizing their material, they reassembled in the common area.

"One important question, Marcus. What is the proper way to use the latrine here?" This candid comment brought a chuckle from everyone.

"Very simple, sir. After you have -er- done your business, use the pads of papers to clean yourself, then just dump the bucket of water down the toilet to remove the residue. It's a simple system."

"So simple even a Roman could use it," quipped Antonius.

"What will we do without our communal sponges?" chuckled Gaius, back into his humorous routine.

"I guess we'll survive somehow." Aulus asked, "You didn't mention your sister earlier as an available translator. Is she not well? We haven't seen her for months."

Marcus answered sadly, "She is well, but she is now a full-time concubine for Ming, and you probably won't see her again. Her translator's duties have been terminated."

"Will you be able to see her?"

"I am her brother, so I can see her from time to time. She sends her best wishes and thanks you for the great friendship you have shown her. She regrets she could not say goodbye."

"We understand," said Aulus. "Please thank her for her help and companionship."

That silenced the group for a moment. Their fleeting views of her on the riverboat revealed a very different person than the happy, outgoing woman she had been on the *Europa*, so eager to teach and learn.

"She was not happy to see Wang Ming again. After the hijacking, once she got over her fear of Ibrahim, she began to think she would never see him again. I have never seen her so happy and optimistic as she was then. She even thought about finding a way to return to Rome with you. Oh well, there is nothing to be done about it," said Marcus.

After another uncomfortable silence, Aulus announced "I have a bit of a treat for you. We have been through no end of adventures and challenges, but now at least we are within a few hundred paces of the Hanaean emperor himself. Maybe tomorrow, or maybe next week or next month, we will meet with him, and we can all go home! I have a bottle of fine Falernian wine, guaranteed to be at least twenty years old, from an ill-fated vineyard on the side of Mt. Vesuvius. Would you gentlemen care to join me?" He introduced a wax-stoppered ceramic bottle, opening it while the rest of the group eagerly searched the living quarters for drinking cups.

CHAPTER 41: REUNION

The following day dawned bright and sunny, though with a cold northwesterly breeze; yesterday's snow for the most part remained. Aulus's living quarters had an outside balcony allowing them to see much more than they had on their gray arrival.

Luoyang sloped upward to the foot of Mount Mangshan to the north, a sheer cliff of yellow granite several thousand feet high. In the distance they could see another walled compound on the northern edge of the city, the North Palace, reserved for ceremonial occasions involving the public, according to Marcus. The South Palace was reserved for the imperial residences and government functions.

The two buildings they had seen on the western side when they first entered the palace compound were the Empress' palace and the women's quarters, respectively. They could see some women strolling in the winter-barren garden.

"Marcia is staying there?" asked Gaius.

"Yes. Ming has a wife and several concubines there," answered Marcus.

"Together? Sounds like trouble to me."

"I think you know the Hanaean symbol for 'woman,' Marcus said, making the symbol in the air with his finger, chuckling. The symbol for 'trouble,' *nuán,* is two women. He keeps his wife separate, but the concubines are together. They actually get along well. Marcia unfortunately is his favorite."

"What happens to her if she stops being his favorite?" asked Aulus.

"Not much. She wouldn't be able to leave, but she would be relieved of his constant suspicions. He is very jealous of her, though she has never given him any reason. Perhaps because she was so young when he took her." Marcus abruptly changed the subject. "Would you like to go out to see the rest of the city?"

"Can we actually get out of here?" asked Antonius.

"It's much easier to get out than to get in. You just have to slide a little door open and ask, and out you go. Getting back in, then you will need your papers."

Aulus replied with a little disappointment. "I have business with Ming today, people to meet and so forth. But go on, enjoy yourself. Tell me all about it when you get back."

The three exited the palace, wearing quilted Hanaean winter garments against the chill, and retraced their steps to the Canglongmen Gate. Marcus drew a sliding panel in the door to make his request to leave, and the door slid open silently to permit their exit into the government area. Marcus pointed out the *Taiwei* office where they had first stopped yesterday. This was not just the 'urban cohort,' but the headquarters for all Hanaean army formations throughout the empire. The *situ* and *sikong* buildings next to it were the ministries of finance and public works, respectively, separated by the Maomen city gate in the eastern wall.

They left the government area behind and came to a marketplace. Here the sights, smells and sounds of a big city emerged, with farmers hawking animals and birds in cages, bushels of wheat and millet, rice from the far south, and many things unfamiliar to the Romans. But the babble of many people buying and selling their goods was familiar, if the language was not.

A number of yellow-robed men, very lightly dressed for the chilly weather, one shoulder bare and their chests exposed to the wind, wandered throughout the market. Some had an Oriental cast to their faces, others black like southern Indians, some almost Western in appearance, all with their heads and faces shaved. They would periodically accost a passerby with a bronze bowl and a mumbled greeting. The person usually smiled and dropped a few copper coins in the bowl, and the strange beggar made some sort of hand motion, bowed with a head nod, and went on his way.

"Beggars all dress alike here, Marcus?" asked Antonius.

"Those are adherents of an Indian religion. The Emperor Ming, Emperor He's grandfather, brought them here after he had a dream, and built them a magnificent temple east of the city, the *Bai Ma Si,* the White Horse Temple, because they arrived on a white horse. They are monks who dedicate their lives to living the life of the Buddha, doing without all the things of the world, living by begging. Emperor Ming was quite an adherent, though he could never give up all the things of the world and go begging with them. The people consider it great good luck to give them coins or food when they beg from them, and the monks can go pretty much anywhere they want… even in the palaces. Look, Antonius, I think you have found a friend. Give him a few coppers."

A monk had come up to Antonius, probably drawn to his western features, and proffered his bowl. "Good luck to yer, lad, an' be off with yer," he said with a smile as he dropped a handful of copper coins into the monk's bowl with a clatter. The monk, himself with western features that would not have drawn a second glance in Rome, bowed and made a blessing motion with his free hand, and said a few words in Greek… not just Greek, but good Greek. Antonius returned the bow with a smile and replied, "I had not expected to hear Greek spoken here so far from the Islands. My name is

Antonius Aristides. May I ask from whence you hail?" Gaius and Marcus listened attentively, though Marcus had no Greek.

"I am from Bactria, and my name is Demosthenes."

"I am pleased to meet you, Demosthenes. I have heard of your country, Bactria of the thousand richest cities,' east of Parthia and I guess, west of here?"

"That is correct, sir Antonius. It is a pleasure to speak with you, but now I must rejoin my companions."

"It has been a pleasure, Demosthenes." Antonius fished a silver *denarius* from his purse and dropped it into the monk's bowl. "Here, treat your friends to a good meal." To his surprise, the monk returned it, almost with an expression of distaste.

"No, I am sorry… we must take no more from the world than we need to survive, and we must not put ourselves in a position above one another. But I forgive your ignorance. Some time, we must meet, and talk about the teaching of Lord Buddha, the Enlightened One. Your simple copper coins are a great prize. May the blessing of the Buddha be upon you and your friends, sir Antonius." He blessed him, smiled and turned away.

"Hmm, that was unusual… he was born speaking Greek," said Antonius.

Gaius was just as surprised. "Right, the last language I expected to hear in Luoyang! Bactria is supposed to be a wealthy country north of India, settled by Alexandria the Great."

Marcus asked, "That was Greek he was speaking? We call them the *Da Yuan*, the Great Ionians, who live in splendid cities. He must be one of them. The Yuezhi, also western-appearing people near them, are quite brutal barbarians, and they conquered the *Da Yuan* some time back. We have fought several wars with them to keep the passage to Parthia open."

"Well, the world is a much bigger, stranger place than ever I imagined," said Gaius.

They continued the tour of the city. Marcus led them to a medium-sized shop, a wood framed building with a foyer or office facing the street, with bamboo screens partitioning off a maze of backrooms. He spoke briefly to the proprietor, an elderly man in black jacket, a pill box hat covering his white hair. Halfway through the conversation, his eyes lit and he burst into a smile *"Da Qin?"* he said, and again *"Da Qin?"* quite excited. Then he slammed his fists together before him and nodded his head in salute to the Romans, and was delighted to receive formal Hanaean salutes in turn from each of them.

Marcus finished the conversation and turned to the three Romans. "Your reputation precedes you. Everyone in town knows that the great *Da Qin* from the West have arrived to meet Emperor He, and he is most honored to have you under his humble roof. '*Da Qin*' is the name they use for Rome, 'Great Ch'in.' They view you as their western counterpart, in the great Yin and Yang scheme of things that maintains balance in the world. You are quite as mysterious to them as our party was to you a few years ago, mysterious men from a place of myth. This is Yi Ren, the owner." Several others workers from the back, clad in light clothing, stepped into the foyer to view the mysterious *Da Qin* strangers.

Marcus introduced the three in turn.

"Yi Ren manufactures bows and crossbows here, along with arrows. The crossbows are under contract to the urban cohorts. The public are not permitted to own them. He also manufactures bows, which civilians use for hunting. Let me show you his work."

They passed through the bamboo screen to one of the back rooms, where a cluster of two dozen or more C-shaped unstrung bows hung from two parallel strings between the walls. They had narrow, leather-bound handgrips in the middle, flaring widely on either side into wide limbs tapering to a fine tip. Each was tagged with an inscription in *Han-yu*. Yi Ren picked up the outermost and laid it on the table, chattering away while Marcus translated. "This is a wood composite bow, made of layers of mulberry and bamboo, wrapped in silk and then lacquered, more silk, then more lacquer. The dangling bamboo indicates the owner's name, and the date for pickup... it takes considerable time to cure. These are all ready for pickup."

Yi Ren took down a bowstring hanging on the wall and expertly strung the bow. Without effort, the C-shape reversed itself into a recurved bow. He picked it up and plucked the string, causing it to emit a throbbing hum. He grabbed a quiver of arrows and stepped through to the backyard, leading them to a small archery range with an array of targets. He put on a thumb guard, nocked an arrow, aimed high to draw the bow and lowered it to the target fifty yards off. He released the arrow to land squarely in the circular bull's eye.

"Nicely done!" said Antonius, and Yi Ren offered him the bow, quiver and thumb guard. Antonius took it and examined it carefully. It seemed similar enough to the familiar Roman military *arcus* that he would probably not embarrass himself, though it had been a year since he last used one. Without fitting an arrow, he drew the bow several times to get its feel, then nocked an arrow, aimed and fired, hitting the target well off center. Yi Ren offered him some advice on his grip, then he drew again and this time came within a few inches of Yi Ren's arrow. The bowmaker clapped delightedly.

"I want to show you something which will really impress you," said Marcus, leading them back inside to the entrance of another room. Yi Ren at first shook his head negatively, and they conversed rapidly. Then Marcus turned back to Gaius and Antonius. "These are military weapons that you shouldn't even see. But since you are *Da Qin* guests of Emperor He, he will demonstrate one to you. But you may not touch it."

Yi Ren stepped behind a blanket and returned with an odd-shaped crossbow. Antonius had seen hand-held crossbows, but this had an odd square hump on the stock, and some sort of u-shaped handle projecting forward from it. Yi Ren went back to the archery range, took ten unfletched arrows and loaded them into the hump, acting as a magazine. He braced the crossbow against his thigh, pulled the handle back, rotating the magazine to cock the weapon and load an arrow. He returned the handle to the forward position, and the weapon launched its arrow to strike home. He pulled the handle back again, reloading and firing, repeating in a smooth rhythm like a smaller version of the *polyboli* on the ships. Within thirty seconds, he had fired ten rounds into the target, each hitting with a solid thunk within inches of center.

He smiled, bowed, and returned to the building to replace the weapon while Marcus explained. "The Hanaeans call that the *lian-yu*. I don't know the Latin word for it, or even if you have something like that."

Antonius answered, "It's a kinda hand-held *ballista*, but like nothin' I've ever seen. The hand-carried ones we have take as long to cock for one round as it took Yi Ren to get off ten. I'd give anything to take one of those … *lian-yu?*... apart and see how it works."

"Not likely," smiled Marcus, as Yi Ren returned. "These are state secrets, you are lucky just to have seen it. I wouldn't talk about it back in the palace." He turned to Yi Ren, chattered some more, and the old man's face lit up again in smiles.

Antonius reached into his pouch and pulled out a silver *denarius*. He pressed it into Yi Ren's hand, and said "Souvenir, Yi Ren. We be thankin' yer very much."

They left the archery factory and stopped by a pharmacy, but Antonius could make out few familiar medications, and Marcus couldn't translate the Hanaean names, so after a few minutes, they resumed wandering, visiting silk vendors and tiny food and pastry shops. Each shop-owner was delighted to have the famous *Da Qin* visit them, and many seated them and ceremonially served hot cups of tea, welcome on a cold day.

As the sun began to settle low over the western wall of the city, they began their way back to the Canglongmen Gate and their quarters in the palace. A hundred yards away, five Westerners, clad like them in Hanaean clothing, were making their way toward them… a tall man, pockmarked with a salt-and-paper beard, and an equally tall bronze-skinned individual, a short slender man with pointed beard and nervous disposition, a bulky black-bearded man, and a fifth they did not recognize.

They had not closed half the distance to the group before the five Westerners became aware of their approach, and a few seconds later, Ibrahim's booming voice called out them: "Gaius, Antonius, Marcus! *Salaam* to you, good friends!" The noisy exuberance drew puzzled stares from the Hanaean shopkeepers and pedestrians, not used to such unrestrained outpourings of emotion. The two groups closed quickly to exchange handshakes and embraces.

Antonius asked. "So yer really serious about becoming a shepherd! When did yer get here?"

"I am, and here I am. By the way, this is my friend Musa about whom I told you. He has contacts that can help me buy a flock and grazing rights. We had just left a bit of a tavern, so let's go back there. The wine is on me."

They turned to follow Ibrahim's entourage, to the bewildered stares of the Hanaeans at the sight of such a large gathering of Westerners.

"When did you get in?" asked Gaius, striding alongside Ibrahim. *I wonder what the bastard is up to? Shepherding, yes that is what he said. But really?*

"A few days after you did. The news of your arrival spread all over town. They call Rome *Da Qin*, some sort of mystical, mythical land of magic and monsters. Having you here is quite exciting."

They reached the tavern, and Musa chatted with the shopkeeper, who went back to get more chairs for the three new guests. "This is it. The rice wine is excellent, a bit like white wine but drier and more crisp."

The shopkeeper returned with a large bottle and eight small ceramic cups, white with blue Hanaean inscriptions baked into the shiny glaze. He poured a cup for each. Ibrahim raised his in toast: "To our most unlikely companionship! So where are you staying?"

"In the South Palace. Nice accommodations," answered Gaius, sipping his wine with a smile.

"And Aulus Aemilius, he is well?"

"He is ecstatic to be here. He and Ming are making the rounds of administrative offices, lining up people to meet. We can't stay out too late because I don't have any idea what tomorrow's schedule might be, and if it involves meeting Emperor He, I'd rather not have a hangover!" laughed Gaius, but offering his now empty cup for a refill.

"And the girl? Marcia, your sister?" asked Ibrahim.

"Marcia's back to being Ming's full-time concubine, but I hope to see her in the next few days. She is no longer part of our party," answered Marcus, his tone implying he didn't want to talk about it anymore.

"And where are yer stayin' here?" asked Antonius, also proffering his glass for a refill.

"On Musa's boat down by the waterfront. Not as nice as your accommodations, but cheap enough." Ibrahim turned to Musa and chatted with him in Aramaic, then Musa explained to Marcus in Hanaean where it was. "I am sorry, my friend Musa does not speak Latin or Greek. We have to use Hanaean as our *lingua franca*."

Marcus explained, "The boat is at the docks just outside the southern Pingchengmen Gate on the waterfront. I know the area."

On the street outside, two Buddhist monks panhandled their way along the street.

"Strange fellows, those!" said Antonius. "Have yer met them yet?"

"As a matter of fact, we have. Musa says it is good luck to give them money."

"Yes. The one we met spoke Greek, a Bactrian. A big world and a small one at the same time, ain't it," said Antonius.

"Both together, indeed!" answered Ibrahim, and they talked, ate and drank for another hour, catching up on events, before Gaius signaled the end of festivities. They headed back along the darkening streets as lamplighters fluttered about like fireflies, lighting paper lanterns.

CHAPTER 42: COMPETITORS

Aulus was acutely aware of the fact that he had now only a single interpreter, and that he had let Marcus take Gaius and Antonius out sightseeing. That left him at the mercy of Wang Ming's rudimentary Latin.

Ming had escorted Aulus on a number of courtesy calls that morning, some inside and some outside the palace, to meet various officials whose names he would not remember and whose titles Ming could not translate in his rudimentary pidgin-Latin. They were apparently important enough for Ming to introduce him, but the only one important enough to remember was Bai Wei, some sort of scheduler for the Emperor, perhaps his personal secretary, chief of staff, chancellor or something along those lines. As Ming put it, "He tell when come see Emperor He."

He led him to yet another office. "You like next, he maybe talk to you. He from *Anxi*." He knocked and entered. A man with Western features and a carefully coiffed beard, clad in a bluish green silk cassock over a pair of white pants, rose, saluted and bowed elegantly to Ming. Ming returned only an acknowledging head nod, which was all he ever did for a foreigner's salute. They exchanged greetings in Hanaean, then the man turned to Aulus and introduced himself in Greek. "I am Cyrus Mithridates, envoy of Ctesiphon. Pleased to meet you." He extended his hand.

Aulus hesitated a moment and extended his own in return; they shared a mutually reluctant handshake. "I am Aulus Aemilius Galba, envoy of Rome. You are far from Parthia, Cyrus. Have you been here long?"

"Long enough to master the language. I have been the envoy of Pacorus II for about ten years now. Welcome to this strange and wonderful land!"

Ming interrupted, and excused himself. "You two able talk, I go. Gai's, you get back to room alone?"

"Yes, yes, no problem, Ming, thank you for the many introductions this morning." Aulus gave the obligatory farewell salute, and got his perfunctory head nod in return. Ming left.

Cyrus gestured to a chair. "Sit, sit. It is a pleasure to have someone to talk with, even if in another time and place we might be sworn enemies. I remember well how alone and lost I felt when I first came here."

Aulus took a seat. Cyrus summoned a servant, spoke to him in Parthian, and sat down on a divan facing Aulus. "I sent for some tea. And I presume you would want some also."

"Thank you. You have been here ten years? How long has Parthia had such close contact with Hanae?"

Cyrus chuckled softly. "Over two hundred years. Remember we are almost neighbors, and the trade route you call the *Via Serica*, the Silk Road, runs through my homeland. We have had diplomatic and trade relations for a very long time."

The servant brought two cups of steaming hot tea, and Aulus took a sip. "How do you feel about your sworn enemy joining you here?" he said with a smile.

"Competition sharpens the wits," replied Cyrus. "I understand you have some very good translators with you. Interesting."

"Rather a piece of luck." Aulus paused, smiling, not wanting to reveal too much without knowing what Mithridates knew.

"How did you come by them?"

"We Romans get around." Aulus did not want to reveal that the Hanaeans had indirectly provided them.

Time to get off this subject. "This tea is excellent. I think we in the west could develop quite a taste for it."

"It is becoming popular in my home as well, but slowly. The Hanaeans maintain a monopoly on its production, so every outgoing bail must pay an enormous tariff and make its way slowly and at great cost by land and sea. It's quite a luxury at home."

Aulus had had many business dealings with Parthians, Rome's fierce competitors in Asia Minor, and had found that managing information was the key to success in dealing with them. Conceal what you know, and ferret out what they know. The victory always seemed to go to the one who managed to stay one or two steps ahead of the other, knowing one or two things the other did not. Right now he wanted to know what Mithridates knew, for he certainly would try to sabotage any relationship between Rome and the Hanaean court before it could emerge.

They kept the verbal sparring match going for the better part of an hour, making small talk about various seemingly inconsequential subjects, probing each other without appearing to pry. At the end, Aulus hoped that what little he had learned exceeded what he may have inadvertently given away.

"So, Cyrus, it has been a pleasure," said Aulus, placing his teacup on the low table in front of them, "but I must return to my quarters. I am expecting my miniscule entourage to return from their tour of the city at any minute."

"The pleasure has been mine. I hope we can resume this conversation sometime soon." Cyrus extended his hand, and Aulus returned the handshake firmly.

Gaius and Antonius returned to their suite a bit after sundown.

"Guess who's in town, cousin?" announced Gaius with a smile.

"Let me guess... Julius Caesar, back from the dead," answered Aulus, with a chuckle.

"Close! Our good friend Ibrahim and a few of his minions."

"That *fellator*! Well, he said he was coming. What minions? And what the fuck is he doing here?"

Gaius laughed, amused at the string of profanity that was more intense than any he had ever heard from his normally staid senatorial cousin. "One question at a time. He is here with Yakov, his inseparable doer of dirty deeds, and Galosga and Shmuel, I think more to hitch a ride than to make sure he stayed out of trouble. He is traveling with another Arab he met in Tianjin who has business here. As to what he is doing here, he told us back in Tianjin that he wants to start his new life as a shepherd, ending as he began." Gaius chuckled a bit more at his cousin's angry demeanor and perplexity.

"That bloody pirate! I should have crucified him to the main mast!"

"He had quite a following among the crew, and I think you'd have had to crucify at least half. Relax, we knew about the shepherding, though I don't quite believe it myself. He said this was where the land opens up enough to support grazing."

"I am still not happy over the 'ransom' you paid out of my funds."

"We negotiated that deal when I didn't even know if you were still alive. He kept his end, got us on our way here, and I kept mine. And it only lightened your chest by a few pounds," Gaius said, eyeing the massive locked chest containing gold and silver for Emperor He.

"Well, you trust him far more that I do, and I respect your judgment. But I want you to understand something. He is not to know anything about what goes on in here, who we meet, what we say. Absolutely nothing. Do not compromise this mission in any way, Gaius Lucullus!"

Antonius and Marcus had watched the stormy session in silence. Antonius decided it was time to intervene to calm tempers. "I'll see to that, sir," he affirmed in his best centurion's gravelly growl.

"Please do so." He exhaled slowly, and everyone stood around in awkward silence. Aulus continued: "Well, that is out of the way. Now you guess who I met today!"

"I have no idea," answered Gaius curtly, still smarting from the rather public tongue lashing he had just received.

"Well, among many others, I met the Parthian ambassador. Fellow by the name of Cyrus Mithridates, and a less trustworthy soul you're not likely to meet. At least he speaks excellent Greek. Ming left us alone, and we spent an hour chatting. I managed to find out a few things he let slip."

"What were those, sir?" asked Marcus, trying to help dispel the still uncomfortable air.

"Well, not only did he not seem to know we were coming until just before we arrived, he apparently didn't know about Gan Ying's mission to Rome with you, Marcus. Apparently this court can keep a secret when it wants to.

And Mithridates has been here ten years and speaks the language quite fluently."

"I know him," interjected Marcus. "He does speak Hanaean very well."

"Well, it's good you know him. Well, or just casually?"

"Casually. He is well above my status in the court."

"Surprised you never mentioned that the Parthians were already here. He said that Parthia has been here for centuries."

"Probably correct. Certainly a long time," answered Marcus. "I thought you knew that, sir, sorry. The two territories are quite close, almost bordering on each other, separated by the *Da Yuan* and the *Yuezhi*."

"No problem. But I have a favor to ask. Make sure you check with Ming to see what he has on schedule for me, before leaving the palace. Ming made a lot of introductions today, but the only name I remember was Bai Wei, he appears to be some sort of chief of staff or secretary to the Emperor, but all that Ming could say in Latin was 'He tell when come see Emperor He.' His Latin is not up to what I need."

"I am sorry, I had no idea Ming would be taking you around so soon. Yes, Wei is the Emperor's appointments secretary, a most important person."

"The others were also, probably. Can you get with Ming to determine whom I saw, and what their positions are in the grand scheme of things, Marcus?"

"I will do so, sir."

Turning to his still-smoldering cousin, he slapped him on the back, and led him to his stash of Hanaean rice wine and a rapidly dwindling stock of Italian wine. "Red or white, cousin? Then you can tell me what you and your pirate scoundrel talked about in town."

CHAPTER 43: DIPLOMATIC INTRIGUE

It seemed that the Hanaean court could keep a secret, after all. They had kept Gan Ying's expedition completely hidden from Cyrus years ago, and Ming's role in it, though he had managed to ferret out its existence a few months after they had left. Just in time for a quick dispatch to Ctesiphon to warn the King of Kings Pacorus II of the expedition's impending arrival, and recommend it not reach Rome.

The Parthian government never let him know what they did in response, and they had chosen not to tell him of the mission's ultimate success in reaching Rome, and Aulus's return mission. Ctesiphon certainly knew that, with the many Parthian agents in Rome and around Trajan's court. In any event, Cyrus had not learned of Ming's successful return with Aulus until a few weeks before their arrival, shortly after they had docked in Tianjin.

He was also surprised to learn that the expedition had bilingual, biliterate translators. He knew some of the Liqian peasants, particularly Wang Ming's concubine Si Huar and her brother Si Nuo, but did not know that they spoke Latin, even had Latin names as well. Cyrus doubted that more than handful of Romans knew even rudimentary words in *han-yu*, and even fewer Hanaeans knew Latin. He had been counting on the language barrier preventing any serious two-way diplomatic contact for a long time. He understood now why, ten years ago, the Hanaean court had brought these rustic but bilingual country bumpkins from Gansu to the palace to be trained in court manners and protocol.

He was not surprised that the Hanaean court had kept all this a secret from him. That was their way. But he was concerned that his government had not kept him informed. No acknowledgement of his warning four years ago, so long ago that he had in fact forgotten all about it. No warning that the mission had gotten through, and a Roman return mission was enroute to Luoyang. Now here he was surprised, with a small but intrusive Roman emissary in his domain, and no clear guidance. He would just have to improvise.

Cyrus went to Ming's office, was admitted and saluted him respectfully. "Welcome back, Master Ming, I hope your trip was not arduous. It has been many years since I have had the pleasure of your company and wise counsel." The liquid vowels of the Hanaean tongue rippled smoothly from his mouth. "I hope sometime, at your convenience, you may share with me your great adventures."

"Now would be fine, Kore-si," answered Ming, using the Hanean pronunciation of his name. "Please, sit and I will have my servants bring us tea." He clapped his hand, and a servant emerged from the shadows, bowed, left, and returned with steaming cups. They both sipped in silence, with Cyrus waiting for Ming to break the silence. It was their custom.

"The moon is beautiful on the open sea," said Ming, poetically.

"It is indeed, Master Ming." Cyrus hoped this poetical diversion would not take too long. "It reflects from the shattered mirrors of the waves."

"Your poetry has improved in my absence, Kore-si."

"It has been my pleasure to try to master your great language with my humble skills."

"You have done well." Another long introspective pause. "We spent a long time on ships, and I had many opportunities to observe the moon at sea."

"The stars are also splendid in the desert, as at sea. Those who have not spent time in either have never really seen the stars."

Another long pause. Ming clapped, and he servant fetched a pot to refill their cups. "You did not come here to share images of the moon and stars, Kore-si." Ming chuckled, in a rare show of well-controlled humor. "You want to hear of my visit to the *Da Qin* emperor."

"Only if you wish to share it with me, Master Ming."

"Ah well, it was an arduous trip getting there. After a long overland trip of many months, we reached your home of *Anxi*. We were surprised to find them expecting us, and your government provided a ship to take us to a port far to the south. Our translators met some *Da Qin* there who provided us another ship to take us north, at the end of which was a magnificent white city on the water, the most beautiful I have ever seen, with a lighthouse visible for many miles. We thought it was Rome, but it was just a way station. In another few weeks, we were in Rome, the capital of *Da Qin*. The Emperor was most cordial to us, and also to our translators. He had a special ceremony just for them, which we did not understand. Si Huar said she and the other translator are descendants of *Da Qin* soldiers defeated by your country a long time ago. At the end, Gan Ying and most of the others returned overland, but to date they have not returned. Very sad, they may have met some misfortune." Another long silence, and more tea. "So do you have any questions, Kore-si?"

"How was your return trip?"

"The Romans built special ships for us. We spent some time in the beautiful white city by the sea, in a land as old as our own, with a magnificent library. There was a bit of a problem at sea, some problem with the shipping master. But it was all resolved, we rejoined, but had to leave one ship behind in India."

"I am glad that all went well," said Cyrus. Then he prematurely broached the subject he most needed to know. "Do you intend a close relation with the *Da Qin* as you have shared with the *Anxi?*"

"That is the decision of the Son of Heaven, not his lowly footservant."

"May I offer my recommendation, Master Ming?"

"Of course, your advice is always welcome."

"Our country has had the opportunity to be in close contact with both your Middle Kingdom and Rome for several centuries now. I cannot say enough about the close trust and affection we have for you and the Son of Heaven and all his ancestors. We have been at peace this whole time.

"We cannot say the same for the Romans. They speak sweetly of peace and brotherhood, freedom and justice, then stab us in the back, intrude on our territories, launch attacks that devastate wide swaths of our territory. They have not been good neighbors to us, or to any other of the peoples around the Middle Sea. I doubt they will be good friends to the Middle Kingdom. They are greedy and ruthless, and will not rest until all the world is enslaved to them. I do not recommend that the Son of Heaven form any close bond with them. Take what they offer, and send them home."

"Your advice is noted, Kore-si. You have always been a good friend." Ming finished his tea, then clapped his hands. "But now I must attend to many things that have been waiting my attention for five years. You must be sure, I will consider your advice."

"Thank you, Master Ming" said Cyrus, saluting with a bow as he exited.

Wang Ming smiled. It seems that the Romans may not have a monopoly on double-dealing. When Gan Ying's party arrived in Ctesiphon, the capital of *Anxi*, they had received a well-prepared and totally unexpected greeting from Kore-si's government, thanks, they said, to a letter sent by Kore-si announcing their itinerary and destination, which had been a state secret, Kore-si carefully excluded from its planning. No matter, ambassadors are expected to poke into things that should not concern them. But then there was the roundabout detour into the Indian Ocean, and their abrupt abandonment by the skipper. "This is Rome, I must return," was his last lie.

Fortunately the translators had located some Roman traders there, astounded to find such an important party seeking transport for an audience with Trajan. They were quickly put on a luxurious northbound ship, and on the way, were shown maps that revealed that the Parthians had sent them thousands of miles around Arabia quite intentionally. He would take Kore-si's warning of Roman double-dealing with very many grains of salt.

Gan Ying had left the *Da Qin* capital almost three years ago to return overland, but they were a year overdue, almost certainly lost. Bai Wei, the imperial secretary, had advised him yesterday to be ready to meet Emperor He in the next few days and tell him of the results of the trip. Gan Ying was the professional diplomat and would have known what to tell the emperor. Wang Ming was uncertain how to do this, especially with the Parthians clearly meddling in this new relationship.

Ming retreated to Si Huar's rooms in the women's quarters. She was dressed in a beautiful blue silk shift, doing something with her hair with the aid of a servant. She rose when he entered and dismissed her servant girl with a gentle wave of her hands. She bowed in greeting: "Welcome, Master Ming!"

"Good day to you, Si Huar. I seek your advice on important matters concerning the *Da Qin*." He sat down on the floor cross-legged in front of a table, and Si Huar sat modestly, knees together, on the other side.

"Shall I have tea brought?" asked Si Huar.

"No, I have drunk far too much tea this afternoon. You are the only *Da Qin* I trust enough to give me an honest answer," answered Ming.

"I really know only what my parents taught me, from what their parents taught them. It is very old, and no longer accurate. The Rome I saw on our journey was not the Rome I had envisioned from our stories," answered Si Huar.

"But if you were to have children, would you continue to teach them Latin and the old stories, as your parents did, and your ancestors before them?"

"But of course!" She paused. "That is not to say I judge my Roman side to be better than my Hanaean side. After five generations, there is very little of me that is still Roman." She giggled. He smiled, and Si Huar offered a shy smile in return. These were things she rarely did with him, and he felt surprisingly affectionate toward her.

"What is it about being *Da Qin* that has made you keep that thought alive all this time?"

"*Da Qin* are much like Hanaeans in many ways, Ming," she replied, omitting the 'master.' Ming chose not to correct her. "We both place high value on honor and honesty. Where we differ … the Roman side allows us to be individuals, to stand out, while the Hanaean side wants us to be harmonious. Inside the people of Liqian, that should be a conflict. But we have lived with it so long, the contradiction is part of our nature." She smiled again. "Do you understand? Am I helping?"

"More than you know." He also smiled, something he also rarely did with her, and the two sat for long minutes, just looking at each other with new understanding. He then reached across the table, took her hands in his, leaned forward and kissed her gently. This girl may prove useful after all.

Later that afternoon, they made love, and to Wang Ming's great surprise, she seemed to enjoy it as much as he did.

CHAPTER 44: THE OFFICIAL PRESENTATION

Wang Ming stood before Bai Wei early the next morning, to find that he was to meet with the Son of Heaven after lunch. He was briefed on dress, protocol, manner of speaking, all of the details critical to that meeting. But Ming had never met the Emperor, or even seen him in person except at ceremonial occasions in the North Palace, from a great distance. He had, on occasion, made presentations to several of the Emperor's most senior officials on matters financial, his area of expertise. But this would be wholly different, and the consequences of displeasing the emperor could be fatal. He did his best to conceal his inner turmoil.

He returned to his quarters in mid- morning, and dressed in his best blue silk robe. He had his servants carefully arrange his black shiny hair around the formal black curled hat. When all was in place about eleven, he decided to visit Si Huar in the women's quarters again, but not for connubial reasons. She could exert a most calming influence on him, and he needed calming.

They exchanged pleasantries on his entry, then with uncharacteristic abruptness, he announced: "I am meeting with the Son of Heaven in a few hours."

"You will do well. I am proud of you, Master Ming," she said, while carefully adjusting the fit of his robe, and tucking away a loose strand of his hair.

"Thank you, but I wish Master Gan Ying were here instead of me. He is the diplomat."

"You will do well," she repeated. "Just try not to say too much. Think of each word before you say it, because it will leave your lips like a bird, never to be retrieved."

Ming found this new relationship with Si Huar stimulating. He had always thought of her as the child he had taken ten years ago, to be raised and disciplined. His stern discipline was paying off now, and she was becoming a useful source of counsel and advice.

They talked about much of nothing for a while. He did not want to sit down, for fear of disturbing his carefully arranged robe. Finally, after about half an hour, he made his departure, and arrived at Bai Wei's reception area probably an hour ahead of time.

Eventually, the bronze door to the Emperor's chamber swung open noiselessly, and Wei whispered, "You may go in now." Ming took a deep breath and entered.

The door closed behind him, and he blinked, adjusting his eyes to the dim interior. Light entered from windows far away, and lanterns hung from the ceiling. More lanterns perched on square stone pedestals. At the far end sat the Son of Heaven on a plain black polished throne, elevated on a shining granite dais. Surrounding the dais was water flowing in a square channel that separated the emperor from his audience like a moat, lamps along its border casting reflected light off its placid surface.

Flanking the emperor were his most senior counselors, fifteen on a side, seated on their knees facing each other across the floor. Before each counselor was a low black lacquer table, some blank paper, ink and a writing brush, all carefully and identically arranged. In one corner, a tall pale green vase sprouted an array of fresh flowers, the only color and curved shape in the room otherwise decorated in shades of gray, black and blue squares. All was silent.

Ming saluted very formally, bowed, swept his robes about him and knelt down. He lowered his head to the floor and remained there in total silence for what seemed like minutes. Far away, he could hear the tinkle of water filling the moat. Finally, the Son of Heaven summoned him. "Wang Ming, my good servant, please tell me of your mission to the land of the *Da Qin*." This was Ming's cue to return to a sitting position, his hands placed properly on his thighs, eyes downcast.

"Son of Heaven, your servant Wang Ming brings you greetings from the Emperor Trajan of the *Da Qin*. He wishes you peace and good health, and has sent his envoys with gifts."

"I look forward to meeting his envoys," replied the Son of Heaven, using the exaggerated and slow intonations of imperial speech. "What sort of place is this mysterious land?"

"Son of Heaven, it is a big land, and I could only see a small part. It is the size of the Middle Kingdom, and the cities that I saw were vast, gleaming with white marble, and filled with people who were clean and healthy. They bring water from hundreds of miles away to their cities, and connect them with fine roads."

"They are not barbarians?"

"They live in cities or farms. They read and write, but not as we do. Their writing is as strange as their speech, and your humble servant was able to master little of either."

"Tell me more about this emperor, Trajan is his name?"

"Yes. Trajan appears to rule fairly and with justice. He is a military man who came to the position by merit. He is widely praised."

"Do they choose all their emperors by merit?"

Si Huar's analogy of words like birds came immediately to mind, for he had no idea how their emperors were chosen, other than Trajan himself; chosen, he was told, to replace an indecisive and unpopular one. Was this the rule? He did not know. And he did not know how the Son of Heaven would respond to ignorance of a question which might reflect badly on his own rule. In fact, he did not know for sure how the Hanaean emperors were chosen! Ming pondered his answer, drew a breath, and thought of Si Huar's birds: "Son of Heaven, I do not know, except for this one case. I will attempt to get a better answer, if you wish."

A long silence filled the room, just the tinkling waterfall far away in the back of the room. Ming's heart thudded in his chest.

Finally, the Son of Heaven answered with just a hint of a smile. "There are few of my servants who have the courage to admit their ignorance of a fact. You answered well. I now will allow my counselors to pose additional questions."

There followed several questions from the counselors, mostly trivial: were the people tall or short? Did they all have beards? These were mostly related to various myths held by the Hanaeans about the people of the west. Wang Ming easily disposed of them.

Then General Ban Chao spoke up. He was the senior military adviser to Emperor He, seated at the head of the right hand column of counselors, the one closest to the emperor. It was he who had organized Gan Ying's expedition. "How was it that you came to be separated from Gan Ying?" The tone seemed accusatorial.

"General Chao, it was by Gan Ying's choosing. We completed our mission three years ago, and it was his desire to return expeditiously home by the overland route. I was to remain in the land of the *Da Qin* while they built three ships for their return mission. I and the five translators were to accompany the *Da Qin* envoys, see them safely through our ports and to the palace here in Luoyang, none of which they could do on their own. He should have returned by now. I fear some misfortune may have befallen him."

"Do you know his intended route?" asked General Chao.

"I do. He gave me his itinerary before he left, which I brought with me, along with a copy of his report. He reached inside his robe to withdraw a paper roll. "I have read his itinerary. His report was sealed and addressed to you."

Without being asked, a servant appeared out of the shadows, and bowing, accepted the rolls from Ming and scurried over to give them to General Chao. The general studied the itinerary intensely, then announced: "I do not know some of the cities named, but he appears to have intended to return by way of the *Anxi* and *Da Yuan*, a very traditional route. Though on occasion bandits beset a caravan." He paused, then continued. "Is there any chance the *Da Qin* may have done Gan Ying harm, preferring you and their envoy to return here, rather than his?"

Ming lingered over his answer. He was suspicious now that the Parthian *Anxi* might have sabotaged Gan Ying's return, not knowing that there was another enroute. But that bird of words, in Si Huar's beautiful simile, was not yet old enough to leave the nest. "I saw nothing but cooperation and interest from all the *Da Qin* people we met, high and low. However, one cannot discount the possibility."

"We will attempt to retrace his route, to determine how far Gan Ying may have travelled and what may have befallen him. I will study his report. Thank you for your answers, Ming."

Ming bowed his head. "Excellency!"

There followed another brief silence, then the Son of Heaven spoke. "If there are no other questions, I have one more difficult one for you, servant Ming."

"Son of Heaven, I will give you my best answer."

"Would you recommend that I meet with the *Da Qin* envoy now, or send them home as unwelcome guests?"

Another long pause while Ming collected the squabbling birds in his mind. "Neither, sir. I have heard from some close to both the Middle Kingdom and the *Da Qin* that they are untrustworthy grasping devils that seek to rule the world, which does not align with the emperor and people we met. Gan Yang's sealed report has not yet been read, which may contain his own insights and recommendations, which are far wiser than my own poor judgments...he is the diplomat, and I am but a financial officer. And there is the question of the disappearance of Gan Yang and his expedition on a well-travelled route."

"Who might have suggested the *Da Qin* might be untrustworthy?"

"Son of Heaven, the *Anxi* have had a close relation with both our people for centuries."

"That they have. And I cannot imagine them wishing to share their relations with us with the *Da Qin*...Servant Ming, you have answered us well. You may leave while we ponder your wise answers."

"Son of Heaven!" Ming rose to his feet, bowed deeply at the waist, and backed out of the room. The bronze door swung open silently to permit his exit.

CHAPTER 45: A NEW FREEDOM

Aulus had avoided his cousin's invitations to join him and Antonius in town the first week in Luoyang. He was expecting an imperial summons at any time, and needed to deal with the logistics of the expedition, using cover letters Ming had provided him that allowed him to send correspondence through the Hanaean post. All he had to do was attach one of the Hanaean cover letters to his Latin correspondence. The two were then given to Ming, who sent them to the port authority in Tianjin under his seal for delivery to the *Da Qin* vessels there. Delivery would take about two weeks each way, depending on weather, but it allowed him to maintain contact with the *Asia* and *Europa*.

Aulus sent his first letter to Lucius Parvus describing the process. Parvus was to attach Ming's covering letter to his response, and the port authorities would seal and deliver it back to the Imperial Palace.

The letter was written in his fine uncial script, bringing Lucius up to date on the journey, and included a coded portion. He underlined one word in the clear text to be used as the key word in a Caesar cipher to decrypt the encoded text at the end, a simple cipher that he and Lucius had often used. Using the key, he encrypted the rest of the message, affirming his intent for them to sail on Ides of April, adding that he expected to be sailing with them. The Parthians could probably break such simple cipher, though the plain text alone would be inscrutable to the Hanaeans. Still, he felt better using it.

That done, he delivered the first package to Ming, who accepted the letters graciously and remarked "Nice day! Why not go out town?"

"I want to be available if Emperor He wants me to have an audience with him."

"Not today, I let you know if he want see you. Go enjoy nice day. Tomorrow will be cold again," said Ming with a rare smile. His Latin was improving, even on occasion using case and tense correctly, even if only the simplest ones. Aulus, in his efforts to learn Hanaean, had found that the language not only didn't have those grammatical distinctions, but the same word could be a noun, adjective or verb. It must be confusing to Ming to master concepts so totally unnecessary in Hanaean. At any rate, Ming's Latin was far better than Aulus' paltry Hanaean.

"I am afraid I let Marcus go with Gaius and Antonius this morning. I should have gone with them."

"Si Huar go town, go with you."

"Si Huar?" Then he remembered, having heard Marcia's Hanaean name before. "Oh, yes, she would be fine! Any problem?"

"No problem. I get for you." He clapped his hands, a servant appeared, and Ming chattered something in Hanaean. The servant bowed and left abruptly."

"Tea?" asked Ming.

"Yes. Please," replied Aulus. Ming clapped his hands again, and another servant brought china cups and a pot of steaming green tea. Aulus sat down on the pillow, trying to match the cat-like litheness with which Hanaeans seemed to sink into a seated posture, legs under them, knees together. Aulus felt anything but cat-like assuming the position, but at least no longer needed to brace himself with his hand to get into it.

They sipped tea, while Ming studied some scrolls. There was no point in small talk, and Ming's working spared them both the embarrassment of staring at each other, trying to think of something simple enough to say that the other would understand.

After about half an hour, Marcia appeared in a green silk robe with a wide floral sash, her hair done up in a bun. She smiled and chatted with Ming, who returned the smile. *Funny, I never saw the two of them smile at each other before.* Marcia then turned to Aulus, and took his hand, Roman-style, beaming.

"Aulus Aemilius, how good it is to see you!"

"We have missed you also, Marcia. You seem to be well and happy."

"We are!" Aulus noticed that she said 'we,' not 'I.' Aulus had not been close to her, as they had been on different ships for most of the cruise; But he could not help noticing, after Ming ordered her return to the *Asia* after their rendezvous, that their relationship was stormy, and she was decidedly unhappy to be back in his company. Apparently their relationship had improved considerably since.

"Ming offered me as your escort and translator, as I want to go out in town today, just to get out of the women's quarters for a while. Have you seen the city of Luoyang yet?"

"No, I haven't. Gaius and Antonius have, and are out in town now with your brother."

Marcia turned to chat with Ming again, then turned to Aulus again. "We have all day, until sunset." She bowed toward Ming, as did Aulus. Ming returned a head nod with a small smile. She turned and led him out of Ming's office. "Let's go!"

Leaving the palace, they found it to be indeed one of those unusually warm days in December, bright sun with high horsetail clouds overhead in a deep blue sky, and a few puffy clouds scudding along the horizon in the light breezes. Other than the leafless trees, it could be springtime, and a few people were milling about the parks and vast white courtyard of the palace, or queuing up to leave by the gates to enjoy the town and riverside parks outside.

Everyone knew this respite from winter would not last long, but it was to be enjoyed, however short.

"You dress well, Hanaean style," remarked Marcia. Aulus was clad in a dark blue wool robe over a lighter blue silk gown and black silk trousers, a black pill box hat on his head.

"My toga would be out of place," he chuckled. "It would attract too many stares. Other than my round Roman blue eyes and my inability to put more than five Hanaean words together in a sentence, I could be taken for a local!" He quipped, then continued. "Things seem well between you and Ming." He was uncomfortable intruding on her private life.

"Very well indeed, better than any in our time together. Ming had to meet with the Emperor last week, and he was quite concerned. He asked for my help to prepare information on things Roman. His meeting went well, and we have been very good together since."

"I am glad he sees you as more of a partner," said Aulus.

"Not really. I am still his courtesan, not his partner. But better to be appreciated than not."

They came to the eastern gate. Marcia spoke a few words through the sliding speakeasy in the door to the guard outside, and the door swung open to permit their exit past the impassive blue-clad guard. They went into the government administration part of town and proceeded north to the market area. Marcia pointed out the army headquarters building, and the financial center where Ming sometimes also worked. Reaching the market area, the streets were crowded with people, bustling about to do their shopping on such a fine day, a delightful hubbub of dogs barking, children playing, and a thousand conversations going on at once.

Marcia took Aulus along on her errands, browsing markets, inspecting produce and haggling for prices, but buying little. "As a lady of the court, I don't normally do my own shopping. But this reminds me of when I was a little girl, going shopping in Liqian with my mother. And when I do buy, I give great status to the shopkeeper."

She purchased a small bag of rice and some fresh vegetables from the stall's shopkeeper, who smiled effusively, bowing repeatedly as he accepted her coins. "Let's get some lunch."

She found a small stall selling cooked meats and rice over charcoal grills. It reminded Aulus of the many *cauponae* food stalls that seemed to exist on every block in Rome. The meat was skewered on a long white stick of some sort, the rice steaming in a bowl with two more sticks. She purchased their lunch, and a bottle of warmed rice wine. Around the stalls were pillows on the ground for seating. Marcia sat down gracefully, Aulus less so, trying to avoid spilling his rice.

"Do you know how to use the *kuaizi*?" she asked, pointing to his chopsticks. "I am sorry, I don't know the Latin word for them. It means 'quick bamboo' in Hanaean."

"I don't think there is a Latin word for them! Anyway, these are one of the first things I learned. You either learn to use these or eat with your hand, as someone told me." Aulus picked up the chopsticks with some familiarity, and deposited most of a lump of rice in his mouth, with only a few grains finding their way to his robe. Marcia giggled, expertly snared a mouthful of rice from her bowl and reached across to playfully deposit it in Aulus' open mouth.

They had finished their lunch, and were halfway through the bottle of wine, when Gaius and Antonius, accompanied by Ibrahim and Marcus, rounded the corner. Aulus and Marcia rose with big smiles. Marcia greeted her brother with a tender handclasp, while Aulus accosted his cousin with a hug, then pumped Antonius' hand in a firm Roman grip. He turned to Ibrahim with a bit less warmth. "I heard you were in town," he said coolly. "Still stalking us, are you?"

Ibrahim smiled behind his salt-and-pepper beard. "Not by intent. I am here to begin the end of my life as I began, as a shepherd. The grazing country begins west of here."

"I understand you have assembled quite a raiding party to capture your sheep!"

"A few, yes. Yakov, Shmuel and Galosga from the *Europa* came along to make sure I didn't get in any trouble, and a countryman I met in Tianjin, Musa. "

"So where are they today?"

"They are off in Musa's boat, fishing. He wanted to tighten the rigging and it is a beautiful day to be out."

"It is a nice day."

Marcia turned to greet Antonius. "My dearest Antonius! It is such a pleasure to see you again! I have missed our long talks," she said with a smile. She clasped his hand warmly.

"*Domina*! My lady! I am hopin' all be well with yer!"

"All is very well!" she answered with a smile. "Tell me all about your adventures!" The six settled down onto the cushions, while the shopkeeper brought more food and wine.

Across the street, in another food stall, Cyrus Mithridates observed the gathering, the flirtatious way that Marcia had fed Aulus a bite of rice, the warm greeting that she had given the rough soldier, and their close and intense personal conversation that seemed to exclude the other four. There could be something to be made of this encounter, he thought.

CHAPTER 46: THE WATCHERS

Cyrus pondered what he had seen in town. The Romans were unremarkable; they went out into the city frequently, though never before with Aulus. But the sixth man caught his attention, tall with an aristocratic bearing that indicated someone used to command... a westerner, obviously, with his well-trimmed beard, but Cyrus had been unable to pinpoint his ethnicity. The man could be from anywhere from Asia Minor to Spanish Iberia. And he was not part of the mission.

It would not be unusual for Europeans to seek out their fellows in such a foreign land, if for no reason other than to speak in their native tongue, and exchange personal observations. Still, it seemed to bear closer inspection.

Cyrus kept a small entourage of Hanaeans who would act as his eyes and ears for a few coins. Never against the Imperial government of course; that could risk a slow and agonizing death for treason and espionage. But harmless information on the reputation of a trader, or in this case, a westerner, was safe and easy money. And Cyrus never betrayed his sources.

As expected, the respite from winter did not last long. The following day, cold air from the harsh northwest returned, borne by screaming winds that sought out every crack in palace or hovel, driving chill rain at a sharp angle. By day's end, rain turned to sleet, then to snow. It was a few days before the weather subsided enough for the Romans to once again venture out. His sources brought in their first reports, none knowing of the others, all reporting very similar stories. The tall, bearded man possessed some wealth, silver coins in his purse, but spoke little Hanaean, and none of the agents were able to determine his name. He was in the company of another man, a boatman who spoke very good Hanaean. His name was Ma, a boatbuilder from Tianjin.

Three others rounded out the party: a short, wiry man, a large black-bearded man, and a person of Mongolian features, both of who had the broad shoulders, narrow hips, and sculpted muscles of fighting men. Bodyguards, perhaps? None spoke any Hanaean.

It seemed unusual that an apparently wealthy man should be staying on a simple boat with three companions, but this seemed less unusual the more Cyrus thought about it. While a few silver coins could buy accommodations at a nice inn for several weeks, the man spoke no Hanaean. Not only would he find it difficult to negotiate quarters, he would be at the mercy of any rapacious landlord who wanted to separate as many silver coins from an ignorant barbarian as he could. Worse, if word got out of a well-heeled foreigner who spoke no Hanaean, he would likely be found in an alley, separated not only from his purse but his life. No, staying in humble accommodations surrounded by friends with whom he could speak, two of whom seemed to be beefy bodyguards, that made perfectly good sense.

What did not make sense was that he and Ma were attempting to negotiate the purchase of a flock of sheep. The boat was not big enough to take a flock back to Tianjin, and there was precious little grazing land east of Luoyang. If taking them back as meat, there were plenty of butchers who would sell prepared carcasses, no need to buy hundreds of live animals on the hoof. One informant indicated that the tall man was actually inquiring about grazing rights, water rights and pasturage, as though he himself intended to become a shepherd.

That was laughable. One only became a shepherd if one were born to the life, and no better alternative was available. This might be a cover for some other activity...espionage? No one looked twice at a shepherd and his flock, but what would he be spying on in the mountains? And the Mongolian. Not unheard of in Hanaean lands, but relatively rare except for wealthy and politically powerful clan leaders and their entourages. And they all spoke at least passable Hanaean. An outcast, picked up as bodyguard? Or a tribal contact man, intended to carry messages back and forth?

Individually, the two threads didn't convey much. But putting together three Europeans with an unlikely cover story, and a Mongolian agent, on friendly terms with the Imperial Roman envoy... this was no coincidence. Nevertheless, Cyrus Mithridates would need more information before taking this before Wang Ming.

After several days of further probes, Cyrus had gained no new information on the envoys' contacts. Nevertheless, he decided to present his information to Ming, in as unfavorable a light as possible, of course, including Si Huar's flirtation, not only with Antonius, but with Aulus himself. Ming politely received the information and dismissed Cyrus, apparently disinterested.

Ming himself had spent the past three years surrounded by foreigners, unable to communicate with most. Had he encountered a fellow Hanaean in Rome, he most certainly would have jumped at the chance to communicate with a fellow countryman. So he was not surprised at the idea of westerners gravitating toward their fellows here. It was entirely understandable. And the Parthian envoy had every motivation to present anything involving the *Da Qin* in an unfavorable light. The information about Si Huar disturbed him though... he had long believed she had adulterous intentions toward the big *Da Qin* soldier. But Aulus? No, the old man was probably a father figure to her.

Nevertheless, it was worthwhile to conduct his own investigation. He dispatched his own agents, while he studied his copy of Gan Ying's report, returned to him by Ban Chao. The report seemed favorable enough:

"The territory of the Da Qin extends for several thousands of miles, with more than four hundred walled towns. There are several tens of smaller dependent kingdoms. The walls of the towns are made of stone. They have established postal relays at intervals, which are all plastered and whitewashed. There are pines and cypresses, as well as trees and plants of all kinds."

Gan Ying had given favorable comments on their politics and honor, corroborating Ming's report:

"Their kings are not permanent. They select and appoint the most worthy man. If there are unexpected calamities in the kingdom, such as frequent extraordinary winds or rains, he is unceremoniously rejected and replaced. The one who has been dismissed quietly accepts his demotion, and is not angry. The people of this country are all tall and honest. They resemble the people of the Middle Kingdom and that is why this kingdom is called Da Qin, 'Great China'.

Finally, he reported favorably on their trade and industry:

"This country produces plenty of gold and silver, rare and precious things like luminous jade, bright moon pearls, Haiji rhinoceroses, coral, yellow amber, opaque glass, whitish chalcedony, red cinnabar, green gemstones, goldthread embroideries, rugs woven with gold thread, delicate polychrome silks painted with gold, and asbestos cloth. They also have a fine cloth which some people say is made from the down of 'water sheep,' but which is made, in fact, from the cocoons of wild silkworms. They blend all sorts of fragrances, and by boiling the juice, make a compound called perfume. They have all the precious and rare things that come from the various foreign kingdoms. They make gold and silver coins. Ten silver coins are worth one gold coin. They trade with Anxi and northwest India by sea. The profit margin is ten to one."

Finally, the report took issue with Parthians, confirming Ming's suspicions of the motive behind the *Anxi* ambassador Kore-Si's dire reports of Roman underhandedness.

"The king of this country always wanted to send envoys to Han, but the Anxi, wishing to control the trade in multi-colored Hanaean silks, blocked the route to prevent the Romans from getting through to Hanaean lands."

The report went on for several more pages, all generally as favorable as the first page. Ming set aside Gan Ying's report, and pondered his own impression of Rome and the other *Da Qin* cities: attractive, well-built, well-run. Obviously wealthy with massive public baths and libraries open to all citizens. He pondered his recommendation while sipping his tea, and decided to await the report of his own agents.

Ming's agents returned in a few days and quickly confirmed much of what Mithridates had disclosed, and went one better than the Parthian's agents: they had engaged the Hanaean-speaking Ma in idle conversation, eventually gaining his confidence enough to ask him directly about his companions.

Ma revealed, without any apparent concern, that his companions had been on the *Da Qin* ships now in Tianjin with the envoys. They were not only acquainted, but close friends.

As for his becoming a shepherd, Ma was amused at his tall companion seeking this line of work, but insisted he was indeed serious, since he had been born a shepherd many years ago in a faraway desert land. Ma had laughed, sharing with Ming's agent his doubts that his friend's enthusiasm would outlast his first Hanaean winter.

The Mongolian-appearing individual was as big a mystery to the Westerners as to the Hanaeans. He was not Mongolian, and one of the agents, fluent in several Mongolian languages, spoke several short common phrases, evincing nothing but a blank stare. Ma, translating for the group, happily informed Ming's agent that the individual had been on the ship its entire journey, and before that had served on many ships from the far western end of the world. It seemed highly unlikely that this man was a Mongolian, and on close inspection, they said his eyes were not right, though his hair and skin color were similar.

The agents' continued their polite conversation with Ma, shared several cups of tea with him and his companions, and then departed.

Ming took their extremely bland report, dismissed them, pondering what they had told him. The tall man intrigued him. He had been on the other ship, the one they called *Europa*. Ming vaguely remembered him from the few times he had been aboard that ship, but didn't recall him being aboard any of the ships at the beginning of the trip. There had been the strange incident in mid-ocean, when the ships broke formation and separated. His Latin was nowhere near the task of finding out what had happened, and he was confined to his cabin along with his translators for about a week. Eventually, they were boarded by a *Da Qin* warship and the shipping master taken off in chains. Aulus had talked rather vehemently of piracy, but Ming thought it was their own ships that had been hijacked. Had the other ship been hijacked as well?

That night, after lovemaking, he asked Si Huar to relate to him the hijacking as seen from *Europa's* deck. While the tall man, whose name she said was Ibrahim, had indeed been a pirate, a bond of trust had formed between him and the two *Da Qin* by the time *Asia* had caught up with them. They had forged some sort of deal to get them to *Ch'in*.

Wang Ming considered these facts overnight, and concluded that the relationship with Ibrahim and the Romans seemed unlikely, but personal. He decided to keep them under general surveillance, but it was time to prepare his recommendation to convey to to the Son of Heaven, based on Gan Ying's report and his own impression of the *Da Qin*.

The following morning, Ming called on Bai Wei to set up an appointment. After the obligatory exchange of pleasantries and a cup of tea, Ming got down to business.

"Excellency, I would like to conclude our business with the *Da Qin*. I have prepared a report for the Son of Heaven on the matter."

"Master Ming, that is most unfortunate. The Emperor is departing early for his yearly tour of the southern lands the day after tomorrow, and he will not return until March at the earliest. We will schedule the *Da Qin's* appointment on his return."

CHAPTER 47: THE HUNTING TRIP

It was a large buck, four feet at the shoulder with nice set of antlers, rooting through the mountain snows in search of food. Fifty yards away, two men signaled one to the other, and one, concealed by a bush, drew his bow and took careful aim. The arrow flew true and struck its target just above the left shoulder. The deer leaped, turning into the deadly pain in its side, and attempted to bound off.

It didn't get far. A few dozen yards, and it collapsed onto its crippled left foreleg. When the two hunters reached it, it was gasping its last few breaths. One of the men dispatched it, slicing its throat with a knife to let the last few beats of its heart pour its life blood onto the snow. Its eyes glazed over in death and then it was still.

The two hunters set to cleaning the deer, and then tied it to a bamboo pole, hoisting it on their shoulders to bring it back to their makeshift camp.

Emperor He enjoyed these hunting expeditions in the Dabie Mountains overlooking the Yangtze River during his winter tour of the south. The tree-covered mountains rolled lazily over the countryside, their pine and bamboo forests home to a wide variety of game. For He, it was an opportunity to drop the burden of empire for a few days, escape sycophantic courtiers, and live like an ordinary human being, alone or with a handful of trusted friends. Even if only for a painfully short time.

Ban Chao, recently returned from the western provinces, was one of those trusted friends. Although the emperor had not had the opportunity to know him well during Ban Chao's duties as Protectorate General of the Western Provinces, he had found his reports and occasional meetings insightful, and noted that he wasted little time on court protocols and self-promotion. And his reputation was enormous; for the last twenty years he had single-handedly led the pacification of the fractious West, defeating the Xiongnu and opening secure routes to the *Anxi* and *Da Yuan*. Now semi-retired with the largely ceremonial title of the Commander of Bowmen Shooters in Luoyang, he was one of the Emperor's closest associates. A frequent hacking cough betrayed his age and failing health.

Emperor He had chosen Ban Chao as one of his companions for his tour of the southern regions and as his hunting companion, both to assess his character in a close personal way, and to seek his advice on the pressing matter of the *Da Qin*.

The emperor and Ban Chao dumped the deer carcass by the fire in their makeshift camp.

"Good shooting, Excellency. That was a long shot and a good one," said Chao. "Right at the shoulder, that cripples them, and prevents a long search for a wounded animal."

"Thanks, but what does it take to have you call me just Zhou?" responded He.

"I appreciate your indulgence, but I very much prefer calling you Excellency. If we were overheard, you would have to execute me."

"Or pardon you."

"We would both lose standing among those who witnessed the indiscretion, Excellency. I can afford to lose standing, or even my life, at my age. You can't. Let's get this deer butchered before it gets dark."

So the most powerful man in *Ch'in*, and his most powerful general, slung the deer up on a tree branch and set to skinning and butchering the animal.

"I can't tell you how much I look forward to this each year. In court, I can't so much as get a cup of tea without ten servants hustling around me, competing for the honor of serving me. Only here do I feel like a human being, doing the things that other human beings get to do."

"I understand. Generals have sycophants, too. And so do governors and inspectors."

"You can chase yours off. Mine set on me like flies. 'Son of Heaven, may I put on your robe?' 'Son of Heaven, may I serve your tea?' 'Son of Heaven, may I help you piss?' You have no idea!" He laughed.

"The pissing part is a bit intrusive, Excellency!"

"I am surprised that when I am lying with Lady Deng, that some courtier doesn't pop out from under the bed and offer to help me put it in!" The two laughed hilariously at the image, and returned to butchering the deer.

When it was all properly partitioned, they stacked it on the snow.

"This will keep until the bodyguards show up tomorrow morning. They will bring some rice paper to wrap the pieces," commented Chao. He introduced a flask of Western red wine. "Compliments of my western tour. The *Da Yuan* make wine in the Western tradition, from grapes. Have a sample while I pile some more wood on the fire, it's going to be a cold night."

"I can match you with one better. Master Ming gave me a bottle of *Da Qin* wine, from the other side of the world. Between those two exotic bottles, and a few more bottles of rice wine, it should be an entertaining evening." The Emperor introduced his bottle, colored glass with a wax seal, embossed in the foreign *Da Qin* tongue. "Falernian, he called it," getting his tongue around the foreign syllables with surprising agility. "Quite old, about thirty years or so."

The fire was soon blazing, Chao's first bottle empty, and some of the deer meat gone to fill their empty stomachs. Emperor He opened the Falernian, and the conversation turned serious, as the two men sat on a fallen log staring into the flames.

"Wine led to my interest in the west," began Ban Chao, taking a swig from the flask and passing it to the Emperor. "The people in the land of the *Da Yuan* said this was the way wine was made in the great civilizations to the west. And judging by the *Da Qin* wine, it seems to get better the further west one travels. This is powerful!"

Emperor He laughed. "Master Ming warned me not to get it too close to flames. It's quite flammable!"

"It is setting my brain aflame already!"

"Well, you need to help me make a decision, before we finish off this bottle." He set it aside and continued. "You have read Gan Ying's report?"

"I have, Excellency. It is a very complete and intriguing report."

"What do you think happened to his party? They should have been back perhaps a year ago. You are very familiar with the area they would have traversed."

"Of course. And I reviewed his itinerary which he had thoughtfully provided to Wang Ming, along with a copy of his report. Almost as though he expected that something might happen to him. We have put down many of the *Yue Zhi* raiders that plagued the caravans there, but like insects, you can never kill them all. It is still a dangerous route. And besides raiders, there is weather, fierce sandstorms, off-season snowstorms. And not all caravan operators are honest or competent. On the other hand, many people have become lost, or been taken captive and detained. Remember one of our first envoys to that land of the Heavenly Horses took ten years to return, acquiring a wife in the process. So... he may be dead, or just delayed. I hope the latter."

"Do the *Da Yuan* know of the *Da Qin?*"

"They do, Excellency, and it is from their accounts that I decided to dispatch Gan Ying westward a few years ago. The *Da Yuan* speak a language of the far west related to that of the *Da Qin*, and they claim descent from a western king who colonized the area with their language and religion. Their name comes from their western homeland, in their own tongue, Great Ionia." Ban Chao stumbled over the unfamiliar words. "They have exchanged envoys and traders with the *Da Qin*. However, the *Anxi* control the western approaches to the *Da Yuan* lands and they are hostile and often at war with the *Da Qin,* so the contact is often intermittent. The translators we provided to your Court for the mission are descended from *Da Qin* survivors of a battle with the *Anxi* a century or so back."

"Amazing that they would keep their culture and language alive for so long, so far from home for so many generations. Do the *Da Yuan* regard the *Da Qin* as civilized and honorable?"

"They do. They say the *Da Qin* are fierce and formidable warriors. They are also great builders, with beautiful well-run cities. Fantastic roads... some say they build the roads their enemies retreat over! Very literate, but unfortunately I found western languages too hard, and their writing system impossible to comprehend. They write sounds, not images as we do."

Emperor He nodded, and broke out the Roman wine. "One more sip, and then the key point." He took a swig of the powerful amber wine, and passed it to Ban Chao, who followed suit.

"Chao, the *Anxi* reside on the land route between us and the *Da Qin*. We have had good relations with them for centuries, but they are hostile to the *Da Qin* and they are essential to maintaining the security of the western end of our trade routes, which are highly profitable to our Middle Kingdom. Do I risk unsettling our long-established friendship with the *Anxi* with an overture to the *Da Qin*?"

"Excellency, it is often useful to have two friends who are themselves enemies to each other. They keep each other in balance, another role of *Chung Kuo*, the Balanced Kingdom," answered Chao, using the multiple layers of word meanings offered by the Hanaean language. "The *Anxi* profit enormously from our trade with the *Da Qin*, and our mutual security in the *Da Yuan* lands is a joint effort. Our new relationship with the *Da Qin* would do no more than hurt their feelings. And any war between the *Anxi* and the *Da Qin* would not affect us. In fact there have been several that went unnoticed here. Trade was not affected."

"Well said, Master Chao, well said. Well, I think I can comfortably invite our *Da Qin* friends to a personal audience in the spring, if they do not become bored waiting for my return and depart for home. And I think I shall invite Kore-si of the *Anxi* to that meeting, just to judge his reaction. Now that the decision is made ... let us finish the wine, and become outrageously drunk!"

The bodyguards arrived at daybreak, and found the Emperor and Ban Chao, each wrapped in blankets and snoring by the smoldering campfire, with four empty wine bottles littering the ground. It took quite some effort to arouse the two.

Back in Luoyang, Aulus received a letter from Lucius Parvus by Hanaean post. Basically, trade was going exceedingly well, and in fact, so well, that they were in danger of depleting their funds: tons of multicolored silk, silver and jade work of the finest quality, even a small quantity of tea, and amphorae of Hanean wine. Deep in the holds were tons of high grade Hanaean iron, prized in Rome for its toughness, ability to take a fine edge when used as weaponry, resistant to corrosion. Parvus expected a twenty-to-one return on investment, less expenses for the ships' maintenance and the crew's share.

Aulus penned a reply, commending Lucius on his fine stewardship, and promising him ten percent on the net return. He advised him to depart whenever weather permitted as they would return via Hanaean vessel. He then attached an encrypted report to be delivered to the *Princeps* via Senator Longus, and a personal letter to his wife Livia, and invited Gaius to do the same; Lucius Parvus would see to it that the letters would be delivered.

Gaius Lucullus retired to his cabin, and pulled his locket portrait of Camilla, studying it carefully. *I wish I had pictures of Gaius Secundus and Lucia. We will have to have them made when I return. If I return. It has been two years since I last spent a few weeks with them, and it will be another year, maybe more, before I see them again.*

He picked up a bronze pen and a sheet of fine Hanaean rice paper, and began to write.

My dearest Camilla,

I hope all is well with you and the children. We have had an unfortunate delay in our diplomatic mission, and we cannot sail with our ships when they depart next month. We will make arrangements to travel on Hanaean ships after our mission is complete, so we should not be delayed more than a few months.

He stopped writing to consider that; it wasn't exactly true. If they did not catch the November monsoon, they might be delayed more than a year.

But it might be more than a year. I wish that I had insisted on time to be with you and the children before I left. I feel like Odysseus on a storm-tossed sea, but it is not Hera that delays my return, but my own pride, the foolishness of putting other things before you, Gaius Secundus and Lucia, who should be the most important people in my life.

He studied her locket, and tried to picture the children. But the picture in his mind was already two years out of date, and might be four years out of date when he returned.

I cannot hold you to Penelope's high standards, for I haven't been the husband that you deserve, but a stranger who sleeps in your bed for a few weeks once every several years, the man who must be introduced to his children as the father they do not remember. All I can say is that if you wait patiently for me, I will try to do better for you when I return.

All my love,

Gaius

Gaius read and re-read the letter, his eyes burning, then left to give it Aulus for delivery.

A week later, Antonius and Ibrahim were seated in Musa's boat with the monk Demosthenes, eating rice with spicy chicken. Musa and Ibrahim's companions were seated back further, engaged in a board game by themselves. Ibrahim had just returned from his brief abortive foray into his new calling. Antonius laughed uproariously as Ibrahim related how, in the biting cold weather, he had hoisted the Hanaean shepherd aloft and shook him after he had had the temerity to try to beat him, before swearing off forever his dreams of becoming again a shepherd.

"I would have loved to see his face!" said Antonius, offering a toast to the ex-pirate. "So what are you going to do now?"

"I think I am going back to Tianjin with Musa. I can join him in his boatbuilding business," said Ibrahim.

"That's more your style, really."

"When I was a shepherd as a boy, we were in the desert. While the desert can get quite cold at night, it is nothing like the cold in the mountains here. It can freeze the flesh off your bones," said Ibrahim. "It makes me shiver to think of it."

"I know what you mean. Up on the Danube, we had lads lose hands, feet, even a whole leg, to cold. Called it frostbite, a good name for it. Well, I am sorry, I know you were serious about being a shepherd," sympathized Antonius.

"That was not to be your path. You will find another," said Demosthenes, raising his right hand in a two fingered blessing. He wore the same yellow robe he had worn a few weeks ago when the weather was warm, with chest bare underneath and one shoulder exposed.

"How the hell do you wear that in this weather?" asked Antonius.

"If you do not acknowledge the cold, you do not feel it," answered Demosthenes with a smile.

"Sounds like Stoic philosophy to me," he snorted.

"What is Stoic philosophy?" asked Demosthenes.

Antonius introduced another bottle of wine and they proceeded to discuss various aspects of Greek philosophy for the rest of the night.

CHAPTER 48: A DOMESTIC SPAT TURNS VIOLENT

Ming's agents continued to monitor the comings and goings of the *Da Qin* in Luoyang, but their activities were so uneventful that it became an opportunity for the well-paid watchers to play board games and consume a lot of rice wine while staying within sight of the envoys and their companions. Unbeknownst to Ming's agents, Mithridates' agents kept similar low-profile surveillance, avoiding their attention... the Imperial Court would take a dim view of Parthian spying inside the Hanaean capital, even if on foreigners. If it weren't for the board games and wine, however, this would be a truly boring surveillance. The tall one had returned, apparently quickly discouraged in his shepherding aspiration by the harsh weather. He and his four companions were preparing to return to Tianjin with the advent of better sailing weather on the river.

In the palace compound, the new-found warmth between Ming and Si Huar had begun to fade. He felt increasingly uncomfortable with her insinuating herself into his business and financial dealings, and she felt increasingly closed out of his life again, so soon after he had allowed her into it. And the other girls in the concubinage, resentful at her sudden ascendancy in his favor, now shunned her as she seemed to be losing stature in his eyes. When she was younger, they had regarded her as a naïve country girl and helped her to fit into palace life. Now they saw her as a threat, the favorite concubine who could wield a vast amount of power over them. As that power seemed slipping through her grasp, they seemed intent on making her life miserable.

"Oh, poor Si Huar! Not warming your beloved Master Ming's bed on this cold winter night... I wonder who is in there with him instead?" one taunted her.

She increasingly sought out the company of her brother Marcus. He made it a point to visit the concubinage as often as possible, afraid that his sister had taken the upturn in her relationship with Ming too seriously, and finding the downturn that much harder to take. His visits were a chance for them to converse wistfully in Latin about their trip to Rome, and Marcus' excitement about his new posting.

"I can't believe my good fortune," said Marcus excitedly. "Zheng Zhong has learned of my skill in Latin, and has given me the task of developing materials for palace diplomats to use in mastering that and other Western languages!"

"Zheng Zhong? The Empress Deng's head of household? What is his connection with that?"

"He is very close to the Emperor, who consults with him often on affairs of state. Language, he feels, limits our influence, since so few Hanaeans speak any Western language and have great difficulty learning them, even more writing them. Antonius has been kind enough to teach me some Greek, and I have an appointment shortly with Cyrus Mithridates, the Parthian ambassador, to learn his language. But enough: how are things with you?"

"Oh, 'harmonious' in that he is no longer beating or insulting me. But I have served his purpose. He isn't unpleasant, just cold."

"I am sorry. You were happier last month than I had ever seen you since we left Liqian."

"Yes, but I don't think the Fates have happiness in mind for me. I hope your new duties with Master Zhong bring you some."

"It is the first time that I saw an advantage in being a eunuch. They have big roles in palace administration."

"Just watch with whom you get involved. There is always someone waiting to stab you in the back, professionally or literally! I don't want to lose you."

Marcus then paid a call on Cyrus Mithridates. "Come in, come in, Si Nuo! I have been expecting you," greeting him in Hanaean. "Zheng Zhou told me of your new assignment and your Latin skills. Have some tea, please, and tell me how a simple farm boy from Gansu province came by such language skills."

"Thank you, I will take some tea." He accepted the tea, but as Cyrus had neither seated himself nor offered him a seat, he drank it standing up. Parthian protocols appeared simpler, and a foreign ambassador, even from the *Anxi*, were inferior in rank to Hanean court members. Which, he presumed, he now was, under tasking from Zheng Zhong. "We are descendants of *Da Qin* soldiers, defeated in your country at a place called Carrhae, and carried off to Liqian." He used the Latin word Carrhae.

Cyrus did not at once follow the abrupt shift from Hanaean to Latin, and answered with a confused "Huh? Where did you say?"

"I am sorry, the place called Carrhae in the *Da Qin* language."

"Carrhae? Really? We know it in Parthian as Harran, Karra in Greek. But that was over a century ago!"

"Our ancestors served as border guards, taking Hanaean wives, but their children, and their children's children, grew up bilingual. My ancestor at that battle was Marcus Lucius, and my Latin name is Marcus Lucius Quintus, of the fifth generation."

"Interesting! We Parthians are very proud of that battle, we inflicted a major defeat on Rome and stopped their advance into our homeland, but I didn't know there were survivors. So that is how you come to speak Latin. Please let's be seated." He motioned to some well-padded, Western-style chairs on the opposite wall. "Si Huar is your sister?"

"She is. Her Latin name is Marcia Lucia, the feminine equivalent of mine."

"Interesting. And do you write Latin as well?"

"Yes, our forefathers preserved as much of our history and literature as they could. It was all from memory, but they wrote it down so it would not be lost."

"I don't speak Latin, unfortunately, but I do speak Greek. Do you?"

"I am learning Greek from Antonius, but I am not yet ready for conversation, maybe soon perhaps. I only know the alphabet and a few courteous phrases."

"Well, perhaps if we encounter words without an Hanaean equivalent, we can try Greek. And we know the Greek alphabet in Parthia, which will allow you to do homework and study in your quarters. Of course you also write Hanaean as well?"

"Yes, and we have had excellent training on the finer points of calligraphy, as part of our preparation for Gan Ying's expedition."

"I have just reached the point where my Hanaean friends don't stop to ask me what I meant to say when they read something of mine!" He gave a hearty laugh through his oily, carefully-curled black beard. He paused and then returned to conversation. "Si Huar is Master Ming's consort?"

"She is."

"She is now in great favor, I understand. She was very helpful in preparing him for his first meeting with the Son of Heaven." Cyrus stroked his beard thoughtfully. "So tell me of your trip to Rome."

Marcus related the story, the endless delays in Ecbatana and Persepolis, then the long sea trip down the Gulf, finally arriving in Rome.

"So you met with Trajan himself, then?" asked Cyrus.

"We did, and he was most enthusiastic about our arrival. And he gave all of us translators papers affirming our citizenship, as it is hereditary, even to five generations. We may no longer look Roman, but we are Romans nonetheless," answered Marcus.

"And what became of Gan Ying? How did you come to be separated?" asked Cyrus.

"He elected to return overland, as he had not enjoyed his sea voyage at all. He said he would prefer a thousand camels to one ship. But he gave us a copy of his report, in case we returned ahead of him."

"Interesting. And was this report presented to the Son of Heaven?"

"It was, by Master Ming."

"How did he take it?" Cyrus inadvertently omitted the Emperor's honorific, normally most impolite, in his surprise at the news of Gan Ying's report.

"I don't know. It was given to us under Gan Ying's seal, and delivered that way to the Son of Heaven."

They then continued on with lessons in Parthian vocabulary and writing. Marcus was struck by the similarities in grammar between Parthian, Latin and Greek. After about an hour, he left with an armful of scrolls to study, and some simple writing assignments.

Cyrus pondered the news of Gan Ying's report. He had heard of the meeting between Ming and Emperor He, but did not know that Gan Ying had provided Ming copies of his report. Hopefully, Gan's bones were bleaching in some Central Asian desert by now, but Cyrus had no way of knowing that he wouldn't show up tomorrow. He had assumed that any reports returning with Ming would be fragmentary reconstructions cobbled together by someone not versed in foreign cultures, as Gan Ying had been.

No matter… the Roman mission had to be sabotaged, but how?

One day in early March, the weather turned warm and sunny with a blustery wind, following a very cold and snowy winter. Marcia decided to take advantage of the day to go into town and shop for new silk robes for spring and enjoy being outdoors without being wrapped up in thick robes. She spent the morning on the eastern side of the city, wandering in parks, tea stalls, and finally in the clothing stalls. She picked out a particularly beautiful pink robe, decorated with birds, trees, and mountain scenes. The dress' artwork itself was good enough to hang on her wall. She accepted the robe in a rice paper wrapping, and paid the shopkeeper a few silver coins. The old woman beamed her appreciation, and Marcia exchanged complimentary bows with her.

As she left the stall, she saw her old friends Gaius and Antonius, enjoying lunch in a food stall, and she hurried over to see them.

They rose to greet her. "Marcia! We haven't seen you since January!"

She smiled happily. "I am so sorry! I don't get to move around the palace much. But it is such a wonderful day! Antonius, how are you?" She extended her hand in the Western style, and he shyly grasped it.

"Fine, Marcia! Been missin' our long talks," answered Antonius. "And the *Han-yu* lessons, such as I remember 'em. *'Mama qí mǎ. Mǎ màn. Mama mà mǎ.'*"

She clapped her hands in glee. "Yer've been practicin'! That's perfect!" she replied in her attempt to mimic his soldier's fractured Latin.

"Yer ain't so bad yerself, *domina!*" Antonius smiled, getting into the swing of the reacquaintance.

"An' I tol' yer before, I ain't yer *domina!*"

Everyone settled into a happy reunion, swapping stories and making the past few months seem as nothing.

Across the street, Ming's watchers noted Si Huar's effusively happy get-together with the *Da Qin* soldiers. After a few hours, they dispatched a runner back to the palace.

About sunset, Si Huar returned to her quarters in the concubinage with her new dress, full of happiness over the reunion with her old friends, only to find Wang Ming waiting in her quarters, stiff and cold, obviously angry.

"And where have you been?" he asked.

"In town, shopping," she replied with a smile, hoping to defuse whatever he was upset about. "I bought a beautiful new spring robe," indicating the wrapped bundle.

"And what else?"

"I met Gaius and Antonius in town, and we talked for a while. I haven't seen them in months."

Ming smacked the left side of her face with his hand, knocking her head around. As she put her hand to her stinging cheek, a tiny trickle of blood from the corner of her mouth stained her fingers. "I told you not to whore around with the *Da Qin* soldiers!" he said, chillingly soft.

Si Huar tried to find her mental quiet place, to endure the beating that was to come. But instead of her quiet place, she found anger at the sudden warming, then refreezing, of their relationship, rage that the abuse of the past ten years was about to resume.

"You animal! How dare you beat me like that!" She rushed at him, slapping him in return on the side of his face. Though it left a red handprint, it did not draw blood. "I am not a whore and you are not to call me that, ever again!" She picked up her package and hurled it at him. It glanced off, but Ming was taken aback by her fierceness. Never had she resisted him before. He grabbed her by the arm, slapped her again, but she struggled free.

Si Huar's neatly coiffed black hair was coming askew, and her blue eyes were bright with anger. She thought of Antonius, how kind and polite he had been to her, and she responded with the Latin profanities she had learned from him. She picked up a small porcelain vase and, grasping it in her right hand, she advanced on him. "I'll kill yer, yer son of a bitch, I'll kill yer, yer hear!"

Ming, bewildered at her aggression, stood stock still, his eyes wide with surprise, and made no motion to resist her clumsy lunge as she aimed for his head, connecting with all the force she could muster, and shattering the vase into a shower of shards.

Ming's head snapped rightwards, his eyes rolling up into his head. He slowly collapsed onto his knees and pitched face forward onto the floor with a gentle thud. A small trickle of blood oozed out of his head at the point of impact and stained the floor.

All anger left Si Huar, and the room suddenly seemed deafeningly silent. She put her hands to her mouth, and sobbed. "Master Ming? I am sorry, Master Ming. Please … get up… get up, please!" But Ming remained still on the floor.

Si Huar whirled and ran out of her quarters, leaving Ming lying there. Fortunately, the residents of the concubinage were at evening meal in a distant part of the building. Her heart thudded, and she considered the consequences of having killed him. Not knowing what else to do, she ran out of the concubinage before someone could discover her crime, and once outside, managed to slow herself to a fast walk so as not attract attention. She headed for the East Gate of the palace and back out into town.

Si Huar had no plan, no hope of escaping punishment. She went to the place where she and her Roman companions had met, what seemed like years ago, though really only about two hours past. To her surprise Gaius and Antonius were still there.

She rushed up to them in tears.

"Marcia, Marcia, yer look like hell! What happened?" asked Antonius.

Across the street, both Ming's and Cyrus' watchers dispatched runners back to their respective masters.

Marcia could do little but sob. "Marcia, please, take a deep breath, and tell us what happened so we can help you," said Gaius.

She took a breath, then blurted out. "I killed Wang Ming!"

"Sit down, Marcia, and tell us what happened." Gaius was trying to calm her down, but he knew there would be little they could do to help if this were true.

"I came back to my quarters… and he was there… he said I was whoring around with you, Antonius… and he hit me!"

"All right, and then what?" asked Antonius, softly.

"I… I usually go to my quiet place when he beats me…"

"We understand… we do the same sometimes, when you know yer gonna take a lickin' an' there ain't nothing yer can do about it. We've been there, both of us." Antonius was soft and consoling. "So then what?"

"I couldn't find… my quiet spot. All I could find was anger. I slapped him back, and told him I wasn't a whore." Gaius handed her a cloth from his tunic and she dabbed at her tears. "I cursed him in Latin," she laughed through her tears. "You would have been proud of me, Antonius! I said, 'I'll kill yer, yer son of bitch!' Just like you would have said."

"Well said, *domina*!"

"Don't call me that!" she laughed, choking on her tears, then continued "I picked up a vase... and ... and... I hit him in the head! It broke, and he went down, and there was blood all over the place... and I killed him!"

Marcia was perhaps five feet tall and around a hundred pounds, and Antonius looked at her. "It's hard enough to knock a man out with a blow ter the head, much less kill him," said Antonius. "Gaius and I have done this a few times. How big was this vase?"

Marcia made a shape with her hands, about the size of a melon.

"That's not a very big vase. Did you hit him with the base or the side?"

"The side."

"That's why it shattered. Where on his head did you hit him? Here?" he said, motioning toward his temple, "... or here?" pointing to the top of his head.

"Sort of in between, here," she said, pointing to the ridge of bone on the side of her skull.

"Not bloody likely you killed him. I don't think I could, with a vase that small. A stone, maybe, if you get a lucky swing in really hard, but with all due respect, *domina*..." he winked at her, "I don't think yer've got the strength and size to do it. You probably just knocked him senseless, as he deserves... Yer really called him a son of a bitch?"

"Yes... but what about the blood?"

"Scalp wounds bleed a lot more than their size warrants. He probably got up with a big headache, maybe a few minutes after yer left. An' it's just as well yer did, 'cause he is probably fixin' ter kill you for real hisself."

"So what am I to do?"

Gaius interjected. "I agree, Marcia, it's highly unlikely you killed him. And Antonius is right, he likely would have killed you if you were still there when he came around. Or hurt you very badly. And he is likely to do that if you go back tonight." It was now well after sunset, and lamps had been long lit along the shops and streets. "Do you have a place to stay?"

"There is an inn around the corner, the Three Horse Inn, I could stay there, but I ran out without my purse, and I have no money."

"Antonius will take you there, and pay for your stay. I will get with Aulus in the morning and see if we can line up Marcus as a translator. Is he around?"

"He is well-connected now, serving Empress Deng's chief of staff. I think that will give protection against Ming."

"Good. Ming's Latin is not up to any involved discussion. Where can I find him?"

Marcia gave some instructions while Gaius scribbled notes on a wax tablet.

"We will meet with Ming tomorrow. We are under Imperial protection as a foreign envoy, and in fact, you also are under Trajan's protection. That may carry some weight against him, your dual status and all. But I can't guarantee anything. If that doesn't work, we may not be able to help much."

"Remind me never to make yer mad! Cold-cockin' a man on yer first head shot, good job, *domina!*" Another wink.

"You two are wonderful. No matter what happens, I am so grateful!"

Gaius departed for the palace to brief Aulus and locate Marcus. Antonius and Marcia left for the Three Horse Inn around the corner. As they went in, Cyrus' watcher team departed at a run.

Ming awoke a few minutes after Si Huar's departure. He shook his head to clear the fog, sending more vase fragments skittering across the black lacquered floor. He saw a small puddle of blood, and put his hand gingerly up to inspect his throbbing head. Other than a rapidly swelling goose-egg and congealing blood, his pride seemed to be the most seriously injured. He got to his feet, and noted that the concubinage was silent. The girls and their eunuch guardians had been going down to an evening meal when he arrived, so the word of this humiliation would not yet be public knowledge, with people tittering behind his back. But that would not last: this was a communal concubinage for the girls of several officials, and in a few days there would be knowing glances from those men. His face flushed at the thought.

He found a basin, a pitcher of water and a towel, and cleaned up his head, washing the blood out of his matted hair and removing a few stains from his dark blue cloak. Si Huar had a bronze mirror by the bowl, so he inspected his wound… no serious damage.

Donning his elaborately curved black headdress, he dressed back some stray wisps of hair, looking not the worse for the incident. He stepped out of Si Huar's quarters into the silent hallway, and departed for his quarters in the eastern palace.

Ming was torn by two emotions: one, anger at Si Huar for her violent attack on his person, and the other, regret at losing the closeness that had briefly evolved between them over the past few months: the *yin* and *yang* of his soul. Ming stood about five foot five, lean, muscular, and well-trained in personal combat; he had seen Si Huar's awkward blow coming and could have easily deflected it, but had not. Why? He remembered being furious at her retaliation, her angry defense of herself, and the fierce *Da Qin* phrase she spat at him just before she landed the blow, something about 'kill,' which he believed she meant. But he was also in awe of her courage, her willingness to risk her life in a hopeless fight. More *yin* and *yang*, opposites pulling at his heart, as he trod across the vast pavilion to the palace, taking the northern stairways to his quarters on the third floor.

Once inside, he dismissed his servants and sat on the floor to meditate, legs tucked straight under him, his hands on his thighs. He concentrated on his breathing to clear the clutter of emotions in his mind, and tried to opine the correct action to restore harmony. Harmony was all; without harmony, there was chaos, as there was now. Should he have her charged with the act of violence she committed? She would likely be executed forthwith, as she had attempted, however poorly, to kill him, and he believed she had fully intended to do so.

Or should he forgive her, and perhaps ask her to forgive him? His anger and jealousy of the *Da Qin* soldiers was the first element of disharmony, the one which triggered it all. His agents had not brought any indications that her meeting with them was anything more than an unplanned friendly reunion, nothing untoward in her behavior. Her disharmony was in response to his. How best to restore the balance? His breathing settled in, his heart slowed, and he felt the conflicting emotions begin to ebb, when his lead agent burst into the room with some urgency.

The man, bowed, hurriedly clasped his hands before him, then blurted out the news. "Mistress Si Huar and the *Da Qin* soldier have gone into the Three Horse Inn in town."

Ming's emerging harmony vanished like a soap bubble and his emotions came raging back. He rose from his seated position, whipped his robe around him, and ordered: "Send a detachment of agents to detain her. Leave the *Da Qin* alone, I will discuss this with the Minister of Justice, and he will determine the proper course of action for foreign envoys."

The agent bowed, saluted and was backing out of Ming's quarters as the *Anxi* ambassador entered. Ming waved his hand dismissively. "Away with you, Kore-si, I have urgent matters and cannot chat with you."

"Well I know, for I have friends who brought me news of a great scandal involving your favorite concubine Si Huar."

Ming's face darkened. "What do you know of this?" he asked angrily.

"Master Ming, my friends have been concerned about the growing closeness between Si Huar and the *Da Qin* soldier, the one called An-dun. We fear the *Da Qin* may be using her to acquire state secrets from you through her. As such espionage might compromise Parthian interests as well, I feel obligated to bring this to your attention."

"Have you proof?"

"Espionage leaves little proof."

"I will discuss this immediately with the Minister of Guards. For now, you are dismissed, Kore-si."

Ming's emotions were once again disharmonious.

Antonius caught up with Gaius returning to the east gate. For months, their comings and goings had become so routine, and their rudimentary Hanaean so comfortable, that they had dispensed with Marcus. They themselves carried the Hanaean scroll pass to the palace compound, and presented it to the guards who just grunted and let them pass. This time, the guard scrutinized their pass with a lamp, as it was well after dark. The guard lifted up a whistle to his lips and blew a shrill piecing blast, summoning ten guards who quickly surrounded them.

"What the hell..." muttered Antonius.

"Stand easy. Just go along with this, there is some misunderstanding and Aulus will have it all straightened out for us. No resistance," Gaius ordered. He smiled at the guards, who didn't smile back. Two guards came up behind each of them, grabbed their hands roughly behind their backs and knotted them with rough rope. Antonius flexed his bonds, testing it... they had done a good job.

"This doesn't look good, sir..." muttered Antonius. A guard cuffed him roughly, indicated that he should not speak, as they were marched into the palace compound. They were taken to a small door at the back of the building that led into the basement stables. A barred cage was at the back, and in it Aulus Galba sat glumly.

Their guards thrust them roughly inside the five-by-five foot cage, lined with straw but without seats. Some filthy blankets were wadded on the floor, and a badly stained slop bucket was positioned in the corner. The guards locked and barred the door, and then silently motioned for Gaius and Antonius to turn around so they could undo their bonds. The men massaged their wrists and stretched, while all but two of the guards departed.

"Good to see you, cousin, despite the circumstances," said Gaius.

"What the hell just happened? I was in my quarters preparing for the Emperor's return, with all indications that our long-delayed meeting was finally imminent. A batch of guards burst into the room, seized me, and dragged me here about an hour ago!" replied Aulus.

"I think I know, sir," said Antonius. "We met Marcia in town today, a very happy girl she was. All bubbly an' like. We had some light eats an' talked fer some time, an' she left about sunset. She came back about an hour later in tears. Wang Ming tried to beat her, but this time she fought back an' beaned him with a vase. Knocked him out, she thought she'd kilt him."

"Did she?"

"I don't know fer sure, sir, but it would be one lucky hit if she had. I think she just knocked him out. We advised her to stay in town. She took me to an inn, an' I paid for her overnight, as she hadn't any money with her. Then we came back an' got accosted by the gate guards when we presented our papers," replied Antonius.

Gaius interjected, "Marcus wasn't with us, so if the guards said anything about charges against us, if such procedures exist here, I didn't know what they were."

"Oh gods, gods, gods! Fortuna has been unkind to our mission. Did anyone witness your meeting with Marcia, poor girl?"

"Sir, we always have minders out in town. They think we don't notice them, but we have nicknames for each of them. We din't do anythin' wrong, so we din't pay them much attention."

"Other than perhaps aiding someone who killed or injured a senior court official? Whatever you did, the court took it pretty seriously. I suspect we may be in serious trouble."

Gaius bristled at the implication. "We helped a fellow Roman citizen under Trajan's personal protection. If she didn't kill him, then her life was in danger if she went back to the concubinage. I take responsibility for ordering Antonius to put her up at the inn, and I'd do it again. Trajan's protection may be the only bargaining chip in our hand, but it is a bargaining chip, if we can find a way to play it. Right now, I suggest we disturb the fleas on the floor as little as possible, and try to get some sleep. Staying awake all night is not going to help us think clearly when morning comes."

He flapped one of the blankets, and clouds of dust and straw debris filled the air as he lay down on his back. Antonius did likewise, and grumbling, so did Aulus.

A few hundred miles upriver in Tianjin, the *Asia* and *Europa* were underway at first light on their return home. They would round the Shandong Peninsula by noon, then head south for Jiaozhi and home.

CHAPTER 49: A NIGHT IN AN HANAEAN JAIL

The *weiwei* Minister of Guards Dong Ch'u and Wang Ming were summoned before breakfast to meet with the *tingwei* Minister of Justice, Feng Chou. The Minister of Justice was the supreme imperial judge, second only to the Son of Heaven himself, and he was not pleased this morning.

Ming and the Minister of Guards entered, saluted formally and bowed, but the *tingwei's* scowling visage did not lighten; he received them standing. "Good morning. You have news for me of an arrest last night."

The Minister of Guards nodded. "The concubine of Wang Ming, liaison to the *Da Qin*, one Si Huar, was detained on charges of attempting to kill him, and of infidelity with the *Da Qin* named *An-Dun*. He was arrested as her partner in infidelity, and the other two *Da Qin*, including the lead envoy, are suspected of espionage and also detained."

If anything, the corners of Feng Chou's mouth turned even more sharply downward behind his trailing gray mustache, but his voice betrayed no emotion. "And you have proof of the espionage?" he asked quietly.

"Master Ming has the evidence, Excellency."

"Master Ming?" he asked, glancing in Ming's direction.

Ming cleared his throat and began, "The agents of the *Anxi* ambassador Kore-si reported..."

"Stop!" the Minister of Justice said, quietly but firmly cutting him off. Ming's Adam's apple bobbled at the rebuke, but he quickly nodded in acknowledgement and shut up.

"Foreign agents are forbidden in the Middle Kingdom, Wang Ming. Of course, we know they are here, but if you are about to report their activities, or even worse, that you accepted a report from them, I will be forced to take action that will have dire consequences for them, and for you. Now, do you have any evidence of the *Da Qin* involvement in espionage... from a reliable Hanaean source?"

Ming paused. "No, your Excellency, I do not."

"Which of you have evidence of the *Da Qin* soldiers' involvement with your concubine?" The question should have been posed to the Minister of the Guards, but Feng Chou fixed his gaze on Wang Ming, and the *weiwei* remained silent.

Ming again answered, querulously, "She and the one called An-Dun were together at the Three Horse Inn."

Feng Chou scrutinized some documents. "Yes, and she entered the Inn at about three hours after sunset, and he was arrested at the gate about an hour later. This does not appear to be strong evidence." Ming accepted his second admonition, staring straight ahead, nodding acknowledgement.

"Dong Ch'u, I have more sympathy for Wang Ming in this matter than for you. You have arrested the entire *Da Qin* delegation based on the slenderest of evidence, most of which appears to come from the *Anxi*, who clearly and frequently have expressed their distaste for the *Da Qin* presence here. Spies of *Anxi* accusing the *Da Qin* of spying? Just yesterday afternoon, we received messengers from the Son of Heaven announcing his intent to meet with the *Da Qin* immediately on his return tomorrow. How shall I explain to the Son of Heaven that they are jailed on *Anxi* fabrications?"

"Excellency, I erred grievously," answered the Minister of Guards.

"You did. You shall promptly order the release of the entire *Da Qin* party with both our personal apologies for the misunderstanding, to be conveyed by you in person. For now they are to be confined to the palace, but they are otherwise to be free to go about their business in preparation for their meeting with the Son of Heaven."

Dong Ch'u nodded in acknowledgement.

Tingwei Feng Chou continued, "Wang Ming, your case against Si Huar has some merit. Shall I pursue charges of attempted murder against her? The lump on your head bears ample evidence, though mind you, there are some in the Palace who feel you deserved it. Many consider your beatings of her to be both unmanly and inharmonious."

"I do wish to pursue those charges, Excellency," answered Ming.

"You are aware of her special status holding documents putting her under the special protection of the *Da Qin* emperor. Therefore, she is a member of the *Da Qin* envoy. Given the sensitivity of this case, if you wish to go forward, I feel it is prudent that I defer her case to the Son of Heaven for his personal adjudication. I expect this case will be heard immediately before he meets with the envoys, so that meeting may proceed most harmoniously. In the meanwhile, Si Huar is to be confined to her quarters in the concubinage, with all necessary provision for her comfort in preparing for her trial."

Ming swallowed hard. He had expected the *tingwei* to try the case. Cases adjudicated by the Son of Heaven were as likely to result in penalties for the accuser as for the accused if the Son of Heaven found fault with their case. And the trial would take place tomorrow, leaving him little time to prepare. But retracting his charges now would make him appear to be a liar before the senior judge.

He acknowledged the decision with yet another wordless bow.

"You are dismissed," ordered the *tingwei*. "*Weiwei*, please return after you have released the prisoners to discuss your handling of this case."

Both bowed and left.

Ming located Si Nuo to act as translator, and hurried with the Minister of Guards along with other senior security officials to the grimy cell in which the *Da Qin* were kept. The two guards snapped erect at the arrival of the high-level entourage, and the three Romans struggled to their feet, brushing off straw and other things they might not want to know about. The *weiwei* ordered the guards to release the prisoners, and they fumbled with keys until the locked cage opened.

This was obviously a formal moment, and although Marcus and the three exchanged glances, they said nothing and asked no questions. Marcus allowed just a wisp of a smile to flicker across his lips, enough to convey that the news would be good.

The *weiwei* said something in Hanaean, with an expression like he had eaten something disagreeable, and Marcus translated: "The Minister of Justice has ordered your immediate release, with his apologies and my own, for this embarrassing misunderstanding. You are to return to your quarters and you are free to move about the palace, to prepare for a meeting with the Son of Heaven in the next several days."

"That is good news," replied Aulus, "though not the way I had been expected to receive word of our meeting with Emperor He. Tell the minister that we accept the apology, and appreciate his hospitality in these temporary accommodations."

Marcus translated. The *weiwei's* face darkened a bit as Marcus gave him an exact translation, but he nodded, and the three left their cell with Marcus and a security escort to their quarters.

"I don't know 'bout yer, but I am ready fer a bath!" chuckled Antonius. "Marcus, I suspect yer'll fill us in on the events?"

"I will, Antonius, I certainly will."

The Minister of Guards, senior leadership and two guards escorted the group to their quarters in the palace. They whirled and departed without a word. Aulus fumbled with the door, opened it, and held it for the rest. "Antonius, why don't you go first for the bath? Gaius and Marcus and I will catch up, but please don't linger, the fleas are feasting on me!"

"Sure, won't be long, I'll warm it up fer yer." Antonius stripped and bundled his clothes up, located a bag, tied them up inside it, and went into the bath off to the side.

"So Marcus, do you know what is happening?" asked Aulus.

"Unfortunately, yes, and that news is not good. My sister faces trial for attempted murder – before Emperor He. She will probably be sentenced to death," replied Marcus. The Hanaean side of his upbringing did a good job of choking back his emotions, but his Roman side allowed much more to show than he wanted.

"We are sorry to hear that. She is under the protection of Emperor Trajan. That's a thread we can pull later as we know more. When is the trial?"

"Probably immediately on Emperor He's return, immediately before your meeting with him. I think tomorrow or the day after. Gaius and Antonius may be called as witnesses."

"Great timing!" answered Aulus, his face contorted in disgust.

"The Minister of Justice would normally hear the case, but he has apparently decided it's so sensitive the ruling needs to be made by Emperor He himself."

Gaius introduced himself into the conversation. "Ming is still alive. Was he hurt?"

"No, and the gossip in the concubinage and among the eunuchs is that he got what he deserved."

"Where is Marcia?" asked Gaius.

"I don't know. I haven't seen her since this whole thing blew up."

"All right, on to us. Do you know what happened to us last night?"

"Other than you were arrested and jailed in unpleasant circumstances? I don't know the circumstances of your arrest. I surmise that Wang Ming got the Minister of the Guards to arrest you on some trumped-up story. I know he and Ming met with the Minister of Justice first thing this morning, and they lost considerable face. The Minister of Guards apologized to you personally. That is unheard of, a minister apologizing to foreigners. Apparently the Minister of Justice ordered him to do so. Your mission is extremely important to the Emperor."

"Nice of him to keep us waiting almost four months, and make us miss our ship home!" interjected Aulus. "So what is our status until the trial followed by the meeting?"

"I was told you are free to come and go within the palace itself. As you are witnesses to my sister's trial, you may not leave the building. Your passes at the gate have been confiscated, so if by any chance you were able to leave the compound, you would not be able to reenter."

Antonius emerged from the bath much refreshed, retired to his room to re-emerge in a few minutes in a Roman army tunic. "Time ter remember how ter dress like a soldier," grumbled the centurion. "Next fer the bath, gentlemen."

CHAPTER 50: A PLAN FOR CLEMENCY

The emperor returned from his southern tour with a great deal more fanfare than on his departure, arriving at Luoyang's south wall by the waterfront with a blast of trumpets and heralds announcing his arrival. He was riding in the rear of an ornate four-wheeled chariot with a low yellow umbrella over him to shield him from the sun and weather, side rails of gold-leaf dragons, with red and green trim. The chariot was accompanied by four very tall and muscular armor-clad Hanaean soldiers whose faces evinced no emotion or even thought; white cloths inscribed with five Hanean characters circled their close-cropped heads. The crowd gawked from a respectful distance as they escorted their equally impassive royal burden, sitting cross legged on purple silk cushions, through the Pingchengmen Gate and then directly into the southern gate of the palace compound. Inside the compound, a single trumpet blast, loud enough to be heard throughout the pavilion, announced his arrival. Long vertical flags of green and yellow, shaped like upraised knife blades emblazoned with Hanaean inscriptions, snapped erect on the parapets.

This done, the procession continued in silence north across the vast compound to the eastern palace itself, where the Minister of the Household stood awaiting him, flanked by six armed guards at the foot of the imperial stairs. He did his ritual obeisance, hands clasped in front of his bowed head, for about a minute, until the Son of Heaven acknowledged him. The *Guangluxun* then stood erect with eyes downcast, while the chariot escorts gently assisted Emperor He in dismounting. He ascended the palace steps slowly in silence, followed by the Minister of the Household and his guards. Inside, he was escorted to the royal apartments, where servants awaited to cleanse him of the dust of the long road trip, and dress him in his dark blue and black silk ceremonial robes. With him dressed, they fitted the ceremonial flat black hat surrounded by dangling jewels on his head. Any movement of his head set the tiny jewels to swinging just inside his eyes' focal range, making him feel that he was in a swarm of insects.

About an hour later, he convened a meeting of his three Excellencies in the throne room for an update on events in the northern provinces during his absence. The three Excellencies sat on cushions on the floor, kneeling on their haunches, also clad in the dark blue and black silk robes preferred by Emperor He. After recapping a rather uneventful winter, the Excellency of the Masses requested permission to call in the *tingwei* to update the Son of

Heaven on recent events involving the *Da Qin* envoys. The Minister of Justice was ushered in.

Emperor He listened impassively as the *tingwei* recounted how the *Da Qin* were wrongfully arrested by the Minister of Guards, based on inaccurate information, kept overnight in an abominable prison, but released the following morning with apologies conveyed in person by Minister of Guards.

"*Tingwei* Feng Chou, you did well to rectify a bad situation. *Weiwei* Dong Ch'u is to be dismissed from his post, imprisoned in that same cell for thirty days, then banished from the palace and from Luoyang. Do you have more recommendations for me?"

"Yes, Son of Heaven. I recommend that you try a concubine for attempted murder. She is also accused of infidelity with the *Da Qin* soldier called An-Dun."

"And why should the Son of Heaven involve himself such a trivial matter?"

"Son of Heaven, the concubine was a translator for the Gan Ying expedition to the *Da Qin*, and returned with their envoy under special protection of their emperor, because she is *Da Qin* by ancestry. I did not feel it wise to allow her consort to execute or otherwise punish her, as would be his ordinary right, nor to pass judgment myself which is also in my purview, on a case of such import to you. If I erred in judgment, it is my mistake." The *Tingwei* bowed his head.

"And who is the consort of this concubine at the center of this disturbance?"

"Son of Heaven, the consort is Master Wang Ming."

The Emperor sat in thoughtful silence, while the *tingwei* and the Excellencies did likewise, their eyes downcast, intently studying the waterway separating them from the Emperor.

At last the Emperor bestirred himself. "And if you were to try this concubine, what sentence might you pass upon her?"

"Son of Heaven, I would show clemency if she has not been unfaithful. Master Ming has a …a reputation for cruelty to his consorts. One certainly has a right to maintain discipline among his own, but many in the court felt that he is excessive, and disturbs the harmony of the court rather than restoring it."

"And if she was unfaithful with the *Da Qin* soldier?"

"She was separated from Master Wang Ming for several months, and I believe she thought her consort dead or lost. I would recommend in that case a symbolic lashing of ten strokes, no more."

"And the *Da Qin* soldier?"

"Son of Heaven, she is an attractive woman and the journey was long."

"I accept your recommendations, *tingwei* Feng Chou. And please convey to Master Wang Ming that he is to refrain from beating his concubines. It is inharmonious for the strong to oppress the weak to no purpose."

The *tingwei* was excused. The Emperor rose from his chair on the dais, sweeping his ceremonial robe around himself in a swirl of silk, and the three Excellencies rose likewise, saluted with a bow, and remained standing while Emperor He departed toward the rear.

CHAPTER 51: THE TRIAL

A few hours after the Romans had cleansed themselves from their overnight stay in prison, both the Minister of Justice and Minister of the Household sent representatives to prepare them for their meeting with Emperor He the following afternoon. Marcus translated.

"The trial will be first," Marcus said with a choke in his voice, as his Hanaean side struggled to control his emotions. "Marcia will enter, then Antonius, you will be called as a witness."

"What is the charge?" asked Antonius.

"She attempted to kill Wang Ming, and a question of infidelity... with you, Antonius."

"That's a crock of manure!" exploded Antonius, disturbing the Hanaean representatives with his emotional rant. "That's a crock and yer know it! If I had seen him strike her, I'd a kilt him mesel', an' saved her the trouble. An' she an' I have never done nothin' but talk, yer know that, too! Tell them that!"

"No, Antonius, I won't. That would make it worse."

"Marcus is right, calm down in front of the Hanaean representatives, or this may affect the trial," said Aulus, trying to calm the furious centurion. "Marcus, what is the procedure here for trials?" He was expecting something like a Roman court of law, with attorneys, questioning, statements and the like.

"It is run entirely by the Emperor. He will ask all the questions, she will answer, he makes a decision. There is no procedure... Marcia will enter first, prostrate herself, and remain that way until the Emperor grants her permission to rise to a sitting position. Antonius, you will then enter, and do likewise. Answer only the questions asked, and do not look at the Emperor. When he is ready, he will render a decision. He will dismiss you, and you rise, back out of the court, keeping your head bowed."

"I ain't ever prostrated meself before any man, an' I don't intend to start now!" growled Antonius.

"What is the likely outcome?" asked Gaius.

Marcus choked again, his Hanaean face trying very hard to remain impassive. "I... I hope her death will be a merciful one!"

Aulus was as angry as Antonius. He controlled the tone of his voice, but his face was livid with emotion. "Is that all from these two?" he said, indicating the two representatives with a head nod.

Marcus exchanged some words with the two, they nodded. "That is all."

"Tell them they are dismissed. And phrase it just that way, the way your emperor would say it! I represent my own emperor here."

Marcus complied and the two Hanaeans' eyes went wide briefly, then they bowed and scurried out.

Aulus declared, "Gentlemen, we have a problem. The solution will probably cost us our mission and our lives, but I cannot let a Roman citizen and a member of my diplomatic mission go to her death on a trumped-up charge with no one to speak on her behalf!"

"I agree!" said Gaius.

"Whatever yer want to do, I am in, sir!" said Antonius.

"What do you have in mind?" asked Marcus.

"We are going to show them how Romans conduct a court of law, and I, as Marcia's attorney, intend to present her case. Erect, of course, and looking the Emperor square in the eye."

"You won't get to say much," said Marcus

"I don't expect to be able to say much," replied Aulus, with a wry grin.

"You will be executed!" said Marcus.

"Yes, and then we will show them how Romans die. We did not come all the way around the world to grovel at the feet of their god-king while he executes a fellow citizen who is innocent of any crime. That is not the message Trajan would want us to present. Gentlemen, I am going to wear my Senatorial toga, and I would like you to be wearing your military kit tomorrow. I want to make a good impression before they haul us off to the killing grounds."

"Marcus, you may wear my toga," offered Gaius, "since I will be in uniform. A bit above your status with an equestrian stripe, but you have earned it."

Marcus gulped, but nodded, his Hanaean side and his Roman side struggling for control.

Aulus produced another bottle of Falernian wine. "What is it the gladiators say, *morituri te salutamus,* we who are about to die, salute you! We might as well enjoy this and several more tonight, because we probably won't be coming back tomorrow."

The following day, they dressed around mid-morning. Gaius and Antonius donned their gear, assisting each other with straps and clips.

Finally, Antonius gave Gaius a punch in the chest, to check for rattles and loose fitting connectors. "*Integer es?* Are you complete?" the centurion asked, in the standard pre-battle checkout.

Gaius returned the punch to Antonius' chest with a laugh. "*Integer!* Complete as hell!" They were both feeling the euphoria that precedes a hopeless battle, which usually evaporates at the moment of contact.

They then helped Marcus with the toga. "There's an art to wearing it," Gaius said. "Just never move your left arm, or we'll have to drape you all over again."

Antonius chuckled, and said, "Yer know, we are in one hell of a fine humor fer people probably looking at the last day of our lives. I hate to ruin the mood, but I've noticed that the further east yer goes, the more creative ways they find to make you die. I got some aconite poison in me medic's *capsula*. Here's a packet fer each of yer. Don't open it until you're ready to take it, it can be absorbed through the skin. But give yerself time, it takes an hour or so."

"Everyone still in agreement on the basic plan?" asked Aulus, half hoping that someone might come up with a more viable alternative. No one offered any.

"I believe the protocol will be that Marcia will go in first, then Antonius. When you go in, we will enter right behind you. I expect the guards may try to force us out or down into a prostration. If they succeed, I will address the emperor from whatever position I am forced into, otherwise, I will address him standing. Make sure you don't have so much as a needle in your military kits, as I understand any weapons in the vicinity of the emperor is cause for instant death," cautioned Aulus.

"We are good, sir. Swords and daggers locked away."

"I'll be wearing the parade helmet Commodus gave me for graduation. It seems fitting. I gave it an extra coat of polish last night." The bronze helmet with its bright red longitudinal horsehair plume glinted in the morning sun as he manipulated the chin straps. He wore a leather breast plate, decorated with several silver *phalarae* awards he had earned for valor in various campaigns. Red leather *pteryges* formed a skirt protecting his thighs, and he wore a bright crimson army cloak.

Antonius was in his centurion's best parade kit with a bright steel helmet mounting a lateral horse hair plume of alternate red and white bands, and bright *lorica segmentata* plate armor heavily laden with his own very numerous *phalarae,* and his red *sagum* cloak.

Aulus wore a bright white toga with broad purple *laticlava* stripe of Senatorial rank, while Marcus wore Gaius' plain white toga over an equestrian tunic with two red narrow strips. Marcus' posture was distinctly Roman, though he was distinctly ill at ease managing the folds of his toga, in fear of it coming undone at some inopportune moment. He moved as little as possible, grasping it firmly in his left hand.

"You look properly Roman, Marcus. You should wear a toga more often," said Aulus, producing one more bottle of Italia's finest. "I think we should share one more glass of wine, to toast our ill-fated expedition," announced Aulus. "It is a bit early, and I don't want to go into this horrible mess inebriated, but I think one glass might steady our nerves."

"Fer me, I'd take the whole damned bottle," grunted Antonius.

The waiting, like that before battle, was the worst part. Gaius and Antonius, having experienced this many times before, knew how to keep the gut-wrenching fear from taking hold. Aulus and Marcus were learning it for the first time.

About noon, two attendants entered the room. They stared quizzically at Marcus, their fellow countryman, clad as a foreigner, and exchanged a few words with him. "It is time," said Marcus.

They were escorted to the anteroom of the throne room, where Marcia was waiting under guard by two soldiers. They caught her eye, but it seemed inappropriate to speak. Shortly, the Minister of the Household emerged. He, too, looked askance at Marcus' unusual attire, but also overlooked it. He chattered rapidly with Marcus, who then said, "Marcia is to go in first, then Antonius."

"Right. But then we all go in. No need to tell him that, however. It will ruin his day," joked Gaius.

The massive door swung open, and Marcia was escorted in. Inside, they could make out the lamps, and rows of robed councilors seated in two parallel rows.

"The emperor is seated on a dais at the back of the room," said Marcus in a whisper. "He is separated from the councilors by a moat of water."

The attendants beckoned Antonius. Aulus swallowed hard to clear the lump in his throat. "Let's go!"

All four strode past the aghast attendants and entered the throne room, fully erect. Their eyes had barely adjusted to the dim interior when two guards by the door attempted to seize them and wrestle them to the ground. They seized Antonius first, and were most unsuccessful, one sent sprawling. There was a rustle of concern among the councilors in the room at this most untoward and threatening behavior, and the attendants could be heard calling for more guards. Marcia lay prone, face down on the blackened stone floor, alone.

The guards, backed by additional ones from the outside, resumed their efforts to quell the unruly intruders, when the emperor motioned them aside with his hand.

Aulus looked the emperor straight in the eye, and began his speech without introduction, fully expecting to feel the cold steel of a blade pass through him before he finished. "Your Excellency, it is the custom and law among our people that every person accused of a crime have available representation before the court. I represent Marcia Lucia, *cives sine suffragio*, a non-voting citizen of Rome, under the protection of our Emperor Trajan, and also, Antonius Aristides, *primus pilus* of the *Legio* XII *Fulminata*, both envoys of that same Emperor and accorded the rights of emissaries throughout the world. Please advise me of the charges against my clients."

Marcus began translating when a voice was heard. "That won't be necessary."

They were puzzled at the source of this well-spoken if slightly accented Latin, when the voice continued. "I have made a point to learn your language." It was Emperor He himself. "What is the purpose of this unseemly entrance into my court?"

"We seek to defend Marcia Lucia, known to you as Si Huar, against false charges of attempted murder and infidelity, and Antonius Aristides of equally false charges of illicit relations with her."

Emperor He pondered the insolence. Fortunately, no one present in court could understand the Latin they were speaking. He had another minute or so to force obeisance and display his power over the *Da Qin*, or the court would perceive him as accepting defiance. That could not be allowed, as it would mark him as weak and lead to his decline and overthrow.

He pondered briefly the cause of this insouciance. Had someone in his court put them up to this trap? One of the Excellencies perhaps, a Minister, or perhaps an ambitious but more lowly person? Or did this come from the *Da Qin* on their own?

One advantage of the dangling baubles from his crown was that they concealed the direction of his gaze. He glanced at the Minister of the Household and noted that he was downcast and visibly distraught. He was responsible for the highly-scripted reception of foreigners in the court, and this was obviously not following his script. And all the Excellencies and Ministers were visibly shocked, not least Ban Chao, whose project this was.

No, more likely the *Anxi* ambassador had been right, the *Da Qin* were power-hungry to rule the world, challenging his authority here in his own court over the concubine of a mid-level court official with a taint of *Da Qin* blood in her veins. He did admit to a bit of admiration for their courage, but they must be brought to heel now.

"It is the custom and law of this land that you enter my court with due respect for me and for the Hanaean people! Whatever customs you follow in your own lands do not apply here. On your knees now, Romans, or accept the consequences of your actions!" This Emperor He spoke with just enough emphasis that the meaning would be clear to his court, if not the words.

Marcus rose to the challenge. "Marcia, stand up. We are Romans!" She rose shakily to stand with her brother, likewise meeting the emperor's gaze. Aulus continued to look the emperor in the eye, neither blinking nor saying anything.

Then Emperor He said loudly, "Remove them to the North Palace for execution!" Twenty-five beefy guards had filtered in during the confrontation, awaiting orders. They moved swiftly, drawing swords with a metallic hiss, surrounding the five Romans. Chains were produced, and they were shackled and led away.

CHAPTER 52: LOVE BEHIND BARS

The Romans were marched in chains out of the palace to the Xuanwumen Gate on the north wall of the palace compound, crossing a bridged walkway connecting the South Palace to the North Palace Compound. They continued to the North Palace, used by the emperor to address the masses in its huge pavilion… and also to conduct public executions. At the back of the palace was a small prison hewn from the rock foundation, its heavy door standing open. Two guards at the entrance snapped to attention as the party appeared, took the prisoners and hustled them down a long interior tunnel to a barred cavern at the end, strewn with straw. The five Romans were unmanacled and shoved roughly into the cave. The guards slammed the bars shut, securing them with a stout-looking padlock. The two guards returned to their posts at the mouth of the tunnel, closing and barring the outer door, then sat down and lit smoky lamps by their table.

The Hanaeans did not waste resources caring for prisoners awaiting execution, just a slop jar for their bodily needs and nothing else. The guards at the top of the tunnel were barely visible from the cave-cell, far back and right-angled off the tunnel.

Marcus called to them in Hanaean, but they did not acknowledge him.

"Well, that went about as expected," said Gaius. "I didn't think anything could make that last cell look better, but it was a first-class *mansio* hotel compared to this. Marcus, did you pick anything up from our escorts about what is going to happen to us?"

"No, nothing. They chatted among themselves, but nothing consequential. We apparently shocked the entire court."

Marcia began to sob. "I… I am so sorry… I involved you in this. Now you are going to die with me. And …I am so sorry."

Antonius gently put his arm around her shoulders. "I think Wang Ming had more ter do with this than yer did, Marcia. And yer didn't involve us in this, we chose ter do it. We weren't goin' ter let yer die alone. At least now they know what Roman honor looks like."

She turned and embraced him, her body shuddering uncontrollably as she sobbed against his shoulder. He stroked her back soothingly. "Be careful, *domina,* yer goin' ter rust me armor if yer keep that up!" They were all still wearing their uniforms and togas from the morning. Gaius had even kept his old Gallic helmet, tucked under his left arm during the court. Antonius' helmet had been lost in the scuffle.

Aulus spoke up. "Antonius is right, Marcia. It was our unanimous decision to challenge the Emperor. If he was going to kill you, he was going to have to kill us all. He made it easy by insisting we crawl into the court on our bellies. I think Trajan would have approved of what we did, though he will never know."

They settled into the cell. In the interest of Marcia's privacy, the slop jar was set far back in the corner, a good place, as it stank from previous users. Everyone sat around pretty much in silence.

Gaius and Antonius found a corner where they could observe the guards. Old military habits called for monitoring for means of escape, however futile, clad as they were in Roman garb with Western visages. They wouldn't get far. But it helped pass the time. The guards whiled away the afternoon on some sort of board game, seated across from each other at a small table under a torch. Every once in a while, the prisoners could hear laughter or groans, or what might be some sort of Hanaean profanity, and the pieces would be removed from the board with a clattering and clinking sound and set back up. About every hour, one or the other would come back to tug on the padlock, but they otherwise ignored their prisoners.

After several hours, there was a knock on the entrance door. One of the guards stood up, went to the door and slid a window open. There were some words exchanged, and the guard lifted the bar to open the door.

Gaius and Antonius watched carefully. Was this the execution party? Was this, in fact, the last few minutes of their lives?

No, it was just the relief watch. The guards talked back and forth a bit, then one of the oncoming guards came back to count the prisoners, tugged on the padlock, and went back up. They exchanged more pleasantries, and the off-going watch departed. The inside bar fell back in place with a thud. The oncoming watch had come in carrying lanterns, and what little light Gaius had seen from outside indicated it was about sunset. "I am guessing they change shifts every six hours or so, Antonius."

"I agree, Gaius, 'bout sundown, me thinks."

The guards produced some bowls of food, and the garlicky smells reminded the Romans they hadn't eaten or drunk since before noon. "Wonder if any of that chow is fer us back here," mused Antonius.

It wasn't. The guards finished their meal, produced a bottle, and began their own board game. "I guess since they figger they're goin' ter kill us, they don't need ter feed us. Waste of food."

The guards continued the lock checks. Gaius had counted them, and guessed they were about hourly.

There was another soft knock at the door. A guard got up and admitted one of the yellow-garbed monks. The monk produced a begging bowl and got the usual copper coins from each guard, smiling and bowing, then he gave them a bottle. They then pointed back to the cell area. One guard raised five fingers and made a gesture indicating that one was a woman, and laughed. He apparently approved of Marcia's appearance. The monk smiled in return and came back to the cell.

It was Demosthenes. His eyes went wide in recognition, and so did those of Aulus, Gaius and Antonius. Demosthenes spoke quietly in Greek, with no apparent recognition in the tone of his voice. "Do not let on that you know me. I bring you food. It is a service we do for condemned prisoners." He produced a tray with bowls of rice, some vegetables and a flask of water.

"Thank you. We thought they were going to just starve us to death," said Antonius with a smile.

"It is why we feed you. They do not feed condemned men. What have you done? The guards say you are to be beheaded in a public execution in five days!"

"I guess our first meeting with Emperor He did not go well. Sorry!"

"There is a rumor in town that you insulted him horribly."

"It seems we did."

"I must go now. I will try to come every night until...," he left the sentence unfinished.

"Thanks for the food," said Antonius.

Demosthenes left, and talked briefly with the guards. They let him out, and the door shut behind him, followed by the thud of the bar. The guards went back to their board game.

"Well, that was unexpected." Antonius passed the food around. It wasn't much, but was enough to quell the hunger pangs. "Looks like those monks do get to go everywhere!"

"Interesting!" said Aulus. "Have you two figured out how to get out of here?"

"Not really, cousin. Short of breaking down our iron cage, overpowering two guards with weapons we don't have, and changing ourselves into inconspicuous Hanaeans, I can't think of one," answered Gaius, grasping one of the inch-thick wrought iron bars in his hands. "Demosthenes says we have five days."

"Well, they told him more than they told us," groused Marcus.

They finished eating, and passed the water bottle around. "Save some fer tomorrow," cautioned Antonius. "We'll be getting' thirsty again before he comes round again."

Their stomachs full, and nothing left to do, they fell silent for a bit. Gaius and Antonius had stripped off their heavy metal armor to just their tunics. Gaius periodically looked at his tiny portrait of Camilla on its thong around his neck, caressing it with his thumb, trying to make out her features in the darkness, wondering how she would feel when he simply never, ever returned.

Talking about their eminent demise seemed to take the sting out of it, huddling together in the center of the cave. All but Marcia had either a woolen toga or army cloak, which they wrapped around themselves against the growing chill. She sat next to Antonius in her silk dress, and he shared his cloak with her.

"I wonder if you feel the pain when you are beheaded?" asked Marcus.

"I suspect not much, if the headsman is any good. It will rip through yer spinal cord, probably more of a shock than anything else," answered Antonius, his medical expertise coming up. "If he misses, and that happens sometimes, it'll hurt like hell."

"Should we take the aconite you gave us?"

"Up to you. Aconite can take a couple of hours of diarrhea and vomiting. Me, I am goin' ter bet on a good headsman."

Aulus injected a philosophical thought. "What about after? What do you think we will find – on the other side?"

"Well, the Epicureans think there are no gods, that we are all random atoms, and when we are gone, it's all over. You get what you can out of what life presents, no more. *Carpe diem*, they say," said Antonius, switching to scholarly Latin, surprising Aulus.

"Our centurion, the philosopher!" exclaimed Aulus.

"I guess I don't need to worry about appearances anymore," replied Antonius.

"Continue, please!"

"Most believe that we linger on, like an echo. That we have some memory of ourselves, but just progressively fade away."

Gaius interjected. "The Christians believe that your spiritual being is immortal, and your body just temporary, that you go to a place of eternal reward or punishment as you deserve."

"Brr, I'll pass on that one, Gaius. I can think of too many things I did that I'd rather not have done, to think about paying for those errors for all eternity. I think I'd rather linger on as a fading echo," said Aulus.

Antonius resumed, "Plato believed in reincarnation, and so does our Buddhist friend Demosthenes. Whatever the gods are, I think they exist, and have a plan, and I don't think they do anything by chance, the way the Epicureans think. You won't see too many Epicureans in the battle line, and anyway, they are way too fat!" Everyone laughed.

"So what is their plan for us?" asked Marcia.

"Damned if I know. What do the Hanaeans believe about the afterlife, Marcus?"

"Mostly it is about this life. You are supposed to live your life honorably and create order in the world around you. That is the gods' plan. We disrupted that order, in their mind, so… here we are!"

"Oh, well. It is getting cold, so I think we should try to catch some sleep. We have five days, according to Demosthenes, to solve all the problems in the world."

As the group disbursed to different parts of the cell, Marcia spoke softly to Antonius. "Do you mind if I sleep with you? I am freezing in this silk, and I find you have a very comfortable shoulder."

"Sure, cuddle up, I'll keep you warm." He stretched out on his back under his cloak, and put his right arm around her. She rolled into his side, put her left arm across his chest, and her thigh over his. Antonius was acutely aware of her soft breast against him and his rapidly stiffening manhood. He tried to put those thoughts out of his mind. He was shivering, but not from the cold.

"Warm enough?" he asked.

"Mmmh, better. Thank you!" she sighed. She traced her fingers along his powerfully muscled biceps. "You have hard muscles."

"My line of work, *domina.*" Her fingers continued their exploration, across his chest and down his rock solid stomach.

"Marcia…" he began, but Marcia put her finger across his lips and shushed him to stifle any further protest.

"I want this, Antonius," she whispered.

It was the softest, most gentle kiss he had ever had, like a flower melting over his lips. Her tongue explored his mouth, his teeth, found his tongue and played with it. Antonius rolled to his right to face her. "Quietly. If the guards hear us it won't go well for you," he whispered.

He embraced her, feeling her body yield under his touch. He cupped her breast, feeling the nipple harden under her silk robe, kissing it through the material, while his hand traced down the side of her body, lingering on her hipbone.

Her hand continued the exploration of his stomach, finding his throbbing erection under the tunic and tracing its length with one finger, making Antonius gasp. The kissing became more urgent, and his hand continued down her thigh until it found the hem of her dress. It continued back up the soft inside of her thigh to her womanhood, wet with anticipation. He entered her with one finger, and it was her turn to gasp.

They continued in this manner for some time.

Gaius and Aulus made no acknowledgement of the activities at the back of the cave, but had positioned themselves with Marcus to keep an eye on the guards, and warn them if one came back for a lock check. One guard was snoring, however, and the other seemed about ready to nod off also.

After what seemed like an eternity of caresses, Antonius entered Marcia, like sliding into a velvet passageway. They moved, they paused, they moved again, in a silent dance of love that neither wanted to end. But end it must, and Antonius' intensity betrayed his impending climax. Its imminence triggered Marcia's, she bit his shoulder to avoid crying out and her body convulsed as she received his seed. Their bodies merged into a white hot ball of pleasure, flowing together until the last spasm subsided and they were spent in each other's arms, gasping, hearts pounding, unable to speak.

Finally, after a few minutes of recovery, Marcia was the first to speak. "Oh, Antonius! Never have I felt what I felt with you! This was – words are wasted trying to describe it!"

Antonius kissed her gently. "*Domina,* I must confess, I have never had a woman who wanted me like you did. I have never before had - made love to - a woman like I did with you. It is a precious gift you have given me – my love."

"My love, my love, you are so right. I do love you, Antonius, and you are worth my life for this." She snuggled into his arms again, and sleep followed quickly for both.

CHAPTER 53: PLANS ARE LAID

Demosthenes found Ibrahim on Musa's boat. He rapped on the hatch door, and Musa opened with a lamp in hand. "Ibrahim, please," said Demosthenes, and Musa turned and called out, "Ibrahim, thou hast an unexpected guest!"

Ibrahim came up from the interior of the cabin. "Demosthenes, welcome! To what do we owe this most unexpected visit?"

"Trouble, sir, great trouble! Your Roman friends are in prison awaiting execution! I just came from talking with them!"

"Which ones, Aulus, Gaius, Antonius.... All of them?" asked Ibrahim.

"All of them and two Hanaeans, one wearing Roman clothing, the other a girl."

"That would be Marcus and Marcia, their translators. I had heard there was trouble in the court today, but this? How did you come to see them?"

"We deliver food to condemned prisoners. We bring wine for the guards and they admit us to the cell area with food for the unfortunates. Tonight was my turn, I spoke to them briefly."

"Hmm, let me get my friend Yakov. He has little Greek, but a good mind. Come into the cabin and sit down." He switched to Aramaic for Yakov's benefit. "My friend, we have a problem. We may need thy keen insight." Yakov nodded attentively, as Ibrahim recounted the situation for his benefit. Yakov and he exchanged a few words, then he turned to Demosthenes. "Yakov wants to know everything you know about this: where the cell is, how you go in and out, what is it like inside, how is it guarded. Everything you know." He took out a waxed tablet and stylus to take notes.

"The prison is in the back of the north palace, the east side. It is a small tunnel with a heavy oaken door. There are two guards."

"Inside or out?"

"Inside. The door is barred from the inside. We knock on the little sliding door, they open it, identify us, and lift the bar to admit us."

"You have papers or some sort of pass to get admission?"

"No, our robes and our begging bowls are our pass."

"Interesting. Continue."

"The guards sit at a small table by the door. There is a pull chain running through a tube to the room above the jail. If they pull that, a bell rings upstairs, and the duty officer will send reinforcements."

"How did you come to know that?"

"One of the guards showed me once. He said if he pulled that, twenty soldiers would appear immediately. He threatened to do that because I was annoying him, but I think he was joking."

"Interesting. Go on."

"Inside, you turn left, go down the tunnel about thirty paces, and the cell is on the left. The people in the cell cannot see much more than the wall in front of them. It's padlocked."

"Who has the key?"

"I don't know."

Ibrahim stroked his beard in thought. "How do you get into the compound itself?"

"I usually use the Dongmingmen Gate on the eastern side. Same as getting into the prison. I come up to the guards on the outside of the gate, beg from them, and ask to go in."

"That simple, really? You little beggars just go anywhere you want?"

"Parts of the main palaces in both North and South Compounds are off-limits, as is the Empress' palace, since all the women are there. Any place where we might run into the Son of Heaven. Are you thinking of getting them out, Ibrahim?"

"Wondering if it is even possible. How were the Romans dressed, Demosthenes?"

"Everyone was in tunics when I went in there, but there were some heavy woolen robes on the floor, with purple stripes, and some military gear, all stacked up in the back. The girl Marcia was in an Hanaean silk dress."

"Roman togas. They must have dressed up for the showdown with the Emperor. I would have liked to have seen it. Please, have some tea while I discuss this with Yakov."

Ibrahim went over his notes with Yakov. Clearly, getting in did not sound too hard, but getting them out of the compound was a serious problem. No disguise would hide their Western faces. Yakov studied Demosthenes closely as he drank his tea. "Master, that man hath Western features, yet he cometh and goeth with freedom. Do the guards count them entering and leaving?"

Ibrahim posed the question to Demosthenes: "No, we often come in as a group and leave separately, or vice versa.

"Do they recognize you by sight?"

"Some do and some do not."

"Tell me, do you often carry bags, or would that be unusual? I have never seen you do that."

"Not often, but we have traveling bags that we use when are on the road to carry food, cooking pots, our razors. And sometimes someone wants to give us a bulky gift, and we will carry it in our traveling bag."

"And the guards – do they inspect your bags?"

"They never have."

Ibrahim went back to discuss this with Yakov. "Thou art insightful, my friend. Thinkest thou that we could take care of the guards and then transform our Roman friends into Buddhist monks?"

Yakov cocked one eyebrow, and gave a wry smile. "Maybe, master, just maybe. If what your friend sayeth be true. Otherwise we shall join our Roman friends on the execution block."

"They may enjoy the company, my friend. Let us ponder this overnight. Thinkest thou carefully of all the missteps. Each one will be fatal, and we have few days to lay our plan."

Ibrahim poured himself more tea, and pondered while Demosthenes waited patiently.

"A few more questions now, my friend. Just hypothetically, of course, if you had to turn our five Romans into Buddhist monks and nuns, how long would it take?"

"Shave their heads, and teach them some basic gestures, blessings and so forth, I guess about two hours. But this would be a great sin against my religion."

"Demosthenes, they are going to die, if you do not do this hypothetical sin. Besides…" he said with a smile, "you might win them over to your Way."

"I will consider it."

"Discuss this with no one, not even the Romans. And tomorrow night, find out where the key to their cell is kept." He dropped a copper coin into Demosthenes' begging bowl. "May I offer you some rice and vegetables?"

Later that night, he discussed the situation with Musa.

"You can use my boat," he promptly offered.

"No, we have been closely monitored, and this will be the first thing checked when they find out about the jailbreak. Better for you to be nowhere around, because if they find you, they will probably question you 'under duress,' removing body parts until you tell them everything. I need you instead to get an oxcart, some cargo as cover, lambs, chickens and the like. You will leave with us, but I think I can get you back in a few days to go home."

"What about you?"

"My lot's with them." He paused, thinking. "I will need some concealment in the oxcart for things that need concealing … their Roman paraphernalia, my cash, some weapons and hunting gear for traveling. And clothes." He handed Musa a string of Hanaean copper coins. "Buy what you need."

Ibrahim would also have to determine where to go, and how to get there. As his mind calculated the planning and deadlines, he realized how he had missed the excitement of planning an operation, evading capture and eluding death… he had been a fool to think he could ever have been happy as a shepherd. To be sure, as that wise man had told him four decades ago, "May God grant you what you most desire." *Yes, thank You, God, Whoever or Whatever You may be, You have truly done so.*

CHAPTER 54: BREAKING FREE

The defiant spit-in-their-eye camaraderie that had marked the Romans' first day of imprisonment had vanished over their confinement, and by the fourth night, fear and anxiety had replaced courage. They were not looking forward to Demosthenes' last nightly visit, which had been one of the bright spots in their existence... tonight, no one wanted to eat.

Antonius' and Marcia's lovemaking had failed them the preceding night, as she was unwilling to engage in what by now seemed like pointless pleasure. She sobbed softly while Antonius crooned her a lullaby from his long-forgotten childhood, tears streaming down his face as well. Today he had gone to the back of the cave and vomited, retching for a long time, although he had eaten little in the past four days. At the evening guard shift, they sat around glumly, not wanting to talk.

Shortly after the changeover, Demosthenes showed up, gave his usual bottle to the guards, and went back to the cell with their meager dinner. "Not tonight, Demosthenes. Nobody is hungry," said Antonius, "and we are not up for talk on this last night."

"This may not be your last night," Demosthenes said in a whisper, although the guards could neither hear nor understand their whispered conversations.

"Yes it is, now off with you. No false hopes, just let it end."

The guards had swilled the bottle he had brought, returned to their board game, then one rolled out of his chair to fall on the floor with a thud.

Demosthenes looked up the tunnel. "That's one," he said.

"You crazy fool! We can't get a hundred yards out of this prison before we are cut down and you with us! Get the hell out of here. There's nothing you can do to help us!" hissed Antonius

"We have a plan." Demosthenes looked up the tunnel at the other guard, who either had not drunk as much of the wine, or had a higher resistance to the opium poppy juice that Ibrahim had put in it. Recognizing something amiss, the guard stood up and staggered toward the bell-pull.

"Oh, no!" Demosthenes gasped, his heart pounding; he had not counted on this. The guard reached for the bell-pull but missed, lost his balance, and joined his comrade on the floor. Demosthenes let out a deep breath. "That's two. I need to get Yakov, and you are out of here!"

"You better have a good plan," said Antonius.

"It's Ibrahim's plan," he said, as he scampered up the tunnel to the door. He opened the sliding peephole and held a lantern to it three times, then unbarred it to admit Yakov, who like Demosthenes, was completely bald and clean-shaven, clad in a yellow robe. He was carrying two big sacks. Demosthenes then rebarred the door.

Yakov looked at the guards sleeping on the floor, pulled out a dagger, and dispatched them permanently with very little blood. He left the dagger embedded in the last one. It was Antonius' Roman dagger that he had given Ibrahim in Tianjin.

Demosthenes recovered the key to the cell from a peg on the wall, and he and Yakov hefted the two bags back to the cell area. They unlocked the cell and produced scissors and razors, some oil, and five yellow robes and begging bowls from the two sacks. "You are going to become our newest followers of the Buddha. Bow your heads while I shave them, and your beard stubble as well. Try not to move, I don't want to leave any bloody nicks. You, too, Marcia, you will become a nun."

Marcia and Marcus were not happy over the loss of their hair, as the cutting of the hair is a great shame in the Confucian tradition, and they were as much Hanaean as Roman. However, this was a small sacrifice for their lives.

It took over an hour to shave them, with only one or two minor nicks. They were careful to gather the cut hair into the bags to leave no evidence of their transformation. Then everyone stripped, put their garb in the bags, and put on the yellow robes.

The four newly-bald monks and one nun stared at each other, and at Yakov. Yakov clearly had already successfully passed himself off as a monk to gain entrance with Demosthenes. "Damn! This might just work," said Antonius.

Demosthenes spent another hour coaching them on proper motions... head bows, blessings, the proper way to beg. If nobody made a mistake, seven might walk out of here, just as two had walked in. They then policed up the cell area to make sure they had taken all their belongings and the incriminating wine bottle. They left the padlock, with key inserted, dangling from the hasp. The idea was to convey the idea that the Romans had somehow gotten the key from the guards, killed them with a dagger that had gone undetected, and escaped, still wearing their very conspicuous clothing. No one would be looking for Buddhist monks.

On the way out, Yakov produced one more item from his bag of tricks, some rope and a hammer and nails. He tied the rope around the ends of the door bar lying on the floor and passed the loop through the speakeasy window. Everyone left and the door was closed. Yakov wrestled the bar back up and in place from outside, tossing the rope back inside and nailing the speakeasy shut. It would take some time for the oncoming watch to get the door open and get inside.

They then headed for the Dongmingmen Gate on the east side as casually as possible, led by Demosthenes, his swaying lantern casting shadows here and there. The palace courtyard was virtually deserted, hours before the next shift change at midnight. They came to the gate, Demosthenes requested passage, and the door swung open; he then presented his begging bowl to the guard, as did the others in turn. Each gave a reasonably good blessing sign, and bowed graciously as the guard dropped a copper coin in each bowl with a smile. They were out! They headed to the upper eastern gate out of the city a short distance away and repeated the process. Outside, an oxcart was standing, loaded with sheep and chickens. Ibrahim, Shmuel, and Musa, all clean-shaven, were seated in the oxcart driver's seat in Hanaean working garb. Galosga, his distinctive long black hair now gone, was standing by for their arrival.

Ibrahim announced, "All right, the hard part is done, gentlemen. I and Musa will drive the first shift. Three of you monks ride, four walk with the off-duty drivers, we'll alternate every few hours. We want to put as many miles between us and Luoyang as we can before daylight."

Marcia, Marcus, and Demosthenes got the first ride. And Ibrahim tsk-tsked the two oxen into a ponderously slow pace.

CHAPTER 55: THE LONG ROAD HOME

The *tingwei* and the *taiwei* Commander-in-Chief jointly led the investigation into the *Da Qin* escape from prison, particularly embarrassing as the Son of Heaven had called for a large assemblage of about ten thousand to witness their execution under his personal observance.

It seemed straightforward to the *tingwei*. The guards had been drinking, perhaps had gotten too friendly with their prisoners over the past several days. The *Da Qin* seized one, killed him and took the key. They then overpowered and killed the remaining guard before he could sound the alarm. A dagger, inscribed with characters in the *Da Qin* script, was found in one of the guards.

The *Da Qin* then apparently vanished into thin air. They did not go out any gate through the palace or the city, so they had to have gone over the fifteen-foot walls, guarded every hundred yards or so by lookouts. The *Dong Ming Sima* provided the battalion guarding these gates... he would have those on watch that night questioned under duress, then executed. The recently-relieved and disgraced *weiwei* Minister of Guards was responsible for this slovenly security, and he, too, would be executed.

A thorough search of the city, starting with Musa's boat docked along the river turned up nothing. The boat was padlocked, but was forced open and thoroughly searched. The owner was not aboard, nor was there any evidence of the *Da Qin*. It would be closely watched, as it would be impossible for the renegades to book any other boat passage back to Tianjin now, with the city fully alert for them.

The *taiwei* ordered fast river cutters to search and inspect all riverboat traffic between here and Tianjin, and cavalry patrols to check all road traffic. He also sent fast couriers to Tianjin to alert the authorities there to detain the *Da Qin* ships.

The oxcart bumped and lurched its way up the road leading north out of Luoyang, toward Mangshan, and away from the Luo River where they hoped the Hanaean authorities would concentrate their search. The advantage of the oxcart, pulled by two massive, flat-horned water buffalo, was the amount of weight the placid animals were able to haul, seemingly effortlessly: four sheep and ten chickens, all in pens stacked on one side, four passengers and three on the driver's bench. The disadvantage was that they moved at a walking pace. The driver had a small torch to light their way, and the five walkers were content to stay in its fitful light. They had covered ten uneventful miles when Ibrahim stopped and pulled off into a very small side road for concealment. "Time to rearrange the cargo and get rid of some stuff we do not want found if we find a checkpoint conducting searches," he announced.

They unloaded the oxcart, setting the complaining chickens and confused sheep on the ground, and dragged the bags of incriminating clothing out. Musa had rigged an ingenious false bottom in the cart, which gave about a foot or so of hidden storage under the floor. It was so tightly made, it was virtually impossible to open from the top, so tightly did it fit against the wall. In the bottom of the cart was a small hole he had drilled. Into this hole he inserted a stout stick, pushed with a grunt, and the back end of the false floor came up several inches, enough for a hand hold to lift it clear. Inside was a stash containing Ibrahim's ransom, now funding their way home, some swords, bows and substantial daggers, and a brace of arrows, none of which some semi-literate foreign laborers accompanied by five monks should be carrying. Into this hidey hole went the bags containing the Roman clothing and military gear they had been wearing, and cut hair. They would dispose of this much later, and much further away. Right now, to anyone who might have come upon this, they appeared to be just rearranging the cargo for a better ride. The false floor closed with a thud, the cargo was put back in place, and the riders clambered aboard to resume their trek.

They were passing alongside Mangshan Mountain, looming dark against the brilliantly starlit sky a few hours before dawn, when they heard behind them the clatter of a group of men on horseback, a cavalry squadron riding hard under torchlight. Their hearts rose to their throats. They tried to act unconcerned... after all they were common laborers giving some monks a ride, with nothing to fear from the authorities.

The men cantered past, without giving a sidewise glance at the oxcart.

At sunrise, they had covered about twenty miles, by Antonius' estimate; he had been counting paces, army-style. There was a small creek near the road, shrouded by bushes. It seemed to be a good place to stop and wash with the bushes affording some privacy, and get some sleep. The former prisoners had slept not at all in the previous twenty-four hours, and besides, they stank, not having had enough water to wash even their hands in the past five days.

The men picked a spot closer to the road. Marcia was afforded the privacy of some bushes further back, but she invited Antonius along. Demosthenes forebade this, as it was already in violation of the rules of the order for *bhikkhuni* nuns to be traveling with *bhukkhu* monks. They were close enough to the great White Horse Temple that they had already encountered some monks, mostly traveling alone, and Demosthenes had the uneasy feeling that those monks found the behavior of his group suspicious. He was going to have to school them very much in rules of behavior. If they were to be exposed, it would most likely be by a passing monk who doubted their authenticity.

They savored the cold, clear water and washed the grime and filth from their bodies. There were some reeds growing by the side of the river that could be fashioned into serviceable toothbrushes, leaving their mouths clean for the first time in several days. They ate a light breakfast of rice, and then passed out into deep sleep until about noon, when they resumed the trek until sundown.

Once past Mangshan Mountain, they turned west, eventually crossing over an arched bridge over the Jianhe River flowing back to Luoyang. On the other side of the bridge, they followed the river through the agricultural communities in the fields along its banks. Other oxcarts trundled past, peasants on foot trundling heavy loads in wheelbarrows, or with seemingly impossible loads on their backs. Dogs barked, birds sang.... It was a good day to be alive. Antonius estimated they had covered another ten miles.

A bit past the villages, the area turned forested. They dismounted and led the oxen down a path to the river in what appeared to be an isolated spot, unharnessed and hobbled them to graze and water themselves without wandering off. Ibrahim, Musa, and the three "peasants" offloaded the animal cargo, cleaned their cages, and provided them some food and water. Antonius broke out his *capsula* from the false bottom, and pondered the cylindrical metal container. Would it be recognizable as a Roman artifact? Other than the cryptic 'LEG XII I COH A. ARIST PP,' he thought not, as he had yet to encounter an Hanaean who understood Western script. He opened the canister and drew out a roll of white linen, and unrolled it to expose his medical kit... pockets containing scalpels, forceps, suture needles and thread, linen bandages, vials of various liquids, packets of willow bark. He prepared to tend blisters. He and Gaius, as well Demosthenes and the four 'foreign peasants,' were used to hard walking, sore but unblistered after thirty miles. Marcus, Marcia and Aulus were not.

"Take care of this, and keep it clean. If it hurts, let me know and we'll call a halt and tend to it. If it gets inflamed, yer may be down for days, and could lose yer foot... or worse!" he cautioned Aulus, tending the last of the blisters. "I'll tell Ibrahim that yer three should ride tomorrow."

"I'm fine!" answered Aulus.

"You are but yer foot is not. Few more days and yer'll toughen those feet up, but I want all three of yers taking it easy tomorrow." Antonius was brooking no argument, as he rolled up his kit and stuffed it back into the *capsula.*

While Shmuel made the fire, Yakov dispatched one of the chickens for the evening meal, but the monks were remaining in character, having only rice and vegetables. Which was fine for Antonius and Gaius, as the Roman army marched and fought on vegetarian fare in the field... meat was believed to bloat a soldier and slow him down. Aulus, Marcus and Marcia thought otherwise.

Aulus approached Ibrahim, and addressed him in Greek, for the first time ever in their relationship. "It seems you've earned the handsome ransom Gaius paid you. Thank you, that was a brilliant strategy you came up with."

"Well, we have a long way before we get out of Hanaean lands," answered Ibrahim with a smile, trying to stroke a non-existent beard. "And the rest of my ransom is under the floorboards and probably a lot more will be spent getting us home. Did you five manage to salvage any money?"

"Just my purse, with a few *denarii* and Hanaean coins. Not much. Hope the good emperor enjoys the gift we left in our room… millions of *sesterces* in gold and silver."

Ibrahim gave a low whistle. "I am tempted to go back and devise a plan to get that out of the palace. Where was your room located?" asked Ibrahim, with a sibilant hiss and grin.

"Please … don't even think of it!"

"Remember, I am a thief at heart!" He clapped Aulus familiarly on the shoulder, and went to see about dinner. Aulus rejoined the other monks.

Demosthenes corralled the monks and acquainted them with the discipline of their adopted lifestyle. This began with fifteen minutes of chants in an unfamiliar language, which they were to have to learn by heart if they were to pass muster with any real monks they should encounter. He showed them how to use his prayer wheel, then they meditated for over an hour before he allowed them to eat. After the spartan dinner, they chanted for another hour before he released them for bedtime, with Marcia dispatched to a private spot. However, Antonius beckoned Demosthenes to join him by the fire before retiring.

"Demosthenes, that was a gutsy thing you did last night, and I am deeply grateful to you for pulling that off. We felt we were already dead, and you returned us to life. We are forever in your debt."

"You are welcome, but I am deeply conflicted about my actions. I have become deeply attached to you five, but attachment is an illusion. Because of my actions and my affection for you, two guards died, violently."

"We spared them and their families torture. And you spared us."

"I know, let me explain….when I was younger, I was a soldier, like yourself, in the army of Bactria. But I grew tired of the killing and bloodshed. I left to follow in the path of the Great Lord Buddha, to break the cycle of *dukkha*, sadness and disillusionment."

For about an hour, he explained the beliefs of Buddhism, and the importance of detachment from the illusions of this life, how actions in this life only perpetuate the cycle of birth and rebirth. Antonius contributed some thoughts from Plato, how this life was indeed only the shadow of ideal forms, imperfectly perceived. But then the long day's trek caught up with them, and they too prepared to retire. They rose, and Demosthenes turned to face Antonius and grasped his shoulder lightly.

"As I said, I am conflicted about this. The beliefs and rules of my order that I have vowed to uphold, say that I have done wrong. And yet... I cannot imagine myself doing otherwise! Once again, I find myself immersed in *dukkha*."

"Later, Demosthenes, we will continue this conversation again, I am sure. But right now... life is a cycle, and what you did must count for something!"

The next morning, Ibrahim bade farewell to Musa, who donned a light pack and headed south toward Luoyang. Musa wished them luck, and he was gone.

Marcia, Marcus and Aulus rode the whole way, while the other "monks" walked behind, practicing their new chants. More cavalry patrols passed them by, and sleepy-looking guards at a checkpoint waved them through with no interest in inspecting their cargo. Well before sunset, they found another secluded spot to camp; Antonius estimated they had covered fifteen miles or so. After dinner, Ibrahim called a meeting of the Greek speakers, Demosthenes, Aulus, Gaius and Antonius, with Yakov at his side.

"I am using Greek because you are the key people in this expedition now, and please pass this on to the others when we are done. First, Musa left this morning by choice. Not entirely his own, because he wanted to continue considerably farther, at least. However, he has a wife, children, and a profitable business in Tianjin, and he has already been absent from them for almost six months. If he came with us, he might never see them again."

Aulus interjected, "What will happen if he is picked up by the authorities in Luoyang and connected with this? We are all known associates of his."

"That is a good point, Aulus, and we came up with a plan several days ago to deflect any attention away from him, and also gives us some cover. Musa bought this oxcart shortly after we learned you had been imprisoned, and he let everyone know that I and my three associates were terrified of being apprehended, and wanted to leave as fast as possible to the east to rejoin our ships in Tianjin. We got detailed directions, maps and all, and Musa gave, as an excuse for not taking us by boat, that he had another business deal to conclude with a customer northwest of Luoyang, then he, too, would be departing downriver. And he does in fact have such a customer, which is where he is heading, to pick up a signed contract for another boat. A dated one. I and my associates "left" the same day we bought the oxcart by the east gate, and waited in the woods for him to join us the following day. He very publicly padlocked his boat, grumbling that we had left him without anyone aboard to keep it secure, and bragged about his new contract to anyone along the dock who would listen. He will return, in a few days, contract in hand, apparently not even aware that the jailbreak occurred.

"No one in Luoyang would expect us to go north into unknown territory." Everyone chuckled at that one. "And if anyone connects those dots, they will look for us to the east, dressed and hirsute as we were when we departed last week. Musa has a packet of aconite, compliments of Antonius, in case he is captured. He will die by his own hand before revealing where we really are." Ibrahim paused to let everyone absorb the gravity of that last statement.

Aulus spoke up. "It seems you have made evading the law your life's work, and have become quite proficient in it. Every expedition needs a leader, and can have only one. You have done an admirable job, and I, for one, prefer to have you continue in this endeavor. Cousin? Antonius? If anyone is not comfortable with Ibrahim continuing in charge of this effort, speak now, and we can pick another."

Everyone agreed that Ibrahim was the natural choice. The amount of careful planning that he had already put into this was phenomenal, and it only became apparent to the three as it was explained to them: careful pieces of deception, planning and execution, all products of a brilliant criminal mind.

"Well, I guess I am stuck with you all. Reminds me of being a shepherd again, caring for stupid damned sheep!" Everyone laughed, and Ibrahim continued. "So one of the things that I have found useful in efforts like this, is to hold daily meetings to dissect each new part of our efforts, and solicit your inputs. Gaius, Antonius, you are familiar with this, having dined with me regularly on *Europa*. And I am sure you do something very similar in the army"

"I didn't realize that was what we were doing at the time, but yes, I understand. We call them staff meetings, but yes, they are the same thing," answered Gaius, in deep interest.

"Gaius, you are the strategic thinker. I need your thoughts and criticism in particular. Antonius, you are the superb tactician. I need to know what's wise and foolish, so Gaius, Antonius, and all of you, feel comfortable with telling me that. Mistakes and omissions are fatal."

"Aye, sir," answered Antonius. "Where are we going?"

"Our next stop is Sanmenxia, which is about ten days away at our current rate, maybe two weeks, according to Musa." answered Ibrahim. "Beyond that is Chang'an. That used to be the capital and is still an important provincial center. Word of our escape will have reached there well before our arrival, so our cover must be impeccable by then. Beyond that is a long road to Kashgar, along a great desert. Very, very far. Demosthenes knows a little about the caravans, having passed through Chang'an on his way into Hanaean territory. Those caravans connect Kashgar with Demosthenes' home country of Bactria. Kashgar and Chang'an are very important cities, so perhaps Marcus and Marcia know more about them."

Demosthenes spoke up, "My home country controls Kashgar and several cities along the north side of the great desert. We will be on friendly territory well before Kashgar."

Marcus added, "We grew up in Liqian in Gansu, which is just a few miles from the road connecting Chang'an to the Turfam area. Marcia and I speak the local dialect."

Ibrahim nodded. "Good! Now, we have two weaknesses: language, and your cover as Buddhist monks. We can't go on relying on Demosthenes, Marcus and Marcia as translators. An Hanaean man and a woman acting as translators is what they expect to see. If the authorities decide to look west in the direction we are going, it will be noticed. We all speak a little Hanaean, and soon we must all speak it much better. From here on, all of our daily conversation, mine included, will be in Hanaean, and if you don't know what to say, use your hands, just as if you were on your own in a village. Expect the barb of my tongue if I hear any language other than Hanaean. The one exception will be these nightly dinners, Gaius' 'staff meetings', which will be in Greek, Latin or Aramaic, depending on who is in the audience, so we clearly understand what our plans are. After that, Demosthenes, Marcus and Marcia will conduct language lessons for everyone for about an hour. I expect in about a month, we all will be reasonably proficient. Does everyone understand?"

Everyone nodded.

Again, Marcus made a point. "The Hanaean you learned around Luoyang and from us is court Mandarin. In the countryside, it will be very conspicuous, especially since we are trying to pass as commoners. So forget what you think you know, you are going to learn our Gansu dialect so we blend in, not stick out."

"The value of these meetings! Marcus, I never would have thought of that. The second thing is, except for Demosthenes, you only look like Buddhist monks. You are going to have to become Buddhist monks, good enough to pass close scrutiny by real monks. Demosthenes?"

"Correct. I have already begun this. After language lessons, we will assemble to perform more chants, meditate, and ponder the truths of your new religion until bedtime – which may be quite late! And you will rise before sunup to perform the morning rituals."

"Well done, Demosthenes. Now does anyone have any questions? If not, we can proceed with dinner, then school."

The following morning, the monks were up well before sunrise, filling the air with their droning chants, seated on their haunches, palms spread, trying very hard to contemplate nothingness... which was harder than it seemed. Thoughts kept intruding.

After a meager breakfast, Antonius checked the blistered feet of Aulus, Marcus and Marcia and pronounced them fit to walk. Then the little caravan was off, led by the shuffling, snorting oxen kicking up dust with their hooves, pulling the creaking oxcart behind.

About mid-morning, Antonius fell in beside Marcia. In a low voice, so his Latin would not be heard, he whispered, "Marcia, I need to tell you... about the time in the cell... well, we were all going to die, but ... but I don't want you to feel obligated to..."

"Antonius, it was the most beautiful thing I ever experienced, despite the circumstances, and I will treasure it always, and carry my love for you in my heart as long as I live. You... you're not obligated either. But I want you to know, Antonius Aristides, that I love you."

Antonius pondered this in silence, then answered, "I have loved many men, the men who served under me, the men I fought alongside of - I mean I would die for them. And I wept when they died, or were hurt. I have never loved a woman that way, but yes, I would die for you. I...we all... chose to do that, and we almost did, so yes, I do love you also." His hand gently touched hers, then briefly held it in a gentle squeeze. It was the most affection they could show for now. He then released it, his own hand hot as though he had been burned.

"*Te amo, Antonie, te amo!*" she replied, smiling but with a single tear trickling down her cheek. "*Te amo!*" She grinned broadly and said, "If we don't switch back to *han-yu*, I'm going to find it hard to continue being celibate with you!"

Antonius chortled, "Right, *domina!*" He then switched to *han-yu*: "Beauty day, Si Huar!"

Marcia looked at him with puzzlement, then figured out what he was trying to say. "Yes, An-dun. It is truly the most beautiful day of my life."

CHAPTER 56: IBRAHIM IN CHARGE

The new *weiwei* Minister of Guards had no illusions about his position. If he did not determine how the *Da Qin* had escaped execution and where they had gone, he would follow his predecessor to the chopping block. This incident was a huge embarrassment to the Son of Heaven, and it could cause major repercussions if they made it back to their homeland.

He went over the files for the tenth time that morning. The guards had reported no comings and goings except Buddhist monks. He examined one report, "About mid-watch, several monks exited the palace.... How many? Several, I didn't count them. More than five." Hmm... midwatch would have been about ten o'clock, late for monks to be begging in the North Palace. He examined another, earlier one from the same guard. "Right after I assumed my watch, two monks requested entry, carrying food for prisoners." It would be nice if he could ask the guard more questions, but unfortunately, he was one of many of the *Dong Ming Sima* battalion executed following the escape.

Yes, that's it! That is why nothing came and went that night but monks, because that was how they left. And the two going in probably overpowered the guards somehow, freed the prisoners and disguised them. Out of character for non-violent Buddhist monks, but then they may not have been monks either. The more the *weiwei* thought about it, the more it looked like a brilliant cover that might serve the *Da Qin* well for weeks ...no one looked at foreign monks.

The report came back from Tianjin that morning. The two *Da Qin* ships had sailed over a month ago, well before the incidents involving the envoys. Wang Ming testified that he had given them use of the postal system and they were free to correspond with their vessels. Ming had seen all such letters, written in *Da Qin*, but one of the envoys had always briefed him on its content. He had not kept any copies. So the *Da Qin* probably knew their ships had departed, perhaps even had directed them to do so. So there was no reason for them to go east! They would be trapped at the ocean, unable to leave for home.

Weiwei Chu Ting briefed the *Tingwei* and *Taiwei* on his findings. Circumstantial to be sure, but it made more sense than anything they had so far discovered. They would redirect their efforts to the west, and focus on parties of five monks or more. They had a two week head start, but Chu Ting expected they would be traveling slow.

Emperor He summoned Ban Chao to a rare private meeting.

Ban Chao was ill, and not likely to live long. He certainly would not be joining his emperor on another southern hunting expedition next year. He had lost considerable weight, wracked by periodic bouts of coughing.

He was apprehensive about the meeting, but if the Son of Heaven wished him to be executed, perhaps it would be better than this lingering death. And he was deeply humiliated that his carefully planned expedition to the *Da Qin* had gone so seriously awry. He entered the throne room, prostrated himself on the cool granite floor until summoned to rise. "Welcome, my friend, please be seated. You do not appear well."

"Thank you, Son of Heaven." There was single cushion close to the moat separating him from the Emperor's dais, with a small table, with a small lamp, paper and writing implements.

"Ban Chao, you are my dearest friend, and the Son of Heaven has few enough of those. I seek your advice, while you are still able to give it."

Ban Chao listened in silence, his gaze focused on the table.

"What should I do with our former guests, the *Da Qin?*"

"They created a considerable turmoil in your court, before all of the Councilors. It was right to order their execution. The Son of Heaven cannot be seen to endure a public insult."

"You are correct, Ban Chao. But was an insult intended? You were present, and you also know the way of westerners better than any man in the Middle Kingdom."

"Their ways are different, Son of Heaven. They do not bow in submission, and the further west one goes, the less common it becomes. Indeed, it becomes a mark of humiliation."

"What of their courts? Their leader spoke of trials, charges and representations. These were terms I did not fully understand."

"May I complement you on your command of their language, Son of Heaven? While I do not speak it, I observed that they appeared to understand you perfectly, and I could detect no hesitation or uncertainty in your speech."

"I have mastered several other languages, including those of the *Yuezhi* and *Xiongnu,* so I am never at the mercy of a translator. Now tell me about their courts."

"I do not know the practices of the *Da Qin,* but the *Da Yuan* say they are similar to their own, and they too place great value on justice, and expect that every man should hear the charges before him, speak in his behalf, and call witnesses."

"This case should never have appeared before me!" Emperor He replied, with uncharacteristic vehemence. "This was a minor incident between a man and his concubine, but because of the *weiwei's* incompetence, it became elevated so that I could not refer it back down to its proper level. Nevertheless, it was my intent to dismiss the girl's case with an admonishment, until the *Da Qin* made a confrontation out of it." Emperor He continued, "It was a very brave thing they did, not allowing one of their own to be executed without demanding that I execute all of them. From there on, I had no choice, with this happening before my court. Now, if they are successful in making their way back to their homeland, they will meet with their emperor, to describe us as unjust and barbaric."

He paused, thinking, then continued. "If I were to send a letter to their emperor, I believe his name is Trajan, could you tell me how such a letter might be delivered?"

"Son of Heaven, I believe if you sent the letter to the *Da Yuan* king, he would know how to send it on. It will probably take a year or more."

"Good. I do not yet know what I want to say but it will be favorable."

"I am not surprised at your offer. Do you intend to free the envoys if they are apprehended before they leave the Middle Kingdom?"

"I do, and I intend to order that they not be harmed if they are apprehended. They have earned their freedom. Thank you, Ban Chao, and mind your health."

Galosga rapidly became one of the most adept speakers of *han-yu*, and even excelled in mastering their script. In less than a week, he was speaking better than anyone else, with a rapidly burgeoning vocabulary. The reason was the simplicity of *han-yu*, and his total immersion in just a single language. *Han-yu* words were short, and the position of the words was always the same. The tones that gave others such problems were familiar to Galosga... though his language used them differently. And the language had no grammar, no endings. He found the pictographic written language not dissimilar in concept to those his people used to inscribe long stories on bark with pictures. He was a storyteller in his home, and had often used bark tablets to keep himself in the story.

For years, Galosga had been regarded as slow-witted by others, due to his inability to communicate beyond the most basic level. He often felt that way, himself. Now he sought conversation with others at every opportunity.

Antonius was the first to hear the strange man's story of how he had come to be here. "So, Gisga," he said, using Galosga's *han-yu* name. "How you come here? Where from?" Antonius' *han-yu* was much more halting than Galosga's.

"Born in mountains, many pines, oak. Squirrels and deer. Nice place, peaceful. I went to trade by seacoast, mountain goods for dried fish, shells. Big ship there by ocean village. Not big like our ship, but most big I see yet. Strange men, like you, not like me. They waved, call me aboard. Think we going fishing, come back that day. But no, land go away, I pull ropes, bail water, weeks and weeks. I tell I want go home, but they don't understand. We come to big city by water. Not big like many seen since, but big to me then. Shmuel says name Gads, Gadet?"

"Gades in Hispania? And weeks to get there?"

"From Gades, another port, new ship. Shmuel says name *Orion*, then Alexandria and our ship."

"Sound like stole you, made you work. Home have name?"

"Etowah. I know name, not where. Like I know name here, but not where." He laughed with gusto. "Have not made joke in many year!"

Shmuel and Yakov were also isolated by language, less so than Galosga, but isolated nevertheless, Aramaic with just a smattering of Greek. This limited their conversation with everyone except Ibrahim. Like Galosga, they found their new common language easy to learn, and allowed them to share their stories with the rest of their party rather than remaining on the fringes.

Shmuel was born to Jewish parents, refugees in Galilee after the Jewish rebellion thirty years prior. In his teenage years he joined a band of Jewish outlaws. Before too long, they had attracted too high a price on their heads, and Shmuel parted company with them, took to sea in the *Orion* out of Tyre, which picked up Galosga in Carthage. He and Galosga had become friends, and eventually signed onto the *Europa's* crew in Alexandria.

Yakov was orphaned as a child in Petra. Living on the streets, he got by the only way he could, as pickpocket and petty thief, acquiring some skill with a dagger. Ibrahim adopted him after the urchin tried to steal the Arab's purse. Now about thirty, he viewed Ibrahim as the father he never knew.

After about a week, the party reached the outskirts of Sanmenxia, "the Gorge of Three Gateways," where two islands split the Huang He River there into parts.

Sanmenxai sat in a flat plane on the Huang He, with mountain ranges to the north and south, built on the southernmost of the two islands. Several graceful bridges spanned the river channels joining the islands to each other and to the mainland.

They camped on the outskirts, and Ibrahim dispatched Yakov and Demosthenes to quietly ensure that the town had not been alerted, and to see what might be available there. They returned at sundown with good news: there was no apparent alert, and there was a small new temple there that might accommodate the 'monks' overnight.

Demosthenes was concerned that the training of his charges might not have been sufficient, that they would be exposed immediately as false monks. This was his *dukkha*, his suffering and anxiety. He contemplated the Eightfold Path: Right Understanding, Right Intention, Right Speech, Right

Action, Right Livelihood, Right Effort, Right Mindfulness, and Right Concentration.

Where had he erred? How had things become so unbalanced, from the supremely peaceful existence he had known just a month ago? Right Understanding? He had seen the reality of his friends' plight correctly, knowing they would die without his help. Right Intention? Taking action and helping them meant disruption and disharmony. Right Action? Two men were dead who had done him no harm, and there would likely be more. Right Speech? He would have to deceive the monks at the temple. His *karma*, his actions, were bearing fruit and the fruit was bitter. But in no way could he have not done same thing over again. For all he wished not to bear this burden, he was also profoundly glad to have saved his friends.

He wished he could discuss this situation with a wise tutor who could guide him in the way of correct action, but even that path was closed to him for now.

The temple was indeed small, a wood-framed building with a wrap-around porch with red columns, a large house given to the order for conversion to a temple. Monks knelt on the porch, studying scrolls, conversing quietly or simply sitting, some in lotus position, their faces devoid of expression as they contemplated existence.

Demosthenes climbed the steps of the porch to the entrance, where he was met by an elder monk, whose bushy white eyebrows were the only facial hair on pale, almost bluish skin. He introduced himself as the abbot.

"May the enlightenment of the Great Lord Buddha be upon you," Demosthenes intoned.

"And on you, my son," answered the abbot.

"I am escorting five *samaneras* novitiates and one *samaneri* female to the Great Temple at Dunhuang. Could the temple accommodate us overnight, as we have walked the hundred miles from Luoyang?"

The abbot answered with a smile, "To be sure, my son. But... a *samaneri* nun traveling with males? That is unusual and a challenge to chastity, especially for novitiates who have not yet quenched the fires of the flesh."

"Yes, that is unusual, but there are so few *bukkhini* nuns in Luoyang, and the roads are dangerous for women traveling without men. I assure you, they are all chaste."

"To be sure. You are welcome here, bring them in."

"Might my friends camp in the compound with their oxcart? They are not Buddhist, but common folk who have graciously allowed us to travel with them and avail ourselves of their oxcart and food."

"No, please, we have accommodations for all, and they may come and go as they please, if they but refrain from loudness, drunkenness or lewd behavior"

"Thank you, abbot. I apologize in advance for my noviates' rudimentary knowledge of the practices of our faith; they are recent converts, on their way to Dunhuang to gain a fuller understanding."

"They are forgiven in advance," smiled the abbot. "Their determination is commendable, as that journey is thirty-six hundred *li*!"

Demosthenes thanked the abbot, and returned to his companions with the news.

"Everyone can stay. It will be spartan, but it will be a cot, not the ground. By the way, Dunhuang is thirty-six hundred *li* from here, and I think Kashgar is about twice as far."

"How far is a *li*?" asked Antonius.

"About four hundred paces."

Antonius considered this. A Roman mile was a thousand paces, about five thousand feet. "That's about fourteen hundred miles!"

"Yes, but quietly, now. Let us all contemplate the meaning of distance." Demosthenes smiled as Antonius grumped and fell silent. It would take at least six months.

Fortunately, the abbot put a premium on silence among his community, and the next two days were spent in silent prayer. They joined in the chants, their sonorous droning coming along quite credibly. After two days of much needed rest, they were on their way again to Chang'an.

CHAPTER 57: A HOME IN THE MOUNTAINS

The erstwhile peasants and monks had paralleled the Huang He River since before Sanmenxia, its levee-banked surface teaming with all kinds of craft, naval riverboats, freighter *chuan*, and hundreds of small fishing boats, the banks lined with villages and docks every few miles. The big yellow river made

a sharp turn north at the junction with the Wei River, and the oxcart had continued on, creaking along the big east-west highway to the outskirts of Chang'an after several more days.

The total immersion in *han-yu* had worked wonders for all of them. Gaius and Antonius started off one morning in conversation that lasted over five minutes before they realized they weren't speaking Latin.

Marcus related the town's recent past as they looked off at the impressively well-walled city surrounded by a wide moat from a low rise. "There was a civil war seventy-five years ago, and the emperor was killed. A large part of this city was sacked by peasant rebels, and much of the interior was destroyed and has not been rebuilt yet. But it is still a provincial capital and a very important place." In the distance they could see the sharply-sloped walls, about four miles on a side and thirty feet high, pierced by three gates on each side. Bridges over the moat connected the city gates to the broad avenues approaching the city.

"Impressive," said Aulus. "It is as big or bigger than Rome, and better laid out."

Ibrahim sent Yakov and Demosthenes off to reconnoiter the city. They returned soon after with a bad report: they had been warned by outgoing monks to avoid the city. The guards were looking for "false ones," westerners disguised as *bukkhu* and *bukkhini*. All western-appearing monks were being detained for "intense" questioning.

Ibrahim quickly called a council of war in *han-yu* to avoid multiple translations. "Yes," he said, "Our cover no good anymore. Si Nuo, Dim, you know area best. Where to go?" He was using Marcus' and Demosthenes' Hanaean names.

"Clearly north," relied Marcus, "But I don't know where."

"Not good. Mountains to north?" asked Ibrahim.

"Yes, quite a few, you can see them from here."

"We should backtrack and cross Wei River bridge we passed a while ago," Gaius added. "Hopefully, caves in mountains, time and place to hide, make new plan."

The broad east-west avenue accommodated three lanes of traffic, each direction keeping to the right, the center reserved for the government post and military. They took a turn to the left to pull the oxcart off into a small market pavilion to reverse direction, with much complaining from the oxen, who stamped and kicked up a cloud of dust. Passersby behind them cursed the inconvenience. They hoped they did not attract too much attention, or that a cavalry patrol did not trot by looking for them. They finally got the cart heading east, and a few minutes later a patrol did come by. Their hearts pounding, they tried to be as inconspicuous as possible, heads down in meditation as they droned their chants. The patrol didn't notice them. Perhaps they were only looking for westbound suspects, as the road was quite crowded.

They kept up a brisk pace and quickly reached the bridge connecting to a much smaller road running northeast toward Weinan about fifteen miles away. At the first dense cover alongside the road, Ibrahim pulled into the brush, and got everyone out.

"Well, that's it, that is as far as this plan will take us. Help me unload the cargo, we need a change of clothes," he said, in Greek for clarity, Antonius translating for Marcus and Marcia.

The crew bore a hand offloading the squawking chickens and neighing goats, and Ibrahim jimmied up the false bottom. Back in the corner was a stack of conical straw peasant hats over neatly folded work clothes, long beige shirts, floppy black trousers, and some multicolored head scarves. Ibrahim looked at Demosthenes, one eyebrow raised. "You said you might have some difficulty taking off your robe and becoming a non-monk. If you don't wish to do that, you can leave the party with our blessing."

Demosthenes thought for just a few seconds, then said, "I am with you. I have compromised so many vows, I will be more honest to say I am a non-monk."

"Good! We would have missed you otherwise!" Ibrahim distributed the clothing and the erstwhile monks stripped with no pretense at modesty, Marcia included. They donned the peasant garb, wrapped their bald heads with headscarves and then put on the wide conical hats, handing the robes to Ibrahim who folded them carefully and put them into the corner of the false bottom. With the false bottom back in place, they reloaded the animals, and Ibrahim took out two shoulder poles and buckets from open storage. "Fill the buckets with anything, dirt, rocks, I don't care, but make it look like we are hard-working peasants."

"Where are we going?" asked Gaius.

"Somewhere else, and quickly." answered Ibrahim, curtly.

Relieved of the need to pray, and no longer caught in a mob of pedestrians, horses and carts trying to gain entrance to Chang'an, they actually made good time. They were on a broad flat flood plain, planted as far as the eye could see in waving fields of yellow wheat and millet, interspersed with lines of carefully tended trees and clustered villages of a few dozen homes. A foot patrol of soldiers marched past; the peasants kept their heads down to hide their faces. All the notice they got was a curt "Out of the way, peasant!" A most welcome insult. In a few hours they were able to backtrack fifteen miles to the outskirts of Weinan.

They skirted around the west side of the mud-walled township. Up until now, as monks and their peasant escorts, they had felt free to mingle with the population, purchase food and exchange pleasantries. They were now acutely conscious of the six shaved heads under the hats and headbands… the mark of a recently released prisoner, according to Marcus, and in the case of Marcia, probably a disgraced prostitute. And their western faces once again stood out.

By sunset, they had covered another five miles, and found a little tree-lined brook under a small bridge to shelter for the night. There seemed to be no houses for a mile or two, and the peasants still working in their fields were packing up their tools to head for home in the fading light.

They were situated on a sandy beach, the oxcart manhandled into cover and the oxen released of their burden. The animals clambered down to the clear, swiftly running water and drank eagerly, then looked for grazing.

"We need talk, *han-yu*, so all talk, all listen, no need cross-talk." Ibrahim said in his clumsy and still-halting *han-yu*. "I sorry, I fail and plan break down. I no have alternative except run. Please all talk, ideas please!"

Gaius spoke up first. "You do good so far, all plans break down, we make do. Problem, we not able to say where from, who we are, where we go, what we do. Must come up with answers to that, until then stay away from people, move fast. Hide in mountains, wait for hair grow back." At that, everyone laughed.

Antonius rubbed his own naked scalp through the head scarf. "Like big goose egg!"

Gaius continued. "No want to add trouble, but food big problem. How to buy now not monks. Just few days food in oxcart."

They kicked around a few more ideas, nothing substantial. They identified more problems than solutions, but at least that was a start. They decided not to start a fire tonight, to avoid attention from late-night passersby, and ate a very light dinner, aware they might have to make rations stretch.

Later, Antonius took Marcia's hand and whispered in Latin, "Come with me." They each grabbed their blankets and went upriver a little way, till the conversation behind them died down.

There was a full moon casting black shadows on a silvery-gray landscape, with a million stars flung across the sky. The Milky Way hung in the sky like a frozen waterfall, tumbling from star to star. In the distance, a dog barked... very far away. Other than that, the only sounds were the babbling of the brook and a gentle sighing of the wind, cooling the warm night. They settled down about fifty yards away from the group, and sat down on a log by the water's edge, Marcia's toes trailing in the water.

"It is a beautiful night, Antonius. I like just holding your hand in the moonlight," she said.

Antonius felt the firm softness of her thigh against his. "I liked makin' love ter yer in the cell, but got to admit, this is more private, at least a little."

She put her head on his shoulder and clasped his hand, playing with his big strong fingers. "Yes, but I never in my life made love with such enthusiasm, a few days from certain death, never mind that my brother and two other people were almost close enough to touch!" She laughed softly. "*Te amo, Antonie, te amo.* It is such a good feeling."

"It's new ter me, Marcia. It scares me and makes me happy, and makes me confused. Please, be patient with me while I learn how this works, *domina.*"

"I am learning, too. I never loved Ming, though a few months ago, I thought I might at least get to like him. You don't mind if I talk about him?"

"He's part of yer life, and hopefully part of yer past."

"Let's hope so. A few months ago, I helped him prepare to brief Emperor He – funny I can say his name now, did you know that would be a death sentence if anyone heard it?"

"Just one of many things they'd like to kill us for! Go on."

"Right. It went well, and he thought it was my doing. But then it did not last. I was afraid I would have to spend my whole life with someone who despised me, that I despised. But with you...I have no words for the happiness I feel, like in the prison when there was no tomorrow for us, and I didn't care."

"Strange feeling for me, too. You know, I have never been friends with a woman, just someone for my needs, nothing more. You, I am afraid I could break you, like fine china in my clumsy hands!"

She laughed, a chuckling happy sound. "You have big gentle hands. For all your strength you are the most gentle man I have ever known. And don't worry, after ten years with Ming, I don't break as easily as you think." She lifted up her head, put her other hand around his neck and kissed him gently on the mouth, a long lingering kiss.

They leaned back on the riverbank, and no, there was no need for celibacy, not tonight, not in the moonlight.

Up at first light, the group hitched up the team and struck across the farmland. In the distance they could see a low range of mountains to the north. Antonius pointed them out to Ibrahim. "There I think mountains we seek, maybe a cave, not too many people," he said in *han-yu*, almost without thinking.

By late afternoon, a few hours before sunset, they reached the town of Tongchuan, identified from signs Marcus and Marcia could read, and fragments of local conversations overheard in passing. Its name meant 'Copper River', situated at the mouth of a valley tumbling down between two ridges, eroded yellow rocks showing through where there were no trees. The town itself was medium sized, maybe ten thousand people. Big enough to provide at least a little anonymity. They passed a small market with vegetables, ducks and chickens hanging from displays in the window, the sweet smell of green vegetables, flour and fresh-baked bread. Their stomachs grumbled, but they kept walking.

After about fifteen minutes, Demosthenes came alongside Ibrahim, perched on the driver's bench of the cart. "Pull up a minute, I have an idea,' he said, in Greek.

"Whoa, Castor, whoa, Pollux!" Of course, after a month, the oxen had names. "What is it?" said Ibrahim.

"We are just about to start up this mountain, and I thought about what we said yesterday, not able to say who we are, where we came from, and what we are doing here. You all may not, but I can, well enough to go back to that market and buy some food."

"So who are you?"

Demosthenes doffed his hat and removed his headband. "I, sir, am a Buddhist, going into the mountains to meditate if am to be a *Bhukkhin* monk. I can say where I am from, and where I am going. So give me a pack and the shoulder pole, I am going to get us some food... oh, and some money, too, a handful of bronze coins should do fine."

"Give it a try."

Demosthenes walked back to the market shop, hoping it was still open. It was, and he entered the dark interior. A matronly woman greeted him "Good day, good day," she said, smiling and bowing. "Come in, please!"

"Yes, I am going up to the mountain to meditate, maybe for several months. I need some food and supplies."

"Meditate? You are Buddhist, your head is shaved, are you a monk?"

"No, not now, not yet." *Not a lie there.*

"My son was going to become Buddhist, he and his friend."

"What happened?"

Her face clouded over briefly. "He died. He was killed in the Battle of Ilkh Bayan up north, against the Xiongnu." Then her smile returned. "That was a long time ago, but his friend Guo Chen did become a Buddhist. They were in Dou Xian's army together during the Xiongnu war. Chen went to Luoyang afterward and became a monk there."

"Guo Chen? Really? I knew him! He was my mentor at the White Horse Temple in Luoyang, he taught me *han-yu*! He was a very respected scholar... I offer consolation for the loss of your son."

"How old are you, if I may ask?"

"Thirty."

"My son was about your age. If you see Guo Chen, please send him my love and tell him to write me, I miss him still."

"I will."

Imagine fate, of all the people to run into, someone with an acquaintance in common hundreds of miles away. Demosthenes had learned much from Guo Chen, in reading and interpreting scriptures, and in coming to understand all the principles of Buddhism.

"So here, let me fill your pack, you'll need flour and vegetables. Meat?"

"Uh, yes, a little, I am finding that part of my calling difficult, I still like meat on occasion"

"My son and his friend had a hard time with that, too, they were always trying to sneak some chicken or pork." The matronly woman chuckled, as she stuffed a goose into the pack. "You need some small pots, some fire materials, always need a little string, here, and I have a blanket. Now let's put several bags of flour and meal in your shoulder-buckets." She handed him a fresh roll. "Eat this on the way, you look hungry. Oh, and here is an axe, you'll need that."

"Thanks, but I don't have much money..."

"You don't need any money, you are a friend of my dead son's lifelong friend. My name is Xian Biyu, and you need anything else, just come down from the mountain and ask. I'll get it for you."

"The blessing of the Buddha be upon you! You are too kind! My name is Dim, and I will pray for you and your son." Dim was his Hanaean name, common enough, and easier for Hanaean tongues than Demosthenes. He struggled to get the bulging pack on his shoulders and balance the heavy shoulder pole across his back. "I must get up the mountain before it gets dark."

"Dim, there is an abandoned house up that road about five miles into the mountain on the left. Hunters use it sometimes, but otherwise it is abandoned. You can stay there, and if anyone gives you trouble tell them Mama Biyu said it was alright."

It took a while for the heavily-laden Demosthenes to lurch back down the road to the waiting oxcart and company.

"You do good!" said Ibrahim.

"I got adopted, I think," said Demosthenes.

The abandoned house was good news, and they set out up the hill, though they had to use torches in the gathering dark to light their way. As the road wound up the hill, it rapidly became much less a road, heavily etched with little runoff gulleys that snared and bound the wheels, and rocks that threatened to break them. After a while, it was necessary for the drivers to dismount and lead the reluctant oxen up the hill, their eyes wide and rolling, their voices bawling in complaint. All too often, everyone had to lean against the side of the cart to keep it from turning over.

But after about two hours of laborious ascent, someone caught sight of a reflection from the house, although set far back in the woods… had it not been for that faint gleam, they would have struggled right by it in the dark. A little path, mercifully smooth, led up to the veranda.

They were expecting a little hut.

This was no hut. Whoever built it had money and liked his privacy. It was rather the worse for not having been inhabited for a long time, but most of the deterioration was in the trim. Wide steps, warped and cracked but still sturdy, led up to the porch framed by thick wooden columns that a long time ago had been bright red. The columns propped up a porch roof that showed no signs of sagging. Peering through empty windows that gaped open on unslung hinges, they noted that the interior seemed spacious, and went in through the door.

Perhaps left by hunters, there were some amenities, an oil lamp on a rickety low table and a bottle of oil. They doused their torches, fearful of setting the place on fire, lit the lamp and let its light guide them through their accommodations. Along the back wall was a fireplace with an attached oven, separated from the living room by a big island for food preparation that had once been lacquered. Candles lined the wall in sconces. Four separate bedrooms debouched off the living area, and one even had a bed. "Looks like we found Antonius' and Marcia's quarters," joked Marcus; Marcia's blush was invisible in the darkness, but she smiled.

Behind the house, a little waterfall cascaded into a small pond, probably a fishpond in its day. Antonius picked up a handful of water, sniffed it, then carefully tasted it. "Seems clean enough."

Also behind was a small cave, a barn for animals. Going inside, they found the remains of pens, with tools, ropes and harnesses hanging, moldering on the wall.

"Looks like someone just walked off and left it," said Antonius.

"Looks that way. I guess there is a story here, but we are not likely to know," said Gaius. "There are no fields up here, no sign of business, maybe he came up here to harvest things out of the forest and went down? Or maybe he had some business or farm in Tongchuan, and just came up here for a retreat. That's what this looks like. He must have been successful at whatever he did, because this was a nice house in its day."

They wrestled the oxcart and oxen into the pen, leaving them hobbled to graze and seek water from the pond. They then retired early, after a long day. Antonius estimated they had covered thirty miles today, a forced march by Roman army standards. They had covered over two hundred miles from Luoyang, and would be needing new shoes very soon.

Marcia and Antonius retired to their private quarters, nude in their luxurious if fleabitten bed, but too tired for anything but kisses, cuddles and sleep.

The morning sun awoke Marcia. It seemed no one else was up yet, and she explored Antonius' body till she got the expected reaction. He threw back the musty blankets and they took in the beauty of each other's body… they had never had the privacy to share their nakedness together. Antonius marveled at her small, firm breasts, hard nipples like raisins in the cool morning. He slid his hands down her flanks and grasped her buttocks, rock-hard from weeks of hard walking. He held her against him, and she was intensely aware of the heat of his manhood against her belly. He then released her to continue to explore her body with his eyes. "Yer so beautiful, *domina,* so beautiful!"

"Yer not so bad yerself, soldier. I am ugly though, without my hair." Antonius playfully ran his hand over her head, bristly with black fuzz trying to grow back.

"I'm naked as a goose egg up there, too," said Antonius, looking into her bright, blue almond-shaped eyes, inside their slight epicanthal folds. She was beaming with happiness.

She took in the sight of his body, broad across the shoulders as befits a swordsman, with bulging biceps and pectoral muscles, all covered with twisty, curly black hair. That hair converged to race down his centerline through his belly button, to explode around his nether regions. His hips seemed impossibly narrow for the rest of him, set on massive thighs and columnar legs.

She playfully twisted the curly hair on his chest, then kissed one nipple, then the other, their bodies intertwined, and then they were one, coursing to the sun and back in long, luxuriant lovemaking. When they were done, they lay spent in each other's arms.

"I don't know why we never tried a bed before, *amatus meus,*" she purred, her tongue exploring the inside of his ear.

"Maybe because we didn't have one?" He turned and kissed her long, then they were taken with a second, more urgent passion.

When that, too, had spent itself, she turned to him, and said, with a bit of seriousness. "Antonius, there is something… it is hard to say."

"Just say it, *domina*."

"There will be times, when we can't do this, not like this. Will you understand when I ask you to wait?"

He propped himself up on his elbow, somewhat concerned. "Why?"

"You don't want another passenger on this trip. There are times when I can get pregnant, and that would be very bad for me, for all of us, and for our new passenger, too, so please, a few days out of the month?"

"Oh, sure! Sure, I can't see you going on a forced march carrying a baby!" They both laughed in each other's arms. In fact, this intimacy was new to him. He knew that women had cycles, and bled once a month, but he had never lived with a woman, never had the intimacy with one to deal with it. In fact, the idea that sex led to babies, while not foreign to him - he certainly knew where babies came from, after all - was never of any concern to him in all his past dalliances.

"Maybe, if we get to where we are going, back to Rome, maybe then… if you want one, that is … I will give you a child, I hope a son that will grow up to be like you!"

The thought struck Antonius dumb. Never had he ever considered the idea of a family, now it seemed like the most logical thing in the world to do. After a long moment he said, "Yes, I would like that. Very much. But first we have to get there! I have worked up an appetite, let's go wake up the others."

She threw the blankets off her long, well-muscled legs and kicked them off the bed. "I think we already have!"

CHAPTER 58: A MOST SERIOUS WOUND

The next week was a refreshing layover. Galosga was a superb hunter, and went out every morning to bring in small game of a variety of sorts, mostly squirrels, but also rabbits, and once, a small deer. He set up a smoke tent to preserve the meat, as he had done on the *Europa* after the storm.

Antonius and Marcia became the host couple, preparing meals and fussing about the house, and everyone was amused and pleased with Antonius' sudden domesticity. The new couple beamed with contagious happiness underneath their sprouting bristlebrush hair.

Everyone's *han-yu* had improved to the point where Ibrahim's daily meetings were mostly conducted in that language, with just infrequent sidebars in the other languages.

On the second day, Gaius addressed his security concerns.

"There are two types of people may stop here. The first type curious, want to know who we are. They must see what expect to see, Dim here meditate. The other type mean trouble, we have to kill, drive off. Preferably kill. If drive off, go get friends, come back. Trouble is, don't know which when show up."

Everyone agreed. Antonius had discussed this plan with Gaius, refining it, so at a nod from Gaius, he picked up the discussion. "Here is plan. Ten people here, seven fighters. Si Nuo no experience, Dim choose no fight, Si Huar woman. So company comes, Dim here inside, Si Huar and Si Nuo in cave behind with animals. Hide. If Dim not here, Si Huar and Si Nuo in house, Han couple look for time alone." Everyone giggled. "I know he brother, just play part!"

He continued. "Rest of us hide outside. Galosga cover road with arrows, you best archer among us. I show good spot in front of house, good cover, arrows reach everywhere. Right side, Ibrahim, Yakov, Aulus, in order. Left side, me, Shmuel, Gaius, in order."

"Here signal. When company comes house, if no trouble, house person says, 'Please come in, have tea.' Loud for all us to hear. Entertain, be nice, everyone else hide till go. All good? Hope that all we ever see."

"Looks like trouble, say "Sorry, I am busy, go away.' Also loud. Galosga take out anyone in front. First two each side come around front onto porch, take from rear in two directions . Last one each side come around back, come in back door, get between house person and bad people. Think this will take out any group, unless big group soldiers show up. Anybody need again in own language?"

No one did. Gaius resumed the lead. "Antonius good plan. Practice after meeting, do it every day, bit different each time, so everyone smooth."

The drills went well, though the first few had some comical moments that provoked Antonius to bawl out his orders like the centurion he was, once even taking on Aulus in Latin, "Galba, hold that god-cursed sword like yer mean ter kill somebody besides yersel'!" The portly senator had lost considerable girth.

Everyone had to take this deadly seriously. Antonius' main concern was bounty hunters, if such things existed here. If Hanaean soldiers showed up, they were not likely to fight them all off, and they would be quickly hunted down if they got away. Still, it was a plan.

Antonius made some heavy wooden training swords, crude but about the right balance. Live metal was not only too dangerous with which to train, but everyone would also pull their thrust at the last minute, to avoid hurting the other – exactly what you don't want to learn to do in a fight. So every day for an hour, the fighters sparred with each other, with Marcus also learning the basics, under the watchful eye of Antonius.

Back in Luoyang, the *weiwei* was again furious at the *Da Qin's* uncanny ability to vanish into thin air. His men had located them at a small temple in Sanmenxia, only a week behind them. It had to be them, six monks and a nun, three westerners dressed as peasants, riding an oxcart. The abbot said their destination was Dunhuang, so they had to go through Chang'an. But they had not, and their shaven heads would be conspicuous in any other disguise. But now their trail was cold again.

The Parthian ambassador followed the search for the Romans through his sources in the *weiwei's* office. Cyrus had hoped the *weiwei's* men would capture them and put an end to it, but with their second disappearance it seemed prudent to send a letter to his government, alerting Ctesiphon that they would likely be transiting Parthian territory on the way back. They must not, under any circumstances, reach the Roman border alive. Being somewhat of an accomplished artist himself, he included sketches of the five that he thought were surprisingly lifelike, and dispatched this under Hanaean postal orders to his homeland via Bactria, with a separate letter to the Bactrian king.

Musa, after a brief detention in Luoyang two days after the *Da Qin* escape, had successfully convinced his captors that this was the first he had heard of it, that he had been out of town on the day of the incident, conducting business with a signed and dated contract to prove it. Ibrahim and his party, he also convinced them, had purchased an oxcart to go back by land, since his departure was uncertain, and they felt they would be dragged into the trouble with their *Da Qin* friends the longer they stayed.

After more questions, they released Musa to return to Tianjin. He was reunited with his wife and son, and set to work filling some profitable contracts for new hulls that would keep him busy for a year.

Demosthenes made another trip into town for supplies, especially vinegar. Antonius had used up his supply, liberally disinfecting all sorts of cuts for the group. So he stopped in to see Mama Biyu.

"Dim, how good to see you! Is all well on the mountain?" Her round face beamed with joy to see him.

"All is well, Mama," he said, but then she fixed him with a quizzical expression, one eye squeezed almost shut, the other eyebrow sharply lifted.

"Who are your friends up there, Dim?"

His heart fell, and he stammered a bit. She didn't give him a chance to answer. "I said you remind me of my son. He didn't lie often, but when he did his face gave him away. You tell Mama what is going on, or I will call the authorities. No one is going to hurt this town!" She was speaking gently but firmly, as to a child.

Yes, Right Speech. That means honesty!

So he sighed, sat down, and related the whole story, about the *Da Qin* and Ibrahim, the prison escape, and the monk disguise, which caused Mama Biyu to cover her mouth while she tittered in laughter, so improbable it was. He told of the weeks behind an oxcart trekking hundreds of miles on foot to Chang'an, to find the authorities looking for them there.

At the end, she said, "I wish you had told me this at the beginning, I could have helped you more. But no matter." She paused, then continued, her voice hard as steel. "Just remember, do not hurt this town!"

As Demosthenes left, heavily laden again with supplies, she sighed and watched him sadly. Her own long-dead son, also Dim, was so like him.

Antonius wandered alone in the woods, pondering Marcia's discussion about pregnancy. For the first time, he remembered the whore in Taprobane, who had caused so much trouble for them, wondering what happened to her. Aulus had said the king slaughtered most of Galle after they left. Did she survive? If he had gotten her pregnant, she might have already delivered. And what did she do with the child? Did she raise it, or leave it on a trashdump to howl its newborn cries to the sky until it died, to become food for dogs?

In fact, he could have many children, living or dead, whom he would never know and who would never know him. Suddenly those dalliances seemed like such despicable waste. And the worst unbidden thought was of his very first woman, when he was just a newly recruited legionary bloodied in his first battle... the reason why he enforced his rule, with hickory stick and if necessary the lash, that no man under his command should ever rape a captive. He remembered her eyes, full of fear, anger, mourning, loathing – and resignation. Then at the end, one of the other soldiers had said, "All right, we're done with you. Pick up your things and go." Not to the slave gangs, not the killing grounds, just to go. He wondered what became of her. How could a man like him deserve such a beautiful gift as Marcia?

His thoughts were interrupted by a clatter of horsemen going by, five men clad in black. They did not look like soldiers, but they did look dangerous. Antonius ran quietly back to the house a hundred yards away.

The black-clad men had almost passed the house when the man trailing behind caught sight of it and whistled to call the others back. They came back up the hill and milled about the road. A little smoke curling out of the chimney betrayed its occupants. The black-clad men left one man to tend the horses by the road, while the rest strode up the pathway.

It took less than a minute for everyone to be in position, Marcus and Marcia inside as Demosthenes was in town.

The bandits clumped up the stairs and hammered on the door. "We need to stay here!" one said. He was not asking

"You are not welcome here!" Marcus bellowed. Galosga unleashed an arrow that penetrated the throat of the man holding the horses; he went down with a gurgling cry. Too late, Galosga was aware of a sixth horseman thundering down the road. That horseman, guiding his animal with his knees, took up a bow and nocked an arrow, aiming at the men bursting out on the left side of the porch. He let fly at the first man, before stopping an arrow from Galosga that knocked him from his horse.

The bandit's arrow knocked Antonius down onto his rump. At first, he thought someone had kicked him in the gut, then he saw the shaft protruding from his stomach. "What a hell of a time ter get kilt," he thought, then his eyes rolled back and he fell backward. His last conscious thought was of Marcia, before the darkness swallowed him.

Shmuel cast not a glance at Antonius as he took charge. The centurion was down, but they had to continue the fight or they would all die. He charged up onto the porch after the four bandits, catching his first man in the side. One down! By this time, Gaius and Aulus had erupted into the back while Marcus and Marcia scuttled toward the cave. It did not take long, perhaps less than a minute, to finish off the three remaining men, taken totally by surprise and surrounded.

Shmuel could see quickly that everyone else seemed unhurt, and yelled for Ibrahim, "Antonius is down! Help me!"

Ibrahim, Aulus and Gaius clustered around the supine Antonius, while Yakov and Galosga checked the fallen bandits. Shmuel rounded up their horses and led them up to the cave.

Ibrahim felt Antonius' neck for a pulse. "He's alive, but I don't know for how long."

Marcia and Marcus had come around from the cave, and when she saw Antonius on the ground, wounded, she put her fists to her mouth and cried out through her tears, "Antonius! No, no! This can't be true!"

Gaius put his arm around her and led her back a bit. "Let the men work on him, Marcia. He's still alive, they'll do everything for him." She turned to bury her face in his shoulder, sobbing, and he soothed her back. A tear was trickling down his cheek, too.

Ibrahim said, "We need to get him on a board. The arrow didn't exit, so the blade is still inside. If we move him carelessly, we'll lacerate what's left of his insides." The men lashed together a make-do litter, put him carefully on it, and carried him into the house.

Meanwhile, Yakov was questioning the one man who remained alive, bleeding copiously from a gashed stomach that exposed his insides. He would not last long. "Who you? Who send you?"

"We were looking for a place to hide. Raid the town ... supplies." He gritted his blood-flecked teeth, and rolled forward over his open belly.

"Where from?"

"Up north... Xiongnu country." He slumped as unconsciousness took him. Yakov debated hastening his death, but Ibrahim might have more questions if the man came around again. He didn't look like he would last long.

He quietly made his report to Ibrahim in Aramaic as the Arab was tending to Antonius. Ibrahim shook his head negatively, focused on Antonius' wound, and Yakov went back outside. He kicked at the wounded man, whose head rolled face-up, its staring eyes indicating that he would not be answering any more questions.

He, Shmuel and Galosga were policing up the dead when Demosthenes arrived from town, stunned at the carnage. "You miss it," said Yakov with a smile. "All over now."

"What happened?" asked Demosthenes, trying hard not to stare at the man with the opened belly. Flies were already buzzing around the bloody wounds in the July heat, finding an easy meal.

"Bandits. An-dun plan work very good, but he bad hurt. Inside."

Demosthenes left his load at the foot of the stairs and ran up inside. Ibrahim, Gaius, and Aulus were clustered around Antonius on his bed. Marcus and Marcia were standing by the entrance to the bedroom, Marcia sobbing, choking, trying to contain her terror that he might die.

"Demosthenes!" called Ibrahim. "I hope you brought the vinegar Antonius sent you to town for! We are going to need it."

Without acknowledging, Demosthenes scrambled down the stairs, and returned with a big bottle. "Can I help? I have had some medical training a while back when I was in the Bactrian army." In Greek; he was going to need medical terms.

"We need all the help we can get. Come here."

"Someone get me Antonius' *capsula*." Demosthenes looked at the arrow wound and gently touched the arrow. "No exit wound, so it must have hit bone, from this angle, a rib. Yes, I can feel the tip, I think embedded a bit." He pulled back on the arrow, no more than a quarter inch. "I think it's free, I can feel it vibrate a bit as it scrapes along the bone. All right, there, I think I found the space between the ribs."

He picked up the vinegar, liberally washed his hands and the shaft of the arrow. Antonius' breathing was slow and regular. "Does he have some opium in his medical kit?"

Gaius unrolled the *capsula* contents, and located a bottle. "Poppy juice, here."

Demosthenes got several swallows of the juice down Antonius' throat. "He's not deeply unconscious, mostly in shock. I don't want him waking and thrashing for what we are going to do next, so give this a few minutes to work."

"And what is it you intend to do, Demosthenes?" asked Gaius.

"We are going to push the arrow through his back, break the arrowhead off, clean it up, and pull it back out."

"Have you done this before?"

"Once." He didn't feel like mentioning that the patient died of massive fever afterward.

Antonius' breathing seemed to slow. Demosthenes checked his pulse, and then said "I think we are ready. Roll him gently on his right side. Very gently, keep him straight. Are we ready?" Everyone nodded.

Demosthenes applied a little pressure to the arrow. "Gaius, tell me if you see it start to dimple where the head is going to come out."

"Yes, there it is."

"All right, Aulus, Ibrahim, hold his shoulders, here it goes!" He pushed hard, the skin stretched and then the sharp head tore through. The unconscious Antonius grunted, then was silent again. Demosthenes kept pushing until about six inches of shaft was exposed.

"All right, the hard part is done. Gaius, take your knife and cut off the head, make sure there are no splinters dangling that could come off inside of him. How is the bleeding?"

"About what you would expect from a skin tear." Gaius knew what he was asking, to find out if there was massive internal bleeding that would follow the arrow out. There was none.

When the arrow was ready, Gaius doused the headless shaft with vinegar, and Demosthenes withdrew it in one smooth motion. Everyone gave a sigh of relief. Gaius handed Demosthenes the arrowhead. He sniffed it. "Good, it smells like blood and meat. I don't smell any shit, so we may be lucky if nothing important inside was damaged."

They cleaned the wounds thoroughly and sutured him up, bandaged the wounds, and rolled him on his back. Demosthenes looked at Marcia, and said, "I think he has a chance. But I will be honest, this is a very serious wound."

Marcia swallowed hard and blinked back her tears. "Thank you, Dim. If you give him a chance, he and I both will fight for it. I am not going to lose him." She paused and continued, "Where did you learn to do that?"

"Like Antonius, I was a medic once." He turned to the group and continued, "All right, let him rest, nothing but water for the next day or so until any inside injuries have had a chance to heal. Let him sleep and pray for no fever. I am going into town for more medical supplies."

Marcia moved a stool into the bedroom and sat beside Antonius, holding his hand.

Demosthenes returned to Mama Biyu's store. "Something bad has happened, Mama. An-Dun is badly hurt and I need more medical supplies if you have any, still more vinegar, bandages, sutures, especially fever medicines and broths."

"What happened?" she asked, her face full of concern.

"We were raided while I was here earlier, by bandits. Our group killed all of them, but An-Dun took an arrow in the stomach. I got it out, but he will probably get feverish and that could kill him."

"You got it out? Yourself?"

"Before I was a monk, I was a medic."

Mama Biyu got a bundle of various things together, and then said, "I am going with you." She went out the back of the store to where a horse and a two-wheeled cart stood. "Get in!" she ordered.

Demosthenes climbed up onto the seat beside her and she clucked the spirited grey into a brisk pace.

"Do you know where it is, Mama?"

"Of course I know where it is. It is my house! My husband built it for us to get away from town, but after he died, I never went up there again. I let hunters use it when they want."

About fifty yards before the turnoff to the house, Demosthenes asked her to stop and he dismounted. Cupping his hands around his mouth he yelled, "Halloo! It is me, Demosthenes, with company, it is all right!" He got back up and Mama clicked the horses on.

"Antonius had set up a security plan, which is why they knocked down the bandits so easily. But everyone will be jumpy now, and I don't want to take an arrow myself."

They pulled into the yard, and Mama surveyed the dead men. She took the headband off one and examined it carefully. "These are the Black Headband gang that has been raiding up and down Shaanxi Province. They are very bad people! Soldiers have not been able to catch them."

"One of our people said they were going to use this as a hideout to raid Tongchuan."

"We are very much in your debt. Far from bringing bad things onto our town, you prevented something very bad." They went up the steps. "These posts need painting badly. And everything else," she said, feeling the peeling red flecks of paint on the column.

"How is he doing?" asked Demosthenes as he entered the living area.

"Sleeping peacefully. Marcia is with him."

"This is Mama Biyu, who has been so kind as to take care of us. These are the people I told you about this morning, Ib-him and Yak the pirates, Simul a rebel from the far west. Gisga, no one knows where he is from, including himself. Gawba and Gais, of the *Da Qin*. And this one is Si Nuo, of Liqian. Si Huar is sitting with An-Dun." Each nodded in turn as they were introduced, and Marcus gave a formal Hanaean bow.

Mama Biyu stretched herself out to her portly five feet, and bowed formally as well. "You have done a great service to Tongchuan. The Black Headband gang has been a scourge to all of Shaanxi, and you kept it from falling on our town again."

Mama Biyu took charge of the domestic affairs, preparing for dinner while the men buried the dead and tended the new horses. After dinner, she joined Marcia at Antonius' bedside. Marcia was speaking rapidly and softly to him in a language Mama Biyu didn't understand.

"May I sit with you, Si Huar? My name is Xian Biyu, people call me Mama." she asked. Mama Biyu had never had any daughters, and she felt very matronly toward the distraught girl.

"Please."

Mama pulled over a small chest and sat. "What is that language you were speaking?"

"It is the language of the *Da Qin*. It is called Latin. He is *Da Qin*."

"I don't understand it, but you seem to speak it very well."

"I speak both Latin and *han-yu*. We are descendants of *Da Qin*." She showed Mama Biyu her eyes. "It is why I have blue eyes, from my *Da Qin* ancestors."

"How did you get involved in this at such a young age?"

And so Marcia related the whole tale of her life, from Liqian to the Gan Ying expedition to Rome and meeting with their ruler, the return trip by sea, the false charge of infidelity and attempted murder. All that she had bottled up inside just poured out like water. At last she finished, telling of her love for An-Dun, and her fears that he would be taken from her so soon after they had come to know love.

Mama Biyu also knew heartbreak; she had buried five sons due to a fever that nearly killed her as well, and lost her sixth son to a far-off war. But now was not the time to share those stories with Si Huar.

"We will make him better, Si Huar, you and me… together."

Si Huar smiled for the first time since she had seen Antonius' prostrate body, and blinked back tears. "Yes, we will, Mama, yes, we will!" She responded warmly to Mama Biyu's motherly concern.

Mama Biyu went back in the morning in the oxcart with Si Nuo to get more furniture and supplies. If anyone asked, she would be restoring the tumbledown retreat. While in her store, she rummaged around in her living quarters for a chest containing memorabilia, found what she was looking for, and added it to the stack of clean linen for bandages, willow bark and poppy juice painkillers, and several herbs to help with fevers.

When she got back, Antonius was feverish and delirious. Marcia was going about in a business-like manner, keeping cold compresses on his head, but she was not fooling Mama Biyu. She knew that if Si Huar didn't stay busy doing something, anything, she was going to break down completely. "Here, see if we can get him to chew the willow bark, it will help with the pain. I will brew up some herb tea that will help the fever."

Antonius, though unconscious, was not totally unaware of his surroundings. Occasionally his consciousness would swim up near the surface and he was aware of women's voices, Marcia's and someone else's, sometimes in Latin, sometimes Hanaean. He was aware of a great pain in his stomach, then he would descend back down into blackness again.

Demosthenes had swaddled Antonius in a makeshift diaper, as the man had no control over his bodily functions. Near the end of the day, he had an odoriferous bowel movement. Marcia notified Demosthenes, who unwrapped him to check the content. Smelly it was, but not putrid; brown, but no sign of blood or pus. "Smells like shit, but the good news is that is all it appears to be, his bowels may be intact. Go outside, Marcia, I will clean up the mess."

"Like hell I will! I'll clean him up. You get me a fresh diaper and take the dirty stuff out!" She rolled Antonius on his side and began cleaning the mess with determination. Mama Biyu joined in, bringing a fresh bowl and more rags.

Antonius remained feverish through the night, but the delirium passed. The incoherent muttering and thrashing went away, and the next morning the fever was gone. He remained peacefully asleep, Marcia's head nestled on his chest. She had not left his side for over a day and a half. Mama, who had slept on one of the cots she had brought, looked in and smiled at the sight with Demosthenes. "I think he's going to make it," said the medic.

"He already has," answered Mama.

Around noon she gave Marcia a package. "I have something for you. Open it." Marcia opened the rice paper wrapping and pulled out a wig with long black Hanaean-style hair. Each strand of hair had been worked through a cloth mesh and tied off. It must have been very expensive and taken forever to make.

"Mama, it is beautiful! Where did you get it?" asked Marcia

"When I was a young girl, I was taken with a fever that caused my hair to fall out, and what was left was very thin and straggly. My mother got it for me so people would not laugh at me. It is just strands of hair. You can do anything to it that you can do with your own hair, curl it up in a bun, whatever you want to do. Till your new hair grows back."

Marcia tried it on. It fit perfectly. Marcia hugged the woman and put her head on her shoulder, "Thank you, thank you, thank you so much! You have been so kind."

About an hour later, Antonius awoke, one eye popping open, trying to focus. After a minute, he moved his head and recognized Marcia. "What happened, *domina?*"

"I think yer tried ter break somebody's arrow but it didn't work," she said, laughing with tears of joy in her eyes.

"Arrow. Gods, yes, I remember, I thought I was dead!"

"You came too close to that for me, *carus meus*. Too damned close." She leaned over his bed and gave him a big hug. "Quit ogling my breasts under my shirt, Antonius! We're back to being celibate for another few days till you're better."

He slapped her buttocks playfully under her trousers. "Sure?"

"Sure. And you know what you said, about loving meaning you would die for someone?"

"Yes."

Marcia kissed him gently on the cheek. "You don't have to prove it, I'll take your word for it. I'd miss you if you died." She cuddled up against his battered body as best she could, with everyone standing around.

Demosthenes, on hearing Antonius' voice, had rushed into the room, followed by everyone else crowding into the bedroom. "Looks like he's better," said Demosthenes.

"Fondling Marcia, yes, he's going to make it!" said Gaius with a smile. "Good job, Demosthenes, damned good job!"

CHAPTER 59: TRAVELING NORTH

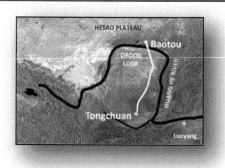

Antonius spent several days recuperating reluctantly in bed. He had, however, insisted on being in the nightly planning councils. "So if I can't get outer this damned bed, just haul yer butts inter me bedroom and hold it here. If yer all gotta stand, maybe the meetings will be shorter!" grumped Antonius to Gaius. And so they all did, but they brought stools, so the meetings weren't any shorter.

Mama Biyu was the only source of local knowledge, and since she already knew almost everything about them, they accepted the risk of having her take part in the meetings. She suggested that they continue north, and offered an itinerary, since they now would be traveling with the horses they had liberated from the bandits.

"About a thousand *li* north of here, the Huang He River bends again to the west and marks the northern border of Han territory. To get there, take the road north, and in two or three days' ride, you should reach Yanzhou. Four or five days later will put you in the area of Baotou on the northern side of the river. After that you'll be out of reach of the authorities, unless they want to send a small army after you into Xiongnu country. The Hans had a big one there once, but ten years ago, they mostly killed or drove off the Xiongnu in the last war and then pulled their army back. The Xiongnu that are left are in small bands now, mostly harmless, but they will still fight to defend their territory. My cousin Xian Bohai has contacts in Baotou who deal with some of the Xiongnu, and he speaks the language and knows some of the chieftains."

"What do we do when we get there, Mama?" asked Ibrahim.

"If they like you and are going that way, they will guide you west for a long way, and you will be safe from Han authorities. And the further west you go, the more western the people are, and your faces won't betray you."

They now had six horses compliments of the dead bandits, short sturdy Mongolians with great endurance, able to live off the land. Mama Biyu got them a four-passenger cart with a closed canopy to keep the weather out, and four more horses, enough for all to ride if necessary, and spare animals if the cart was in use. She found a peasant family who gratefully accepted their oxcart and oxen, and made sure the travelers had plenty of clothes, bedding, food, medical supplies and herbs, and rice wine. How Mama Biyu did all this while attracting no attention they did not know; she had her ways.

Since none of the ten had ridden in at least a year, everyone decided to refresh their riding skills. Galosga pointed out: "I never ride, never see horse before this side of water. None at home."

"Really?" Ibrahim. "No horses at all, or just none tame?"

"Never see any, wild or tame. Here I see people ride, so yes, I learn, you help."

The next interesting discovery were the stirrups on the saddle, heavy leather straps with an iron bar across the bottom. "Those are called *ma deng*, 'horse something-or-other'. I don't know the Latin word for it," Marcus said.

"There may not be a Latin word for it. I've never seen such a thing before. Looks like a good idea for getting on, but why so heavy? Once you are on, they would just be swinging back and forth, banging your legs and the horse," commented Gaius, in Latin.

Marcus chuckled, also replying in Latin. "You keep your foot in them while you are riding. You are serious...you really don't have these back west?"

"Never saw one before in my life." All of the westerners shook their heads in the negative.

So Marcus demonstrated, swiftly mounting the horse in one easy motion, then with his feet firmly in the stirrups, demonstrated the ease with which he controlled the animal, dancing it around in tight turns, getting it to rear and paw the air while he easily kept his seat.

They each eventually mastered the stirrup. Galosga began his riding lessons, working up to a nervously stiff but steady canter after a few hours, and learning how to care for his beast. Everyone discovered how hard riding is to a butt not used to it. They rode an hour or so each day, following the lightly traveled road up the mountain and back down, both to toughen their rears and develop bonds with their mounts.

Ibrahim's ransom money was holding out well, but since it was a significant sum, it seemed prudent to divide it up among them, a lighter load and more secure distribution. To keep clinking coins in the saddlebags from attracting unwanted attention, Ibrahim used a smuggler's trick: they melted beeswax in pots and dropped the coins in them, and after they cooled they wrapped the wax blocks in rice paper. Not only did this keep the coins from clinking, but a casual inspection would show only beeswax, though the weight might give them away if hefted. If they needed some coins, they could just carve some out with a knife, and pat the wax back.

Demosthenes pronounced Antonius fit to travel, with no fever for the past several days. However, he was to spend the first few days in the cart, which provoked more grumping, but finally acquiescence.

Xian Bohai arrived with Mama Biyu for dinner the last night, his horse prancing and tossing its head as he pulled up in the front yard. He was about forty years old, five feet or so, lean and wiry with skin like yellow leather from many years out of doors. He sported a dashing long mustache whose black strands hung down six inches beside his mouth, ending somewhat below the chin. His riding hat covered black hair ending in a long braid, thrown over his shoulder and down his breast. He seemed utterly at home on the back of his lively black horse, much taller and much more graceful than their Mongolians. Dressed for action, he had a sword and a bow crossed on his back, with a quiver of arrows slung on the saddle pommel.

"So these are the great criminals I am supposed to sneak out of the Middle Kingdom. An unlikely looking lot, they!" He said with a big laugh as he scanned everyone clustered on the porch. "The columns look nice, cousin Biyu, when did you repaint them?" he said, changing the subject, admiring the freshly-painted porch and elegantly bright red columns.

"You can thank your passengers. They insisted on doing something for me!"

Bohai slipped out of the saddle, fluid like quicksilver pouring from a ladle, befitting a man whose saddle was also his home. "Well, it looks like they don't expect something for nothing then, that's a good sign. Who's in charge of this motley crew?"

"That be Ib-Him," volunteered Aulus. "I Gawba, this one Gais, An-Dun, Si Huar, Si Nuo, Dim, Yak, Gisga, and Simul." Each bowed as he was introduced.

"Good, you speak passable *han-yu*. How about the others?"

"We all speak some," said Ibrahim, warming to the man's blunt humor. He extended his hand, and Bohai took it in a firm grasp. "Everyone in charge of something, but I am head thief, pirate, so I lead lawbreaking part."

Bohai guffawed. "I've heard you did a good job of lawbreaking. Did you really insult the Son of Heaven and get out with your heads still attached?"

"Seem so. Gawba tell that story, he was one who did," Ibrahim said, smiling.

"Over wine, after dinner, we tell. Over much wine!" said Aulus.

"And six dead Black Headbands. I want to hear that story, too, over still more wine. We ride with hangovers tomorrow at first light!"

Bohai enjoyed the stories of their imprisonment and escape, and then it got around to their trip across the Indian Ocean in *Asia* and *Europa*, Aulus's relentless pursuit, the firefights in Galle and in the Straits of Malacca. Although he had never been on a ship, nor even seen the ocean, Bohai found this fascinating, and he had his own stories to tell. The rice wine had flowed freely, but they were in fact up at first light, hung over as promised.

After saying farewell to Mama Biyu, they set out down the rough mountain road back to Tongchuan. Mama Biyu wiped away a tear as she thought of her long-dead son.

Bohai broke them up into three groups, separated by about half an hour, smaller groups attracting less attention than big ones. Aulus, Gaius and Ibrahim rode in the lead with Bohai. Galosga and Demosthenes rode in the middle with the cart, Shmuel driving with Marcia and Antonius as passengers, the spare horses in trail. Marcus and Yakov brought up the rear. There was at least one fluent *han-yu* speaker in each group.

The men's hair had begun to regrow, but they wore riding caps to conceal its still sparse length, and Marcia was wearing her wig. All of the men except Galosga, who oddly enough had no facial hair, had begun beards, Ibrahim's its usual salt-and-pepper, Aulus's streaked with white, everyone else's dark.

The plan was to ride till around noon, then switch off two of the riders. As they cleared Tongchuan and the road opened up to the north, Bohai challenged the lead group. "Let's see what you are made of!" he cried as he tsk'ed his horse into action and kneed the stallion to a burst of speed, taking off in a cloud of dust. Aulus, Gaius and Ibrahim laid low about the horses' necks and did likewise. Gaius slapped his horse with the reins to urge more speed, as did Aulus and Ibrahim, though Bohai rapidly outdistanced them. It was an exhilarating ride in the clear early morning air, and eventually, they caught up with Bohai under a tree, his horse drinking water from a small creek. "Not bad. Those little Mongolian ponies can't keep up with Longma, no matter how hard you ride," he said with a smile, slapping the black horse's graceful black neck. "He is a *doyuanmo* from *Da Yuan*, a heavenly horse indeed! Still, you put all you had into it, so good work!"

Two days of hard riding brought them to within a day of Yanzhou, where the Yan River joins the Hwang He in its southbound journey, picking up the fine powdery grit of the Loess Plateau that gives the river its characteristic color and its name – the Yellow River, so thick with fine grit it was sometimes more like a fast-moving mudslide than a river. They stopped for the night and camped in an eerie, uninhabited landscape of wind-carved steeples of not-yet-eroded dirt, above flat alluvial plains.

After most of the rest had retired, Marcia and Antonius retired a hundred yards away for privacy, and much later, they lay naked on their backs on the cool grass in the warm August night, their bodies savoring the afterglow of their lovemaking. The sky was moonless, and there was no human light except the banked campfire, far off by the rest of the group. Their eyes had long ago adjusted to the darkness so they had no trouble seeing by the preternaturally bright starlight from a sky frosted with stars. A shooting star drew a thin ruler-straight white line across the sky, vanished, and a few seconds later, another big one flared and broke up, leaving a trail of red, blue and green fragments tumbling in its wake, each winking out at its own pace.

Marcia sighed and hugged Antonius' biceps, holding it firmly to her chest. "Looks like the gods are cheering us on, they are putting on quite a show!" she said.

"They are indeed." he replied.

"The shooting stars are all coming from the same place in the sky – there. I wonder why?"

"That's the constellation Perseus, I don't know why... We found a shooting star, many years ago when I was a young soldier in Germany."

"What happened?"

"That bright one we just saw flaring is called a *bolidus*, and one like it fell all the way to earth, about two miles from our camp. Big boom before it hit, then a bigger one when it hit the ground, a few seconds after the flash. Like lightning and thunder, I guess. It started a fire, so we all got our *dolabra* shovels and went over to see what it was. Knocked over a bunch of trees, dug a big crater. We dug in the crater, and we found a fist-sized chunk of iron that looked liked it had come out of a forge, too hot to touch."

"Amazing! Jupiter's thunderbolt?"

"If it was, he either couldn't aim or he had it in for the trees, because he missed us."

"So what are we going to do when we get to Rome, *carus meus?*"

"If we get to Rome. It's a long way and we just got started... I don't know. I can't imagine Trajan will be too happy with how this mission went, but Aulus thinks he will approve of what we did. My next tour should be *praefectus castrorum,* prefect of camps, but I don't know if I want to do that."

"Why not?"

"In case you haven't noticed, I am quite taken with being around you, and helping you make babies someday, if you want. I followed the eagles for twenty-six years and I've had all the adventure on this trip I need."

Marcia snuggled against him, fitting her body into the curve of his. "So what you want to do instead?"

"I don't know. I could teach swordsmanship, or go into medicine, since I am a medic. I could do what my father did, tutor upper class brats, as long as I could cuff them when they got uppity. Or I – we – could teach *han-yu.*"

"We? You and I teach together?"

"Why not? You know the language, and can write it, you even know Hanaean poetry. We could be a good team."

"You know what I love about you, *carus meus?* You always make me want to do more than I think I can." She kissed his shoulder tenderly.

"You've already done more than any woman I ever met. Let's see... taken from home, concubine at twelve, trained in the Hanaean court, bilingual in

Latin and *han-yu*, left for a world jaunt at sixteen, crossed all of Asia overland to meet Trajan in Rome, then back again by ship, survived a hijacking, bad storms, two firefights, been sentenced to death, was in a bandit attack that left six dead, and a now you're on a journey to take tea with the savage Xiongnu. You haven't lived a dull life, *domina mea*, not at all!"

"Mmmh. Thank you. Do you mind if I talk about Ming?"

"There are things you need to talk out. So speak."

"He always made me feel like nothing. Our first night when I became his concubine ... is it all right to talk about that?"

"Go ahead."

"He came in, took off my clothes, lifted up his cloak, and got on top of me without saying a word. He was... in me long before I was ready, it hurt, and he just finished, got up, arranged his cloak, and said, 'I'll see you tomorrow night.' I had no one to talk to. I didn't know the other concubines, and they were much older than me."

Antonius put his arm around her, and she sobbed a bit into his shoulder, then continued. "He always made me feel worthless. Just that one time, when I helped him to meet with the Emperor, he was happy, and I was worth something for a while. Then, it went back to the way it was, and when the beating started again... I had been treated with respect for the first time in my life on the *Europa* by everyone, and especially by you. I wasn't going to go back to being nothing again, and if I had to break that jar on his head again, I'd do it, but harder!" She laughed through her tears.

Antonius laughed with her. "Yer'll never be nothin' again, not as long as I am around."

"And you almost weren't! I thought I had you forever, then I almost lost you, when I saw the arrow in your stomach. I don't know what I would have done without you."

She hugged him, then she sat up. "There is something I need to talk about, Antonius. Back in Tongchuan, when the fighting was going on, I was in the barn with Marcus. And if you had lost that fight, Marcus... he wasn't going to let me be taken alive. You know what would have happened."

He nodded; he had given Marcus a dagger during the pirate raid last year, to kill her to prevent her capture.

"They would have had their way with me, and when they were done, they would have killed me or made me their slave. That can never happen again, Antonius. I need you to teach me how to fight. If I am going to die, I want to die by your side, not hiding somewhere waiting helplessly for whatever comes next."

"*Domina*, you don't know what yer askin' fer. You're a woman. I can teach yer how to use a knife, sure, but fight in the line... yer can't do that! Yer'll just git yersel' killed."

"Antonius, knowing how to use knife is a start, but it isn't enough. Even if I had a sword, and knew how to use it, those bandits would have just overpowered me. I might have gotten one or two, but in the end... I don't ever want to feel helpless, ever again." She collected her courage, preparing to defy him for the first time. "When you train the men tomorrow, I'll be there. Just think of me as another soldier."

"I don't think I can picture that." He put his arm around her and they cuddled as the sky blazed with shooting stars, until sleep took them.

CHAPTER 60: THE WILD SAVAGES OF THE NORTH

Back in Luoyang, the *weiwei* noted the report from Shaanxi province about some disturbance near Tongchuan involving some itinerant strangers and a local bandit group. Details were scarce, but those who had seen the strangers described several of them as bald, accompanied by a woman. He was sure it was the *Da Qin*.

The *Da Qin* must have become aware of the search mounted for them in Chang'an, and bypassed the city. A local trader had procured a cart and a large amount of food and fodder, too much for a man known for traveling in small groups in his dealings with the Xiongnu up north. So perhaps the *Da Qin* were heading north to Xiongnu lands.

The news was too late for the *weiwei* to use, and the Xiongnu area too wild and inhospitable to follow them. But if the *Da Qin* were to come to ground in the Middle Kingdom again, it would likely be in Liqian, the translators' hometown. The frigid howling winter winds from the North Asian plains would certainly blow them south again. That, and family ties.

Marcus was formally inducted as part of Antonius' little 'army,' along with Aulus, a few days after leaving Tongchuan, having successfully completed Antonius' essential training drills. They could now take regular watches with the group, rather than acting as reserve back-up. Marcia took great pride in her brother's induction; he had not even been allowed to own a sword as an Hanaean. But after the ceremony she abruptly turned away from the camp and walked off several hundred yards.

Gaius watched her departure, noting that she looked a bit downcast. *Trouble with Antonius? I doubt that. I think she is finding the training harder than she expected. Maybe now is the time to get that foolish notion out of her mind.* He followed discretely. She was sitting on the ground, her knees drawn up to her chest, quietly contemplating the world.

"Marcia?" he asked. "Do you mind if I join you? You look concerned about something." Latin seemed appropriate, if she had something difficult to express.

"No, Gaius. Please, sit."

"First, congratulations on your brother." Gaius said, seating himself cross-legged beside her, and picking up a dry weed on which to chew. "He made great progress, starting with no experience at all. And he handled himself well in his first fight last week."

She smiled. "Yes I am very proud of him."

"He is a good man."

"Thank you."

"But I think there is something else on your mind, as well. Can I help?"

She sighed. "Yes. My training… it is not going well."

"It's taking you longer than you expected?"

"Yes. I am clumsy, slow, and it seems that, my sparring partner, whoever it is, just casually bats my sword out of my grasp and sends it flying. I have been practicing for weeks, and it's not getting any better. Do you think I am a fool for trying to do this?"

The answer Gaius gave was not the discouragement he intended to give. He asked rhetorically, "Do you think you are?

She paused and smiled. "I expected you to tell me I was."

"It's certainly going to be harder for you than it was for Marcus."

"Then I guess I will have to work harder. Thank you, you remind me of my father, what I remember of him. He always encouraged me to do the hard things."

Gaius laughed ruefully. "Being a father and a husband are the two things I haven't done well. I haven't been with my family for two years and I don't know when I will again. My children won't remember me."

"They won't forget you. I never forgot Papa, and they won't forget you.

"Thank you. And let me give you a tip. Drill a hole through the pommel of your sword, run a leather lanyard through it and grasp the sword through the loop. If someone knocks it loose, it won't go flying. Old army trick."

She laughed, a bright cheerful laugh that took the tension out of her. "I'll do that!"

"Well, I'll be off now. Good luck!" *Well, that didn't work out like I expected.*

About a week out of Tongchuan, the party reached the Hwang He, now flowing east through the Baotou region of the Hetao plateau. From the higher hillcrests, they could occasionally glimpse the Ordos Desert's barren terrain behind them to the southwest.

Several months had passed since their heads had been shaved to make their escape, and much of everyone's hair had grown back. Marcia, without Mama Biyu's wig, could now pass as a twelve year old boy with scraggly locks, though her hair was still a far cry from the three-foot-long black silken tresses that had previously adorned her head. And Demosthenes, after a great deal of meditation and introspection, had decided to let his hair regrow also. His shaved head had symbolized his rejection of the things of this world, things and friends which he now, however reluctantly, embraced. It was more honest to no longer pretend to ascetic detachment, though it saddened him greatly to leave that life behind.

From a hill overlooking the Huang He valley, Bohai, Gaius and Ibrahim surveyed the countryside. Like most of the Huang He's long course, the river here meandered through a broad flat alluvial plain several tens of miles wide, dotted with the yurts of various groups of nomads and their flocks and herds. Here was the border of Han control, tenuous at best, with a constant ebb and flow of nomadic herders across it from all directions.

Bohai was a smuggler, and he knew many ways to cross the Huang He without having to answer too many questions from the Han officials who pretended to exercise control over this area. His band of refugees was hot cargo.

Bohai sat in his saddle and pointed ahead. "We'll turn west along that road there, about a mile from the river. About five miles on, there we will find a reliable and not too curious ferryman."

On reaching the location, they indeed found a ferry, a flat-bottomed boat with railings to contain animals, big enough to hold ten or so horses. Bohai exchanged some brass coins with the man for his trouble, and two trips got the party and their cart across.

"The band we are looking for are on the other side of Yin Mountains up ahead," he said, pointing to the rilled hills looming ahead.

On the north side of the mountains was a treeless grassland watered by streams. Bohai identified an encampment in the distance as their target, and they began a descent to the steppe below.

They neared the camp about nightfall. Horsemen clattered up to the group several hundred yards before they reached the camp, clad in leather breaches, wool jackets, and black conical hats, a sword and a bow crisscrossed across their backs. Some carried long spears at the ready under their armpits, the shafts decorated with feathers or animal pelts. Their skin was like worn leather from years in the steppes and deserts, but the Romans recognized among them familiar round eyes, aquiline noses and light hair. One of that group was a powerfully-built red-haired woman, well-armed with a forbidding expression. Others in the group had more familiar Asiatic visages, almond brown eyes with epicanthic folds, their skin, too, was burned brown by the sun. They halted about twenty paces from the group and waited.

Bohai trotted off to greet them alone, pulling to a stop ahead of what appeared to be their leader, to greet him in their own language. Bohai seemed to allay the party's suspicions, as the leader smiled and raised his hand in greeting, relaxing a bit in his saddle. Those with lances lowered their butt ends to the ground. Bohai turned and signaled to the group to come forward, and the group's mounted riders and the cart proceeded to the encampment. Outside the encampment, horses, goats, sheep and camels grazed, under the attentive eyes of herdsmen, aided by dogs.

The encampment consisted of about thirty white felt yurts, each about twenty feet in diameter and ten feet high. A larger one in the middle, decorated with various flags, pelts, and symbols, was apparently the leader's tent. As the group passed into the camp, dogs barked and children ran up to stare at the strange visitors. Men stared sullenly at their Hanaean clothing, clearly not happy to host such visitors.

They trotted to the large central yurt and dismounted when their escorts did. Bohai beckoned them into the big yurt. They were followed by five of their escorts, including the big woman, who stood about six feet tall.

The inside was illuminated only by light from the open door, which showed a man seated at the rear in an intricately carved chair, overlaid with gilt. Like the others, he was clad in felt leather breeches stuffed in calf-length boots and a felt shirt, under a blue silk vest. Bohai greeted him again in Xiongnu with some familiarity, they exchanged some words, and then he turned to Ibrahim. "Introduce yourselves. This is *Shanyu* Bei of the Huyan clan of the Xiongnu. He speaks *han-yu*, as do most of the people here, though reluctantly... they are fierce enemies."

Ibrahim introduced himself first. "I am Ibhim, son of Yusuf, a nomad of the sea, leading my companions here to safety in the west. Aulus?"

"I am Aus Gawba of the *Da Qin* far to the west. I led a diplomatic expedition to Emperor He, who treacherously imprisoned us, and would have executed us were it not for Ibhim. My cousin Gis is my second in command, An-Dun my strong right arm, and our translators Si Nuo, and his sister Si Huar. We all five owe our lives to Ibhim's companions, Dim, Yak, Simul and Gisga." Each bowed in turn as they were introduced. "Dim is a most heroic follower of Buddha, Simul, Gisga and Yak fearless fighters from the west. And Bohai has been our most gracious escort to your lands."

The *Shanyu* greeted them. "Welcome to the sad remnants of the once-proud Huyan clan of the Xiongnu. Once we would cover the plains with our numbers, but after the battle of Ilkh Bayan this is all that is left, just a few thousand. Please, we are poor and informal here. Have a seat on the pillows on the floor, as we do." He clapped his hands. "Food and *kumis* for our guests!"

He returned to his guests. "You wish to return west to the land of the *Da Qin*?"

"That is our intent, sir," replied Aulus.

"You are fortunate then, as we are beginning our final trek south to better weather, but we will not return to this, our home, ever again. We are too few to continue living here. We will rejoin the other clans at Dzungaria to the west, between the Tien Shan and Altai Mountains. You are welcome to travel with us. We will be leaving in a few days to trade at Yinshuan and then Liqian in the Qilian mountains, then on to our destination."

Marcia's heart leapt. She interrupted, "Liqian? In Gansu?"

"That is the one, why?" answered the *shanyu*.

"That was my home. And Si Nuo's. We have not been there for ten years."

"Then that is fortunate!"

People came in carrying bowls of food, goat and beef, some leafy vegetables of an unidentifiable source, and white *kumis*. Bohai excused himself to bring in some bottles of rice and grape wine, gifts for Bei's clan. Bowls of *kumis*, wine and food were placed in the middle of the circle and everyone reached in.

The *kumis* kept coming. Although it was not strongly alcoholic, it was plentiful. The wine, while not plentiful, was strong, and reserved for the hosts, a rare treat for them.

"What is this white wine?" asked Aulus of Bohai. "It is sweet, almost like almonds."

"Fermented mare's milk," answered Bohai, causing Aulus to choke in mid-swallow.

The tall woman came to sit beside Marcia. She sat down cross-legged, in such a manner that her tight-fitting felt leather breaches left little to the imagination, a posture Marcia found unladylike. But that was from her upbringing in faraway places where ladylike behavior had meaning. The woman seemed even more powerful up close than at a distance, her ruddy hair framing a green-eyed face. She still wore her sword and bow across her shoulders, a fine scar running along her right forearm.

"You are from Liqian, then. Are you and your brother Han?"

"We are descendants of *Da Qin* soldiers many generations back. My ancestor gave me my blue eyes, and the women on my mother's side gave them their shape. My brother and I both carry his *Da Qin* name, him Marcus, me Marcia."

"How did someone from such a small place in Gansu attract the attention of He the Horrible?"

"We speak both *Da Qin* and *han-yu*, and Emperor He's people took me, my brother and others to Luoyang to be trained as translators. I was twelve, he was twenty; we never saw our families again. I would like to see them, if they are still alive, or learn what happened to them."

"Perhaps you shall. For now, I am glad you and your brother are not full-blooded Han. As you were taken from your family at Liqian, so they took my family from me at the same age. I despise the Han." She straightened up and left without further words. Not once had she smiled.

Bohai walked up to Marcia as the woman strode off. "Looks like Hina likes you."

"She certainly didn't sound like it. How can you tell?"

"She talked to you. She's one of their best fighters, but not very sociable."

"How did she lose her family?"

"After the battle of Ilkh Bayan, thousands upon thousands of Xiongnu were killed, captured or driven off. She never knew which fate befell her family, and became a fighter at a very young age to avenge them. And she has avenged them, several times over."

"How do you, as an Hanaean, trade with them, if they are so hostile to your people?"

"Same as you, I am not full-blooded Han. My grandfather was Xiongnu, Xubu clan."

The following morning, the clan arranged entertainment for the guests: horseback riding and archery. The men along with Hina fired at various targets from a full gallop with deadly accuracy, culminating in hitting a stationary target through a small swinging ring, impaling the ring.

Also included was a game played on horseback with a dead goat. The object of the game was to snatch the carcass from whoever had it and run with it through one of two goal posts, with a great deal of cheering and betting from the enthusiastic crowd. There seemed to be no other rules, and the game continued until the carcass disintegrated from rough handling.

Antonius sauntered up to Gaius, and made a proposition: "Gaius, I think you and I oughter put on a demo of Roman swordsmanship."

"You're on, Antonius!" answered Gaius.

They made the announcement in *han-yu*, and the clan gathered around the two. Their wooden training swords were brought out, which caused some amusement among the Xiongnu. Antonius explained that wooden swords allowed more aggressive training that could result in death or injury if they used real swords, which mollified their skeptical audience a bit.

The two men distributed their swords for the Xiongnu to examine. Short and broad, less than two feet in length, all the swords were virtually identical, no guard, leather-wrapped wooden grips. Antonius had painstakingly made these out of the toughest wood he could find, carving and sanding them until they were a near perfect replica of a Roman *gladius*, about two feet long and perhaps two inches wide.

Bets were made, and the game was on.

Gaius and Antonius engaged in a round of well-rehearsed parries and thrusts which went on about five minutes, and ended up with the heavier, bearded Antonius taking advantage of a poorly-executed sword shift by Gaius to his left hand. Antonius charged, kicked Gaius' feet from under him, and ended up straddling him with his wooden sword tip at Gaius' throat. This elicited a round of cheers, and then Antonius called out the rest of their party in turn to spar with him, ending with Marcia. She was overmatched, basic maneuvers poorly executed. He quickly knocked her sword from her grip, spinning on its lanyard around her wrist, his point at her throat. The crowd cheered loudly, which caused Marcia to flush angrily as she glared back at the crowd.

Then Hina stepped into the ring, proffering Antonius a steel Xiongnu sword. Antonius cast aside his wooden sword, and she tossed the blade to him across the five feet separating them. He caught it easily by the hilt, and she withdrew hers from across her back with a deadly hiss. She descended into a crouch, her green eyes bright, and beckoned with the fingers of her left hand. "You and I, real swords!"

The crowd went wild.

Antonius and Hina circled, crouched, sizing each other up. Then they exchanged thrusts and parries, the metal swords clanging like bells. The two were warming up, breathing easily through wolfish grins.

The two were well matched, but decidedly different in size and style. Antonius was full and brawny, black-bearded and perhaps fifty pounds heavier than Hina, though none of it fat. He fought with force and precision, with a dogged determination to wear her down through blow after fearsome blow.

Hina was a well-muscled Amazon of a woman, lithe and whippet-like, making up in speed and agility what she lacked in shear power. Parry and thrust, thrust and parry, their ringing blows beat out a slow, deadly rhythm throughout the camp.

Antonius saw his opportunity, and presented a vicious overhead stroke that would have cleft Hina in two, but she quickly presented her sword crosswise across her face to block it. This stopped the deadly downstroke, but left her locked in the contest of shear strength that she had thus far avoided. Immobilized, her sword locked in the horizontal parry, she had to resist the inexorable downward pressure of Antonius' sword. She braced the flat side of her sword against her left hand, but his strength and gravity were against her, forcing her downward. The veins on her arms stood out in etched relief against the straining muscles.

Hina executed a high-risk pirouette from that awkward position, gracefully sliding out from underneath the downward press, and her sword hissed free. Relieved of the pressure of the defensive parry, Antonius' sword sliced forcefully through empty air where only seconds before the woman's body had been, staggering him momentarily off balance. But Hina was not quite in position to take advantage of the new situation. Completing her pirouette, she stepped backwards to assess the situation. She recognized the aching fatigue in her right arm, and began a retreat to change sword hands, fumbling with the thong securing the sword to her wrist. As she began her switch, Antonius, in a sudden burst of speed, brought his sword up in a slashing attack from below. The woman's sword, not yet secured to her left hand, spun free, whirling scythe-like through the air, spectators scattering to avoid its deadly blade. The woman, now defenseless, continued to back up, stumbling over a pot someone had left near a yurt at the perimeter of the field. Antonius completed the attack with a swift kick, taking her feet out from under her and dropping her gracelessly onto her back. Antonius' sword struck like a serpent, thrusting its single fang into the hollow of her throat.

"I think you should watch your feet, or some Han bastard will take your head off for a souvenir!" He mocked her in *han-yu,* poised for the death blow. Antonius chuckled at her discomfort as he stood over her. "I think that was a night pot you stumbled over." The acrid smell of stale urine filtered up from the foul pool of liquid in which the young woman lay.

But the game was not yet over. Antonius was spread-legged, straddling her with the sword tip at her throat. While he savored victory, Hina brought her left foot up in an arc directly into his crotch. All signs of amusement left Antonius' face as the air left his lungs with a "woof", and his chest muscles struggled ineffectively to bring in another gulp of air. Hina had time to aim and concentrate her next blow, coiling her legs up to her abdomen and launching them into Antonius' exposed belly, rocking him backward. Antonius' sword clattered uselessly from his hand, and he was driven by the force of the blow to collapse on his back.

Hina slipped a nine-inch dagger from her scabbard as she leaped to her feet, continuing with one fluid motion to straddle the man's chest. She laid the dagger blade-edge across the hairy throat, the tip at the spot directly below the point of the jaw where the carotid artery throbs.

"Turnabout, *Da Qin!*" she hissed, "You should not be so quick to celebrate your victory!" She grinned wolfishly, and continued. "Hmm, I like this beard. Perhaps I should remove just a bit of it, starting say...here, as a souvenir" as she dug the knife point delicately into the skin, drawing just a drop of blood.

"Arggh...Hina! You already poured piss all over the campground. Will you now spill my blood on it, too?"

Hina stood up, sheathed her blade, and proffered a hand to Antonius, who took it, and she hoisted him to his feet. "That was a good match, not many men can last as long as you did," she said, shaking off grass and debris from the ground. Someone from the crowd had retrieved her sword and handed it to her, which she returned to its scabbard.

"Hina, I have not been bested in many years. You did well," answered Antonius, smiling ruefully and massaging his testicles.

"It seems that I will need a change of clothes. Perhaps you will accompany me to my yurt?" she said, softly so as to not be heard by too many people.

"Ummh, Hina, I'm honored, but... I am taken now," he replied, nodding toward Marcia.

Hina strode over to where Marcia stood. She had been close enough to overhear the exchange. "Ah, the girl from Liqian! It seems you have a loyal companion. That's rare, keep him satisfied, or I will seek him out again later!"

With that, Hina walked off, still in search of male companionship, as fighting of any kind usual left her quite lustful. It was the Xiongnu custom to request companionship from visitors who might bring new blood into the well-inbred clan lineage. Her eyes fell on Galosga, the second-largest besides Antonius. They exchanged a few words, and the pair went to her yurt.

Inside the yurt, Hina wasted no time. "We will be alone for a while," she said. She stripped off her fouled clothes and threw them in a corner, then pressed her body full against Galosga's, her mouth on his in a wet but very sweet kiss that lingered a long time. She thrust her pubis against him, feeling him rise to meet her advance. They stood that way for several minutes, locked in an embrace, exploring each other's bodies. Then she broke away, peeling up his shirt over his head, kneeling to pull down his pants and cast them off his feet. She took his erect manhood in her hand and admired its length, licking it and then taking it fully in her mouth.

Galosga moaned in pleasure, caressing her red hair.

Hina released him, grabbed his hands and lay on the ground in front of him, legs spread to reveal her womanhood. She pulled him down to her, saying "Let's go! I need you now!"

Hina made love like she fought, fiercely. In fact, it was not lovemaking at all but sheer physical rutting. Galosga felt that he was mating with the same tiger he had watched earlier besting Antonius, as she twisted and turned under him in a frantic search for relief. With a great deal of concentration, he hoped to bring her that release before his own.

He succeeded. Her movements became more insistent, more urgent, her breathing more rapid, until she arched her back under him and cried out in a paroxysm of pleasure. He could feel the pulsating pleasure rage through her body, and he kept moving gently until she began to go limp. She was wet with sweat, breathing like she had just run several miles.

He let her savor the afterglow for several minutes, then he smiled and said, "It is my turn now. You enjoy, I ride you." He thrust into her gently, feeling her tremble with each slow stroke. It was lovemaking as Galosga understood it, but it seemed to be new to Hina, for she trembled, building to a second climax. He kissed her on the mouth, one hand found a breast, the other cupped her butt. She began to return his thrusts with her own, and as the second wave broke over her, Galosga gave himself over and spent himself inside her, over and over, and yet over again, until they both lay limp, depleted in each other's arms.

It was a long time before either wanted to move, each savoring the contractions of residual pleasure where they were coupled together. When at last they were capable of speaking, she whispered into his ear, "I chose wisely. I beat one man in battle, but you have beaten me on the bedroll. No man has ever done that."

"I have never made love to a *huldaji* before," gently kissing her on the nose. His lip was bleeding and swollen from some intense kiss.

"What is that?" she asked.

"It is a word in my language; I don't know the word in *han-yu*, but it is a large cat, about the size of a man, that roams the mountains, very wild and fierce."

"That is a tiger. And yes, a tigress is my *persona.*"

"Well, I have heard you roar, *huldaji*, and I have heard you purr. I like the purr better."

She snuggled up against him, and they half-dozed for a few minutes. Then Hina propped herself up on an elbow, and tapped his almost hairless bronze chest.

"So how long have you been riding, strange man? You look awkward on horseback."

"Only a few weeks. We don't have horses in my home."

"No horses?"

"None."

"Perhaps you learn to ride while you are with us."

"I have much to learn."

Galosga's straightforward answer took Hina aback. Another man might have been insulted, or blustered, or gotten angry. He knew he rode poorly and had no problem admitting it.

"Perhaps I could teach you." She was breaking a long-standing rule, to rut once with a stranger and then let them go their way, having nothing to do with them afterwards in any way. She enjoyed the way they reacted to being cast aside after having been used for her satisfaction.

"I would like that." He paused to rummage around in his pouch, and drew out a flint arrowhead, and handed it to her to examine. "And many other things are different there. No metal… we make our tools out of stone. Like this. We farm, but we don't have livestock."

She examined the curious object in her hand. "So where is this strange land, Galosga?"

"If I knew, I would go back there."

"How did you get here then? Surely the wind didn't blow you here to land in my arms."

Galosga repeated the story of his kidnapping and impressment, and arriving in a land of marvelous cities with wondrous things he had never before seen. "I learned I was a 'deckhand,' someone that works on the ship. It was not until I learned *han-yu* that I found a language that I could speak easily. I feel like I am speaking like a child, but everyone understands me, and tells me I speak the best of all the *Da Qin*."

"You do. An odd accent, some words a bit strange, but good for a stranger."

"So tell me your story, *huldaji*."

"I am what I am, a fighting woman. I live in the here and now, and there is no story."

"There is, but it is painful to you. Maybe later."

"Maybe not."

She levered herself off the blankets, rummaged through her belongings to find clean clothes, slid on her black breeches, slithering them up to her waist, and tying them with a thong. She reached down for her shirt, and pulled it over her ample breasts.

"That was enjoyable. But you must go now." The door between Hina and other people was slamming shut. She wanted to get back to the casual laughter of the camp, get drunk on *kumis*, and be ready to pack out tomorrow for their final trek. "Get dressed!" she said abruptly.

Galosga stood, and kissed her fully on the mouth. "It was enjoyable, but I will leave you to yourself," he said, holding her struggling in his arms. Then he turned and walked out of the yurt without a word.

He was about ten yards outside the door when she put out her head and broke her own rule. "Would you like to ride with me tomorrow? First light before breakfast?"

"My tent is over there," he said, pointing in its direction, but not turning to look back. "Slap on the side of it tomorrow morning."

CHAPTER 61: A VISIT FROM A GHOST

The clan celebrated the evening before their departure on their final trek from the Hetao plateau. There was abundant *kumis*, and various meats roasting on spits in the encampments: familiar ones, like sheep, goats and yak cattle, and to the Romans' surprise, an occasional horse. A big bonfire after dark sent sparks shooting high into the heavens, drums, clanging cymbals, stringed instruments that played a wailing tune as the singers sang monotones through their throats, in a drone almost like that of a bagpipe. It reminded Gaius and Antonius of German tribal festivities along the Danube, and Galosga of events at home.

The clan reverted to their native Xiongnu language, and for a while, the Westerners wandered throughout the encampment, sitting to listen to storytellers tell stories that they couldn't understand, but enjoying the animation that went with them, partaking freely of *kumis* and the various foods proffered them. After a while, they found their way back to their tents around the large oxcart for which they had traded their Tongchuan horse cart. The oxcart, drawn by two yaks, would stand up better on the roadless steppes, and with much better payload for tents and supplies, protected from the weather by its canvas shelter over the bed. They had bought or traded for heavier Xiongnu clothing, woolen felts better suited for the rapidly cooling fall weather, and some heavy winter gear as well, because that season would set in soon, and harshly. The oxcart freed up two more horses for riding, and they garnered two mares and a stallion from the clan to round out their little herd to thirteen, mounts for all plus spares.

Bohai was off socializing with the clan, so that left the ten of them alone, conversing cross-legged around the fire.

"Looks like we can sleep in tomorrow," announced Gaius. "They are going to leave about noon. It's going to take a couple of hours for them to drop their yurts and load them on camels, but all we have to do is drop a couple of tents."

"Yes, everything that can be loaded, we already got packed up today. Just bedrolls inside," said Antonius. Turning to Galosga, he said with a grin, "So how did the Tiger Lady treat you this afternoon?"

Marcia, seated next to him, elbowed him in the ribs in mock consternation. "What a question! That's none of your business!"

"Seems the Tiger Lady made it everybody's business. There was nothing subtle about the way she hauled him off!" answered Antonius, guffawing and slapping his leg.

"Well, it's a good thing she didn't haul you off. I would have killed her." She snuggled against him. "Put your arm around me, it's getting chilly. And thanks for turning her down."

"I think she would have killed you first if you would have tried. Remember, she beat me, and it's been a long time since any man beat me. So, Galosga, how was it?" said Antonius, putting his arm around Marcia. She put her head on his shoulder and snuggled dreamily.

Galosga thought a minute before answering, "She is very physical in all things."

Everyone erupted in laughter, Ibrahim spewing a mouthful of *kumis* at the unexpected understatement. "I'll bet she is that!" he laughed. He turned to Antonius. "But that was a cheap trick she pulled on you, kicking you in the nuts when you had her dead to rights."

"The fight isn't over until your opponent knows it's over. I was getting such a good laugh at her taking a piss bath that I forgot she still had lots of fight left. My mistake, and she capitalized on it. There is only one rule in fighting, be the one who walks away. If that had been for real, I'd be dead. She's a damned good fighter, and I'll fight alongside her anytime."

They swapped another couple of stories, then retired to their tents early, having decided they needed to replace them with a yurt before the winter set in, and not quite sure how to do that… perhaps Bohai would have some suggestions.

Hina had stayed with the riders from her own ten man *arban*, swapping crude jokes, laughing the harsh, barking laugh that fighting men everywhere use. Her men sought details on her adventures with Galosga. She also took some ribbing for being turned down by Antonius, which had never happened before. Their unit had also packed out already, so she had a few hours to get her ride in with Galosga in the morning, something she had wisely chosen not share with the men… no man had ever gotten a second bite of Hina's apple before. And Galosga wasn't going to get one, either. Just a riding lesson. She retired early, and had the yurt to herself before the rest of the troop came in.

Hina normally fell asleep in a few minutes. Not tonight. Too many things had gone out of control today. The fight with Antonius was unexpectedly difficult, one she had almost lost. His turndown was another, though as she later watched him with the Han girl, she realized what she didn't know then, that they were lovers, which brought back memories she didn't need to recall. If she had known, she wouldn't have asked him. Oh, well. And Galosga. Turned down by the man she had beaten in battle, the man who accepted her had beaten her on the blankets. Galosga was an interesting character, and she regretted having shut him down at the end. But she had not shared her 'interesting stories' with anyone for eight years now, and she was not going to start now.

So sleep did not come.

There is a part of the mind that puts together pieces of understanding from scattered fragments. So when she heard a voice that she knew so well, had not heard in so long, and could not possibly be hearing now, she did not know if it was a vision, or her imagination.

"Hina, it's been a long time." The voice was so clear that she looked around the yurt, lit by the outdoors campfire, but there was no one inside.

"Get out of here, you demon, you cannot have my soul!" she said angrily, unsheathing the dagger she always kept ready at her bedside.

"I am no demon, Hina. But *Tengri* the skygod allowed me to come to free you of yours."

"You're dead, Mayu," said Hina numbly, wishing she could see him and touch him.

"I am dead, and the last sight I saw was you aiming an arrow at my chest. I welcomed that arrow as I would welcome a kiss from your sweet mouth."

"You must be his spirit, because no man knows that." She put her hands to her mouth to stifle a gasp. Could she be going crazy? The other nine men filed into their yurt to take their beds, laughing, joking and scratching. They didn't seem to notice her talking to empty air.

"They can't see us. They only see you asleep, and cannot hear us."

"I am not asleep! Why are you here?" she asked.

"I have a request, no, an order, that you must make a decision tonight. Either let go of my memory, or take that knife of yours, drive it into your chest and join me. "

"How do I do that, to let go of you?" She rolled the knife around in her palm, seriously considering the second alternative. To be with Mayu again! Forever, with *Tengri* in the sky!

"That's not the alternative I want you to choose," the Mayu spirit said, reading her mind. "You know our people cannot afford to lose another fighter, especially one like you. After all, I taught you everything I knew. You went on to excel in all. I want you to continue doing that."

"So how do I let you go? Especially when I don't want to ever let you go."

"You never told anyone what happened that day. That is your demon. You allow yourself no friends, so there is no chance you might accidentally share it with them. You can't be whole until you tell that 'interesting story,' as that most curious fellow Galosga called it."

"You saw... what we did?" gasped Hina. "I am sorry ... I didn't want to hurt you."

"You can't hurt me, and yes, I can watch what you do. I actually like Galosga, better than some of your other choices. I would like you to share with someone what the *Da Qin* Antonius and Marcia share, what we once shared."

"I don't know if I can tell him all of what happened that day."

"Then tell parts of it. Eventually it will all come out. You know how pus builds up in an infected wound, that has to come out or you will die? That story is infecting your soul, and the only way you can lance the infection is to talk about it."

She felt his hand on her thigh. "Goodbye, Mayu. I will always love you!"

"And I will always love you. Heal yourself, and heal yourself soon." And he was gone.

She lay on her back, heart thudding, knowing she would try. Everything had come together, a ride with Galosga in the morning, this vision. But how could she tell anyone what happened that dreadful day? Maybe Galosga would be a good choice after all; he would only be with them a few weeks.

Galosga heard the slap on the tent side a little before daybreak. Shmuel, his tentmate, rolled over and groaned sleepily, "What the hell is that?"

"Nothing for you, go back to sleep. My riding partner," answered Galosga as he cast the blankets aside and got into his clothes in the crisp chilly September morning. Shmuel made snuffling sounds into his black beard and pulled the covers more tightly about him. Galosga crawled out the tent entrance to find Hina waiting, holding the reins of her horse.

"I want to be back for my *arban's* packout, but we have maybe four hours," she said.

Galosga prepared his horse, harness, blanket, and saddle, carefully cinching the saddle in place. Hina inspected his work. "A little tighter, Galosga," she said, feeling the cinch strap. "Too loose, and you will slide back and forth on the animal, uncomfortable for him and throwing you off balance. Too tight and he can't breathe easily."

Galosga re-cinched animal and offered it to her inspection, and she tugged again. "That's better. We're going to take a slow start to get the horses warmed up, then I want you to gallop hard by yourself while I watch, and see what you can do to improve. Then we are going to ride like hell for twenty minutes. Stay with me as best you can. Try not to fall off, I don't want to bring you back slung over your animal's back."

They trotted out of the camp, taking care to avoid the various obstacles in the morning half-light. Then outside the camp, Hina pulled up her horse to a halt and patted him lovingly on his black neck. "This is Eagle, for the way he flies. What is your horse's name?"

"Gahlida. It means 'Arrow' in my language. Same reason, straight and true."

"Good, you seem to have some affection for him. Now, see that rise over there, about a mile away? I want you to gallop there at a comfortable speed, but don't try to go too fast. I will be alongside watching you."

Galosga clucked his horse into action and bent over the animal's neck. Their speed built up until they were clattering over the steppes at a fairly brisk pace, faster than Galosga had ever ridden, in fact. Hina galloped alongside, closely observing him.

When they reached the rise she had indicated, Galosga reined in the horse with a little clumsiness; the animal wanted to continue running.

"Not bad for a beginner," said Hina. "You need to get lower onto your horse's neck, right into his mane, and stand up a bit in the stirrups to take your weight off his back. He will go faster, and you will be able to keep your balance better. Now, back to where we started!"

She whirled Eagle around and the horse leaped away, followed by Gahlida with Galosga very low across his back. Galosga improved with each lap. After several repetitions, Hina thought he was ready. "Just follow me, don't try to beat me, because you can't and you might hurt yourself, or worse, the horse. Hyaaah!" and she was off.

The grass and rocks flew by in a blur below them, rocks and dust in the two horses' wakes. "Hyaah!" he said, imitating her cry, slapping the reins against the horse's neck. The animal responded, and the distance between him and Hina at least stopped opening; she was now a good hundred yards in front of him. After about twenty minutes, she wheeled Eagle around to a walk, Galosga joined her and did likewise. "Good job!" she said, still without any hint of a smile."You stayed with me. What was his name again?"

"Gahlida."

"Yes, Gahlida the arrow! Good name for him." She slapped Gahlida's sweaty neck, then slid off Eagle. Galosga also dismounted. "There is a little spring over here, where they can get some water."

After tending to their horses, they dropped the reins over the horses' necks to lie on the ground; they had been trained to tether this way, because there was little beside grass on the steppes, no trees to which to tie them.

"Sit!" She sat down cross legged, pulled out her waterskin and took a swig, then handed it to Galosga, who had likewise seated himself beside her. He, too, drank, and handed it back. She rummaged in her pouch and found the flint arrowhead he had given her. She offered it back to him. "I forgot to return this to you yesterday."

"Keep it," he said. "I have other mementoes of home. Think of me when you touch the arrowhead."

""Thank you, I will." She had been gathering her thoughts throughout the morning ride. She still had a lump in her throat, as she thought of the story she had to tell, and the racing of her heart had nothing to do with the horse ride.

"You wanted to hear my 'interesting story'. I must ask you some questions first."

"Of course," Galosga nodded.

"Do you, your people, believe that spirits of the dead can visit us?" she asked.

"Yes, we call them spirit walkers. Some people have the power to summon them, but that can be dangerous. Some sprit walkers are evil, some are good."

"Next question, have you ever loved someone?"

"Yes," he answered, "I left a wife and three children back home. And yes, I loved them, and still do. She was my partner in all things, and I know she was unhappy when I failed to return."

"If you could not get back, would you want her to take another?"

"Yes, my children need a father. When a person has been gone for a year, my people have a ceremony. Everyone gathers in the longhouse, remembers the missing man, and performs rituals to quiet his spirit. Then the wife is free to marry again. I hope she did."

The lump in Hina's throat was becoming thicker as he spoke. She hoped she would not shed a tear. She had not done so on that day so long ago, and had never cried since. Her men joked that she was incapable of tears.

"One more question: An-Dun's *Da Qin* name is Antonius, and Si Huar's is Marcia, are they not?"

"You mispronounce them a bit, but yes, that is correct, why?"

Hina's heart hammered. "Last night, I was visited by the spirit of a lover long dead, and he mentioned those two names to me. I knew them only by their Hanean names. He mentioned you by name, and said I should tell you my 'interesting story' to heal myself. Are you ready?"

"Please."

"Parts of this are horrible, and I have never shared these things with anyone before. Please do not share this story with anyone else, please. I must trust you … and trust does not come easily to me." Galosga nodded, and she continued.

"I was not born to Bei's clan, but to another. This was about the time of a great battle called Ilkh Bayan. Before that battle our encampments numbered tens, even hundreds, of thousands of people, vast cities on the move across the steppes. In that battle, the Han allied with some of our Xiongnu brothers from the south and almost wiped us out. The remaining clans left and did not return. Bei's clan is all that is left here, and we, too, are leaving today. "

"I was twelve when the Han came to our encampment. My father saw them coming, miles away. He ordered me to run, while my older brothers took up arms to fight alongside him. He said, 'Run like the wind, Hina, run, and don't take a horse because they will see you! If the encampment is still here tomorrow, come home, if not, go north to find another clan. Now run!' And I ran, hearing the screams of people behind me. Even then, I was fast for a scrawny little girl. I covered about five miles until I could run no more, and turned around. And already, a tall plume of black smoke was rising from the encampment, rising until the wind whipped the top of it and spread it over the grassland." She closed her eyes to visualize the memory.

"So I ran and walked, always north, the rising sun on my right, and the star that does not move ahead of me at night. Do you see that star where you grew up, Galosga?"

"Yes, we call it Yona the bear star, the same as the *Da Qin*, who call that whole group of stars the Little Bear. Continue."

"I didn't sleep for three days, didn't eat, drank water from mud puddles, until I found Bei's clan. They cleaned me up and brought me before him; he was a leader, but not yet the *shanyu*. I told him what had happened to my people, and he said that it was happening to all the clans, the Han were bent on wiping us out, or forcing us to go away west. He said he would find a family for me in the clan."

She paused. "I said no, I want to be a fighter!" Me, a scrawny little girl with bumps for breasts, barely five feet tall, and I had not yet had my first bleeding! Bei laughed, and turned to his lieutenant Mayu. Mayu was commander of a *zuun* company of a hundred men, and trained the new would-be fighters. 'Mayu!' he said, 'Can you make a fighter of out of this little waif?' He said 'No,' and my heart fell. It was not unheard of for women to become fighters alongside men, but it was very rare. Then he went on. 'If she is a fighter, I can make her a better one, but if she is not one now, I have nothing to work with. Girl, are you a fighter?' 'I am!' I answered. He went on, 'I am forming up a *zuun* of new recruits next week, if you want to fight, be there.'

"So I became a fighter. The boys were my age, and most just wanted to fuck me. One after another learned not to ask. I had to be better than them at everything I did, and I was. I was fourteen and a young woman when I – we – went to our first battle with the Han, a little skirmish of about fifty on a side. I killed my first man that day. In fact, I killed three. Have you ever killed someone, Galosga?"

"Yes, it is not pleasant."

"No, it isn't. I thought that I would be happy, having killed them, but all I could remember was their eyes, surprised, hurt, then fading out. The boys didn't seem to mind, but I did. They went to bed, and I stayed by the fire, my arms around my legs, holding them up against my chest, staring into the fire." *Amazing how much I remember of these things I thought I had forgotten.* "Mayu came and sat beside me. He didn't say anything for a long time, then he said, 'Killing your first man isn't easy. And it never gets better.' He put his arm around me and just sat there. I wasn't scrawny anymore, about the size I am now, and later that night, we made love for the first time. He took my virginity, before I knew what it was, so gently.

"But we were not supposed to do that. He was my commander. We had a tradition among our people that those who are close, like brothers, are not supposed to be in the same *zuun*, because they will fight for each other and not their hundred. But Mayu and I were in love, like Antonius and Marcia." She sighed and closed her eyes, visualizing her and Mayu side by side with Antonius and Marcia. *Yes, it was like that. Their light seems to burn bright, like ours once had.*

"So one day we were out on patrol, just the two of us. This time there was a Han patrol out, and we were ambushed." She stopped to consider her words. *You don't have to tell it all at once, Mayu had said.*

"I got away, but they wounded Mayu and knocked him from his horse. I got away, tethered my animal, and came back to see if I could free him. There were five Han soldiers, blue padded shirts with armor, conical helmets… they tied him to a bush and used him for target practice. It was horrible." *You don't have to tell it all.*

"I couldn't take it anymore. I took down two of the five with arrows, then charged in. I don't remember drawing my sword, or fighting. The next thing I remember was blood all over me, not mine, and three men dead by my sword. And Mayu, my love, dead with an arrow in his chest."

"I buried him, cut off the Han ears and left their bodies to rot, and rode back to the encampment. I went into Bei's yurt, and he asked where Mayu was. I said we were ambushed, he was killed, and I threw the ten ears on the floor of the tent, said he was avenged, and left."

"I have never had another friend or lover since. I can't. You are a good man, Galosga," she said tenderly, putting her hand on his arm, "but I have nothing to offer you."

"What you have given me, Hina, I will treasure. You are a powerful woman, to have lived the life you live. And that is more than just an interesting story."

"Thank you. Mayu's spirit said last night that telling this story would be like lancing a boil."

Now squeeze the boil and push the rest of the pus out, Hina.

Go away, Mayu!

Do it, it is time, it will only hurt a little, then it will heal.

She took a very deep breath, exhaling it in a very long sigh. "All know that part. Now there is the part I have always kept hidden. You will not think well of me when I tell that part, but I must." She took another deep breath, paused and continued.

"Mayu and I went on patrol together often to be alone and make love. We were shirking our duty, but… we were in love. I invited him to make love that morning, and he turned me down, then a little later, he said it didn't look like we were going to find any Han, so why not? But the Han almost rode over us, we barely had time to get up and on our horses. He was knocked off before he could mount." Her eyes were beginning to burn and she rubbed them hard. *"We can tell this without tears! Damn you, Mayu, help to get through this without tears!*

"They not only used him for target practice, being very careful to not hit anything fatal, but then they gelded him like a horse, they held up his man parts and laughed, then threw them in the dirt! My first arrow was for him, he was hurting, the blood pouring down between his legs, and he would never again be whole. He smiled… when he saw me aim for his chest. He mouthed the words 'I love you!' as I shot him." A tear trickled down her cheek.

Good job, Hina! I will always love you, but I think I will leave you two alone now.
I will always love you, too, Mayu. Thank you for making me do this.

Eight years of dammed up emotions broke in an instant. She gasped, sobbed and seized Galosga with all her might, burying her head in his shoulder, hanging onto him as though her life depended on it. She cried for Mayu, she cried for herself, she cried for crying, and she cried for not having cried a long time ago.

"Let it out, *huldaji*, let it all out. It's been in there way too long." He stroked her gently. Finally, the sobbing subsided, and she rested in his arms.

CHAPTER 62: THE MIGRATION BEGINS

Galosga and Hina returned to the encampment by midmorning. They had not made love after her cathartic storytelling; it would have seemed anti-climactic. He just held her for a very long time until she went to sleep in his arms. They rode back slowly in silence. On arrival, they each went to their respective yurts, with the simplest of farewells.

Hina's *arban* had nearly completed dismantling the ten-foot yurt, her traveling bags and bedroll stacked neatly outside. She was greeted by Hadyu, her second-in-command. "Good morning!" he said cheerily. "We moved your stuff out so we could start early. Good ride?"

"Yes, it was, indeed, Hadyu, a very good ride,' she said as she dismounted and rearranged her clothing.

"Is the Tiger Lady maybe taking a mate?" he asked with a grin. "You have never taken the same man twice."

She punched him on the shoulder in mock anger, and said with the faintest of smiles, "We had a good ride. Leave it at that."

"Something is up! I thought I saw her smile!" he said to his fellows.

Me, take a mate? He'll be gone in a few months, going west to try to get back to his home in the mountains. But, still, why not? Nearly every other person in the whole thousand has a 'mate,' either a wife or a partner, except me. Well, I will think on this later.

She turned a hand with bundling the big yurt and its support poles, which was reduced to a reasonably small package to be loaded onto a complaining camel.

When Galosga got to the *Da Qin* encampment, he also took some kidding from the group. "I'm sure you are worn out after a morning with Hina, so we put you in the oxcart to recover!" quipped Shmuel.

"No need, Shmuel, just a good ride!" he said, laughing.

Ibrahim had procured a white yurt for the group to replace the light two-person tents for the winter. Still bundled up, it had already been loaded onto the oxcart, over the folded two man tents they had been using. The oxcart was fairly large, about five feet wide and ten feet long. It was big enough to haul all their belongings and several passengers, sheltered from the weather by a circular white felt canopy stretched over bamboo half-circle ribs over the wagon bed.

After midday meal, Bohai bid the *Da Qin* party farewell and headed south back to Tongchuan, after dropping off one last package of goods to the *Shanyu*.

The migration began. While the group was a tenth the size of what had been the usual Xiongnu encampment, thousands of people and tens of thousands of animals on the move at once is still an impressive sight. Gaius and Antonius, part of the southern perimeter security, had galloped up to a rise, on the watch for Han, hostile Xiongnu, or bandits.

They conversed in Latin, now so seldom used that they were afraid they might forget it entirely. "Look at that line! Must be five miles long!" said Antonius.

Five hundred slow moving oxcarts, each with several horses in tow, and as many heavily laden camels, made up the center of the moving mass, with hundreds of people, dogs and goats milling among them on foot. The white canopies of the oxcarts dipped and lurched rolling over the rough roadless steppe grassland. Following them was a herd of horses, with riders whipping back and forth around the unmounted animals, directing them with whoops, whistles and calls, keeping them generally moving in the same direction. Ahead of the convoy were thousands of camels, sheep and goats. Some of their herdsmen were on foot, some on horseback, using dogs to shepherd the animals. From a mile away, Gaius and Antonius could hear the barking dogs, screaming children, calls of the herdsmen, bells of the sheep and goats, and complaining grunts from the camels, the cacophony of a small city on the move.

On either side, more mounted guards, uniformly clad in beige and black, cantered along beside, riding in a never-ending wheel clockwise around the center body of the migration, their flags snapping in the crisp early October air.

"I thought our oxcart days were over," said Gaius, shifting in his saddle. "They'll be lucky to make ten or fifteen miles a day!"

"Aye, an' a few more of them than us when we were on the road. They do this twice a year and cover thousands of miles in both directions."

"Tough people!"

Back in Luoyang, the *taiwei* military commander had received intelligence of *Shanyu* Bei's imminent departure from the Hetao plateau on his route west. This was be the last one, as indications were the Huyan clan had decided to join the rest of the beaten northern Xiongnu around the Altai mountains thousands of *li* to the west. Good riddance. Bei's clan was the biggest of the few remaining holdouts. The *taiwei* gave orders that they be allowed to trade enroute at Bayan Nur, Yinchuan, and Liqian, with further stops to be determined by the weather. They were not be molested by the army unless they launched raids; the band was too minuscule to cause much trouble.

Since they were stopping at Liqian, he notified the *weiwei*, as the minister of guards had dispatched Wang Ming to Gansu Province, against the chance that Si Huar and Si Nuo might attempt to contact family there. And if so, they would lead them to the other *Da Qin*. The Son of Heaven had issued strict orders that they not be harmed if found, and returned for consultation with him and then freed to return home. Si Huar was Ming's, to do with as he wished.

Gaius and Antonius found the daily routine to be not at all unlike a Roman army route march, in which the troops might cover twenty miles in a day while engineers scouted ahead for a suitable campsite. The Xiongnu seemed to follow a similar pattern, at night re-erecting their yurts in predetermined secure locations, in the morning taking them down to move on.

The two, with their military experience, had been invited to participate in *Shanyu* Bei's planning sessions, conducted in *han-yu* for their benefit. There was, however, little for them to contribute. The Xiongnu knew the terrain intimately, and their skirmishing plan left the soldiers little to improve upon, hundreds of riders constantly circling the main body to protect against any intruder.

But Xian Bohai's last package, dropped off in the morning, was something of considerable interest.

Bei produced some packages wrapped in rice paper. "Bohai left twenty of these for us this morning. He said they were very hard to come by. They appear to be a disassembled crossbow of some sort." The *zuun* company commanders peered at the parts, as did Gaius and Antonius.

Antonius picked up the large rectangular box, eighteen inches long, six inches wide, and two inches thick. The long thin top was open, and the box was hollow inside. A small round hole about an inch in diameter penetrated the front side. The other pieces were a two-foot crutch-like stock ending in a curved brace about six inches long, an unstrung and unmounted bow, and a fist-sized paper wrapping containing small metal parts.

"I think I know what this is, Bei! I saw one of these up in the bowmaker's shop in Luoyang, remember, Gaius? He demonstrated it, but wouldn't let us touch it. A state secret."

"Yes, I think you're right, Antonius. It's disassembled, but that's what it is. He called it a *lian-yu*, a continuous crossbow, or something like that. Did Bohai provide arrows?"

One of the *zuun* commanders opened a paper package to disclose several hundred arrows. Antonius picked one up. "Yes, that is what they are. No fletches, very small dart-like point. Bei, do you have someone here who works on crossbows? We don't know how to put one together, but he can probably figure it out, if we show him where the strange pieces go."

They summoned the bowsmith, and he quickly had one assembled in working order.

"It's too dark now. We'll try this out tomorrow, but it looks right. That bowmaker worked it like this," Antonius said, bracing the crutch-like bar on the end of the weapon against his thigh. "And he got off ten shots about as fast as I could count... one, click-clack, two, click-clack, that fast. You have a hell of a weapon here. If we can train some people to use these, together they can get off about a thousand shots a minute. Not too accurate, no fletches and no way to aim, but it will sure make someone put their heads down. You might want to have your arrow smiths make up some more arrows though, you'll go through that pack in a few minutes."

They agreed for a test firing the next day. After the meeting, Hina approached Antonius. "May I join you at your yurt?" she asked.

"Sure, come with us and share dinner and some *kumis*," answered Antonius. "You don't have reputation for socializing, though."

"In your case, I will make an exception. I find you all interesting. Antonius, you and Marcia remind me of some people I once knew." *And once was!*

They arrived at the yurt, where Marcia and Demosthenes were preparing dinner outside for the group. Everyone else, including Galosga, were out.

"Hello, *domina*, looks like unexpected company."

Marcia wiped sweat from her brow and ran her hand through her scraggly black hair. Although the weather was cool, the fire was not. She put down the ladle, wiped her hands on her trousers, and came over to extend her hand. "Hello, Hina. Still talking to me?"

"I am always happy to talk to you," she said with a shy smile, her first in many years, accepting Marcia's in a firm soldier's wrist clasp.

"Even after my terrible display of swordsmanship? Your people seemed to be very pleased that I lost so fast."

"Actually the opposite. They expect me to fight, as they expect any of their men to fight, no matter the odds. But for someone like you to choose to fight when the odds are all against you, that is high courage, especially if you lose. They were cheering for you, Marcia"

"That makes me feel better, but I still can't fight."

"We will talk about this later. I am hungry."

They sat down to eat and drink, then as the sky turned dark, they shared more *kumis*.

"I want to talk about Marcia. I understand what you are doing, and Antonius, you want Marcia, if she has to fight, to be able to defend herself."

"I'm not sure I want her fighting at all. It's her idea, but I think she can only get herself killed. I keep trying to show her that it's out of the question," answered Antonius. Marcia sat silently, clasping her knees to her chest as they talked about her.

Hina shifted her attention to speak to Marcia. "You remind me of myself a long time ago. You're not as big, but you are as stubborn, and I like that."

"Thank you, but I agree with Antonius, it seems hopeless."

"Antonius, you are teaching Marcia how to fight like a man, and she will lose to a man that way, every time. Almost every man a woman fights will have the advantage in weight, strength, reach and experience, like you over me. And if you hadn't gloated over your victory before you had it, you would have beaten me."

She turned back to the girl. "Marcia, I would like to teach you to fight like a woman. I had to learn that the hard way, without a woman to guide me. But you have me to help you."

"I think I would like that."

"I don't think you will like it at all. I am going to teach you the art of fighting, and it won't be fun. It will involve pain, getting knocked down, hurt to the point of crying, getting back in the fight when you don't think you can." Hina turned back to Antonius. "You and she are lovers, and you can't do that, though you know, as a soldier, exactly what I mean."

"She's right, Antonius, I have seen you use your centurion's hickory stick quite routinely on your troops, and I can't see you using it on her, no way," added Gaius, smiling.

"What is different about fighting as a woman?" asked Marcia.

"Many things. If the man is the bigger and stronger, you are the faster and lighter. And you must anticipate what he is about do, before even he knows it. Antonius probably understands some of what I am saying, but not all."

"You make sense, Hina. Do you want to take over her training?" asked Antonius.

"No, I want you to continue the sword drill, it's a good strength and agility training. Teach her the science of fighting, I will teach her the art. And the camp loves to watch. It's the fun part of training, and at least some training should be fun.

"This pain... blood or broken bones?" he said, fixing Hina with a suspicious gaze.

"Not very much blood, nothing needing more than a bandage. Bruises, not breaks, mostly not intentional," she said, with another uncharacteristic smile.

"I think you sound like a centurion," using the Latin phrase. "That's what I am, a leader of many men. That's what you should be some day. I have had the same concerns, so what you say is good. If she insists on fighting, I want her to be good."

Marcia agreed with some enthusiasm, "Yes, I'll do it. When do we start?"

"Good, I want to do our training out of the sight of the clan, on the road tomorrow, after Antonius finishes some work with my *arban* and my mid-morning patrol. You continue with the wooden swords, and enjoy them. And be careful, Antonius, she will put you down someday!"

"It would be my pleasure to take a fall from her, Hina. Some more *kumis?*"

"Please." Antonius led them into the yurt against the gathering chill, and brought out leather sacks of the liquor, while Marcia and Hina sat cross-legged on the floor. Marcia had adopted that style from her, finding it much more comfortable to sit for a long time that way.

Hina accepted the sack from Antonius, who joined them on the floor. She took a swig and passed it to Marcia. A fire, fed by pungent dung, illuminated the yurt adequately. Around the wall were sleeping rolls. "So, Marcia, have you ever been beaten in your life?"

Marcia laughed heartily, and Antonius sprayed *kumis* through his nose in a guffaw. "Several times a month, since I was twelve. No broken bones, but a chipped tooth, more bruises and black eyes than I could count. It is the reason the Hanaean government is searching for us!"

"Well, that is not the answer I was expecting. Your husband?"

"My consort. I was brought from Liqian to be trained in court *han-yu*, along with my brother Marcus, and several others, because we were fluent in *Da Qin* and *han-yu*. I was the only girl, so they put me in the concubinage and assigned me to the tender mercies of Wang Ming, who beat me regularly. Mostly I think he just enjoyed it. My brother, they... settled him down. But it allowed him to visit me in the concubinage."

"May *Tengri* strike the bastards dead! I thought you were a piece of palace fluff, with the way your polished court language shows through, but you and your brother have been through hell. Did you ever see your family after they took you to – where?"

"Luoyang. No. We were not allowed to write. Even when we passed Liqian on our way west six years ago, we were not allowed to stop and see them. I don't even know if they are still alive, but that is why it is important for us to go to Liqian."

"You and I are the same age, and have similar stories. When I was twelve, my encampment was burned, and I never knew if my family escaped, were captured, or were killed. I became a soldier, you became a concubine. So how did you and Antonius come to meet?"

So Marcia rehashed the whole story, leaving Luoyang at sixteen with the Gan Ying expedition, in tow behind Wang Ming, the trip to the *Da Qin* capital, the long sea voyage back and her freedom for a few months from Wang Ming, chatting with Antonius alongside the ship's rail." She took Antonius' hand and squeezed it in both of hers. "He was painfully shy," she said with a smile. "He didn't know what to do with me, was always afraid he would insult me. He put me on a pedestal like a fine statue, far above his station. No one had ever made me feel like that."

"So you became lovers then?"

"No, we didn't become lovers until we were falsely accused of it, and I was accused of trying to kill Wang Ming, which was true. We made love for the first time in a filthy jail cell in the North Palace, sentenced to death, with my brother, Aulus and Gaius keeping watch so the guards didn't notice. Antonius says making love in a yurt with nine others is almost as bad." She laughed, and Antonius sort of harrumphed. If the light had been better, Hina would have noticed him blush.

"There certainly is no privacy in a yurt. I live with the nine men of my *arban*, myself." Hina was enjoying this, but unsure how to deal with it. She had never been on close personal terms with any woman: most she intimidated, some she made jealous, and a few thought that with her mannishness, she was after them. She had never had a conversation with a woman or a man this intimate. These people seemed to just welcome her into all their secrets.

Marcia continued with the story of the jailbreak, Tongchuan and her near loss of Antonius. "It was in that cave, while the fight was raging, that I realized that if they lost, I would go back to what I had been. And I was helpless. I don't ever want to be helpless again."

"Well, you two have some very interesting stories to tell. More *kumis*, Antonius?"

He refilled her bowl, and she continued. "When I wanted to become a fighter, my trainer was asked if he could make a fighter out of me. He said no, but if I was a fighter, he could make me a better one. I would say the same about you. We will start tomorrow."

Galosga came in to join them around the fire, along with Marcus, while the other six, made their pleasantries and headed for their bedrolls. Hina passed Galosga the sack of *kumis*. "You have some interesting friends, Galosga."

"I do indeed, *huldaji*, I do indeed."

Marcia offered a suggestion. "You are welcome to sleep here tonight, Hina. If we can keep it quiet here, I am sure you can too." She giggled a bit and gave her a knowing glance.

"Let me tell my second where I am, and our plans for tomorrow, and I'll be back. Try to stay awake till I get back, Galosga… and thank you, Marcia."

The following morning, Hina awoke early to the warmth of Galosga beside her. He was lying on his side, facing away from her. She turned to snuggle her naked body spoon-fashion against his, caressing his broad chest; she kissed his shoulder. In all of her sexual escapades, she had never slept with a man, not even with Mayu. She wished she had time to rekindle the fires that had burned so bright last night, but everyone would be rising very soon to strike camp, and she needed to be with her *arban*. Yes, she did indeed seem to be taking a mate, for as long as she had him.

And this yurt brought back memories of a time when she was a child with a family. She was becoming very comfortable with all of these people, they were like family. She also feared that familiarity. *No, not now, not yet. I am not ready for it.*

Galosga grunted, and she kissed his shoulder again. "Time to get up. I have to look after my *arban*."

"And we have to get up also." He rolled her around and kissed her once last time on the mouth, a wet languorous kiss, holding her soft breast against his chest. "Till the next time, *huldaji*."

CHAPTER 63: LEARNING TO FIGHT LIKE A WOMAN

Antonius and the two *arban* squads stayed behind as the encampment departed. They could easily catch up with the plodding migration after checking out the *lian-yu* weapons Bohai had surreptitiously delivered to them. They had set up some bails of hay as targets to assess their range and accuracy.

Target shooting was not an option, explained Antonius; the fletchless arrows reduced the accuracy, and the thigh-mounted firing position prevented aiming at anything other than the general direction for the arrow to fly. He loaded ten arrows into the top of the rear-hinged wooden magazine on the stock of the weapon, pointed it in the general direction of the targets, and worked the magazine to arm, load and fire it in a single fluid motion. The mechanism released the arrow with a thunk, to fly in a high arc and land in the vicinity of one of the targets a hundred yards down range. Antonius then worked the action rapidly, firing the remaining nine arrows in about ten seconds. "That's all there is to it," he said, handing his weapon to Hina for her turn at firing.

Hina stepped forward, loaded under Antonius' supervision, then fired off ten rounds.

"This is a nice weapon for the way the Hanaeans fight, Antonius. They drag thousands of peasants from their villages, put this in their hands and in a few weeks a line of them can lay down enough arrows that they have to hit something. This is the way we fight." She took her bow from behind her back and ten arrows from her quiver, nocked one and drew her bow, holding the remaining arrows in her bow hand. She aimed high at the sky then brought it down to the aim and released it. The target visibly shuddered under the impact. She took another arrow, then another, until she had fired all of them. Not as fast as the *lian-yu*, but when the group came up to the target, the ten arrows were buried to their fletches in the straw; an open hand easily covered their impact points. The *lian-yu* arrows protruded from the ground around the target. None had hit.

"All we can do with this weapon would be to waste arrowheads, and arrowheads are precious." She shook her head, and her *arban* agreed. "Let's see if we can sell them to some Hanaean rebel warlord, he probably pay a fair price for these *lian-yu*.

The riders mounted up to surge after the migration. After their rendezvous, Hina went for an uneventful mid-morning patrol, returning in the afternoon to find Marcia, and the two rode off for their first training session.

They began with a bit of serious riding. Marcia was going to need more work than Galosga. As a concubine, she had ridden little, and lacked Galosga's confidence with animals.

After a few miles, they dismounted, leaving the Mongolian ponies to tether themselves. The first order of business was conditioning, and they started with a hard run; a hard run for Marcia, that is, followed by strength exercises. The girl was in good condition, but she needed much more work to prepare herself for a long, drawn-out fight. Finally, they were ready for the first training bout. Marcia was breathing heavily, sweating slightly despite the fall chill.

Hina began with a lecture. "First, and foremost, you are a small girl. If there is any way for you to avoid a fight with a man, do so. If you decide to fight, be prepared to kill him. You must always be emotionally ready to do so." Marcia nodded. "Now, for the best rule of fighting like a woman: there is a golden moment when a man will not take you seriously as a fighter because you are a woman. If you can kill him then, you will save yourself a lot of trouble. Usually, it comes at the beginning of the fight."

Marcia nodded again.

"Always expect the unexpected. Are you pregnant now?" asked Hina.

Marcia was taken aback by the discontinuity. "No, I am not. Why…" She didn't get to finish her question before Hina whirled and struck her full force in the belly, knocking the wind out of her and doubling her over. Marcia's eyes squeezed shut in agony, arms around her midsection, struggling to draw a breath. After several seconds she wheezed in a gulp of air and painfully straightened up a bit. "You bitch!" she groaned. "What the hell did you do that for?"

"Expect the unexpected. If you react like that in a fight, you will be a dead woman. We were trained to make our stomach muscles a solid shield for our guts. You will get that training. And you must expect, endure and even welcome pain in a fight. Let that pain light your anger, and let your reason focus that anger into white-hot fury to destroy your opponent."

The rest of the afternoon, Hina and Marcia exchanged blows with their hands, as the smaller woman learned to evade and deflect blows. "Never take your eyes off your opponent's eyes. His eyes will tell you where he will hit next. And your own eyes will never reveal your next intended strike. Your hand can find its target without you staring at it! Again!"

On the way back, Hina rode off with Marcia's horse in tow behind Eagle, leaving Marcia to run after her, watching the galloping horses disappear into the distance. She had no idea how far she might have to run, but she would drop dead before admitting defeat. Fiercely angry with Hina, she struggled on, mile after mile, *Let your pain light your anger, let your reason turn that anger to white hot fury... you bitch!*

Finally she caught up with Hina, horses standing at ease drinking from a little rivulet. Hina smiled and tossed her a waterskin. "Don't drink it all in one gulp, you'll throw it up! And flop down for a few minutes, you've earned it. Playtime is over, you can relax!"

After about fifteen minutes and most of the waterskin, Marcia began to feel like she might survive the day. They mounted up and trotted leisurely back to camp.

"You did well today. You are tougher than you look, for a piece of palace fluff," said Hina, mockingly.

"You bitch!" said Marcia, spitting out the words as she had done throughout the grueling day. Then she reconsidered; she had got about as good a compliment as she would get from Hina... *that bitch...* and she managed a weak smile. "Thank you. Does it get better?"

"No, it gets worse. Much worse. But you'll do fine."

"Will you be staying with us again tonight? You are welcome."

"I would like to, but the men in my *arban* don't get more than one night a week with their families, so I can't allow myself more personal time than they."

"Galosga will miss you."

"And I him. And all of you."

The training continued for about six weeks, several times a week, whenever Hina's other duties permitted. Meanwhile the migration crawled the five hundred miles to the outskirts of Liqian, passing through the lush green hills of Bayan Nur and the outpost of Yinchuan on the way. Hina had not intended for the training to be as intense as it became for Marcia, but whatever she demanded of her, the slip of a girl rose to meet and exceed her expectations. At the end of several weeks, Marcia had not only mastered basic self-defense with hands, feet, teeth, club, knife and sword, but without realizing it, was moving on into serious combat. She mastered knife-fighting, Hina's recommended fighting style for her because of her diminutive size. "A sword is useless if man rushes inside your reach and pins your arms to your side," she explained. "But if your opponent uses a sword, you must also."

Hina was impressed with her spunk and courage, and her willingness to reach higher and higher levels. She was also intrigued with the idea that this girl, so much smaller than Hina in strength and size, might yet become a credible fighter in her own right. So over the next several weeks, she expanded the regime.

Marcia learned to fight with both knife and sword together, to fight with either hand, and to change hands in mid-fight in case of injury. She learned archery, both standing and from horseback, and finally at last clinging to one side of the horse as a shield and shooting under the horse's throat, hitting the target without falling off. The many preceding attempts at this tactic had not ended well, but each time Marcia got herself up out of the dirt, remounted and tried again. Not bad for a girl who, a few months earlier, had trouble staying upright in the saddle.

During each session, Hina ensured that Marcia hated her intensely, but at the end of each session, that mockery and fury evaporated, and they rode back, chatting idly.

Hina had never been around women much the past ten years, much less had a female friend. She found it comforting to be able to discuss "women's things," things no one had taught her, about how her body functioned and how to care for it.

She would deliver Marcia, exhausted, to her yurt after each session, where the girl promptly collapsed onto her bedroll, often too tired to even wash off the sweat of her exertions. If Hina were on her weekly visit, she would stay up and talk with the men.

Antonius was impressed by the depth of training she was giving Marcia, which went far beyond what he had expected, and it was showing up in his own training with the group; Marcia had just won her first training bout, against Yakov. They compared styles, finding that they both did much the same things to their new people, for the same reasons. Like Hina, he was curious how far Marcia would go, and like Hina, he was concerned she might someday put herself in a situation beyond her ability.

Hina also liked the other soldiers, the standoffish Gaius, the scholarly Demosthenes, and the rebellious bandit-turned-deckhand Shmuel. They all related to her on a soldierly level, and seemed to take no notice of her sex. They swapped stories, shared experiences, and laughed at each other's outrageous jokes or stories.

Hina liked Aulus, with his stories of Rome, the Senate, politics, and business ventures that spanned vast oceans, though these were things beyond her comprehension. She had never been to a city, except passing by them in the distance on her travels. She had no idea what it might be like to live in one, or the splendid houses like he described.

She was also intrigued by the fatherly Ibrahim and his rascally adopted son Yakov, although she had never seen the sea and had only a vague idea what a ship might look like.

Finally, there was Marcus, shy quiet Marcus. She knew his carefully-guarded secret, having learned it from Marcia, a secret he shared with her dear dead Mayu.

She began to feel very warm inside, as something inside, long frozen, thawed. Yes, indeed, for now, she had a family in these people, and she would miss them very much when they went on their way. *And thank you, Mayu, for helping me find them.*

And of course, there was the ever-strange, ever-wonderful Galosga, the man whose name inexplicably meant, 'he who fell'. He who fell from the stars into her life.

During one of those meetings, the men convinced Hina to introduce her "mate" to her other family, her *arban*. She had been reluctant to do so, but Antonius pointed out that they might consider Galosga a distraction to her, and therefore a threat, unless they met him.

So she took him around the *arban* the next day, expecting sniggers and jokes from her men, aged between fifteen and eighteen. But Galosga was a giant among these men, fully six feet tall like Hina, broad-shouldered and well-muscled.

Hadyu greeted him with a big smile, clasping Galosga's shoulders with both hands. "Welcome! So you are the Mongol who finally tamed the Tiger Lady! Tell us how you did it."

Galosga returned the shoulder clasp with a laugh. "The man has not been born that can tame the *huldaji*. She is as wild as ever!"

That got it off to good start. The men were as intrigued with him and his stories as she had been. She showed them the stone arrowhead and they shook their heads in amazement.

While her men gathered around her new mate, her *zuun* commander walked up. Would he be displeased with this relationship?

"So this is your mate, Hina?"

Hina tried to look defiantly into his emotionless, cold eyes.

"He is."

The commander's brown eyes crinkled a bit around the edges in his leather face, as just the barest of smiles crossed his lips. "It's about time, Hina. We are glad to see this."

"Really?" she answered, puzzled.

"Hina, you have been like a bow with a bowstring an inch too short. Such a bow looks fine, but you never know when it will snap or shatter when you draw it. We have watched you become a fine fighter, but we all have been concerned that you were too tightly strung... since Mayu. It looks like this man has done a fine job of restringing your bow."

"Yes, he has, and the other *Da Qin*…they have become like family to me."

"Everyone needs family, a place to unstring their bow completely. What will you do when they leave?"

"I'll find another mate, another family… I think I am ready for that now," she said. Galosga and the *Da Qin* would be hard to replace.

"Good… by the way, you have had that *arban* too long, and it's time to move Hadyu up to command it. There are some *zuuns* coming open, and your name has been mentioned to the *shanyu*. No promises, though."

She smiled broadly, for the first time in years. "Yes, sir!"

The migration traded in Bayan Nur, then south to Yinchuan for more trading, where they sold the twenty contraband *lian-yu* for a dozen silver coins, which they promptly melted down for jewelry. They traded animals, wool and leather goods for wood, precious on the treeless steppes, jewelry, iron, both finished products and raw metal ready for smelting, tools and occasionally contraband. Occasionally, someone picked up a bride for a son, or gave away a daughter, as marriages within the clan were frowned upon.

The Xiongnu believed the best fighters became possessed by the spirit of a particular animal *persona* unique to them that gave them its characteristics. Hina's *persona* was the steppe tiger, long, lean and powerful. When she got into her battle crouch, knees flexed, back slightly bent, arms extended with sword in one hand, dagger in the other, she looked the part, stalking, side-stepping slowly, about to spring on its prey, green eyes glowing with a predatory light.

Marcia sought her *persona*. She recalled a big feral cat that had invaded the concubinage. She had laughed as Marcus and the other eunuchs struggled to evict the unwilling cat. The animal puffed itself up as big as it could get, hissing angrily through its open mouth, baring its fangs. It raked the first man to reach for it, leaving four bleeding scratch marks across his forearms. The last man had gotten too close to the angry animal, and a furry bundle of squawling, spitting fury launched itself onto his face, then departed the concubinage in a high-speed zig-zag. Yes, that would be her *persona*. And when she got into her battle crouch against Hina, an angry hiss and growl came from her mouth. Unlike Hina, her dagger and sword played back and forth, constantly seeking a target. Yes, she was ready to leave her claw marks on any man who challenged her.

As they neared Liqian, Hina made a gift of the small light sword with which Marcia had been training.

"Marcia, I killed my first man with this when I was fourteen. Use it wisely."

They rode back to the encampment, discussing the upcoming trip to Liqian, Marcia's hopes for her family to still be there, and a lot of very intimate things. "Did you have any sisters, Hina?" Marcia asked. The woman had never discussed her lost family, and Marcia hoped this would not be a bad question for her.

Hina smiled; she did that more and more these days, no longer self-consciously. "No, I was the baby, with five older brothers. Even ... before then... I preferred riding with them instead of working with little girls my age." But then her darkness settled in.

"It's all right," said Marcia, and she let the rhythm of the hoofs fill the silence for a few minutes. Then "Marcus is my only brother. Would you be my sister, since I don't have one either?"

Hina brightened up again. "Can you put up with me?"

"Gladly." Marcia swayed gracefully in the Xiongnu saddle to the clip-clops of plodding hoofs. "You and Antonius are so much alike, you two could be twins, born to different mothers many years and a continent apart. Both of you so hard and stern on the outside, and so full of love inside it burns you up," she said with a laugh.

"Seems incestuous, your sleeping with your sister's twin brother."

CHAPTER 64: HOMECOMING

Liqian was a small village of a few thousand people, on the north side of a flat grassland in the shadow of Mount Wudang. The grassland was broken up in spots with orderly rows of tall slender trees, dividing parts of it into rectangular checkerboard patterns; further out, it was treeless. The plain was well-watered by rivers flowing out of the snow-capped Qilian range of mountains to the north.

The Great Silk Road passed a few miles south of Liqian, but the town was too small to offer much in the way of accommodations. Caravans did stop in Liqian for its one claim to fame, fine red wines made from grapes.

The Roman settlers found the Hanaen rice wine tasteless, and had acquired some grape plantings from a passing caravan from Shiraz in Parthia. They planted them on the hills to the east of their settlement, to make a fine red wine quite acceptable to Roman palates. Those hills were now covered with carefully tended grapevines, from which they now made both red and white wines. The vineyards bottled the wine in wax-sealed glazed ceramic jars, emblazoned with Hanaean characters on one side bearing the town's name, and "SPQR" underneath a six-teated she-wolf on the other side, the foster mother to Romulus and Remus.

The town looked forward to the biennial Xiongnu migration, because those of that ethnicity could renew family ties, marry off sons and daughters, and catch up on clan news, mostly bad now in the years following the battle of Ilkh Bayan. And everyone looked forward to trading various things for fresh livestock.

Wang Ming was in the provincial capital of Lanzhou, about a hundred miles east of Liqian, in the company of thirty military representatives of the *taiwei* commander-in-chief, and they, too, were awaiting the arrival of the Huyan clan. They had reason to believe that the *Da Qin* would be traveling among them, as it would be almost impossible for them make the trek alone. However, they were under strict orders from the *taiwei* to approach the clan under a flag of truce, inquire of the *Da Qin* presence, and invite them to return to another meeting with the Son of Heaven. They were not to detain them, under orders from the Son of Heaven himself.

Ming had no issues with allowing the *Da Qin* to come and go as they saw fit, they were of no concern to him. But the bitch Si Huar was his concubine, and he would take her back to Luoyang, regardless of some faraway *Da Qin* warlord thinking she was his subject. She was Hanean by birth, and his by law. He contemplated ingenious ways to make her life miserable, in revenge for her whoring around, for trying to kill him, and for causing him to lose face.

The Huyan clan had paralleled the Hwang He River on its western bank from Yinchuan, taking advantage of the good grassland on that side, and followed the river to where it emerged from the mountains past Zhongwei as churning, white-water rapids. They continued east on the plains to Wuwei, where they stopped to plan the approach to Liqian. The clan had done this many times, so there was nothing new, but it would be their last.

Liqian would greet the arrival of the migration with their customary town fair. The clan would pitch their encampment a mile or so south of town, clear of the town's herding and farming areas. They would pitch some yurts in the center of town as a bazaar to exchange wares, sit around, tell old stories, and sing old songs accompanied by the *morin khuur*, the square, two-stringed horsehead fiddle.

Gaius and Ibrahim assembled the *Da Qin* group to discuss their strategy. If any place were under surveillance, the translators' hometown would be the one. Ibrahim would send Yakov along with the clan's advance team, to assess the situation. If the authorities were actively looking for them there, he would return to warn them, and they would decamp, move off quickly, to rejoin the Xiongnu at some prearranged date and place. Gaius would not risk all their lives for a family reunion, however bittersweet it might be for Marcus and Marcia to come this close and not see their family. Some letters, written in Latin and delivered through the Xiongnu to their parents, would have to suffice, expressing their love and assuring them that they were alive and well. And the Xiongnu would accept a letter back in return.

On the other hand, if the town were quiet, then a meeting might be arranged, best done here in the camp. They wanted as few townspeople involved as possible, because tongues would inevitably wag, and the authorities would eventually learn of their presence here and be in hot pursuit. There was only one road west, with the rugged Qilian mountains on one side and the desert on the other.

Antonius had written a rather cryptic letter in Latin for Marcus and Marcia to their family and sealed it with a red wax seal embossed with the six-teat she-wolf. He signed using his last name, which he was sure the Han authorities neither knew nor could pronounce.

Yakov rode in with the advance team, and after a few discrete questions found that there no authorities in town, no one inquiring of the *Da Qin*, no strangers. Just the regular outsiders who came in from neighboring villages to take part in festivities. So Yakov then executed the next step.

It was the custom of the advance team to visit many of the houses to inquire of their interest in trade goods, so that the clan could have an ample supply of the items most in demand. So a visit to the Liu Shiu family, as their surname was pronounced in *han-yu*, would not be unusual, and Yakov could slip inside for a brief private conversation. That was likely to be emotional and should not be held where others might see. They arranged that call to be the last.

When they reached the house, a matronly plump woman in her fifties answered the knock, her black hair tinged with gray, done up in a bun. She was dressed in black peasant clothing of no particular shape.

She said curtly "I am not interested in anything," and turned to close the door.

Yakov could see Marcia's face distinctly in the woman's fine oriental features, delicate epicanthic folds that narrowed her eyes without imparting too much of a slant. But Marcia certainly got her blue eyes from her father, this woman's were brown. He spoke his carefully rehearsed Latin phrase: "*Ave, Vera!* Hail, Vera."

She squinted at him suspiciously: "*Quis es? Te non cognosceo!* Who are you? I don't know you."

Yakov returned to *han-yu* and said, "I am sorry, that is all the Latin I know. I have a message from some people very special to you. May I come in?" He handed her a scroll sealed with the stamped figure of a wolf.

Still suspicious, she beckoned him in. She looked long and hard at it.

"Is your husband home?" asked Yakov.

"No, he passed away last year."

"I am sorry to hear that." She kept fingering it, trying to guess the contents.

Obviously Roman, the young man had used Latin, so... what? Finally she broke the seal and rolled it open. There, written in a fine uncial script was a letter she had waited a decade to see:

"*Dear Marius Lucius and Vera Lucia,*

We hope this letter finds you in good health. I have had the pleasure of traveling with acquaintances of yours, M. et M. L., who send their regards and would like to see you at the earliest opportunity.

A. Aristides,

PP, Leg XII Ful I Coh

Vera Lucia put her hand to her chest, and suddenly felt very faint. There was a roaring in her ears, and the whole world seemed to come to a focus on this fine piece of paper in her hand. 'M. et M. L.' could only be Marcus and Marcia, her long lost children. In the company of a Roman centurion. She was Hanaean, but she had been around things Roman for the thirty years she had been wed into the Lucian household. The man's script was good, and the abbreviations after the man's name were familiar. Why had her children not written personally?

All of a sudden the horror of that day came back to her, the men holding her husband at bay with drawn swords, Marcus fighting, being beaten, Marcia and herself screaming as the two were taken away by force, to serve some purpose, somewhere, and nothing heard afterwards. Were they dead or alive, free or in jail? Now this…

"Young man, if this is a trick, we will run the whole encampment into the desert!"

"It is no trick, Vera. Marcia asked me to give you this." He handed the woman a small pin. "Marcus and Marcia have escaped from Luoyang, but are in considerable difficulty with the authorities, so communication must be careful. They are in the Xiongnu camp with Antonius, the letter's author, and with a Roman *legatus* and a Senator. We have transportation if you wish to go there. But do not tell anyone of this until we are gone."

The pin was a gift she had given Marcia on her tenth birthday. She turned it over and over in her hand, tears running hotly down her cheeks. "Yes, let's go," she said, clutching the pin firmly in her hand.

Yakov's horsecart was waiting outside, loaded with cases of wine. They helped Vera in, then Yakov clicked the two horses into motion and they clattered off to the encampment. Vera kept staring at the pin, expecting Marcia to materialize from it.

They reached the encampment, perfunctorily challenged by Hina's *arban* gate guard. Yakov rolled up to the *Da Qin* yurt, dismounted and helped Vera down and into the yurt. Inside were Marcus and Marcia, flanked by the whole *Da Qin* contingent and a tall woman.

All were dressed in nearly identical style, Xiongnu beige winter felt coats over shirts, and black breeches stuffed into tall riding boots. All were armed with swords and daggers.

Amid great shouts of "Mother!", "Marcia!" and "Marcus!" the three collided in a loud, tearful hug. There was not much talking, just patting of backs, sobbing and kissing, as ten years of separation fell away. In the course of this, they learned they had missed their father by a year, with his unfortunate death. After about five minutes, they finally separated. Marcia spoke in *han-yu*, "Mama, not everyone in here speaks Latin. We use *han-yu* so we can all talk, but we will speak Latin together later, when it is just us, all right?"

"Fine. But Marcia… you are armed? Are you a warrior of some kind?" Marcia had both a bow and sword crossed across her back, her dagger on the right side. And her small body rippled with new-found strength.

"Becoming one. My friend, Hina, she is Xiongnu, she is the warrior, and soon to be, well, sort of a centurion among them. Commander of a hundred men. She taught me what little I know of fighting."

"She doesn't do herself justice, Vera Lucia. She is the best fighting woman in the camp, after me," said Hina, proud of her protégé.

"I am the only fighting woman in the camp after her! Introductions, now! I will save the best for last. Mother, this is Senator Aulus Aemilius Galba, who leads this expedition, and *legatus* Gaius Lucullus, hopefully to command a legion when we get back. Yakov whom you met, Ibrahim, Galosga, Shmuel our rebel, and Demosthenes, they all saved our lives." Each nodded in turn as they were introduced. "And now for the best part, Mama, my future husband, if you approve, Antonius Aristides, *primus pilus Legio XII Fulminata!*"

"Future husband! Really!"

Just then the happy reunion was disrupted by one of Hina's men bursting in, running up to her. "Han soldiers on horseback, flag of truce."

"Excuse us," Hina said, and she exited the yurt at a clip.

"What is happening?" asked Vera.

"Nothing good," answered Antonius. "There's a price on our heads. You stay inside with Marcia and Marcus." Marcus drew his sword and held it ready.

The Hanaean troops pulled up by the encampment perimeter and remained on horseback. There were about thirty, all military except one well-clad civilian. The *shanyu* approached them on foot. The commander of the Hanaean squadron greeted him. "Long live *Shanyu* Bei of the Huyan clan. I bring you greetings from the Son of Heaven, who wishes you the best of good fortune on your journey to your new home in the Altai Mountains"

"He is the reason we are making the trip," answered the *shanyu,* acidly. "To what do I owe the pleasure of your company?"

"We have reason to believe that there may be a party of *Da Qin* traveling with you. We have a message for them."

The *Da Qin* party was gathered out of sight in the center of the compound, but well within earshot. Marcia had left her mother's side to stand alongside the men. At the last phrase, each of them, including Marcia, drew their swords simultaneously, the hissing of steel reaching the squadron commander's ear. "You may put back your weapons, please. The Son of Heaven has pardoned you, and ordered that any who harm you are to be executed. That is my message."

Aulus looked quizzically at Ibrahim, Gaius Antonius and Aulus. "Can we trust the bastards?"

"Does it matter?" answered Gaius. "Thirty men are not going to run down a thousand Xiongnu today, and if they intend to take us tomorrow, they'll come back with what they need. Let's go see what they have to say, since they know we are here."

Aulus and Gaius strode out to stand beside the *shanyu.* "I am Senator Aulus Aemilius Galba, representative of *Imperator Caesar Nerva Traianus Divi Nervae filius Augustus, Optimus Princeps,"* Aulus intoned Trajan's full name and titles in Latin, then in *han-yu,* "Emperor Caesar Nerva Trajan son of the Divine Nerva, the August one, Best Ruler," which came off well despite his Gansu country dialect.

"I see we will have little need for translators," said the commander, turning toward Wang Ming. Then back to Aulus, "You speak very well. May I commend you?"

"You need not. Please state your case," answered Aulus. He saw no merit in being polite. He hoped to goad them into showing their hand early if this was a trick.

"The Son of Heaven sends his respects, and would like to offer you his hospitality to resume the discussions that were so unfortunately interrupted last spring."

"You may tell the Son of Heaven that we have experienced his hospitality, and that of the *shanyu* here, and of the two, I much prefer *shanyu* Bei's. He has yet to sentence us to death, which was the cause of that 'unfortunate interruption.' I will, however, convey his respects to Emperor Trajan upon my return to Rome, and if he so wishes, my emperor may send a return delegation. I hope they fare better in Emperor He's court than did mine. I presume that I am in fact free to return to Rome, or is your intent to drag me back to Luoyang in chains like a common criminal if I refuse his offer to return voluntarily?"

There was brief but audible intake of breath by the commander at the mention of the Emperor's personal name, a great and potentially fatal insult. Aulus had made that choice knowingly and willingly. But the commander recovered, and continued, "You are under the Son of Heaven's personal protection in whatever you choose to do."

"Tell the Son of Heaven that we respect and appreciate his offer, and are forever in his debt. We will, however, return to Rome, and give our Emperor a favorable report on his great kindness." Aulus had indeed mastered some of the intricacies of Hanaean diplomatic language.

"A significant amount of gold and silver was found in your quarters after your departure. The Son of Heaven wishes you to know that it will be returned to the next delegation from your great nation, to do with as they see fit. I thank you, sir, and you are free to go about your business. Please accept a record of safe passage for the rest of your journey." A black–clad soldier scurried up to Aulus to put a sealed Hanaean document in his hand, then the commander whirled his horse about and the group rode off.

"Well, I'll be a son of a bitch, did Emperor He just pardon our asses?" hissed Antonius, as Aulus and Gaius came back and the riders vanished in the distance. Marcia quickly translated the document, confirming it was indeed their safe passage under the orders of the Son of Heaven.

"Looks like it, and they aren't going to spend the half million sesterces we left in our quarters, either. An unexpected touch of honor there."

"Looks like it," said Gaius. "Well, let's get back to the family reunion."

Inside, Vera was distraught. Marcia walked up and hugged her. "I was so afraid they were coming for you and Marcus, and I would lose you both all over again," her mother said.

"They won't take us so easily this time, Mama. Remember, I am the second-best fighting woman in the encampment."

They broke out the wine, took a case from the wagon, and gave the rest to *shanyu* Bei to distribute among the camp. "Watch that stuff, Bei, it's much stronger than that horse piss you drink. I don't want your men to get too high and wide too soon, all right?" cautioned Antonius.

Marcia picked where they left off. "So… Mother, what do you think of my choice of a husband? Do you approve?"

"I do, but when and where are you going to be married?"

"We were thinking of Rome, but now, the situation has changed. How about as soon as we can arrange it? Here with you! Besides, all of my friends are here, and they will be scattered to the four winds when we get to Rome. Antonius?"

"The sooner the better, *domina*," he said, in Latin, with a big grin. And turning to Ibrahim, "Security for the wedding? Looks like it may have gotten simpler. Anyone who wants to come can come, it looks like. Camp, town, everybody."

Aulus offered to officiate. He opened a flask of wine and started filling cups to toast the bride and groom.

Ibrahim smiled and nodded. Then he turned to Yakov, pulled out a pouch full of jingling coins and said in Aramaic, "Son, returnest thou to the winery and procurest all that they have. Methinks they will need much wine. Make as many trips as thou deem necessary."

CHAPTER 65: NIGHTMARE'S CONCLUSION

The upcoming wedding, so quickly announced, set the whole village and encampment abuzz, everyone wanting to take part in the momentous event. Liqian was marrying off one their own to a real Roman, a centurion at that, officiated by a Roman Senator. The Xiongnu were sharing the joy of the band of strange traveling companions they had come to know and love. Mama was, of course, ecstatic, though uncertain about Marcia's developing warrior skills under the tutelage of Hina, truly the most fearsome woman she had ever met, though also the most charming. She endeared herself to Vera by also calling her 'Mama,' because, after all, she was Marcia's 'sister.' And sisters played an important role in Xiongnu weddings.

It was going to be a Roman wedding, of course, but there were going to be a lot of other undercurrents. Galosga went hunting for deer, since among his people, the groom was supposed to provide venison. Ibrahim was setting up a makeshift Arabic *sewan* tent to roast goat for his part of the wedding feast. And of course, there was going to be good Liqian wine, lots of good Liqian wine. Yakov and Shmuel were trundling back and forth to town bringing it in by the cartload, as well as various items from the Lucian household.

Included in the lot were four togas, Marcus' old one, their father's, and two others on loan from his friends. Aulus had disposed of his and Marcus' clothes, and Gaius' and Antonius' military gear, outside of Luoyang. They set about finding some chalk to whiten them.

Mama contributed her own wedding dress, stored away thirty years, a cream *tunica recta* tied with the Knot of Hercules, with a flame-colored veil.

Marcia had her own duties to perform, to dedicate her childhood toys and locket to the *lares,* gods of the household. Her mother assured her that her toys were in her room, exactly where she had left them ten years ago. As this was going to be her first visit to the town and home where she grew up, she wanted to go alone to savor the memories.

It was a warm November afternoon, warm enough to dispense with the heavy jacket. She removed her weapons, but then reconsidered, fitting her dagger down her back on a throat lanyard. She wasn't comfortable completely unarmed now, though perhaps that was just pride.

She rode her horse into town, trotting slowly through familiar streets. She needed no guide, as she had burned the memory of home into her mind years ago. Here on this street along the southern edge, yes, that was Sulpicius' house, her Latin teacher. If she closed her eyes, she could hear the laughter of children running down the hill to master the complexity of Latin grammar. She smiled as she remembered the time she had struggled with the difference between the objective and dative cases until he hit her on the back of the head, saying "dative, dative, dative!", trying to ram the difference between the two into her mind.

Her home was along the same road that ran east and west along the edge of town, until it turned north to ascend a small hill. And there it was, seated far back amongst the tall familiar pine trees, away from the other houses. She tethered her pony at the bottom of the hill.

She followed the steep stone walkway that curved up and around bushes, once carefully tended, by a tree that bore the initials ML that she had carved when she was child, still there, welcoming her home. She put her fingers on the letters. "Thanks for waiting," she whispered.

She reached the wide, steep set of stairs that led to the wraparound porch, the deck well above her head as she started up the steps. She caught familiar scents she had not smelled in years, the smell of her mother's cooking, and that unmistakable scent that is home, made up of all the things a family uses in their own unique mix. She inhaled deeply, feeling at peace at last. She went inside to the common area, overlaid with an intricate Hanaean rug. A large table made of heavy wood planks sat in the middle, surrounded by stools… so many meals had she taken off these planks, so many stories. Here in the corner was a rocking chair where she would snuggle into her father's lap. And here in a scroll basket beside it, waiting for her, was his copy of Ennius' history that he would read to her, always reminding her at the end, '*Memento, tu es Romana,'*… Remember, you are a Roman girl. She touched the chair, setting it to rocking.

Hello, Papa, I am sorry I missed you. I have so much to tell you. I'm getting married. I heard, Marcia. Congratulations. He is a good man.

Her room was on the back, off to the right. Mama had not changed a thing since Marcia was taken. There at the foot of the bed was her toy box. She opened it, finding on top her wax notebook, and she leafed through the wooden pages. These were her last Latin lesson notes! And here was a set of bamboo strips, inscribed with an Hanaean poem. Mama gave her that for her twelfth birthday, just before they came for her.

She was rummaging through her chest of memories when she heard footsteps on the porch. Who? Mama? Marcus?

"Si Huar!" Stand up when I come in." That voice and that name she never wanted to hear again. *Take a deep breath to control panic, Hina had said.* She remained sitting, facing away from the voice, staring, deliberately unresponsive, into her toy box.

"Si Huar is dead, Wang," she answered, deliberately insulting him by using his surname. "That girl died in a prison cell in Luoyang. You may call me Marcia." She composed herself, quietly closed the lid, and gave a quick shrug of her shoulders to make sure the dagger was handy. *Glad I decided to bring that.* She put her hands on her thighs, stood up, still facing away, then slowly turned around.

She had been with very masculine, weather-beaten men for the past six months. She was surprised how effeminate Wang Ming now looked, with smooth skin, soft hands, an expensive blue robe with a black outer cloak, his hair done up in a black headpiece run through with pins. He used makeup, and he stank of perfume.

"Is that your whore name, now? I will call you by your civilized name, Si Huar, and beat you until you remember…" He had started forward, his hand raised to strike her, but in one fluid motion she recovered her dagger from its back scabbard and it gleamed in her right hand, pointing at his midsection. He stopped abruptly, his hand still raised.

Never fight with a man unless you are willing to kill him.

"No, Wang, not today, not ever again. Those times are over. Go home to Luoyang and leave us in peace here."

There is a golden moment, when a man will not take a woman seriously in a fight. If you kill him then, it will save you a lot of trouble later.

Wang Ming dropped his upraised hands to draw his own dagger. Marcia got into her fighting crouch, sidestepping around him, trying to keep him off balance, her dagger weaving back and forth. He followed her movements carefully.

His eyes, never take your eyes off his, they will tell where he will strike.

A sidewise shift of his eyes betrayed him. Marcia blocked it with her left forearm, pivoted and slashed at his silk robe, ripping the fabric but not striking meat.

He attempted another lunge, but again she evaded him, this time raking his left arm, drawing blood where the shorn silk had fallen away. The fight was on now. He was better, much better than she had expected. She had thought that once she showed her teeth, he would slink off in fear, but this was going to be her first real fight, and it could only end one way, with one of them dead on the floor. Her confidence waivered. This was not a training bout.

Suddenly he slashed fiercely across her upper chest, deliberately aiming for her breasts. His knife hit meat on the upper slope of her left breast. The pain and burning was intense. For a moment, she thought sure she was going to die here in her childhood home.

Let the pain ignite your anger, and let your reason focus that anger to white hot fury.

Her cat *persona* took her spirit. She hissed, which turned into a deep-throated growl, and she slashed back wildly left to right across his stomach. This one cut through more silk, which fell away to expose a deep bleeding cut. She thrust the dagger up toward his face, aiming for his eyes. A lucky turn of the head saved his eye, but she laid his face open in a deep cut from cheek to jowl, which began to pour blood.

Her fighting rage was upon her now and she remembered nothing of the rest of the fight, thrust, parry, dodge, pivot, it was a carefully-rehearsed choreography that she had done thousands of times with Hina, and it was working.

Wang Ming sought to end the fight early and rushed her, arms outspread. *A man will always seek to embrace you, to immobilize you, arms against your sides.*

It was a stupid move and Marcia executed its counter. Wang Ming's rush was clumsy, leaving his midsection exposed, and Marcia's nine-inch dagger sank its full length into his gut.

A gut wound is fatal, but not quickly so. Do as much damage to him as you can while the knife is inside.

Marcia cut sideways, meanwhile working the knife blade up and down inside him as she cut. She heard the zipping of skin and muscle giving away against her blade. Wang's eyes got very big, and he shuddered under the pain. She stepped back and withdrew her knife, watching a small loop of green intestine pop out through the gash. Wang saw it also, fumbling with it with both hands, trying to push it back in. He groaned, bent over, then glared at her. "You bitch!" he cursed. Then his legs folded up under him, and he sat down with a thud on his haunches, still holding his midsection. A trickle of blood flowed out the right corner of his mouth, mingling with the blood of his tattered left cheek.

Marcia wiped her knife, but remained on guard. There may be fight left in him, or he may have friends coming to his aid. She looked down at her own breast, bleeding profusely. She put her hand over it, applying pressure to staunch the flow. Then she knelt down beside him, as he shuddered convulsively. "I am sorry, Ming, I didn't want to do this. I wish…"

"Go fuck your barbarians, whore!" he cursed at her again, then fell back. His breathing became more ragged and rattled as his lungs filled, then with a final spasm he was still, his unblinking eyes staring at the ceiling. Marcia reached over and closed them, "Be at peace now, you poor, troubled man." She was surprised how long it had taken him to die.

She sat there, not moving, for a long time. Somewhere far away, a dog barked, birds sang. She held onto her wounded breast, feeling the warm blood ooze through her fingers. The pain was intense now, throbbing. She thought of all the stupid mistakes she had made, all the things that Hina had taught her that she had forgotten.

She was beginning to feel sleepy, light-headed, perhaps she should just lay down and stretch out, when there were footfalls on the porch. Wang's friends, she thought, as she struggled to her feet, wobbling, almost unable to stand, but at least she would die on her feet, fighting to the end. Antonius and Hina burst in. "Marcia, what the hell…" said Antonius, then he saw the prone body of Wang Ming on the floor. "Hina, get some water and some clean rags. Hurry!"

He lay Marcia down and lifted up her shirt to expose her injury. The knife had sliced a gash about an inch deep and five inches long through the top of her breast. Well-supplied with blood, it bled heavily, but there did not appear to be any penetration of her chest. "Any other wounds?" he asked.

"Some scratches, just that one," she said sleepily.

"Good. That is an ugly cut, but not serious. You'll heal, and the breast will be fine. I'll see to that. Remember we are getting married this week." She smiled wanly, but she was woozy, in shock, pale and clammy. He put a box under her feet, and bandaged her injury.

"Who is that man?" asked Hina.

"That's the man who used to beat her. Looks like he won't be doing that anymore."

"How did he find her here?"

"He was with that bunch of Hanaean troops yesterday. Looks like he thought to take her back. She will tell us about it later."

They wrapped her in a blanket and helped her down the stairs to the horses. Antonius was hoping this had not attracted attention, because a death involving someone from the court would stir up a lot of trouble. Ibrahim could deal with the cleanup. Fortunately, it seemed half the town was out in the Xiongnu encampment, meaning fewer witnesses, but perhaps too many when they arrived in the camp. Antonius put her up on Hina's horse, Hina behind her holding the bandage over Marcia's damaged breast.

As luck would have it, there was a rowdy game of *buzkashi* 'snatch the dead goat' going on outside the encampment that had attracted the attention of the Xiongnu and the most of the curious villagers of Liqian, leaving the encampment almost deserted. They got her into the yurt unseen, where Mama and Marcus were sitting with Demosthenes, Shmuel, Yakov and Ibrahim.

Mama cried out, "Marcia, Marcia, what happened?" She flustered over her bloody daughter. Marcus hovered solicitously and helped lay her out on the floor.

Antonius said, "An accident, Mama. I need to take care of her. Hina, tell her what happened, and swear her to secrecy. Ibrahim, we have a dead body at the Lucian house that needs to go away, details from Hina. Demosthenes, my *capsula*, clean linen, and vinegar."

Antonius scrubbed the injury thoroughly, opening it up to examine it for bits of cloth or thread. Marcia was conscious but silent throughout, flinching a bit as he washed the gaping cut with vinegar. Then he sutured up the wound with horsehair thread. She bit her lip with each suture prick, but bit by bit, the wound was closed. "All right, Marcia, good as new, looks like the wedding is still on," Antonius said, bandaging the wound.

Demosthenes had prepared a glass of wine and poppy juice for pain and to help her sleep. The wound would be painful, but it would heal nicely, and probably not even leave much of a scar... if it did not get feverish. Would it still work as a breast, producing milk for future children? Antonius didn't know, he had never dealt with this kind of injury.

Yakov and Shmuel had already made several trips to the Lucian household that day, so one more did not attract attention. They rolled Wang Ming up in the blood-stained carpet, and cleaned up the mess that remained on the floor and furniture. They carried the carpet out, the lifeless Wang Ming inside, and dumped it in the back of their cart, taking his non-descript Mongolian pony in tow.

They drove out of town heading west. When they came back, the carpet, with Wang Ming inside, was not in the cart. Unless someone saw them, Wang Ming was unlikely to ever be found.

CHAPTER 66: A MAGNIFICENT WEDDING

The next morning, Marcia awoke about sunrise, groggy and sore, having slept about twelve hours. She touched her bandaged breast and recoiled in horror, remembering the ugly wound Wang had inflicted on her. She felt carefully around the sore mound, feeling its familiar shape and softness under the wrapping… still attached, that gave her some relief. She remembered Antonius treating her, like in a dream. Antonius was lying beside her, but not too close, not wanting to jostle her in the night. "Good morning!" he announced cheerfully, and got up to get her some water to rinse her mouth.

"How are you feeling?" he asked, handing her the water and a brush.

"Like my horse threw me, and then walked all over me."

He knelt down beside her while she nursed her bowl of water. "I'm going to lift up your shirt. I want to inspect the badge of honor you got yesterday."

She lay back down and he exposed her breast to undo the bandage. He gently palpitated it. The breast felt normal, warm but not hot, firm but not hard. The sutured wound along the top was black with dried blood along the sealing lips of the wound, but nothing fresh, no oozing moisture or pus. The little black horsehair sutures stood up like little insects marching across her breast, twenty of them. He washed down the wound with some vinegar, noticing that the chill fluid made her nipple crinkle. *Good sign, looks like she has sensation there.* Then he re-bandaged her wound and pulled her shirt down.

"Looks like yer healin' fine, *domina*," he said. "Let me get you some breakfast, an' yer can tell me all about it."

Everyone was awake now, and Demosthenes and Hina came over and sat beside her, so Antonius switched back to their mutual *han-yu*. "What would you like to eat?"

"Just some bread, that would be fine."

He got up, fetched a slice of barley bread and brought it over with more water. She ate just a little, but slurped down the water thirstily. She handed the water mug back. "Some more, please?"

He refilled the mug from the water sack. She asked for help getting into a sitting position, and Antonius piled some pillows behind her. "So it looks like you gave better than you got, Marcia," he said, arranging the covers around her. It was chill and they had not yet started the dung fire to warm the yurt; Yakov and Shmuel were working on that.

Mama and Marcus came over to see what was going on. "How are you, dear?" said Mama, looking very concerned.

"Antonius just checked, and said I was healing fine. Tired and sore, but all right."

"What on earth happened to you? Antonius and Hina told me you had been in a fight with a bad man... and killed him?"

"That is right, Mama. He was a bad man at court. I was assigned to him as his concubine when we got there, and he was not nice."

"But you were only twelve! That's too young!"

"I had to grow up fast. I told you about the trial, and about our escape..."

"Yes."

"He was the man who made the false charges. He was with the troops who came the day before yesterday, I guess to take me back. I wasn't going. He didn't like that."

"So he cut you?"

"We cut each other quite a bit. I ...." She turned to Antonius, "Does she know...?"

"She knows she must not talk about it to anyone. Go ahead," said Antonius.

"I ... in a fight, you really don't remember much, it was all a swirl, but when it was over, Wang was on the floor, and I had killed him." Turning to Hina, she said with distress, "I was a mess! I did everything wrong, and forgot everything you taught me!"

"Your first real fight is always a mess, but it looks like you did fine. You remembered to be the one left standing, and that's the only rule that counts." Hina smiled and patted her arm. "You and I can talk about this later. Mama, that is what happened, and she put up a very good fight, I wish I could have seen it. He was quite a bit bigger than she is, and she took him down."

"Was he a bad man, then?" Mama asked.

"Not always, but sometimes, and very bad yesterday," answered Marcia, settling back into the soft pillows.

"Just remember what we talked about, if anyone comes around inquiring, he came back looking for Si Huar, she wasn't there, and he left," said Antonius. "Don't mention his name or admit you know it. You don't know where he went, but you thought he might be going east. Remember, he was an official in the court, and people may be wondering what happened to him. They don't play nice, as you learned ten years ago, Mama." He had carefully rehearsed this cover story with Ibrahim yesterday, and then with Mama. She had to follow it.

Shanyu Bei came in to check now. Antonius had also told him what happened, as it affected his clan. He was happy to see she was doing well. "How was the fall from your horse yesterday?" he said with a chuckle.

"Fall from a horse, I... oh, yes, stupid of me, I took a careless chance riding too fast!" A big grin brightened her face.

"Happens to all of us," he said with a toothy smile. "Get well soon! Is the wedding still on, Antonius?"

"I'll confirm tomorrow, but looks like it's still on. She'll be fine." Turning to Marcia, Antonius said with mock reproof, "Try to stay on your horse, next time." She giggled.

The next day Marcia was up and about. Hina wanted to take her back to the house, to 'exorcise the demons,' if she felt up to it. Marcia agreed, and they rode slowly back.

Marcia felt quite a bit of trepidation as she climbed the old stone stairs again, as though Wang might jump out from behind a bush and grab her again, but she quelled her fear. Inside was much the same as the other day, but the rug she had known from childhood was gone. She remembered that both of them had bled out on it. Other than that, everything was the same. She went over to her father's chair and set it to rocking.

Hello, Papa.

Hello, Marcia.

That thing I wanted to talk to you about...

Your learning to fight?

You approve?

I couldn't have done better myself. Is that Hina with you?

Yes. My sister.

She is a good sister, she taught you well. And don't worry about Wang Ming anymore. His spirit will never bother you again. No one beats my daughter and gets away with it, this life or the next!

Thanks, Papa! Are you coming to the wedding?

I wouldn't miss it.

The rocking chair seemed to be gently rocking by itself. For a minute she could see him, tall, lanky, bronzed skin furrowed by lines, crinkles around his barely Asiatic eyes, straight nose, pointed chin. And piercing blue eyes, just like hers. She bent down to kiss him, but her lips caressed nothing but air.

That's all right, Marcia, I felt that anyway. Memento..."

"Yes, I know, Papa, Romana sum. I am a Roman girl. See you in a few days at the wedding.

'I'll be there.

The rocking chair slowed to a halt. Hina was watching intently. "It's all right. You're not the only one who talks to the spirits of dead loved ones. That was my father Marius, and he and I were having a chat," said Marcia.

Marcia went back to her toy box, picked up some suitable offerings, and placed them on the altar for the household *lares*. She bowed her head and said some prayers. Then she took Hina on a tour of the small house, showing off her and Marcus' rooms. Like her own, her mother had kept it ready for his eventual return. She went in to her parents' room, but noted with great dismay that the bed was missing. "Oh!," said Hina. "That was supposed to be a surprise. So try to be surprised when you see it again."

"Bed? Where in the hell are we going to put a bed in a yurt, Hina?"

Hina smiled knowingly. "Don't ask any more questions, Marcia."

The wedding came a few days later. Antonius removed the bandage, but left the stitches in. Nothing would show to reveal her wound. Fortunately, the weather continued unusually mild for late November, as the Mediterranean clothing of the Roman wedding would not be suitable for an Hanaean winter.

Galosga had returned with three deer draped across the back of his extra horse. It was the tradition of his people that the bride and groom exchange gifts, venison from the groom, and *selu* from the bride. *Selu* didn't grow here, he had substituted a sheaf of wheat. The deer were roasting alongside the goats in Ibrahim's *sewan* tent, slowly turning on spits over firepits, emitting mouthwatering smoke over the crowd. The *sewan* was packed with tables holding bowls and white bottles of Liqian wine, sacks of *kumis,* and more bottles of Hanaean rice wine.

Hina acted as sister to the bride, while Gaius would act as brother to the groom. Hina's *arban* would be the escorts, required by Roman custom to carry the bride to the new domicile. It was Xiongnu tradition that the father of the groom provide the couple a yurt, and Bei had taken that role, providing them their very own yurt and a camel to carry it. They could consummate their marriage in privacy! Mama had put her own bed inside the yurt as the *ān chuáng* wedding bed, covering it with new red bedsheets and decorating it with fruits, nuts, dates, persimmons, and sprigs of leaves. The bed would be going back to the house when they left because it was far too big to travel, but it was theirs until the migration resumed.

Marcia wore the wig provided months back by Mama Biyu, and Hina, under Mama's supervision, combed it four times in the Hanaean tradition the night before, for togetherness to the end, for a hundred years of harmony, for a houseful of children, and for longevity. The two women then fussily but carefully arranged Marcia's black tresses in the correct style with a proper bun. Mama prepared little cakes for all of the *Da Qin* party, Hina's *arban*, and everyone in the *shanyu's* yurt.

The wedding day arrived. Aulus had written up the contract, laying it out on a table weighted by a stone against an errant gust of wind, awaiting signatures from all who wished to sign, in whatever language they wanted to sign it in. Everyone else crowded in behind as Bei ordered a horn blown, and silence fell on the encampment.

Antonius and Marcia walked up to the table, flanked by Hina on Marcia's right, and Gaius Lucullus on Antonius' left. Antonius and Gaius were clad in chalk-white togas, as was Aulus. Marcia wore the cream-colored *tunica recta* with the *flammaeum* orange veil, a girdle about her waist fastened with the Knot of Hercules, all given to her by her mother. Hina wore a red silk robe over her black felt pants. Mama beamed proudly, beside Marcus in his own toga.

Aulus rose to speak before the crowd in *han-yu.* "Is there any nation that we have missed today? This is the most unlikely wedding I have ever officiated." A titter ran through the crowd. "I have taken the omens, and they are auspicious, as they should be. If any two people were fated by the gods to be joined together in harmony and peace, it is Antonius and Marcia. Let us call upon all the gods of all our people to bless this couple: Shangdi, of the Han people, Tengri of the Great Blue Sky of our Xiongnu hosts, Adonai of our Jewish partner, El of our Arab friends, Buddha of our heroic Demosthenes of Bactria, and *Se-lu* of Galosga, the ancestral mother of his people. Finally I call upon all our Roman gods, especially Jupiter Optimus Maximus, Juno, the goddess of marriage and women, Bona Dea, the goddess of fertility, Fortuna, who has smiled upon this pair more times than I can count, Venus, the goddess of love, who has also blessed them, and Vesta, the goddess of the hearth. Now let us pray silently, in our own languages and customs, to these deities for Antonius and Marcia.

A hush fell upon the crowd. Antonius was lost in thought at the unlikeliness of this union. Was it just a year and a half ago, when he would stand by the rail of the *Europa,* watching the bow wave cresting like a team of horses racing the ship in echelon? Afraid she would come, and he would stammer and embarrass himself? Afraid she would not, and he would miss the company of a woman who had no business associating with him? He remembered teaching her his soldier's Latin, and all its profanities, her teaching him his first words of *han-yu.* He remembered missing her, after Wang Ming had taken her back to the *Asia,* and his fury, discovering that he had beaten her. At no time did he ever think that this unlikely friendship would end in a wedding like this, before thousands of people on the way out of the land of the Han. *Yes, thank you, Fortuna. And all of you gods.*

Aulus was speaking again, reading the contract, but the words were not reaching Antonius in his reverie. Gaius and Hina went forward, along with Mama and everyone in the party, to sign it. Gaius and Hina returned to each present an iron ring to the bride and groom. Antonius fumbled with the ring, fitting it on the third finger of Marcia's left hand, she smiling shyly. Then she fitted her ring on his finger, and intoned the ancient words *"Ubi gaius est, gaia sum."* Gaius, not the ubiquitous Latin first name, but the ancient meaning of generic men and women. 'As you are my guy, I am your gal.' And with that, they were wed.

Everyone cheered, someone put a bottle of Liqian wine in Antonius' hand, he raised it in toast and everyone cheered again. Then Hina's *arban*, acting as escorts, lifted Marcia up between the shoulders of the two biggest men, and the rest surrounded Antonius, following Marcia to the nuptial tent. They carried her into the yurt, smiled, bowed, and left, closing the door flap behind them. Marcia and Antonius were on their honeymoon.

Antonius reached out and took Marcia's hands in his. They smiled and just kept repeating "husband" and "wife." Then he got down on one knee, fumbling with the complex Knot of Hercules while she stood looking down at him. After a few minutes she smiled and said in mock impatience, "Aren't you ever going to get that damned thing undone?"

"I'm doing my best, *domina*. Anyway, tradition says yer supposed ter be protesting, demanding more time."

"That tradition is for virgins, which you and I are certainly not! I'm protesting that I want you on top of me very soon, ravishing me in the manner I have come to enjoy!" She caressed Antonius' big shoulders and ruffled his hair, doing nothing for his concentration.

The knot finally fell away. He lifted off the *flammaeus* off her shoulders, then the *tunica* up over her head. He shed his bulky toga, and Marcia did the honors for his tunic. They drank in the sight of each other's nakedness, which had been a rare luxury to them. Antonius reached and cupped her injured breast very gently. "Is it all right? Not sore?"

"Not sore. Don't get too energetic on that side, or you'll tear my stitches."

"I won't"

Marcia was a slender girl, but her size concealed taut power that she had gained over the past six months. Gone was the slight palace softness that had cloaked her body when they started this trek. Her stomach was hard and lean, with just the barest of bulges below her navel, indicating her womb, then plunging downward, curving inward to the pubic line, where it disappeared into black curly hair, resting on well-defined thighs and calves able to run for miles. Taking his gaze up to her shoulders, they were wider than her slender hips, her biceps not bulky, but showing clear muscular definition. Her breasts were firm, ending in small nipples behind dark aureoles.

Antonius lifted her wig off gently, fumbling with the pins holding it in place. He mussed her short hair, which he had begun to like, causing her to laugh.

Living with ten people in a twenty foot yurt, nakedness amongst themselves had been common but not sensual. Everyone generally ignored various exposed body parts and bodily functions, the only means for privacy in such close quarters. And at night, when Antonius and Marcia came together to share the pleasures of each other's bodies, the two were usually partially dressed and careful to not awaken the others with their scuffling and sighs. The ability to just drink in the sights and smells of each other's naked bodies was a rare treat.

Antonius reached behind her back and drew her to him. This girl was the toughest and the gentlest, the hardest and the softest person he had ever known. Their lips met in a deep kiss, each other's tongue searching for its companion.

They consummated their marriage with great abandon and gusto. Several times.

CHAPTER 67: ONE MOVES ON, ONE STAYS BEHIND

While Marcia and Antonius enjoyed the privacy of their own yurt, and the townspeople and the Xiongnu got rip-roariously drunk in the encampment, Mama and Marcus returned home for some quiet time together, a little before sunset. He helped her up the steep walkway and into the house, lit a fire in the oven/fireplace on the back wall,

while she set about preparing him tea. He went into his room, looking around its familiar environment so long unseen. He shrugged off his toga and hung it back up on its hanger where it had been for ten years, scattering a fine patina of chalk dust on the floor. His simple Roman tunic was a bit light for the gathering chill of evening, so he rummaged through the chest for other clothes left behind ten years ago, and changed into an Hanaean-style wool shirt and linen pants. Experimentally, he stretched himself out on his bed. Yes, everything was as it had been. Almost.

Mama called from the common area, "Marcus, I made us some tea."

He took a seat at a stool around the big raised table in the center, where Mama had placed a small steaming cup of tea. The fire crackled in the back wall, shedding light and heat, as a cast iron kettle chuckled and steamed. Yes, he was home. "Thanks, Mama. It has been a long time."

She touched his hand, her almond eyes staring into his blue ones, and smiled wistfully. "Too long," she said. Inside, she was wrestling with the fact that she would be losing her children again, this time forever, as they headed west. Marcia, so happily wed, could not stay, and she did not want to beg Marcus to stay, however strongly she wished he would. At least she could die at peace, having seen what proud, strong people her children had become. "So tell me all about Luoyang," she asked her son.

Marcus did tell her, about the beautiful city, the palaces and parks along the Luo River. He talked a lot about Marcia, how they had been strong for each, "The rock and the pebble," she used to call themselves. The long two-year trip to Rome, the magnificent city dwarfing Luoyang, the new immense

Flavian Amphitheater and imperial palaces on the Palatine Hill overlooking the Circus Maximus, the meeting with Emperor Trajan. Then the long trip back, the magnificent ships, the hijacking, reluctant alliance, and ultimately friendship between Ibrahim the pirate with Gaius and Antonius, and Marcia's budding friendship with Antonius.

Then about her departure to the *Asia* with Wang Ming and isolation so complete her own brother barely caught a glimpse of her, and finally the return to Luoyang... the trial, the death sentence, jail, the escape, and the long trip home.

Mama listened intently. Marcus had omitted only one thing, his castration. He had not shared that story with her, nor with his traveling companions, and never would.

It was getting dark, and it was Mama's custom to retire early, so she bade her son goodnight, kissing him gently on the forehead, and retired to Marcia's room... her own bed being in joyful use right now by the newlyweds. "I am going to sit up a while, Mama," said Marcus, lighting a few oil lamps. "I think I want to read some of Papa's scrolls."

Marcus went over by his father's chair. He remembered Marcia telling him of her imagined conversation with him. He gently set the chair rocking. *Hello, Papa.*

Hello, son, welcome home. The mind could play tricks, but this did seem almost real.

Do you mind if I sit in your chair now? The rocker had been reserved for the *paterfamilias*, off limits to everyone else.

You're the man of the house now, it is yours to sit in.

Marcus remained standing. *I guess I am – sort of.*

There was a long silence, then: *Marcus Lucius Quintus, I am going to tell you this once, and once only.* Father never used Marcus' full name unless he was angry with him. *What happened to you ten years ago was cruel and unjust, but it is over and can't be undone. Testicles predispose you to manhood, but they do not make you a man, your actions do. You are more of a man by half than many that have a fully-functioning pair, and I am very proud of you. Now sit yourself in the man's chair now before I get really upset with you.*

Yes, sir! Marcus took his seat. *Thanks, Papa, I have a real hard time talking about that...*

Understandable.

Marcus rummaged through the scroll basket and picked one out, the *Annales* by Ennius. Of course it wasn't the authentic Ennius... soldiers did not carry a library along with them in the field. When his ancestors settled here five generations ago, they decided to record all they could remember, to preserve their *Romanitas*. *Memento, Romani sumus,* Remember, we are Romans, they said to each other. They set up a senate, elected consuls, and the educated ones wrote down everything they could remember, stories, Plautus' plays, and of course, Ennius' history. Every Roman schoolboy had been drilled in his *Annales*, having had it beaten into their heads by their tutors at an early age. It was all the founding myths of Rome, how they had cast out their king, set up in place the *res publica*, the public business, insisting that *leges non reges habemus:* we have laws, not kings.

It's not like that in Rome anymore, Papa. They have the Principiate, ruled by the Princeps Optimus, the Best Ruler. To call someone a republican is to accuse them of treason, for believing that power comes from the people, not the princeps.

I know. But we had a good long run with that idea. And someday, someone somewhere will rediscover what we did, and build on it, and keep the idea going.

He read the words on the scroll, well over a hundred years old, and felt connected to his ancestor by five generations, Marcus Lucius of the III Cohort, who had so narrowly missed his own execution. If those men had not recorded their *romanitas* and passed it on with their language, then Marcus and Marcia would just be Hanaeans with unusual blue eyes from some long-forgotten foreign ancestor. And the Gan Ying expedition might not have taken place without translators fluent and literate in both Latin and Hanaean. And there would have been no return trip by Aulus, and Marcia would not be married to Antonius. He might also still have his balls, too, but maybe there is a purpose in that, too, though hard for him to see what it might be.

You're deep in thought, son

Feeling connected, like I never have been before. The gods weave a magnificent tapestry of threads that direct our lives.

And we help weave them too, with our choices. Like their choice to preserve their Romanitas.

Is this ... are you... real? Am I really talking with your manes, *your ghost?*

It's real enough to me, son, said his father's shade with a laugh. *But I can't stay much longer. I can't explain, but some time from now, my echo will finally die out, and you will call, and I won't be able to be here for you.*

I am thinking, I might want to stay, to not go back to Rome with Marcia. That will be hard for both of us. What should I do?

You are a man now, sui manus, in your own hands. You'll have to choose. I would suggest talking to Marcia first, though. Well, even shades have to sleep. Enjoy Ennius.

Marcus read the familiar text for several hours. Considering it was written from memory, it was not badly done. Marcus had brought back a copy of the real *Annales,* along with a copy of Livy's new history of Rome, *Ab Urbe Condita,* From the Foundation of the City, considered the most comprehensive history to date. He had hoped to somehow get the books to his father, but they were back in his quarters in Luoyang, and his father was dead.

Marcus set the scroll aside, poured himself a cup of wine, feeling more at peace with himself than he could remember. He fell asleep in the chair.

The next day, he went to meet with a childhood friend, Frontinus Quintilian and their other old friends, the gathering prearranged during the wedding. They had been inseparable as youths, their pranks probably contributing to several of the grey hairs streaking their fathers' heads. It was a most enjoyable gathering, and he retold his story again to a group of men who had never been fifty miles from home, about the magnificence of Rome with its magnificent white marble buildings, much more than the tales of Rome on which they had been raised. This had indeed been a momentous journey that few men had ever done, and he began to grasp its magnitude, and to take some justifiable pride in what they had done. Enroute, he had never felt the accomplishment, living it one day at a time. But in the retelling, the scope manifested itself, reflected in the eyes of the listeners.

It was disappointing, though, as theirs was probably the last generation in Liqian to retain the dream of Rome. The younger children had no interest in Latin, and Rome to them was somewhere between a great exaggeration and a complete myth. Sulpicius was dead, and no one had bothered to continue his Latin school.

Marcus rode back to the encampment, to find Marcia outside her yurt tending a fire.

"Hello, sis. How is the consummation going?" asked Marcus with a big grin.

"Oh, about as well as can be expected. How is Mama?"

"Doing well. So is Papa."

"You talked to him, too?" she asked quizzically.

"I think it really is the old man's *manes*. But a friendly one."

"Yes, he is a sweetheart. I think he couldn't bear the thought of missing our return."

"Marcia, I have something to discuss, very important," he said, as he dismounted, sliding easily off the horse. He sat down on a log by the fire. "Marcia, I think I might want to stay here, and not continue on." His heart pounded, she would be very shocked at that.

She sat in silence for several minutes, sitting very straight, staring into the fire. Then finally, just a simple, "Why?" Her voice quivered a bit, betraying her reaction.

"This is home to me, sis, in a way Rome can never be. I got together with Frontinus and the gang, and the past ten years just fell away. And Mama, she needs someone to care for her. I have been happier the past two days than I have ever been, I feel like a dried up plant whose roots have just found water again."

"What would you do here?"

"Well, old Sulpicius has died, and his school is closed. I have picked up much improved grammar from being in Rome. I could reopen his school, and try to rebuild the dream. And maybe learn Parthian, some other languages, too. They thought I had a talent for them back in Luoyang."

Marcia sat, continuing to stare into the fire, the silence palpable between them. Finally, her eyes brimmed over with tears. "I can't imagine life without you, brother, you have been my rock and I've been your pebble our whole lives together."

"Nor I without you. You're the reason I didn't kill myself ten years ago, when I cried for hours into your skinny shoulder, after they 'settled me down'." His eyes were hot, near to overflowing also. "Papa said I should discuss my decision with you first."

"That's nice of him," she said, choking on her tears.

"If you want me to come with you, I will."

Marcia struggled to get her emotions under control, and neither said anything for another few minutes. Then Marcia wiped her eyes and spoke. "I can't ask that of you, brother. It's just that I will miss you terribly." She turned toward him and buried herself in his arms, sobbing uncontrollably, her whole body shuddering. "I love you, brother!"

Then Marcia pulled away and tried to recompose herself. "We are leaving day after tomorrow. In my toy box, there is a little Hanaean bamboo poem, Mama gave it to me on my twelfth birthday. Would you bring that please before we leave?"

So Marcus packed out his belongings from the tent and returned to the house. The next day, the group gave him a great going away. Aulus determined that there might be a way to communicate with Marcia, if Marcus could find people on a westbound caravan going to Roman territory to carry a sealed letter. All they had to do when they arrived would be to drop off the letter to any Roman government or military person, and it would be in Aulus's *cubiculum* in Rome a few weeks later, delivered by the *cursus publicus* Roman government mail. Aulus gave him his seal to use for the letters. It was a long shot, but better than nothing.

The next morning at daybreak, the massive encampment broke up their yurts and set out, encumbered by their flocks and herds. Marcus had spent his last night in the communal yurt, rising to see them off.

His staying behind put a damper on Marcia's spirits for several days. This did seem to be a better choice for him, but gods, she was going to miss him!

That night they encamped in the Zhangye area, then got underway again at first light, passing through brilliantly colored rock formations. Broad parallel stripes of red, yellow, white, green, brilliant turquoise blue, violet, each nearly equal in width, looked as though the gods had a draped a brilliantly striped blanket over the rolling mountains. The road meandered along the side of these magnificent multicolored cliffs for miles and miles.

Hina rode up alongside Marcia, her body rolling easily in the saddle with the motion of Eagle between her thighs. "Beautiful, isn't it? I have always loved crossing these mountains."

"Yes, they are beautiful," answered Marcia, but without much enthusiasm.

"Missing our brother, my sister?" asked Hina, sympathetically.

"He's my brother, and yes, I am," she answered curtly, then retracted it almost at once. "I'm sorry, that's unkind. You're trying to be friendly, and I am being nasty because I am miserable. Yes, I am missing him. We hope we might be able to exchange letters, but realistically, he is lost to me forever."

"He made his choice. And you have put up with my bad temper more than once, for less reason. How is your battle scar coming?"

"Antonius took the stitches out yesterday, and other than itching a lot, it looks like it's fine. Antonius wants to rub some cream onto it to keep the scar soft, I can't imagine why."

"Men!" she laughed.

Hina made her excuses and rode off on Eagle. She was newly appointed by the *shanyu* to head up a *zuun* of a hundred men, and they would be riding out ahead as scouts in front of the migration by several miles, wary of the Han fort at Jiuquan two hundred miles ahead.

It was December, and the nine-hundred mile transit from Liqian to Turfam was made miserable by the weather, taking almost two months. At one point, fierce westerly winds brought in a blinding sandstorm from the Taklamakan desert, which, combined with daylong subzero temperatures, forced the migration to lay over for a week, huddled in their yurts around dung fires and wrapped in blankets.

They reached Turfam in mid February, and mercifully, temperatures stayed above freezing most of the day. The migration would lay over for several days here, to allow the animals and people to recover from the arduous trek. Here was the departure point for the Xiongnu. They would be continuing to Dzungaria hundreds of more miles to the north, between the Tien Shan and the Altai mountains, while Aulus's party would find a way to continue west. It would be another sad parting of the ways.

CHAPTER 68: TWO MOVE ON TOGETHER

Hina was ambivalent about Galosga's imminent departure with the *Da Qin* group. He had touched her heart and healed her soul the way no other man ever could have done, and she would miss him deeply. The "mating" had long since moved past the physical, and she could enjoy sitting quietly with him during her fertile periods, when she normally would not allow any man close to her, and Galosga in turn accepted these periods of intimate abstinence. She fondly remembered one such time when the fierce desert winter relented, sitting alone with him under the night sky, his arm about her shoulders for warmth, telling her the names of the stars and constellations in his own language, and their legends among his people. She trusted him completely, and she would certainly miss him.

On the other hand, she wanted to end this dependency on him, and go back to being the self-sufficient woman that she had been before. She had her *zuun*. Only two other women in the oral history of the clan had been warriors, and only one had risen to lead men, and that just an *arban*, generations past. She looked forward to winter's abatement when she could begin to train her men in earnest, put her stamp on their style of fighting. She was blazing unknown territory. That part of her looked forward to seeing Galosga on his way, back to the faraway west to find his mysterious wife and children. But that part would miss him also.

So she was a bit disconcerted to find that he intended to continue on to Dzungaria with the Huyan clan, and request adoption by them. He mentioned this while riding alongside her on a day when the temperature and the wind permitted conversation.

"Galosga, you can't do that! You must find your way back home to your family!" she protested.

"I can do that, and intend to do so." She hated it when he simply refuted her, without argument. He waited a minute and continued. "I talked to Ibrahim, who has sailed all over the world. He has never heard of any land over the western sea. He said it would be a dangerous trip, trying to find an island, even a big one. We could miss it by a hundred miles and sail right by without seeing it. Still, he offered to accompany me to Gades, and if he couldn't find a ship that would make the trip, he would buy one and try himself."

"So that is your way back."

"It is not. I would not risk Ibrahim's life and his fortune on a dangerous trip like that."

"You're a fool!" she retorted. "I can't stay mated to you if you come along. You will be on your own."

"Perhaps I am a fool, and perhaps I will be on my own. But I am not coming because of you. I have told you of my world. I have been in the world of the west. I was in a city called Alexandria. It must have more people in it than in all my world together, and they have things I don't even have names for. I can't live in the west, or east in the Middle Kingdom. Your people are as much like mine as any I have seen. What you have here that is new to me, I have learned to use. Animals that you herd, not hunt, metal, horses. You taught me to ride, and I enjoy the feel of a horse under me. This is my new home, the Huyan clan are my new people. Here I will grow old and die."

"Well, you'll have to do that without me." And she ran off as she usually did when the conversation didn't go her way, spurring Eagle to a gallop and whirling away.

He just kept Gahlida cantering on.

Hina wound up at Marcia's yurt, and scratched at the felt door. Marcia admitted her, the inside illuminated with half light from outside. "Well, hello, stranger!" Marcia greeted her cheerfully.

"I need to talk, Marcia. Galosga insists on continuing on to stay with the clan."

"We knew that. He feels very comfortable with your people, and with you."

"He's got to continue on with you. He needs to go back west, and find his way home to his wife and children."

"That path is not open to him. But it's not them you're worried about, is it?"

"What do you mean?" she asked, feeling on edge.

"You want to send him on his way, so you can go back to being the tough woman you used to be. But that tough woman is as dead and gone as my meek little Si Huar, and neither of them are ever coming back, Hina. You two share a love for each other that is as special as that between Antonius and me, and I think it frightens you."

"Love! Now there is a word out of mushy Hanaean poetry!" scoffed Hina.

"You know, you and I are the luckiest women in the world," smiled Marcia. "Most women, be they Roman, Hanaean, or Xiongnu, get about as much choice in their male partner as I did when Wang picked me ten years ago. Roman marriages are made by parents for business ties, politics, or status. Yours are made for clan alliances. And we who get picked, we get the privilege of fucking them when they want to fuck, cleaning for them, cooking their meals, and raising their children. If we are lucky, we get someone we can be comfortable with. If we're not, we get to put up with beatings, and with their chasing around after other women. You and I, we got to choose the men in our life, and we both chose well."

They both fell silent while Hina pondered this, finally getting to the crux of her problem. "I can't give him what he needs, Marcia. He needs a family and children. I can't do that... I can't head up a *zuun* and be more than his mate, someone who warms his blanket once a week or so. And that is not fair to him. Maybe I could find him another woman who could." But as soon as she said it, she realized how hard that would be, also... for her. The idea of him being to someone else what he had become to her?

"Hina, Antonius and I have talked a great deal about what love is and the different ways it shows itself. He says that the highest form of love is the kind that makes you willing to sacrifice something important, even your life, for someone. You have laid out your choices nicely, and those are the two on the table. You have a lot to think about to choose the one that is right for you, and I can't help. However, I have a few bottles of Liqian wine left over. Would you help me empty them?"

"Thanks, Marcia, I think I will."

So they killed several bottles, not bothering with cups, just passing the open bottle back and forth till they both got a little tipsy, talking about nothing important.

Then Hina asked, "Can you do me a favor? Can I have your yurt for a few hours, and you go find Galosga and bring him here? We need to talk."

"You have a lot to talk about, you can have it all night if you like. Antonius and I will bunk up in the communal yurt." She left to find Galosga.

When Galosga came in a half-hour later, Hina was sitting cross-legged on the blankets. "Please, sit, Galosga," she said, indicating the place opposite her. "I can talk about things easier with you than any other man, but I still have trouble with some things.

"First, I am sorry for trying to tell you what choice you should make about where and how to live your life. The reason I treasure you so much as my friend is that you never dictate to me, and I should not do so to you. I did, and that was wrong. If you wish to join our clan, I will not only accept it, I will speak to the *shanyu* in your behalf. Can you forgive my unkindness?"

"There is no problem, *huldaji*, I understand your moods better than you, I think. Yes, I forgive you for that very small thing."

"This next one will be difficult, and I have asked Tengri to guide us in the path that best suits his will. Galosga, you who fell into my life, continuing as my mate is no longer fair to you if you are to remain here permanently. Either I must become your wife and the mother of our children if you want me, or I must help you find a woman more suitable for you. You deserve a family to replace the one you lost."

"You know I would prefer to stay with you. But I cannot ask you to give up your *zuun*." Galosga smiled at her gently.

"And I don't want to lose you to another woman. I have grown very fond of you." She laughed nervously. She paused, then continued. "Marcia told me that the highest kind of love involves sacrificing something precious for the one you love. Both these choices involving my sacrificing something I value above all else: the one, my status as a warrior to be your wife and the mother of our children; the other, to give you up to another woman. Either way," she was trembling a little now, "I have earned the right to say I love you, Galosga."

She took his hands in hers, leaned forward and kissed him tenderly. She then rested her head on his shoulder.

"It took you long enough to understand that, *huldaji.*" He stroked her hair gently, and waited so long in silence that she was afraid he wasn't going to return the expression. The man could be maddeningly taciturn. Then "I love you, too. I have since the day you let me heal your heart."

Almost with a sigh of relief, she straightened up and leaned back upright.

"So I have asked Tengri to help us make this decision. You know, I think, this is my fertile period."

"Yes, and I am honored that you allow me near you."

"If your seed quickens me tonight, then you will have to put up with my foul temper the rest of your life, because that means Tengri intends me to be your wife, and my role as a warrior must be second to that. I would like to be wed when we get to Dzungaria, if that is all right with you, and keep my *zuun* until then, if that is all right with the *shanyu.*"

"That is good," he said with a smile.

"And if I don't quicken, then you can breathe easy, because I will find you a woman worthy of you, and you will be rid of me forever…after I attend your wedding. I will settle for standing in as your sister."

She stood up and beckoned him to rise. "We have the yurt to ourselves for the rest of the night, and more privacy than we have had since our very first time. There aren't ten other people in here with us." She laughed shyly, embracing him, pressing her warm body firmly against his full length, and they shared a long, wet, languorous kiss, their tongues exploring, hands roaming each other's body. Then she broke away and stood waiting.

Galosga slipped her shirt off over her head, revealing his flint arrowhead on its lanyard between her full breasts. "I will treasure this forever, no matter what happens," she said, caressing it tenderly. She gave a little choking sob. "Damn you, you taught me to cry again!" She hugged him again, burying her head in his shoulder to shed a few tears.

They unclenched again, and Galosga knelt down to pull her boots off, then her trousers down and off her feet. He stopped to nestle his nose in her triangle of brown black curly hair gracing her prominent mound, savoring her tangy musk.

He then stood and stripped off his clothes and stood before her. Her heart pounding and her mouth dry, she took his hands. "Let's see what Tengri has in store for us." She lay down and pulled him down and into her with no preliminaries. Galosga put no effort into restraining himself as he usually did, and when his seed filled her, she exploded in a paroxysm of pleasure like none she had ever experienced, arching her back to receive him more fully. Her body convulsed again and again, and she clung to him until the last shudder left her. She was panting, her heart hammering, sweating despite the chill, as she cradled him in her arms. He was whispering something to her in his own language. She nuzzled his ear with her lips.

They rolled off each other and lay on their backs, wordlessly. She studied the intricate yellow and green design on the decorative centerpiece in the middle of the roof covering the smoke hole, reflecting the fire below. The enormity of what she had just done suddenly hit her. *Oh Tengri! We will do what you choose for us!*

Two days later, she knew, as many women know, but can't explain how they know, that Galosga had quickened her. She was riding Eagle when just the faintest of twinges in her lower abdomen told her she was no longer alone. *Hello, little stranger! I hope you find your new home to your liking!* She thought, patting her lower belly. At the same time, her mouth went dry, and she felt a lump in her throat. *Well, it's done, and it can't be undone.*

And two days later, her very regular course failed to arrive. She visited the shaman to determine what she needed to do.

The migration was gearing up to depart, yurts being loaded onto carts and camels, and she would be leading her *zuun* out on patrol shortly. She and Galosga rode up to Marcia's yurt to say goodbye, and to share the news.

"Thanks for the talk the other day. I needed to hear what you had to say," said Hina from horseback.

"Have you made your decision?" asked Marcia.

"I made it that afternoon."

"I thought you did. Our cycles have been in synchronization for months," she said with a knowing wink.

"We asked Tengri to guide us, that if I quickened, it would be his choice that I be Galosga's wife. Well, I'm pregnant, scared for the first time in my life, and I can't go back and change my mind. That's how I wanted it, and that is how I had to have it. I gave him the most precious thing I had, my status as a warrior, and now we have a future together."

"Being scared of new things is good for you," said Marcia. "I am happy for you. Father Galosga looks pleased," she added, glancing at the big man, as his face split with a broad smile. He didn't smile often, but when he did it was as bright as any lamp.

"How about your *zuun*?"

"The *shanyu* said that I can take them to Dzungaria, if I feel able. Two or three months. After that, nobody knows. I am a fighting woman, now I am a pregnant fighting woman, always breaking new ground! The *shanyu* said he will find more suitable duties for me, so I don't have to carry my baby into battle and nurse during a fight."

"Good luck to you and Galosga."

"If it's a boy, we'll name him Antonius, if it's a girl, Marcia."

"I'll return the favor and call ours Galosga or Hina. We'll let everyone know that the strange names belong to the most marvelous people we ever knew." She then switched to the Xiongnu that she had learned. "May *Tengri* bless you, and the great blue sky smile upon you."

"Not bad! *Bona dea te benedicat.* May the Good Goddess bless you!"

"I will miss you, and think of you always." Marcia put her hand on Hina's taut thigh, gently and affectionately. "Good luck, sister."

"And to you, sister! Hiyaah!" She wheeled Eagle around and tore off at a gallop, followed by Galosga, both turning to wave farewell. They were riding off into unknown worlds, something both of them were good at doing, each having done it several times.

Antonius walked up beside Marcia and put his hand around her shoulder. "Looks like they got things figured out."

"Yes, indeed. They are going up Dzungaria and raise tiger kittens," said Marcia with a smile.

"I'll believe it when I see it," said Antonius.

"You just did. She's a couple of days pregnant."

CHAPTER 69: THE CARAVANSARY AT TURFAM

Turfam, whose Hanaean name *Jiaohe* meant 'River Junction', was located between two small rivers that converged just southeast of the city. It was built on the arid, elevated flat top of a mile-long mesa. The city overlooked the plain below, lush agricultural land rich in grapes and melons, well-watered by the rivers and an irrigation system extending out about twenty-five miles. It was a nicely built city, the capital of the Jushi kingdom on the periphery of the Middle Kingdom. Long under Xiongnu dominance, it had been conquered by the Han armies more than a century ago, but now was under Bactrian control, administered by the Xiongnu. This suited Aulus and his friends just fine.

The Roman party was encamped just east of the rivers' confluence on a vast treeless grassland below the town, empty of other travelers following the departure of the Xiongnu.

The bitter winter weather had lifted briefly for a peek at an early spring. It was a tolerably warm day, with brilliant sunlight highlighting the whites of the dusty ground and the yellows of the winterbitten shrubs and grass. Mornings were frosty, but quickly warmed up so heavy winter coats were unnecessary. In the mild weather, everyone did some sightseeing, while Marcia took her turn to guard the camp.

Locals told Aulus, Gaius and Antonius about their *karez* irrigation system, which the three found fascinating. It kept the area agriculturally productive, despite being just a few dozen miles from the Taklamakan Desert. One man offered to take them up to see it. They accepted eagerly since, even by Roman standards, it sounded like impressive engineering. They rode eastward several miles to the mountains, where vertical shafts had been sunk down hundreds of feet into the mountain. A slightly sloping horizontal tunnel linked the bottoms of the shafts, forming a conduit to lead collected mountain rainwater to the fields below, making the desert bloom even with the very modest precipitation of the area. Their guide led them into one of the horizontal shafts with a torch to light the way. The builders had sunk the vertical shafts every few hundred feet to keep the air from stagnating and suffocating the excavators. Below ground, the water never froze in winter, and the clear, fresh water bubbled happily on its way to the fields. There were hundreds of miles of such tunnels. As impressive as any Roman aqueduct, though almost invisible.

Ibrahim went down to the caravansary about a hundred yards from their camp with Shmuel, Yakov, and Demosthenes.

The caravansary was a very large hexagonal two-story yellow brick building, circled by a wide dirt perimeter road link to the three highways intersecting there. Near the caravansary perimeter there was a large fenced area with several gates, stalls, and water troughs for animals.

On each side of the caravansary's first floor were double-doored gates big enough to accommodate a fully-burdened camel, opening into an interior courtyard perhaps fifty paces across. The group entered inside through the one open door on the north.

Around the courtyard interior, businesses occupied rooms in the perimeter, including a tavern, a bath house, a kitchen and a bakery, rich with the smell of baking bread, all open and doing some business. There were large store rooms chained shut, and offices of some sort. The interior of the courtyard was filled with frameworks for merchants' stalls, most vacant, but some sheltered by multicolor awnings over tables covered by local produce and merchandise, fruits, melons, baskets and baskets of grapes and local raisins, a very good local wine, and felt clothing and rugs. A few locals examined the goods or chatted idly with the few remaining vendors.

Ibrahim, taking Demosthenes with him, went off to see if he could find someone who knew anything about caravans. Demosthenes had learned Greek as a boy, but his birth language was Bactrian, and he was pleasantly surprised that most of the locals spoke a dialect that he could understand. And they understood him.

Ibrahim found the office that served the various enterprises operating out of the caravansary. Some of them spoke *han-yu*, though not well, and the local dialect was very different from the now-familiar Gansu dialect.

Ibrahim asked for someone named Alisher, whom the Xiongnu had recommended to him. They pointed toward a man at a table, studying some maps. Alisher, the manager of one of the two enterprises here, was a short stocky man of Eurasian appearance, about fifty or so, clean shaven with a mustache, longish dark hair streaked with gray, and happy dark eyes. Mercifully, he spoke excellent *han-yu,* though he exchanged pleasantries with Demosthenes in their own language. He described himself as a *Yue-zhi*, a Kushan in Bactrian.

"*Shanyu* Bei of the Huyan clan recommended you. I and my associates need to get to *Da Qin* territory, but we have no idea how to do that," said Ibrahim, simplifying their predicament down to the basics.

Not only had the *shanyu* recommended Alisher to Ibrahim and Aulus, he had also filled Alisher in on their situation. Alisher responded happily, "Let's go the tavern to discuss this over a bottle of wine!"

In the tavern he acquainted Ibrahim and Demosthenes with the details of how the caravan system worked. The man's knowledge was encyclopedic; he had begun working in this enterprise under his father, and had led caravans as a youth. His grandfather had built this caravansary.

"You have a long way ahead of you, my friend," said Alisher. "About five thousand *li*, six months to a year. But I made the whole trip all the way, not once but twice. I swam in the sea you call the Middle Sea, just so I could say I did. Both trips took more than two years"

Ibrahim mentally converted the *li*, about two thousand Roman miles. "Quite a trip! How did you do it?"

"No caravan goes all the way, not more than a year roundtrip, usually a lot less. You have to know your route like the back of your hand, and the territory and markets. And your drivers want to see their families again."

Ibrahim thought how similar this was to oceanic trading.

Alisher continued. "We base out of key cities like Turfam here that provide caravansaries like this one. I work three caravans out of here, one down to Chang'an and back along the way you came, one north to Dzungaria, where your Xiongnu friends are heading, and one southwest to Kashgar, which is where you are going. Each is about a six months round trip, except for Chang'an which is a bit longer."

"How big are the caravans?" asked Ibrahim.

"Usually about five hundred animals, some supply wagons, a few hundred people as animal guides, and special people like carpenters and wheelwrights to repair wagons. And a few dozen guards."

"What about tag-alongs like us?"

"We take on travelers if we trust them, for a few silver coins per person. That buys you security, and someone you can trust who knows the area, routes, and languages. It's good for us, because the bigger the group, the less interest the bandits have in robbing us. Each of those animals carries about five hundred pounds of merchandise, and you help load them up every morning and unload them every night. If you are any good with weapons, you can help out with security. You provide your own wagons, food, animals, and shelter."

"Sounds like we need a lot of food and supplies for six months," said Ibrahim.

"Not really. Going to Kashgar, you will stop at Korla, Kucha, and Gumo, and several smaller towns, usually not more than week or two on the road. You can load up with supplies at each stop, and they have baths, bars, and inns like the one upstairs. My crew has priority for rooms, but you can rent any left over, or camp out around the building.

"What about beyond Kashgar?"

"I have one arriving from Kashgar this week and turning around in a few days to head back. If we agree to do business together, I will be happy to assist in arranging your next leg, and give you a reduced rate if you use one of my partners going west from there," offered Alisher.

"Interesting. We would like our route to go through the city of Bactra, because Demosthenes needs to return home," said Ibrahim.

"From Kashgar," Alisher answered thoughtfully, "the most popular route is to Samarkand through the Ferghana Valley, but that is slow. The caravans stop at all the big trading centers at Khogand, Bukhara and Samarkand, and all the smaller ones in between. There is a lot of buying and selling on that route, and they don't leave each city till they are full. You will spend a lot of time just waiting to move on, and Bactra would be a detour."

Alisher took a sip of wine and continued. "I have a partner in Kashgar who runs shorter routes to Bagram, as soon as the snows clear out of the high passes. From Bagram you can go alone to Bactra. The distance is short, the countryside safe, and you will travel much faster."

"Well, I think I need to discuss this with my friends, but this sounds interesting. I think everyone is in a hurry to get back."

"So tell me about your friends," asked Alisher, pouring Ibrahim more wine.

"Well, besides Demosthenes here, there are seven more. Aulus Aemilius Galba, Gaius Lucullus and Antonius Aristides are *Da Qin*, Marcia is Antonius' wife, and Shmuel and Yakov are my companions. They all speak Gansu *han-yu* and the *Da Qin* speak Greek."

"Well, this is about the limit for the Gansu dialect. Bactrian will be understood everywhere from here to Parthia, so you will depend on Demosthenes, or learn it from him. Greek is widely spoken west of Kashgar." He paused and looked Ibrahim squarely in his eye. "And you are what to these people?" asked Alisher pointedly.

"I am their humble guide," answered Ibrahim.

"Your friends are far from home. How did you come to be here?" asked Alisher.

"We came by ship, at Tianjin. Due to unfortunate circumstances, we missed the ship and it left without us. And the *Da Qin* are on a mission of discovery, to learn lands and people that are new to them, so they decided to return overland," answered Ibrahim, evasively.

Alisher expected him to be evasive. The *shanyu* had described Ibrahim as a man of few words, who would never tell a stranger more than absolutely necessary. His companion Aulus would be the one to fill in the details if Ibrahim approved of the listener.

Alisher accompanied Ibrahim to the Roman encampment to check out their gear and livestock. Everyone was out except Marcia, guarding the encampment. She was wearing her Xiongnu felts, her bow, sword and shield on her back, dagger at her waist, looking formidable except for her smile as she greeted the pair happily.

"This is Marcia, Antonius' new wife. They had quite a wedding in Liqian a few months ago." Turning to Marcia, Ibrahim introduced the beaming

Alisher, who bowed. "This is Alisher, who has explained how we are to get home."

"Honored!" answered Marcia.

"Also! I had not expected such a well-armed newly-wed!" quipped Alisher.

Ibrahim interjected. "She was taught to fight by one of the Xiongnu warrior women. She is not someone I would want to go up against alone, and we are all very proud of her." He patted her affectionately across the shield.

"Quite an unusual skill. I have heard some of the Xiongnu women do take up arms, though not often," answered Alisher.

"I was taught by Hina. We actually became quite close, like sisters."

"Hina, yes, she was the one I had in mind! I talked with her last week when they were here. If you trained under her, you trained under their best, and I would not want to be the person trying to raid your camp! She spoke highly of you as well."

Ibrahim and Alisher went off to inspect the Roman equipment. Their transportation consisted of two camels, two oxen, the covered ox cart, and a good string of horses, with additions from their Xiongnu hosts, consisting of one rambunctious stallion and fifteen mares, enough to give each horse a day off. The stallion kept the mares in line, making the string easier to manage. Only Marcia could ride him, but he was her favorite mount. These were tough Mongolians, good for the mountains, cold weather and rough forage, and able to keep up a good pace. Alisher checked each animal carefully, pronounced them fit, and the cart sound. They could purchase saddles and pack gear for the camels that would allow them to be ridden as well as to carry baggage.

At the end, Alisher made an invitation. "So… when your friends return, would you please invite them to my house in Turfam tomorrow afternoon for dinner? I would like to meet them and let them know what adventures they have in front of them. If everyone agrees, we can close the deal then," asked Alisher.

"To be sure!" answered Ibrahim. They exchanged directions to his house, and then Alisher strode off to the caravansary alone.

The mention of Aulus's name and Liqian triggered something in his memory. Back in the caravansary courtyard, he strode toward one of the double doors on the southwest side, and unlocked the chain with a key from a massive keychain around his waist. The dark musty storeroom was packed with sacks, rolls of silk covered with protective cloth, cases stacked to the height of a man, each tagged with a red ribbon, all the goods going to Kashgar and points west.

Just inside the door was a cubby-holed box, partially filled with papers, scrolls, Hanaean bamboo scripts, and other documents. Alisher rummaged through the shelves until he found what he was looking for.

Alisher examined the document. It was a rolled-up piece of paper, sealed with an impressive *Da Qin* seal, and addressed to Senator Aulus Aemilius Galba in Latin, Greek and Hanaean. He would deliver it to the man in person tomorrow. He put it in his pocket, closed and relocked the storage room doors, and went back to the office.

Gaius, Aulus and Antonius returned about sunset, to share in the news about the caravan, and they made plans to meet with Alisher the next afternoon.

Gaius and Aulus retired to the yurt early after dinner and a long day, having ridden about thirty miles. Antonius stayed up a bit, and found Shmuel sitting alone by the outside fire, looking somewhat morose. He had gone through more bottles of wine than normal, drinking by himself. Antonius decided to sit with him and chat, under the pretext of practicing his little-used and much-abused Aramaic. "Art thou missing Galosga, my friend?" he asked.

"Huh?" answered Shmuel. "Oh, yes, I am. He was a good friend, but I am glad to see him pair off permanently with Hina. She was a good match for him."

"She was, and the Huyans are a good match for him also. Our world is too different for him. How long didst thou know him?" asked Antonius.

"I was on the *Orion*, my first little ship out of Tyre, when he joined us in Carthage on some ship from Gades. They had kidnapped him, treated him pretty badly, and passed him on to us in trade. He couldn't talk to anyone, they didn't pay him anything, and they pulled ugly pranks on him. I took him under my wing and protected him from the worst of it. But he did not need not much protection. The man was big and very strong. The fire of his anger may start slowly, but it burns brightly.

"One man went too far one night and pulled a knife on him. No one saw Galosga's hand so much as move, but then suddenly, he had the man by the throat, and his feet six inches off the deck. I had been teaching him some Aramaic, and he said just one word: 'Drop!' The fellow dropped that knife, Galosga kicked it to me, and he shook the man like he was a sack of feathers. Then he said one more word, 'No!' and dropped him. The man scuttled off. They backed off a bit after that."

"I believe they would," answered Antonius, chuckling.

"So he and I became very close, even though we could hardly talk. The rest of the crew called him the dummy. He could understand, I think, more than he let on, but he did not like to embarrass himself. Except with me." Shmuel smiled and continued. "So when we got to Alexandria, Hasdrubal was recruiting crews and signed us both on to the *Europa*, for a ridiculous amount of money for a deckhand. I vouched that I would handle any language problems with him, that he was very smart, strong and hard-working, so they took him, too.

"Thou shouldst have seen his eyes in Alexandria! Like nothing he had ever seen in his life, the lighthouse, broad streets, temples, the Library. It wasn't until he got to speaking *han-yu* that he could tell me how different his world was from this one," said Shmuel.

"So what wilt thou do when we go back to Rome? Art thou going home to Galilee?" asked Antonius.

"That is what saddens me. Antonius, I am an outlaw, with a price on my head and crucifixion in my future. I think I will probably drop off in Parthia somewhere. I would love to see my family in Capernaum, but probably never will again," answered Shmuel.

"What didst thou do?" asked Antonius.

"I was born five years after thy people destroyed our temple, laid waste to our land, raped our women, sold most of us off into slavery, and took our temple treasure and sacred articles to Rome," said Shmuel bitterly, taking another swig of wine.

Antonius interjected. "*Legio XII* took part in that fracas, though well before my time under the eagles."

Shmuel continued. "When I was sixteen, I fell in with a band of zealots that promised to finish the revolution and throw you Roman bastards out. What they actually did was rob and kill a lot of travelers on the road to Caesarea. I shipped out of Tyre as a deckhand to disappear. I am a wanted man, so I cannot go home again." Another sip of wine and he cast the empty bottle aside.

"When Ibrahim and Yakov headed out to Luoyang to start over as shepherds, I went along. I had done some shepherding when I was young, so I thought I could help. He had been a good skipper, and we all spoke Aramaic. Galosga was going to follow me to hell itself, if that was where I wanted to go, so … here we all are! One big happy criminal family!" he laughed, but with a bitter edge.

"And it's a good thing thou art. Without thee we would be dead! I think I can help thee. I can get thee a pardon in return for all that thou hast done for us," said Antonius.

"How wouldst thou do that?" asked Shmuel.

"When we get to Roman territory, thou art my prisoner, so no one else can take thee from me. When I get to the authorities, I will tell them that thou saved the Roman mission, including the Senator, and that thou hast earned a pardon."

"What if they do not grant it?" asked Shmuel, encouraged but skeptical.

"Senator Aulus is on speaking terms with Emperor Trajan. They will grant it," answered Antonius. "If thou wish it, Senator Aulus can get thee citizenship for that deed as well. No one can crucify thee after thou art a citizen!" He paused for a moment for effect. "Citizens must be beheaded if they misbehave, as it is more kind!" he laughing, slapping Shmuel heartily on the back. "And if you do misbehave, I'll do the beheading personally!"

"God bless you!" said Shmuel, thunderstruck at the offer. "Then I could go home?"

"Anytime," answered Antonius. "He produced another bottle of Turfam wine. "You are empty. A toast to you!"

CHAPTER 70: THE CARAVAN MASTER

The next day, the Roman party left Shmuel in charge of the camp and took the wagon to the caravansary to use the bath house and get new clothes before going on to Alisher's home. Their Hanaean peasant garb was no longer appropriate for this area and their Xiongnu felts were ripe with sweat, their own and that of their horses.

The caravansary was preparing for the Kashgar caravan's arrival, opening up shops in the inner courtyard, merchants setting up early to get the best spots. Locals also milled around the stands, vying for local goods and merchandise before the caravan arrived to clean it all out.

The Romans took a soak in the wooden bath, then persuaded the proprietor, with the help of a few copper coins, to close the facility momentarily so Marcia could bathe in privacy.

Refreshed, the group found a stand selling a local garb called a '*salwar kamis*,' a long shirt over baggy trousers, apparently universal for both men and women here. The difference between work clothes and dress clothes seemed to be in quality of fabric and amount of decoration. They each, including Marcia, bought several sets of linen work clothes, beige trousers and off-white shirts, good traveling shoes, a wide flat woolen hat called a *pakool*, and a wrap-around blanket.

In addition to the traveling clothes, the men each purchased a nice silk *salwar kamis* for the afternoon, each choosing a slightly different color trousers, white shirts, a dark sash to serve as a belt, an embroidered dark vest, all intricately and individually embroidered, a plain black pillbox hat and dress shoes.

All of the men went around behind the stall to change into their fancy clothes, then bundled their bulky felts together with their new purchases, and put them all in the waiting wagon bed.

Marcia saw several local women wearing dresses of an unusual style that she found attractive, so she and Antonius went in search of a dress merchant. She found one such dress on a stand fronting one of the stalls built into the wall, underneath the uplifted door. The skirt came with an accompanying white blouse and vest, all of shimmering silk. She lifted the blue filigreed skirt off its hanger and held it against her waist. "Look at this, Antonius! This is so beautiful!"

"It certainly is, *domina*. Try it on, and the other things with it."

The proprietress helped her select a set of about the right size, and Marcia took them into the back of the booth where the woman had rigged a privacy screen; local women bought here frequently, and they needed to try things on. Marcia needed to get out of the serviceable but rough winter felts she had worn since Liqian, washed not nearly as often as they should have been.

After a few minutes, she stepped back out.

The skirt was shiny turquoise blue with a white hem, delicately embroidered with red, green and white threads to form flowers and birds. It fell to mid calf, widely flared, and had some sort of silken undergarment beneath. The blouse was plain white shimmering silk, and the vest dark blue, also intricately filigreed. She spun around and the skirt swirled with her. "*Pulchra est!* This is beautiful!" she cried delightedly in Latin, acting for once like a little girl.

"And so are you, *domina,*" answered Antonius, then back in *han-yu* to the proprietress. "How much?"

The woman named a price and Antonius handed her some coins. "Include a hat and shoes as well," he said. She smiled and put an embroidered black pill-box hat on Marcia's head at a jaunty angle, and handed her a pair of embroidered silk shoes, whose tips came up in a point. Not very practical for walking, but definitely pretty.

"Antonius, it's beautiful, but when are we going to wear all this again?" she wailed. "I don't need it!"

"Sorry, *domina,* you're stuck with it. We've all got one nice dress rig, and who knows when we might need it again? Bundle up the felts and take them with you before I burn them," he said. "I don't get many chances to spoil my bride, do I?" he said with a wink. If these clothes ever got back to Rome, they would be quite the talk, and the price was ridiculously cheap. She was fun to spoil.

"Oh, Antonius! *Te amo!*" she said, smiling and taking his arm, her old well-worn winter clothes bundled up under her arm.

The now well-dressed Roman party toured the caravansary, admiring the jewelry, cooking equipment, and glazed pottery. Little cooking stalls offered competition to the eatery, roasted goat, *nan*, melons, and the yellow raisins for which the area was famous. It was, as it almost always was, clear and sunny, and the sun was providing a bit of warmth now in March.

In the afternoon, the Roman party took the cart with their bundles back to Shmuel in the camp, along with some wine and food they had bought for him. They then rode out to Turfam, across a bridge over the river, and up one of several sloping roads built onto the cliff face from rammed earth overlaid with stones and gravel. The road was about twenty feet wide, stone stairs laid on the inboard side for pedestrians. The cart clattered its way up the cobbled surface, swaying and lurching. There was not much on the outboard side of the road to prevent their plunging a long way down to the river below, just a slightly elevated wall that would not stop a panicked horse.

At the top, the city wall grew up vertically from the edge of the cliff face, indented into a hollow square that served as a courtyard in front of the entryway. The road debouched onto the courtyard, the gate on their left. Its massive wooden doors stood open, guarded by a none-too-alert sentry, absentmindedly waving everyone through without looking too closely at any of them.

Inside the wall, they found Alisher's residence easily enough on the perimeter road, a two story whitewashed adobe building, the second story overlooking the wall. Two rows of neatly cut logs protruded from the walls at the tops of each story, providing both decoration and support. From the roof, black smoke curled up, tangy with the scent of roasting meat.

They tethered the horses to a hitching post and Ibrahim knocked on the red-painted door. Alisher answered. "Come in, come in!" he said, waving them in. "Welcome to my humble house! You have adopted the local dress very well."

Humble the house was not. The rough whitewashed walls held silk tapestries depicting various Hanaean scenes, while on the floor under their feet lay thickly padded carpets woven with incredibly intricacy, some in blues, golds and whites, others black and gold. Padded sofas and chairs lined the walls, and here and there were statuaries from various countries. Aulus noticed one that was almost certainly Greek, or a very good copy. A bronze horse, with a bluish green patina, its nostrils flaring and mane and tail flying with the wind, was frozen for all time delicately balanced on a single hoof in mid-gallop on a black lacquered table in the middle of the room. And a bronze idol of the god they called Buddha rested somnolently in the corner, smiling beatifically, hand raised.

"Introductions, please," said Ibrahim. "This is Aulus Aemilius, Gaius Lucullus and Antonius Aristides of the *Da Qin* army, of whom we spoke yesterday, and my adopted son and business associate, Yakov of Petra. Antonius' wife Marcia and our traveling companion Demosthenes of Bactria you met yesterday."

Alisher bowed in the Hanaean style. "Pleased. And Marcia... you look beautiful. You are not armed today?"

"I am off duty," she replied with a bright smile, with a hint of a polite Hanaean bow.

A tall woman entered the room, wearing a dark blue *salwar kamis* with a floral pattern. "And this is my wife, Farahnaz. Her name means 'Joy,' and she has truly been a joy to me." Alisher bowed by way of introduction, sweeping his hand before his wife. "Unfortunately, she does not speak *han-yu.*" Demosthenes took the opportunity, offering a blessing on their house in Bactrian, delighting her. She bowed and took his hand, smiling. Then Alisher beckoned them toward stairs at the back of the room. "A pleasant surprise! Come upstairs, and we can dine on the roof."

The stairs opened onto a square open area on the second floor, its elegant polished wood floor overlaid with more intricate carpentry. A parallel set of stairs led to the roof through an open hatch, admitting sunlight, reflecting on pastel-colored vases at various points around the room. The second floor was apparently sleeping quarters, with one room at one end and several at the other. Alisher gestured toward the multiple rooms in passing. "These are my sons' rooms. They are all grown now with their own homes and families, but my son Jamshid is staying with us. He is taking the incoming caravan back to Kashgar, and rode out to meet them today."

They climbed to the flat white adobe roof. A raised wall about four feet on the perimeter provided protection against falls over the edge, and over that wall they could see a spectacular panoramic view in all directions... the grassland, with their tents, and some yurts they had not noticed sitting like mushrooms every few miles in clumps of one to five. The east-west highway ran like a brown slash across the grassland as far as the eye could see, and far to the southwest, a faint yellow glare marked the beginnings of the Taklamakan. The Flaming Mountains to the east and the snow-clad Tien Shan range to the north completed the view.

The rooftop was populated with a cabinet and a table under an awning, and weatherworn wooden chairs clustered around a big firepit; a goat on a hand-cranked spit over a glowing fire dropped occasional spatters of grease that hissed as they hit the flames, adding aroma to the air. "I love to come up here to just sit and watch the view. And it is warm enough now to do it during the day, though I fear March has some more cold days for us. It always does. Sit!" He motioned to the chairs in the center, and beckoned to one of the white-robed servants, unobtrusive on the perimeter, who went to the cabinet and extracted some wine and cups. He returned with a tray and distributed them amongst the guests.

Demosthenes exchanged some pleasantries with Fahranaz, then turned to the Romans. "Besides Greek, we speak Bactrian at home. I am pleased to hear it spoken here."

"You didn't pass this way when you left Bactria?" asked Alisher.

"No, we went south through Qandahar, Purushapura, and then on to Tibet, for Buddhist studies. I didn't know Bactrian had penetrated this far north."

"Mostly in the last fifty years," Alisher said. "The Han tried to control this area, but it is too far from their center. The local people, myself included, speak Tocharian, but outside our clan, everyone else speaks Bactrian, all the way to Parthia, north to Sogdiana, and south to northern India. So traders use it out of necessity. In Bactria they speak Greek as much as they speak Bactrian, and use the Greek script for both languages. Our King Vima Kadphises in Bagram mints his coins *basileus basileon*, the King of Kings!" said Alisher.

Demosthenes, Alisher and Farahnaz exchanged a few words, and the smiles and gestures indicated to the Romans and to Ibrahim that there would be no language problem as long as Demosthenes was with them.

Returning to *han-yu*, Alisher continued. "As a merchant I use many languages. Tocharian at home, Bactrian, *han-yu* and Parthian at work. A little Greek, but not well, I am sorry, though I can read it a bit. So enough about me. Tell me how you came to be here." He addressed Aulus, since he knew from the Xiongnu that he was the senior man among them.

Aulus launched into the whole story, the Gan Ying expedition, and the Roman mission in response. He pulled no punches, not omitting the hijacking and eventual alliance-turned-friendship with Ibrahim, the disaster in the Hanaean court, Ibrahim's role in their escape and eventual link up with the Xiongnu, and the wedding at Liqian, though omitting the death of Wang Ming. The whole story took about half an hour.

At the end, Alisher smiled at Ibrahim. "Your friend keeps secrets well. He told me you were just explorers, out to see strange new lands and have great adventures. Which you certainly seem to have done. I have one problem: if you are still at odds with Luoyang, they could seriously hurt my Chang'an route if they wish to retaliate against me for helping you."

Aulus had brought along with him their letter of safe passage they had been given in Liqian against just this eventuality, and handed it to him. "For whatever reason, Emperor He has had second thoughts, and his representatives gave us this in Liqian." He handed the roll to Alisher, who read it and reread it.

"Hmmm," said Alisher, scrutinizing the seal for authenticity. "It's not like Emperor He to change his mind like that."

"Well, we were not there when it happened. But happen it apparently did. His emissaries in Liqian wanted us to return to his court as his guests, but at that point, we declined. He gave us safe passage anyway." Aulus paused, and continued, "Ibrahim did not lie to you, but he will not tell more than what he thinks a stranger needs to know, and his discretion has more than once saved our lives. But I thought you needed to know all about us, so you could choose whether to have us aboard or not."

"I appreciate your honesty. And for that, I will be happy to have you join us, if you wish. I don't think I've ever had such a distinguished and strange set of fellow travelers!"

"I do so wish," answered Aulus, producing a clinking purse and putting it on the table. "Tell me about the connecting caravan to ... where? Bagram?"

"Well, my partner Behzad in Kashgar runs a route to Bagram through the Pamir Mountains beginning in May when the snows clear in the passes. So let's see, travel to Kashgar will be two silver coins per person, and you will pay Behzad an additional one silver coin each."

Aulus counted out sixteen *denarii*. Alisher accepted them and put them in his pocket. "I will write you a letter of introduction for Behzad, and tell you how to find him. And speaking of letters, I believe this is yours. It came in from Liqian with the last caravan from Chang'an. Most unusual!" He handed Aulus the scroll.

Aulus examined the unbroken seal, and saw his name in Latin, Greek, and some Hanaean characters. "Actually, I think this is yours, Marcia. From Marcus." He handed her the scroll, and she took it with unsteady fingers. "You may wish to go off with Antonius to read it in private. You may share it with us, if the news is good."

He turned toward Alisher. "This letter is from her brother who remained behind in Liqian, with instructions to write and deliver it as best he could. It looks like it worked!"

Antonius and Marcia went off to a corner of the roof, hoping the letter brought good news, but afraid that it might not. She fumbled with the seal and unrolled it, reading it softly aloud:

Ave, dearest sister.

I hope this letter finds you, Antonius, and all of our beloved party in good health, and by the time this reaches you, safely back in Roman territory. Mother and I are in good health, and she sends her regards. She regrets that she never learned to write Latin well, but I convey her words to you.

Authorities from Lanzhou came here inquiring about our mutual friend. His absence has been noted, and they wished to know his whereabouts. We conveyed the information that you had provided, which seemed to satisfy them. I think we can permanently close the door on that most unhappy part of your life.

As for my life, it has taken a most unexpected turn. My friend Frontinus' cousin Mei was abandoned by her husband because she was barren. She was living with Frontinus' family, at some burden to them, because it is difficult for a woman at her age, a bit older than me, to support herself. We found we shared a common interest in poetry and languages, and she is now residing in your never-again-to-be-used room with Mama and me. She is aware of my condition, and we find it no impediment to our happiness and pleasure. So, while the Lucian line may come to an abrupt end with me, I am sure that you and Antonius will happily make up for our inabilities, if you have not already done so. I do not know if we will wed, or simply reside together here at our home, but for now, in a manner that I never expected, I feel that I am, once again, a whole and complete man.

I have not heard from Papa, I believe his spirit is finally at rest.

Looking forward to your reply, no matter how many years it may take, I remain your loving brother.

Marcus.

Marcia read and reread her brother's letter, her eyes brimming with tears. When she finished, she turned to hug Antonius and sobbed happily into his shoulder. "Thank you, thank you, thank you, gods!" she repeated over and over again, then to the group around the fire, "The news is all good!"

They returned to take their place by the fire, and recapped the gist of the letter for everyone, Demosthenes translating for Farahnaz, who smiled at Marcia's obvious delight.

"With that, I think we should toast our lovely lady's great good news!" Alisher said, raising his cup for everyone to join in. "So now, Marcia, would you explain to me how such a lovely Hanaean lady came by such blue eyes, a *Da Qin* name, and a proud husband?" he asked, his mustache quivering with amusement.

With that, the business part was obviously over, and fingers reached for the greasy goat meat and *nan*. The talk went on till late at night, about themselves, the Carrhae legions, life in Rome, Liqian and Luoyang, about Turfam and its irrigation system, about life and history in this part of the world. They went home with moonlight silver on the grasslands below, taking special care not to drive off the sloping roadway down the cliff face. Once down, they let the mares find their way home to their stallion at camp.

Back in Luoyang, the *tingwei* reviewed the report from Lanzhou. The military cavalry squadron had returned without Wang Ming, reporting that he had stayed behind to recover his concubine and bring her home with him.

However, two months had passed and Wang Ming had not yet returned. The *tingwei* had directed the provincial government at Lanzhou to launch inquiries, beginning in Liqian. None of the townspeople recalled him by name, though a handful recalled a well-dressed man inquiring about the Liu Shiu family, the family name of Si Huar and Si Nuo. Inquiries at the Liu Shiu residence revealed that Si Huar's brother had remained behind to care for his aging mother. Both said that Wang Ming had come to the house to ask Si Huar to return with him. She had refused, and he had left after some words. They did not know where he went, though they believed he was going east. Si Huar and the *Da Qin* named An-dun subsequently had an elaborate wedding at the Xiongnu encampment that brought almost all the town out for the festivities. None of the residents had seen Wang Ming in the camp, and there were no altercations before, during and after the wedding.

The *tingwei* determined that Wang Ming was most likely the victim of robbers, accident or illness somewhere on the long road back to Luoyang. He concluded that the missing man's fate might never be known, and that further inquiries were not warranted.

The next day the *tingwei* presented his report to the Son of Heaven, after a briefing to him and the full council on Xiongnu relocation and pacification. As was his want, the Emperor sat in silence for a long time after the conclusion of the *tingwei's* report, to quiet his mind and to focus his thoughts for the proper solemn response. Then he replied. "*Tingwei* Feng Chu'o, you have done well. I am pleased to learn that Si Huar has been wed to An-Dun. She has gained a courageous and honorable husband, and I hope he brings her the loving kindness she deserves."

He made another long pause. "Harmony in the world begins with the family, and spreads out to create harmony about them. There is no greater responsibility that a man has, than to maintain harmony within his own family, with discipline if necessary. However, there is no greater disharmony than for a man to misuse that responsibility to inflict cruelty for the pleasure of cruelty. Wang Ming did this, as we all knew, and we did not correct his behavior, which led to more disharmony. Because of this disharmony, a very important initiative, ably executed by Ban Chao on my behalf, was brought to naught. So I charge you to ensure that no one in this household ever again cruelly disciplines a member of their family, wife, child, or slave. I charge you to correct those who break this rule."

Another long pause. He thought of the bold *Da Qin* in their strange garb, seizing the honor to defend one of their own, at whatever cost they might incur for doing so. He remembered the portly ambassador's gray eyes, fixed on his own, simply because it was so rare for him to see anyone's direct gaze. Among his advisors, only the *tingwei*, Ban Chao and a few others, had ever had the courage to do this, and only in private council. And he was about to lose Ban Chao: the man's failing health had precluded his attendance today. However badly the *Da Qin* had violated protocol, they had shown the highest courage and honor.

CHAPTER 71: THE ROAD TO KASHGAR

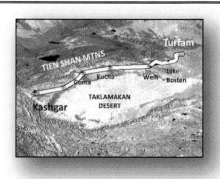

Three riders heralded the arrival of the caravan from Kashgar, riding in hard to dismount at the caravansary, handing over their sweating, snorting horses to the livery boys. The riders sought out Alisher to let him know that the caravan from Kashgar was two days west, giving him a list of the quantity and destination of the various cargoes and passengers. After reading the list, Alisher asked a few questions, then gave them a bundle of silk ribbons of various colors. They remounted to rejoin the caravan after a quick meal at the small eatery.

The caravansary came alive over the next several hours. Merchants came down to stake out the remaining locations, setting up their stalls under multicolored awnings in advance of their merchandise. Carts began rumbling in with wine, food and supplies for the tavern and bakery. People cleaned out the newly-opened accommodations upstairs. Alisher's people began inventorying goods in the storage areas for the caravan's return trip, cross-checking to make sure nothing had been misplaced.

The night before the caravan's arrival, everything was waiting for them. The bath house normally ran only one bath, but could bring up five for a caravan. All were hot and steaming, the air thick with the pungent smell of smoke from the shiny black rocks called *mei* used for fuel. Everyone took advantage of the baths, and the proprietor offered an hour reserved for women.

After baths and a small meal, the Roman party returned to their camp to bundle up their gear to prepare for traveling, and all moved into Antonius' and Marcia's yurt, planning to sell the smaller communal one.

They each inventoried the beeswax-sealed cash, with Ibrahim's and Aulus's showing knife marks where some coins had been dug out to reward Mama Biyu and Bohai generously several months back for their help, and more for the Xiongnu and Alisher. Everyone else's beeswax stash was intact. They decided to dig out two to five silver coins each, and trade them off with Alisher in the morning for copper and brass ones. Silver attracted too much attention.

The caravan arrived mid-morning the next day, turning north off the main road, lined with merchants and townspeople gawking at their arrival. Such arrivals were festive affairs, bringing news of faraway places, men returning home after months on the road, and an opportunity to buy and sell.

Children held their parent's hand or sat on their father's shoulders, to wave at the fascinating entourage of camels, horses, donkeys, carts and wagons, escorted by fierce-looking armed horsemen... who broke into smiles at the opportunity to wave their swords in mock threats at the children. Camels, with seemingly impossible loads, slumped along uncomplaining, their tails swishing at flies, and occasionally leaving a little fertilizer behind for the farmers' fields. Carts creaked and lurched, horses carried heavy loads or riders.

One by one, each load entered the south gate, Alisher's people directing the organized chaos inside. Young boys working for a few copper coins led the animals to the color-coded storage areas matching their ribbons where waiting men unloaded them, and the boys led them to the paddocks back outside. By noon, all the animals were contentedly grazing in the paddock, and the bath house was full of grimy drivers and loaders refreshing themselves after many days on the road. More men nursed drinks and meals in the adjacent eatery and bar, waiting their turn for a much needed hot soak.

Antonius and Marcia quickly sold off the extra yurt and some of their Xiongnu summer clothing that morning. The brass coins they earned from that sale were promptly handed over to a merchant selling camel tack: two saddles, high in front and back to fit between the animal's two humps, with two big saddle bags and a rump pack that looked like they could carry several hundred pounds, if the camel didn't mind both a rider and a load.

For lunch they dined in the little eatery: goat with *nan* bread and bowls of Turfam's famous yellow raisins, dried in the heat of the sun, washed down with the town's equally fine wine. They bought supplies, bottles of wine, and big wheels of *nan*, each about two feet in diameter and an inch thick, golden brown with a white fluffy inside. *Nan* was standard caravan fare, requiring no preparation, and it would keep for months. Supplemented with camel milk, it was extremely nourishing. Alisher had advised them there would be three layovers on the trip to Kashgar, about six weeks depending on weather and time spent in the cities along the way.

The Roman party met with Alisher's son, the caravan master Jamshid. He was stocky, a bit shorter than Antonius, swarthy and dark-haired with a bushy beard, in his forties. His complexion was fair but leathery from exposure to the harsh weather for most of his life. First, Aulus asked about languages enroute, to add to what they had learned from his father.

"Yeah," he said, with a decided western drawl to his *han-yu*, "By Kashgar nobody speak *han-yu* except few merchants, travelers like you. They speak *yue-zhi*, more *yue-zhi* further west you go." He exchanged a few words with

Demosthenes in Bactrian, and they shared smiles at some mutual comprehension. "You friend here speak western *yue-zhi*, I understand pretty well what he say. Get better, go further west."

"Well, that sounds promising. Dim, do you think you can teach us Bactrian so we are not lost if you are not with us? The way we learned *han-yu?*" asked Aulus.

"I would be happy to try," he answered.

Then Antonius addressed Jamshid. "We want to participate in security, if you can tell us what you want us to do."

"Sure," answered Jamshid. "Ride patrol, swords, bows. You fight horseback?"

"All of us."

"Tomorrow after breakfast. Bring horses and weapons. Must go now, thank you for helping." He shook hands with Antonius in a wrist clasp, then again with Aulus and Ibrahim. He turned and headed off to tend to caravan matters.

When everyone got back to their encampment, loaded with bags of purchases on a borrowed handcart, the Roman camel novices tried their hand at riding the two camels, to the merriment of Ibrahim, Yakov, Demosthenes and the local observers who gathered around to give unasked-for advice. Their efforts to entice Claudius and Claudia to kneel so they could mount greatly annoyed the two camels, who began to make grunting noises, their mouths furiously chewing something nasty they had brought up from their stomachs just to spit it at the unsuspecting Romans. Eventually everyone got on, went several times in a circle, stopping, starting, turning, and dismounting, without falling off. Afterwards, the camels were happy to go back to doing whatever camels do when humans are not annoying them.

Antonius and Marcia retired early, claiming to have something to discuss. The rest of the group stayed outside to drink and talk, and to give them privacy since they would soon no longer have any, once again sharing a common yurt until warmer weather. However, at one point, Marcia stormed out the tent, looking very angry, and headed off briskly for a long walk.

"Looks like whatever they were discussing did not go well with her!" remarked Gaius.

"About time they had a disagreement. They've been married for three months now!" laughed Aulus. Gaius topped off Aulus's cup, while he drank the rest out of the bottle. They talked about various things, their wives and Aulus's future family, until Marcia returned, still looking sullen. They gave her a few minutes to retire, and then went in themselves.

The next morning, Marcia awoke, reaching for Antonius, only to remember that she had, for the first time since they had become lovers, voluntarily slept apart from him on a separate blanket. She thought regretfully about their argument. *He was only being protective. I should not have said what I said.* Everyone was stirring. She reached for her felt breeches, pulled them on under the blanket over her chilled thighs, straightened up and wriggled her shirt on over her head. Now, somewhat dressed, she cast the blanket off and put on her leather riding boots. Antonius was up by now, rearranging his clothes. He had apparently slept in them.

She went up to him. His breath was bitter in the morning, but hers was probably no better. Softly, she said to him, "I am sorry for last night. I said some nasty things to you."

"No matter," he answered, but without his characteristic smile.

Marcia reached for her shield and sword on the hanger, and slipped her arms through the straps to fit it on her back.

"So yer going ter do it." He stated this, not as a question.

"Yes." Her heart thudded, fearing that this would kick life back into the embers of last night's argument.

"Why?"

"*Carus meus*, once I watched you take an arrow in the gut, and nearly die, while I was off helpless, hiding in a cave. I told you that I don't ever want to feel helpless again. That is why I learned to fight from you and Hina, and that is why I have to do this now. It's what I have to do." She watched him intently, hoping that he would understand.

"They are going to try you mercilessly, Marcia. And I can't do anything ter help yer. And they may not even give you a chance, just throw you out. You understand that?" She studied his eyes intently, seeing that he was genuinely concerned. She nodded.

"Please, if it looks hopeless, just come back ter the yurt and wait fer us. Don't fight a hopeless battle with them."

"I promise." She hefted her sword in its scabbard behind the shield, secured the straps in front, and strung her bow. That too, disappeared into the shield, and she strapped on her dagger at her waist. Antonius did likewise. They turned to face each other, and he took her by the shoulders and finally smiled, lighting her heart. "Yer look fearsome enough, *domina*. Go show 'em what yer made of!" He kissed her tenderly on her forehead.

The eight showed up at the appointed place a little after sunrise, even Dim casting off the last vestige of his monkhood; he had joined Antonius' training exercises months ago. Everyone wore the loose-fitting *salwar kamis* except Marcia, wearing the more tightly-fitting Xiongnu summer felt. She preferred that because the looser *salwar* might distract her, and she had no intention of being distracted this morning. Her gut tightened, the way it did whenever she faced a challenge like this.

Jamshid greeted the eight, and introduced them to his regular guards. Speaking in *han-yu*, he said "These *Da Qin* volunteered to help our guards so you get more time off. Three are experienced soldiers, and all are veterans of many fight. They not speak *yue-zhi*, so speak *han-yu* please so understand. We let them show us what they do, see if good as they say."

All of the men were looking intently at Marcia, obviously wondering what the hell she was doing here dressed up like a fighter. One of them, a bearded man clad in black, pointed his finger at her and said, "Who's that, a twelve year old boy or a girl?" Everyone guffawed. There was a chorus of catcalls, rude gestures, whistles and what were probably obscene comments in *yue-zhi*.

Antonius had tried to explain last night, as Hina had also explained months ago, that men will not easily accept a woman as a fighter. This was her challenge to meet; no one could do it for her. Or she could just go back, beaten before she had a chance to try.

Marcia waited until the hubbub died down, then accepted the challenge pleasantly. "My name is Marcia Lucia, wife of Antonius Aristides. And yes, I am a woman, despite the fact that he is of Greek descent!" That brought guffaws from the group, as she poked fun at the Greek reputation for pederasty which had reached even this far east.

But the man in black was not amused. He loudly proclaimed, in fairly decent *han-yu*, "I am not trusting my life to a goddamned Hanaean bitch!"

Marcia walked up to face him at arm's length, hand on hips, legs spread, her Xiongnu hat at a jaunty angle. She was still slightly smiling, though her heart was pounding. *Why did this have to be so hard?* Then she said, politely but firmly, loud enough for all to hear, "My name is Marcia Lucia, not 'goddamned Hanaean bitch'."

It got very silent. Marcia fixed her eyes on his, but out of the corner of her vision she could see everyone break ranks to circle around them, anticipating an impromptu fight. She sized him up; he outweighed her by fifty pounds, taller by six inches. She was anticipating a rush, but she saw his eyes glance briefly to her right, and heard his dagger hiss out of the scabbard. "You'll piss yourself at the sight of steel, bitch!"

A flick of his eyes betrayed his next move, a swipe across her midsection which she evaded with a nimble back step, letting the blade pass harmlessly through air. She drew her own sword with her right hand, her dagger with her left and crouched for the fight. She was vaguely aware of the crowd yelling and cheering... not for her. *Time to be loose now, girl, be ready! Time to be the cat!*

She saw his next strike coming also, this time from right to left. He again failed to connect, leaving himself extended and off-balance. She slammed her sword down on his blade, sending it clattering along the rocky dirt. She then brought the sword tip up to the hollow at the base of the disarmed man's bobbling Adam's apple. She hissed softly, so only he could hear. "The last man to try to kill me is buzzard food. Do you want to be next?" She applied a little pressure to make sure he understood, dimpling the skin but not drawing blood. Then, louder so everyone could hear, she repeated, politely with a slight smile. "My name is Marcia Lucia. I don't believe we have been introduced. Your name?"

"My name ..is...Farhad." A very long pause. "...Marcia."

"Pleased to meet you, Farhad!" She withdrew the sword from his throat to trail position, sheathed her dagger, then returned the sword to its scabbard with a solid thunk.

She retrieved his dagger, handing it back to him hilt-first, then said, again loudly so everyone could hear, "Thank you for the practice!" She turned her back to him, showing appropriate disdain for any remaining threat, and went to stand beside Antonius.

Antonius took her hand in a little squeeze, and whispered, "You did well, *domina.*"

"Thank you, *carus meus.* I never did that stroke with a real sword. I was hoping I didn't take off his hand!"

Antonius chortled. "That is good, he is the head of Jamshid's guards!"

"Oh!" She felt her gut tighten again, realizing she may have just made a very bad mistake. *Good choice, that!*

Jamshid invited any others to challenge Marcia. There were none. They went through several hours of exercises, archery on foot and on horseback, some sword drill, dagger work, and hand-to-hand against Jamshid's men. Marcia did well in all except the hand-to-hand. She held her own as best she could, but men had the advantage over her in size and weight. Nevertheless, she could punch and take a punch, and never quit until she was hopelessly pinned down. The Roman soldiers found the men average but enthusiastic fighters and brawlers.

Before lunch, Jamshid broke off the demonstration. "I satisfied they good enough," he said, to a rumble of assent and affirmative head nods. "Pick one of the *Da Qin* as partner."

One by one, the seven men were picked, beginning with the massive Antonius and ending with the older Aulus. Marcia's heart fell as each choice passed her by until she stood alone, but she had one last card to play. She walked up to Farhad, and quietly announced: "Farhad, I want to earn your trust, and there is much I have to learn from you. May I be your partner?" She looked him squarely in the eye, hoping she did not sound pleading.

Another silence fell on the group as they awaited Farhad's response. He looked her in the eye and said, "Yes. But carry your own weight."

Marcia extended her hand, man style. It hung there in the space between them for several seconds. Then he clasped her arm by the wrist, and she his. "Don't let a man get close enough to fight you with his hands. You're no good at that," he said with just the wisp of a smile.

The addition of eight to the twenty-man guard team was a welcome improvement. Farhad, the head of guards, briefed their organization. The watches would consist of four two-person teams, one *Da Qin* per team, one team in the van, two flanker teams on either side, and one in the rear. The day shift would begin an hour before departure and last till the nightly stop, the night shift from an hour before the stop until departure, to give a little overlap during the dangerous dawn and dusk periods. Going from ten to fourteen teams meant each team had a day watch, a night watch, and the third day off.

A few hours ahead of departure, Marcia and Farhad pulled their first watch together, Marcia on a black stallion, Farhad on a dun mare. They both wore black scarves around their necks and lower face against dust. "*Lroud pid tao*, peace be upon you," she greeted him in halting Bactrian.

"*Lroud pid tao*, peace be upon you also. That is a lot of horse there. Are you sure you can handle him?" he answered in rippling Bactrian.

She patted the animal gently on its sleek neck. She hadn't understood all he said, but she caught the word 'horse'. She reverted back to *han-yu*. "Sorry, that is all the *yue-zhi* I can manage right now. The horse, yes, men find him headstrong and willful, but he likes me. Whatever I want him to do, he's doing it before I tell him. His name is Excelsior, 'Ever Onward' in *Da Qin*. Anyway, I thought you would feel better if I brought a pair of balls with me, even if they aren't mine!"

Excelsior nickered happily, pawing the ground. He liked the attention, and Farhad snorted at the joke. "Not bad, not bad! Let's ride, I want to be a few miles ahead before the caravan gets started. Keep it at a trot, it's going to be long day, and I don't want to wear the animals out. Hyuu!"

Behind them, the caravan began loading up the animals and wagons with green-tagged baggage for Kashgar, exiting through the south gate to line up with the rest. After an hour or so, Jamshid blew his horn, and the caravan began to move out. Townspeople once again turned out to watch the early morning departure, their children waving excitedly at the people and the animals. The caravan was on its way.

The road wound through a green grassland oasis west of Turfam, then south to the low foothills of a tongue of the Tien Shan Mountains jutting out into the desert. Marcia and Farhad had been idly chatting till well past noon, Turfam now miles behind them. Farhad found her life fascinating, that she had gone all the way west once, come back by sea, and was now going west again. Perhaps he had underrated her. "So are you going to join the *Da Qin* army when you get home?" He was only half-joking, such things might indeed be possible there.

She laughed. "No, Farhad, I don't think they're ready for that, and I want to be Antonius' devoted *Da Qin* wife, making babies for him. I am looking forward to that, I've had enough adventure."

"Well, I am sure that you will do that very well also. So how did you learn to fight? You surprised me. You were better than I expected."

"Antonius and another woman taught me. Antonius wasn't happy about it at first, but he has gotten over it."

"Have you been in many fights?"

"Just one."

"And how did it turn out?"

"He's dead."

They rode on quietly for a while. Then Farhad picked up the conversation again. "The men don't want you on the team. They don't trust a woman in a fight."

"I know. I expect to earn your trust, and theirs."

"It won't be easy. Now we are out of Turfam, let's keep an eye open for trouble."

The gravel-strewn road rose gently up through sparse sagebrush to a pass through the foothills. From that vantage point they could see an incredible distance. Far to the east, across expanses of barrenness, one could see thirsty grasslands suckling much needed moisture from the first rainstorm of spring, billowing white clouds with shadowy gray bottoms against the darkening eastern sky, purpling above a skirt of hazy rain. To the north, the rugged white-capped Tien Shan Mountains rose to staggering heights even at a distance of fifty miles, the gold of the evening sun on their flanks contrasting with black cliff shadows. To the south, the landscape gave way to the Taklamakan desert, a vast sea of sand slowly ebbing and flowing in the wind at a pace measured in days to weeks. The pass ahead led into rugged black mountains, following a twisting pass, but the road itself did not appear difficult.

Jamshid called a halt for the night, and drivers began unloading the animals while others set up tents. Marcia and Farhad groomed their horses for the night, washed the dust from their faces and hands, and found the rest of the guard detail. The off-duty teams had prepared meals for the off-going day watch.

The next morning, the caravan cleared the pass and descended back down to the arid plains. Marcia and Farhad had the night watch. She should have had the next two days off, but Farhad informed her that he needed her to fill in on another team the next day. And at nearly every one of her next days off, Marcia was called on to ride with other partners to 'fill in for people taken ill or injured,' until Farhad no longer bothered with an excuse. Most of her partners barely tolerated her, others went out of their way to make the duty miserable. Aulus, too, was often tagged for these extra duties. She knew that Farhad, however nice and apologetic he seemed, was playing them both. She resented it, but said nothing.

Marcia was beginning to feel the wear, especially when two back-to-back night watches meant she had to sleep during the day while in transit. She tried sleeping in the jolting, jerking wagon just once and found it miserable, constantly awakened by each lurch and bump. She found that the camels Claudius and Claudia, on the other hand, had a soft, swaying gait that lulled her to sleep. Riding a camel felt like sitting in a rocking chair, with a sliding roll forward, then a gentle bowing up and a rock backward. It could be very soothing, and with the increasingly warm weather, she easily went to sleep riding. Fortunately, the camel tended to follow the animal in front, so Claudius and Claudia kept to the track, whether its human baggage was awake or not.

Outside of Kucha, Marcia and Aulus stumbled back to their yurt from a day watch, well after dark. Their partners had delayed them long enough that they had missed the courtesy meal the off-duty watches prepared for everyone else. The rest of their party had retired early, but left the fire banked.

"Marcia, I have some *nan* in my pouch and a little wine left over in my winesack. Would you join me for a bite before we retire," he asked her in Latin.

"I'd love to, Aulus Aemilius. The bastards are making sure we don't get to eat, as well as not sleep," she said, settling onto a stone set up by the fire. "I understand why they are putting me through hell, but why you? You're old enough to be their father."

Aulus handed her some *nan* and the winesack. "In fact, I am old enough to be their grandfather. That's their problem, that and I am not a very good fighter."

Marcia took a sip of wine and wolfed down the bread. "Not true! Gaius said you did very well at Tongchuan, killed one of them."

"He is very kind. I was terrible."

Marcia laughed. "First fights are like that," she said, remembering her own with Wang Ming, and what Hina had told her.

"Maybe. But be careful, some of them really don't like you."

"They have made that clear…because I am a woman," she said, taking another sip of wine and handing the sack back.

"Yes, and because you are better than most of them."

"Are you going to quit? That's all you have to do, just not show up tomorrow."

"No. Are you?"

"Wouldn't give the bastards the satisfaction. I am going to win this one. Well, we need to be in the saddle before sunup, so…" She extended her hand, then changed her mind and grabbed his shoulders, pulling him down so she could give him a peck on the cheek. "See you in the morning, Senator!"

Several weeks later, outside of Gumo, guard duty suddenly became more than routine. Marcia was riding flankers again with Farhad, engaging in small talk, when it happened.

"Yes and ... wait. Do you see that over there? Behind the hill, a little dust cloud?" she said.

"Probably a dust devil," he answered.

"I've seen it several times now. It's lasted too long, and there's not much wind."

"Let's go check it out. Men riding this far off the road will not be up to any good. They are probably bandits, scouting us to pick off stragglers, rustle animals." They clucked their horses into a brisker pace, holding their bows by the grip with arrows ready to notch.

The dust was coming from a band of ten mounted riders, all clad in baggy black Hanaean garb, heads wrapped in cloth so that only their eyes were exposed. "They look Han from their dress, and far from home. That means trouble. We're going to pull up about seventy-five yards from them, let them know we've seen them, and hope they wander off for easier pickings. Be ready!" Farhad directed.

As they closed the distance, Farhad hailed them in *han-yu*, but one of the gang unleashed an arrow that buzzed wickedly through the air between them. Marcia didn't wait for directions; she hurriedly said, "You take the front, I am going to flank them on the left, ride around behind them to draw their aim off you. Hiyaa, Excelsior! Ride, boy!" Excelsior whinnied excitedly, and set off at a dead run gathering speed, his hooves drumming rhythmically. Farhad yelled something behind her, but she didn't hear what he said.

Riding into her first combat was exhilarating. She leaned forward in the saddle, pressing her thighs tightly against the animal's heaving sides, rising slightly in the stirrups to the rhythm of his thundering hoofs as dry brush flew by at a dizzying speed. Thus balanced, she let go the reins, notched an arrow, aimed and fired, then another and another, some, she thought, striking home. An arrow buzzed over her head in response, followed by a second. Marcia rolled far over to shelter on the other side of Excelsior's flanks, hoping against hope she didn't fall at this speed. She could smell Excelsior's sweat, feel his chest heaving with each breath, the dust, pebbles and clods of dirt flung up from his hooves stinging her face. Hoof beats drowned out all sound. Secure in her grip, she leaned forward to peer under the horse's throat heaving up and down above her head, notched an arrow and let it fly, then several more from this position, until her legs began to burn from the effort of holding her weight. She grabbed the pommel and pulled herself back upright, finding herself just twenty-five yards from the group, slightly to the rear.

She took the reins, encouraging Excelsior to lay on still more effort. Several men were down, the rest beginning to mill around, disorganized, some still dismounted. She drew her sword and drove into the three men on foot, dropping one with a crunching slash to the shoulder. From the corner of her eye she saw Fahrhad charge into the remaining bandits, sword drawn and swinging. The last of the bandits wheeled about, galloping off to the north, leaving their fallen in the dirt. She counted four down. The fight was over.

She gently pulled Excelsior to a walk. He blew noisily, tossed his head and slowed. It was suddenly very quiet, except for the blowing of the two horses. "Good boy, Excelsior, you're a good boy!" she said, patting his sweaty neck as she rode up to Farhad, feeling exhilarated.

But Farhad's face was livid with anger. "Don't ever ride off on your own again like that, woman, or I'll put an arrow in you myself! Understand?"

Marcia flushed. She had expected praise, not a harsh admonishment. She nodded, not sure what she had done wrong, no idea what to say.

"I'm your boss, and you left me alone not knowing what the hell you were doing!" But then the anger left his face, replaced with a slight smile. "But nice work, after I figured it out! I was afraid I had lost you when you disappeared from the saddle. Xiongnu trick, but I never saw it done before."

"I had to bust my butt a lot of times before I got the hang of that. And never did it at that kind of speed! And I'm sorry... I wanted to be in that fight."

Farhad tossed her a waterskin. "You were. Drink some water, and wash the dirt off your face. Then let's find some water for the horses. And make sure the bandits don't circle around and come back at us."

The bandits did not return. Several hours later, the memory of the hum of arrows, some missing her by inches, the face of the man she had cut down, made her realize how close she had come to death that afternoon. She suddenly felt so chilled her teeth chattered.

Farhad and Marcia returned to Gumo, where the caravan had already arrived. The story of Marcia's exploits in the encounter with the bandits made for good campfire stories. But the back-to-back watches continued.

After Gumo, they cut north through a well-watered rolling green plateau, rising several thousand feet. Here was the first forest they had seen since leaving Liqian, tall pines against the sharp gray cliffs of the Tien Shan Mountains seeming so close they could be touched, steamy white clouds wisping over their snow-clad peaks. It was April, but they were glad they had kept the Xiongnu winter gear... it was quite chilly, even in the day, and snow lay on the ground, though not a solid layer in the sunlight.

Finally the walls of Kashgar came into sight. Two years since they left Roman territory, and they were now maybe halfway home.

CHAPTER 72: LAYOVER IN KASHGAR

Marcia stepped into the bathhouse and stripped off her riding felts, rancid with sweat. She eased herself into the hot bath, pausing for a moment to let the heat loosen aching muscles, then settling down all the way to her chest. A small shelf next to the tub held a bottle of scented oil, a ball of soap, and a wet washrag.

Marcia had always been fastidious about her hygiene, but the two months since Turfam had made that all but impossible. The long days and nights of shift after shift without a break had left her little privacy in the yurt to tend to her personal needs, and the cold weather made splashing icy stream water on bare skin really unpleasant. She knew... she had tried it several times. It was better than nothing, but not to be enjoyed. But that was over, and a hot tub and a thorough scrubbing seemed like a really good idea.

She washed her hair, then laid back and let the steam curl around her head. Antonius had given the bath attendant a bottle of wine and some coppers, telling him to find something to do for an hour, so she had plenty of time. Bless his sweet heart, Antonius knew how badly she needed this. Maybe because, sleeping with her, he knew just how rank she had become!

She examined the scar across the top of her left breast. It had healed nicely, leaving just a white line, barely visible. She hoped the injury had not damaged its ability to make milk, but no matter... she had two. And the need for that was still far off, though maybe when they got to Roman territory... mmmh. The hot bath made her mind wander.

She twisted the iron wedding ring on her left ring finger, the one with the nerve connected to the heart, they said. Her mother's ring, given by her father Marius, now hers.

How much her life had changed in the past year. Last year, she had kowtowed herself on the floor before the Son of Heaven – Emperor He, she corrected herself, let's not deify the man. She replayed the memory of that day, recapturing all her feelings then. She was not afraid he would condemn her to death, she was afraid he would not, and send her back to the concubinage and Wang Ming. She had decided, there on the floor, that if he did that, she would kill herself. Though she didn't know how, or if she could. There had been a disturbance behind her, muted calls from the guards, and Aulus and the men bursting in. She heard him addressing the Emperor, angrily demanding her right to a trial as a Roman! She heard the Emperor respond in Latin, surprisingly good, and the Senator saying that if she were to die, they would all die with her. For the first time in her life, she had not been some insignificant insect, but a person worth dying for. She had hoped it would not come to that, though it almost did.

She thought of that night when she took Antonius into her for the first time, with her brother, Gaius and Aulus watching to warn of the guards' approach. Sex with Wang Ming had been, at best, not too unpleasant. But that night she had exploded in such ecstasy that she had bitten Antonius on his shoulder to avoid crying out.

She smiled and touched herself under water, not for satisfaction, but just to see if she would be ready this afternoon, despite her aching fatigue. Her nipples came erect, little hard raisins seated on their crinkled aureoles, surrounded by a little ring of goosebumps. Yes, she would be ready. More than ready, as her schedule, besides making bathing a rare opportunity, had severely restricted their opportunity to make love.

She thought about Hina and Galosga. She wondered how her sister's pregnancy was going, whether she stayed on with her *zuun*, of which she was so proud. They must now be where they had been heading, up north far away from the Han. She thought how much alike she and Hina were, though their lives had taken such different paths, both losing their families and having a harsh introduction into adult life even before they were women, neither forming any close friends, male or female. Hina had given her so much self-respect and confidence! And now Hina was stepping into the world of women for the first time, as confidently as she had stepped into the world of men a decade ago. Marcia wished she could talk to her again, but that was impossible. Their paths had merged, radically altered each other's lives, then separated, never to meet again.

She thought of Marcus, his new love Mei, and Mama. Individual thoughts cascaded into a maelstrom of disconnected thoughts and then … "Hey, *domina!* Are yer goin' ter stay in there till yer melt?" bawled Antonius from the entryway. She shook herself awake. She had fallen asleep, long enough for the water to lose some of its heat.

"Coming, love. Just enjoying a long hot soak!" She got out, dried, and put on the clean *salwar* that she had brought, bundling up the stinking felts for a well-deserved washing.

Aulus had bought three rooms upstairs for the group: one for himself with the other Greek speakers Gaius and Dim, whose Hanaean name had become his nickname, one for Ibrahim, Yakov and Shmuel, the Aramaic speakers, and one for the newlyweds Antonius and Marcia. Each room had four beds, the first beds for everyone in a year, except for Marcia and Antonius on their honeymoon. Aulus had arranged storage for unnecessary baggage, so the rooms were not cluttered. Marcia put her arm around Antonius' waist as they climbed the stairs, leaning slightly on him. "Yer want ter be takin' a nap, *domina*? I can wait, yer know."

She smiled and turned to kiss his shoulder, "No, love, I can't wait another minute, I've had to wait too long for you." Then she giggled. "But if I start snoring, just finish without me!"

"Right, *domina!*" They reached the room on the corner of the second floor. Antonius tugged the door open, leaving it open for light… the room had no windows. He took down a lamp from a wooden shelf and fumbled with flint and steel to strike it aglow. Four beds covered with blankets and pillows faced outward from the back wall, one loaded up with their personal stuff. A small chamber pot sat in the corner, and a wooden table held a washbowl and water jug. The lamp flared into brilliance, and he closed the door. "I've seen bigger army cots! Give me a hand, girl, and let's drag three of these together so we can have room to enjoy oursel's." Together, they maneuvered the remaining beds side by side. Antonius pushed experimentally on one. "Feels like wood underneath, but no matter. It's not the ground!"

Marcia reached up, put her arms around his neck and pulled his face down to hers for a long, lingering kiss. Their bodies pressed firmly against each other and she felt his manhood rise against her belly. *No, not too tired at all!* They spent several minutes clinging together, their tongues sparring with each other, their hands roaming over the expanse of each other's bodies. Antonius slipped a hand under her *salwar*, creeping up the expanse of her bare back to explore the length of the hollow of her spine. His other hand joined it to explore her shoulder blades, then wandered off to find her breasts.

"*Te amo, Antonie! Te amo!*" Such a simple phrase, repeated so many simple times, and still as profound as the first time she said it on the road outside of Luoyang, when they should have been dead but weren't. Antonius gently lifted the *salwar* over her head, and she slipped his off in return, then his breeches, letting them settle in a pile on the floor along with hers. Antonius reclined on the bed and she straddled him, feeling him enter her at once.

She rode him quickly, her excitement building into rapid thrusting as she tried to make up for the last few weeks, until the heat in her loins exploded. She pressed herself hard against him, trying to keep the pleasure going, then collapsed on his chest, panting and gasping. She kissed his throat, feeling his scratchy bristles against her lips. "*Iterum, te amo, carus meus!* Again, I love you, my dear!" Antonius stroked her gently to bring her down, then began moving himself, slowly at first, until he too convulsed inside her. They lay together, still coupled, stroking and caressing each other. Then she rolled off onto her back. "Whew! You kept me awake, not a bad trick. I can't believe how tired I am. And angry about the bastards. All those extra shifts, me and Aulus! And they went out of their way to make them longer. Bastards, all of them!"

Antonius put his arm around her shoulder and cuddled her. "They were testin' yer, *domina.* And yer did good. It's what men do, when they get a new one and they aren't sure he is a fit for the group. They rag him low and cunning, try to get him to quit. You especially. I warned yer about that. They just wanted to make you quit."

"I know." she asked, burrowing into his shoulder and putting her hand across his hairy chest to play with his nipple. "Bastards! I did everything I could to prove myself."

She yawned, and rolled off to lay over on her side into a ball, facing away from him. "I'm going to get some sleep now. Don't wake me for dinner!"

Marcia's anger continued to simmer, but simmering soon turned into snoring. Antonius took a short nap, then got up, dressed, tucked a blanket over the sleeping Marcia, and slipped out quietly to join the others.

About an hour later, there was a loud banging on the door. The racket slowly penetrated Marcia's consciousness, though she tried to ignore it. Whoever was banging kept it up. She shook her head, got up, and wrapped a robe around herself. Oh, yes, and grabbed her dagger. She went to the door and yelled through it. "Who the hell are you?"

"Marcia, it's Farhad! The guards and I are going down to the bar and have a drink to wash the dust down. Would you and Antonius like to join us?" Farhad asked through the closed door in Bactrian. "Unless you're too tired."

Like hell, I'm too tired! "You men double my shifts, I learn how to not need sleep! Antonius is out, but I come. You men need lessons drinking!" she responded in her broken Bactrian. The unlikely invitation abated her anger a bit, but she remained suspicious of more ragging. "Give me moment."

She slipped back into her *salwar kamis*, tucked the knife into its scabbard, and left a wax tablet for Antonius that read 'Drinking with the guards, back when I get back, Love, M'. She opened the door to find all twenty of the guards clustered around the narrow walkway, many looking like they had already started drinking. "We go!" she announced, now enthusiastic.

"Hey, you don't stink anymore!" said Farhad.

"Took bath. You should try one."

The bar owner was a Hanaean about fifty, a bit portly in a red gown with black belt, washing utensils in a bowl when the entourage arrived. His thin eyes crinkled with glee as he smiled at the group, anticipating a profitable night. He had set up tables and chairs inside and out so everyone could sit, with a brazier nearby to keep the evening chill at bay and give some light. Boxes filled with several jugs of wine sat inside, indicating the bar would not run out. The men boosted Marcia up onto one of the tables, gave her a cup of wine, and the proprietor distributed cups to all the men. Farhad proposed a toast. "Marcia, you took all the shit we could give you, and you never quit. Here's to the toughest Hanaean bitch I ever rode with!" The rest of the men chimed in and downed their wine.

Emotions surged up inside her. *They are actually accepting me! Oh, girl, don't cry, not now!* "Well, here to sorriest bastards I ever rode with! You guys all right. Here!" She raised her cup, quaffing it in a single swallow. She held it out for someone to refill. "I get sloppy drunk tonight. Keep up with me!"

The party went on, periodically exploding in howls of laughter. Marcia recounted stories of Hina, seeking mates for her one-night stands. "Oh, pick me, pick me!" said one man, laughing uproariously.

Another asked if it was true that the Xiongnu gave their wives to strangers. "Well, you know, many cousins in encampment. Need fresh blood not related to them!"

"So did you ever see that?" asked one.

Marcia thought a minute and decided to improvise on a ribald story she had learned from Antonius. "Well, one time man come to camp, *shan-yu* give him his wife for night. Next morning, *shan-yu* say "Well, how was it?" Man answer, "Was great! She like too. She scream '*na rushna! na rushna!*' Means 'You great!', or something, in Xiongnu?"

Marcia paused for effect, then continued. "*Shan-yu* set down his *kumis,* look at man and say, 'Means wrong hole!' That caused the whole group to double over in laughter.

Antonius got back to the room about ten, found Marcia's note and smiled. He dozed a bit, until a rap on the door about midnight. He opened the door to find the guards clustered around Farhad, carrying Marcia limp in his arms, one arm trailing, her head lolling on his shoulder. Some of the men carried lamps.

Antonius looked at her. "She all right?"

"She will be tomorrow. Late tomorrow, maybe tomorrow afternoon. Your wife can drink as good as she rides," answered Farhad with a smile. "How do you keep up with her?"

Antonius laughed, took the comatose Marcia in his arms, and looked down at her lovingly. "Hard sometimes. Thanks, men, means much to her, you no idea how much." He turned and went inside.

The Roman party spent thirty days in Kashgar, located at the western end of the Taklamakan desert on a high fertile plain, well-watered by three large rivers flowing out of the Pamirs to the northwest, surrounded by lush fields of rice, wheat, nut and fruit trees, melons and pasturelands. To the southwest, the massive snow-clad peaks of the Kunlun Range reared toward the sky. Kashgar was located at the junction of highly profitable caravan routes connecting with *Ch'in* to the east around the Taklamakan Desert, Bactria through the Pamir Mountains to the west, Sogdiana in the Ferghana Valley to the north, and India and Tibet to the south. The wealthy city boasted a cosmopolitan population of several hundred thousand speaking a babel of languages, various dialects of *han-yu*, Bactrian, Parthian, even a little Greek, plus many more that the Romans could not recognize.

Kashgar was a manufacturing center for weaving, clothing, carpentry, pottery, iron and bronze work, all locally made in the industrial center. The Romans were quite taken by the coppersmiths, who swiftly and elegantly fabricated complex cooking utensils and teapots from flat sheets of copper, bending them around wooden forms and hammering them into shape. The smiths fabricated extensions for handles and pouring spouts, soldering them to the pot over a flame. When the basic utensil was completed, the smiths smoothed and polished the gleaming copper until no trace of the hammer dents remained, and the formerly battered copper gleamed like a mirror. Antonius bought Marcia a teapot as a souvenir.

Nearing the end of their stay, they were ready to move on. Jamshid had introduced them to their caravan master Behzad and their new caravan leader Kambiz. A few days before Kambiz was ready to begin the trek west, he called a meeting with his drivers, guards, and Aulus's party in the caravansary, conducted in Bactrian. Fortunately, a combination of forced immersion and Dim's patient tutelage for several months had left them conversational, if not fluent.

Kambiz started with the situation. "I sent riders ahead last week to scout the passes. The snows are mostly gone and roads are fair, though a bit mushy, so we will leave at first light two days from now. I want to make good time on the plains, because going through the pass will be slow," said Kambiz. "You Romans, watch your animals and yourselves at the top of the pass. Mountain sickness will make you dizzy and light-headed. Watch your animals' footing. Drivers, we will be going with light profitable loads, mostly bulk silk for Bagram. Make sure it is tightly wrapped against the weather and getting dumped in the mud. I don't want to lose any cargo due to mishandling. Mehrzad, security."

Mehrzad, head of the guards, was short and stout, with a bushy black beard and thick dark eyebrows that joined in the middle, and a drooping mustache. He wore a dark cloth wrapped around his head, a dirty green. "Too early for bandits, riders checked out the upper reaches of the Alay Valley, very few people up there yet, but bears and wolves are up, and hungry after winter. We have some volunteers for this trip. These eight," he said, turning toward Aulus's group, "come highly recommended by Farhad, many of you know him. They are all good fighters, three of them professional soldiers in their own lands, and three adventurous sailors. And the only one to actually fight on their last trip is the woman, Marcia." There were groans and catcalls, and a few obscene remarks.

Mehrzad let the hubbub die down. "She was Farhad's partner on her last trip, and she killed three men in that fight. He said she rode like a hound from hell! He suggested that any one you want to test her, feel free, but don't pull a knife on her... she has a short temper about that!" He beckoned Marcia to step forward.

Marcia, wearing her riding felts and fighting gear, did so, smiled sweetly, and bowed ever so slightly before the men. She straightened up, extended her arms held low, palms out, signaling her invitation for a challenge, but still smiling. The men looked skeptical but there were no takers. Most knew and had ridden with Farhad on other routes, and knew he didn't hand out praise like that lightly. After a few moments, Marcia dropped her arms to her sides and stepped back next to Antonius.

Kambiz stepped up before the men. "So do you accept these volunteers? Any objections, let's hear them!" There were none, though some grumbled about a woman.

So on the appointed day, the Romans said goodbye to their beds, packed up their gear, and were mounted and ready in the caravansary before the sun crept over the horizon. Marcia was outside with Excelsior prancing restlessly, taking first day watch with Mehrzad. The rising sun cast long shadows in the flat terrain.

The caravan was much smaller than their last, about a hundred pack animals, more horses and mules than camels. The beasts were loaded up, and the procession slowly formed up outside the north gate. Then Kambiz blew a blaring note on his horn, and the whole group moved off around the sandy bluff to the north, then west to the Irkeshtam Pass.

CHAPTER 73: ACROSS THE IRKESHTAM PASS

The caravan traveled all morning through pleasant grassy terrain along a small river, Marcia and Mehrzad riding point and making small talk. About noon they turned directly west, along terrain that was mostly arid sagebrush country, until nearly at sunset, the road began to slope up between two mountains, 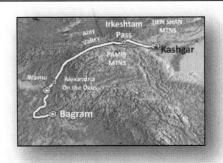 corrugated by cliffs on either side. The road crossed a stream in a pine-filled meadow, and Kambiz turned to follow it, calling a halt a bit later. Marcia and Mehrzad bid farewell, as did Aulus with his partner, and they returned to their respective camps.

The other six in the Roman party were off-duty and had set up all the tents. They were busy cooking dinner when Marcia and Aulus showed up. The two took care of their horses, then tethered them to the rope rigged for that purpose.

"How did they treat yer, *domina*?" asked Antonius solicitously.

"Not bad, not bad at all! And I am off for three days, if they keep their promise. I see you set up the tent," she said with a sly twinkle. "Privacy tonight?"

"We'll be back in the yurt in the mountains, so we might as well take advantage of it while we have it."

The next morning they began the ascent into the pass. Antonius was on duty, riding point with Ardavan, a nineteen year-old youth, unshaven except for a wispy mustache, with dark curly hair. They, too spent the morning in small talk, Ardavan fascinated with Antonius' adventures along the Danube and Syria, a world away from the young man's life. The caravan continued ascending into the mountains throughout the morning, the route lined with slender aspens. The mountains loomed over either side of the trail, grey and forbidding, their wrinkled flanks like grey blankets tossed aside by the gods. Gray clouds scudded over their tops like wisps of wool. By noon, the air turned chill and windy, the vegetation had dried up and turned to scrub, and it stayed that way until, again about sundown, the caravan camped in another tree-lined spot lined with a few mud-brick homes. Marcia, who was off duty, had pitched the tent again.

The Irkeshtam Pass was a rising valley about five miles wide at the bottom, between two ranges of mountains on either side. The well-worn road down the middle of the valley became more difficult at the higher levels, dodging around projecting mountain flanks, as the valley narrowed to a mile or less. Still, it was by no means difficult, though animals and men labored for breath at the top with just a little exertion. Clouds now completely obscured the tops of the mountains and a foggy mist chilled the air. The wind kept up a restless moaning, a constant backdrop to the sounds of the animals, their bells, and muted conversations. By afternoon, the slope turned downward, the valley widened again to several miles, and the air began warming. The wind through the aspen and pine trees made their branches shiver. The road ran along the banks of the Vakhsh, a wide meandering mountain river flowing westward alongside the road in a valley green with spring grass.

The going was easy through the relatively unpopulated area. Only a few nomadic yak herders had yet made it up to the summer pastures this early, and they offered friendly waves and occasional attempts to barter supplies in a language not Bactrian. And on one occasion, an eastbound caravan lumbered past them, heading for Kashgar. Kambiz and Mehrzad conferred with their counterparts, but neither train stopped to commingle. Other than that, it was simply boring, one overnight stop after another, each much the same as the last. There were no caravansaries in the few tiny villages along the route, so to break the monotony, Kambiz took a two night stand-down once a week. This gave everyone a chance to relax, sing, drink, and get a good night's sleep without the rigors of early morning packouts, and rest the animals as well.

It was during one of these stopovers that Aulus, Gaius, Antonius and Marcia found themselves sitting around a late night fire. Ibrahim had camp watch that night, everyone else having retired early.

Aulus was introspective. More properly, he was staring into the fire, brooding over the outcome of the trip.

"Quiet tonight, cousin?" asked Gaius.

"Rather. Feeling a bit uneasy about what we will find when we return," answered Aulus.

"We've talked about that before. If you hadn't done what you did, we would have left you alone in the anteroom and charged in without you," said Gaius. Antonius turned around to pay attention to the exchange.

"I hope Trajan sees it that way."

"Well, if he doesn't, what of it? He isn't the kind to put our heads up in the forum for that," answered Gaius. "I think something else set you off today. What was it?"

Aulus gave a long sigh. "While we were out on patrol today, my partner Rozi said he'd heard I was some kind of important person. And you know, all the things I thought were important a year ago, my money, my position as Senator and as ambassador, all those things… they are worthless out here. I used to spend more money in a few hours than I have spent all last year! Now, I am probably the least important person in the group."

"Arrgh, Senator, that's not true an' yer know it," Antonius growled. "Yer took a stand back in Luoyang on a snap, and yer made a damn good call. An' when it came time to getting' out of Luoyang, yer had the sense to put Ibrahim in charge. That man was born ter be outside the law, an' he's good at it. An' after yer put him in charge, yer never second-guessed him. So relax, yer'll get a chance to be up front, and yer'll be good at it again. Besides… yer've lost fifty pounds, look and fight like a soldier and ride like a Xiongnu! That's what's important here!"

Aulus gave a chuckle. "Thanks, it's good to hear that, Antonius. I think I was feeling sorry for myself. Yes, I have done some things I never expected to do. I remember buckling on a sword back in Taprobane when we were on your tail. I put it on because I had to do it for show, but I damned sure did not want to have to use it. Probably would have cut myself!"

"Considering yer haven't spent yer life learning how ter use it, yer getting' pretty good at it. So relax and enjoy the break in responsibilities!" Antonius leaned back, reached for a wine flask, poured himself a cupful, and reached for Aulus's cup. "Here, Senator, good fer mountain sickness, that's what's ailin' yer."

"Me, too!" said Gaius, offering his cup. "You know, Aulus, Antonius and I are more like common soldiers now than the *legatus* and centurion we were. And we take a lot more orders than we give. We do here what we have to do to survive. So cheers! We just take care of each and see that we all get home."

The group fell silent, and Gaius rumbled around in his pouch to find his locket, and fingered the image of Camilla in the flickering firelight. Marcia noticed and leaned over to observe. "She's beautiful. Your wife?'

"Yes, that's Camilla. And she is my wife, if she'll have me when I get back."

"Why wouldn't she?" asked Marcia

"Do you realize that you and Antonius have probably had more time together since Luoyang, than she and I have had in, let's see, ten years of marriage?"

"Your duties?"

"Always my damned duties! Duty kept me away when my children were borne, both of them. She or they could have died, maybe both, and I wasn't there. Duties for this trip, couldn't come home… I hadn't seen her and children for a year, was planning to be gone and out of touch for a year. It will be four years when I get back, maybe more. She was good about it, she understood. And someday I will have to understand when she has taken a lover because I could never be there. I envy you and Antonius."

"She won't take a lover, Gaius," said Aulus. "We know her."

"Others have. Or she may just want to divorce me when I come home. Duty! I haven't done my duty by her, and I never have."

Marcia edged closer. "You love her enough feel this way, and she knows that you feel that way. We women… we have duties too. Mainly it is to support our men, so they are free to do what they must to protect us. That's my duty to Antonius, Hina's duty to Galosga, and Camilla's to you."

"I know that if I get back from this damned trip, I will take a hell of a lot better care of her than I have. Give me another swill of that mountain sickness wine, Antonius!" He wiped his burning eyes on his sleeve. "Time for me to quit feeling sorry for myself."

The Alay valley widened out into a green alpine meadow a good five miles wide. Here at the warmer lower elevations everyone felt better. The nomad herdsmen became more numerous, their white yurts clustering on the grassland like mushroom fields, surrounded by their herds of yaks, goats, sheep and, occasionally, impressive-looking horses. And it was in this pleasant but isolated upland valley that the caravan spent the next several weeks, until the mountains closed in again. Through these rock corridors the caravan followed beside the Vakhsh as it turned into a plunging mountain torrent, until the trail opened out of the Pamir foothills into mountain glens to the Oxus River.

They crossed the Oxus by a magnificent stone bridge not far from the ruins of the fort of Alexandria-on-the-Oxus, built by Alexander himself during his conquest half a millennium ago and destroyed two centuries back, according to Mehrzad. They followed a lush river valley through green vineyards heavy with ripening grapes and yellow–green wheat fields rippled by the hot August wind blowing in off the arid Arian desert plain. Warnu emerged like a pearl in the distance set in the center of greenness, a city of white limestone and marble buildings.

Here they reached their first caravansary since leaving Kashgar, and Kambiz gave his men and animals a much needed week-long break; they had been on the road for two months, six weeks of it in the Pamirs.

Warnu was a cosmopolitan city, with separate quarters speaking Aramaic, Greek, Bactrian, and *han-yu*. Everyone in the group wanted to hear their birth language spoken by someone with whom they hadn't been traveling for two years.

The week in Warnu passed uneventfully, sightseeing during the day followed with evening meals in town, each group savoring the return to more familiar sights, sounds and surroundings. Then the caravan resumed its route south, through Baghlang and Sirkh Kotal, each a few day's easy journey apart, with short stops in each. Then it was back up into the mountains of the Hindu Kush and down to Bagram, 'Alexandria on the Caucasus'.

CHAPTER 74: BAGRAM AND THE BACTRIAN KING

As the Roman party was preparing to offload their baggage outside Bagram's large caravansary, an officer, flanked by several other soldiers, stepped up to them. Although Gaius and Antonius recognized neither the uniform nor the badges of rank, it was clear, in the international language of all soldiers everywhere, that this man was an officer, with considerable authority. He wore a peculiar beaked helmet, a horizontal visor protecting his eyes against the glare of the sun, above which sat a bronze snake rearing mouth open, ready to strike, a shallow neck guard and cheek pieces secured a black chinstrap. He was clad in a thickly quilted linen tunic covered with metallic disks, giving way to a light-weight knee-length linen kilt. He was clean-shaven, with moderate length brown hair, slightly curly. The soldiers behind him were similarly clad, but had the shields at the ready, hands on their sword pommels.

The officer called out in Greek, "Senator Aulus Aemilius Galba!"

Aulus had been facing the troops as had they all, and answered slowly, "That is I. To whom do I speak?" He held himself with as much *gravitas* as was possible, considering he was taken completely by surprise.

"I am Boni Megarion. The king requests the presence of you and your party of ten in the palace."

Aulus wondered whether Boni was name or a title. It meant 'guard,' so it could be either. "We are honored for the invitation. However, we are eight, not ten. Please give us a few minutes to unload and refresh ourselves to be ready for such a visit, because as you can see, we have just now dismounted after a long day's ride." *How the hell did he know the number that had started this trip? Does he have everyone's name?*

"My men will take care of your baggage. You may refresh yourselves at the palace, where you will find appropriate attire." He consulted a paper list he produced from a pocket. "Point them out to me: Gaius Lucullus, Antonius Aristides, Si Huar, Si Nuo and five traveling companions, and identify the missing ones, and why?"

Aulus indicated each in turn, introducing Ibrahim, Yakov, Shmuel and Demosthenes by name. "Our fifth traveling companion wed into the Xiong-nu and continued on with them to Dzungaria in the Altais. Si Huar prefers her Latin name Marcia Lucia as she is now married to Antonius. Si Nuo is her brother, who remained in Liqian to care for their aging mother. Let me commend you on the accuracy of your information about us. Please allow me to consult with my friends, as they do not all speak Greek."

"To be sure." The man made a virtue of military taciturnity.

Aulus assembled the group around him and addressed them in Latin. "Ibrahim, I know this is not your favorite language, but please translate into Aramaic for your companions. I want this man, Boni Megarion, to hear as little of this as possible." He paused and continued, "All right, it seems we are expected, and invited to a reception in our honor with the king. Let's all hope that it goes better than our last meeting with an eastern potentate! He wants us there immediately with bathing and clothes - I hope! - provided for us at the palace. They are going to take care of our baggage, but I suggest we ride, to keep our beeswax as secure as possible. We haven't been told to disarm, so let's keep them to hand until told to do so. Questions? Keep them simple, because I don't have many answers."

The Latin speakers shook their heads in the negative and murmured agreement. Ibrahim translated into guttural Aramaic for Yakov and Shmuel, and Marcia translated for Demosthenes.

Aulus turned back to the officer. "We would like to ride, if possible."

"To be sure." *Talkative, that one.*

The soldiers began unloading the pack animals. A wagon came out of nowhere, discharging more soldiers to lead the animals off to the paddock, and to help load the baggage.

Inwardly, Aulus was fuming, but it seemed to be futile to protest. "Where are you taking our baggage?" he asked the impassive Boni.

"To the palace. You will be staying a while."

Kambiz rode up and talked quickly with Boni in Bactrian. He obviously was as surprised as Aulus, and less interested in not making a disturbance. The exchange was heated, but in the end, the outcome the same. Kambiz turned to Aulus. "You seem to have attracted royal attention. I am sorry, but he is not at liberty to discuss why, if he even knows. If I don't see you again, it has been a pleasure having you ride with us." *If he doesn't see us again... encouraging note!*

So they saddled back up and followed Boni and his men to the city. Bagram was circled by a brick wall with towers at each corner, laid out inside in a grid of cobble-stoned streets, with frequent colonnades, parks, temples, and fountains. The palace was the large white marble building at the center of town, a classic Greek-style building with a gabled marble roof supported on eight columns, surrounded by a green park studded with shade trees.

Marcia cantered up alongside Aulus on Excelsior, rocking gracefully in the saddle in her sweat-stained felts. "I thought you should know...We were here before on my first trip west several years ago. Dim says the king's name is Vima Kadphises, the same as we met."

"Any reputation on him?" asked Aulus. "Bloodthirsty, arbitrary, or just hard-headed?"

"Dim said he has a reputation for being easy-going," she answered.

Aulus shook his head. "He must be having a bad day."

Marcia smiled and said, "I remember the meeting was formal in the Hanaean style. None of our group had either Bactrian or Greek."

"Well, we will see."

Marcia wheeled Excelsior around and fell back to ride with Antonius.

Ibrahim was the next to ride up. "Well done, Aulus," he said quietly in Latin. "They let us keep our weapons, which is a good sign, though I presume they will make us get rid of them before we go into the palace."

"Or maybe they expect to execute us with them."

"He expected ten of us, so the information he has comes from Luoyang. And despite it all, we seemed to be on good terms with Emperor He as we exited on safe passage," offered Ibrahim.

"Well, if Emperor He can change his mind once, maybe he changed it back again." Aulus was very much not in a positive mood.

"Play it by ear, my friend. The gods would not have thrown such an unlikely pair as you and I together just to have us die to no end."

"Those the gods would destroy, they first make mad. But yes, we are the most unlikely of friends, you damned pirate, and we both have had a hell of a run, even if this is as far as we get!" Aulus felt his stiff face smile, and a chuckle leave his lips unbidden. "You never get discouraged, do you?"

"Not possible in my line of work. Always another rich merchant to take down!" He whirled his horse off to leave Aulus to continue alone.

Boni's troops led them around toward the back of the palace, leaving the wagon with their goods parked at a side entrance. The riders continued around back to an entrance into the basement stalls, rich with the odor of horses, hempen rope, leather, manure and hay, the rough wood glowing amber in the light of oil lamps high on the walls. Perhaps fifty stalls lined both sides, and as the riders entered a number of grooms clambered up out of the hay in which they had been waiting, ready to receive the animals. Everyone dismounted, relinquishing their mounts to the grooms, giving special instructions as necessary in Bactrian.

Marcia patted Excelsior's nose. "Good boy!" she said, producing a little sweet which his velvet lips happily nibbled up. "We'll see you later! Be nice to these boys!" He whinnied and stamped his foot as she departed. At the far end of the stalls was a door to the basement of the palace, entering onto a stone-walled room with a flagstone floor, at the far end of which was a barred gate. Aulus's heart was thudding in his chest. He hissed to Ibrahim, "Damn! Looks like a prison to me!"

"I'm not sure it is. I think they would have disarmed us by now. Take a deep breath and assume the best."

Boni confirmed Ibrahim's opinion. "This is the armory. Please remove your weapons. Senator Aulus, we will provide you an inventory so you may retrieve them on your departure, but weapons are not allowed beyond this point."

Aulus' sigh of relief was audible. "Certainly!" he said, though feeling very uncertain as he unbuckled his sword and dagger. Demosthenes translated for the others.

Another soldier appeared on the other side of the barred gate, unlocked it from the inside, and sat down a low table with an oil lamp to record the weapons. "Name, please," he asked.

"Aulus Aemilius Galba."

Boni handed the man Aulus's weapons, and the information was duly recorded on two scrolls. The rest of the party followed suit, ending with Antonius and Marcia.

"Hsst, *domina,*" he cautioned Marcia in Latin. "Don't try to slip in your shoulder rig. They'll probably pat us down."

She reluctantly lifted the weapons lanyard from around her throat and put it in her pile. "Marcia Lucia!" she said to the attendant.

Antonius was right. There was a quick pat down of all to make sure no one had tried to conceal a weapon; even stockings were checked for small knives. The attendant handed a copy of the inventory to Aulus, then Boni led them up the stone steps to the main floor through a massive pair of wooden doors guarded by two impassive soldiers armed with spears. They emerged onto a gleaming marble hallway, with a white ceiling, yellow marble with white veins on the walls, and grey floors. A series of polished and intricately carved doors ran along each side, and a larger door sat at the end. Carved white marble sconces held lamps that gave the windowless passage a warm glow. Boni knocked on one of the doors and five servants appeared clad in white tunics.

"These are our guest quarters," announced Boni. "Senator, this is yours." He opened the door to display a large, well-laid out accommodation, lamps already lit and clothes laid out on the bed. Aulus looked in, nodding approvingly, but stayed outside to make sure everyone else was properly set up.

"The bath is through the large doors at the end of this hallway," continued Boni. "There are robes and dress clothes in your rooms, and the servants will take your traveling clothes and have them washed for you. I will come in an hour to take you to the king. If there is anything you need, the servants will take care of them for you. Do you have any questions?"

"Thank you for your hospitality," answered Aulus, extending his hand.

Boni took it and nodded. "You're most welcome." He turned on his heel and exited back down to the basement.

Aulus turned to the group and announced in *han-yu*, their other *lingua franca*, "Looks like if we are to be imprisoned, at least the cells are more comfortable than the last one in Luoyang!" This provoked some chuckles and smiles from all. "See you in the bath in a few minutes. I, for one, desperately need one!"

The servants escorted everyone to their assigned rooms. Only two minor problems emerged: Marcia and Antonius were assigned separate accommodations, and Marcia preferred western garb rather than the Hanaean robes in her room. The first problem was instantly corrected, and the servants set off in search of an appropriate *stola* for her... apparently they had a stash of Roman clothing, and probably clothing for every other major empire around them. Bagram Palace seemed to be a crossroads of civilizations.

There were white linen robes on hooks in each room, and a few minutes later everyone clustered around the bath, a grey-tiled waist-deep pool full of water about twenty feet long in a red-walled room that added to the warm feel. Bowls of multi-colored balls of lavender-scented soap lined each side; brass pegs for clothing and shelves of white towels lined the walls. Antonius and Marcia retired to one end for a modicum of modesty to shed their robes and ease into the warm water, while everyone else did likewise at the other end.

Once the group had soaked and scrubbed off the sweat and grime of the past few weeks, they relaxed in the warm steamy water until Marcia and Antonius began cavorting like children at the other end, splashing each other and giggling. Antonius poured water over her head, and she threw herself on him and dunked him. Gaius watched them, and turning to Aulus with a grin, dragged his hand along the surface of the water to splash his cousin. Before long the rest of the men joined in, their laughter and splashes echoing hollowly in the room. It was a welcome respite from the rigors of the past months on the road.

Back in their rooms, they found clothing of the appropriate rank and style hanging in their closets, along with mirrors, razors and combs. Fully refreshed and re-groomed, they reassembled in the hallway to await Boni. Aulus, Gaius and Antonius were clad in togas and tunics, each thoroughly chalked to a dazzling white and appropriately marked, Aulus's with the broad Senatorial purple stripe, Gaius' tunic with a narrow equestrian purple stripe, Antonius' plain. Marcia wore a white ankle-length silk *stola* with a modestly opaque weave elegant in its simplicity, and a translucent yellow silk wrap. Demosthenes wore a white silk *chlamys* tunic while Ibrahim, Yakov and

Shmuel wore multi-colored robes with headbands. *Whoever knew we were coming knew a lot about us,* thought Aulus.

Boni arrived and escorted them into an open interior court, illuminated by the wide open colonnaded entrance which soared fifty feet high. Along the top of the side walls, grated windows admitted more light, and above their heads, lamps suspended on hoists from the ceiling provided additional illumination. The pungent scent of burning incense filled the air, but Aulus could not determine the source. Across the black marble floor, a variety of people came and went about whatever important business brought them to the palace.

There was a red marble ceremonial throne, vacant, at the back of the court, flanked by unlit gold braziers on either side, and four dark green Corinthian columns from floor to the vaulted ceiling. Boni passed around the throne wordlessly, and led them to a wooden door guarded by two soldiers with spears who snapped erect at his approach. He spoke softly to them and they faced inward to admit them.

Inside was a white room, lined with comfortable looking brown leather couches. A wizened old man in a white tunic with a beard to match was working at a table with an assortment of scrolls, ink and writing implements. The man stood when they entered, and he and Boni spoke softly, their heads together. Boni pointed toward Aulus, the man nodded attentively, then Boni turned and left without saying goodbye.

The man stepped swiftly around his table with a scroll and introduced himself in Greek. His manner reminded Aulus of a twittering, restless bird. "I am Rustam, the chief of protocol. You will be meeting with King Vima and it is my job to make sure it all goes smoothly. You are Senator Aulus Aemilius Galba?"

"Yes."

"And I trust your accommodations are satisfactory?"

"For the few minutes we have been in them, they seem very much so."

"I would like to go over the spelling and pronunciation of each of your party." He handed the scroll to Aulus, while Aulus scrutinized the list and handed it back.

"Now titles. You are a Senator, and what brings you here?"

"I am the ambassador to the Hanaean Emperor, returning home."

Rustam scribbled some notes next to the name, then asked, "Who is next, in order of seniority?"

"That would be Gaius Lucullus, legate of *Legio XII Fulminata,* last operating in Syria three years ago. He is head of our military delegation. Next would be Antonius Aristides, senior centurion of the same legion, and his wife Marcia Lucia, also our Hanaean translator."

The old man smiled and bowed at the two. "Charming couple, congratulations!" He returned to his scroll. "Next?"

"Hmm…" Aulus considered his next answer, then said, "Ibrahim bin Yusuf, my shipping master, traveling overland with us for personal edification, and his son Yakov of Petra, your countryman Demosthenes, of Bactra and finally Shmuel bin Eliazar, a friend."

Rustam repeated each name. Aulus was impressed with his pronunciation, particularly of the Aramaic names. "Excellent. Do you speak Latin and Aramaic as well as you pronounce it?"

"Ah yes, in my humble work it is necessary to manage many languages."

"In what language will our meeting be conducted?" asked Aulus.

"For you, in Greek."

"Not all of my people speak Greek well, but we all speak Bactrian with various degrees of facility. Could we conduct the meeting in that language, so we do not have the distraction of simultaneous translation?"

"How well do you speak Bactrian?" asked Rustam, switching abruptly to that language.

Aulus hesitated a moment, mentally shifting linguistics. "Ah… yes. Not nearly as well as I want, only five months speaking. But think we make ourselves understood, if accent and grammar not embarrassing."

"Excellent! Only five months and you do quite well. The king would actually be most pleased to do that, as there are many in the court that would like to see our language used exclusively for government instead of Greek, which they consider foreign."

"For clarity, I may go back to Greek sometimes."

"He will not mind." He paused a moment to change topics. "You will be meeting in the King's private chambers, through that door over there. I will announce you one at a time, in the order of seniority you gave me, then you go in, and stand right to left in the order you came in. When the King gives you permission to be seated, take your seats in the chairs provided. Let him lead the discussion. At the end, if he asks you to stay for wine, you have done well. If he asks you to stay for dinner, you will have done very well indeed!"

"I thought it would be Hanaean style, with bowing and so forth. Marcia Lucia was part of Hanaean party, pass through here heading west six or so years ago, and she said much more like Hanaean court, than what you say."

Rustam scrutinized Marcia closely, then suddenly smiled broadly. "I do remember you! There are few women that participate in royal meetings, and I remember your face, though you are now dressed in Roman style… because of the wedding?"

"One of many reasons," answered Marcia.

"Truly beautiful you are, Marcia. We try to adapt our meetings with foreign nations in a style to which they are accustomed. The Hanaeans expect a great deal of formality, we give them that, the Parthians some, and the Romans chafe at any. This has been tailored for you, Senator. So do you have any questions?"

"None, and thank you for the thorough preparation," answered Aulus.

"I must go into the inner sanctum and prepare King Vima for the meeting. I will be back in a few minutes and then this will begin. Will you excuse me?"

"Certainly, go about your business," answered Aulus. Rustam smiled and exited through the door into the king's private chambers, clutching his scrolls.

Aulus gathered Ibrahim and Gaius about him, barely able to contain his pleasure at how well this meeting was progressing. "This is going far better than I expected when it started!"

"Just remember, cousin, tread lightly. Let's congratulate ourselves when it is over," said Gaius, with Ibrahim nodding in agreement.

Rustam returned after about ten minutes. Aulus had time for one last question for him. "What is the king's preferred address?" asked Aulus.

"Initially, in Bactrian, it will be *Shaonan Shao*, in Greek, *Basileus Basileon*, 'King of Kings.' After the initial exchange, you may use just 'Your Excellency.'"

The door opened. It was time. Rustam entered into the throne room and announced, "Senator Aulus Aemilius Galba of Rome!"

Aulus walked in, stopped next to Rustam's right as directed, and proclaimed, "Greetings to *Shaonan Shao* Vima Kadphises, King of Bactria of the Thousand Richest Cities, from *Imperator* Caesar Nerva Trajan, Son of the Divine Nerva, Son of Augustus the Best Ruler." As he said this, he hoped he was not putting Trajan in competition with the Bactrian King.

Rustam likewise announced each of the party in the agreed order, who each greeted the *Shaonan Shao*, and then took their place to the left of the gathering group.

Aulus surveyed the private throne room. More marble, the beautiful yellow that appeared to be the same as that of their quarters. The throne was black, with gold armrests held up in front by gargoyles, glaring red faces with gilded eyes and protruding triangular tongues. Along the wall stood a statue of Buddha to the king's right, and a statue of a very anatomically correct naked woman to his left. Behind the throne was an intricate tapestry depicting various hunting scenes, in whites, greens, browns and black. White sconces held lamps casting a steady illumination. To the king's left, a tunic-clad man sat at a table, apparently acting as a scribe, taking notes on a scroll.

Aulus also scrutinized the king. His features were sharp, with a precisely trimmed brown beard just edging the line of his jaw, and brown eyes that never once took their gaze off Aulus. He wore a simple silver diadem on curly hair with a hint of gray at the temples, and was clad in silk, an outer robe of purple edged with gold and silver trim, over an elaborate green and white *salwar kamis*. He sat unmoving with his hands along the arm rest, almost a part of the throne.

"Greetings and welcome to my kingdom, esteemed travelers." He paused for effect. "Aulus Aemilius, please relate to me the story of how you came to be here, especially how a notorious pirate came to be your shipping master. My empire has maritime interests through our ports at the mouth of the Indus, and he is known there by reputation, if not yet by predation."

Antonius had once told Aulus about a trap constructed to kill or injure soldiers: a pit, lined with sharpened stakes, broken swords or spears, overlaid with a thin mat and covered with leaves and brushes. When an unwitting soldier stepped on the mat, he fell through to be impaled on the waiting sharp objects. Aulus's heart thudded while he paused to consider how to back off the imaginary mat creaking under his weight before it gave way. *They seem to know everything about us. So let us give them the truth and not omit any details.* He took a deep breath.

"Your Excellency, I apologize for my bad Bactrian, I only speak a few months. I praise your people for finding important facts. Yes, that is Ibrahim bin Yusuf, most notorious pirate in the eastern Mediterranean and also now our closest friend, who has saved our lives many times. Your Excellency's permission, I let my friend speak for himself, how this began with hijacking and ended with friendship." The king gave him an almost imperceptible nod, and Aulus continued, "Ibrahim, your story please. Tell all, from Alexandria." *Ibrahim is quick on his feet, he will realize what I am saying. Lies will likely be fatal.*

Ibrahim paused to collect his thoughts, then spoke "Your Excellency, I am that man. I scout ships, take but the weakest, leave rest to thrive. Like wolves. Three years ago, I learn of Aulus's mission through his shipping master, Hasdrubal. Very rich ships, lot of gold and silver. I plan to take one ship early." He summarized the planning and execution, Hasdrubal's perfidy and his countermove, then paused for effect. Aulus attempted to gauge the *Shaonan Shao*'s willingness to believe this, but saw only interest. "Continue," said the king. He had not moved a muscle since they first came into the throne room.

Ibrahim described Gaius' and Antonius' resistance, then the storm. "The worst I had ever seen. I released them to help fight the ship through it. I went overboard, and Antonius rescued me."

"And why might he do that?" asked the king.

"Your Excellency, with your permission, I want him to answer."

"Granted."

Antonius spoke up, "Your Excellency, that night, he was the only person who could save the ship. And I – we – have all had many reasons since to be glad I saved him."

"Thank you, Antonius. Continue, Ibrahim." Aulus thought he detected just the glimmer of a smile on the king's thin lips, but he wasn't sure.

He talked about their truce and eventual alliance. "Hasdrubal's treachery wrecked my plans to dispose the ship's wealth in Africa. I could not go there, because it was no longer secure, and I could not continue on without their assistance and cooperation. So, our relationship went from an uneasy truce, to an alliance negotiated by Gaius Lucullus. "Your Excellency, that is how I went from being the man who hijacked one of their ships, to the man who is honored to have them call me friend. It is in your power to have me executed, or to hand me over to the many people who would like to execute me, as you wish."

Aulus spoke up, this time without waiting for the king to give him permission to speak. "Your Excellency, on one other occasion, we put all our lives on the line to protect one of ours from an unwarranted execution. If it is necessary to put our lives again on the line for our friend and colleague Ibrahim bin Yusuf, who has himself saved our lives and is responsible for our arriving here safely, then we shall do so again, gladly."

Aulus waited in silence while the king studied him intently. Then King Vima said, "And what do you intend to do with this notorious pirate when you return to Roman territory?"

"Your Excellency, I intend to seek a full pardon and citizenship for him from Emperor Trajan, for extremely valuable service to the Principate."

At last the king smiled, and even chuckled a bit. "Well, let us hope the rest of your story is as interesting as its beginning. Thank you, Ibrahim. You have not committed any crimes in my empire, at least any of which I am aware, and I see no need to hand you over to others, as your friends speak so highly of you. Aulus, how did you come to be reunited with the rest of your party?"

Thank the gods Ibrahim handled that so well. Aulus related their rescue at Masirah, the decision to continue on with *Asia* and *Africa*, the *Africa's* detachment to return home at Muziris, and then learning of the *Europa's* location in Taprobane. "We got there to find she had sailed, but apparently there had also been some sort of internal war, and Galle had been devastated."

"Yes, about two years ago. Something about a Roman invasion. Was that you?" There was that hint of a smile again.

"Your Excellency, we may have been the excuse."

"Interesting. And what happened when you got to Luoyang, Senator Aulus?"

"Your Excellency, at first nothing. I thought we would meet with the Emperor shortly after we arrived, but nothing happened. Then he went south for the winter, and we did more of nothing. We could not meet with any of the ministers, or observe the army, or travel outside of Luoyang, until we met with him."

"Who was the Parthian ambassador?" asked the king.

"Cyrus Mithridates, if my memory is correct."

"It is. He is a scheming bastard, always cooking up intrigues. He was posted here for several years and I was glad to see him become Emperor He's problem. And of course, he no doubt became yours. Emperor Pacorus of Parthia is not happy to see Rome establishing friendly ties with the Han Empire. I also have a presence, official and otherwise, in Emperor He's court, and I assure you, Mithridates was behind much of your troubles."

I wonder if he will elaborate on that later! "Your Excellency, thank you. Just prior to Emperor He's return, there was an incident involving Marcia Lucia, Si Huar by her Hanaean name. She was at that time concubine to our Hanaean delegate returning with us by sea, and in Luoyang she was falsely accused of infidelity and attempted murder of her consort. As she had dual status as a Roman citizen by ancestry, I felt obliged to defend her before Emperor He. He felt otherwise, and condemned all of us to death."

"And were these charges false?"

"Infidelity? Absolutely. Attempted murder? She was attempting to defend herself while being beaten."

"Hmm… my sources indicate that Emperor He was not happy to have her case disrupt proceedings with you that he felt were of far greater importance. They say he intended to pardon all of you at a large public ceremony. He was impressed with your sense of honor, though not with the way you challenged him before his court."

"He did not share that plan with us while we were in his jail, your Excellency. "

"The one thing that my sources could not find out was how you managed to just walk out of prison and the North Palace, unobserved."

"We can thank Demosthenes and Ibrahim. Demosthenes was, at that time, a Buddhist monk, who found us imprisoned. Since Buddhist monks have free run in Luoyang, after he and Yakov overpowered the guards, he had us put on yellow robes, shave our heads and just walk out, begging our way to a waiting oxcart, arranged by Ibrahim. We left town chanting and praying. I think we picked up ten or fifteen copper coins escaping."

For the first time, Aulus saw a full smile light up King Vima's face. Then the king slapped his knee and laughed loudly. "That is the most outrageous story I ever heard! And no man in his right mind would make up a concoction like that, so it must be true!" He continued laughing, wiping his eyes, and when finished, he was visibly less formal. "Come, come! I am a terrible host, and have had you standing this whole time. Sit down!"

King Vima clapped his hands and servants appeared with silver goblets, distributing them to each and filling them to the brim from silver pitchers. "Drink up, our best Kapisan wine! To my Romans and their friends!" He lifted his glass in salute, and everyone rose.

Aulus returned the toast. "To our most gracious host, *Shaonan Shao* Vima Kadphises!" They then reseated themselves. Aulus found the wine to be a delightful red, dark and full-bodied. He noted it had not been watered.

King Vima continued his questioning, though now less hostile. He fixed his gaze on Marcia and smiled broadly. "And you, Marcia, you are a charming beauty, Hanean face, but blue eyes, a Latin name and Roman garb. And a Roman citizen, no less."

Marcia flushed, but did not lose her control. She smiled and said, "Your Excellency, we have met before, though I doubt you remember. We visited you about six years ago with Gan Ying's party going west."

"With the Gan Ying party?" King Vima thought for a moment, his hand pinching his bearded chin thoughtfully, eyes screwed shut. Then he smiled and said, "Yes, yes! I do remember, for there was but one girl in that party. I remember that distinctly. That was you?"

"That was me, your Excellency. I was not allowed to say much, and in fact could speak neither Greek nor Bactrian."

"And you were just along as concubine?"

"No, sir. I and my brother, and eight others from my home in Liqian, were translators, since we were fluent in Latin and Hanaean since birth. One of us for each delegate. I, of course, was my consort's translator."

"How did that unique combination of languages happen?" He leaned forward, interested.

"In Liqian in Gansu province. We are descendants of Romans captured by Parthians, and given to Hanaeans as mercenaries. We kept our language and traditions for more than a century. My father used to tell me, *semper memento, romana es,* always remember, you are a Roman girl." She smiled wistfully at Papa's memory.

"So Gan Ying made it to Rome, and you with him?"

"Yes, Your Excellency. And met with Emperor Trajan."

"I see!" He paused. "What happened to the Gan Ying expedition?"

"Your Excellency, I don't know. We were a party of thirty, ten delegates and translators, and ten military escorts. Five of us translators were given to Senator Aulus for his expedition, along with my consort as government representative to guide him through the Hanaean ports. The rest returned overland. They had not yet reached Luoyang when we left."

"I don't think they will." King Vima, in contrast to his formal stiffness, was a very animated talker informally, constantly moving his hands, grabbing the throne's arm rests, or stroking his beard. "I also, of course, have a presence in the Parthian court. They made it to Ctesiphon, ummh, five years ago, and met with Emperor Pacorus. They never crossed into my territory. I was very interested in how it went, as I had a hand in setting that expedition up. Do you know Ban Chao?"

"Not personally, your Excellency. He is a very senior counselor to Emperor He."

"His senior military man. Fifteen years ago, he was very active here in Bactria as Hanaean western military commander, running a cooperative campaign with me to quell some of the more obnoxious nomadic tribes in the area. We met frequently, and I told him about the great empires to the west, Parthia and Rome, and I suggested to him that they should get acquainted with Rome. I said it was like China, but bigger, *Da Qin* I think is the Hanaean phrase."

Aulus interjected. "That is what they call all Romans now, *Da Qin*! So that is how the name got started!"

"Perhaps! But the Gan Ying party apparently met with some misfortune. I wonder what he would have told Emperor He about Rome."

"His report was very favorable. He gave my consort a copy, in case something happened to him, and my consort gave it to the Emperor."

"Very good!" he paused, waved a hand, and a servant refilled his cup. He took a sip and continued, this time losing the animation, and fixing Marcia with an intense look. "So how does your consort feel about your marriage to Antonius?"

Marcia paused and took a deep breath. "Your Excellency, he no longer cares what I do, and I no longer care what he might think." Aulus noticed the very hard edge to her voice.

The King turned his gaze from her to look around the room studying each in turn. Everyone had fallen quite still and silent. Then he refocused on her again. "Wang Ming journeyed to Liqian with the party bearing your official pardon. Did you discuss your marriage with him then?"

Another long pause. "We did."

"He never returned to Luoyang. Do you know where he went?"

"I don't know what became of him," she said, much too calmly.

"Travel can be dangerous." King Vima relaxed a bit, and so did Aulus, screwed tight along this line of questioning. *What the hell does this bastard know? One more push and she may just say she killed him and is glad she did.* The undercurrent of movements that goes with normal conversation resumed. "You will be happy to know that Wang Ming's cruelty to you was a scandal in the court, and the subject of an imperial edict last year. Cruelty toward spouses, concubines and children is inharmonious, and should not be tolerated. So your suffering was not without benefit. Antonius, you are a lucky man! To a long, happy marriage!"

"Aye, sir, aye and surely! Your Excellency!" Antonius raised his cup, then pecked his wife on the cheek, to the delight of King Vima and everyone else.

CHAPTER 75: THE PRINCESS

Formal introductions out of the way, King Vima became considerably less formal, chatting casually with Aulus's entourage about various points of interest on their trip, the state of affairs in Rome when they had left, and their observations of Luoyang. Servants quietly circulated around the room with silver jugs, each uniquely and ornately engraved, making sure that no one's wine cup remained empty for more than a few heartbeats. Marcia, however, nursed just a single cup, uncharacteristically silent and withdrawn into herself. She studied the naked goddess on the wall, noting that her cup had an identical engraving, also anatomically correct. She had never thought of it until now, but of all the female sculptures she had seen in her travels, they had all been sexless, the pubic region completely blank. This one, however, had her pudendal slit carefully inscribed, surrounded by carefully etched pubic hair.

King Vima noticed her studying the goddess. "My dear Marcia, that is our fertility goddess Anahita of the Pure Waters. She rides a chariot drawn by four horses, Wind, Rain, Cloud and Sleet. Our scriptures describe her as 'the great spring, the life-increasing, the herd-increasing, the fold-increasing who makes prosperity for all countries, wide flowing and healing'. She is also our warrior goddess, an odd role for a goddess."

Antonius spoke up. "I am married to one of these warrior goddesses, Your Excellency!" Marcia very much did not want him to bring that subject up, and quietly pinched his arm in silent protest, too late, for the King had already focused on Antonius' praise.

"A warrior bride, you say? Taught by you, I suppose?" King Vima asked.

"And others. Tell us your story, Marcia."

"Well, it is a long trip, Your Excellency, and a woman must be prepared for all things," she answered, with a great deal of reluctance. This line of conversation was too close to Wang Ming, and what the king knew, or didn't know, about his disappearance.

Antonius looked at her with some concern. She had never before been reticent about her fighting skills. "She can take care of herself, your Excellency. Quite handily."

"That is good," said the king, and returned to the topic of the goddess. "I am sure you men have noticed that Anahita is, shall we say, a complete woman in all respects? I don't understand the Greeks at all. They will depict statues of men with all their paraphernalia, but leave women a blank slate, as though they fear that orifice from which we all came, and to which we return from time to time to share in the pleasure of creation."

Marcia smiled wanly, half listening to the conversations swirling around her, seeing Wang dying on the floor, cursing her to the end. The scar on her breast began to throb.

Rustam reentered the room, tapped Aulus on the shoulder and quietly whispered, "Senator Aulus, do you prefer to eat reclining, Roman style?"

Aulus snorted, "Rustam, it has been so long since I ate that way, I don't think I would remember how! Seated is fine, please."

Rustam nodded, and spoke with one of the servants, apparently the head steward. The steward left, and returned with ten more servants carrying a large table, which they placed on the floor lengthwise between the king and Aulus's party. They left and returned with an ornately carved gilt chair with violet cushions filigreed with gold and silver, positioning it at the head of the table. These maneuvers were executed silently with well-rehearsed military precision, with barely a disruption of the ongoing conversations. Other servants put nine three-branched candelabras on the table, lighting each with a burning taper to burn with a whiff of sandalwood.

The steward indicated that the Roman party should rise, while servants repositioned their chairs, four on either side of the king, while other servants brought in carts loaded with dishes and linens, covered dishes, and silver jugs of wine.

When all was in place, the king stood and stepped down from his throne to take his seat. He clapped his hands. "Sit, let's eat," he said, "You have had a hard day and long trip!"

When everyone was seated and the servants were preparing to distribute the first course, the king spoke up. "I would like to set your minds at ease before we dine, as that aids digestion. It was necessary to interrogate you a bit at the beginning, because while apparently the Son of Heaven Emperor He has belatedly come to hold you in some esteem, my fellow King of Kings, the *Shahanshah* Pacorus of Parthia does not, and considers you to be enemies of the state. I did not take this seriously, as he considers all Romans to be enemies of his state, but then you introduced a known pirate as your shipping master! I had to determine quickly whether to offer you my hospitality, thereby sticking a finger in Pacorus' eye, or ignore Emperor He's request and turn you over to him. As you can see, you have won my confidence, and here I am seated next to your bloody pirate!" He raised his cup. "Here's to you, Ibrahim."

Everyone raised their cups, "Hear, hear!"

"Now, Demosthenes, my fellow countryman. You are from Bactria, and a Buddhist monk, are you not?" the king asked amiably, directing his gaze at Demosthenes.

"I was, Your Excellency, but I fear I lack the detachment necessary to pursue perfection by that path," Demosthenes answered softly, studying the dregs of wine in his cup intently.

"I thought your hair was a bit long," laughed the king. "What happened?"

"I was taught that perfection lies in inaction, lest action invoke a *karma*, a consequence that demands further action, each action taking one further from the path of enlightenment. Yet had I not taken action, all of my friends to your right would be dead. But also because I took action, two guards were killed, I had to lie to protect my friends, and took up arms again. If I could replay those decisions, I could not choose to do otherwise. Inaction, it seems, has its own *karma*, and for me, that *karma* would have been worse than the *karma* of the action I took. I am still a follower of Buddha, but the path of a *Bodhisattva,* one seeking enlightenment, is closed to me for this lifetime. Perhaps in my next life!" He raised his glass, and the king did likewise.

"You took up arms again, you said," asked the king, leaning forward with both arms crossed on the table. "You once before took up arms?"

"Yes, Your Excellency. I was a soldier with the Lions of Bactra, a medic and a fighter."

"A fine unit, one of my best!" responded the king gleefully.

Antonius interrupted. "Your Excellency, I might add, he is a damned fine medic. He saved my life from an arrow in my gut two years ago. I am also a medic with the Roman army, but I don't think I could have done as well by him."

"Very good!" said the king, directing his gaze toward Antonius on the right. "How did that happen?"

"We were two months out of Luoyang in Shaanxi. Our monks' disguise had been discovered so we found a place to hole up to let our hair grow out. Bandits raided us and we fought them off, but I took a hit. He took care of me, just a little fever for a few days."

"Marcia was also shaven?" he asked, smiling.

"She was, your Excellency, bald as a goose egg! But I loved her anyway."

The banter was good, but it was bringing back too many memories for Marcia: the shock and horror she felt when she saw the arrow protruding from his belly, believing him dead. The long days while he lay unconscious, her sitting beside him, telling him stories, holding his hand, certain that he would shortly give a sigh and breathe no more, so soon after she had known love with him. The cups were refilled, except for Marcia's. She had taken only a few sips, in fear that her increasingly black mood might get out of control if she drank too much.

Dinner was served, a feast that would meet the highest epicurean standards of Rome. Duck, stuffed with oranges, apples and nuts, whole pig stuffed with sausages for entrails, large trout from the mountain streams, roast goat, and of all things, so far inland, oysters and clams. King Vima was particularly proud of these, brought live from Barbaricum at the mouth of the Indus, traveling hundreds of miles overland in seawater chilled with ice from the Hindu Kush.

Marcia sampled the oysters, raw and fresh, but she had little appetite. The visions in her head wouldn't go away. She was sitting on the floor in Liqian, next to the dead Wang Ming, herself bleeding, looking at the ugly wound she had made in his stomach. But she couldn't hate him. Suddenly she felt her gorge rise and with a great deal of effort, restrained herself from becoming sick. The room spun, faded, then she was hearing nothing but a distant voice in Latin.

"*Domina! Domina!*" The voice echoed in her mind. She knew that voice, and it drew her back slowly.

"*Domina!* Are you all right? What's the matter?" she heard Antonius' voice as the room swam back into focus. *No, thank the gods, I am not in Liqian. What's the matter with me?* She became aware that all eyes in the room were on her.

"I am sorry, Antonius. Sorry! It's like a nightmare, but I am awake, seeing all the bad things... You, almost killed, Ming dead on the floor," she whispered in Latin, keeping it from the king at least.

Antonius understood at once. He took her hand. "Hold my hand firmly, *amorata mea*. Focus on me. It happens to many people, they relive a fight in broad daylight, blots out what's going around them."

She nodded. "That's what happened."

"Just keep holding my hand, and focus on me. I have had this too, sometimes still do, but it's frightening the first time it happens. Focus on me, and drink your wine. It will help."

She took a big gulp.

"Good girl! Just keep holding my hand, and it will pass." She squeezed his big hairy paw as hard as she could, feeling the rough calluses.

Antonius was aware of the king saying something in Bactrian. He shifted linguistic gears to answer. "I am sorry, your Excellency, we were speaking Latin and I missed your question."

"Certainly. I was hoping she was all right. Do you need a doctor?"

"Er, no," he said, cobbling together an explanation that would deflect further questions. "It's a ... a woman thing, Your Excellency. She is fine."

Marcia gave Antonius a crosswise look, then understood.

"She's not pregnant, by any chance?" asked the king, with concern.

"No, Your Excellency. Just a little discomfort."

The king clapped his hands to get a servant's attention. "Some mint tea, for the lady, please. My wife's preferred remedy. She swears by it." The servant silently went out and returned shortly with a hot steaming cup.

Marcia took the cup, nodding thanks, and brought it to her lips, inhaling the sweet scents of peppermint, spearmint and some other things she couldn't identify. She took a sip, swallowed, and almost immediately her mood began to lift. "Thank you, I think this will do nicely!" She thought, *This is not monthly cramps, but the tea works with whatever it is, anyway.*

Antonius said softly into her ear in Latin, "We'll talk about this more later, I'll not drink too much so we can. If it comes back, just squeeze my hand, and I'll make it go away again."

She nodded. "The tea is miraculous, Your Excellency. I feel better already. Let's not waste this banquet worrying any more about me!"

"We are glad you are feeling better, young lady. I was concerned."

"Thank you, and please thank your wife for me," she said, nibbling on a chicken leg.

This restored everyone's mood and the gentle hum of conversation resumed. The king turned his attention to Aulus. "So, Senator, where do you go from here?"

"Your Excellency, we were hoping for your advice on that. So far, we relied on caravans to get this far, along with a brief sojourn with the migrating Xiongnu. Our next destination should be Bactra, Demosthenes' home. That is west of here, not too far, I understand?"

"Just a few days. In fact, I have a military convoy going there at the end of the month, and if you all don't mind being my guests until then, you are welcome to travel with them, under my safe passage. From Bactra, you will want to go to Aria, also not far, the convoy commander can no doubt connect you with another convoy going there. It is also not far, but that is the limit of Bactrian territory, after that it's Parthian territory. They are looking for you by name."

"Is there a way around Parthia?" asked Aulus.

"Not by a route you would want to take. You would have to go around the Caspian Sea, which is a long way through nomadic territories. The nomads, if they like you, will protect you with their lives. If they don't, they may eat you and make a drinking cup out of your skull. There are no cities there. Best take your chances on the Parthians."

Gaius nodded in agreement. "*XII Ful* was based in Baku a few years ago, and it's about two or three days' sailing to cross the sea, and nothing on the other shore when you get there. We had a few navy patrols go there for curiosity, or to drop off scouting parties to keep an eye on the Parthians' flanks, but there isn't much worth seeing. Hunting, maybe."

"So, Your Excellency, advice on outwitting the Parthians?" asked Aulus.

"Easy. I have people here whose job it is to get people in and out across borders without being identified. Those beards are new?"

"They are, your Excellency. Shaving is a luxury on a caravan."

"I imagine so. So don't shave them. Clean-shaven gills mark you as Roman before you open your mouth."

Ibrahim had been listening intently. The king shifted his attention to him. "I suspect you might know some tricks of your own."

Ibrahim smiled, stroking his pointed salt and pepper beard, now with a little more salt and a little less pepper than when he left Luoyang. "Your Excellency, I have some ideas. I'll be glad to offer them to your people."

"I am sure you do, my dear scoundrel, and I am sure you will!" he paused and turned his attention to Aulus, who had noted the scribe taking note of this discussion.

"So, Senator, from Aria, you will go northwest to Hyrcania on the southern coast of the Caspian, from there, hug the coast line, until you get to Roman Armenia. About fifteen hundred miles from here. Anyone of you speak Parthian?"

Ibrahim answered up. "I and Yakov speak it passably well, and also Aramaic, spoken commonly there. Parthian is not too different from Bactrian."

"That's very good. If you keep your identity under wraps, you should be able to slip right on through. You can either travel alone or in a caravan, whichever you prefer, but it will not be the difficult traveling you had getting here, through desert and mountain country. Cities, inns, you should be fine. I presume you have money?"

"We have Roman gold and silver coins," answered Ibrahim.

"My treasury can change them for Bactrian and Parthian coins that will attract less attention. Be aware, tensions are starting to heat up with Rome there. My people think Pacorus is casting his eyes on Armenia again. But no one thinks war with Rome will come for several years," said King Vima.

"Thank you, we will be alert. If I may ask, if war came between Rome and Parthia, whose side would you be on?" asked Aulus.

"You may. I would be on the Bactrian side. We depend on trade continuing to flow, and our taking sides in your war would disrupt that trade. If I took your side, Pacorus would come to settle scores with me afterward, and Rome has no reach to protect me from that. So, pragmatically, I will remain neutral, go on keeping the worst of the nomads off his eastern flank, and continue trading with both of you. Though, if I have to employ smugglers to get goods to and from Rome, the wartime prices may not be those to which you have become accustomed."

"I appreciate you honesty, your Excellency. We will convey that to Trajan."

"With my regards. Please join me in my private quarters at noon tomorrow for lunch, and we can continue business then, and I may have some more items for us to discuss. For now, I would like to concentrate on enjoying our fine wine, and sharing jokes and stories!"

The servants cleared away the plates, brought out an iced desert, and story swapping began, the hijacking, the firefight at Galle, the small boat pirates in Malacca. The stories slowly turned to ribald jokes, with Marcia first rehashing the one about the traveler among the Xiongnu sharing the *shanyu*'s wife for the night. The punchline 'wrong hole,' brought down the audience, the king included, and set the tone that they need not be overly concerned with Marcia's sensibilities.

Antonius closed with one he insisted was a true story from his Syrian tour. "You know, your Excellency, we use camels in the Roman army. One-humpers, not two-humpers like here. I was showing this brand new subaltern tribune - he couldn't have been eighteen or nineteen, but full of his aristocratic self - I was showing him the lay of the camp, how watches were run, and we got to the camel paddock. I was explaining we used 'em for transport and such. And he dug me in the ribs and whispered, "Question, centurion! When you and your men need a woman, what do you do around here?'

"And I says, 'Sir, mostly, they come down here at night and take a camel…' and he got really red in the face, kind of shocked, and said 'Not while I am in charge! Any man that does that, I'll have him flogged!' And he turns on his heels and struts off.

"So a few weeks later, well after sundown on the first night watch, there's this hell of a racket from the camels. I and the centurion of the watch grab some boys, torches and weapons to go down and see what's up. Rustlers? Wolves?

"So we all show up and there's our young tribune standing behind a camel, who is very upset with what the boy is trying to do, making a big fuss. The men start laughin' so bad, they dropped their torches. I was afraid they'd set the hay on fire, and the tribune was turnin' red as a beet. I said, 'Son, I think you need to step back from the camel before she bites you!'

"So he does, and then glares at me, real angry, 'Centurion, you told me you men come down here to take a camel when you… when you…'

"You didn't let me finish, son! I was going to say … 'to ride into the town a few miles from here where they got a fine brothel.' At that point, I lost it and doubled up laughing also. I have never laughed till it hurt, but that hurt!"

The king was nigh unto doubling over himself, as was everyone else, howling with laughter at what must have been an outrageously funny incident … except, of course, for the young tribune. All the king could get out was a gasped "True story? True story?"

Gaius chimed in, "True story! You can imagine the nickname the lad got in the officers' mess. A few months later, he was reassigned to the governor's staff in Caesarea, and that was the end of his military career!"

"Oh, I should hope so!" The king was laughing so hard he was almost crying. He took a couple of deep breaths, readjusted his crown and said, "And nothing can top that joke! Excellent evening, thank you for accepting my hospitality, and I will see you at noon tomorrow for lunch." Rustam had silently reappeared in the room from wherever he had been waiting, himself still chuckling over the last joke. "Please escort my guests to their chambers, Rustam, and thank you for preparing such an excellent banquet on such short notice."

"I am honored, Your Excellency." He gave a small bow and motioned the party toward the door, while the king departed through another.

Quite a lot of wine had been consumed, and Aulus needed some assistance, a bit wobbly and bleary-eyed. The rest were just happily drunk. Per his promise, Antonius was not, and Marcia had drunk only a few cups. She opened the door and Antonius followed her in. During their absence, servants had moved in a second wooden clothes closet and a bed more suitable for two, nicely cushioned, leaving two oil lamps lit on the wall on shelves on either side. These gave off a bright steady glow, pleasantly scented, for a golden ambience. An air vent somehow brought fresh air into the windowless room, occasionally making shadows dance on the walls.

"Good, I was afraid I was going to have to fight you for the bed, the other one was certainly not for two!" she said, slipping off her cloak and the long *stola* and hanging them in the closet. She did a quick inventory of the other clothes, several *salwar kamis,* another *stola* of a different color, a heavy robe for the bath, and several tunics of different styles. She was still wearing her under tunic, much shorter and more translucent than the cotton one Antonius was wearing, having happily shed his toga and hung it up.

"Damn, it's been years since I've worn a toga. Hmm, my coming of age ceremony, before I joined the army, but I left that one home. I bought one for this mission, which I guess is still in Luoyang, but never wore it once. I'm not even sure if I got the folds right," he growled.

"You looked fine, *carus.*" She sat on the bed, her legs folded up under her, with a generous amount of thigh exposed under the short silk. "So, what the hell happened to me this evening?" she asked, as Antonius clambered onto the bed from the other side to sit facing her.

"Is this the first time yer've had anything like this?" he asked, looking at her intently. He held both her hands in his on his lap.

"I've had bad dreams, but nothing when I was awake," she answered.

"Like I said, I've had I guess, hundreds of young soldiers go through the same thing. Yer mind recoils at killing a human being, and yer first one is especially hard. Yers was especially hard because yer knew him, and maybe cared for him a little."

She nodded. "He wasn't always bad. There were times he made me smile."

"And that's all right. And the other, about me almost getting killed, well, that one will come back for a while too. The good news is, the more yer talk about these, the better it gets, and one day they'll be just memories, yer can take them out of their little box in yer mind, look at them, turn them around, and just put them back. They won't hurt much, or be scary. But that will take a while. Right now, they are like boils in yer mind, yer have ter keep lancing them and squeezing them till they dry up. But don't do that alone. Have me, or someone else with yer, when yer do that. But don't bury them. Yer saw what that did ter Hina."

"Galosga helped her a lot."

"He may have saved her life. We had a soldier, lost his best friend in battle right next ter him, an' a couple of years later, he went mad and tried ter kill everyone in his tent. They had ter kill him, and if they hadn't, we'd have had to execute him, 'cuz he did kill one of them. Sad." He paused. "But enough gloomy stuff from me. Do yer feel better?"

In answer, she grabbed Antonius around his neck, kissing him so hard she could feel their teeth clicking together. She was desperate for him, rolled onto her back on the bed and pulled him onto her and into her, no preliminary cuddling needed or wanted. She wrapped her arms around his neck and buried his bristly black beard in her shoulder, legs tightly around his waist, and thrust hard and urgently against him, desperate for release. She was normally very attentive to Antonius during their lovemaking, as he was to her, but tonight he was just an instrument for her. It might have been a minute, it might have been five, but when release came, she arched against him strong enough to lift him up, her body convulsing under him.

She lay gasping, her body suddenly limp, her heart pounding, breath ragged, the last aftershocks of her pleasure rippling through her flesh. "If this is how these bad daydreams are going to end, I am going to have to dig up those memories pretty often," she purred, rubbing her cheek against his whiskers.

The next morning, servants brought them breakfast in their rooms, *nan* and yogurt with juices and tea. And overnight, their personal baggage from the stable appeared, stashed in the hallway for each to pick out their personal belongings. Marcia brought hers and Antonius' into the room. She went through her bundles, searching for the beautiful dress and jacket that Antonius had gotten her in Turfam. That seemed to fit her mood for the morning.

Properly dressed, everyone waited for Rustam's summons in Aulus's room, making comparisons between these and their accommodations back in Luoyang, deciding that both were definitely imperial quality. And Antonius, no stranger to heavy drinking, opined that King Vima was definitely a heavy drinker.

"Are you sure he was drinking the same thing we were?" asked Aulus.

"Aye, I was watchin' fer that old trick. Speaking of us drinkin', Senator, how's yer head this morning?" he laughed, thumping Aulus's head playfully.

"It's still on my shoulders, but sometimes I wish it would go away."

Antonius fished a few pieces of willow bark out of his purse and handed them to Aulus. "Here, chew on these a while. It'll help yer head. Roman army hangover cure, willow bark."

About midmorning Rustam summoned them to the king's private chambers. They went through the throne room, now completely restored to stately elegance after last night's festivities, and through another door that opened into his private living quarters.

The large living room, with white marble walls and light gray floors overlaid with intricately woven carpets depicting geometric patterns and hunting scenes, was richly but subtly furnished with contrasting brown leather sofas, chairs and small black lacquered tables. A life-size black statue of the goddess Anahita faced the entrance, silently welcoming visitors. Various other plain white marble rectangles held a Buddha contemplating the universe, other small statues, or lamps. Silver circular plaques hung on the walls above the lamps, carved with Greek maenads and other mythological creatures.

The room was brightly illuminated by daylight through large Egyptian glass windows and a broad opening in the far wall admitting daylight from a large sheltered balcony. Silk curtains in pastel colors of mint green and orange billowed in the wind, their weighted bottoms preventing them from floating free. King Vima was on the balcony, leaning over the marble railing to observe his kingdom. Rustam led the party out to him, and King Vima turned to greet them, simply clad in a Greek tunic and slippers, no crown.

"Good morning! I hope you all slept well!" he boomed, taking Aulus by the arm and shaking his hand strongly, then keeping it in his grasp.

"The wine certainly helped," answered Aulus, smiling.

"Very good! I like the view from this balcony," he said, beckoning them forward to the sun-splashed railing to look down at the garden. It was a hundred yards on a side, surrounded by white brick walls, with immaculately trimmed bushes forming almost a maze, interspersed with a variety of multi-colored flowers and trees. Pathways meandered throughout the area, with benches and occasional statuary. A gardener in a brown tunic was tending the yard below, an apron stuffed with tools around his waist, a watering can at his feet.

The king inhaled a deep lungful of air. "I love the smell of the garden in the morning. But it is going to be hot today. Come inside. I have something I want to show you that I think you will find most interesting," said the king, leading them back into the living quarters. Along one wall, above a long rectangular table holding several lamps, was a giant map of the world.

Aulus's jawed gaped, as did everyone else's as he took in the scope of the map, truly a map of the whole world. At the far left was the familiar shoe-shape of the Mediterranean, boot-shaped Italy, the cow's head shape of the

Black Sea, the shrimp-shaped Caspian. The Red Sea snapped at Egypt like a serpent, jaws open at the northern end. The triangular shape of India, then the unfamiliar shapes of the east, ending with the Hanaean coast. The sea was a light blue, the land yellow. Rivers meandered in blue, what might be roads were in black.

Gaius leaned over to examine the legends. Towns were labeled in Greek. On the left he found Rome, Damascus, Jerusalem, Caesaria, Alexandria, Myos Hormos… where their journey began… On the right, he found what he thought was Tianjin, Luoyang, and Chang'an. Here they were lettered with both Greek and Hanaean characters. "Marcia, you can read these, is that Luoyang? Right there?" he asked, pointing to a spot a bit inland on a river.

Marcia looked. The lettering was small but distinct. "Yes, that is Luoyang!" she said excitedly. "And that's the Huang He River, Sanmenxiang, Chang'an. Tongchuan is not marked, but it must be about here, these little triangles are the mountains." Her finger followed the loop of the Huang He north around the Ordos loop, then back down and west. "Wuwei, yes and Liqian! It's not marked either but it has to be right here, in the mountains west of Wuwei. And Dunhuang, here's Turfam, Kashi, that is Kashgar!"

"And we are here," said King Vima, proudly, pointing to Bagram, just south of the cluster of triangles that marked the Hindu Kush. "I commissioned this map about ten years ago, to assemble the best picture of the world from both Roman, Parthian and Hanaean sources. The European side is from one of your mapmakers in Alexandria, and the eastern side from Hanaean mapmakers. Though I never expected a party that would actually have required all of this to depict their trip."

Amazing!" said Gaius. "I worked with the Alexandrian navigators on the *Europa*, and the European side looks just like one in their portfolio. Yes, and I never thought I would see a map big enough to encompass it all!"

He turned toward the map, locating Ctesiphon on the Tigris River, then following the river north. "We were fronting Dura Europos, here, went to Alexandria, up the Nile to cut over to Myos Hormos, then Eudaemon."

Ibrahim chimed in. "The big island off Eudaemon is Socotra, here, and Hasdrubal took you north up to Masira, where the Romans relieved you of him, then you coasted down India, while we went to Taprobane. Then through Malacca, and we rendezvoused about here, then up to Tianjin. Yes, it's all here, and looks like a fine piece of work!"

And Antonius joined in. "My wife here is the veteran. She is over halfway through her third trip!" Marcia blushed a bit.

"That is an accomplishment, young lady. There may not be another person in the world who has ever done that."

"I was just along for the ride, your Excellency," she said modestly.

Aulus chimed in. "It gives a Roman a sense of humility. We like to think of ourselves as the center of the world, but we are really about to fall off the edge of it into the Great Ocean. You, sir, on the other hand, are truly at the center!"

"That's why I commissioned this map, because we truly are the bridge between east and west. And north and south, as well," he said, pointing to India and the Ferghana Valley to the north. "Senator, I will have a copy prepared for you to take back, as a gift to Emperor Trajan. I hope he will not feel that I am trying to displace him as the center of his universe!"

He waved them away from the map toward a low table, around which some sofas and chairs clustered, and invited them in to take a seat. A servant quietly entered the room, bent down to take some whispered instructions, and left. The king announced, "I ordered up some tea. I suspect after last night, that would be preferred to wine, am I right, Senator?" He smiled broadly at the sheepish Aulus.

"I tried to keep up with you glass for glass, but I lack your royal capacity. I got quite drunk trying."

Antonius chimed in. "I am making you an honorary centurion in the Roman army, your Excellency. You are welcome to drink in our mess anytime."

Tea was brought, and the King got down to business. "We are a forgotten empire, and I want to make an offer which you are free to accept or not. I would like you to stay here thirty days or so, until that military convoy leaves for Bactra, and until we work out a plan for Parthia. During this time, you have free run of my ministries, the army, the countryside, whatever you want to see or do, except for some few things which may be closed to you. At night, several times a week, I would like to entertain you as my guests with the culture of Kushana... plays, concerts, poetry readings, philosophical and religious discussions, and so forth. As I have no scheduled senior visitors, you are welcome to stay in your quarters. If on the other hand, you wish to leave early, that is your choice."

Aulus answered, "I think I speak for all, Your Excellency, that we would like to accept that opportunity. And we do need to figure out how to get through Parthia safely, now that we know they are looking for us."

"We will talk to my minister of state this morning about that. He will have some ideas for cover. Rustam will let you know when and where. And bring Ibrahim along. He will probably have some thoughts as well.

"Now, if you have all finished your tea, I want you to meet my family. I have been waiting for my daughter, but she isn't back yet. She left this morning before I could tell her you were coming, so she will be a bit... rough when she comes in. She was out riding, her favorite pastime." He led them through another door, where a short, dark-haired woman was standing, with a boy in his early teens. "My wife Cassandra and my son Kanishka."

Cassandra was wearing a long blue silk robe, her hair carefully done up in a bundle, a slender, attractive woman about forty, with penetrating brown eyes. Kanishka wore a red robe of similar length. He carried himself well, but he did not yet shave.

"Pleased to make your acquaintance, er…" Aulus was uncertain of the correct address.

"Cassandra, please," she said with a smile that put everyone at ease.

Aulus introduced everyone in turn.

There was a clatter on the stairway on the patio outside while this was going on, and a young woman burst into the room, dusty, sweaty, and wearing very casual riding gear, also sweaty. "Mom, Dad, glad to …" she paused, putting her hand to her mouth, seeing the finely clad guests. "I am so sorry! I didn't know we were expecting company. I'll go change!"

Aulus intervened to set the young woman at ease. "Not at all, young lady, unless your father insists. This is the first time we have been clean and dressed up in months of traveling, so be at ease and join us. We are guests in your home."

The king added, "Please, stay! I especially want you to meet Marcia, who is, I think, my favorite of this bunch."

The young woman stepped up to Marcia. "Glad to meet you, I am Ranisa." she said, taking Marcia's hand in an almost masculine handshake. Marcia could feel the calluses of the girl's hand, not your average soft princess. Wearing a plain beige linen *salwar kamis,* she smelled of sweat, her own and that of her horse.

Marcia smiled. She instinctively liked this straightforward girl, and returned the firm handshake grip for grip. "Marcia Lucia, and this is my husband, Antonius Aristides."

"You're an interesting combination. Hanaean features, blue eyes, Bactrian speech and clothes, Roman name and Greek husband. Is there an interesting story here?" she said, twinkling.

"Several! He is Roman of Greek descent, a centurion with the Twelfth Legion."

"Pleased," she said, turning to give Antonius a firm handshake as well.

"My daughter Ranisa, horsewoman of great excellence," said the king. "She has little patience for palace protocol, but she keeps me honest."

Ranisa was introduced to each in turn, and was somewhat taken in awe of the gracious pirate Ibrahim, but she gravitated quickly back to Marcia. "So… about those stories?" she said, leading Marcia off to a corner to put their heads together.

At the end of getting acquainted, Marcia made her an offer. "If you're riding tomorrow, I would like to join you if you don't mind."

"I ride pretty hard," Ranisa cautioned. "Most of the women who have ridden with me think 'riding' means cantering for short distances, not galloping to the mountains.

"Good, you might be able to keep up with me then. See you at daybreak. Meet in the stables?"

"Looking forward to it."

CHAPTER 76: KIDNAPPED

Ranisa and Marcia reached the mountains a few hours after sunrise following a most enjoyable ride, a brisk gallop outside the city to warm the animals up, then just letting the animals have their head. Marcia was wearing her Xiongnu summer gear, Ranisa her beige *salwar*.

"I thought you were expecting to take the lead, Marcia?" Ranisa asked with an exultant smile. Her mare had stayed ahead of Excelsior consistently with every gallop.

"I think Excelsior was much more interested in watching your mare's rump, and thought running headlong away from her was a very bad idea. Typical man!"

"Aren't they all? My favorite lake is off to the left around those trees."

A little pathway turned off the main dirt road, and after a few hundred yards opened onto a blue lake, lined with trees splashed with the beginnings of fall colors, interspersed with dark, almost black pines. Ranisa led them up to a pile of big grey granite boulders, on the other side of which was a deep quiet pool, overhung by a willow.

"This is my favorite spot. Here I can hunt, fish, or just lay around and watch the animals and birds. I wish Dad could marry me off to some poor farmer. I could live like this, take care of his horses, have his babies, help build his house, I'd be happy... but I don't think Dad needs a political alliance with some poor farmer, or even a rich one. What are you and Antonius going to do when you get back to Rome?"

"Well, the latest plan is that he wants to leave the army, go back to his home town and pick up tutoring, like his father did. And maybe the two of us teach the languages we've learned, Hanaean and Bactrian... there may be a lot of people interested in that, if we salvage this trip. And have lots of babies; I am looking forward to that part. But Antonius is a little afraid of change. All he knows is the army, what he has done for twenty-five years, and he is afraid he doesn't know anything about teaching."

"From what little I've seen of you two, if I had to be married, it would be like you two."

"Thank you. And you and I are a lot alike. But I wasn't always like this. I was an Hanaean concubine until a few years ago. You think your court life is restrictive? Try that. Sewing, singing, flower arranging, that's good, poetry, yes, and don't forget about learning to please your man, who doesn't give a damn whether he pleases you or not... everything else, off limits." But Marcia was smiling; the words no longer had any bitterness in them. "Tell your father what you want in a man. I think he will try to give you what you need."

"Hmm. I might do that. I am a bit rebellious and headstrong, but he has been good about not forcing me into marriage. He tried once, but let me off when I objected. The man was over sixty, his children twice my age, and here I am not yet twenty!" Ranisa stood up and stretched. "I am sweaty as hell. Do you mind if I strip down and take a dip in the pool?"

"If you don't mind if I join you."

The girls stripped out of their clothes and edged into the chilly water, eventually standing waist deep, splashing the water around their chests and face… and playfully, on each other, cavorting like water nymphs.

"That is an ugly scar on your breast, Marcia. How did that happen?" said, Ranisa, noticing the hairline wire scar threading across the top of Marcia's left breast.

"Knife fight." She was going to let it drop but remembered Antonius' advice. "My consort was trying to take me back to Luoyang, right before my wedding to Antonius."

"What happened?"

"He's dead."

"Antonius?"

"Me."

"Oh!"

Ranisa was silent for a while. "I'm sorry I asked."

"It's all right." Marcia splashed some water under her armpits, then scooped up a handful to drink. "This is cold, clear water. Where did you learn to hunt and fish?"

"Uncle Boni," answered Ranisa.

"Boni is the king's brother?" asked Marcia, with some surprise.

"No," answered Ranisa with a smile. "He is the head of Dad's palace guards. He is sort of my adopted uncle, since I was nine or ten. Taught me to ride, shoot, fish, hunt, dress and butcher game, make fire from wet tinder, the good stuff. I was desperately in love with him when I was about fourteen, but he wasn't having any of that. That is why my father trusts him."

"He wouldn't take advantage of you?" asked Marcia, smiling with one eyebrow cocked.

"No, he wouldn't let me take advantage of him!"

They got out, dressed, and Ranisa produced a little lunch from her saddlebag, some wine, *nan* and grapes. Then they hitched up to head back, hoping to be back before noon.

They headed down hill to the flat plain at a brisk gallop, pulling up to give their horses a breather after about a mile or so. Marcia heard riders behind them and saw about five or ten riders coming fast, raising a cloud of dust.

"Company!" she said, putting her hand on her dagger. "I wish we hadn't ridden our horses so hard."

"Probably all right," said Ranisa, but she put her hand on her dagger as well. *I hope Boni taught her how to use it!*

Two riders blew by them in a cloud of yellow dust, then whirled around to face them, their mounts pawing the ground. Several others, Marcia guessed about five, pulled in behind them. One of the two in front was tall and thin, looked to be about fifty, mounted on a black horse. The other was a short stocky guy with really bad teeth, mounted on a gray, who did the talking. "Hello, girls! Out for a ride?"

"We are," answered Marcia, keeping her eyes fixed on him, but alert for any other movement around her.

"Can be dangerous out here. Why don't you ride with us so we can protect you?" He had several rotten teeth in his mouth, ringed by a scruffy beard.

"We're fine."

"I said it is dangerous! I wasn't asking you."

Ranisa started to edge her horse through the blockade. "We are not answering you! Out of my way, I'm the king's daughter!" she said, in her most imperious voice.

"Oh, and I thought you were Aphrodite," he said, with a mocking leer, bowing low with a sweep of his hand. He straightened up and then ordered, "Get off that damned horse now!"

Marcia could hear the horses behind her pawing the ground. She kneed Excelsior, who reared, neighing fiercely, kicking the air in front.

Bad Teeth slid out of the saddle and drew his sword, getting dangerously close to the flailing hooves, yelling, "Get that damned horse under control, or I'll cut his head off!" The tall thin man had also dismounted, and leveled his sword at Ranisa's animal.

Marcia reined him in. "Good boy, Excelsior, good boy. Steady now, they won't hurt me." She patted his sweaty neck and he nickered affectionately back, but his ears stayed low on his head. *There's no doubt they will kill the animals if they have to, and we will need them if we get a chance to escape later.*

The tall thin man seemed to take charge now. "Both of you, off your horses, and hand over the little apple peelers on your waists, hilt first"

Marcia handed over her dagger, as did Ranisa. "You're making a big mistake! My father will have his whole army looking for you!" said the girl, in her most haughty voice.

Bad Teeth continued to mock her. "I don't think daddy's little princess would be out and about looking like a peasant girl. Where is your bodyguard?"

Two men grabbed the girls from behind, pulling their arms behind them and coiling rope around their wrists, leaving about a ten foot length behind as a sort of leash. They then gagged them with dirty rags, and roughly mounted them on two of their horses. "We'll bring their animals in tow. That black stallion will fetch a good price after he is gelded," said the thin man.

Bad Teeth swung into the saddle behind Marcia, and secured her leash to a saddle ring. "Don't try to jump off, or I'll just drag you along behind me.

Bad Teeth smelled as bad as he looked, and it wasn't too long before his hand around her waist began to explore things. *Don't give him any reaction. Focus on what is going on. I think the Thin Man is in charge, they call him 'Boss'.*

One of the riders pulled alongside them. "Hey, Anteater! You got the Hanaean bitch! She's cute!"

I wonder how Bad Teeth came by that name?

Back at the palace, King Vima was beginning to become nervous. Aulus's party was gathered for lunch, but neither Marcia nor Ranisa had returned. "It's not like her," he fretted. "She knows I don't like her riding alone." Cassandra sat beside him, holding his hand, looking worried, but saying nothing. She kept glancing at the outside stairs, hoping Ranisa would burst through in her usual ebullient fashion, but she did not.

"Well, she's not alone," said Antonius, offering some encouragement. "Marcia is the next best thing to me out there with her. She is a damned good fighter. They may have had some mishap, a thrown shoe or something. Give them another hour."

"I will, but I am going to alert Boni now. If they don't show up soon, we are going to go out after them while there is light." He motioned for a servant. "Take this lunch away and you servants enjoy it, Cassandra and I are not in the mood for eating right now. Send for Boni."

Antonius snagged some grapes and bread before the tray disappeared. The king went off into his quarters with Cassandra.

Aulus looked concerned. "Antonius, you're not really that unconcerned, are you?"

"No, I am concerned as hell, but he didn't need to hear that. I am sure hoping it's some minor accident, but I agree, if we don't hear anything in an hour, we ride. Let's get into our gear. I'll go down to the stables and get the horses ready."

About an hour later, the entire group assembled in the stables in fighting gear. The king appeared with Boni, both clad in white linen uniforms with breast plates and riding helmets.

"Let's mount up," said the king. "The rest of the men are outside."

They led their horses, snorting and stamping, outside where five more mounted riders awaited them. Boni introduced one to the king as Berzad. "Your Excellency, he is our finest tracker, nicknamed 'Sniffer' for his ability to read the road like a book. If the girls can be found, he will find them."

Berzad dismounted and inspected the road out of the stable, and eventually announced, "Two horses, early this morning, one unshod."

Antonius nodded. "That would be Excelsior, Marcia's Mongolian stallion. No shoes."

Berzad nodded. "Good. That clue will help a lot."

They exited the north gate, riding beside the road so as to not disturb the tracks. Berzad verified that Excelsior had come that way heading north, along with several other shod horses, normal for a busy road. There were no indications he had returned that way.

After about an hour and half, constantly verifying that they hadn't lost the trail, they came on a heavily disturbed area in the road ten miles north of the city. Berzad waived everyone off to the side. "Five to ten horses here, milling around. Hmm, Excelsior reared, his hoof prints landed hard several times. These are fresher, much fresher than the ones we have been following, just a few hours old. They were intercepted by several men on their way back." He scanned the sky, watching a single buzzard wheel in the updrafts. "That bird is looking for something to eat, but sees nothing. There are no bodies around here, so they left together."

Another mile up, they found Excelsior's northbound morning tracks, overlapping some southbound tracks. "He was galloping southbound, walking without a rider northbound."

Boni pointed northward. 'About a mile or two that way, there is our lake where we used to go." As soon as he said it, he tried to catch himself. "I taught her to fish and hunt there."

The entrance to the lake was unremarkable, two horses went in, two came out, one shod, the other unshod. They had begun a gallop before joining the main road, probably for fun, Berzad opined, for there seemed to be no indication at this time of pursuit. "That is probably why they didn't try to escape the group that rode up on them. They'd already exhausted the horses, and knew they wouldn't be able to outdistance them."

North of the lake, the group of five to ten horses and Excelsior continued on, not riding hard. Two horses, both shod, were heavily loaded, Excelsior and one other shod horse carrying no one. "The girls were riding double on two horses with men, Excelsior and the Princess' mare in tow," said Berzad

Near sunset, the horses had turned east onto a small trail that led up into the mountains. Overhung with brush, they found several strands of long black hair that looked like Marcia's. The trail was harder to follow on the rocky ground, and light was failing when Berzad called a halt. "I won't be able to follow the trail without a torch, and that will alert them that we are following. And we might step all over their trail in the dark. I suggest we camp here, dark, no fires, and quiet. They could be fifty yards away, or five miles."

They dismounted and tended the horses, while the king, Boni, Berzad, and Aulus' party huddled to assess the situation. The others took a light dinner with the soldiers, and began to unroll their sleeping blankets. Without a fire, it would be chilly.

Boni volunteered that they were probably not far away. "They start up the Salang Pass tomorrow, so they will start early and ride eight to ten hours. I suspect if the kidnapping went down around noon, they stopped for the night before sunset, and not moving fast, so... twenty or twenty five miles. We stopped a lot to check the trail, but in between rode hard so I guess twenty or so miles for us. So we're close."

"Why do you think they took them? Is this political?" asked the king.

"I don't think so," answered Boni. "For one thing, there is almost no unrest about anything. All local issues. Kidnapping the king's family is a big step, and not likely to turn out in any opposition's favor. Even if they do the worst. Especially if they do the worst." Everyone understood what he meant, and were silent a bit. "I don't think they know who they have."

"Ranisa would have told them."

"And Ranisa doesn't look like a princess right now. They probably didn't believe her. We have had a number of girls go missing over the past few years, so many that the authorities started looking into the cases more closely. We thought it might be some demonic individual preying on lone girls, but this looks like organized group. Probably selling them into slavery. Which means they want them alive and reasonably healthy. This gang may give us a lead into the other disappearances, so we want to leave at least a few alive when we find them."

"Thank you, Boni. We will get her back, and Marcia for Antonius." King Vima paused for a little water from his leather bag, and passed it around. "Berzad, what time to you want to start tomorrow?"

"Let's saddle up the horses at first light," he said, taking a sip from the king's waterbag and passing it on. "Thank you, your Excellency."

"No, I must thank you. No one else could have gotten us so close so fast."

They sat in silence for a while, each thinking their own private thoughts about the missing girls. Then the king spoke up again. "Boni, did you know Ranisa loves you?"

"And I love her, as though she were my real niece. She calls me Uncle Boni." He smiled fondly, the starlight barely catching his wistful look.

"And as a woman loves a man, Boni."

"Your Excellency, I have done everything to discourage her. She is royalty, and deserves a marriage to royalty. I have nothing to offer her, and... I swear, I have never taken advantage of her feelings!"

"And I know you haven't. She has also told me that. Have you noticed she is a hard-headed woman? Her idea of marrying into royalty is to 'refuse to be a marriageable pawn on my royal chessboard'. That's one of her more polite expressions on the subject." He paused, then choked up. "I am sorry... I miss her so much, and love her so much." The darkness hid his tears but did not stifle his sobs. And it hid Antonius' tears, his fists clenched at his helplessness, unable to defend Marcia or even find her.

Where the kidnappers had left the road to enter the trail, there was a low-hanging leafy tree branch. One would have normally ducked to clear it, but Marcia instead stood up as best she could with Anteater pawing her waist, and let her head go straight through the branches, shaking her hair as she did. She felt the twinge of hairs being pulled out. Hopefully, a good tracker might notice.

The kidnappers halted a bit before sundown, a few miles into the hunting and smuggling trail. The girls were taken down, their leashes tied to two trees, sufficiently far apart that they could not collaborate on working each other's knots loose. Other than that, they could stand, stretch, and lie down, as best one can with hands tied behind one's back. Anteater undid their gags long enough for them to rinse their mouths, dry, dusty, and foul tasting, with several mouthfuls of water, then he fed them some bread. Then the hated foul gags went back on.

Marcia listened, hoping to pick up as much information as she could.

"...have a little fun with them!" The men cheered, "Yeah, nice pieces! I want the 'princess!'"

The Boss was having none of this. "The buyer in Baghlang wants his goods clean and undamaged. If these girls get the price I think they will, then I'll buy you all a romp with both of them. Break them in right for their first night on the job. But leave them alone till then. He checks, and if they're already used, the price goes down by half or more."

Goods, that what we are, just merchandise to be sold. The good news is we're going to Baghlang, three or four days' ride. The bad news is we're going to be sold into a whorehouse and gang-raped when we get there. Antonius, I hope you are in a hurry!

Many thoughts came unbidden. *I'm coming into my fertile period! This can't happen. How would Antonius deal with me if I got pregnant by these animals? Would he still want me after other men have had me? What if we were never found?*

Hina's counseling took over from her momentary panic. *Take a deep breath, let reason control the panic. Deal with what you have now, and that is three days to get you and Ranisa out. Don't panic, because she is much more terrified than you.*

Rock and pebble, she thought of Marcus, her and her brother in Luoyang. *Well, this is more pebble and pebble right now, but I have to keep her spirits up.* She caught Ranisa's ashen face, she too had heard the men's conversation. Marcia gave her a big slow wink, and as much of a smile as she could manage with a dirty rag in her mouth, and slowly shook her head negatively. *No!*

She explored the knot securing the rope around her wrists. The hemp rope was raw and scratchy, but she worked it. Try as she could, she could not find the knot, but she counted five loops around her wrists, and the leash wrapped three times around the bundle between her wrists. She tried to visualize the knot in her mind, turn it around in her head to see how it could be undone. She found a granite rock and sat down in front of it, trying to saw the rope against it without moving enough to attract attention. It was a new rope, and would take a while. Ranisa watched her, and got the idea as well.

The sun went down, the men built a fire about fifty or a hundred feet away from where the girls were tied, ate, drank and talked, mercifully not about them. Finally, after it had gotten quite dark, the Boss told Anteater: "Go take care of the girl's business. Get 'em up, walk 'em around to go pee, then give them some more water. Tell 'em we leave the gags off unless they get fussy. Fussy, they go right back on. And give them some blankets for the night."

"They've been real quiet. Not like the last couple. Screamed and cried all the way to where we were going. Even behind the gags."

Anteater came up to Marcia first. He tossed a blanket down beside her, untied her leash from the tree branch, and helped her to her feet. Pins and needles tormented her legs as the circulation came rushing back, but in a moment she was able to take some uncertain steps. He led her off behind a bush, then crouched down in front of her to pull down her pants, spending entirely too much time doing so. Then he stood, and Marcia mercifully squatted to relieve herself, long overdue. She stood, he crouched again, and she could see the leer in his face from the reflected fire glow. "I think I'm goin' to have some fun anyway, you and me. Nobody can see us behind this bush. Been wantin' some of you all day!" he said, knocking her feet out from under her. She landed with a thud, her pinioned shoulders agonized by the awkward fall onto her back. He climbed on top of her, trying to pry her knees apart, struggling with his *salwar* bottoms.

Marcia looked up at his face. She could smell, no, taste his foul breath, like rotting garbage. His face loomed over her like a rising moon in the dark, his bulbous nose… she arched her back for leverage and whipped upward, smashing her forehead into his nose with a satisfying wet, squishy crunch. He pulled back and howled in agony. She recoiled and launched a second lunge, missing his nose, but hitting him in the mouth. She felt a sharp pain in her forehead, but heard a distinct crack, hopefully from those rotten teeth of his. He howled again, rising to a sitting position, and raising his balled fist to strike her. *All right, I know the drill from here. Quiet place, quiet place, let it all go on around me.* She smiled to herself at her small victory, waiting for the retaliatory blow to land.

It didn't. Out of the darkness a hand grabbed Anteater's paw, pulling him erect, whirling him around to receive a fist solidly on his damaged nose, which cracked loudly. He howled yet again, this time in extreme agony. *If I didn't break his nose, it certainly is broken now!*

It was the Boss, and he was angry, yelling at him in a loud voice. "I told you to leave the damned girls alone till they were paid for! You think I was just talking? Get back to the campfire!" He spun Anteater in that direction and launched a swift kick to his backside that sent him tumbling. Anteater scrambled back up to his feet and scuttled back to the campfire, making little sobbing noises.

The Boss helped her to a sitting position, took her gag off and gave her a water bag. She took a mouthful, spat the taste of the rag out of her mouth, and then took several more swallows. "Thanks," she said, uncharacteristically polite to her kidnapper.

"If you girls are quiet, the gag can stay off. Are you – uh – done yet?"

"Yes."

He helped her to her feet, lifting her trousers back up modestly from behind without ogling or groping. "Let me see your wrists," he said, as though she could offer them to him for inspection. He loosened the knot a bit and she could feel pins and needles there also, as circulation returned to them. She would have been grateful, but she had just heard him planning their gang rape a few days hence. He led her back to her tree, retied her leash, and then took care of Ranisa. He then went back to the campfire, leaving the girls to talk quietly.

"What was that all about?" asked Ranisa.

"Anteater thought he would get a free sample. Got a broken nose, and I hope some broken teeth!"

"Good job, girl! Tomorrow, I am going to convince them that I really am the king's daughter. They'll have to release us then."

"To the wolves they'll release us. If you convince them you are King Vima's daughter, they'll know they are dead men. They can't take us anywhere we could be recognized, they can't let us go because we could identify them. They'll have their fun, then dump our bodies where they can't be found, and go back and get some safer girls. Be a farmer's daughter, a merchant's daughter, think of something, but don't for all the gods be the king's daughter!"

"Right, I will!"

"I don't know about you, but I am going to get a little sleep. G'night, Ranisa."

Anteater's howl carried a great distance through the night-silent woods, to where the rescue party lay in darkness, preparing to sleep till daylight. "What the hell is that, some sort of animal?" asked Antonius, cocking his head to the noise. The howl was followed quickly by one shorter and sharper, more like a bark.

"Nothing I've heard before," said Boni.

A few seconds later, a third howl echoed through the woods, longer, and ending in a sobbing sort of sound. This was immediately followed by angry words, something about "…leave the damned girls alone!"

Both were on their feet. "We found 'em!" said Antonius, "Everyone up, quietly."

Antonius and Boni assembled their men and geared up, no need for bows, too dark, and shields would be an encumbrance getting quietly through the woods.

"Boni!" said Antonius in a hoarse whisper. "They are not more than a few hundred yards off. Let's get everyone in a bit closer, then Gaius and I will scout all the way to their camp. We need to see if the girls are there and all right, how many we are up against, and if they posted guards. We'll signal, and I'll send Gaius back with details. Owl hoot, they're there. First frog, count the croaks for the men, second frog, count croaks for the guards. Then we rush them!"

"Good, let's go!" answered the king, speaking for Boni. "Try to identify the leader, and keep as many alive as possible. I want to know what they intended!"

The group entered the woods slowly and carefully, moving like smoke through the branches. Their eyes had not seen light since sunset, so the trees were perfectly visible just by starlight. At some point, Antonius signaled a halt. "Gaius and I from here on. We'll be slow, very slow, so don't get impatient. The two of us can crawl into their bedrolls if we want. Ready, *legatus?*" Antonius had not called Gaius by title in a very long time.

"Ready!" Gaius wasted no time, squatting to stretch out on his belly, and Antonius went down beside him. The two slithered off into the darkness, silent as serpents.

After few minutes, they crested a low rise, and looked down into the kidnappers' camp fifty or so feet below. The fire was banked low, intermittent tongues of fire licking around red logs, casting dancing shadows around the area. Six men lay around the fire, wrapped in blankets, a seventh sat off by himself, doing something with his face. There were no guards that they could see. A hundred feet to the right of the fire, they could see the two girls, apparently trying to sleep, separated by several feet. The girls' hands were behind them, in what looked an uncomfortable position, probably bound. "They look all right," whispered Antonius. "Guards?"

Gaius replied softly, close to Antonius' ear. "I don't think so. I counted horses over there to the left. Nine horses, seven men, two girls."

"Makes it easy." Antonius cupped his hands around his mouth. "Ooh-hoo! Ooh-hoo!" he hooted loudly. One of the men stirred at the noise, but rolled back over into his blanket. Antonius counted to one hundred to himself, then croaked out "Korax! Ek-ek-ek-ek-ek-ek-ek- Korax!" and repeated it. A frog's croak, indicating seven men. He repeated it, then a final "Korax!" followed by nothing. No guards. Nobody below them stirred.

"Gaius, go back, and get 'em. We'll take the kidnappers to the left, have Boni secure the girls on the right."

A few minutes later, Gaius scuttled back in beside Antonius, behind him the rest of their group. "All right, to your left," hissed Antonius. "On three! *Unus, duus, tres... Gladies stringete, oppugnate!* Draw swords, charge!" Antonius bellowed at the top of his lungs, and all the rest yelled "*Oppugnate!*" as they burst out of hiding, charging down the hill trying very much to look like the Furies from Hades. The kidnappers, confused, struggled with their bed rolls, groping for their swords. Three of them, unlucky enough to actually get them to hand, died quickly in a shower of blood, one killed by Demosthenes, the other two by Aulus and Gaius. The rest had swords pointed firmly at the hollow of their throats, their eyes wide with fright. The one sitting off by himself had tried to scuttle away, but Antonius grabbed him from behind and hoisted him erect.

In the meanwhile Boni's men and the king charged in, circling around the girls. The king and Boni freed Ranisa and helped her to her feet. She promptly hugged her father, then whirled around to hug Boni. Boni seemed taken aback, his arms outspread, his sword angled safely away from her, as she buried her head in her shoulder.

The king smiled in the firelight. "Boni, in the name of Ahura Mazda, would you please kiss Ranisa? It's all right!" Boni did, and Ranisa returned it passionately.

The other soldiers had freed Marcia, helping her up. She rubbed her wrists to restore the circulation, and stepped carefully, her legs numb, limping up to Antonius. He was holding Anteater erect, his hand firmly around his throat.

"Well, Antonius! I see you met Anteater!" Anteater's nose was hugely swollen and purple, streaming blood. Below that, he had a badly split lip and his two incisors were bent backwards, covered with blood. "Did I do all that to you?" she asked, mockingly sympathetic. He struggled against Antonius' grip, making an ugly face as best he could, and she continued. "Anteater, please meet my husband, Antonius Aristides. And *carus meus*, this is Anteater. He is the man who tried to rape me!" Antonius tightened his grip on Anteater's throat, looking as though he might rip the man's head off. The man made a choking groan.

Marcia continued. "Anteater, you took my dagger from me yesterday, which was a special gift from a special person. Would you please tell me where it is?"

He snarled, and spat a bloody gobbet that splattered onto her shirt.

"Antonius, his teeth are hurt. Please hold his mouth open for me." Antonius jammed the hilt of his dagger into the corner of Anteater's mouth, forcing it open. Marcia reached into his mouth and grabbed one of the loose front teeth, twisting it, wiggling it, then removing it with a slow yank. Anteater squeezed his eyes shut and grunted with the pain. She repeated the process with the second tooth.

She wiped her bloody hands on her shirt. "Now, about that dagger, Anteater." Her expression was that of barely-contained fury. "You have a lot more body parts to remove, and the king is not going to care what sort of shape you are in when he executes you."

Antonius loosened his grip to allow the man to speak, and Anteater lisped. "There, my bedroll," nodding in the direction of the fire.

Demosthenes had come up to join them, wiping his bloody sword on his clothes. "I'll get it, Marcia." He went back, rummaged through the bedroll and returned with her dagger.

Marcia accepted it and slid it into her scabbard. "I'm done with this maggot, Antonius. Do whatever you want with him." She turned around to join Ranisa with her father and Boni.

Ranisa greeted her with a hug. "Father," she said, uncharacteristically formal, "She kept me alive. When I heard what they were going to do with us, I thought I would have to find a way to kill myself, and looked over at her. She gave me a big wink, and shook her head 'No.' Marcia, I love you! Are you all right, though? Anteater took you off and… I am sorry."

Marcia rubbed the little cut on her forehead where Anteater's incisors had gouged a cut, reddish and growing purple around the edges. "This was as far as he got!" Taking Ranisa's hand and turning to the king, she said, "Your daughter was incredibly brave." Marcia noticed that Boni was holding her other hand. "Your Excellency, that tall thin man that Gaius is tying up is the leader, the one they called the Boss. You have some questions for him?"

The king certainly did.

CHAPTER 77: THE OTHER GIRLS

The Boss, whose real name was Burz-Ormuzd, was not hesitant in answering Boni's questions. Since he was very aware now that Ranisa really was the king's daughter, it was a question of whether he would face a swift death, or a painfully slow one.

Burz-Ormuzd was from a noble family in Bagram. Never married, he had a life-long addiction to prostitutes, and had long wondered why so many were ugly, deformed or slow-witted. In discussions with the owners of various brothels, he found that attractive slaves were extremely high-priced, and quickly bought up by rich bidders for their private stables. Brothels depended for the most part on daughters sold by their own families because they were unmarriageable, along with the occasional good-looking girl who had managed to lose her virginity at an inopportune and public moment, or had become pregnant out of wedlock.

Burz-Ormuzd had arranged a deal with several brothel owners for a regular string of good-looking girls at a cheap price, which he procured using a band of thugs to kidnap them from around Bagram. A fraction of the price of a pretty slave to the brothel owner, but still a handsome price to him. And, being literate and a meticulous keeper of records, he had a list of names, the brothels who had purchased them, and their prices, going back several years... over twenty girls, waylaid as Marcia and Ranisa had been, but not so fortunate as to be rescued.

He did not get the swift death for which he had hoped in making his confession, but the list he provided would help recover his victims.

The next day, the king had an earnest discussion with Gaius, Antonius and Aulus, first to offer thanks for their assistance in rescuing his daughter, and then to the very personal question of her marriage options. "She is dead-set against any marriage other than to Boni, but Boni is a commoner, and that would cause an imperial scandal. I don't see a way around that."

Aulus offered a suggestion. "Your Excellency, in Rome we have a tradition of adoption that easily breaks class barriers, and even provides for imperial succession sometimes. Do you have such a law or tradition here?"

"We do, but it is so infrequently used I am unfamiliar with how it works. I will have Rustam look into it."

It turned out that Bactrian law was not significantly different from Roman law: adoption made the adoptee a member of the adopting person's class. Accordingly, a few days after his daughter's kidnapping and recovery, he summoned Boni to his family quarters. He met with him and Ranisa on the patio, with Cassandra by his side.

"Boni, you and Berzad have earned a great reward for rescuing my daughter, but I have something more than just money to offer you. Nobility is more than a social position. Many of the nobility are anything but noble, and yet many commoners, such as yourself, are very noble. Therefore, I would like to adopt you as my nephew. This would make you a noble prince of my family line, though with no right to succession. How do you feel about that?"

Boni paused to take a long breath. "That would be most generous, but… but what responsibilities come with that position?"

"Just to continue to act nobly in all things, as you have always done. Do you accept?"

"I… yes, I accept."

Cassandra smiled. She knew where this was going as she and King Vima had worked this out in the finest detail.

"One of the best demonstrations of your nobility has been your conduct with my daughter. Although she has set you above all men since she became a woman, you have never abused my trust in your conduct with her, for the simple reason that she could not wed you because you were a commoner. I know you explained this to her repeatedly, to her great frustration. But now there seems to be no impediment to a marriage between you two, except your own wishes. As I have been an abject failure in arranging my daughter's marriage to date, I will step out with Cassandra while you two discuss the matter. When we return, you can tell us your decision. And, Boni, whatever you decide, you are still a prince of the realm."

The king stood up to go, along with Cassandra, but Ranisa beckoned him to stay seated. "Dad… Most Excellent Father," she said, correcting herself to address him formally. "Please stay while we discuss this. Boni, there is no man I have ever wanted but you. If you would have me, I am yours."

"And I am yours. I guess that settles it after all these years?"

In response, she seized him in an embrace and kissed him, while her father and Cassandra looked on smiling. When they finally released each other, King Vima said, "Of course, one of the nuisances of a royal wedding is that you have little choice of the format or the guest list. We will have to have the kings of Samarkhand, Bukhara, and Khojand of Sogdiana, Purushapura, everyone who can make it, ambassadors from the Han, Persia, India… of course, Senator Aulus can stand in for Rome."

"Knowing in advance what your decisions would be, I took the liberty of advising Rustam about this, and he believes the wedding can take place within sixty days. Senator Aulus and his people have generously agreed to remain to represent my colleague Trajan at this most auspicious gathering. Mind you, we will all come to hate Rustam in the next few weeks, as he will dictate every detail of your wedding and allow neither Cassandra and I, nor you two, any say in how it is to be done. He is a stickler for detail, hence his position as my chief of protocol. Anyway, welcome to my family, my nephew and future son-in-law. You have waited a long time for this!"

In the next few days, using the kidnapper's list, Boni's people were able to locate several of the girls abducted from Bagram in Baghlang. Boni organized the expedition to free those girls and bring them home. Ranisa and Marcia insisted on going along to help the girls. The expedition brought along a large covered cart to carry them in comfort over the Salang Pass to home. The brothels were to be closed and the owners turned over to the local authorities to be punished for illegal enslavement, the nearest statute that seemed to apply, as free women had been sold into involuntary servitude.

The Palace of Aphrodite did not live up to expectation. The brothel consisted of a first floor bar and waiting area, where customers could wait their turn or brag of their prowess afterwards. It reeked of beer, bad wine, vomit and urine. The furniture was rickety, the room dimly lit. What once had been some sort of tapestry dangled in tatters from the ceiling, blown about by stray puffs of air from the open door. The appearance of Boni, in his white uniform, flanked by Ranisa and Marcia, at the entrance did not evoke a respectful response from the fat man behind the bar, making a pretense of wiping it down with a filthy rag. "What der yer want? We paid our bribes. You need some more money now?"

Boni quietly walked up to the proprietor, grabbed him with both hands by the shirt collar, and wheeled him out from behind the bar. He put his face close to the man and hissed. "Gamanig is your name?"

"Yes!"

"Does the name Burz-Ormuzd mean anything to you, Gamanig?"

"Yes... yes, he comes here... sometimes. What has he done? I can help!" he stammered, sensing this was more than the usual shakedown by the authorities.

"I believe you can. I have a list of girls he sold you, illegally, into servitude. He has been executed, but you can help me find them." He put the list in Gamanig's trembling hands.

"Armaghan, Delaram, Firoza..." Gamanig read all the names on the list. "Yes, they're all here. Except for Gulnar... she -uh- died a few months ago."

"How?" asked Boni, his steady eyes boring into Gamanig's shifty ones.

Gamanig had a long ropy mustache that twitched as he talked. "Accident. With a customer."

"He beat her to death?"

"N-no, just hit her harder than he should have. He didn't mean to."

"Did you report the death?"

"No. She was just a whore. It happens."

"It shouldn't just happen. Besides illegal slavery, we will add murder to the list. Get the girls." Boni signaled his aide by the door, who brought in the other guards. "Take these men to where the girls are. And kick your 'customers' out. This shithole is closed, now!" One of guards took him by the scruff of his neck and led them upstairs.

Marcia and Ranisa were appalled at the conditions. Twenty tiny rooms, no larger than closets, held tiny beds where the girls both slept and serviced their clients. A pool of urine from an overturned chamber pot spread over the floor of one cubicle. A few clients were being hustled out... and the girls! Filthy clothes, scrawny, under-nourished. Dark eyes that had seen too much sadness and had no hope of seeing happiness ever again. How could a man pay to use one of these poor girls? Ranisa took the list and called out the names. "Armaghan, Delaram, Firoza, Mahdokht, Parween... we've come to take you home to Bagram. The rest of you will go to your homes elsewhere, the local authorities will take you there. My name is Princess Ranisa, and this is my friend, Marcia Lucia. If there is anything here you wish to take, bring it, but we will feed you and give you fresh clothes. This life is over for you."

She was surprised at the reaction. "Oh, please, no! Let us stay. We're safe here! Our families... we have no families anymore," wailed Parween. The other girls joined in, a chorus of tearful pleading.

Boni whispered in her ear. "They are afraid their families will throw them out on the streets, or sell them into another brothel. Or maybe stone them, or flog them to death before their neighbors. And they are right, they have shamed their families."

"They have done nothing of the sort! Their families most certainly will not do any of those things!" Ranisa set her jaw firmly, her eyes bright with determination.

"And Delaram's husband. She is -was- married."

"She still is, Boni." Turning to the girls, in her most maternal manner, she gathered them together. "Enough foolishness, girls. You have done nothing wrong, and nobody is going to hurt you again. My father King Vima says so." He hadn't yet, but he would, somehow.

Across the street was a little inn with a bath. Marcia went off to the market to buy some clothes for them, while Ranisa commandeered the bath, kicking the men out for an hour while the girls got a chance for a much needed scrubbing. Marcia showed up as they finished with the clothes, hairbrushes and some snacks. Cleaned and dressed, the girls looked much better than they did earlier. They then took the girls to a little eatery, where they wolfed down food hungrily. Ranisa wondered how long since they had had a good meal.

They billeted the girls in the inn, three to a room because of the number, and Ranisa and Marcia also shared a room. Boni and the men stayed at facilities run by the local authorities.

The next day, they loaded the five Bagram girls up in the cart for the trip home, the girls still unconvinced there would be any welcome for them. Boni, Marcia and Ranisa rode, contemplating how best to handle the reconciliation.

"My father will manage this reconciliation," said Ranisa.

"How?" asked Boni.

"I don't know yet. But he has to do it."

A few days later, when Bagram came into sight, Ranisa announced she would head on alone to make the necessary arrangements, that they should meet her at the palace stables on their arrival. She left at a brisk pace.

Ranisa's plan had come into her head on the way in, at least the broad outlines. At the stables, she put her horse in the hands of the stable grooms and rushed upstairs to locate Rustam. "We have some unexpected guests of honor, Rustam. The girls we rescued must be put up immediately in the distinguished visitors' quarters. Bathed, fine clothes, you know what to do.'

"Wait a minute, Your Ladyship! Only your father can authorize these rooms and he hasn't…"

"He will. I'm going upstairs now to make arrangements. There are five girls and their families, five rooms." She gave him her most winning smile. "Thank you, I knew you could handle such a high priority thing on such short notice, you are wonderful at that, Rustam."

"But…"

"I'll be back in a few minutes with more instructions from my father."

Rustam attempted to make another protest, but she was already on her way into the living quarters, where she cornered her father on the patio.

"Dad, you have always stressed the importance of justice in ruling the kingdom."

"Yes, and welcome back, by the way. Did you find the girls?"

"Yes, and there's the injustice. The second injustice. The first was their being taken from their families. The second is that their families will reject them." She was breathlessly blurting all this out, the thought only vaguely in her head and the solution evading her.

"Slow down, slow down. What do you want me to do?"

"I am going to put the girls up in the distinguished visitors' quarters, and when they arrive, I will have Boni fetch their families here. And then…. I don't know, Dad! But we have to arrange some sort of reunion, so these girls don't get thrown back out on the street. Don't you see? Their families think they're nothing but cheap whores now. They'll feel disgraced by them and the girls will end up freelancing in the parks and back alleys, until someone kills them or they kill themselves. And all we did for them will be wasted."

Tears welled up in her eyes. "I'm sorry, Dad, I haven't thought this through. I know what I want to happen, and I am afraid it won't, and it will be ugly, and they'll be hurt again!"

"Your heart is pushing you to help these girls, but that won't be enough to overcome their families' feelings of shame and anger. If we are to succeed, we need to use our heads, not our hearts. We need a strategy, we need the right words. Let me think how we might do this. How much time before they get here?"

"The girls will be here inside an hour, several hours more to locate their families and get them here."

"Close to dinner, then?"

"Yes."

"Have you told Rustam about this yet?"

"Yes, he's flustered, but getting things ready. I think. I told him five rooms, but we need to keep them separate until we can bring them together."

"That's good. They can stay overnight."

"Yes, I told him to expect that."

"When the girls are refreshed and changed, have them brought here. Cassandra and I will entertain them while their families arrive and freshen up in their rooms. When the families are ready, have them assemble in the private throne room for the reunion, and we will bring the girls in. Tell Rustam to put on an unexpected dinner in the private throne room for … let's see… guessing four per family, plus the girls, plus… dinner for thirty at sunset. Are any of the girls married?"

"One. Delaram. She's terrified of seeing her husband again. She's afraid he will kill her. Worse, maybe that he won't."

"Get Antonius and Marcia. Antonius can give a husband's perspective. Now, relax, breathe deeply, and sip your tea, while I think deep thoughts on what I might say."

The girls arrived and were settled in, told they were to be guests of the king, and Boni dispatched soldiers to locate and bring in their families. The girls were brought into the king's private quarters, where they were welcomed by King Vima, Cassandra and Ranisa and made to feel at ease as best they could, just a few days removed from being filthy whores of no value, living in squalor. Now they were guests of royalty in a magnificent palace. King Vima then removed himself to his study, where he scratched notes on a scroll, trying to capture the key points he would need to make.

Antonius and Marcia arrived, and Marcia introduced the girls to her husband. A few minutes later, Rustam announced that all was ready in the throne room.

The girls filed in and there were five happy reunions… no one had told the families what had become of them. They knew only that they were fresh, clean, and healthy in appearance. The girls, on the other hand, were obviously awkward and uncomfortable. There were tears and hugs, the little bits of catching up, then all were seated to hear the King speak from the throne, Cassandra standing to his right with Ranisa and Boni, Antonius and Marcia to his left. Everyone waited in silence, while he paused for effect.

"I have gathered you together, my most honored guests, because I owe you a great apology." He paused for a long time. That statement got their attention.

"Our philosophers, from Plato in Greece to our own here in Bactria, tell us that men create governments of various kinds to provide for security and justice for the people. Security, so that you the people can go about your business without fear. Justice, so that nothing precious can be taken from you. I have failed you in both regards. I failed to protect your wives and daughters, and nearly failed to protect my own daughter and her friend. A great injustice was done to you and to your girls. Your wives' and daughters' most precious possession, their freedom and their dignity, was taken from them. Shameful things were done to them, as might also have been done to Princess Ranisa and Marcia Lucia, the wife of a Roman diplomat. Shameful things were done to your girls, but I want to emphasize, not by them. The shame of this tragedy is mine alone, and for that I beg your forgiveness." Another long pause to let this settle in.

"It would be an even greater injustice now, if you were to punish these girls for my failings and the sins of their captors. These are the same girls who left your homes a long time ago, happy and full of hope. They are home at last, but they are injured and sick of heart. They need to heal, and I need your help to heal them. There will come a day when they no longer dwell on the terrible days they endured in captivity in Baghlang, but that day is not today, and will not be tomorrow. Ahura Mazda, the creator of all things good, has brought these girls home. Let us all rise to His challenge and heal these beautiful children so that one day they may smile and laugh again without shame."

There was not a dry eye in the audience. He continued, "If it will be difficult for parents, it will be incredibly difficult for husbands. For that, my friend Antonius Aristides, diplomat of Rome, will speak to them, as he nearly shared your fate when his wife Marcia was taken." He beckoned Antonius to speak.

"I am a soldier, and as a soldier, I spent a lot of time with prostitutes. And I never thought about how those girls came into that life. Now I know that none chose that life, that all were forced into it, and I regret every coin I spent in those places, making some man rich off their suffering. What would I have done, had Marcia actually made it to Baghlang, been taken by other men, used against her will? How would Marcia react on her return to me? Would we be able to be husband and wife again? I would like to think that we would overcome all difficulties, but I know that it would be the hardest thing we ever did, and I don't know if we would succeed. All I can ask is that you try, as we would have tried... harder than anything else you have ever tried... to breathe life into that spark of love that still flickers in your hearts for each other.

"And I speak to both parents and husbands. We dealt once with some of our soldiers captured by the enemy. Like your daughters, they were forced to do unspeakable things until we recovered them. Like your girls, they were in shock, and tried to keep their memories of that time sealed. We had to get them to talk, to tell us things we didn't want to hear, to say things they didn't want to say. Because only through that, could they heal. You will have to do the same. Don't do it tonight, nor tomorrow, but soon. These girls must tell you what their life was like, and you must listen, because only that way can the poison come out and the wound heal."

Antonius nodded, and the conversation returned to King Vima. "I know that some of you will try, and despite your efforts, fail to get back to where you were before. For those, do not cast your girl out, but bring her here. I have made arrangements with the Buddhist monastery, with the Christian communities here, and others, to take your daughters in and care for them if that proves impossible for you. They will have a loving home if it should be impossible for you provide one for them."

He paused, and signaled Rustam. "Enough serious talk! Let us feast our daughters' return. Stewards, fine Kapisan wine, then dinner!"

Musicians and singers came out to play lilting songs of family, while the stewards circulated to provide everyone wine, and by the end of the night, there were some shy smiles.

To announce the wedding, fast riders were dispatched to the farflung cities of Bukhara, Samarkhand, and Khojand five hundred miles to the north. Changing riders and horses at way stations every twenty or thirty miles, they could cover one to two hundred miles a day. The riders also brought the news to nearby Baghlang, Sirkh Kotal, Warnu, Bactra, and Purushapura within Bactria. Within a week, kings and nobility were gathering their entourages together for the long trek to Bagram.

While the preparations for the wedding went on, the king provided both education and entertainment to Aulus's party several nights a week in the palace theater. The theater was located on a hill in the park surrounding the palace, a semicircular array of stone seats around the play area and background *scaena*, with excellent acoustics that allowed the barest whisper to carry to the backmost seats up on the hill.

The entertainment included music, ranging from Greek melodies to a variety of hauntingly beautiful Kushan songs. It also included plays, mostly Greek ones familiar to the Romans, but also, to the Romans' delight, a few plays by Plautus, performed in presentable Latin. There were philosophy discussions, mostly in Greek, of both the classical well known schools of Plato, Epicureanism and Stoicism, and local philosophies heavily influenced by Buddhism. And there were religious debates, from a wide variety of contending faiths: Hinduism, Buddhism, Zoroastrianism, Judaism, and the small Christian community, all conducted in a very informational and non-proselytizing manner. Most of these were in Greek, so Shmuel and Yakov generally excused themselves from the events. Marcia relied on Antonius' quiet translations of the Greek, though she was trying to master the language.

During the day, the Roman party toured the temples, academia, libraries and markets that made up the hub of Bagram. The exigencies of the upcoming departure, however, limited their purchases mostly to clothing, traveling supplies, and food.

Ranisa went out after a week to invite the girls from Baghlang to her *proaulia* feast ahead of the wedding day. It was also an opportunity to see how they were faring, readjusting back into their newly-resumed lives. Most were doing well, although in some, she thought she felt some tension. But they were all still under their families' roofs, so that was a good sign. She saved Delaram for last. Her husband's face was dark and sullen the night of the reunion.

Delaram lived in a poor but well-kept neighborhood of craftsmen, in a mudbrick house with an adjoining shop. Ranisa stepped up to the door with some trepidation, but it was open to admit a breeze through a woven curtain that offered some privacy. She could see Delaram on the inside as she knocked gently on the frame. "Delaram? It's me, Ranisa. Are you busy?"

"Your ladyship!" said Delaram, dropping whatever she was doing and rushing to the door. "At your service!" she said, bowing low.

"Straighten up, Delaram. Our shared experiences make us closer than sisters. Please, call me Ranisa," she said, taking Delaram's hands in both of hers and smiling. "All is well?"

A two-year old toddled up to peer shyly out from between her mother's legs, sucking her thumb. A five-year old boy looked at Ranisa curiously, standing by the table where he had been helping his mother prepare vegetables. "These are my children, your lady... er, Ranisa. This is my daughter Rukhshan, my youngest, and over there is my little helper Kanag. We were making lunch for his father, who is out in the shop working." She turned toward him. "Kanag, would you go get your father, and tell him Princess Ranisa is paying us a visit?" The little boy scampered out a door at the side of the room.

Delaram continued: "I missed them terribly. I thought I would never see them again. Yes, things are going well... very well." She dabbed at a tear with the rag in her hand, choked up a bit, but quickly regained control. "Very well."

Kanag came back in, towing his father by the hand. "You have met Wano, my husband," she said, facing Ranisa.

The man rubbed his dirty hands over his sawdust-covered leather work apron, then self-consciously through his tousled black hair. "Your ladyship…" and he began to bow, as both girls tittered a bit.

"She has asked us to call her Ranisa, as we have a close personal bond," said Delaram.

He smiled a bit shyly at first, then letting it widen across his face. He took her hand firmly in his, "Well, Ranisa, we don't often have royalty come to call here in our home. Welcome, our house, such as it is, is yours."

"Wano, I came to invite you to my *proaulia* wedding feast in a few weeks. I wish I could give you a specific date, but my father and mother are still arranging and rearranging the schedule and guests. All of the women and their families are invited as our honored guests. You may not know this, but you had a hand in my getting married."

"How's that?" asked Wano.

"Boni was the man in charge of my rescue. He had been a commoner, though he was head of the palace guard. My father adopted him as nephew, which made him a prince, and … well, it is what we wanted for a long time, but could not have."

"Well, congratulations!" said Wano. "May I offer you some wine? It's by no means as good as your palace wine, but it's all we can afford."

"That would be wonderful."

Wano came back with a leather wineskin and some clay cups, filling each, and handing one to Ranisa and one to his wife. "We owe you and the King of Kings a great deal. To King Vima!"

"It looks like you are doing well."

"The children are glad to see her back. The soldier was right," he said. "It was hard for her to tell me things, and harder still for me to hear them," he said, pointing to a damaged cabinet on the wall. "That happened the first time she told me about things. Now, I just keep big sticks around, and when we talk of that I break them. We don't have furniture to spare!"

"We have bad days," said Delaram. "We have a Buddhist friend who takes us to temple sometimes. It helps to just sit silent, and contemplate, to try to understand that all things have a purpose and a meaning. Yes, we owe you all a great debt."

Ranisa stayed with the family for a while, marveling at how resiliently they had rebounded, from something she honestly thought was unrecoverable. Then she bid farewell and left, very happy with how well the impossible was turning out. Without her father's help, everything Boni had predicted would have happened, maybe even worse.

The *proaulia* was held a week before the wedding, before the massive entourage of visiting dignitaries descended on the palace, a family feast for the bride before the wedding, just friends and close relatives… in this case about a hundred of the king's extended family and the local governors and kings from the surrounding provinces that Ranisa knew only slightly.

The ceremony was held in the broad grassy park surrounding the palace, ringed by trees flaming gold, yellow, red and orange in the peak colors of October, matching the brilliant yellow fall sun. Multicolored tents had been set up on the lawn, a narrow one a hundred yards long, open on all four sides and bedecked with flags, sheltered the bridal party guests. King Vima, Cassandra, the king's son Kanishka, Ranisa and Boni, were seated on portable thrones in the center, and their family and friends, seated at two very long tables to either side of the thrones. The right hand table seated the king's immediate cousins and their families, the left hand one seated Cassandra's extended family, and at the far end were seated the girls with their families and Aulus's party. The commoners were ill at ease with royalty, self-conscious of their dress, speech and manners. However, Aulus's party was a good match for them. They made the families comfortable, and their accented Bactrian made the commoners feel more at ease. Soon they were talking comfortably across the table about various things of little import…mostly their travels and adventures, the commoners' jobs and experiences. Antonius and Marcia were seated opposite Delaram and Wano, and Antonius was very pleased to see the signs of affection flitting between the two. Gaius seemed distracted however, studying his cameo of Camilla.

In front of the guests' tent, opposite the thrones, was a small tent sheltering a black marble statue of Anahita in front of which stood a small table, a lit candle flickering in the wind and burning incense.

Behind the long guests' tents were three smaller tents. The center one sheltered singers, lyrists and flutists, whose pleasant tunes and lyrics spilled like a waterfall on the social gathering. On either side of the musicians' tent were two long tents, one of which sheltered the cooks preparing lamb, pheasant, goat, cow and pig, the pleasant smell of wood smoke and cooking meat permeating the air. Bowls filled with multicolored spices covered the tables, and servants were busily dicing huge piles of vegetables. The other tent sheltered a long table, piled with gifts for the bride and groom.

Servants in white Greek tunics circulated among the guests, never letting the silver goblets remain empty for too long.

Rustam, in an orange silk tunic, emerged from the kitchen tent which had become his command center for orchestrating the activities. He came up unobtrusively behind King Vima's throne and whispered something. The king nodded, Rustam politely backed away and the king stood and clapped his hands for attention. "Honored guests!" he said in Greek. "It is time for the *proteleia*, the time for my daughter Ranisa to offer up the toys of her girlhood to Anahita." The audience fell silent. "Ranisa, please rise."

Ranisa rose, standing straight, looking splendid in a long white silk dress that reached her ankles, contrasting with her raven black hair. She had a child's doll in her right hand.

"Ranisa, are you ready to leave your childhood behind, and take up the life of a woman?"

"I am, Most Excellent Father," she answered, staring straight ahead.

A servant appeared from behind her and stood at her left, silver scissors in hand. He took a length of the shining black hair, and cut off an inch or so. Ranisa held out her left hand, and he placed the cut length in her open palm.

"Are you ready to offer the treasures of your childhood to Anahita, as you embark on your life's journey as a woman?"

"I am, Most Excellent Father."

The king nodded, and she walked straight ahead to the statue of Anahita. She dropped the cut hair into the flame of the candle where it vanished in a puff of smoke. She then lay the doll on the table, backed away and bowed in prayer, her arms across her chest. She remained this way for a minute. Then she straightened up, clapped her hands... once, twice, three times, slowly, then backed away and returned to stand in front of the king.

King Vima raised his hands. "I give you my blessing, Ranisa Princess of Bagram!" Ranisa bowed before him, arms once again across her chest. "May Ahura Mazda, the Creator of All, and his Bountiful Spirits, guide and protect you through the trials of life."

Ranisa remained bowed, then straightened up. "And may they guide and protect you also, Most Excellent Father." She then returned to her seat. The audience applauded loudly.

Dinner was then served. Servants in white tunics hefted plates piled high with the meats that had been cooking so fragrantly in the kitchen tent. Whole pigs, surrounded by baked apples and pomegranates, grease oozing through the crackling skin, partridges surrounded by small quail, venison, beef, large fish. Four of each of these large trays were placed on the guests' tables, and another small squadron of servants, armed with serving knives, one arm covered with a white towel, went from guest to guest, inquiring of their preference, took their plate and returned with their meal. After the plates were filled with food, the servants fell in behind the guests..

The air was filled with the buzz of table conversation as the guests ate. After dinner, Rustam stood before the king to announce the presentation of gifts. One by one, servants brought forth a gift, stood before the bride and groom, while Rustam intoned the name of the giver, and their particular best wishes for the couple. The gifts were given in order of seniority, and most were lavishly expensive gifts of little utility, of the kind to remind others that that the giver possessed such great wealth that he could distribute it freely:

the king of Khojand, not yet arrived, had given a string of the famous "heavenly horses" of the Ferghana Valley, and the king of Bukhara had given a gold statue of Anahita. Others gave jewelry, intricately engraved plates, books of poetry and so forth. The Roman party was next to last, followed by the girls' families. Aulus had given them a gold ring, engraved with the Hanaean symbol for love, Gaius a string of pearls, and Ibrahim a silver necklace with an interwoven silver knot design. Demosthenes, Yakov and Shmuel had collaborated on a very well-made silk shawl, with an Hanaean dragon motif. Antonius gave Boni a *gladius* sword with leather scabbard, carefully made by a local sword maker to Roman specifications. The pommel had a gold-plated eagle and SPQR in the center, surrounded by a silver ring bearing his abbreviation, ANT ARIST PP LEG XII FUL. Marcia gave Ranisa a nine-inch pearl-handled dagger. Enclosed in the scabbard was a personal note: "Don't wear this until you know how to use it!"

The girls' families were last. Rustam intoned: "From the families of Armaghan, Delaram, Firoza, Mahdokht, and Parween, commoners of Bagram, a dress for Her Ladyship Princess Ranisa of Bagram, with their undying gratitude."

At the reunion some weeks earlier, the king had left small purses in each family's room containing silver *drachmae* worth more than a year's wages. They had used a part of this to purchase bolts of the most expensive filigreed silk they could find. The silk alone had cost one of the five bags of coins. They had then collaborated to stitch together a beautiful dress, a diaphanous gold-filigreed light blue floor length gown, bound at the waist with a purple silk girdle, and a silver-filigreed white *himation* mantle, made by their own hands.

The servant stood, dress in hand. Ranisa broke with tradition. She stood to touch the beautiful dress. She paused for a moment and then said, "I shall wear this for my wedding. All of the gifts given today are of great value, but the people who gave us this gift, gave us their hearts."

CHAPTER 78: THE WEDDING

The wedding itself was held a week after the *proaulia* on a crisp clear day in late October, when the King of Khojand arrived, the last of the most senior royalty. The wedding was held in the amphitheater in the park, which held a thousand people comfortably. Its excellent acoustics allowed the highest rows, reserved for the most junior guests, foreign delegates and invited commoners, to hear the proceedings clearly, with almost the same clarity as the kings and their entourages at the bottom. The Roman party was seated in the upper rows, along with the Hanaean and the Parthian delegations, and the girls' families.

In the lull before festivities, while the last of the bottom rows were being filled, Marcia conversed freely with the Hanaean delegate Dong Qin, while Aulus followed their court *han-yu* as best he could. He determined that Emperor He was in good health, but that the Son of Heaven's beloved military adviser Ban Chao, grand architect of the outreach to the *Da Qin*, had passed away. Dong Qin made no mention of their difficulty in the court, it having seemingly vanished as though it never happened.

As the conversation with the Hanaean party reached a lull, the Parthian ambassador injected himself. "And how are you, my Senator Aulus?" he said, in Parthian-accented Latin that always reminded Aulus of a snake's hiss. "I am Dariush Aspathines, servant of *Shahanshah* Pacorus, colleague of my associate Cyrus Mithridates in Luoyang, whom you met."

Feeling the opportunity to pass undetected through Parthia slip through his grasp, Aulus responded wryly, "We have met." Then, deciding to tackle the central issue head-on, he added, "The most excellent Pacorus considers us to be enemies of the state. To what do we owe this honor?"

"A misunderstanding, to be sure," said the Parthian with a sibilant hiss. "A consequence of the slow communications between Ctesiphon and Luoyang. Subsequent messages from Cyrus corrected the impression that you were under a sentence of death by the Son of Heaven, so we no longer feel obliged to detain you on his behalf."

"That is nice to know," answered Aulus flatly. "I presume then, that we can expect safe passage as diplomatic envoys?"

"To be sure, nothing less for Pacorus' dear colleague Trajan."

"And Pacorus' dear colleague Vima Kadphises as well. We carry messages from him to Emperor Trajan, which I am sure he would like to see reach their destination." This was, of course, a bluff, but one that could become reality, if he could get a moment with King Vima.

"Hmm." The long pause indicated that the bluff may have worked, at least for a moment. Dariush seemed caught off-guard, but recovered quickly. "But of course. Nothing less. Perhaps an armed escort for your safety? Parthia is safe, but like anywhere else, there are always bandits waiting to prey on the careless wayfarer."

"Yes, of course, and there are the bandits you know, and those you do not." Aulus expected any Parthian escort would escort them straight to Hades, of course through a most unfortunate accident. "I will consider your offer... but look, the services are about to begin!" The amphitheater fell silent, providing a welcome break in this conversation. The passage north around the Caspian Sea through skull-drinking barbarians was looking more and more attractive.

The wedding itself was a simple affair, conducted before the colonnaded *scaena* of the theater with King Vima, Queen Cassandra and Kanishka seated. Prince Boni, in his splendid stiff white dress uniform, stood proudly erect with Princess Ranisa in her beautiful dress, the white mantle floating like a cloud above the sky-blue gown. Representatives of the major religions of Kushana stood before four statues of their respective gods, two each flanking either side of the royal family. Musicians with pipes, lyres, harps, and drums were seated quietly in front of the *scaena*.

The ceremony was over in fifteen minutes or so, conducted in Greek. It consisted of a public pronouncement of the marriage between Prince Boni and Princess Ranisa, followed by invocations for the blessings of the Hindu Shiva, of the Buddha, of the Zoroastrian Ahura Mazda and his Bountiful Spirits, and finally an invocation by King Vima himself for the blessings of Anahita on the couple. All of this was followed by the couple ceremonially drinking a bowl of wine. That done, the musicians struck up lively tunes in celebration, tables were brought out for the feast, and beginning with the lowest rows, the guests came down to congratulate the royal family.

Aulus's party took advantage of the commotion to encircle the girls' families, who were standing around, shy and uncertain what to do.

"Come on down, people, stay with us and we will guide you through the steps, you're all doing fine," said Aulus, taking Wano by the arm to escort him down, with Delaram on the man's other arm and Marcia beside her. Gaius, Antonius, Ibrahim, and Demosthenes each took one of the other four families in tow, while Shmuel and Yakov tagged along behind. After a considerable wait, they all worked their way up the long line to congratulate the happy couple. Princess Ranisa smiled brightly at the families, taking each of their hands in hers warmly, personally thanking them for the beautiful dress.

Aulus then steered them to the king, whom they reached just after Dariush Aspathines made his obeisance. The Parthian lingered in earshot, so

Aulus played another bluff card. "Yes, and I need to meet with you at your opportunity, your Excellency, to discuss our mission on your behalf to Emperor Trajan," he said, clasping the king's hand in his.

King Vima looked puzzled, and Aulus, as unobtrusively as possible, cocked his head ever so slightly in the direction of the Parthian. "Mission? Oh, yes, it has been a busy day, yes, yes, we must discuss this. I will send Rustam to your quarters when I am free. Yes, that is very important to me." At that, Dariush turned and walked away.

The Roman party and the girls' families had been required to relocate their quarters to one of the many guest houses in the palace park after the *proaulia*, as the guest rooms closest to the king had been preempted by the arriving royalty: status was measured by proximity to the king. However, the guest house, if anything, was more luxurious than the palace accommodations: ten airy rooms with Egyptian glass windows, a common area with a fireplace, a kitchen and bath, and of course, plenty of servants. It easily accommodated the group, with each family assigned their own room. They indulged themselves in luxury for the entire week.

The morning after the wedding, Antonius was in his room, beginning the task of packing out the leather panniers for their departure, trying to convince their spare gear and acquired trinkets to go into the traveling bag that refused to hold everything. On his third attempt at repacking, there was a knock at the door, and Wano came in.

"Good morning, Antonius. Packing out, I see."

"Trying to. The damned stuff won't all fit."

"I ... uh.. want to wish you well on your trip, and again ... thank you for all you and everyone did for us. The King, his concern for us…"

"No problem, lad," he said with a smile, clapping him on the shoulder with a big friendly hand. "All is working out well?"

"Better than I ever expected. Can we talk, or are you busy?"

"This will wait. Talk!" said Antonius, casting aside the recalcitrant pannier and plopped down onto a chair.

"I wanted to talk to you especially… I almost didn't take your advice, the first night."

"Hmm, not surprising."

"We went back to the room, there were two beds. She took one and I pointedly took the other. I spent a sleepless night, so mad, figuring out all the different ways to tell her that she had to go, being mad at you… What almost happened to Marcia didn't happen, but did happen to her, and how were you to understand?"

"I gathered from your face that was how you felt. What changed it?"

"We got to back to our house. My mother had been taking care of the children, as she had been since ... Delaram's disappearance. When we walked in, Kanag, my little boy, his face lit up like the sun, and he screamed 'Mommy! You're home!' He rushed over, grabbed her legs and hugged them and said 'Don't ever go away again!' And little Rukhshan, the two year old, I think she recognized her. Delaram started crying, my mother hugged everyone, she started crying, the children cried, and so did I, and any thought of kicking her back out vanished. All because of a child."

"Sometimes children are wiser than us adults, Wano."

"Anyway, I wanted to thank you… for your words."

"Words are nothing, Wano. I don't know what I would have done, if it had been Marcia. You were the one who made it happen."

"Actually I think it was Delaram. That first day home, she went back to being their mother, like she had never left. Being my wife… took longer. She wanted there to be no doubt if she became pregnant, so she insisted we wait. But last night… well, she is my wife again as well as the mother of my children." Wano smiled shyly, revealing a hidden truth.

Before Antonius could comment on this private revelation, Ranisa entered the room with Marcia and Delaram. "Wano! I wanted to see all the families before I left, to thank each of you personally again for the beautiful dress. That was amazing."

"The women did it, and our seamstress neighbor. She couldn't miss the chance to work on such beautiful fabric, a gift for royalty. Delaram modeled, since she is about your size. Us men tried to stay out of the way, and not spill anything on the fabric. But I thought you would be with Prince Boni this morning?" answered Wano.

"He is packing. We are going to our favorite lake, for a week of hunting and fishing. Where our love began, and doing what we love. I hate to leave so soon but I need to catch the others before they leave."

"I think they are all still here, enjoying their last bit of royal luxury for a while," said Antonius. Ranisa left with Delaram and Wano.

Antonius turned to Marcia, saying in a mock accusatorial tone, "How in the hell am I goin' ter git all yer stuff in this pannier, *domina*? Did yer have ter buy everythin' in the whole damned marketplace?"

"Shush, *carus meus*, I'll take care of it." She took the pannier and began removing its contents, spreading them on the bed. "You need to put the big things in first."

"I packed it four times, somethin' always won't fit. Have yer seen Gaius and Aulus?"

"They're right behind us. Met with the king on urgent business over breakfast, something about Parthia. By the way, he and Queen Cassandra regret they won't be able to see us all off. His schedule is packed, seeing the royal departures off. Protocol, he said."

At that moment, Aulus came in along with Gaius.

"This is our pass, along with other things, unless King Pacorus is more treacherous than even I believe," said Aulus, brandishing a leather scroll container. "The Parthian envoy was present when King Vima gave us a message to convey to Trajan, offering his services to prevent another tragic war between Rome and Parthia over Armenia. He gave Aspathines a blunt message for Pacorus that should we fail to make it through Parthia, not only would he not intercede, but if war should come, he may be unable to protect Parthia's eastern flank. Unless Pacorus is ten kinds of fool, we'll go through Parthia without any trouble."

"I'll believe it when we are out of Parthia and back in Roman territory. Marcia, how are you doing?"

"Done, *carus meus,*" she said, deftly closing the last leather strap on the pannier. "But you get to heft this thing."

The next day, on a crisp November morning, the Roman party departed for Bactra with the military convoy.

Far away in the Altai foothills, Hina had developed a new-found respect for women throughout her pregnancy. The morning sickness of her early months had been limited to right before breakfast, so it had not interfered with her duties as *zuun*, and disappeared as her pregnancy began to show. However, about midway through, the old crone who had been guiding her through the experience put her ear to Hina's distended belly, listening carefully. Not satisfied, she shook her head and listened a second and a third time.

She had heard two distinct heartbeats. Hina was carrying twins, a very bad omen: few twins survived, and often killed the mother as well. There were, the old woman said, potions that would cause this pregnancy to pass away, and they could try for a more propitious one in a few months.

Hina would have none of this. The children were an answer to her prayer to the Sky God, as much as they were of Galosga and her. To reject them was to reject His answer. She would carry them to term, and if it was Tengri's will that she would die in the birthing yurt rather than on the battlefield, no matter. The old crone shook her head, warning her that she had, in her entire life, seen only one set of twins born alive, and the mother survive as well. Hina told her to prepare to see it happen again.

Hina's labor was a little early, as is usual for mothers bearing twins. When her water broke at sundown early in November, flooding the earth floor of the yurt, she sent Galosga out to fetch the birthing women and the old crone. While she waited, she lifted up her smock and tied it, leaving herself bare below the waist, and rigged the birthing pole across the top of the yurt to support herself during labor. She felt the exhilaration that comes before battle, and patted her rotund tummy, "Not too long now, little people, not too long at all." She smiled and wished her sister Marcia could be with her... she hoped all was well with her and Antonius, wherever they might be on their long journey home.

The women arrived and began to brew the traditional soup, a concoction of various herbs, meats, and mare's milk that took four hours to prepare. Not only was this soup supposed to be restorative to the delivering mother's strength, it also served to mark the progress of delivery... if the child had not come by the time it was ready, more ingredients were put in to extend the process another four hours.

Just as the soup was set on the fire, the first contraction came, a feeling much like a very intense and long-lasting gas pain. Hina clung to the overhead pole, but this contraction did not seem as bad as she expected, nor the second nor the third. The fourth one, however, took her breath away, and behind her eyes, screwed shut in concentration, dazzling lights flashed in a kaleidoscope of colors. As that wave passed, she panted a bit. The women applauded her efforts.

However, the soup reached its four hour time, was prepared, prepared again, and prepared yet again by the time the sky was beginning to turn gray with dawn. The crone had been periodically checking her insides with her long bony finger, feeling for something that had not yet happened. Hina could tell the mood among the women was becoming somber. Each contraction seemed to be just another futile effort to expel that which could not be expelled, and she began to contemplate the idea that the old woman might have been right, that this might be her last day alive.

Enough! Thoughts like that had no place in battle and no place in her birthing yurt. As the next contraction took her to heights of agony, she groaned loudly, in determination and anger at the children's intransigent refusal to emerge from her straining belly.

Outside, Galosga had been sitting around the fire near the yurt, chatting with the men in his patois of *han-yu* and newly-acquired Xiongnu, drinking *kumis*. His presence in the yurt was bad luck, so he could not be there with her, just as he had not been with his first wife during her labors. But he had become concerned over the past several hours. No stranger to childbirth, his other three children had been born in just a few hours, and as he heard Hina's latest agonizing groan, he began to wonder, too, if this was to be her last day. He also knew that twins were extremely difficult. What would life be like, without his beautiful, strong, brave *huldaji*? He could not imagine life without her, and began to pray to Selu, the Corn Goddess. She was far away, but could she not help? Were not the spirits all-powerful?

Inside the yurt, as the last contraction trailed off into uselessness, the crone fingered Hina's inner parts, then inserted what seemed to be her whole hand, feeling around for... what? Hina had no idea, but she had lost all sense of modesty hours ago. Suddenly the old woman smiled, inserted her hand still deeper, and then looked up and said, "Hina, your womb is open, and I feel the head! You are ready and the baby is ready, so on the next contraction, push with all your strength!"

Hina nodded, wondering what the hell the old woman thought she had been doing. The contraction came and the crone sat on the ground between her legs, while the other four women supported Hina, offered her sips of water, patted sweat from her brow, and offered her signs of encouragement. As the contraction peaked, she felt something shift, then a burning between her legs. She gasped for breath and bore down against the contraction. All four women dropped to the ground, doing something between her thighs, and she heard a high thin cry. The enormous pressure lessened considerably.

"The head is out, keep pushing!" She pushed and she felt the rest of the baby, crying lustily, slither out into the women's hands. "It's a girl, Hina, it's a beautiful girl!" said the old woman with wonder. "Now on the next contraction, push again for the next one. This will be easier, because your daughter has opened you up."

She pushed and the second one slithered out quickly, howling lustily. "It's a boy, Hina. You have a boy and a girl, your gifts from Tengri, like you said." Two of the women helped her down from the pole to a sitting position, lifted up her smock to expose her breasts, while the other two cleaned and wrapped her newborns. They put an infant against each nipple, where they proceeded to nurse noisily.

Hina was vaguely aware that they were cleaning up the bloody mess around her bottom, and she was aware that something else slid out, almost effortlessly. The afterbirth, they told her. The old woman inspected it and declared it whole. She squeezed blood from the two umbilical cords into a bowl of *kumis*, swirled it around and put it to Hina's sleepy lips to drink its coppery tang. "To put back what has been taken out of you," the crone said with a smile, supporting her head while she nursed her babies.

Someone had put a blanket over her, and Galosga came in, all smiles. "I knew you would do fine," he said in Xiongnu, then adding "*huldaji.*"

Hina felt the exhilaration and exhaustion that comes after a hard fought battle. She smiled at Galosga and her babies. "Meet your new son and daughter, Galosga. Antonius and Marcia."

CHAPTER 79: A RELIGIOUS EXPERIENCE

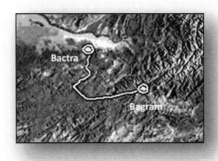

It took a little over a week to cover the two hundred and fifty miles to Bactra, traveling at a good pace and staying at well-placed military forts not more than two days apart. While not offering the palatial luxury they had enjoyed in Bagram, the facilities were clean and comfortable, and the food good. November was bringing very cold nights that made the Romans' yurt distinctly more comfortable for the intermediate stops between forts than the two and four person tents the soldiers shared. Evenings found them a popular destination for the off-duty soldiers to sit inside by the warm fire and share stories.

Bactra was an unusual layout. Whereas most of the Greek cities of Bactria were laid out on carefully aligned north-south and east-west grids, Bactra was laid out as an octagon, with eight broad avenues radiating from the center and connecting to gates at each point of the outermost ring, thence to highways that ran straight as an arrow shot in each cardinal direction. Inside, the interior streets formed concentric octagons.

The convoy entered Bactra by the southeastern gate, and proceeded through a park at the center of the town filled with evergreen pines. They passed through the north gate, ending up at a fort overlooking the city from an elevated mound several hundred feet high. From the fort's walls, looking down into the city, it looked like an archer's target, the green park they had crossed the bull's eye.

The group got accommodations there, individual rooms adjacent to the commander's quarters, similar to a *praetorium* in a Roman camp. The quartermaster assigned them each a single room on the second floor, well-lit by windows protected by translucent oiled leather admitting light, but keeping the heat in and the wind out. Large hanging lamps hung from the center of each ceiling, and a small fireplace along the back wall provided heat. The rooms were above the officers' mess on the first floor and the officers' bath, a large hot pool inside with an outdoor *frigidarium* cold pool for those so inclined.

With everyone settled in, refreshed and with some of the baggage unpacked, the group settled in for a light lunch. Demosthenes, in between bites, announced his eagerness to go out in town to locate the family he had not seen for a decade.

Ibrahim offered to accompany him. "I'll go with you, Dim. I'll be happy to meet your family. Have you heard from them? Do you know where they live?" Alone in a strange town is a bad idea anywhere, he knew, but alone in one's hometown after a long absence can put one in particular danger, tripping down the streets of childhood memories, instead of paying attention to one's surroundings. After all, what can happen in one's hometown?

"Thanks, Ibrahim, and no, I know where they lived, but I don't even know if they are still alive. I left for Tibet ten years ago, and we haven't been able to communicate."

"Can you find your old neighborhood?"

"Blindfolded! Let's go. It's on the eastern side, close to the wall."

Perhaps blindfolded, he could have found it more quickly. After an hour and a half fruitlessly searching for his old neighborhood, Demosthenes announced in frustration, "It has to be one of these streets!"

The problem was that the houses were nearly identical, working class structures of mud brick, wood frame windows shuttered against the November chill. And besides the big octagonal roads that formed the city's bull's eye, there were innumerable unpaved roads concentric with them, and hundreds of little alleys, each lined with its own cluster of look-alike houses. Racking his brain for landmarks, Demosthenes remembered there was a market, with a butcher shop next to a blacksmith and cutlery shop. If he could find that cutlery shop, the owner's name was Warazan, then he could find his old home. After a few minutes of questioning passersby, he located it, and there was the blacksmithery with a display of fine knives hung under an awning. Old Warazan was sitting around the smithy's fire, huddled in a dark winter cloak with a cloth around his head, continuing on to wrap around his neck. His thin face sported a bristling grey beard.

"Warazan? Remember me? Demosthenes Kaneoios. I used to live here, many years ago, and come to your shop all the time."

Warazan looked at him with unlinking rheumy blue eyes, then he smiled and exposed his few remaining teeth, dark stained. "Demosthenes! Yes, I remember you! You used to want to be a blacksmith like me when you were a lad, but your family wanted you to get an education. You went off to become a monk?"

"Yes, and I did, I went to Kashmir and Tibet, then to China."

"But you're not a monk now?"

"It is a hard life. Many things I could sacrifice for perfection, but not my friends. It's a long story …but right now, my family? Do they still live… let's see, down that street and around the corner? I am ashamed to say, I almost couldn't find my own home!"

"They do, young Demosthenes, but… your mother passed away two years ago."

"Oh." Odd the thought did not stun him. "And my father?"

"He is well. You need to go to him."

"I do. Thank you, and I will be back."

Demosthenes retraced the familiar steps back to his boyhood home, Ibrahim tagging along behind, his black robe rustling. He stepped onto the stoop and knocked at the door.

His father, a wizened thin old man with a grey bristling chin, one eye gone milky white and unseeing, opened the door. He squeezed the bad eye shut, trying to focus the working eye. "Demosthenes!" His mouth flew open in joy and surprise, revealing just a few stumps of teeth. "Demosthenes, you've come home! Come in!" He opened the door wide. "And your friend?"

"His name is Ibrahim, father," said Demosthenes, stepping into the dim room. If his father's eyes were failing, he thought, there might not be much need for candles. "We have had quite a trip! And Ibrahim, my father Kaneias."

"Sit, and tell me of your adventures!" His father beckoned them to some cushions in the room, and the two seated themselves. He poured some hot tea into cups for them, then he, too, sat down. "You're no longer a monk?"

"No, I am not. I hope you are not disappointed. There were things I could not accept."

"Well, I am no longer Buddhist. We … I am sorry, did I say that your mother passed away two years ago?" asked Kaneias.

"No, but Warazan told me. I saw him on the way… what happened?"

"A fever took her, but it was swift. I miss her, but old age was very painful for her. She is, I hope, in heaven now with Lord Jesus."

"And who is he?" asked Demosthenes.

"Your mother and I became Christians, followers of Jesus the Nazarene, a few years ago. So we are no longer Buddhists, as you are no longer a monk. What caused you to change your mind? You were very enthusiastic ten years ago."

"I was. But I learned that inaction is a form of action as well, with a *karma* of its own. My inaction would have let my friends die, which I could not accept. And I found myself further and further from the Way, until I realized that I could not follow it anymore. Perhaps in a later life, when I am more ready."

"Or perhaps that is not the Way for you. We met a group of Christians here, and found a better Way to salvation and perfection. Your mother, bless her, was baptized right before she fell ill, and I with her."

"I am traveling with some Romans, and I have heard them talk of Christians, but I have no idea who or what they... you... are."

"We will be meeting tonight to talk about the blessed Paul, and his trip to Rome, his shipwreck..."

Ibrahim's intake of breath was audible, interrupting Kaneias in mid-sentence. "Paul? Of Tarsus? Perhaps forty years ago?" asked Ibrahim.

"That would be right. You have heard of him?"

"I sailed with him briefly right before his shipwreck. If is the same person. We sailed from Caesarea to Myra, and he was wrecked on Malta. I am sorry, those names mean nothing to you."

"But they do! It is all written down, though as you say, to us they are faraway names. Did you meet him?"

"Yes, he sought me out, we talked, though I was but an ignorant deckhand. He wanted me to come with him, but it was too much to ask. He changed ships in Myra and was shipwrecked later in a storm. I never learned what became of him, if he survived."

Kaneias crossed himself. "I see the hand of God moving through you, Ibrahim. He has brought you along this strange route for the past forty years for a purpose. What is your faith?"

"I put my faith in skill and cunning, Kaneias, rather than any belief. I hope there is no afterlife, because if there is, I merit nothing more than punishment, which I hope at least won't be eternal as some believe," Ibrahim chuckled, stroking his beard.

"You have done evil, as all of us have, but you have also done good." He paused to sip his tea. "Listen, some friends will come by tonight to discuss some of our scriptures, and the topic tonight – here again, the hand of God at work! They will be bringing the scrolls to read of Paul's journey to Rome. Will you stay? Everyone will want to hear your story, and you can find out what finally happened to your friend Paul." Kaneias' one good eye scrutinized him intently, hoping to pry out an affirmative answer.

"I would be honored. Demosthenes, I did not mean to turn the conversation away from you toward me," Ibrahim smiled, sipping his tea and gesturing to Demosthenes to take over the conversation.

Ibrahim and Demosthenes returned to the fort to let their friends know they would not be returning in the evening but would remain overnight at Demosthenes' family home, then hustled back. Ibrahim stopped by a little sidewalk seller of meat pastries to buy a dozen or so hot sandwiches of thin *nan* around a spicy center of lamb, and a good-sized jug of wine. He expected the guests tonight might wish something to eat, and Kaneias did not look up to preparing much in the way of a meal. When they arrived, they found the small house crowded.

Warazan was among the people present. Demosthenes wondered just how popular this Christian cult had become in Bactra.

Kaneias accepted the meat pastries and wine and distributed it among his guests. He then introduced Ibrahim. "We are honored tonight to have among us someone who knew the Blessed Paul and conversed with him, before an angry wind blew him onto Malta." The crowd of about fifteen huddled about him, waiting to hear him speak.

Ibrahim began his story. "I was a deckhand on the *Astarte*, clad in rags and barely able to speak Aramaic, when a man came aboard in Caesarea, under escort by a Roman officer and some soldiers, with two friends. I took little note of him. He was of some high position, and we were forbidden to socialize with passengers."

Ibrahim's relating of the story brought those few days him back to him vividly, as though yesterday.

I leaned against the rail, letting the warm ocean breeze dry the sweat from my fatigued body. It was late afternoon, and I had been on duty since well before midnight, getting the ship ready to sail on the morning tide, then rigging her for open sea. The Astarte was an ill-cared-for tramp freighter, whose owners put as little money into the ship and crew as possible. And that included not hiring enough hands, and working those they had impossibly hard. The boatswains drove the crew to exhaustion, allowing the ones no longer capable of working the opportunity to sleep for a few hours, then rousting them out again for more work. The captain was an ill-tempered alcoholic Greek, a pig by nature, and he had disappeared below to sleep off the flagon of wine he had consumed in the afternoon. I wanted desperately to sleep, but the opportunity to do nothing for a just a few minutes was rare. I took the moment to watch a school of green and gold flying fish burst out of the crest of a blue Mediterranean wave, their wing-fins buzzing like locusts as they hummed through the air a foot or so off the water, straight as arrows in flight, to reenter the water after half a ship length with barely a ripple.

I became aware of a man next to me. It was the passenger, well-off by his carriage and dress, wearing a well-cut, multi-colored robe and a turban, their colors still bright and the weave good. Unchained for now, and behind him the centurion guarding him lay down on a pile of rope with a sigh, hands behind his head, preparing to doze in the sunlight. Whatever the man had done, the centurion did not seem overly concerned with guarding him.

"Beautiful day," the man said in Greek, a language which I had not yet mastered.

"Sorry... no speak... well," I replied.

"Oh, I'm sorry..." said the man, switching to Aramaic. "Is this better?"

"I thank thee. I know only a few words of Greek."

"Thou lookest tired. My name is Paul. Paul of Tarsus. Thy name?"

"Ibrahim. Of Arabia. And what didst thou do to earn thy escort?"

"It's a long story that began before thou wert born. We are all prisoners of something or someone. I am a prisoner of the good Julius there," Paul said, cocking his head toward the soldier, who had begun to snore loudly. "And thou... what imprisoneth thee?"

I felt uneasy talking to him. Fraternizing with the passengers was strictly forbidden, since real or fictitious claims of stolen money or valuables invariably resulted. I cast a glance furtively to the quarterdeck, but the cybernetes *on duty at the tiller did not appear to pay any attention to us.*

"This ship! This cursed ship! The owners don't know how to run a ship. With decent repairs and a good crew, she could turn twice the trips she does. But they pay little or nothing for either. This was supposed to be our last stop at Myra, and us to be paid off tomorrow and done for the season. But the captain decided to pick up just one more load. Thou feelest how warm it is for October? Mindest thou, there will be a gale from hell itself in a few days when the weather changes! And he knoweth that. This barge cannot take much pounding."

"So why not just get off in Myra? Thou art not a slave, art thou?"

"No, of course not. But they pay not till the season's over. I would winter over without enough coins to fill up my hand. And next season, the word would be out on me, no berths for ship-jumpers. No, thou art right, I'm a prisoner of the ship, the same as you of that Roman." I looked off into the endless blue of the Mediterranean, touched with whitecaps.

"But our worst taskmaster is ourselves. The things we want, the things we think we must have. What are those things, Ibrahim of Arabia?" the Jew continued, eyeing him closely.

"What I'd really like is a ship like this, of my own. Not that I'll ever get one, being just a simple deckhand. So really, what earned thee thy escort?"

"I am a follower of the Way of Jesus, and I fell into a religious dispute with my fellow Jews. A dispute that could have ended in my death. Somewhat unfairly, I was the one charged with a crime. Now I'm on my way to Rome to appeal my case before the Emperor Nero himself, and bring the Way to him."

"The Way? What is that?" asked Ibrahim.

And Paul explained it to me. The story of a Jewish holy man named Jeshua, and one God and one Way for all the people of the world. About sin and forgiveness. Much of it I could not comprehend, since the Way was intertwined with the holy book of the Jews. I knew some of the stories from that book, similar to stories of my people. But I could neither read nor write then. Religion was little more than prayers to gods and goddesses that I scarcely understood, offered mostly in times of danger like magic spells. Paul's words droned on in my ears as I began to nod sleepily, even while standing. Paul noted this and ended the discussion, sending me off to a few hours of blessed sleep.

We managed to talk for a few minutes every day for a week until we reached Myra. That last day, we whiled away an hour or so, before I had to catch a brief nap before a night to be spent making preparations for entering port. At the end of the discussion, Paul added, "Why not comest with me, young Ibrahim? Forget the ship. Forget wintering over in Myra. Breakest thou thy chains."

I had been drowsing off, just half-listening. So casually had Paul said this, that I awoke from my reverie. "Huh? I am sorry. Come... with thee? To Rome?"

"Thinkest thou on it. We will disembark tomorrow. Give me thy answer then. Get some sleep, post your watch." Just then, the centurion came on deck to find Paul. He said something in Latin to him, and Paul laughed. "My guardian Julius is hungry, so it must be dinner time. Think on it." He turned and left, going forward down to the galley.

I went below and found a flea-infested pile of dirty rags on which to sleep. But sleep didn't come. Go to Rome? I could disembark in Ostia, as a passenger, not as a ship jumper. Next season, I could find a berth on a fine Roman freighter, where I could earn five to ten times what I made on these eastern tramps. Fine ships, fine crews! And Paul seemed well-to-do, even as a prisoner. But what did the strange Jew really intend for me?

Ibrahim helped wrestle the Astarte safely into her moorings at daybreak, a hundred yards from a huge Alexandrian grain freighter whose tall masts cast long shadows over the dockyard in the rising sun. It was time to make my decision. Follow him? Where? Why? Why did this man take such an interest in me? What on earth was this man talking about? Yeshua not only raising others from the dead, but raising himself? Sin, forgiveness and salvation? Crazy talk!

Paul stood at the quarterdeck with his two friends and the soldiers, once again in chains. I thought of just avoiding him, but no, he had been nice enough company. I walked up to him, and outrageously took his manacled hand in mine, calling him by name for the first time. "Paul, I thank thee for our talks. I did not understand most of what thou said, but I will think on it. As for now, I will remain with my ship. Good luck to thee on thy trip to Rome."

"I thought thou might not yet be ready for the Way, Ibrahim. But thou wilt be, someday. Until then, may God grant thee thy greatest wish. And thou wilt do very well in that endeavor. Good luck to thee, young man, and God be with thee." With that, the centurion took Paul by the arm and escorted him down the gangplank.

With that, Ibrahim returned to the present. "Paul took passage on the big grain freighter next to us. And within a few days, a fierce storm blew up, casting it a wreck onto Malta, and blowing me into command of my first ship, a twenty year old pirate, knowing nothing about navigation or seamanship, or even piracy! But I found people who could teach me and I learned. And I learned Greek, well enough to read the philosophers and the Septuagint Bible in Alexandria. But I also killed scores of people, financially ruined hundreds more, and committed every sin in that book, and some for which there are no names. I did not become worthy of the trust Paul had in me, I spurned it."

There was a great silence in the room. Then Kaneias looked at Ibrahim with his one good eye. "We are honored to have you among us, you who were blessed by Paul," he said. "You are no more sinful than I, or any in this room, or even the Blessed Paul. But more on that later. I would like to share the story of the rest of Paul's journey."

And he related from memory the account of Paul's sea voyage, boarding the ship Ibrahim had identified as the *Astarte* at Caesarea with companions Aristarchus and Luke, with stops at Sidon and a change of ships at Myra, in October around the Day of Atonement. From there, the ship attempted Cnidus, but winds being unfavorable, went southwest to Fair Haven in Crete. There they made the fateful decision to make for the better harbor at Phoenix, but a gale blew up and they struggled fourteen days against it to Malta where they intentionally ran the ship aground. Ibrahim listened intently, hearing his own account repeated, followed by a very good description of the next leg. Warazan finished his account, then said, "I am not a sailor, nor am I familiar with these places. Ibrahim, can you shed some light on this story?"

"That type of storm is called a *Euraquilo*, a northeaster, the same as the one that struck my ship. And yes, I have stopped at all the places mentioned, many times. Fair Haven is a bad place to winter over for a big ship, anchored out and exposed to the waves, so I understand why they tried to make the shelter at Phoenix. What became of Paul afterwards?"

Kaneias answered, "He went to Rome and was imprisoned, awaiting his trial that never came. A few years after he got there, there was a huge fire that destroyed a large part of the city. Nero blamed the Christians for setting it, and killed thousands of them, many horribly. Paul, a citizen, was beheaded. His companion and fellow apostle Peter, who also had come there, was crucified."

They talked until the dawn was breaking, about sin and the forgiveness of sins, about eternal life, and love as the supreme sacrifice. Ibrahim had long ago rejected any notion of an afterlife, other than perhaps a vague fading out of one's existence after death. Likewise, he rejected the idea of a god, or gods, as other than some vague powerful entity that might cause everything to begin, but otherwise be no more concerned about his life than the sun or the moon. To conceive of a god that cared, implied a god of justice, and a god of justice would then mete out punishment as well as reward, and Ibrahim knew full well what he merited. But he felt strangely drawn to these people, and he remembered what Paul had told him decades ago, "You are not yet ready for the Way. But you will be." And the various events in his life had steered him to this place and time, to this humble mud house in Bactra and a belated reunion with his old friend Paul, long dead, with the implacability of an ocean wind. But could his sins really be forgiven? It was on this that his 'faith', as they called it, fell short.

Demosthenes did not seem to struggle with the new faith at all. The idea that he was required to interact with the people around him in love and sacrifice, rather than attain some sort of total detachment of the world, had come naturally to him. He was to reject the things of the world, the fame, the praise, the money, the power... but not the people. He had been imbued with Greek philosophy in his education, as well as Buddhism, and understood Plato's analogy of the reality of the world of the senses as shadows cast on a cave wall; in fact, he used that as the foundation of many of his Buddhist meditations. And his father had told him that he could retain his Buddhist ethics and meditations with his new beliefs.

At dawn, Warazan, who seemed to be the leader of the group, announced that this was their day of worship, and of rest thereafter. The two newcomers were welcome to observe but not participate. Bread and wine were put on the table, and the group sat around it with Warazan at the center. They sang some unfamiliar hymns to Jesus as to a god. Warazan spoke a few words on the gift of their visitors, praying that God would provide them the answers they sought. He then shared a ceremony of bread and wine.

CHAPTER 80: TREACHERY AND DEATH

The group left Bactra after about a week, traveling with a caravan for Aria and the Parthian border at the Hari-Ruud River. Demosthenes remained behind and was missed, but having been reunited with his father and his extended family, they knew he would be in good hands.

The five hundred mile trip was among the worst they had experienced in two years of traveling, loess sand plains and open desert, bitter cold in January with biting winds that easily penetrated even the Roman party's winter fleeces and traveling yurt, and occasional blinding snow. Marcia wished she could grow a beard like the men to protect her face. She made do with a woolen scarf wrapped entirely around her face and ears, leaving only her eyes exposed. At the worst of times, her breath froze on the cloth in a white frost.

The caravan consisted of mounted horsemen or wagons towed by either horses or camels, trying to maintain a pace of twenty or so miles a day, weather permitting. The caravan was laden mostly with foodstuffs for exchange among the villages and cities enroute.

The road was interspersed with various small towns: Faryab and Maynama were the largest, providing the luxury of overnight indoor accommodations, but many of the smaller villages only supported the caravan drivers, and sometimes not all of them. Not even the Roman yurt could keep out the frigid wind when they were forced to camp overnight in the icy weather.

Antonius had resumed training the group with the wooden swords. They had not drilled in almost a year, though they had provided security for caravans for several months. But two months of luxurious living in Bagram, and another month in accommodations almost as good at the fort in Bactra, had left their muscles soft and their reflexes slow. Antonius proceeded to whip them into shape quickly, in the event they had to fight off bandits enroute. However, unlike with past caravans, they were not part of caravan security. The short winter days allowed for an hour of drill before dinner, conducted inside their yurt due to weather.

Marcia, alone of the group, had been quietly doing some practice on a new move of her own. A charging attack with a sword had almost always left her vulnerable. She always stepped backwards, often losing her balance and with it the bout. She thought she had a counter to that move now, and she looked forward to using it in this night's practice. She drew Gaius as her sparring partner, and they squared off inside the yurt, lit by the center fire. Lamps were not yet lit, in case one should be upended and set their shelter and all their belongings ablaze.

There was the usual initial checking, a clacking of swords, testing thrusts easily parried, just warming up. She watched Gaius' eyes. He didn't give away much, because as an experienced fighter, he understood eye control. But she had learned through sparring with him that he always took in an audible gasp of air before doing something dramatic. That warned her that something was coming, though not where, so she was ready when she saw the lunge materialize, and she executed her counter while his sword was still enroute toward her midsection. She pivoted lightly on her left foot, spinning clockwise, drawing both arms and her sword tight in against her body to make herself spin faster. She had made a quarter turn when the point of Gaius' sword passed through the air where her gut had been at the beginning of the stroke, leaving him extended, surprised and off-balance. His momentum carried him forward, and he was behind her when she flexed her butt into his side, just enough to further unbalance him. As she completed her turn, she extended both arms and her sword to slow her spin, saw Gaius' exposed back where she expected it, and administered a sharp delivery across his spine, knocking him to his knees. Had it been live steel, she likely would have sliced him in two.

She sheathed her sword and graciously extended her hand to help him up, smiling.

"Damn, woman! Where the hell did you go? You vanished like smoke!" he said, struggling to his feet. "That hurt!" he rubbed the small of his back, while everyone else in the yurt laughed.

"I've been working on that move for months. The lunge was the one move that I couldn't counter if I couldn't parry it. Anyone else?"

Shmuel stepped up beside the fire, and they set off with the usual preliminaries. Shmuel's eye control was not as good as Gaius', she saw his lunge coming but chose not to parry, spun and cut him down quickly.

Antonius nodded his approval. "Good move, *domina*, damned good move. I think it would work even on me."

"You're too easy, *carus meus*. You always pull your strokes with me!" she laughed, wiping her forehead with a rag. Even in a chill December, a yurt with a fire and seven people exercising in it warmed up fast.

They sparred for a few more rounds, then broke for dinner. "We all got some catching up to do. Let's hope we don't meet some real bandits before we are back in shape!" said Antonius.

Antonius broke out some homebrew *kumis* that was a close approximation of the real thing, a wheel of *nan*, a bowl of walnuts from Bactra, and some dried meat, smoked and salted in the style Galosga had taught them. "Never thought I would enjoy being back in the yurt, but I actually like this better than sitting around the castle. Never been one for aristocratic society," he said in Bactrian.

Marcia elbowed him in the ribs playfully, munching a handful of *nan*. "You did quite well, *carus*, you didn't embarrass me much… except maybe with that awful joke about the camel!"

"We were all drunk, the king included!" he responded defensively, while everyone laughed. "Anyway, he made it easy to be around him. If I have to be around the upper classes, I'd as soon be around King Vima as anyone else. Very normal sort of man. And Cassandra and Ranisa. Real people, no airs. Just like you, Senator!" he said, grinning at Aulus; It was the first time in a very long time that he had addressed Aulus by his title.

Aulus was struggling with the tough smoked meat, chewing furiously, unable to answer for a minute. Finally he gulped down his mouthful with a bowl of *kumis* and wiped his hands on his grimy riding shirt. "Well, yurts don't lend themselves to much in the way of social distinctions! But good camaraderie. Speaking of camaraderie, that was quite a ceremony with Dim's family, and you, too, Ibrahim. He must have had every cousin, uncle and aunt in Bactra come to that. What was the occasion?"

"We were baptized into our new faith. It seems to be quite the solution for both of us, forgiveness of my sins for me, a chance at perfection for him," said Ibrahim.

Shmuel interjected, "It reminded me of a *mikvah* bath, a Jewish cleansing ceremony. I went through that at a synagogue a few months ago in Warnu. I'm not sure sin has the same meanings between the two faiths, although Ibrahim's new faith sprang from mine. But I enjoy feeling Jewish again."

"What was the occasion for Dim? That was rather a sudden change from Buddhism to … what? Being Christian?" asked Marcia.

"It was," answered Ibrahim, sitting cross-legged across from her. "As you know, he was really tormented about having failed as a monk. His family had been quite proud that he had chosen the Buddhist way when he left, and he was afraid they would feel he had shamed them when he returned as a lay person. Only they had all become Christians in his absence, so it was a natural thing for him to follow them. And he got to keep many of his Buddhist beliefs and practices. which aren't too dissimilar at all from Christianity. Detachment from material things, he never had a problem with that. It was more of a struggle for me."

"Why was that?" asked Gaius. He got up to fetch a flask of wine, and returned to sit before the fire.

"Mostly philosophical. If God is justice, then how can He forgive sins without holding the sinner accountable? That seemed contradictory to me. And certainly I knew what accountability for my sins meant. I preferred to deny an afterlife, rather than face it!"

"So what changed your mind?" asked Antonius.

"They finally convinced me that God is infinite mercy as well as infinite justice, so He can dispense however much of either as He chooses. So I decided to take a chance on the new faith. And I thank Dim for introducing me to both this faith, and to some of his Buddhist beliefs. In many ways, they are very similar. Like Buddhism, not much in the way of rituals, no long list of things to do or not do so the gods don't get upset and smite you. Just to not worship other objects as gods, which I don't do anyway. It's a very, well, philosophical God, not like the ordinary gods that just seem to be the personification of jealousy and pettiness."

Aulus cleared his throat. "Well, I hate to change the subject, but before we retire to our bedrolls we need to discuss what we do when we reach Aria and Parthian territory. Ibrahim, while you may have your sins forgiven, you still have great insights into evading authorities that you gained by a lifetime of sinning. What are your thoughts about how best to cross Parthia?"

"I suggest we do it openly," answered Ibrahim, sipping his wine. "The Parthians know who we are, the Parthian ambassador almost certainly sent word back on us, and there is no way to enter Parthia except through Aria. They will have a good description of us. King Vima made it very clear to their ambassador that our reaching Rome is critical to avoiding war, that we are carrying messages from him to Trajan, and that if we don't deliver them, that could seriously jeopardize relations between Ctesiphon and Bagram. Pacorus has to balance his petty jealousy about our relations with the Han, against a real threat of war with Rome, with his backside exposed or even threatened if he provokes King Vima. I think we should go, pick up a caravan in Aria to the Armenian border, and keep our fingers crossed. Trying to skulk through is likely to make us look more suspicious."

"My thoughts also, but I wanted to hear you say it. Yes, Armenia it is. King Vima said that the *XII Ful* is back in Baku covering the border, and after checking his maps, the shortest and easiest way is through Hyrcania along the Caspian Sea, well away from both Ecbatana and Ctesiphon. We may be traveling under some protection, but I don't want to get too close to the centers of Parthian power. Does anyone have any other ideas?"

Ibrahim offered a suggestion. "I'll send Yakov and Shmuel into Aria with the caravan's arrival group to check on the situation there."

"And if it's not good?" asked Gaius.

"We don't go putting our heads on the chopping block by showing up. We hold off on the Bactrian side of the border while we figure out another way home."

Everyone agreed with the plan. More wine was poured and stories told, before one by one, they each went into their bedrolls.

Hasdrubal enjoyed his new calling as master of the caravan in Aria. When he left Hormirzad a few years ago, he had connected with an east-bound caravan. The caravan leader Dariosh had found the urbane and well-educated Hasdrubal a welcome companion, and they had spent many nights discussing the intricacies of running the operation, so remarkably similar to running ships. When they got to Aria, Hasdrubal found himself working with Dariosh in the caravan office. A year later, Dariosh died of an illness, with the help of a very inconspicuous poison procured by Hasdrubal. Dariosh's son would have inherited the business, but had little skill or interest in it, and Hasdrubal offered the grief-stricken son a considerable amount of money from his ill-gotten stash. It had been a good business for the sailing master from Tyre, and he seemed secure for the rest of his life.

So he felt a moment of shock, when, from his office inside the caravansary, he could hear a man talking to his staff outside. The man's Nabataean accent seemed familiar. Hasdrubal craned his neck to catch a glimpse of the man's thin face and pointed mustache. He scratched his head, wondering why the face and voice should raise such alarm bells in his head, when he remembered from three years ago... Yakov, Ibrahim's weasel-faced henchman. This could not be possible! What in the name of all the gods could that scum be doing here, how might he have gotten here?

Hasdrubal listened intently to the conversation. The man was trying to line up passenger accommodations with his staff to wait for a caravan to Armenia. *No. This is a coincidence.* Then he heard the name 'Yakov' and a shiver went down his spine. *I must scrutinize this passenger list!*

"We are quite full right now," Hasdrubal said, from within his cubby hole office, interrupting the conversation. *I don't want him to see me, if it is him.* "Bring me the list and I'll see what I can do. No, just you," he said, indicating his servant. "He can remain outside." The man brought in the list of names.

Hasdrubal's gut wrenched as he read the familiar names. *Aulus Aemilius Galba, Gaius Lucullus, Antonius Aristides...* some Jew and a female Roman name that he didn't recognize... *Yakov and Ibrahim! How the bloody hell they might have wound up here, in my office, of all places? One word by them to the authorities and he would be as good as dead.* "No, too many, we are full."

"But, sir, the entire second floor..." argued his servant.

"We are full! Do you understand, for them we are full." He said softly, picking up the little dagger he always kept handy on his desk. "Full!"

"Yes, sir!" The servant scuttled back out to convey the bad news to Yakov and his companion, whom Hasdrubal vaguely remembered as a deckhand on one of the ships.

"Have them let us know where they are camping when they arrive, something may come available between now and then," Hasdrubal offered politely from his office.

Yakov and Shmuel rejoined the caravan a day later with the news. Thankfully, there seemed to be no alert for Aulus and his party among the Parthian border guards. Yakov had accosted several in various taverns around Aria and they admitted to no unusual alerts, even after his plying them with generous amounts of beer and wine. The group would most likely have to camp alone outside the caravansary, but the yurt would be fine, if they could engage the bathing facilities there.

They arrived two days later. As instructed, Yakov walked in to inform them of their location a few hundred yards out, while everyone else headed toward the baths and the markets. That night, after several flagons of the good local wine, everyone collapsed into a sound sleep, the banked fire casting flickering shadows among the goods and baggage carefully organized inside.

Marcia stirred against Antonius, his body warm through her cotton shift, her body still damp from the quiet but intense lovemaking of a few hours ago. This long trip, this long, hateful, exhausting trip, was nearly at an end, and she could see the end, a house with Antonius, children, the little duties of being a wife and mother... she dreamily thought of what that house and life might be like.

A little noise outside brought her to momentary wakefulness. She lay still, listening... an animal stirring outside, perhaps, as she relaxed blissfully against her husband, his buttocks firm against her thighs. So soon, that peaceful life!

The door to the yurt was ripped open, the glare of a torch filled the interior, the patter of men bursting in, angry words hissed in the dim light. A hard hand grasped her wrist away from Antonius, jerking her unceremoniously to her feet. Another man put his sword to Antonius' throat and ordered him up. She heard him growl acquiescence as he rose to join the others, all with swords directed at them. She counted seven men, one for each of them.

She shifted her shoulders, feeling the weight of her dagger between them. Antonius had teased her endlessly about sleeping with it when they were on the road. Right now, it was their only weapon against the gang.

An eighth man stepped into the tent with a commanding air. In Greek, he said, "Welcome to Parthia, Ibrahim and Aulus! And all your friends. It has been a long time." The voice was vaguely familiar to Marcia.

No one said anything for a minute. Then Aulus spoke up, "I see you have taken to camels, Hasdrubal. Fitting companions for you. Smelly and full of fleas."

"Now my good senator, let's not make the last few minutes of your life unpleasant." Hasdrubal walked up in front of him, looked him in the eye, spat in his face, and delivered a ringing slap across Aulus's face that would have knocked him down two years ago. Aulus recovered, glaring at the man, a trickle of blood at the corner of his mouth in the torchlight.

"I am going to kill you all tonight, but not here. It would be messy, so near my new business. He walked over to where Ibrahim stood. "And Ibrahim, my old friend, I have a special treat for you. You will beg me to kill you." He likewise slapped Ibrahim hard across the face.

Then Hasdrubal addressed his accomplices in Aramaic. "Take them to the place you prepared, and keep them under the sword the whole way, no escapes. The Hanaean girl is yours after we are done with the others, but then she dies too. No witnesses. Frisk them for weapons, then put out this fire. We can come back for their animals and belongings when we are done."

Marcia had learned just a smattering of Aramaic and Greek, not enough to follow everything that Hasdrubal said, but enough to understand.

The thugs searched everyone for weapons, easy enough since they were all in night clothes, but did not search Marcia. *Deep breath, girl! We have a chance. They didn't take the woman seriously either. Eight against one, but it is a chance.*

They filed out of the tent in single file, one man behind each captive, sword at their backs. Marcia brought up the rear as they stepped off into the darkness, their eyes not yet adjusted to the night, blinded by the flaring torch the lead man carried.

It's not eight to one. The man behind me is the last in line, so it's one on one against just him. I take him, and the man in front of me covering Antonius, that's just two to one. Then Antonius and I each have swords, against six. I need to let them know what's up.

Marcia mentally prepared herself to become hysterical. First she began sobbing uncontrollably. Then, in *han-yu*, she began screaming, but not so loudly they might restrain her, "Oh, they think they're going to kill us all! But we're not going to die!"

"Shut up, bitch!" The man behind her said, heavily accented but close enough for her to understand. He prodded the small of her back with his sword.

"We're not going to die!" she screamed. "Be ready to fight!" She wailed, she was wringing her hair, fully hysterical now. She heard the man behind her laugh in amusement. She kept up the act until her guard was completely at ease with a helpless, hysterical woman. Then she pivoted on her right foot, spun clockwise in the darkness as she released her hair to recover her dagger with her left hand. As she came around, she buried it in the man's kidney. Taken totally by surprise, he let out no more than a "woof!" at the impact.

Marcia kept him impaled, twisting her dagger inside him, then reached for the hilt of his sword, prizing it easily from his unresisting fingers. She jammed the point of his sword into the hollow of his throat. A jet of blood, black in the darkness, erupted and he went down to his knees, gurgling. She withdrew both blades, and turned to face Antonius' guard, who was just now turning to see what was going on behind him. She delivered a slashing blow with the sword to his left side below the ribs. He went down thrashing, as she recovered his sword and passed it to Antonius. She then took up a position against Antonius' back. A third man charged her, and he too went down.

The whole melee was over in a minute. The guards were thugs, only moderately competent with a sword, and taken completely by surprise. Antonius clapped the bloodstained Marcia across her shoulders. "We owe you, *domina*! I hope none of that blood on you is yours!"

"I don't think so! Nothing hurts!" She smiled, breathing heavily.

"Check yourself. In a fight, you might not notice."

The fight was all over, except for Hasdrubal and Ibrahim, squared off around the guttering light of a dropped torch. Ibrahim had a sword, Hasdrubal only a dagger, so the group gathered to watch the inevitable conclusion. It was obvious that Hasdrubal was not familiar with fighting, his slashes clumsy and his parries weak. Ibrahim was toying with him. Suddenly Hasdrubal lunged in desperation, grunted as he impaled himself on Ibrahim's waiting sword point, and went down.

Ibrahim withdrew his sword from Hasdrubal's abdomen, put his hand to his own chest where a spot of darkness had blossomed, and went down on his knees to sit on his haunches, gasping. In his final act of desperation, Hasdrubal had stabbed Ibrahim in the chest. Someone dragged away the thrashing Hasdrubal, then everyone gathered around Ibrahim. Antonius lifted Ibrahim's tunic over his head and laid him down to check on him. The wound in his chest just below his left nipple was not bleeding profusely, but it hissed and bubbled with each intake of breath. Antonius put his hand directly over the wound, which seemed to help Ibrahim's labored breathing. "You're going to be fine, Ibrahim. You're too much of a scoundrel to die yet," Antonius said.

"You're a liar and you know it, Antonius my friend. That is a sucking chest wound and you can hear it. But keep your hand there for a minute, so I can say some things. Yakov?"

"Yes, father," answered the slender man.

"You have to get these people, our friends, through Parthia. I've taught you everything, so take care of them, please. I am proud of you, my son."

"Yes, father," he answered huskily, trying not to let his voice break, tears trickling down his cheeks.

"Gaius, Aulus, Antonius. I told you all a long time ago that I wanted, someday before I died, to find true friends, people who would die for me, for whom I could die." He stopped to make a gagging cough, bringing up a gout of blood. "I have found my friends, and I go to my death satisfied. I look forward to the afterlife Paul promised me. If it exists, I will watch over you from there, my friends." He paused for another coughing bout. "Antonius, you can take your hand off my wound now, I am ready."

"No, wait, my friend," answered Antonius. "I can patch you up." Antonius' voice choked up, and tears were running down his face.

"No, you can't, and you know it. I love you, I love you all. So take your hand away and let me go to what awaits me."

Ibrahim took Antonius' hand and gently lifted it away, and the sputtering hiss from his wound resumed with each intake of breath. He gasped, unable to talk, but smiled, waiting patiently with everyone watching silently, while he inexorably suffocated. At the end, his eyes grew wide, he smiled, and with one last rasp, took his final breath. Antonius gently closed Ibrahim's staring eyes.

Marcia sat down beside the man, taking his lifeless hand in hers. Tears burned her eyes and rolled silently down her cheeks. She didn't try to wipe them away. The idea that this man, their father figure, the mastermind of this trip, would no longer be there to cheer them on with an unlikely joke, to listen to their stories and tell one of his own, confident, great yet always humble. This could not be, but it was. He seemed asleep, she wanted to shove him, tell him to quit playing games and wake up… but his chest neither rose nor fell. He would not be getting up ever again, and she prayed to the strange god he had so recently adopted that He would accept Ibrahim into the afterlife he had so reluctantly come to believe in.

Everyone else either stood or sat silently, thinking their own thoughts for several minutes until Yakov took charge, remembering his father's orders. He coughed silently and wiped the tears from his eyes. "Goodbye, my beloved father. Now, all of you, he would not want us all to be killed, standing around mourning for him. Shmuel, Hasdrubal said something about taking us somewhere prepared. There may graves or a pit ahead prepared in advance that will accept their bodies as well as it would have ours. Go see if you can find it, take the torch. Antonius, get us some more torches and a shovel. I'll bury my father here."

People starting moving. They checked, there were no horses. Hasdrubal and his men had come on foot, nothing to get rid of but their bodies.

Shmuel returned a few minutes later. "There's a shallow grave, six feet wide and twenty feet long. The dirt's all piled up, even had shovels there. They saved us some trouble."

"Good, Antonius, go help Shmuel with the bodies. Everyone else, I need some help with my father's grave," said Yakov.

After a few hours, they had disposed of the bodies, and laid Ibrahim in a deep pit, wrapped in a white shroud. They all gathered around him. Shmuel offered the final words. "I share the same god, and many of the same beliefs he came to have. So I will pray for him as my people pray: *Yit'gadal v'yit'kadash sh'mei raba.* May His great Name grow exalted and sanctified in the world that He created as He willed. May He give reign to His kingship in your lifetimes and in your days, and in the lifetimes of the entire Family of Israel swiftly and soon," the mourning prayer of the Jewish people from whom Ibrahim's new faith had sprung.

Yakov, as his son, picked up a handful of dirt and cast it into the pit, then lost his composure and sank to his knees, sobbing. Marcia comforted him, hugging him to her, while everyone else grabbed a shovel and filled in the grave. They stacked a layer of rocks over it as a kind of monument.

Gaius also cried, hard choking sobs, for in the past two years, he had come to regard this wise and gentle man as his father as well.

By now, the first streaks of gray were beginning to appear in the east. Yakov had recovered, and was once again taking charge of his father's unlikely crew. "We need to be moving. Hasdrubal had some position with the caravansary, I thought I recognized his voice last week, and he will be missed. We want to be well on our way when they find the graves, and well off the road. So break camp and quickly!"

They mounted up before sunrise with the supply wagon lumbering along behind them, following a smuggler's trail a few hundred yards off the road, rather than risk border guards.

After several days and no pursuit, everyone seemed to relax a bit. The trail followed a ridge line that offered fair passage to the wagon and a good view of the road below so they could find their way. After a few more days and still no pursuit, Yakov decided they could risk limited time on the road. He periodically deployed two or three riders for directions and supplies from the village markets as needed. There were quite a few Aramaic and Greek speakers here, and with difficulty, they could also exchange information in Bactrian, similar enough for some mutual understanding.

Late in the afternoon, Antonius rode ahead to scout out a spot for the night's camp, when out of the side of his eye he caught a flash of color in a ravine. He looked, but did not quite see it again; was it a person on the move? The wind stirred and he saw it again, some sort of banner. He rode down carefully, dismounted and stepped into the ravine to investigate.

It was a faded yellow banner, the vertical feather-shaped ones used by the Hanaeans, with Hanaean characters, cocked upright against a tree. Several other banners lay strewn about on the ground. They looked like they had been there for a very long time, as had the bones strewn about them. Obviously, animals had been in amongst the remains. Few skeletons were intact, but he counted twenty skulls. Also swords, some still in their scabbards; they had been taken by surprise. Helmets and other items, no wagons. A good-sized party of Hanaeans met with some foul play here.

Antonius rode back to break the news. "You're not going to believe what lies ahead!" he told Aulus and Yakov from horseback. "Looks like a band of Hanaeans were ambushed a few years ago just a few hundred yards ahead." He pointed in the direction from where he had just come.

Marcia overheard this and walked up, "Why do you think they are Hanaeans?" she asked.

"Hanaean banners with characters on them, yellow"

She put her hand to her mouth. "Gan Ying's banners were yellow!"

While everyone else was still talking, Marcia started off on Excelsior, following Antonius' well-marked trail in the wild winter grass. She found the site and was down examining it when everyone else rode up.

"This is Gan Ying's expedition! That is his banner, 'Western Harmony'! She cast among the wreckage, looking for anything she might find. These were people she knew, five she had grown up with in Liqian, had traveled with them all for years and knew their names, though time and animals had left no one identifiable. Her eyes fell on a leather tube, also carrying the 'Western Harmony' symbols. She picked it up, opened it and extracted a paper roll. She was reading the Hanaean script, her lips moving silently, when Antonius came up beside her.

"This is Gan Ying's report. He made a copy of this for Wang Ming, in case something happened to him… it seems something did," she said bitterly. "I helped Ming prepare for his presentation of it to Emperor He."

Antonius put his arm around her shoulders. He had an arrow in his hand. "Parthian army arrow. I pulled it out of one of the rib cages. This was treachery, to make sure they never got back."

This discovery heightened their sense of danger, despite the absence of any apparent pursuit. Once again they stayed off the roads and avoided inns, while the fluent Aramaic speakers Yakov and Shmuel purchased what supplies they needed in towns. Parthian cavalry patrols clattered by on the roads below them, but did not seem to be actively searching for anyone. Nevertheless they stayed in concealment, weapons ready, until they passed.

A few weeks travel found them in the Elburz Mountains of Hyrcania, just a few hundred miles from the *limites* of Rome, the border and safety. They camped off road, but set nightwatches against the huge wolves lurking in the dense forest.

Gaius took the midnight watch with Marcia, but did not feel like talking. Marcia was seated across the fire from him, cross-legged in the style she had adapted from Hina when wearing trousers. *I used to find that somehow offensive, but no longer. She is like Anahita, the goddess from Bagram, proud to be a woman. I wonder what Camilla will think, though.*

Marcia said something, jarring him from his revery. "I'm sorry, my mind was elsewhere. What did you say?"

"Just that yer mind goes wanderin' more an' more, the closer we git to the *limites*," she answered colloquially with a grin, then switched to formal speech. "Even Aulus is looking forward to going home, though he fears having to admit failure. You used to be the most cheerful of the lot at the worst of times. What is bothering you?"

"Camilla. I am worrying about what I will find when I get back. Someone in my bed, raising the children that I didn't have time for?"

"Did she ever say anything in her letters to make you think something was wrong?"

"No, never. Always cheerful, what the children were doing, work around the garden. Never complaining. Of course there haven't been any letters in either direction for the last two years," he said with a chuckle.

"Ah, that's better. I got a laugh out of you. How did you come to be married?"

"Oh, typical Roman wedding. Uncle Mercator wanted to cement a business relationship with her father, and she was part of the deal. She was fifteen and I was twenty five, home on leave, so we married and spent enough time to get her pregnant with Gaius Secundus, then I had to go back up to the Danube. Came back the next year to meet him. Then the next year, long enough to get her pregnant with Lucia Camilliana... and back to the eagles for that birth, also!"

"That is a hard life. I imagine all soldiers' wives put up with that."

"The troops, like Antonius, can't get married. Tribunes, like I was, can, but most don't. Those that do, try to keep their wives close by, but that can be rough living. And the frontier can be dangerous... thousands of women and children were butchered in Britannia forty years ago during an uprising. I didn't want her there." He paused to stare thoughtfully into the crackling, low-burning fire. "Enough of me, you have done an admirable job of whipping Antonius into a devoted husband. I thought I'd never see that!"

"That's it, I got another smile from you! We are making progress with your mood. Yes, he has, but the gods know I am not the person he first met in Alexandria three years ago either. Not at all."

The horses began nickering nervously, interrupting their introspection. Gaius shoved a torch into the fire to light it and grabbed his sword. "Marcia, go wake the others! I think we have wolves again!"

CHAPTER 81: HOME AT LAST: ROME, 103AD

Lucius Julius Maximus, *legatus* commanding *Legio XII Fulminata,* sat behind the worn campaign desk in his curule chair in front of the finely-crafted leather *mappa mundi* from Alexandria. Across from him sat Aulus in his senatorial toga, Gaius Lucullus and Antonius Aristides in uniform, all freshly-

shaved, their faces still red and raw. Marcia Lucia wore her splendid *stola.* The layout reminded Gaius of his departure three years ago, but this meeting was in the gray stone *praetorium* of the legion's permanent fort in Romana, near the 'The City of Winds,' Baku on the Caspian Sea. Lucius Julius' close-cropped hair had gone a bit gray around the temple in the intervening few years. The tanned leathery skin around the commander's eyes crinkled a bit as the he examined Gan Ying's report to the Hanaean emperor, neatly printed in translation in Marcia's delicate miniscule script. The indecipherable Hanaean original lay on the desk, along with a Parthian army arrow and a bag of silver and gold coins of various denominations and nationalities.

"So the Parthians ambushed them a couple of years ago?" he asked.

"It appears to be so," answered Gaius. "Definitely a Parthian arrow, army issue."

Aulus added, "The Parthians very much did not want a relationship to develop between Rome and Luoyang. They were almost successful in detouring Gan Ying and preventing him from reaching Rome, and they, I think, stirred up our problems in Luoyang. And Kadphises in Bactria sent a strong message to Pacorus not to interfere with us."

Aulus continued with the final bit of his two hour report, delivered impromptu and without notes. "So after we discovered the Gan Ying massacre, we decided to avoid the roads and inns. The trip was uneventful, except for the damned wolves in Hyrcania."

Lucius Julius chuckled. "Yes, they gave their name to that place south of the Caspian Sea. 'Werka' is the word for wolf, approximated in Greek as Hyrcania, the land of wolves."

Antonius interjected. "Bloody big barstids, sir, and bold, no fear. Come right up ter our campfires, twenty feet away, and just look at us, they eyes glowin' in the firelight."

Aulus continued. "But other than that, uneventful. And damned glad to be back on Roman soil. The only thing I don't understand is how Hasdrubal wound up driving camels in Aria. The last time I saw him he was heading to jail in Masira to await execution."

Lucius Julius smiled. "How he got to Aria is anyone's guess. But he didn't stay in jail in Masira for long. He broke out, apparently helped by one of his guards, whom he killed right afterward on the beach. Bashed his head in, dumped the body at sea, but it washed right up. Titus Cornelius put out an urgent report among all the military commanders because of his high status, access to large sums of money, piracy and the hijacking of your imperial mission."

Just then, the commander's orderly entered the back of the room, stood at attention and saluted, arm across his chest. "The documents you requested, sir!"

Lucius Julius waved him in. "Come in, come in, lad." The young man strode stiff as a spear to the commander's desk and presented him two scrolls. The commander unrolled and scrutinized them, then waved him off. "Thank you, lad, and express my thanks to the *librarii* for their quick turnaround on these."

"Yes, sir!" He saluted again, arm across his chest, and left.

Lucius Julius handed the documents to Aulus. "Here are the pardons you requested on Yakov bin Ibrahim and Shmuel ben Eliazar. And express my congratulations to them for their efforts. Do you know where they intend to go?"

"Shmuel wants to return to his mother Devorah in Galilee, and Yakov wants to return to Petra. And when I get back to the Senate, I intend to introduce motions for citizenship."

"Admirable, Senator." The commander paused, then continued, "Interesting report! I had not intended this adventure to become such a monumental challenge when I detached your cousin Gaius and Antonius three years ago!"

Aulus answered with a smile. "It was quite the adventure. And thank you for the pardons. Whatever those two did in the past, they certainly made up for it on this trip! I think everyone had a hand in saving everyone else's life at least once. Marcia, most recently!"

The commander eyed Marcia, trim and elegant in her white silk *stola*. "You are quite the talented young woman, Marcia Lucia."

"Thank you, sir, but I think I am done with fighting for a while," she answered demurely.

"As are we all," added Antonius with a smile. "And I am greatly honored that you offered me a slot as *praefectus castrorum*, sir. But I've been followin' the eagles fer most of my life. I want ter spend time with me lovely wife now, and hope to be raisin' yer some young legionnaires shortly. Bein' as how raisin' a family an' following the eagles, they don't mix well."

"I fully understand, Antonius. Well, you will exit your service with equestrian status, back pay for the past three years and a generous bonus for this task. Where do you intend to take your land settlement?"

Antonius switched from his coarse Latin to the polished rhetoric which the commander had never heard him use before. "I intend to become a tutor in my home of Aquileia, as my father before me. The usual studies, Greek and Latin rhetoric, the philosophers, but also perhaps teaching Hanaean and Bactrian to those interested."

"Antonius, you surprise me! Your speech is elegant... how come you never spoke like that before?"

Antonius reverted to his old speech. "An' as yer know, sir, a soldier has ter fit in among his messmates. Don't pay ter be puttin' on airs."

"Agreed. Well, good luck to you and your beautiful wife. Expect a lot of visitors to your new academy wanting to learn what you have learned." He turned to Aulus with a smile, "By the way, Senator, I looked in this bag, you said it was what was left of the ransom paid to Ibrahim. But odd, I didn't see anything in there but beeswax. Why don't you take this beeswax and distribute it among your group as you see fit, as you paid the ransom out of your own money. Over and above the *honorarium* we will be paying Gaius and Antonius."

The commander picked up another document from his desk. "Gaius, I have nominated a posting for you, awaiting Trajan's confirmation, to command the *Legio II Traiana* in Dacia, after an appropriate time at home with your wife and family. That is a brand-new legion, fitting out to settle the mess in Dacia. Their king Decebalus is up to his usual treachery, despite getting mauled several times while you were gone. Trajan is preparing to throw half the Roman army along the Danube against him, and *II Trai* will likely be the tip of that spear."

"Honored, sir," answered Gaius.

"Very well, then, I won't take up any more of your well-earned rest and relaxation time. There is a military escort waiting to get you to Trapezus where a fast packet ship leaves for Rome in about a month. Good luck in Rome with Trajan!" Lucius Julius rearranged some papers and writing instruments on his desks, and the group took their cue to depart.

The only sad part of departing was Marcia's farewell to her faithful Excelsior. The small packet had no accommodations for horses on such a long trip. However, he was going to stud duty with the *XII Ful's* cavalry wing, a job he would surely enjoy. She gave him his last apple, he nickered softly, ears twitching as she rubbed his velvet nose, then she turned away and left quickly, hoping not to burst into tears with the hostlers watching.

In the fall of the year, the fast packet docked at Ostia to discharge its passengers. Gaius departed to Neapolis for a long overdue reunion with his wife, accompanied by Antonius and Marcia to meet Gaius' family. Everyone would return to Rome to be present at Aulus's presentation before the Senate *curia* and Emperor Trajan. They had received word via the Praetorian Guard that the *Princeps* Trajan would be expecting them to accompany him as his guests on the imperial dais in the Senate for Aulus's presentation.

After that, Gaius would return home for a few months of leave before departing for his new command in Dacia, and Antonius and Marcia would depart for their new home in Aquileia.

Aulus's freedman and financial advisor Lucius Parvus greeted the Senator in Ostia with two pieces of good news and one piece of bad news.

"Yes, sir," he said enthusiastically. "The voyage was a financial success beyond our wildest dreams. The *Africa*, returning early laden with Indian trade goods, paid off most of the creditors alone. The *Asia* and *Europa*, laden with exotic silks by the ton, Hanaean iron ingots in the bilge for ballast, thousands of board feet of exotic bamboo of various diameters... we are still counting the profits but it is huge, Gaius! Huge! We doubled our investment, at least."

"And..."

"Livia delivered a beautiful baby boy, now three years old."

"I know, I heard via Gaius. He received several letters at the fort that his wife Camilla had written him over the past several years, many about young Pontus Aemilius Galba! I can't wait to see him. I hope he isn't afraid of strangers!" Aulus paused. "And the bad news?"

"Your political rivals in the Senate are furious that you not only failed to meet with the Hanaean emperor, but you so thoroughly displeased him that you were condemned to death and had to escape like a common criminal. They want the government's share for the expedition refunded, including the money for the ships, since the mission was an abject failure... as they say, an exciting and interesting tale, but not what they paid for. If they succeed, we will be severely in the red, and we may lose the ships."

It was a glum ride back to Rome, bouncing along in the luxurious carriage. The affable Aulus thought he had few political enemies, but success seemed to manufacture them. The story of his expedition had preceded him, based on stories in letters from soldiers of the *XII Ful*, feeding into the Roman gossip mill. Various concoctions, featuring battles with fierce beasts, an attack by a whole army of Amazon warriors... *Hina would love that one*... and a fierce battle against hordes of giant Hanaean warriors. These were the stories found in the *Acta Dialis* 'Daily Doings' gossip sheets posted in the various *fora* in the city. He might be a folk hero, but to his fellow senators, he was an abject failure.

He was also an object of jealousy, as the first Senator to openly engage in business as head of his trading enterprise, since Senators were restricted by tradition to farming enterprises only. Not that they observed this rule; they set up *latifundia* factory farms growing a single crop employing thousands of slaves, businesses in everything but name, or set up shadow companies, run by their freedmen, to skirt the tradition against earning money in the trades. They got the profits, the freedmen took the risks. Aulus had had the courage to break with that tradition.

Aulus was also not the same man who had left Rome three years ago. Three times, twice at the hands of Hasdrubal and once at the hands of Emperor He, he had faced what he knew to be certain death. Twice, at Tongchuan and at Aria with Hasdrubal's thugs, he had fought in deadly combat, killing his opponents. He had lost fifty pounds, and while not as thin as Gaius nor as burly as Antonius, three years on the road had hardened him into a very physically fit fifty year old, a match against people half his age. He missed the life he had lived the past three years, constantly on the edge while traveling, and despised the cheap political theatrics to which he was returning. His political enemies were a nuisance, not a threat.

Back in Rome, Aulus had a most welcome reunion with Livia in their home on the Aventine Hill, and a first meeting with his son. He played rolling carts with young Pontus Aemilius until the lad was ready for his afternoon nap. The lad seemed to hit it off with the new stranger in his young life that they called 'Papa.' Aulus then retired with Livia for their own nap, a long-overdue passionate welcome home.

Afterwards, as they lay side by side, watching the shadows of the trees sway across their ceiling with the wind in the afternoon heat, Aulus decided he must bring Livia into the seriousness of the situation.

"Love, there may be trouble in the Senate. I could go from stupendously wealthy after this trip to not much of anything. And if my enemies have their way, I may not be a Senator."

Livia turned to him and put her cheek against his, her arm across his chest. "You'll still have me, *carus*. As we said when we married, '*Ubi gaius es, tua gaia sum*' You are my man, and I am your girl. We'll get by."

"We may even lose this house."

"Didn't you live in tents for years? We can do that."

"You have no idea what living in a yurt is like! But thanks. Worse comes to worst, maybe we can go back to Bactria. It's a beautiful country, lovely mountains, and King Vima might find a use for me. Or we could go up to Aquileia and help Antonius with his academy."

"That's a beautiful city... as long as I have you." She rolled over and kissed him warmly and wetly, to indicate that her abstinence of the past three years was far from sated.

The next day Aulus met with Titus Flavius Petronius, his most trusted colleague in the Senate, and recounted the events in the Hanaean court. His old friend shook his head. "No matter how you pitch it, you put the life of an insignificant person above the mission. It may have been noble, but it was also stupid, and cost you the meeting with their Emperor. And that, your enemies will argue, is what they paid for. You didn't deliver, and they want their money back. They also think that you may have put your financial interests above Rome's, since you did make a huge amount of money. Sorry, Aulus Aemilius, but this is going to be hard to sell."

"What if Trajan personally intervenes?"

"Not likely, given his deference to the Senate. He could, and then I think they might back down. But I don't think he will. The best way out of this mess is to lie. Paint Emperor He as a scheming devil, a barbarian."

"No, I will not. I am going to tell it exactly as it happened, and if the truth is not good enough, then so be it."

Back in Neapolis, Gaius turned the cart into the path circling a plane tree in the front yard, reined the horses up into a stamping halt, blowing noisily. He was assisting Marcia out of the cart when Camilla and the two children burst forth. She practically knocked him down with her embrace, to the great amusement of Antonius and Marcia. Several house stewards came out to take care of the cart and horses.

When Gaius and Camilla finally completed their first kiss in many years, he then embraced his children, Gaius Secundus, now a gangly teenager, and Lucia Camilliana, a shy twelve year old with budding breasts. "You two have grown so much!" he said, "And I missed you so much. I have so many adventures to tell you. Look, these two are my friends, Antonius my centurion and his wife Marcia Lucia, like a new uncle and aunt to you." The children shook hands with each and made a polite bow.

Gaius' little villa was home to both Camilla and her mother Servilia, who stayed with her during Gaius' prolonged absences. Servilia came out in gardening clothes and an apron, a spry, graying woman of about sixty. She introduced herself to everyone with a firm handshake. "Thank you for getting my wayward son-in-law home and back to his wife, at least for a few months. Then he'll most likely be dashing off again for some new adventure somewhere. Pardon my hands, I was tending my garden. The servants think I am doing their work for them, but I like tending my vegetables and flowers myself. Keeps me young."

The villa was actually a small farm on the outskirts of Neapolis, with a good view of the ominous Vesuvius across the valley. There had been some damage thirty years ago from the massive eruption, long ago repaired, and the ash left the land fertile, though Gaius had reservations about living within sight of the monster volcano that had killed his family. They adjourned to the atrium inside the house, sitting beside a small fountain and a number of well-tended plants. Servants brought drinks and snacks, while everyone caught up on events near and far.

That night, after a dinner spent mostly discussing the wilds of Further Asia, the Bactrian mountains, and camels, everyone retired for the night. Behind closed doors, Gaius took Camilla in his arms. "I am so sorry, *cara mea*, so sorry." He kissed her tenderly.

"For what?" she looked concerned in the candlelight, as though he was about to reveal some devastating secret.

"For never being here when you need me."

She laughed, relieved. "You have never not been here for me, Gaius, and you never will not be here. I keep you in my heart always." She laced her arms around his neck, drawing him to her for a long-overdue reunion.

A few weeks later, Gaius, Antonius, and their wives returned to Rome to Aulus' house on the Aventine Hill, opposite the massive imperial palace on the Palatine Hill overlooking the Circus Maximus. They were to help prepare Aulus for his presentation to the Senate, and to observe that presentation from the imperial dais as Trajan's guests.

Aulus was skeptical of his reception by his fellow senators, but was surprisingly nonplused at the possibility that it could be a disaster. His colleague Titus Flavius assisted, patiently hearing each version of Aulus's speech in the atrium while everyone else looked on. He contented himself with critiques of its form and style, having long ago given up trying to alter its content.

In the off-moments, the women went shopping in the city, Livia providing maidservants to carry parcels, and a grim-looking ex-gladiator named Rufus as bodyguard. Marcia was overwhelmed with the cosmopolitan markets, hearing a babble of languages from around the world, some of which she understood. It was with a great deal of surprise that she encountered an Hanaean merchant with a long trailing mustache dealing directly with some silk merchants. He was speaking a Shaanxi dialect of *han-yu* through an ineffective translator.

Marcia stepped in to introduce herself, to the great amazement of the Hanaean gentleman, whose eyes brightened at her fluent Gansu. They exchanged pleasantries momentarily, him complimenting her on her unusual blue eyes, she inquiring of events near her home. The decimation of the Black Headband gang was still big news in Shaanxi, and he knew their old friend

Xian Bohai, 'a delightful smuggler,' which caused them both to laugh. She took over the Latin translation with the silk merchant, displacing the man's former translator, a Parthian with but a smattering of both Latin and *han-yu*. Marcia helped the man close a good deal for the silk, assisted him in the calculation of currencies, and closed with his promising to look up her brother when he passed through Liqian on the way back, and also to give her regards to the Xian family.

Camilla and Livia looked on in amazement through the rapid-fire linguistic interchange.

"Amazing!" said Camilla. "Yes, of course, you were a translator."

"I was many things, Camilla." She just smiled, and returned to admiring the sights of the city, the hustle and bustle of the crowds, the rumble of the carts, the smells of charcoal and cooking foods at the various *caupona* food stands, the reek of beer, stale wine and urine from the *taberna*. She had, of course, been to Rome six years ago with Gan Ying, but then she had been forbidden to interact with any of the people, or to even go out alone. But that was so long ago.

On the day of the presentation, they met in the atrium of the Aulus house, newly-minted civilian Antonius resplendent in his new toga, the thin purple stripe on his white linen tunic denoting his new equestrian social status. Gaius was dressed in his best parade field equipment, leather polished to a glossy shine, brass gleaming mirror-like. Marcia wore her fine *stola* from Bagram, with red ribbons criss-crossing the front as a girdle and an orange silk wrap. Camilla wore yellow silk, and Livia a dark green that favorably complemented her red hair and green eyes. They left on two litters borne by burly black Nubians via the *Vicus Longus*, the Long Avenue, alongside the eastern end of the half-mile long race track of the Circus Maximus. They turned left on the *Clivus Scauri*, lined with meticulously manicured slender black pines spaced exactly a hundred feet apart like a botanical colonnade to ascend to the eastern entrance of the Flavian Palace on the Palatine Hill. If the golden-domed Temple of Jupiter Optimus Maximus, on the Capitoline Hill across the *Forum Romanum*, was the home of the gods in heaven, the Flavian Palace was the home of the gods of the earth in its magnificence.

The bearers lowered the litters by the entrance to the Basilica on the north side, and they were challenged by a spotlessly-clad Praetorian Guardsman. Gaius introduced himself and the members of his party, and quietly stated they had a meeting with *Princeps* at the third hour of the morning. The soldier checked his list, then summoned an escort who led them in to the enormous *Aula Regia* Royal Hall, a massive interior colonnaded hall sixty feet high, made entirely of marble. Fading off into the distance, men in togas and servants in tunics went about their business, the occasional footfall or raised voice echoing in the colonnaded space. The escort led them to a waiting room off to the side to await the Emperor.

Gaius carefully placed his bronze helmet, with its newly-mounted red horse hair plume, on a table to avoid the least smudge on its glistening polish. Antonius looked at it admiringly, waiting for the *Princeps* to arrive. "Well, *legatus*, yer lookin' rather fine but fer that old-fashioned helmet of yours. How in the hell did yer keep that all the way from Luoyang?"

"The only thing I did keep," Gaius smiled, ruffling its red plume. "I would be damned if I was going to leave Commodus' gift buried on the side of an Hanaean road somewhere! Everything else was replaceable, but not this. I wrapped it up and buried it in whatever wagon we were using to carry baggage. I just never mentioned it."

"It's a fine piece, and still takes a great shine. I'm glad yer was able ter keep it"

In the distance a mechanical waterclock began to bong out three prolonged sonorous chimes, echoing hollowly in the vast chamber. At that instant Trajan entered, accompanied by a tall slender woman, her hair done up in an elegant crest, followed by two very senior Praetorian Guardsmen. Trajan was clad in military garb, though the metalwork was white enamel and the leather breastpiece the color of cream. The white helmet, held under his left arm, had a purple plume, and the cloak was also imperial purple with white and gold tracery on the hems. He went straight to Gaius Lucullus and grasped him firmly by the hand in a military handshake, as though he were his commander rather than the emperor of all Rome. "Gaius Lucullus! So glad to see you! I hear you have accepted your posting to my new legion. The Senate did me the honor of naming it after me."

This was the first word that Gaius had that his posting to *II Trai* had been confirmed. "Yes, sir, Your Excellency! I look forward to doing honor to your name."

"Very well, then. Please introduce me to your friends."

"Sir, this is my former *primus pilus* of the *XII Ful*, Antonius Aristides, and his beautiful wife Marcia Lucia, to whom you affirmed citizenship five years ago on her original Hanaean mission. Livia Luculla, my cousin and Senator Aulus Aemilius's wife, and my wife Camilla."

Trajan greeted each one in turn, also introducing his wife, the *Augusta* Pompeia Plotina, with a comfortable familiarity, despite being one of the most powerful men in the world. He seemed to be a source of tightly-disciplined energy, so characteristic of professional military men. To Marcia, he asked with a smile, "You have a beautiful name, the same as my mother's! Are you the young lady that fought off hordes of Amazon warriors among the barbarians?"

"Your Excellency, not everything you read on the *Acta Dialis* is true. I did know one warrior woman among the Xiongnu who taught me many things. We became as sisters."

"That must be a remarkable story, Marcia, of which I want to hear more, after Senator Gaius Aemilius' presentation. I have chosen to walk to the Senate *Curia* to give the public a chance to see you all. Despite the *Acta Dialis*, or maybe because of it, you are the heroes of Rome today!" He had a big, booming laugh that was pleasant to hear.

A few moments later, another guardsman entered, saluted with his hand across his chest in a solid thump, and announced: "Your Excellency, your lictors are ready."

They exited the anteroom into the main floor. Formed up were twelve lictors in two rows, carrying the bound ax-handle *fasces*, the symbol of magisterial power and strength through unity since the founding of the Republic half a millenia ago. Trajan adhered to the Republican prohibition against mounting the axes themselves within the City walls. The ax heads were the symbol of *imperium*, the power of life and death; not all his predecessors had obeyed this prohibition, symbolically or in fact. Behind the lictors was a squad of Guardsmen in parade regalia, led by the *imagifer* carrying an image of Trajan on a tall pole surmounted by the Roman eagle and emblazoned with SPQR, *Senatus Populusque Romanum*, the Senate and the Roman People, the symbol of Roman power since time immemorial. Two Guardsmen carried circular horns around their shoulders, and behind them two more carried drums; the remainder provided security for the emperor.

Trajan led his guests into the midst of the two columns, Gaius on his right and Antonius his left, the women behind, the ranks at the rear closing around them. At a word from the *imagifer,* the Guardsmen began to march, exiting the west side of the Flavian palace. The trumpeters gave a blast on their horns, the drummers began a rippling cadence, and the emperor and his entourage began the descent down the *Sacra Via* through the Forum. Crowds began to gather amid chants of "Trajan! Trajan!" He waved over the heads of his Guardsmen at the crowd, telling the nearer people that he was accompanied by the Hanaean party of Senator Aulus Aemilius Galba. As this word spread, the chant changed to "Trajan and the New Jason and his Argonauts!" until by the time they reached the steps leading up to the *Curia* at the foot of the Capitoline Hill, over ten thousand people had crowded into the Forum, their cheers thunderous.

Aulus had departed his house on foot with Titus Flavius Petronius, to be seated in the *curia* well before the third hour when Trajan was to depart the palace. Trajan drew huge crowds for his public appearances, and if the senators were caught in the Forum, the *Princeps* might arrive in the Senate before them. They walked in silence, the portly Petronius wheezing slightly at Aulus's brisk pace. When they reached the steps, the last of the senators were entering when the sound of trumpets brayed from the palace, signaling Trajan's imminent arrival. Like the surf on a beach, the soft susurrations of the people on the Via Sacra began to rise as they gathered to greet the popular *Princeps*. Then, almost like a triumphal procession, the murmur rose to a roar. The two senators could hear the chants, "*Ave*, Trajan and Jason! Trajan and Jason, *Io Triomphe!*" Aulus smiled, Jason being the Greek explorer and his Argonauts who had charted the Black Sea a millennia ago in search of the Golden Fleece.

"Whatever, the Senate thinks of you, the crowd approves of what you did," said Titus.

"They may, Titus Flavius, but in the end it will be what the Senate thinks that matters."

Aulus and Titus crossed the elegant marbled floor to take their seats in the middle row on the left side of tiered benches. Aulus looked at the marble statue of Victory at the end of the hall, vividly painted with windblown brown hair, piercing blue eyes, an upraised silver sword in one hand, an olive branch in the other. *Wish me luck, Lady Victory. Only you can help me now!*

The other senators greeted him, some curtly, some with a bit of warmth. "Welcome back, Aulus Aemilius. You have been missed these past several years." That was the warmest greeting he got, and it came from the bloated Lucian Septimius Pontus, his most ardent foe.

"It is good to be back, Lucian Septimius," Aulus answered simply. He just could not bring himself to fear these overweight pigs of men. Instead he was amused by their pretentions, not regretting having shed his own somewhere in the wilds of Asia. These men were not the senators of old, they were parasites.

Trajan, with Gaius Lucullus and Antonius, strode in with military precision, followed by their wives and Aulus's Livia. The Senate rose respectfully as they crossed the floor to the dais in front of the Statue of Victory. Livia caught his eye as she seated herself behind the men with Marcia and Camilla. She had never been in the *curia* before.

Trajan turned to address the Senate, his powerful parade ground voice echoing through the *curia*. "Be seated, please! Thank you all for assembling at my request on this exceptionally warm day in October, to hear the report of Senator Aulus Aemilius Galba on his mission to Hanaean lands, and many other interesting lands and kingdoms.

"We are in the company of three ladies, and I wish to explain their unusual presence here today. Marcia Lucia is a member of this mission, and a veteran of the previous mission by the Hanaeans here five years ago. Her citizenship, and those of their other translators, was affirmed before this body as descendants of the lost cohorts of Carrhae. She is Aulus Aemilius' translator and now the wife of Antonius Aristides. It did not seem fair to admit his wife, and exclude the beautiful wives of Senator Aulus Aemilius and Gaius Lucullus, the beautiful ladies Camilla Sempronia and Livia Luculla.

"And having thus trod upon our hallowed traditions," he said with a slight smile, "it was impossible then to exclude my own wife, the *Augusta* Pompeia Plotina, though she eschews the title you so generously granted her three years ago."

A quiet titter of respectful laughter spread through the *Curia*.

"*Dominae*, please rise and introduce yourselves to this esteemed body." The three women rose, and bowed politely to both sides of the aisle, then seated themselves. "As *Princeps Senatus*, the First Man of the Senate, I wish to set the rules for this presentation, so this report can be completed in an orderly manner. Any Senator may interrupt Senator Aulus Aemilius for a question, but please raise your hand to be acknowledged by Senator Aemilius Lepidus Scaurus, our senior Senator. After receiving your answer, you may ask one more question for clarification. After that, the floor returns to Senator Aulus Aemilius, or to another Senator recognized by Aemilius Lepidus.

"And now, the *Princeps Senatus* yields the floor to Senator Aulus Aemilius Galba." Trajan seated himself on his ivory curule chair.

The Senator got up to go down to the center of the *curia*, to address the body from the floor. He stood silent for effect, and in the waiting silence, the muted noise from the huge crowd outside the building penetrated the hall. Then, in his best oratorical voice, he began his presentation, beginning with the Gan Ying report. "As you all know, five years ago, this body received Gan Ying's mission, and it was his mission that launched my own in return. He provided their emperor, Emperor He, a report on our people. Marcia Lucia assisted in its presentation before Emperor He, but was not privy to its contents. However, through a combination of Parthian treachery and incompetence, we have come by the original report that was to be presented to the Hanaean emperor by Gan Ying, and I would like now to read it into the record."

Aulus read Gan Ying's report, noting that emperors were selected by merit, and discharged when things go wrong. "Not strictly true, as we all know, but this aptly describes the accession of *Princeps* Trajan, which had just taken place," he said, interrupting himself for the aside. He continued, noting that the Romans were "tall and honest," with favorable descriptions of their cities, civilization and architecture, even putting them on a par with the Hanaeans. The report concluded that 'The king of this country always wanted to send envoys to Han, but Parthia, wishing to control the trade in Chinese silks, blocked the route to prevent the Romans getting through to China.' How far they went in blocking this route will shortly become clear!"

Aulus went on to describe the shipbuilding in Myos Hormos, and then the voyage of the *Asia, Europa* and *Africa* down the Red Sea to the open ocean. These massive ships, of unusual design, had performed flawlessly.

"As you know, this voyage was the victim of treachery from the outset. My shipping master, Hasdrubal of Tyre, conspired with the notorious pirate Ibrahim bin Yusuf to hijack these ships, laden with the treasure of the Roman people. But we were successful in handing Hasdrubal over to Roman authority for execution, and Gaius Lucullus, detached *legatus* of *Legio XII Fulminata*, and Antonius Aristides, *primus pilus* centurion of that same legion, not only thwarted Ibrahim's plans and recovered the *Europa*, but also turned him into a valuable ally! I commend their efforts!"

Lucian Septimius Pontus raised his hand to be acknowledged by Senator Scaurus. The wizened old man, white headed and gaunt, nodded his acknowledgement, and Pontus formed his question. "Did not *Legatus* Lucullus ransom the *Europa* from Ibrahim?"

"He did, and that was a wise move. Ibrahim's own plans had been disrupted by Hasdrubal of Tyre, and he had no place to go with his huge treasure. A ransom allowed him and his centurion to continue their mission and eventually rejoin the *Asia*. I should like to remind you, that a ransom was paid to rescue Julius Caesar from the clutches of pirates."

"And he came back to crucify them. For clarification, how much was the ransom?"

"One hundred thousand sesterces."

A shocked murmur went through the Senate at the sum. Aulus Aemilius produced a bag of coins and shook it, letting it jingle. "I have about half that amount, forty thousand or so, returned to us by Ibrahim on his death. Most of that was spent on our journey home, freely by Ibrahim as we had no money. It was Ibrahim's bequest that we four should share in his ransom, but I will not do so until an accounting has been made of our trip."

He continued on, discussing the firefight at Galle where the *Europa* and all her treasure could have been lost to a foreign king, but for the courage and honor of Ibrahim in defending their ship. And likewise their perilous transit through the Straits of Malacca. "That ship was carrying fifteen million sesterces, twenty tons of gold and silver in ballast in her bilges, and the ship was worth that much as well. Ibrahim's loyalty to us, once brought around by my two companions, was unquestionable, and essential to our success. A few tens of thousands of sesterces to preserve tens of millions? That is a good return on investment, not a shame."

Senator Aulus recounted the early detachment and return of the *Africa*, a decision made when the *Europa* was believed lost, in the hope of achieving some small profit margin, and then the pursuit of the *Europa* over thousands of miles of sea, to ultimately rendezvous and jointly make landfall in Tianjin, and inland to the capital of Luoyang.

"And there we encountered treachery from the representative of King Pacorus II of Parthia, one Cyrus Mithridates, whom we believed had a hand in delaying our meeting with Emperor He for months. We determined the Hanaeans had an excellent imperial post the rival of our own. It was made available for our use, so we were in constant communications with our ships. When it appeared that we could not make our necessary departure date I directed the two ships to detach on the Ides of April, two years ago, bearing letters on our status. It was our intent to remain and return via Hanaean ship to India." He paused for effect.

"Marcia Lucia was then the concubine of a member of the Hanaean court, who was our official liaison. But the Parthians played on the jealousy of his weak mind, convincing the man that Marcia was unfaithful to him with Antonius Aristides, a false charge to which we can all attest. He beat her in her chambers, she retaliated, and he claimed she had attempted to kill him. She was brought to trial before the Emperor, just hours before we were to meet with him." He paused again. The senators were all following this intently.

"An Hanaean trial is not like a Roman trial. One is placed before the judge, in this case Emperor He himself, in an abject position, questioned, and the sentence announced. There was no guarantee of witness, or any opportunity to defend one's self, except as granted by the judge.

"As Trajan noted earlier, Marcia Lucia's citizenship was affirmed during her first visit to Rome, as *cives sine suffragio*, citizen without the vote, but with all other rights which make Roman citizenship valued throughout the world. Gentlemen of this august body, I could not allow a fellow citizen to go to her death without at least ensuring her a fair trial. I interrupted her trial, as her representative, and was immediately joined by Gaius Lucullus, Antonius Aristides, and her brother, Marcus Lucius Quintus." He paused again, then continuing with increasing fervor, "I could not do otherwise, and would so again today without hesitation." He paused, then delivered the conclusion in an angry shout echoing in the chamber. "If there was to be one Roman unfairly condemned to death, then we would all die together!"

There was a long silence, and then scattered sounds of approval. But then Lucian Septimius Pontus raised his hand, was recognized, and asked his question. "That was very noble of you, Aulus Aemilius, very noble indeed, but you also had a duty, and duty requires sacrifice. It would seem that the life of a mere woman, five or six generations removed from being a real Roman, would be a modest price to pay for a successful mission to the Hanaean emperor."

On the dais behind Trajan, both Camilla and Livia, seated on either side of Marcia, each took one of her hands and squeezed it gently. This was the point that it would get ugly.

"I am sorry, Lucian Septimius. Your question?"

Lucian Septimius rose to his feet, his face turning purple, his triple chins waggling as he spoke with vitriol. "It's not a damned question, it's a statement! Your foolish 'honor' cost the government tens of millions in *sesterces!* You not only did not meet with the Hanaean emperor and represent us before him, you almost got yourselves killed!"

Apparently this was the feeling of the majority of the body, because Trajan's ground rules were now quickly forgotten as dozens of senators rose to their feet to decry Aulus, demanding their money back and condemning him as a fool, and worse... the word 'traitor,' 'faithless' and 'greedy' could be heard among the many epithets they hurled at him. Senator Scaurus tried ineffectively to regain control, but the meeting had disintegrated into chaos. Aulus stood silent and impassive... this was the ending he had expected. *What fools! How easy to speak of sacrifice for a mission, when someone else must make the sacrifice.* Aulus was the only one who noticed that the *Princeps* had risen, and was calling for everyone to be seated.

Finally, in a commander's voice intended to heard above the chaos of battle, Trajan roared, "Seats, gentlemen, seats!" As heads turned toward him, he said again in a slightly lower voice, "I have something pertinent to this discussion that I would like to read into the record."

Everyone quickly returned to their seats. Embarrassed silence reigned over the *curia* as the *Princeps* unrolled a scroll. "I received, last year, long before Senator Aulus Aemilius returned with his party, a personal letter from Emperor He regarding his conduct in the court. This letter was sent by Hanaean courier overland thousands of miles, personally to me.

"To Emperor Trajan of Rome, greetings. I hope by now that your faithful servants Aulus Amelius Galba, Gaius Lucullus, Antonius Aristides, Marcia Lucia whom we know and love as Si Huar, and her brother Marcus Lucius Quintus, whom we know and love as Si Nuo, have returned safely to you. I wish to commend these people to you for having such a high sense of honor, that they would cast all things aside to defend the least of their own. Such honor has been an inspiration and a topic in our court since their departure. We look forward to a long and strong relation between our two peoples, if such honor is common among all of you.

"Following their departure, we determined that some belongings and a large quantity of money were left behind. This has been placed in safekeeping, to be returned to your next envoy, whom we look forward to seeing. Be well!"

Trajan remained standing in silence for over a minute while the *curia* pondered the Hanaean emperor's message. Then he turned to Senator Scaurus. "Are we ready to continue, Aemilius Lepidus?"

"We are, your Excellency. Lucian Septimius, do you have a follow-on question?"

Pontus looked like he had eaten something foul. He just shook his head.

"Does anyone else have a question for Aulus Aemilius Galba?" No one responded. "Then you may continue, Aulus Aemilius."

Aulus looked up again at Lady Victory. *Thank you for turning the tide in my favor.* He almost felt he saw her wink and give him a secret grin, in a way that reminded him very much of Marcia. He reopened with a joke to relieve the accumulated tension. "You will notice," he said, "that the good Emperor He, who styles himself as the Son of Heaven, omitted the part about condemning us all to death!"

Polite chortles of laughter rippled through the assemblage. The audience was now his, and this was storytelling now, no longer oratory. He recounted Ibrahim's and Demosthenes' roles in their daring escape, the fight with bandits in Tongchuan, the Xiongnu and Hina, Marcia's transformation, the wedding at Liqian and the Emperor's pardon, the caravans, the warm welcome in Bagram by King Vima Kadphises, the near-disaster at Aria with the treacherous Hasdrubal and the sad death of Ibrahim. There was the discovery of the remains of the Gan Ying expedition and the evidence of Parthian treachery: he produced the Parthian army arrow and held it aloft for all to see. Finally, the wolves of Hyrcania, then the welcome return to Roman Armenia. The telling took an hour; by the end even Lucian Septimius was paying rapt attention, hand on his ponderous chin.

In closing, Aulus invoked the Parthian nemesis. "At every step of the way, the hand of King Pacorus II of Parthia was set against any relationship between Han and Rome. He misdirected the Gan Ying expedition thousands of miles overwater, stranding them in Eudaemon Arabia, when they had been only a few hundred miles from our border overland. He then treacherously ordered the Gan Ying overland party wiped out on their return through Parthia, after meeting personally with them." Aulus again held the arrow aloft for all to see. "This arrow is proof of their treachery!"

"But Pacorus II was unaware that some of the people, and a copy of Gan Ying's most favorable report on Rome, also accompanied us on our mission, and this report was presented to Emperor He, with the able assistance of Marcia Lucia.

"Our unexpected presence in Luoyang disturbed their envoy greatly, and he did everything he could to poison the court against all things Roman. When that failed, he tried to discredit the virtuous Marcia Lucia and Antonius Aristides. Our Roman unity foiled that plan, though we risked all to do so!" He paused rhetorically, to allow murmurs of assent from the curial assembly. He noted that even Lucian Septimius was nodding his approval.

"When we reached the court of King Vima Kadphises, the King of Kings of Bactria, he had received two conflicting requests: one from Emperor He, requesting that he extend his hospitality to us and assure our safe passage through his lands, and another from King Pacorus demanding our heads! Fortunately, he chose to grant Emperor He's request, thereby, as he so aptly put it, 'poking a finger in Pacorus' eye!'" The audience, including the staid *princeps*, erupted in laughter at that. When the laughter died down, he continued.

"King Vima Kadphises made us his official emissaries to Trajan, offering to mediate the emerging dispute over Armenia, and head off a looming war. He made it quite clear to the Parthian envoy that his neutrality in that war, should it come, should not be taken for granted by King Pacorus, if anything should befall us in that transit." The audience erupted in loud cheering at that.

"We delayed long enough to ensure that King Kadphises' message was conveyed to Pacorus. So therefore, although we exercised considerable caution in transiting Parthia, the greatest threat we faced were the famous wolves of Hyrcania! With that, my report is complete and I thank you for your attention. Are there any questions?" The *curia* was silent.

Aulus continued. "As there are no questions, then I should like to introduce two motions before this august body. Aemilius Lepidus?"

"Proceed," said the old Senator.

"One is a motion for full Roman citizenship for our traveling companions, Yakov bin Ibrahim of Petra, and Shmuel bin Eliazar of Galilee. These men, though of lowly stature, were steadfastly faithful in ensuring our safe return. They have given great service to Rome, and deserve Rome's greatest reward, citizenship.

"The second is rather *pro forma*. And that is a posthumous pardon, and full citizenship, for our dear and valiant friend Ibrahim bin Yusuf of Jiddah, may his newfound god grant him peace." Aulus choked back his tears, but his eyes still burned and blinked fiercely. "I only wish he could stand by us in this body. He may have been a pirate, but he was a man of noble honor, and I am proud to call him my friend. Is there any discussion on these motions?"

There was none, and both carried. Then the *Princeps* Trajan stood. "Aemilius Lepidus, I wish to introduce a motion."

"Certainly, Your Excellency."

"I would like nominate Aulus Amelius Galba to be *consul* beginning in January of next year, his fellow *consul* to be Titus Flavius Petronius. Is there any discussion?"

There was none, and that too was carried.

EPILOGUE

Aulus Aemilius Galba had a successful though uneventful term as *consul* with his friend Titus Petronius. Though the position of consul in the Principate was now largely ceremonial, it was still the high point of the *cursus honorum*, the Roman career path. He declined several post-consular governorships to return to sea with the *Asia, Europa* and *Africa* for a second trip to the land of Han, and a much more cordial meeting with Emperor He.

Antonius and Marcia, now happily pregnant, returned to his home town of Aquileia, and with the assistance of Lucius Parvus, temporarily on loan from Aulus, and some of Aulus's clients there, opened his schools of philosophy and languages, dedicated to his father.

Gaius Lucullus had a distinguished command as *legatus* of *Legio II Traiana,* which engaged in a number of battles in the final war against Decebalus in Dacia which broke out the following year. He returned to the long-suffering Camilla, who had waited out the war in nearby Byzantium, to find himself elevated to Senatorial rank.

Yakov opened an orphanage in Petra, seeking out street urchins as he had once been, to raise and educate in the tradition of his adopted father.

Shmuel settled down to a quiet life in Galilee, tending to his mother Devorah.

And far away in the Altai mountains, Hina and Galosga conceived another child, a boy whom they named Attila. His descendant and namesake would make that name resound through history.

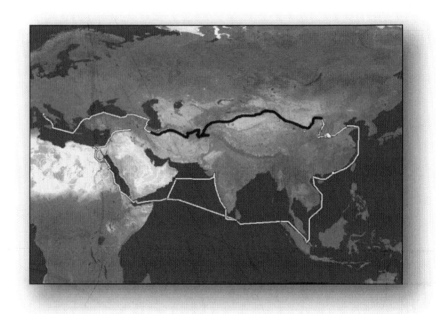

The Journey

ABOUT THE AUTHOR

This is the first full-length novel by Lewis McIntyre. His first work, a short story *Come Follow Me, a Story of Pilate and Jesus*, was released in January 2017. Lewis McIntyre was born in Asheville, NC, and graduated from the Naval Academy in 1970, serving as a Naval Aviator until his retirement as a commander in 1990. He continues to serve the Navy as an engineer at Patuxent River Naval Air Station. He lives with his wife of thirty seven years, Karen, and three cats, in La Plata MD.

Made in the USA
Las Vegas, NV
28 March 2023

69804475R10321